Love in the Time of Hate

Love in the Time of Hate

In the Mirror of Urdu

Rakhshanda Jalil

London · New York · Sydney · Toronto · New Delhi

First published in India by Simon & Schuster India 2024

1 3 5 7 9 10 8 6 4 2

Simon & Schuster India
818, Indraprakash Building,
21, Barakhamba Road,
New Delhi 110001.

www.simonandschuster.co.in

Simon & Schuster: Celebrating 100 Years of Publishing in 2024

Hardback ISBN: 978-81-970426-2-1
eBook ISBN: 978-81-970426-9-0

Typeset in India by SÜRYA, New Delhi
Printed and bound in India by Replika Press Pvt. Ltd.

This volume is dedicated to my mother Mehjabeen Jalil
who has steadfastly believed in the power
of love and forbearance

Saat sanduqon mein bharkar dafn kar do nafratein
Aaj insaan ko mohabbat ki zarurat hai bahut

Stuff all the hatred in seven boxes and bury it deep
Today, humans need love more than anything else

—Bashir Badr

Contents

II. PEOPLE

III. PASSIONS

IV. PLACES

Introduction

I am 60 years old and confess to a crushing fear, one that weighs my chest with an inexorable weight and makes it difficult to breathe sometimes. Yes, with all my privileges—of education, of class, of having friends in 'high places'—I feel scared, more scared than I have ever been in my entire life. I must also confess to an almost persistent depression, like a low-grade fever, over the past many months, that doesn't quite halt the daily rhythm of life; it just slows you down by its continuous, relentless presence in your life making you feel sad and somehow empty.

I suspect I am not alone in this. I feel this fear and depression among a great many Muslims in urban India. I hear it in their silences. I sense it in their steadfast refusal to get drawn into political debates. I notice it in their stoicism in the face of virulent hate swirling about in school and college Whatsapp groups as well as RWA/housing society group chats. I spot it in the hastily withdrawn social media posts drawing attention to some recent communal outrage or atrocity. I recognise it in their zeal to distance themselves from instances of *any* sort of violence, be it a Muslim man killing his Hindu girlfriend and chopping her into pieces or a Muslim man killing his non-Muslim partner in a business dispute.

If my own fear and despair and that of others like me, is so palpable and pronounced, what of those Muslims who are doubly marginalised by their poverty and illiteracy? Or vulnerable because they don't have the safeguards and barriers, however flimsy, that 'people like us' have in our gated communities and cushioned lives? What of those who live on the edge of survival because they must perforce go out into the real world every single day to eke out a living? What of the plumbers, electricians, painters, carpenters, maids, and sundry service providers who don't give their real, Muslim-sounding names for fear they will not be hired? Or the vegetable vendors who festoon their carts with saffron flags after every call to boycott small Muslim businesses? Or the biryani vendors, kabab sellers, quilt makers, car mechanics who have traditionally plied these trades for generations but now fear for their lives? What of the meat sellers whose makeshift stalls happen to be along the routes taken by the *kawariyas* during every monsoon? What of the imams and naib imams, often from the poorest of families, who are hired by Wakf boards to serve as custodians of small, isolated mosques surrounded by hostile neighbours?

I don't 'look' like a Muslim so, to an extent, I am safe. Unless called out to chant 'Jai Shree Ram' to profess my Indianness, I am largely safe. But what of my name? How can I camouflage that on a railway booking chart? Or hide it when asked to provide proof of identity? While my first name can afford some benefit of doubt for it might pass as a Parsi's, my surname is a dead give-away. When push comes to shove in the New India that is Bharat, not even speaking English will give me an exit pass if a mob baying for Muslim blood were to *gherao* me. All my so-called privileges can be brought to naught by a crowd of lumpens. The realisation is chilling.

And if I were a man? Imagine, over 75 years after partition and after reading all the gory stories penned by Saadat Hasan Manto and other chroniclers of communal violence, having your pants pulled down to check whether you are a *katua* or not? But what if I did 'look' like a Muslim? What if I chose to offer *namaz* perfectly peacefully and quietly while sitting on my berth in a train? Worse still, what if I had a beard, wore a *topi* or a *hijab* and indeed 'looked' like a Muslim? What if I worked as an imam in a mosque? So what if I had just assured my family that all was well, that I was safe given the police presence all around me?* What, then? What if I, as an Indian, have been conditioned to believe that the tattered fabric of secularism will be held up no matter what? The violence in Gurgaon in July-August 2023 proved that these are no longer hypothetical scenarios. This is a lived reality for countless Indian Muslims.

Jab mulle kaate jaainge
Ram Ram chillainge

When the Mullahs are slaughtered
They will shout: Ram! Ram!

Or:

Hindustan mein rehna hoga
Jai Shree Ram kehna hoga

If you want to stay in Hindustan
You'll have to chant Jai Shree Ram

And '*Goli maro saalon ko...*' (Shoot the buggers...) by someone who is now a union minister are no longer isolated instances of random, unrelated, personal biases and prejudices. They are dog whistles. They are a clarion call to a large, restive majority

---

*https://indianexpress.com/article/cities/delhi/naib-imam-killed-in-gurgaon-mosque-had-assured-family-of-enough-police-security-8872138/

that is being brain-washed to believe they are second-class, nay 'seventh-class' citizens, in their own land. They are part of a larger narrative, a grand design.

Since we have clearly turned into a nation of 'whatabouters', each of these hate-filled, terror-inducing slogans will be instantly and viciously countered with those raised by the PFI or other fringe minority outfits. When rapes, murders, corruptions, scams, and scandals are thwarted in Parliament by elected representatives of the people by instances of whatabouts, how can these rising incidents of bigotry and hate not be similarly countered? It's easier to come back with counter-accusations, to point fingers, to obfuscate, to fling more filth, to parry hate with hate than it is to understand fear, to acknowledge militant, muscular majoritarianism, to call out the elephant in the room.

As we spiral inexorably downwards, as every fresh instance of bigotry is outstripped and outdone by even bigger, bolder, more blatant, more bare-faced occurrences, we don't seem to pause to think of the consequences. This rampant whataboutery—both at the political and the individual level—is exhausting, predictable and eventually empty. It will derail the India we have known and loved—probably forever. In an attempt to put up some sort of bulwark, however feeble, however ineffective, however flimsy in the face of formidable forces, I have attempted to put together this collection of essays. You may say I am a dreamer but in John Lennon's immortal words, 'I am not the only one.' I hope at least some of you who read this book will join me.

Several essays in this volume were written at different times on different occasions, some triggered by topical events, others written in response to an impulse arising from deep within, a few written especially for this collection. However, all of them nevertheless have one singular quality in common: they look in the mirror of Urdu, more specifically Urdu poetry. Like divers diving deep into the oceans in search of rare pearls, these essays bring up pearls of poetry, beautiful, luminous, heart-warming fragments of thoughts and ideas strung on the twine of love. Hence the title 'Love in the Time of Hate'.

But why Urdu, you might ask? I counter with: Why not Urdu? What better representation will one find of a pan-Indian language, one that is not confined to a state or a region but one that is willing to be embraced and owned by anyone who wishes to do so? Moreover, here is a language that has honed itself over centuries to reflect not one or two or three concerns but a range of topics and themes not to mention tones and tenors. Given the catholicity of its concerns, given the fidelity with which it has been reflecting the good, bad, ugly, indifferent face of society, given its dogged refusal to be tied down to a caste or community or state, it seemed a good idea.

What Mirza Ghalib had once said for the spoken word, can well be said for Urdu poetry:

Dekhna taqreer ki lazzat ki jo uss ne kaha
Main ne ye jaana ki goya yeh bhi mere dil mein hai

Such is the deliciousness of speech in what he says
That I understood everything to be what is in my heart

For, indeed, the Urdu poet has written something for every occasion, every sentiment, every impulse that flickers through the human heart. There may be plenty one might disagree with, but there is always something to be found on nearly every subject. Nothing is beyond the pale, nothing is sacrosanct or unquestionable.

Some years ago, when I had first set myself the task of looking into the mirror of Urdu to see how the Urdu poet has viewed the 'other', I set out on a journey of discovery. My sense was that poets seldom, if ever, fall victim to bigotry, prejudice, and narrow mindedness; a propagandist or publicist might, but not a poet. And the Urdu poet, in particular, has always been known for his/her liberalism and eclectism. Even in matters of religion, he/she has always spoken for *qaumi yakjahati* and *muttahida tehzeeb*, on communal harmony and the co-mingling of cultures.

There are love jihads and there are love jihads. Mine turned into a labour of love—that eventually took the form of fortnightly columns for an online portal—to present the range of concerns contained within Urdu literature. I found myself on a self-appointed crusade to excavate how diverse the concerns of the Urdu poet have always been, and how Urdu poetry is NOT poetry by Muslims for Muslims about Muslims, nor is it chiefly concerned with the travails of the *shama* and the *parvana* (popular tropes of the candle and the moth) or the *gul-o-bulbul* (the rose and the nightingale that came to Urdu poetry from classical Persian poetry) as is often erroneously assumed.

My search yielded delightful results: I found vast amounts of poetry written by Hindu and Sikh poets on Eid and Milad-un Nabi as also large numbers of soz, marsiya, naat, manqabat (each being a form of devotional poetry) on subjects culled specifically from Prophet Muhammad's life or the early years of Islamic history such as the events pertaining to the Battle of Karbala. In equal measure, these explorations revealed large numbers of Muslim poets who have waxed eloquent on Holi, Diwali, Janamshtami, Guruparab, Christmas, Basant, Rakshabandhan, not to mention many heart-warming poems on Ram, Krishna, Shiv, Guru Nanak, Buddha, Mahavir, and Isa Masih (as Jesus Christ is referred to in Urdu).

Many of these poems on religious figures are grouped under headings such as 'Hamarey Mazhabi Rahnuma' (Our Religious Guides) in anthologies such as the two-volume *Hindustan Humara* edited by Jan Nisar Akhtar; others are seeded in collections such as Maulana Hasrat Mohani's many odes to his beloved Krishanji Maharaj which find pride of place in his *Kulliyat* (Collected Works). Still others are stand-alone texts such as Khwaja Dil Muhammad Khan's delightful verse translation of the *Bhagvad Gita*, titled aptly enough *Dil ki Gita*, first published in 1944 from Lahore. Of the several hundred versions of the manzum (verse) Ramayana in Urdu, some of the best known are *Ulfat ki Ramayana* and *Rahmat ki Ramayana*.

With time, the broad topics revealed themselves to me, often prompted by real-life events, tremors in the seismograph that is the present-day Indian political and social milieu, sometimes jogged by the passing of a much-loved pan-Indian figure such as Dilip Kumar or Lata Mangeshkar. Some were triggered by my travels, some by newspaper headlines and quite a few were written in response to small, everyday increments of change. With time, I could also discern a fairly natural pattern; I found I could group these diverse essays under four broad headings: Politics, People, Places, Passions. Running through them is a common current: of love for this, My Land, My India.

What you hold in your hands now is the result of many years of explorations; sometimes mindfully and purposefully, sometimes serendipitously discovering hidden facets. Over the years I have marveled afresh at the love and tenacity of purpose of the Urdu poet: love for his/her motherland, its richness and diversity and his/her relentless, almost missionary zeal to express that love. It seemed important, and timely, to pluck these scattered thoughts and place them between the covers of one volume, especially at a crucial time in our history as a nation, as a people. Writing this book is, also, an attempt to staunch the fear and depression I alluded to earlier. For, in looking back, and in looking into the mirror of Urdu, these essays also show the way forward. And finally, what better way to counter fear than with inclusion? Or hate with love?

Rakhshanda Jalil
New Delhi
April 2024

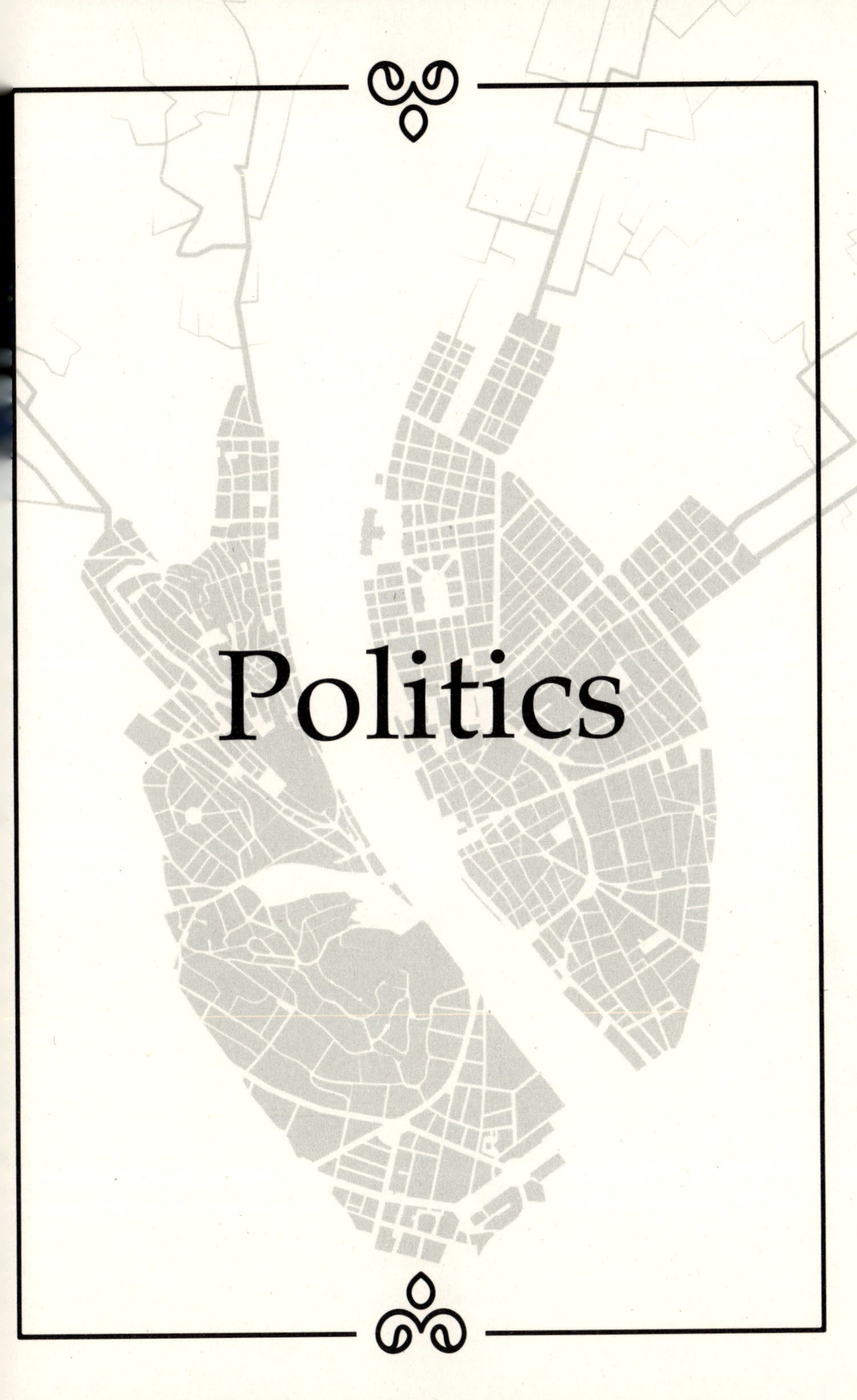

Politics

1. Creeping Normality and the Tragedy of Gradualism

Creeping normality (also called gradualism, or landscape amnesia) is a process by which a major change comes to be accepted as 'normal', even 'acceptable' if it happens slowly through small, often unnoticeable, increments of change. A change that might otherwise be viewed as objectionable if it were to take place in a single step or short period is seen as quite all right—as we living in the 21st century India can bear witness to the slow-building horror some of us have felt over the decades. Slow, small, seemingly insignificant events, beginning with the country-wide Rath Yatra of 1990, kept adding a layer of 'normal' till we have reached this stage of the New Normal where blatant bigotry, bare-faced communalism and publicly-aired prejudices are considered perfectly all right.

The American scientist Jared Diamond, describes 'creeping normality' in his book written in 2005, *Collapse: How Societies Choose to Fail or Succeed*, and gives the remarkable example of the natives of Easter Island who, seemingly irrationally, in just a few centuries, chopped down the last of their trees, wiped out their rich ecosystem, drove their plants and animals to extinction, and saw their complex society spiral into chaos and cannibalism. As Diamond writes, 'I suspect, though, that the disaster happened not with a bang but with a whimper. After all, there are those hundreds of abandoned statues to consider. The forest the islanders depended on for rollers and rope didn't simply disappear one day—it vanished slowly, over decades.'

How has the Urdu poet looked at gradual changes, so gradual that they creep up unannounced as a fait accompli? As Shaz Tamkanat admits, often there's a self-denial that this will not happen, not to me, not now at the very least:

Abhi kyun kar kahun zer-e-naqab-e-surmagin kya hai
Badalta hai zamaane ka chalan aahista aahista

Why should I say what is under the grey veil
The ways of the world change slowly, slowly

And Ateeq Asar is ruing the gradual absence of trustworthy voices which is possibly an early warning signal of the dangers that lie ahead, a warning that goes unheeded:

Utthe jaate hain dida-var sabhi aahista aahista
Ye duniya mo'tabar logon se ḳhali hoti jaati hai

All the connoisseurs leave one by one
This world empties of wise men slowly

And the much underrated but marvellous poet, Asad Badayuni, who died tragically young, speaks as though he has foreknowledge of what the future might hold. As is often the case in Urdu poetry, it is implied, obliquely, rather than stated directly and the references to roses and thorny bushes is implicit rather than explicit. In a sher eerily reminiscent of what happened at Easter Island, he writes:

Ye dharti ek din banjar zamin ban jaaegi jaanan
Gulaabon ki jagah lenge babool aahista aahista

This earth will turn into a barren land one day, dearest
Thorny trees will slowly and steadily take the place of roses

Sometimes, the poet draws solace from placing the blame squarely on Time and, therefore, absolving himself of all culpability as, for instance, in this sher by Shahryar:

Waqt teri yeh ada mai aaj tak samjha nahi
Meri duniya kyun badal dii, mujh ko kyun badla nahiin

Time, I have never understood this trait of yours till today
Why have you changed my world, but not changed me

Coming back to where we started, to gradualism and creeping normality, it is never about pulling down one advertisement that offends someone's sensibility, renaming one road, removing one book from a syllabus, issuing one letter of apology, retracting one seemingly benign statement, dropping one member from a committee…and so on and so forth in a long list of solitary acts. It is rather about the cumulative impact of these solitary acts of omission or commission. It is about the Sorites Paradox (also known as the Paradox of the Heap). Imagine a heap of sand, from which grains of sand are methodically removed, one at a time. One might think that removing a solitary grain here or there makes no difference to the heap. But what if this process is repeated over a period of time with persistence and regularity? What if only one grain remains from the original heap? Will it still be a heap? If not, when did it change from a heap to a non-heap? Was it that first time, when the first solitary grain was removed? These are questions we in India need to ponder.

Naushad Noori, one of the most remarkable Urdu poets from Bangladesh, draws our attention to the Mound of the Dead and the lessons to be learnt from it. An ardent supporter of the Bangla language movement and the creation of a new country based on linguistic and cultural affinity rather than religion and jingoistic hyper-nationalism, Noori seems prescient, pointing towards the disaster waiting to unfurl in this poem titled 'Mohenjodaro' written in 1952:

Ho sakta hai, koi toofan
Ho sakta hai, koi darya
Ho sakta hai, koi faateh
Ho sakta hai, koi lutera
Shehr-e-tamaddun dhool ke neechey
Dhool ke neechey boli bhasha
Aur issey tarikh-nawees
Log kahein murdon ka teela

Koi vaba to phooti thhii
Koi bala to tooti thhii

Mere shehr ke rehnewalon
Apni Pothi, apni Gita
Apni apni lok kathaein
Apni apni geeti mala
Apna apna harf-e-tahajji
Apni apni boli bhasha
Pattey, patthar, poste, papyrus
Tambe, lohey par likh rakhna

Wahi vaba phir phooti hai
Wahi bala phir tooti hai

It could have been a storm
Or a river
Or a vanquisher
Or a plunderer
That buried an entire civilization
Under a mound of dirt
Languages and dialects

Under a mound of dirt
Today, the historians call it
The Mound of the Dead

Perhaps an epidemic broke out
Or a calamity fell upon it

O people of my city
Hold on to your Gita and Pothi
Your folk tales and fables
Your songs and ballads
Yours letters of the alphabet
Your languages and dialects
Inscribe them on copper and iron
And on leaves, stones, skin and papyrus

That same epidemic has broken out again
That same calamity has befallen

However, those of us who are impatient for change might do well to remind ourselves of Firaq Gorakhpuri who has the last word when change, especially revolutionary change, manifests itself:

Dekh raftar-e-inquilab, Firaq
Kitni aahista aur kitni tez

Look at the speed of revolution, Firaq
So slow and yet so swift

2. Religious Intolerance: Love in the Time of Hate

When a militant muscular right wing forces jewellery brands to pull down advertisements showing inter-faith marriages, when the bogey of 'love jihad' acquires the status of gospel truth, when it is easier and far more expeditious to regurgitate hatred and lies than it is to talk of love and truth, it is time to peer into the mirror of poetry. For, there comes a time in the history of nations when they need their poets most; not the politicians, nor the policy-makers and publicists but the poets who are true visionaries. For, it is the poets who can remind people of the essential values that hold them together, or as the American writer Ursula K. Le Guin put it so pithily, because poets are the 'realists of a larger reality'. For us in India, that time is NOW lest the clamour of the strident illiberals drowns out the voices that have always pointed towards the larger reality and the greater good and the bloody tide of unreason sweeps away the India we have known and cherished.

In Urdu, the poet has consistently been the voice of optimism and hope, pointing towards a better future. When the country emerged from a bitter fratricidal war, licking the wounds inflicted by brother upon brother, neighbour upon neighbour, Majaz wrote:

Hindu Muslim Sikh Eesai aman ke moti ro lengey
Khoon ki Holi khel chukey hain rang ke dhabbe dho lengey

Hindu Muslim Sikh and Christian shall weep pearls of peace
Having played Holi with blood they'll wash off the coloured stains

One would have thought, if nothing else, a nation so scarred by communal hatred, so battered by storms of communal frenzy, would have learnt its lesson. If nothing else, partition should have driven home the lesson for every Indian that hate begets hate. If nothing else, We the People should have resolved to never allow the evil within to resurface. Instead, we stoked the fire and kept its lambent flame alive while the poet kept cautioning, trying to show the way as in this sher by Anand Narain Mulla:

Main faqat insaan huun Hindu Musalmaan kuchh nahiin
Mere dil ke dard mein tafreeq-e-eemaan kuchh nahiin

I am only a human; not a Hindu or a Musalman
The sorrow in my heart is not separated by dogma

Or in this by Qateel Shifai who is alluding to a force that benefits from keeping the two communities forever at loggerheads:

Hum ko aapas mein mohabbat nahin karne detey
Ik yahi aib hai iss shahr ke danaon mein

They do not let us love each other
That is the only defect in the wise of this city

Qaumi yak-jahti (national integration), *insaan-dosti* (love for humanity), *watan-parasti* (love for the nation) remained popular themes in the years following the partition. The Urdu poet bent backwards to keep the flag of secularism flying high as is beautifully expressed in this sher by Hafeez Banarsi:

Sabhi ke deep sundar hain humaare kya tumhare kya
Ujaala har taraf hai iss kinaare uss kinaare kya

Everyone's lamps are pretty; not just yours or ours
The light is everywhere; not just on this shore or that

Special songs and lyrics were written especially for children to instil the 'right' values from an early age, such as this geet by Shafiuddin Nayyar:

Pyaaraa Hindostaan hamaaraa pyaaraa Hindostaan
Jaan fidaa hai iss par apna dil iss par qurbaan

Our dear Hindustan, our dearly beloved Hindustan
We lay down our life for it, sacrifice our heart for it

However, as the relentless juggernaut of communalism began to drive a wedge between communities, reopening old wounds, the thread that bound diverse communities together began to snap and the tapestry of shared living showed fresh tears despite constant darning, the poet became, by turns, hopeful and hectoring. A victim of communal violence himself, Bashir Badr whose home in Meerut was looted and set on fire, urged his fellow countrymen to bury hatred far, far out of sight:

Saat sanduqon mein bharkar dafn kar do nafratein
Aaj insaan ko mohabbat ki zarurat hai bahut

Stuff all the hatred in seven boxes and bury it deep
Today, humans need love more than anything else

And Nida Fazli spoke of the consequences of building picket fences of religious identity:

Koi Hindu, koi Muslim, koi Eesai hai
Sabne insaan na hone ki qasam khayi hai

They are a Hindu, or a Muslim or a Christian
Everyone has taken an oath not to be a human

Till quite recently, Hindi cinema too has done its best to constantly hold up models of pluralism and multiculturalism be it art-house cinema or mainstream films. From the early days of Nehruvian India film lyricists such as Sahir Ludhianvi were at pains to insist:

Tu Hindu Banega na Musalman banega
Insaan ki aulad hai insaan banega

You will not grow up to be a Hindu or a Musalman
You are the child of a human and you shall be a human

Kaifi Azmi was showing the pitfalls of growing religiosity, pointing the potholes that would turn into craters and eventually eat up the entire road ahead:

Basti mein apni Hindu Musalmaan jo bas gaye
Insaan ki shakl dekhne ko hum taras gaye

Ever since Hindus and Muslims have come to live in my neighbourhood
It has been an age since I saw the face of a human

Whenever the flames rose high, after an Ayodhya or a Gujarat, a Mumbai or a Moradabad, the poet wrote a dirge to a lost time, but the sub-text was always that the clock can be turned back, still, there is time, yet, to set things right as in this poignant poem by Ajmal Sultanpuri:

Musalman aur Hindu ki jaan
Kahan hai mera Hindostan
Main uss ko dhundh raha huun

The life of Hindus and Muslims alike
Where is my Hindustan?
I am searching for it

The German Lutheran Pastor Martin Niemoller wrote the confessional 'First they came...' as atonement and acknowledgment of cowardice and the silence of the majority—after the fact, that is, after the silent majority in Nazi Germany had allowed unimaginable horrors to be perpetuated upon certain targeted sections of the community. In much the same way Javed Akhtar is reminding poets and writers—NOT Urdu writers alone, certainly NOT Muslims only—of their responsibility and exhorting them to bear witness by the very act of writing and recording before it is too late:

Jo baat kehte darte hain sab, tu woh baat likh
Itni andheri thhi na kabhi pehle raat, likh

Jin se qaseede likkhey thhay woh phenk de qalam
Phir khoon-e-dil se sachche qalam ki sifaat likh

Jo roznamoon mein kahin paati nahin jagah
Jo roz har jagah ki hai, woh waardaat likh

Jitne bhi tang daire hain saarey torh de
Ab aa khuli fizaon mein ab kainat likh

Jo waqeyaat ho gaye unka to zikr hai
Lekin jo hone chaahiye, woh waqeyaat likh

Iss bagh mein jo dekhni hai tujh ko phir bahaar
Tu daal-daal de sada, tu paat-paat likh

To speak of that which everyone is fearful, of that you must write
The night was never so dark ever before, write!

Throw away the pens with which you wrote the odes
In praise of the true pen dipped in the heart's blood, write!

The narrow circles that confine you, break all of them
Come under the open skies now, of a new creation, write!

That which finds no place in the daily newspapers
That incident which happens everywhere every day, write!

That which has happened finds mentions
But of those that should have happened, write!

If you wish to see spring return to this garden
Call out from every branch and on every leaf, write!

Postscript: Watching an old movie, *Judgement at Nuremberg* (1961), I am struck anew by the terrible consequence of those who knew yet chose to remain silent as terrible changes were being wrought in civil society, in the executive, the judiciary and in almost every sphere of life in Nazi Germany. An American judge presides over a tribunal in post-war Germany in the trial of four German jurists accused of 'legalising' Nazi atrocities. Prescient with lessons for us in India, it makes compulsive viewing.

3. Stupid vs. Evil: Who is More Dangerous?

Stupid people can be more dangerous than evil ones. So argued Dietrich Bonhoefer, a Lutheran pastor who lived through the worst excesses of Nazi Germany and was deeply troubled to see ordinary Germans turn against the Jews who had lived in their midst for centuries, throwing stones at their homes and businesses, harassing and humiliating them and eventually becoming silent and unprotesting witnesses to the escalating hate pogroms against them. A founding member of the Confessing Church that resisted the Nazi government-sponsored efforts to unify all Protestant churches into a single pro-Nazi German Evangelical Church, Bonhoefer's vocal opposition to fascism eventually cost him his life; he was arrested in 1943 and executed in the Flossenbürg concentration camp in April 1945.

Being unaffected by reason, Bonhoefer argued, stupid people can be neither fought against nor argued with; in his letters from prison, he wrote, 'One may protest against evil; it can be exposed and prevented by the use of force, against stupidity we are defenseless. Neither protests nor the use of force accomplish anything here. Reasons fall on deaf ears.'

In the swirling tide of hate sweeping across New India, in the flood of scurrilous, often entirely inaccurate whatsapp messages, youtube videos and social media posts, Bonhoefer's words carry an ominous warning and a bone-chilling portend of disaster waiting to unfold.

While the scale and spread of stupidity is amplified manifold in this age of information technology and easy access to social media, stupidity masquerading as power is by no means a new phenomenon. Going by Urdu poetry, which is the mirror in which this volume of writings attempts to view the world, the poet has time and again spoken out against *jihalat* (ignorance compounded by boorishness), *himaqat* (stupidity) and *nafrat* (hate).

Altaf Husain Hali, who formed a bridge between the classical poets such as Ghalib and his predecessors and the modern poets of the 20th century, wrote:

Aalim ko hai ilm apni naadaani ka
Jahil ko nahin jahli kuchh apne khabar

The intelligent man knows of his ignorance
But the foolish man is unaware of his foolishness

A latter-day poet such as Tufail Chaturvedi warns:

Nafraton ka aks bhi padne na dena zahan par
Ye andhera jaane kitnon ka ujaala kha gaya

Don't let even the shadow of hate fall on your mind
This darkness has gobbled up the light of so many

With his tongue firmly in his cheek, Mohsin Bhopali asks:

Jahil ko agar jehl ka inaam diya jaaye
Iss hadisa-e-waqt ko kya naam diya jaaye

If the ignorant are given a prize for their ignorance
What name would you give to this accident of Time

Saghar Khayyami too resorts to humour to make a penetrating observation on the wedge that has divided society and the stupidity that lies at the heart of this hatred:

Nafraton ki jang mein dekho to kyaa kyaa kho gayaa
Sabziyaan Hindu huiin bakra Musalman ho gayaa

See what all has happened in this battle of hatred
Vegetables have become Hindu and the goat Muslim

But who is to blame for this escalating hatred? Mohammad Saleem Nashtar is unequivocal in saying the blame lies with both warring groups:

Khud-bakhud nahiin haael nafraton ki deevaarein
Kuchh khataa tumhaari thhi kuchh khataa hamari hai

These walls of hatred have not come up between us on their own
Some part of the fault was yours and some part is mine too

When the goblet of tyranny and hatred spills over, the poet has cautioned and counseled as in this sher by Muzaffar Razmi:

Yeh jabr bhi dekha hai tariḳh ki nazron ne
Lamhon ne ḳhata kii thhii sadiyon ne saza paaii

The eyes of History have witnessed this coercion
Centuries bore the brunt of the mistakes made by moments

As for governments, they come and go for they are elected by the people. Nida Fazli points to the transience that is at the heart of any elected government no matter how popular. Governments can be changed but what about the people themselves?

Hukuumaton ko badalnaa to kuchh muhaal nahiin
Hukuumatein jo badaltaa hai woh samaaj bhii ho

It isn't impossible to change governments
As long as there is a society that changes governments

To return to Bonhoeffer who said: 'The ultimate test of a moral society is the kind of world that it leaves to its children.' That is the question that troubles me the most: What kind of world are we leaving for our children? A better, or worse one, than the one we inherited? A divided one, or a united one? A monochromatic one, or a pluralistic colourful one? For as Sarshar Sailani said:

Chaman mein ikhtilat-e rang-o bu se baat ban ti hai
Hum hii hum hain to kya hum hain tum hii tum ho to kya tum ho

It is the intermingling of colours and fragrances that make a garden
If there's only us there can be no us and there can be no you if there's only you

So why not take heart from this sher by Bashir Badr as we set foot in a New India:

Naye daur ke naye khwaab hain naye mausamon ke gulaab hain
Ye mohabbaton ke charaagh hain inhein nafraton ki hawaa na de

These are new dreams of a new age, new roses of a new season
These are lamps of love, don't stir them with the breeze of hatred

And to those who insist on fanning the fires of hatred, here is this gem by Sahir Ludhianvi:

Nafraton ke jahaan mein hum ko pyaar ki bastiyaan basaanii hain
Duur rahnaa koi kamaal nahiin paas aao to koi baat baney

In this world of hatred we have to set up habitations of love
Staying away is no big deal, coming closer is the real thing

Party considerations aside, perhaps there is something to be said for setting up a *mohabbat ki dukaan* (a shop of love) in bazaar of hate (*nafrat ka bazaar*) where the only currency is abhorrence, detestation, loathing and fear.

4. Electoral Politics and the Bugbear of Democracy

❧

With campaigning for the 2024 Lok Sabha elections reaching a particularly brutish crescendo and elections in general coming to mean far more than simply the exercise of individual franchise in a democratic system, it might be useful to see how the creative writer and poet, especially in Urdu, has interpreted and analysed the electoral process.

Plato had wanted poets banished from his republic because they could make lies seem like truth. PB Shelley, on the other hand, thought poets were the 'unacknowledged legislators of the world'. In the light of such pronouncements, let us see how our Urdu poets have viewed our political scenario, especially people's power to vote.

Akbar Allahabadi, a trenchant critic of 'modernism', takes a jibe at the fledgling electoral systems being installed within a larger colonial enterprise, alluding here to the first-ever general elections held in British India in 1920 to elect members to the Imperial Legislative Council and the Provincial Councils, in this somewhat tart observation:

Scheme ka jhoolna woh jhooley
Lekin yeh kyun apni raah bhooley
Qaum ke dil mein khot hai paida
Achhey achchey hain vote ke shauda

Let others swing on the swing of the 'Scheme'
But why have they strayed from the beaten path
A flaw has entered the heart of the people
The best among them are enamoured by the vote

Akbar's younger contemporary, Zareef Lakhnavi, is similarly dubious about the 'benefits' of municipality elections in a satirical poem called 'Shaamat-e-Election' (The Calamity of Elections). In its engaging portrayal of an elitist man crossing the hitherto impenetrable socio-economic barrier in search of votes, the poem can be seen as an early portrayal of social engineering that India would witness in the decades after Independence. It talks of the 'high' going to the 'low' begging for votes, of asking for votes in the name of being co-religionists among a litany of other woes concluding with the rueful question:

Iss tarah ke voter aur member hon jab iss qism ke
Kahiye iss municipality se kisey rahat mile

If the voters are such and the members are like this
What relief can such a municipality expect?

One of the earliest commentators on the socio-political scenario in Pakistan, the India-born satirist Dilawar Figar takes a jibe at female representation:

Apiya jo ab ke qaumi election mein hain khadi
Mardon ki rahnumai karega zamana kyaa!

Now that Big Sis is standing for the elections
How will the world show the way for men!

Taking a cue from Ghalib's famous line, *Ik Brahaman ne kaha hai ke ye saal achcha hai* ('A brahmin has predicted that this will be a good year'), our very own humourist Popular Meeruthi is predicting:

Meri qismat ka sitara hai chamakne wala
Mere baare mein ye voter ka ḳhayal achchha hai
Iss bharose pe election mein khada huun main bhi
Ik nujumi ne kaha hai ki ye saal achchha hai

The star of good fortune is about to shine brightly
It's a good thing that the voter thinks well of me
And with that good faith I too am standing for election
An astrologer has said this will be a good year for me

And elsewhere, hinting at the menace that lies beneath the veneer of democracy with political leaders relying upon the services of specially-hired thugs, he writes:

Ek leader se kaha ye main ne kal ai 'Papular'
Tu election mein agar haara to kya rah jaaega
Apne ġhundon ki taraf dekha aur uss ne yuun kaha
Jis diye mein jaan hogi woh diya rah jaaega

I said to a leader yesterday, O Popular
What'll happen if you lose in the election
He looked at his hired goons and said
The lamp that has life will remain lit

With his tongue firmly in his cheek, Nashtar Amrohvi is declaring:

Nahin parva ki leader kaun achchha kaun ganda hai
Siyasat meri rozi hai election mera dhanda hai

I don't care which leader is good or which is bad
Politics is my profession and election my trade

On the money spent on electioneering by individual candidates, here is Arshad Mir's woeful lament:

Election ab bhala kaise ladenge hum raqibon se
Kamai to uda daali hai saari ishtiharon par

How will I fight the elections with my rivals
I have spent all my earnings on advertisements

In a short poem entitled 'Makhmasa' (meaning 'puzzle' or 'riddle'), a contemporary poet Inayat Ali Khan is asking where does one go when an election means choosing between a rock and a hard place:

Pahunch gaye hain election ke phir dvaare par
Tumhi batao mire bhai kis taraf jaaen
Idhar miyan hai udhar maai kis taraf jaaen
Idhar kuaan hai udhar khaai kis taraf jaaen

We have again reached the doorway of elections
You tell me, my brother; where should we go
A husband here, a mother there; where should we go
A well here and a cliff there; where should we go

In a poem entitled 'Wasiyyat' (Will), Kaifi Azmi is asking his son to give his heart, his eyes, even his *khuddari* (self-respect) after he dies but never, never give his vote to 'them', meaning the dark forces that are tearing away at society:

Jo woh phailaain daaman ye wasiyyat yaad kar lena
Unhein har cheez de dena par un ko vote mat dena

If they beg you remember this Will of mine
Give them everything, but do not give them your vote

The poet and film-maker, Gulzar, who had made the film *Mere Apne* (1971) about gang-warfare and political campaigning that exploits unemployed youth, writes this haiku-like piece on post-election horse-trading and the scenes witnessed in some state assembly elections using the analogy of rogue roosters and hapless hens:

Badey mustande murghe thhe gali ke
Bacha ke rakhna mushkil ho gaya thha murghiyon ko

Kabhi sab tokri mein rakh ke ooper eent rakh detey
To charrh ke eenton par woh bang detey thhey
Unhein darbon mein band kartey
To darwaazon pe dastak aaney lagti thhi
Bason mein bhar ke le jaate hain ab
Unhein ab hotalon mein band rakhtey hain

Koi 'ego' nahin inn murghiyon ki
Faqat voting mein aa kar andey detii hain!

The roosters in the alley had become such rogues
It was becoming difficult to keep the hens safe

When the hens would be put under baskets with a brick on top
They would climb atop the bricks and crow
When the hens would be put in coops
They would begin to peck at the door
Now they are taken away in buses
And kept locked up in hotels

These hens have no 'ego'
They only come during voting to lay eggs

The poet from the Jamia Millia Islamia neighbourhood who adopted the university's name as his nom de plume, Asrar Jamayee who passed away in 2020, penned 'Leader ki Dua', a spoof on Sir Muhammad Iqbal's famous poem 'Dua' (Prayer); except that this prayer is not addressed to the Lord but to Iblis (Satan):

Paida dil-e-votar mein woh shorish-e-mahshar kar
Jo josh-e-election mein danka mira bajva de

Create such a fear of Doomsday in the voters' heart
That it may beat my drum in the frenzy of election

Asra Rizvi, a modern young poet, draws our attention to the arrogance and appropriation of political power that is far more sinister than the pomp and splendour of election rallies, the flower-bedecked stages, the loudspeakers and bombastic speeches filled with high rhetoric and empty promises:

EVM bhi mera hai
Sab neta nagri meri hai
Ab koi nahin kuchh bolega
Aur koi nahin munh kholega

The EVM too is mine
The city and all its leaders are mine
No one shall say anything now
No one shall open their mouth

A long satirical poem directed specifically at elections entitled 'Main Nashe Mein Hoon' (I'm Intoxicated) by Syed Mohamad Jafri (who migrated to Karachi from Bharatpur, India but what he has to say about elections in Pakistan could well be true of us in India) takes a sharp penetrating look at the state of the nation, rocked as it is by protests, empty sloganeering, false promises and processions where nothing is free, not even fame that can bring in votes (*shohrat to muft vote dilati nahin hai kuchh*):

Iss qaum ki falah hai jaam-o-subu ke beech
Tum intiḳhab ja ke lado hav-hu ke beech
Dushnam aur balvon ke aur du-ba-du ke beech
Jaise ki koi baitha ho bazm-e-adu ke beech

The welfare of this nation lies betwixt the glass and jug
While you go and fight your elections amidst hue and cry
Between abuse and riots and confrontations and tete-a-tetes
Like someone sitting in an Assembly of Rivals

In yet another poem, titled 'Election', the same Jafri paints a picture that has become all too familiar: a state and society in the throes of elections, of leaders behaving like wrestlers in a wrestling pit, of scuffles breaking out among rivals during processions, when grand sales are announced at shops selling votes (*voton ki har dukan pe hogi grand sale),* when only those people matter whose names exist in electoral rolls (*zinda hai woh ki jis ka register mein naam hai*):

Saaqi sharab de ke election hai aaj-kal
Barseinge vote jis mein woh saavan hai aaj-kal
Jamhuriyat ke paanv mein jhaanjan hai aaj-kal
Ye mulk uss ke naach ka aangan hai aaj-kal

Pour me some wine for it's the time of election these days
It's the season of rains when votes will shower these days
There's a tinkling anklet on the feet of democracy these days
This country has become a courtyard for its dance these days

And:

Hasil karenge laakh tariqon se vote ko
Paani hii ki tarah se bahaenge note ko

We will gain the votes though lakhs of different ways
We will pour wads of money like flowing water

In a New India when the air is rent with talk of 'Tukde-Tukde Gang' and cries of '*Jab Mulle kaate jaayenge*' or '*Goli maro salon ko*', jibes of votes-for-cash and empty sloganeering seem benign, almost genteel. Only time will tell what the poetry of tomorrow will depict.

5. *Pandrah Agust*: The Dawn of Freedom

Any talk of 15 August invariably takes us back to that muggy monsoon day over seven decades ago when a nation came into being after a long and bloody partition. The events of 1947 were witnessed by some of the finest writers who saw and commented on what they had experienced, in many cases, at first hand. For many, those experiences coloured what they wrote. For the progressive poets and writers in Urdu, especially those who were members of the Communist Party, partition and the freedom that came in its wake was a 'false freedom'. Taking the Party's line, many poets spoke of the sense of inadequacy, the squandering of dreams that the dawn of freedom ushered in. By far the most famous, and most quoted, comment on the partition is contained in 'Subah-e Azaadi' (Dawn of Independence) by Faiz Ahmad Faiz:

Yeh daagh daagh ujala yeh shab-gazida sehr
Woh intezar thha jiska yeh woh sehr to nahi

This patchy light, this night-bitten dawn
This is not the dawn we had been waiting for

There was a great deal of questioning among poets, writers and thinkers about what was, still, for many the bitter fruit that had ripened on the vine of partition. For instance, here is Akhtarul Iman voicing the disquiet and despair of an entire generation in his 'Pandrah Agust' (15 August):

Yahi din hai jiske liye maine kati thhi inn ankhon mein raatein
Yahi seeli aab-e-baqa, chasma-e-noor hai, jalwa-e-toor hai?
Issi ke liye woh suhane, madhur, rasbhare geet gaye they maine?
Was it for this day that I had spent so many sleepless nights
For this damp water of eternity, this stream of light, this mountain of miracles
Was it for this I had sung all those sweet, melodious songs?

With time, however, the poet and the writer began to take note of the immense possibilities of social transformation that freedom from colonial yoke allowed a new nation finding its feet and taking the first steps towards a post-colonial modernity. Even those who clung to the progressive fold increasingly found little reason not to join Jawaharlal Nehru's rousing call to join the nation-building project. When the Prime Minister talked of building the new 'temples' of India—namely, the schools, colleges, dams, factories—the poets and writers responded with full-throated abandon. The film lyricists, in particular, helped in spreading the idea of independence and the possibilities it offered. The IPTA (Indian Peoples' Theatre Association) poet Prem Dhawan wrote:

Chhorho kal ki baatein, kal ki baat puranii
Naye daur mein likheinge hum milkar nayi kahani,
Hum Hindustani, Hum Hindustani...

Forget about yesterday, yesterday is old news
Let us together write a new story in this new age
We are Indians, we are Indians...

Even after Nehru's death, the vestiges of a buoyant, optimistic Nehruvian India, committed to secularism and social justice continued to be found. In KA Abbas's *Saat Hindustani* (1969), for instance, we see the film lyricist Kaifi Azmi exhorting his fellow countrymen and women—almost in Soviet style—to move forward and build a new and prosperous India.

Faasle sab dilon ke mitaatey chalo
Apne seene se sabko lagaatey chalo

Move forward, removing distances between hearts
Meet others, embrace them as you move forward

Firakh Gorakhpuri, the quintessential *ghazal-go* (a writer of ghazal in the classical mould), is optimistic about independence and all that it entails. Even his choice of words is indicative of a bouncing effervescence and youthfulness:

Lahu watan ke shahidon ka rang laaya hai
Uchhal raha hai zamane mein naam-e-azadi

The blood of the country's martyrs is showing results
The name of freedom is bouncing in the world

For Arsh Malsiyani, the fervour for independence and all the joys it brings remains unadulterated in this nazm entitled '15 Agust' written in 1949. The poet speaks of the much-awaited day of independence and how everyone should come together amidst cries of 'Jai Hind' but he is also ruing how the spirit of service has become listless:

Jab ḳhurshid-e-azadi ki phooti thhi kiran woh din aaya
Jab qaid-e-qafas se chhute thhe murġhan-e-chaman woh din aaya

The day has come when the rays of the sun of freedom burst forth
The day has come when the birds of the garden were released from cages

Nazeer Banarsi, who wrote several nationalistic poems and was extremely popular in his day, also wrote a poem entitled '15 Agust', using imagery culled from pastoral and romantic poetry. Here he is speaking with unabashed hope and optimism of drawing courage for new directions:

Ghata hai ghanghor raat kaali faza mein bijli chamak rahi hai
Milan ka siina ubhaar par hai birah ki chhati dhadak rahi hai
Hawa jo masti mein chuur ho kar qadam qadam par bahak rahi hai
Kamar hai har shaḳh-e-gul ki nazuk thahar thahar kar lachak rahi hai

The clouds are dense the night is dark and lightning streaks the air
The breast of union is rising and the bosom of separation heaving
At every step the mad, intoxicated wind is losing its way
The delicate bough of every flower-laden branch is bending

In recent times, the most definitive poem on 15 August can be said to be the one penned by Javed Akhtar and recited on 15 August 2007 at the very place in the Parliament from where Jawahar Lal Nehru declared India's independence from the British Empire on 15 August 1947. Also entitled 'Pandrah Agust', it stresses the historical importance of that very spot from where the centuries-old black night was defeated. It also reminds us of how we, as a nation, had vowed to heal the wounds on our collective psyche. All the oppressed who were 'without a tongue', have found a tongue in the decades since that day; today, they ask questions and demand answers. While much has been achieved, a lot still remains to be done as Javed Akhtar says in this lyrical, joyful yet cautioning poem:

Hai waada ḳhud se nibhana hamein agar apna
To karvaan nahin ruk paae bhuul kar apna
Hai thodi duur abhi sapnon ka nagar apna
Musafiron abhi baaqi hai kuchh safar apna

If we are to be true to the promise we made ourselves
Then our caravan must not ever stop even by mistake
Our city of dreams is still a little afar
O travelers, the journey still remains

Perhaps the best way to celebrate 15 August each year would be, as this poem shows us, to bear in mind that independence is a goal not a destination; it is always a journey towards a greater good.

6. The Migrant Workers' Exodus and the Idea of Home

A goods train trundled past a railway track early one morning in Maharashtra during the peak of the corona pandemic killing 16 men.* Many, on social media, reacted with shock and wonder: But why were they sleeping on the tracks? Why not beside the track or anywhere else? This, to my mind, encapsulates the distance between those who have homes, beds and a roof over their head and those who don't, those who can wonder and pontificate from the safe confines of a home over the compulsions of those who set out on long journeys home when work dries up virtually overnight in cities and they undertake these perilous journeys because the cities have suddenly become hostile and alien to them and going back home is imperative, no matter what the cost. During the terrible weeks of the summer of 2020, thousands of men, women and children undertook the long walk home in the sweltering Indian summer carrying nothing with them save the 'idea' of a home that they had left behind in their villages.

---

*https://timesofindia.indiatimes.com/city/aurangabad/maharashtra-train-runs-over-a-dozen-migrant-workers-in-aurangabad/articleshow/75614987.cms

The exodus of migrant workers triggered memories of other mass migrations of human populations over the years brought about by Acts of God such as drought, famine, floods or man-made disasters such as, most notably, the Partition of 1947 or other more localised communal outrages and riots such as the exodus of Kashmiri Pandits from the Valley. But the spontaneous, unplanned mass migration of migrant workers during the COVID-19 pandemic stands out from all others. It was fuelled by a host of socio-economic factors such as loss of livelihood, inability to pay rentals or buy food or maintain social distancing and observe basic hygiene by those who are the most disenfranchised and marginalised. That they are vital in keeping the very same socio-economic machinery propped up and working that discarded them at the time of peril is both ironic and tragic.

This blithe disregard for workers is grotesque and inhuman, and far more tragic than the casualties of the corona virus. It is also new. There was a time when poets sang rousing songs about workers' rights, films eulogised their labour and skill, writers—especially those affiliated with the influential literary grouping known as the Progressive Writers' Association—wrote stories about mill workers and labourers and popular culture was aware and sensitive to the 'working class'. When and how did we change? When did the worker and labourer leach out of our creative imagination? When did we yoke the word 'migrant' to the 'worker' thus robbing them of the dignity of a home and a life in our midst in our cities? When did we de-legitimise their very existence, forcing them to flee?

That it wasn't always so is borne out by the vast amount of poetry, especially in Urdu, celebrating the worker and the farmer. It is true that much of it is hagiographical and eulogistic painting the worker in impossibly glowing colours and making him a veritable hero or an angel such as this sher by Munawwar Rana:

Farishte aa kar un ke jism par ḳhushbu lagaate hain
Woh bachche rail ke dibbon mein jo jhadu lagaate hain

The angels come to dab fragrance on the bodies
Of those children who sweep the floor of trains

Or, pitted in a binary with the capitalist who is wicked and clever, the worker is invariably simple and innocent as in this verse by Muhammad Iqbal from his poem 'Khizr-e Rah' (The One Who Shows the Way):

Makr ki chaalon se baazi le gayaa sarmaaya-daar
Intihaa-e-saadgii se khaa gayaa mazdoor maat

The capitalist wins the game with his wily tricks
The labourer loses due to his extreme innocence

And the same Iqbal, addressing God, also wrote:

Tu qaadir-o aadil hai magar tere jahan mein
Hain talḳh bahut banda-e-mazdoor ke auqat

Yes, You are Powerful and Just but in Your world
The state of the labourers and workers is bitter indeed

The idea that the workers live relatively simple lives compared to the complicated lives of others better endowed than them is also a recurring motif in a great deal of Urdu poetry that romanticises the life of the labourer, such as this by Munawwar Rana again:

So jaate hain footpath pe aḳhbaar bichha kar
Mazdoor kabhi neend ki goli nahin khaate

They sleep on the footpath on a newspaper
The labourers never need a sleeping pill

During the 'high noon' of the Progressive wave that rippled though Urdu poetry, there were many poets who dreamt of a 'red tide' that would wash over all ills and oppressions, removing injustices and inequalities when the red flag would herald a new morning, a 'red morning' (*surkh savera*) such as this by Ali Sardar Jafri:

Phootne wali hai mazdoor ke maathe se kiran
Surḳh parcham ufuq-e-subh pe lahraate hain

A beam of light shall burst forth from the worker's forehead
Red Flags are billowing in the horizon of the morning

Others such as Firaq Gorakhpuri thought independence would bring in a new morning for the working classes:

Banaaenge nai duniyaa kisan aur mazdoor
Yahin sajaaenge diwan-e-aam-e-aazaadi

The workers and farmers will create a new world
Together they will decorate the free Hall of Public

Possibly no one has captured the sheer helplessness of the workers fleeing the cities that Gulzar, the bard of our times, has in two searing poems written in real time as the tragedy was unfolding before us in two poems entitled 'Migrants: COVID-19', Part I and Part II, the second bearing the subtitle 'Batwara' (Partition):

Mahamaari lagi thhi
Gharon ko bhaag liye thhe
Sabhi mazdoor karigar
Mashine band hone lag gayiin thhin sheher ki saari
Unhiin se haath paaon chalte rahte thhe
Wagarna zindagi to gaon hii mein bo ke aaye thhe

Woh aur do acre zameen ya paanch acre
Kataayi aur bowaii sab wahiin to thhi
Jawaari, dhaan, makki, baajri—sab
Woh batwaare chachere aur mamere bhaiyon se

Fasaad naale par, parnalon pe jhagde
Lathait apne, kabhi unke
Woh nani, dadi aur dadu ke muqadme
Sagaii, shaadiyaan, khalihaan
Sookha, baadh, har baar aasmaan barse na barse
Mareinge to wahiin jaa kar jahan par zindagi hai
Yahan to jism laa kar plug lagaye thhe

Nikaale plug sabhi ne
Chalo ab ghar chalein ab—aur chal diye sub
Mareinge to wahiin jaa kar jahaan par zindagi hai

The pandemic raged
The workers and labourers fled to their homes
All the machines ground to a halt in the cities
Their hands and feet moved with the machines
For, they had planted their lives back in the villages

That acre or two of land, or perhaps five acres
The sowing and the harvesting were all back there
Jowar, wheat, corn, bajra—all of it
Those divisions with the cousins and brothers
Those fights at the canals and waterways
The strongmen, hired sometimes from their side and
sometimes from this
The lawsuits dating back to grandparents and grand uncles
Engagements, marriages, fields
Famine, flood, fear: will the skies rain or not?
They will go to die there—where there is life
Here, they have only brought their bodies and plugged
them in!

They pulled out the plugs
'Come, let's go home'—and they set off
They will go to die there—where there is life!

And 'Migration, Covid-19—II, Batwara':

Kuchh aise karvaan dekhe hain saintalees mein bhi maine
Ye gaon bhag rahey hain apne watan mein
Hum apne gaon se bhaagey thhe jab nikle thhe watan ko

Hamein sharnarthi kah ke watan ne rakh liya thha
Sharan dii thhii

Inhein inki riyasat ki hadon pe roke dete hain
Sharan denein mein khatra hai

Hamaare aagey peechhe tab bhi eik qaatil azal thhi
Woh mazhab poochhtii thhi

Hamaare aagey peechhe ab bhi eik qatil azal hai
Na mazhab, naam, jaat, kuchh poochhti hai

Maar deti hai!

Khuda jaane ye batwara barha hai
Ya woh batwara barha thha

I had seen similar caravans in '47 too

They are fleeing to their villages in their own country
We had fled from our village setting out for our country

Calling us refugees, our county had kept us
Given us refuge

They are stopped at the borders of their states
There is danger in giving them refuge

Then, too, there was a murderous Death around us
It asked us our religion

Now, too, there is a murderous Death around us
But it doesn't ask us our religion or caste or name

It simply kills!

God knows if this Partition is great
Or that one was greater

In the years ahead, images of the hopeless, hungry, tired men and women carrying the old and the infirm as well as the very young, exhaustion and despair writ large on their faces, robbed of dignity and pride during the worst days of the migrant exodus will haunt us as we claim our place in the comity of nations.

7. *Har Dil Tiranga*: The Tricolour in Every Heart

The Har Ghar Tiranga campaign aspires to bring the National Flag, literally, into every Indian home. But the *tiranga* has seldom been absent from our thoughts; if anything, love for the *tiranga* has been hiding in plain sight in a great deal of Indian poetry, specifically Urdu poetry. Virtually from the day it was first hoisted, the poet has written paeans in its praise, invoking the sacrifices of countless Indian men and women that made possible its first unfurling in Free India, embodying the hopes and aspirations of a fledgling nation. Among the most often used adjectives to describe its *dhaj*, a word that defies easy translation and goes way beyond the English equivalent for 'appearance', are *shaan* (splendour or style), *nirala* (unique), *azmat* (glory) making the *tiranga* a veritable embodiment of peace and harmony (*amn-o-aman ka paikar*), a lasting symbol of freedom (*azaadi ki nishani*) and a symbol of national identity (*Bhaarat ki pehchaan*).

Shamim Karhani, who wrote many a qaumi geet (nationalistic song) in the early years of independence, also penned a beautiful poem on the *tiranga*, likening the saffron in it to the colour of ripe mangoes, the white to the pristine snows on the Himalayas and the green to the tender saplings growing in the fields of rural India:

Jan-baazon ke paak lahu ki yaad dilane wali
Jangal ki aankhon ki surat sabz hai teri dhari
Jaise dhaan ki pahli konpal sundar komal pyari
Aur Ashoka chakr mein amn-o-rahat ka ujyala

Reminding us of the pure blood of the bravehearts
The green border is like the green eyes of the forests
And as lovely as the first green shoots of tender paddy
With the Ashoka Chakra embodying the light of peace

Vaqar Khaleel, the poet from Hyderabad in a long poem on the tricolour, says such indeed is its majesty that even the mighty Himalaya bows its head before it (*uncha jo hai Himala woh bhi to sar jhukaya*):

Amn-o-aman ki rangat veeron ke ḳhoon ki laali
Iss mein jhalak rahi hai mazdoor ki bahali

The colours of peace, the red of the martyrs' blood
Reflects here and the better days awaiting the workers

Saadat Nazeer writes:

Sachchai aur dharam ka mazhar
Chaand sitaare sadqe tujh par

A testament of Truth and Righteousness
The moon and stars offer themselves as sacrifice to you

Others have written of the fluttering tricolour that fills the air with peace, harmony and goodwill, the frisson of deeply-felt emotions that are excited upon spotting it. For Masooda Hayat, the flag embodies what it means to be an Indian:

Jhanda hii tauqeer-e-watan hai
Jhanda hii tasweer-e-watan hai
Jhanda hii taqdeer-e-watan hai

The flag is the honour of the nation
The flag is the portrait of the nation
The flag is the destiny of the nation

Many poets have written nationalistic poems especially for children; of these Shafiuddin Nayyar has written some of the sweetest, such as *Jhanda uncha rahe hamara,* which uses words a mother might for her child so brimful it is with a pure, unadulterated love while also stressing that that the tricolour belongs to ALL Indians and not a chosen few:

Sab se achchha sab se nyara
Rang tiranga pyara pyara
Qaum ki ummidon ka sahara
Des dulara jag ujyara
Dil ki thandak aankh ka taara...

Des disa dikhlane wala
Hosh mein hum ko laane wala
Josh se dil garmane wala
Khidmat par uksane wala
Qaum ki nayya khaivan hara...

Jab jhanda lahraega yeh
Man ki jot jagaega yeh
Apnaiyat phailaega yeh
Preet ki reet sikhaega yeh
Prem ka sagar prem ki dhara

The loveliest and fairest of all
The dearly beloved tricolour
This prop for the nation's hopes

The nation's darling, beacon for the world
Gives comfort to the heart, this light of our eyes

It gives direction to the country
It brings us back to our senses
It warms our heart with passion
It rouses us to service and duty
It is the rower of the nation's boat

When this flag flutters in the wind
It lights the lamp of our heart
It spreads a sense of belonging
It will teach us the habit of loving
For it's an ocean of love, a stream of love

Postscript: I am no poet and can, at best, rely on simple words to relay real, first-hand, truly-felt emotions. I have never felt prouder to be an Indian nor closer to tears upon sighting the Indian flag than I did while performing the Haj in 2012. As a Guest of Allah—one of over 3 billion people who come to the Baitullah, the Holiest of Homes for the annual Haj—the entire experience was a humbling one. To be a tiny speck in the vast ocean of humanity from the far-flung corners of the Muslim world is an over-whelming feeling and yet in the midst of it all I could feel my heart swell with pride upon spotting the Indian tricolour fluttering tall and majestic at the camps for Indian Hajis at Mina and Arafat. That rush of emotions at the sight of the *tiranga*, thousands of kilometres away from home and country, remains among my most cherished memories.

8. The Male Gaze: How Men See Women

While it can be argued that the 'beloved' is a bit of a conundrum in Urdu poetry, for it can refer to not just the lay or the divine lover but, equally, it can refer to a man, woman or child. However, when it comes to the 'woman', there is no ambiguity. She appears in all her resplendent glory, her manifold beauty, her many guises: temptress, seductress, tease, beguiler, goddess, teacher, mother, daughter, and yes occasionally, companion and fellow traveler. Sometimes, the 'she' in a seemingly romantic ghazal, especially of the Old Masters, might appear to be about a woman whereas couched in the vocabulary of the ghazal (the ghazal itself being an amatory ode meaning 'talking to women'), it could be about *tasawwuf*, or mysticism where the 'beloved' is God.

The woman has been both subject and predicate in a great deal of writing by male writers. In Urdu poetry she has, of course, been the subject of vast amounts of romantic, even sensuous imagery. Be it muse or mother, vamp or victim, fulsome or flawed, there has been a tendency among male writers to view a woman through a binary of 'this' or 'that' and to present women as black and white characters, often either impossibly white or improbably black. Since men are not expected to be one or the other but generally taken to be a combination of contraries, such a monochromatic view inevitably results in women being reduced to objects, of being taken to be 'things' rather than 'people'. That this objectification of women, and the consequent dehumanisation, effectively 'others' half the human population seems to escape many writers, even those ostensibly desirous of breaking stereotypes or those who see themselves as liberal, even emancipated men. Films, television and media have traditionally aided and abetted the idea that women are objects to be pursued and eventually won over like trophies or prizes. Literature has fed into the trope that women are bona fide objects of sexual fantasy, or blank canvases on which men can paint their ideals, or even empty vessels into which they can pour their pent-up feelings and emotions.

Feminist theoreticians would have us believe that there is, and always has been, a traditional heterosexual way of men looking at women, a way that presents women as essentially sexual objects for the pleasure of the male viewer. The feminist film critic Laura Mulvey in her seminal essay 'Visual Pleasure and Narrative Cinema', written in 1975, termed this way of seeing as the 'male gaze'. Mulvey's theory was based on the premise that 'an asymmetry of power between the genders is a controlling force in cinema; and that the male gaze is constructed for the pleasure of the male viewer which is deeply rooted in the ideologies and discourses of patriarchy'. Within a short span of time, the expression slipped into accepted usage and moved seamlessly across medium: from film to literature to popular culture. Today, we use the term loosely to describe ways of men seeing women and consequently presenting or representing them.

Coming to Urdu poetry, let us begin with Altaf Husain Hali who, at the turn of the 20th century, formed a bridge between the traditionalists and the modern poets and who, for all his hortatory zeal, was exhorting fellow-men to see women as prized possessions and repositories of grace:

Tum ghar ki ho shehzadiyan mulkon ki ho abadiyan
Veeraan dilon ki shaadiyaan
Eimaan salamat tumse hai
Ai maaon, behnon, betiyon, duniya ki zeenat tumse hai

You are princesses of our homes, prosperity of nations
The harbringer of happiness to desolate hearts
Our faith is intact because of you
O mothers, sisters daughters you are the grace of the world

Allama Iqbal, too, presented a somewhat similarly flattering though 'flat' representation of women:

Wajud-e-zan se hai tasvir-e-kainat mein rang
Isi ke saaz se hai zindagi ka soz-e-darun

The existence of women fills the world with colours
She is the instrument that creates the innermost songs

Coming to the progressives and their well-known penchant for offering support and solidarity to women, here is Kaifi Azmi in a long poem entitled 'Aurat' (Woman) exhorting the woman to rise up and throw away the shackles of modesty and tradition, discard false notions of shame and elegance that have kept her a willing captive and walk beside the man, as a comrade-in-arms, as a friend and fellow-traveler:

Utth meri jaan mere saath hi chalna hai tujhe

Arise, my love, you have to walk beside me

In much the same vein, Ali Sardar Jafri is discarding the age-old notions of romance symbolized by Laila-Majnu, Shirin-Farhad and scores of others from history and mythology when he holds up the example set by himself and his partner Sultana:

Har aashiq hai Sardar yahaan, har mashooqa Sultana hai

Every lover here is a Sardar, every beloved a Sultana

Then there is Sahir Ludhianvi, raised by a divorced mother, acutely aware of the inequities faced by women and one of the most vocal advocates of women's equality who has written a great deal on women, the suffering they have faced at the hands of men as in this sher:

Aurat ne janam diya mardon ko mardon ne usey bazaar diya
Jab jii chaha masla kuchla jab jii chaha dhutkaar diya

Woman gave birth to men while men gave her the bazaar
They crushed and trampled her or rebuked her at their will

In an early take on modernity, Majaz is asking:

Bataoon kya tujhe ai hum-nashin kis se mohabbat hai
Main jis duniya mein rahta huun woh iss duniya ki aurat hai

What shall I tell you, my friend, of her whom I love
She is a woman of that very world in which I live

Here's Shakeel Jamali taking a seemingly benign view that is more than likely to rile a modern-day feminist:

Abhi raushan hua jaata hai rasta
Woh dekho aurat aa rahi hai

The road is about to be illuminated
Look, a woman is coming this way

Munawwar Rana's penchant for writing poems about the mother continues with this sher:

Chalti phirti hui aankhon se azaan dekhi hai
Main ne jannat to nahin dekhi hai maa dekhi hai

With my own eyes I have seen the call to prayer
I have not seen heaven but I have seen a mother

To conclude, let me rest my case with these words by Milan Kundera in *The Book of Laughter and Forgetting*:

> The male glance has often been described. It is commonly said to rest coldly on a woman, measuring, weighing, evaluating, selecting her—in other words, turning her into an object…What is less commonly known is that a woman is not completely defenseless against that glance. If it turns her into an object, then she looks back at the man with the eyes of an object. It is as though a hammer had suddenly grown eyes and stared up at the worker pounding a nail with it. When the worker sees the evil eye of the hammer, he loses his self-assurance and slams it on his thumb. The worker may be the hammer's master, but the hammer still prevails. A tool knows exactly how it is meant to be handled, while the user of the tool can only have an approximate idea.

While a woman is certainly no tool, nor should she know how to be 'handled', there is something to be said for returning the gaze, of looking back. Perhaps if more women were to turn a steady gaze back at the beholder, there is no knowing what the seeing eye will see.

9. *Lal Salaam*: The 'Red' Influence in Urdu Poetry

By the early-20th century, the impact of socialist thinking was not instantly widespread, though the theme of exploitation—both by the colonial government and its collaborators—had begun to figure quite largely in Urdu prose and poetry. It was not till the October 1917 revolution that the floodgates of socialism and communistic ideas opened into India finding their way into vernacular literatures and a home, ready and waiting, especially in Urdu.

The Russian Revolution opened a window to the future. It triggered new debates on state and society. Some of these debates found expression in the establishment of the Communist Party of India (CPI) in 1925, which, in turn, provided a fertile ground for Left-leaning writers to gain a stronghold and eventually led to the formation of the Progressive Writers' Movement (PWM) a decade later. However, there were existing liberal and enlightened trends in Urdu literature prior to the formation of the Progressive Writers Association (PWA); the PWA was, if anything, a logical extension of what was already being debated from social platforms and also increasingly, being written about by Urdu writers.

Saadat Hasan Manto wrote an entire play entitled 'Karl Marx' and several Urdu poets wrote poems entirely devoted to him. Here is Wamiq Jaunpuri writing a paean in praise of Karl Marx:

Marx ke ilm-o-fatanat ka nahin koi jawaab
Kaun uss ke dark se hotaa nahin hai faiz-yaab

There is no match to the knowledge and wisdom of Marx
Who has not benefitted from his proficiency and understanding

The first Urdu translation of the *Communist Manifesto* had been serialised in Maulana Abul Kalam Azad's widely-read weekly newspaper *Al-Hilal* by 1927; the translation was done by Maulana Adur Razzaq Malihabadi (1889-1959). Musheer Kidwai, the *taluqdar* of Gadia in Barabanki district, influenced by the rising tide of socialism in the west, wrote a pamphlet called *Islam and Socialism* (London, 1913) which attempted to prove this radical connection through references from the Holy Quran and the Hadith. Many other scholars and theologians subsequently attempted to prove the link between socialism and Islamic tenets; they did so by stressing that while the Prophet's socialism was 'ethical', the modern breed of socialists were 'materialists' who attacked capitalism but espoused agnosticism.

'One of the great paradoxes of the history of Islam in the twentieth century,' according to Humayun Ansari in his seminal work, *Pan-Islamism and the Making of the Early Indian Muslim Socialist*, 'is that many of the first Muslim socialists were men who at earlier stages in their lives had been devout Muslims, often passionately involved with the fate of Islam throughout the world.' Why should this be considered a paradox? Is Islam so antithetical to the notion of socialism? Are a Muslim and a socialist a contradiction in terms? Not really. After all, both Islam and socialism preach equality and brotherhood and advocate an egalitarian society. The best example to illustrate this point is the remarkable and varied career of a man like Hasrat Mohani. A romantic poet in the classic ghazal tradition (remembered today for his sweetly sentimental *Chupke chupke raat din aansu bahana yaad hai* immortalised by Ghulam Ali), journalist, politician, parliamentarian and freedom fighter, Hasrat Mohani was impressed by the Russian revolution and carried its imprint on all his later writings. It was Hasrat Mohani who used the slogan 'Inquilab Zindabad' as a rallying cry at a trade union rally in Calcutta in 1925. A practicing Muslim his entire life, he liked to call himself an *ishtraki musalman* (socialist Muslim). Having been a member of CPI, then Muslim League and finally the Congress in his political career, Hasrat asked:

Gandhi ki tarah baith ke kaateinge kyun charkha
Lenin ki tarah denge na duniya ko hila hum?

Why sit at the spinning wheel like Gandhi?
Why not shake the world up like Lenin?

Sir Muhammad Iqbal introduced modern philosophical concepts, gleaned from his study in Europe, and vastly broadened the scope of the existing intellectual discourse among educated Muslims, keeping it all the while tethered to its quintessentially religious moorings. In his passionate protests against the capitalist and imperialist forces, he propounded the message of socialism couched in Islam:

The capitalist from the blood of workers' veins makes
    himself a clear ruby;
Landlords' oppression despoils the villagers' fields:
    Revolution

And

> What is the Quran? For the capitalist, a message of death:
> It is the patron of the property less slave

As the PWM gained momentum and many known Communists came to be identified with the PWA, we begin to see a change in the tone and tenor. Overtly communist ideology is no longer hidden behind a fig leaf of socialism. We have Ali Sardar Jafri, a long-time member of the CPI, declaring Lenin as the keeper of the 'red tavern':

> *Jisne har qaum ko har mulk ko sairaab kiya*
> *Surkh maikhaane ka woh peer mughaan hai Lenin*
>
> He who nurtured every country and nation
> Lenin is the tavern-keeper of the red tavern

In response to those who were 'fearful' of communism Jafri wrote a long poem entitled 'Mere Azizon, Mere Rafiqon' (My Dears, My Friends) asking why they are afraid of the hopes and aspirations he had for all of them:

> *Meri communism kuchh nahin hai*
> *Ye ahad-e-haazir ki aabru hai miri...*
> *Meri communism zindagi ko*
> *Haseen banaane ki aarzu hai*
> *Ye eik masoom justuju hai*
>
> My communism is nothing else
> But the dignity I want for the times we live in
> My communism is a desire
> To make our world beautiful
> It is an innocent quest

In *Surkh Savera* (Red Dawn), a collection of poems published in 1944, Makhdum Mohiuddin, a known communist who was active during the Telangana agitation, is confidently asserting:

Iss zameen maut parvarda ko dhaaya jaayega
Ik nayi duniya naya Aadam banaya jaayega

This death fostering earth shall be destroyed
A new world and a new Adam shall be created

Kaifi Azmi, in a poem entitled 'Roosi Aurat Ka Naara' (The Call of the Russian Woman), is portraying the extent to which events in Soviet Russia have impacted the Indian imagination:

Jalatii hui saikdon gulistan
Chaman par mere phatt padi hay khizaan
Gira kar har eik shaakh se bijliyaan
Uttha kar har eik gul se surkh aandhiyaan
Khizaan ko chaman se nikaloongi main
Watan saaf tujhko bacha loongi main

Setting hundreds of rose gardens afire
Autumn has burst upon my garden
Flinging bolts of lightning from every branch
Raising red storms from every flower
I will drive out the autumn from my garden
I will save you surely, O country of mine

And here is Abdul Majid Zahid interpreting the message of tomes and treatises in words that the common man can understand:

Nai subh chaahte hain nai shaam chaahte hain
Jo ye roz-o-shab badal de woh nizaam chaahte hain

We want a new morning and a new evening
We want a rule that can change this day and night

Others, while not members of the CPI who were known sympathisers or fellow-travelers include: Josh Malihabadi, Akhtarul Iman, Krishan Chandar, Rajinder Singh Bedi, Sahir Ludhianvi, Jan Nisar Akhtar, Majrooh Sultanpuri, Ismat

Chughtai, among scores of others. And then there was Manto, always the contrarian. While a great deal in his vast and varied ouvre is about the 'common man', the 'small person', the most disenfranchised, Manto chose not to be identified either with PWA or with communism: '*Mujhe naam-nihaad Communiston se badi chid hai. Woh log mujhe bahut khalte hain jo narm-narm sofon par baith kar daraanti aur hathaude ke zarbon ki baatein karte hain.*' (I get very irked by so-called Communists. Those people who sit on soft sofas and speak of the blows of hammers and sickles trouble me greatly). A dying political force worldwide, communism lights up parts of the Indian political spectrum still; that speaks of its resilience and the enduring appeal of Marx's message to the toiling masses.

10. The Perils of Populism and *Hum-Sab* vs. I, Me, Myself

Every now and then one gets invited to speak at panels and discussions, at litfests and other public platforms to hold up the minority card. There was a time I would agree but increasingly now, I have come to believe that in a democracy it should not be left to the minorities to speak up for themselves for they alone can no longer hold aloft the tattered pennant of secularism; the majority *must* speak for and about the fate of the minorities. All mention of fear, silencing and marginalisation, of bullying and lynching, any criticism of the easy and almost blithe tossing about of obnoxious coinages such as 'love jihad', pointing out the nonchalant normalisation of hate crimes—can not and must not come from Muslims alone. It's time for all Indians to speak up for *'hum-sab'* rather than live in our self-made islands of 'I', 'Me', 'Myself'. What is just as important is for all Indians, and not just the much-derided 'libtards' and 'sickulars', to dig their heels in against the sweeping tide of populism and a growing sense among the average Indians who feel their concerns have been disregarded for far too long by established elite groups.

Let us see how the Urdu poet has interpreted the idea of commonality, of finding and making common cause, of speaking up for each other. First and foremost, there has been a sense of ownership of everything in this fair land that is Hindustan. Nida Fazli speaks for many when he says:

Eik hii dharti hum sab ka ghar jitna tera utna mera
Dukh sukh ka yeh jantar-mantar jitna tera utna mera

This one Earth, our home, is as much mine as yours
This observatory of joys-sorrows is as much mine as yours

The fiery activist-poet from Hyderabad, Makhdoom Mohiuddin, too, speaks for working together towards a common goal:

Hayaat le ke chalo kainaat le ke chalo
Chalo to saare zamaane ko saath le ke chalo

Take along all of life and all of the created universe
When you move forward take along the entire world

It's against this sense of being completely invested in the country, and the world, that the growing divide and 'othering'—so evident in recent times—has to be seen. The Mumbai-based Sayyed Riyaz Raheem gives voice to a quiet discontent that nags away at the heart of a section of the population:

Bahut kuchh kaam hum sab kar chuke hain
Dilon mein ghar banaanaa rah gayaa hai

We've all done much work and achieved a great deal
What's still left is to create a place in people's heart

That those whose job it was to keep us on the right path actually misguided and led us astray is voiced by some poets such as in this sher by Krishna Mohan:

Bhatak ke raah se hum sab ko aazmaa aaye
Fareb de gaye jitne bhi rahnumaa aaye

Led astray from the path we saw everyone's true worth
All the leaders who came only gave us deceptions

Though, of course written in another time and context, there's this sher by Momin Khan Momin, brimful with regret for a lost world of togetherness:

Kabhi hum mein tum mein bhi chaah thhi kabhi hum se tum se bhi raah thhi
Kabhi hum bhi tum bhi thhe aashna tumhein yaad ho ke na yaad ho

Once there was liking between us, once there were paths between us
Once you and I were friends, whether you remember it now or not

It seems worrying, to me, that we are becoming an increasingly self-referential and insular people. We seem to think we are the only functioning democracy and our public positions are peculiar to us. In any public discourse on populism, we invoke a set of totemic images drawn from, let's say, the partition, or successive elections, communal riots, Ayodhya, Mumbai, Gujarat and so on coming to recent events around cow slaughter or 'love jihad'. Perhaps we need to look outside and draw lessons from other peoples and other histories. So let me allude to two examples from recent history, both from outside India.

The first is the rather obvious case of Hitler and the rise of fascist forces that tapped into a populist sentiment in a Germany that was on its knees after the Treaty of Versailles and a people who were looking for a way to feel good about themselves after a humiliating defeat. Hitler, who didn't have a majority in the German Reichstag, went on to form a one-party dictatorship based on totalitarianism and autocracy. From vitriolic beer-hall speeches, he went on to build a certain mass appeal relying upon an oratory based on hate and opposition fuelling an existing, though not widespread, public sentiment. The outcome is too well known to be discussed in any detail. But it bears some reflection for us in India how far a popular sentiment based on hating the 'other' can go and how the silence of a majority can, eventually, be so damning for the majority themselves.

The other example I have in mind is that of Vaclav Havel, the last president of Czechoslovakia and the first president of the Czech Republic. Here's a man who was an extremely well regarded playwright, essayist, memoirist, born into a wealthy and influential family, a man who brought together politics and culture in many imaginative ways, a man who enjoyed great popularity in his own country, a man of moral authority, a public intellectual such as few politicians can aspire to be. He also had the ability to go against popular sentiment when he felt it was required.

A populism that is devoid of moral authority, if it begins to operate outside the rule of law, then yes, populism can be a threat to democracy. Let me end by quoting Vaclav Havel, though out of context because he said it for post-world war Czechoslovakia but I want to use it for populism in a democracy such as ours: 'We are all responsible; we are all guilty.'

11. Increments of Change: Renaming Gardens, Streets, Cities

❧

'A rose is a rose is a rose is a rose,' wrote Gertrude Stein, the expatriate American novelist, playwright, poet and aesthete as the opening line in her book *Geography and Plays* (1922). Elsewhere she noted, 'Civilization begins with a rose...It continues with blooming and it fastens clearly upon excellent examples.' While much of Stein's fine writing is forgotten today, the first line is often quoted in the context of meaning 'things are what they are'. Perhaps Stein was playing on Shakespeare's famous quote 'A rose by any other name would smell just as sweet' and giving it a modern riff.

In a rare moment of sanguinity one is reminded of these lines as the juggernaut of renaming continues to roll across India. The roses in the erstwhile Mughal Gardens will smell just as sweet in the newly named Amrit Udyan inside the Rashtrapati Bhawan in New Delhi. As will the Chahar Bagh pattern of laying out gardens that inspired the Mughal Gardens continue to evoke images of the Four Gardens of Paradise. Unless, of course the rose bushes are pulled out and replaced by sacred tulsi and ayurvedic herbs. And the Chahar Bagh layout demolished and refashioned according to a new design sensibility that distinguishes between a Muslim Paradise and a Hindu one. Both of these scenarios are entirely possible in the India we live in.

However, in less sanguine moments one asks oneself where this renaming will take us. And more importantly, what will we be left with as this systematic weeding and plucking, this relentless refashioning and renaming, this dogged erasure and obliteration continues? Will we be richer or poorer as a people? The blithe souls amongst us maintain we will still be who we are even if, in the days and weeks and months ahead, our Mughal Parathas and Murgh Musallams are renamed or the entire 'Mughlai menu' from most restaurants serving 'Indian' cuisine is rechristened. After all, did the skies fall after Allahabad was renamed Prayagraj or Mughal Sarai was named Deen Dayal Upadhyay Nagar? Where renaming is yet afar, a minor alteration or a change in pronunciation can also do the trick as in Ahmednagar being called 'Naggar' and dispensing entirely with the Muslim-sounding Ahmed reminiscent of its founder Ahmed Nizam Shah I. The more pragmatic amongst us justify all such changes as being in keeping with the true spirit of a place or thing and therefore not merely justified but also more democratic.

Only a few are left to worry over small, seemingly unrelated events creeping up on us. As when a major jewellery brand is forced to take down an advertisement showing inter-faith marriages in the face of a muscular majoritarianism's ire over the bogey of so-called 'love jihad'. Or, when a popular clothes brand is similarly forced to pull down its Diwali poster because of the use of Urdu-sounding words in its promo that are seen as a 'deliberate attempt at Abrahamisation of Hindu festivals' leading to a social media backlash and, as is the norm now, a trending #Boycott. Examples such as these are too numerous to be recounted. And save for mild tut-tutting and expressions of dismay in the echo chamber of social media handles of friends with similar inclinations, causes nary a flutter in the India that is Bharat. In the years ahead, hopefully, these changes that have crept up on us gradually, so gradually in fact that we accept them as a fait accompli, will be studied by social scientists.

In the meanwhile, let us see how the Urdu poet views this business of *naam badalna* (name changing). Khalid Malik Sahil says:

Baaz auqaat tira naam badal jaataa hai
Baaz auqaat tire naqsh bhii kho jaate hain

Sometimes your name is changed
Sometimes your imprint also changes

Placing the changing names of cities in the larger social context, Ajay Sahaab, a modern poet, asks:

Wahi bhooke wahi aahein wahi aansu hain Sahaab
Shahar ka naam badal jaane se badlaa kyaa hai

The same hungry people, their sighs, their tears, O Sahaab
What has changed after changing the name of the city

But how is one to deal with the changing of names of dearly beloved places for purely short term political gain and expediency? With anger? With despair? With hopelessness? No, Kaleem Aajiz shows the way:

Ye vaaz-e-wafadaari Aajiz na badal dena
Woh zaḳhm tujhe denge tum un ko ġhazal dena

Don't change your clearly evident faithfulness
They will give you wounds you give them a ghazal

Postscript: Within hours of the renaming of the iconic gardens in Rashtrapati Bhawan came news of another Mughal Gardens in Delhi, a small lawn in front of the Vice Chancellor's office in the University of Delhi, being renamed Gautam Buddha Centenary Garden. The university administration was at pains to clarify that it was not a coincidence but had been in the works for some time. They need not have bothered with a clarification. Of course, it isn't a coincidence. It is part of a larger design. A plan. A blueprint. A road map…

Post-postscript: I first visited the splendid gardens in Rashtrapati Bhawan formerly known as Mughal gardens as a wide-eyed nineteen-year old. I had won an essay competition on the topic 'Nehru and his Contribution to the Asiad Movement' organised by the *National Herald*. It was a momentous occasion: A new pair of jeans was bought from an indie brand and a shirt from Janpath, from a kiosk that sold 'export surplus'. The entire family went, crammed in the family Ambassador, to clap and partake in the special day. A cash prize and certificate was given by the-then incumbent of Rashtrapati Bhawan, Giani Zail Singh, in a charming ceremony hosted in the gardens followed by High Tea served by white-gloved waiters in elaborate livery. The benevolently smiling Giani ji, the splendor that was the Mughal Gardens in the late afternoon sun of a balmy winter, the last vestiges of a Nehruvian India that was the *National Herald*…Today, everything is irretrievably lost in the mists of time.

12. On International Human Rights Day: *Azaadi, Baraabari, Waqaar, Huqooq*

The Universal Declaration of Human Rights, proclaimed by the UN General Assembly in Paris on 10 December 1948, has been translated into 500 languages. I have a framed copy of the Urdu version of Article 1 of the Declaration gifted to me by the fiery activist Kamla Bhasin. It occupies pride of place on my wall; I glance at it several times a day as it reads:

> *Tamaam insaan janam se baraabar aur azaad hain. Sab ka yaksaan waqaar hai. Sab ke yaksaan huqooq hain.*
>
> All human beings are born free and equal with equal dignity and equal rights.

While this Declaration has inspired scores of human rights treaties across the world, the spirit behind it has also inspired generations of Urdu poets. Vast amounts of poetry have been written on the four pillars that support it, namely, *azaadi* (freedom), *baraabari* (equality), *waqaar* (dignity), and *huqooq* (rights). By extension, copious amounts of poetry have also been written on all that violates these or attempts to diminish, dent or demolish these four pillars, namely, *zulm* (oppression or violence), *jabr* (compulsion, coercion or force), *sitam* (outrage or injustice).

Let us begin with Faiz and his enduring call for *azaadi*:

Bol, zubaan ab tak teri hai
Bol, ke lab azaad hain tere
Ab tak sutwaan jism hai tera
Bol, ke jaan ab tak teri hai

Speak, for your lips are free
Speak, for your tongue is still yours
Your supple body is still yours
Speak, for your life is still yours

In much the same way, Makhdoom Mohiuddin the fiery poet from Hyderabad, made his declaration against those who murder justice and equality in his nazm 'Chup Na Raho' (Don't Be Silent):

Jab talak dahr mein qaatil ka nishaan baaqi hai
Tum mitaate hii chale jaao nishaan qaatil ke

Till even a trace of the murderer remains in the world
Keep removing every trace of the murderer from the world

While the trigger for the above nazm was the brutal assassination of Patrice Lumumba, the first democratically elected Prime Minister of Congo, in January 1961 it can be read, over 50 years, later as a rallying cry against any suppression of human rights. Just as these oft-recited lines by Sahir Ludhianvi, also written in white heat over Lumumba's execution, can today be disengaged from their time and circumstance and read as an anthem of resistance against all forms of *zultm-o sitam* (tyranny and injustice):

Zulm phir zulm hai badhta hai to mitt jaataa hai
Khuun phir khuun hai tapkegaa to jum jaaegaa

Tyranny is but tyranny; when it grows, it is vanquished
Blood, however, is blood; if it spills, it will congeal

A pacifist, Sahir also wrote how and why war is justified when it is against oppression and a means to end violence:

Hum amn chahte hain magar zulm ke ḳhilaf
Gar jang lazmi hai to phir jang hi sahi
Zalim ko jo na rokey woh shamil hai zulm mein
Qaatil ko jo na tokey woh qaatil ke saath hai

We want peace, we are against violence
But if war is inevitable then so be it
He who doesn't stop the tyrant is part of the tyranny
He who doesn't check the murderer is with the murderer

Several contemporary poets have written directly on human rights and the need to speak up especially addressing minorities who find themselves swamped by an aggressive, muscular majoritarianism. Mohammad Habeeb 'Habeeb', a modern poet from Dhule, writes:

Qaleel aap nahin aur hum kaseer nahin
Huqooq sab ke hain yaksaan koi haqeer nahi

You are not few and we are not many
Everyone's rights are equal, no one is lowly

Alluding to the Amendment of the Citizenship Act that led to country-wide protests in 2019, Rashid Taraz asks:

Shahriyat ke jahan aiin se chhin jaaen huqooq
Aisi tarmeem se kya mulk sanvar jaega

Where the rights of citizenship are snatched by the law
Will the country benefit from such an amendment

Ruing the calamity that befalls those who ask for their rights, Sohail Akhtar speaks up for all those who find themselves beleaguered and battered for voicing their concerns:

Zara si baat jo chhedi huqooq ki hum ne
Utha ye shor ki jageer chahte hain hum

Barely had we raised the subject of our rights
When furor broke out that we were demanding the entire fief

True equality can come about only when there is respect, respect for one's own self but also for the other. When some people are in a seemingly unequal position and the 'other' who is superior is seen as the enemy, even then respect must be the fulcrum of the relationship as Javed Akhtar says here:

Mujhe dushman se bhi ḳhuddari ki ummid rahti hai
Kisi ka bhi ho sar qadmon mein sar achchha nahin lagta

I expect self-respect even from my enemy
No matter whose, a head should not lie at one's feet

And finally, Ghani Ejaz reiterates the equal rights enshrined in the Constitution when he writes:

Hum ko dastoor ne baḳhshe hain baraabar ke huqooq
Koi kamtar na siva hum bhi nahin tum bhi nahin

The Constitution has granted us all equal rights
No one is inferior or superior, neither us nor you

13. *Ehtijaaj*: The Poetry of Protest

Poetry, it has been said, flourishes when all else withers. When political chaos mars the ordered tenor of everyday life, when the social fabric tears, when corruption and poverty become rampant, when in the words of William Butler Yeats 'the Centre does not hold', it is, usually, the poet's finest hour. And so it was in the last years of Mughal rule in India. From the middle of the eighteenth century, events conspired to give plenty of fodder to the Urdu elegist's mill. There was the decline and dismantling of the Mughal empire with each successive incompetent ruler, the sack of Delhi by Nadir Shah (9 March 1739), the series of invasions by Ahmad Shah Abdali, the Marathas and Rohillas, the establishment of British control over Delhi in 1803, and the most cruel blow of all—the annexation of Awadh in 1856—followed by the Ghadar a year later. With each fresh catastrophe, the Urdu poet evolved a vocabulary to express his angst, clothing his bewilderment, anxiety and sorrow in a time-honoured repertoire of images and metaphors. Some favourite synonyms for the Beloved—*sitamgar, but, kafir, yaar*—now began to be used mockingly for the powers-that-be as the poet began to speak truth to power—sometimes directly but often obliquely, indirectly, mockingly.

The tradition of protest (*ehtijaaj*) is an old one in Urdu poetry; it predates the relatively modern concept of formal, organised protests. The Urdu poet chose to fall back on existing poetic traditions to express their angst; it is true that the sharpness and vigour of modern protest poetry is missing in early Urdu verse but a political sub-text runs through even seemingly poignant, pathos-laden poetry. One of the earliest examples of such poetry is this sher by Raja Ram Narain Mauzoo, replete though it is with all the conventional tropes of Urdu poetry but is nevertheless an indictment of the murder of Nawab Siraj-ud Daula of Bengal by the British in the Battle of Plassey in 1757:

Ghazala tum to waqif ho kaho Majnun ke marne ki
Diwana mar gaya aaḳhir ko virane pe kya guzri

O gazelles, you know. Tell us how Majnun died?
The mad lover died, but what happened to the wilderness?

Majnun, the legendary lover of Laila-Majnun fame, becomes here a metaphor for Siraj-ud-daula who fired the imagination of many Indians by his heroic resistance to the British. While animosity for the British was becoming increasingly evident in Urdu poetry well before 1857, the *ghadar* was a watershed insofar as hatred for a tyrannical foreign rule coalesced with mounting frustration at one's helplessness. It was 1857 really that caused a burst of political consciousness to seep out and colour Indians' understanding of the world. It changed our ways of seeing the world and by extension it changed our literature. Political events changed literary sensibilities like never before and *ehtijaaj* and *hubb-e watani* (love for the nation) became common, often intertwined, themes as far as Urdu poetry of the early 20th century was concerned.

That protest takes different forms is evident from this sher by Haseeb Soz:

Ye intiqaam hai ya ehtijaaj hai kya hai
Ye log dhuup mein kyun hain shajar ke hote hue

Is it revenge or is it protest, what is it?
Why are these people in the sun despite the tree

Kalim Ajiz, the poet from Patna, speaks of the 'hidden hand' of the tyrant in this oft-quoted sher:

Daaman pe koi chhint na ḳhanjar pe koi daagh
Tum qatl karo ho ki karaamaat karo ho

Not a speck on your garment nor stain on your dagger
Is it murder you do, or perform a miracle?

In a completely forthright manner, Nida Fazli is asking:

Rahegii waaadon mein kab tak aseer ḳhush-haali
Har eik baar hii kal kyuun kabhi to aaj bhi ho

For how long will prosperity be imprisoned in promises
Why is it always Tomorrow; surely it must be Today too

And elsewhere Nida Fazli is declaring why protest is inevitable when there there is want and scarcity:

Har ek ghar mein diyaa bhi jale anaaj bhi ho
Agar na ho kahiin aisaa to ehtijaaj bhi ho

In every home there should be a lit lamp and food to eat
Where it isn't so there should be protests

Munawwar Rana directs the question to himself:

Kya mujh mein ehtijaaj ki taaqat nahin rahii
Peechhe ki simt kis liye hatne laga huun main

Do I no longer have the strength to protest?
Why have I begun to shift towards the back row?

That fear and tyranny go hand in hand—just as protest and fearlessness also does—is evident from this sher by Shamsher Khan:

Ye baat sach hai tumhein zulm mein mahaarat hai
Ye baat bhi to haqeeqat hai main nahin darta

It's true that you have mastery over tyranny
But it's also a fact that I am not scared

And in a world where the boundaries of right and wrong are blurred, who will protest against the wrong-doers, as is the dilemma posed in this sher by Mohsin Naqvi:

Sunegaa kaun magar ehtijaaj khushbu ka
Ki saanp zahr chhidakta raha chameli par

But who will listen to the fragrance's protest
For the serpent kept spewing poison on the jasmine

14. What Men Would Want Women to Wear, and Why

A woman wearing ripped jeans cannot be a good role model, not for her own children or for society, so opined a certain Chief Minister in a remark that soon went viral.* The storm that erupted on social media over the minister's outrage over ripped jeans is a reminder of the excessive importance given to clothes, especially women's clothes and what constitutes decent attire for women. Outrageous and offensive though the remarks were, they have rekindled debates on what women should and should not wear. As elsewhere in this volume of essays, we shall attempt to view this debate through the mirror of Urdu poetry and seek answers in the words of male Urdu poets, both past and present, to glean a 'majoritarian' view on *libaas* (dress/clothes) and what women should, and in some cases, should not do with it.

As always, the views range from provocative to traditionalist, sometimes operating from a space of benign patriarchy to,

*https://www.indiatoday.in/india/story/tirathrawat-ripped-jeans-controversy-all-you-need-to-know-1781166-2021-03-19

occasionally, inciting outright rebellion against accepted best practices; but this essay will be confined to the male gaze, to how men see women and, more to the point, how they would prefer to see them dressed. As to how women see matters of dress, let's keep that for another occasion.

Let us begin with the *aanchal*, especially the *udta hua aanchal* (the billowing veil) that both conceals and reveals tantalising glimpses, that is at once a sign of modesty and a source of much speculation as to what lies behind, is the subject of profuse amounts of Urdu poetry. Even a liberal, feminist poet such as Ali Sardar Jafri falls back on the old, romantic trope of the *aanchal* and the mystique of its falling:

Apne udte hue aanchal ko na rah rah ke sambhaal
Husn ke parcham-e-zar-taar ko lahraane de

Don't constantly fix your billowing veil
Let the gold-threaded pennant of beauty flutter

The *aanchal* is invoked, time and again, for the spreading night or the clouds that cover the moon as also for something pure that has now been soiled (*maila aanchal*) or poverty and want (*phata aanchal*). Then there's also *maa ka aanchal*, a mother's veil that is at once evocative of shelter, warmth, safety, nurturing.

Mushafi Ghulam Hamdani speaks of the allure of the female form beneath the outer raiments:

Yuun hai dalak badan ki uss pairahan ki tah mein
Surḳhi badan ki jaise chhalke badan ki tah mein

Such is the lithe body beneath the folds of the dress
Like the red glow of the body gleaming from beneath

Then there's the ultimate male fantasy embodied in this sher by Akbar Hameedi:

Libaas mein hai woh tarz-e-tapaak-e-aaraaish
Jo ang chaahe chhupaanaa jhalak jhalak jaae

Her clothes have such a style of embellishment
The parts she wishes to hide glimmers 'n glimpses

And this by Jan Nisar Akhtar:

Maanaa ki rang rang tiraa pairahan bhi hai
Par iss mein kuchh karishma-e-aks-e-badan bhi hai

Agreed that your colourful attire adds to your allure
But the magic of your body's outline, too, adds to it

Of all the many items of women's clothing, the greatest amount of poetry is to be found on the *angiya* (a brassiere or short fitted blouse or bralette worn under a diaphanous kurta). Sample this sher by Munir Shikohabadi with its delicious play on words:

Shabnam ki hai angiyaa tale angiyaa ki pasina
Kyaa lutf hai shabnam tah-e-shabnam nazar aai

The dew of sweat beneath this angiya made from dewdrops
What joy to spot dewdrops beneath a layer of dewdrops

Nazeer Akbarabadi, the 'bazaar-poet' from Agra, has written with great naturalness on not just the female body but left us with a catalogue of women's ornaments, toiletries and cosmetics popular in the 18th century in poems such as *Pari ka Sarapa* and *Chitvan mein sharaarat hai aur seene bhi chanchal hai.* Here are the last lines from *Saraapaa husn-e-samdhan goyaa gulshan ki kyaari hai*:

Bhare joban pe itraati jhamak angiyaa ki dikhlaati
Kamar lehngey se bal khaati latak ghunghat ki bhaari hai

Proud of the prime of her youth showing glimpses of her angiya
Her sinuous waist beneath the lehnga, her face hidden behind a heavy veil

The *choli* finds itself centre stage in the popular male imagination, be it songs from popular Hindi cinema or conventional Urdu poetry. What the *angiya* was to an older generation that fantasised over the glimmering inner wear visible through a pearly, diaphanous outer garment, the visible in-your-face blytheness of the *choli* is for the latter-day poet, and the more *chust* (snug) it is the better! The *choli* finds itself added to other appendages as in *choli-daaman ka saath* (meaning to be inseparable from something or someone), *chaak choli* (slit or torn), or *bheegi choli* (damp with perspiration or the colours of Holi). Even a classicist such as Mir Taqi Mir has this to say about the *choli*:

Guundh ke goyaa patti gul ki woh tarkiib banaaii hai
Rang badan ka taab dekho jab choli bheege paseene mein

As though the petals of the rose have been kneaded
See the colours of her body when her choli is drenched in sweat

Another item of women's clothing that finds profuse mention in Urdu poetry is the *dupatta*. Used as much to dab tears of helplessness as to cover one's head with modesty, for the poet it's a tantalising length of fabric. Ideally, though, it must keep 'honour' safely hidden within its folds as unequivocally declared by Mardan Ali Khan Rana:

Abru aanchal mein dupatte ke chhupaanaa hai bajaa
Turk kyaa mayaan mein rakhte nahin talvaaron ko

It's only right to keep honour hidden in the hem of a dupatta
After all, don't Turkish soldiers sheath their swords in scabbards

Dagh Dehelvi takes a jaunty sally at the *dupatta* that reveals in a vain bid to conceal:

Yeh sair hai ki dupattaa udaa rahi hai havaa
Chhupaate hain jo woh siina kamar nahin chhupti

In this excursion the breeze lifts the dupatta and ends up
Revealing the waist as she tries in vain to cover her chest

Much like the hectoring minister of the recent ripped-jeans debacle, here's an unknown poet wagging the metaphorical finger at women and telling them how they should wear their *dupatta*:

Dupatte ko aage se dohraa na odho
Numudaar cheezeen chhupaane se haasil

Don't wear your duppata folded in the front
Things that should remain hidden become visible

Taken together, this sampler highlights the objectification of women by men, even some of the finest minds of their age and shows how deep patriarchy cuts. It takes a lone voice, such as a Majaz (cited elsewhere in this volume), who can incite women to turn the beautiful veil on their foreheads and refashion them into pennants reminiscent of the standards carried into battle.

15. *Zabt-Shuda Nazmein*: The Colonial Impulse Behind Banning and Proscription

Writing the Preface to the catalogue of books proscribed by the Government of India, B C Bloomfield notes:

> ...the British normally banned publications for two main purposes: first, they promoted criticism of the British administrations; and second, they promoted religious and/or racial strife. The proscription of publications for moral or sexual reasons seems almost never to have been the case...*

A study of the catalogue in the British Library reveals how—taken together—the books, pamphlets, periodicals, newspapers, handbills and posters in all the major Indian languages proscribed by the British government in India provide an invaluable

*Publications Proscribed by the Government of India: A Catalogue of the Collections in the India Office Library and Records and the Department of Oriental Manuscripts and Printed Books, British Library Reference Division, Graham Shaw and Mary Lloyd (eds.), (London: The British library, 1985).

printed archive. There is ample material here for the study of the Indian freedom struggle during its last four decades. The collection at the British Library constitutes perhaps the largest accumulation of primary literature and ephemera relating to the Indian independence movement. There are similar, but smaller collections in the library and files of the Home (Political) Proceedings of the National Archives of India and the state archive in Kolkata. The editors of the catalogue write:

> From the establishment of a commercial publishing and newspaper industry in the 1780s up to the Mutiny of 1857, the British authorities in India fluctuated between tightening or loosening their powers restricting the production of books and newspapers…by the turn of the century the two main categories of proscribed publications had been established: criticism of the British colonial government coupled with increasing demands for self-government, and expressions of communal conflict fuelled by inter-sectarian and inter-religious controversy.*

Since our frame of reference for this volume of essays is Urdu poetry, let us look at the contents of three remarkable books: *Azadi ki Nazmein* (Poems of Freedom) compiled by Sibte Hasan in 1940; *Zabt-Shuda Nazmein* (Banned Poems), compiled by unknown persons possibly working while 'underground' later revived by Khaliq Anjum and Mujtaba Husain in 1975; a selection from the National Archives of India edited by Rajesh Kumar Parti entitled *Ashob* (meaning variously upheaval, affliction, tumult, lament).

All three books have poems specifically written on the subject of independence from foreign rule, some going back

---

*Graham Shaw and Mary Lloyd (ed), op. cit., Introduction, p. vii.

to the Revolt of 1857, their contents vary in tone from woebegone to belligerent; some are written in the melancholic *shehr ashob* (literally meaning 'lament of the city' but often carrying a political undertone) tradition whereas others adopt a more rousing tone but the current running through all three collections is clearly a desire to throw off the imperial yoke, a listing of the ills under British rule and employment of a range of metaphors from the traditional to the modern, some showing the way to contemporary poets.

Now let us look at a sampling to understand what brought their contents under the imperial scanner. Let us start with Ram Parshad Bismil who was executed for his role in the Kakori Conspiracy Case:

Desh par qurban hotey jao tum ai Hindiyon
Zindagi ka raaz-e muzmar khanjar-e qatil mein hai

Keep sacrificing your life for your country, O People of Hind
The secret of Life is hidden in the murderer's dagger

And in another oft-repeated nazm:

Sarfaroshi ki tamanna ab hamare dil mein hai
Dekhna hai zor kitna baazu-e qatil mein hai

The desire for rebellion is now in our heart
Let us test the strength in the murderer's arms

There are several poems addressed to Bhagat Singh, his courage, his youth, his mad desire for freedom. Many poems are by virtually unknown poets others who were relatively well known in their own time but have got lost in the mists of time such as Partap Chand Azad, Tika Ram Sukhan, Gurmukh Singh, some with just a first name to evade detection. The topics range from *charkha*, *swadesi*, *khaddar/khaadi,* Gandhi, Nehru, Jallianwala Bagh, *baaghi jawan* (rebellious youth), turmoil in the Punjab (several bearing the title 'Punjab ka Hatyakand'), and overlaying everything a sometimes crystal clear, sometimes inchoate desire for *inquilab* (revolution). Several are directly addressed to topical events such as the Lahore Conspiracy Case, the Kanpur Mosque Case, Rowlat Act, Montague Reforms, Simon Commission, etc.

These collections contain several poems with rousing titles such as 'Chalo Jail-khaney, Chalo Jail-khaney' (Fill the Jails, Fill the Jails) by anonymous poets urging ordinary people to fill the imperial jails to bursting: *Karo thodhi himmat, na dhoondo bahaney* (Show some courage, don't look for excuses)! Others make outright calls for rebellion, for bloodshed, for sacrificing one's own life if need be, as in: *Gulshan-e watan shaadaab kar de baarish-e-khoon se* (Make verdant the garden of your country with the rain of blood) or this:

Hain abhi tayyar mar-mitne ko mastaane bahut
Likhe jaayengey hamare khoon se afsaane bahut

Many daredevils are ready to give up their life
Many stories are going to be written in our blood

Others adopt an angry, hectoring or exasperated tone as in: *Ai khasta-bakht Hindi kab tak tujhe jagayein* (O ill-fated people of Hind, how long must we awaken you) written on the Meerut Conspiracy Case; others admonish the *firangi* as here:

Baaz aa ab to jafa se ai firangi baaz aa
Phoonk daalegi hii tujhe ye sharar-bari teri

Desist from this oppression O firangi, desist
This playing with fire will destroy you

Still others talk of how death is preferable if the country doesn't get *mukammal azaadi* (*poorn swaaraj* or complete freedom and not the sop of Home Rule). Zafar Ali Khan in 'Mazalim-e-Punjab' (The Victims of Punjab) mocks the excesses of the

British and jestingly praises the delights of Martial Law and the brutality of men like General Dwyer. In 'Shola-e-Fanoos-e-Hind' (The Spark in the Chandelier of Hind), he goes on to wish that all the drops of the martyrs' blood may be used to decorate the walls of the *qasr-e-azadi* (the fort of freedom).

Josh Malihabadi calls out British hypocrisy in unequivocal terms in 'East India Company ke Farzandon Se' (To the Children of the East India Company) dubbing the British mere traders (*saudaagaraan*). Adopting a similar tone, Majaz writes in his 'Bidesi Mehman Se' (To a Foreign Guest):

Musafir bhaag waqt-e be-kasi hai
Tere sar par ajal mandla rahi hai

Run, O guest, it's a time of helplessness
Death is hovering over your head

In fact, almost all the major Urdu poets of the time—Majaz, Makhdoom Mohiuddin, Jan Nisar Akhtar, Shamim Karahni, Sardar Jafri—find their poems banned; it would appear that to be proscribed is seen as a badge of honour, worn with pride and courage by these men. Listing his 'Majburiyan' (Compulsions) in a short poignant poem Salam Machhlishahri says he has no problem with romantic poetry or beauty or earthly delights but he cannot enjoy any of them in Ghulamabad (Enslaved Nation) and so he must perforce write in an angry, fiery tone:

Abhi Hindostan ko aatishi naghmein sunane do
Abhi chingariyon se barg-e-gul rangeen banaa ne do

Let me sing these crackling fiery songs to Hindostan
Let me colour the flower's petals with my embers

16. *Meri Zameen*: Poetry on Earth, Land, Country, Ground

Zan, zar, zameen—meaning women, wealth and land—have been considered the root cause of all strife. Men are willing to lay down their lives protecting them. Of the three, however, more wars are fought over *zameen*, used variously to refer to land, country, earth or ground. How, then, can it be absent in literature? In Urdu literature, *zameen* is sometimes *zaalim* (cruel), sometimes *tang* (narrow), sometimes so loving that it fashions manacles around one's feet and sometimes that very love can prove to be a chimera, a false dream. Sometimes the land turns into a field of death, stained with blood. Sometimes it holds out the promise of new beginnings, of starting over, of building on a clean slate.

Intizar Husain's trilogy, *Basti*, *Naya Ghar* and *Aagey Samandar Hai* speak of the lure of the land, telling the stories of those who undertake the arduous *hijrat* (migration) to a new homeland, one that has been promised to them as the Land of the Pure. Khadija Mastoor's Urdu novel *Zameen* too is set against the backdrop of the partition with its protagonist Sajida, one of the millions who have set out in search of a new homeland, a new *zameen* that will be theirs for ever more. The trials and tribulations of the crossover, the difficult life in the refugee camps, the lying and the cheating of the early days in the promised land are depicted with brutal honesty.

Coming to poetry, the notion of one's own piece of land has been dealt with by many poets. Nida Fazli would have you believe that the idea of complete ownership itself is flawed as in this sher:

Kabhi kisii ko mukammal jahaan nahiin miltaa
Kahiin zameen kahin aasmaan nahiin miltaa

No one anywhere ever gets a complete world
Sometimes they don't get the land, or the sky

Others believe that the only piece of land that can truly be one's own is the grave—the proverbial *do gaz zameen*—in which one sleeps the eternal sleep under mounds of earth till one is awakened on the Day of Judgment. As Ganesh Bihari Tarz says:

Ye mahal ye maal-o-daulat sab yahiin rah jaainge
Haath aaegii faqat do gaz zameen marne ke baad

These palaces, this wealth and goods will all stay here
All you will have is simply two gaz of land after death

The idea is elaborated by Shad Azimabadi thus:

Bataa hudd se sivaa hum paanv phailaain kidhar jaain
Faqat do gaz zameen apni hai aur saaton falak teraa

Tell me, where should I stretch my feet beyond my bounds?
Only two *gaz* of land is mine; the seven heavens are yours

Bashir Badr rues that life has dealt him a poor hand by giving him land that is even less than the size of a grave:

Zindagi tu ne mujhe qabr se kum dii hai zameen
Paanv phailaauun to deewaar mein sar lagtaa hai

Life, you've given me even less space than a grave
When I stretch my legs my head strikes the wall

The idea of sleeping the eternal sleep in one's own land, of getting the proverbial *do gaz zameen* (enough for a corpse to fit in a grave) finds its most poignant expression in this immortal sher by the last Mughal emperor Bahadurshah Zafar who was doomed to spend his last years in exile in Rangoon, far away from his beloved Hindostan:

Kitna hai bad-naseeb Zafar dafn ke liye
Do gaz zameen bhi na milii kuu-e-yaar mein

How unfortunate is Zafar, for his burial
He did not get even two gaz of space in his beloved's street

The same *do gaz zameen* can become a metaphor for space in the beloved's heart as in this sher by Jigar Moradabadi:

Mujh ko nahiin qubuul do-aalam ki vusatein
Qismat mein kuu-e-yaar ki do-gaz zameen rahe

I shall not accept the vastness of the two worlds
As long as fate has two gaz of land in my beloved's street

Rahat Indori displays his typical insouciance when he says:

Woh jo do gaz zameen thhii mere naam
Aasmaan ki taraf uchhaal aayaa

That two gaz of land that was marked for me
I have flung it up towards the sky

Turning away from the morbid view of *zameen* to the more pleasant ones, here is Shahryar voicing the wonder that beauty on this earth can be:

Gardish-e waqt ka kitna bada ehsaan hai aaj
Yeh zameen chand se behtar nazar aati hai humey

What a great favour the turning of Time has done to me
This earth appears better than the moon to me

And because in Urdu poetry, for every argument there is a counter argument, here is Kaifi Azmi talking of the futility of finding a better home/land:

Main dhuundtaa huun jise woh jahaan nahiin miltaa
Naii zameen nayaa aasmaan nahiin miltaa

I can't find the world that I seek
I can't find a new sky or a new land

And, taking the pairing of *zameen* and *aasman* further, Ameer Minai remarks:

Hue naamvar be-nishaan kaise kaise
Zameen khaa gaii aasmaan kaise kaise

How the well known have been rendered nameless
How the earth has swallowed countless skies

17. Gender, Violence and Communalism

The abduction, gang rape and murder of an 8-year-old girl, Asifa Bano, by six men and a juvenile, in January 2018 in a village near Kathua in Jammu and Kashmir showed, yet again, the inescapable link between communalism, communal violence per se and violence against women or, as in this case, even very young girls and minors.* The victim was from the nomadic Bakarwal community; the main accused was the priest of the temple where the assault took place over several days.

Always more vulnerable to violence than men at any given time in any community, during communally charged times violence against women peaks and acquires an even more sinister form. Why is this so? Why do the bodies of women and girls become sites for violence when an overwhelming need for revenge, retribution, reprisal is coupled with a blind, monstrous anger? Psychologists and sociologists will no doubt have their explanations. As a student of literature, as a literary historian I want to point out that this is not a new phenomenon; it has

*https://www.bbc.com/news/world-asia-india-43722714

happened in the past and the creative writer has been quick to seize this aspect of violence when linked to gender and religion.

Let us look at the violence against women in a purely communal context—starting from the partition years and coming to contemporary times—as reflected in literature because literature holds up a mirror to society, it shows the good and the bad in equal measure; it also—sometimes through excess and rhetoric and exaggeration—shows us the beast that lurks within. But in portraying such violence literature also shows us possibilities of redemption. And so, in these dark times, there seem to be lessons to be drawn from modern Urdu literature.

The stories of Saadat Hasan Manto, Krishan Chandar and Rajinder Singh Bedi come instantly to mind: Manto's 'Khol Do' (Open It), Bedi's 'Lajwanti' and Krishan Chandar's novel *Ghaddaar* (Traitor) and the collection *Hum Vahshi Hain* (We are Savages). Of these, perhaps Manto's 'Sharifan' deserves closer study—not merely for its depiction of the bestiality that can overcome otherwise decent human beings when communal passions run high but also because Manto's Sharifan is only a few years older than Kathua's Asifa. That a story written 70 years ago is still relevant to us in India today is both shocking and tragic. What is more, in Manto's story there are extenuating circumstances though rape as revenge was as political then as it is now; Manto, like others of his generation, clearly holds the circumstances responsible, the time of madness that many of his peers allude to in their writings. Kathua had no such fig leaf.

Bedi's 'Lajwanti' draws attention to the issue of abduction as does Amrita Pritam's Punjabi novel *Pinjar*. We know that approximately 100,000 women and girls were abducted in 1947 though estimates vary as so many of these abductions went unreported and unacknowledged. It was simpler for families to pretend that their daughters, sisters, wives had been killed rather than acknowledge that they may well be alive but living either as sexual slaves or wives albeit in 'enemy' families through forcible conversions. The underlying reason—whether men forced women into unpaid labour coupled with sexual abuse or took them as forced wives—was the impulse to subsume, transform, or remove all traces of the other community, especially in places where the two communities had lived together for centuries. The desire was to shame and corrupt 'rival' religious communities through explicit demonstrations of sexualised violence, including rape and mutilation. In their seminal study *Borders and Boundaries*, Ritu Menon and Kamla Bhasin detail cases in which women's breasts were tattooed with symbols of their attackers' religion. Several attacks on women's bodies included men gouging out or carving political slogans, such as 'Pakistan Zindabad' (Pakistan Forever) or 'Jai Hind' (Long Live India) into a living woman's skin—demonstrating the ways that women's bodies became living sites of war. Warring factions also mutilated women's bodies as a way of asserting domination over a section of the population that had almost overnight become hateful and intolerable. Menon and Bhasin write about the graphic testimony that a doctor in Sheikhupura, in Punjab, gave to the government's fact-finding team. The doctor cited 'amputation of breasts of women', adding that 'six such cases of chopped-off breasts were brought to the refugee camp and all of them proved fatal.'

Partition studies have also told us that *jathas* or groups of men worked in a highly organised and carefully planned manner to waylay caravans of refugees, called *kafilas*, travelling across the newly created border or ambushed villages and hamlets of one community with the express intention of killing all able-bodied men and abducting all women and girls. We get graphic accounts of the activities of such organised attacks in novels such as *Ghaddaar*, accounts that are corroborated by historians. By the time things settled down shortly after partition, efforts were made by both countries to repatriate these abducted women and appeals were made by leaders most notably Gandhi ji—Muslim women were to be sent to Pakistan and Hindu and Sikh girls were retrieved from Pakistan and sent to India to be rejoined by their families but in many cases met with shame. Rajinder Singh Bedi's short story 'Lajwanti' is written in response to precisely this call to take back abducted women—back not just into home and hearth but also into the hearts of their men. In September 1947 both Jawaharlal Nehru and Pakistani Prime Minister Liaquat Ali Khan vowed not to recognise the forced marriages that resulted from abductions and both countries ratified this agreement in the Inter-Dominion Conference in December of the same year which established the recovery procedure. However, within a few short months, by January 1948, the process of recoveries slackened and eventually ended as the officers on the two sides were busy totting up the figures and expressed their displeasure when the figures of abducted women did not match the numbers of recovered women thus showing that the enemy had once again had the upper hand! In recovery as with abduction—or for that matter violence—the driving impulse was one-upmanship.

The linking of sexual violence with notions of shame and honour has been repeatedly picked up by writers of the partition generation. In recent times, Gulzar's debut novel *Two*, published in 2017, deals very sensitively with the issue of sexual violence in a communal context and the toll it takes on a woman's mental health and its long-term consequences. Researchers such as Urvashi Butalia, Kamla Bhasin, Ritu Menon have talked of the silencing of the trauma in the early decades after partition and how suppressed memories scarred women for the rest of their lives. Oral testimonies and survivors' accounts are still surfacing; memoirs, autobiographical essays, interviews, etc are still recording some of these experiences and contributing to our understanding of communal violence against women in the years leading up to the partition and immediately thereafter.

Regrettably, violence against women in communally charged times did not end with the partition and the coming of independence. It continues; each time a communal riot breaks out women are the worst victims of the worst excesses. Be it Gujarat or Kashmir, Assam or Uttar Pradesh, women have been subjected to violence as a measure of revenge, reprisal, teaching a lesson and so on. Now that the enemy is within and there is no third party to blame for the divide and rule as was often the simple, formulaic approach of many partition generation of writers, contemporary writers have become more circumspect. They do wish to draw attention but are careful not to indulge in blaming any one community; they draw our attention to genocide and communal violence but prefer to use an obliqueness and allusion bordering on political correctness. The rawness of the partition generation is missing in contemporary fictional accounts save for an Asghar Wajahat writing his sharp haiku-like 'Shah Alam Camp ki Roohein' or Gulzar writing about the atrocities committed by the paramilitary forces against women in Kashmir in the guise of internal security in a short story such as 'Search'.

While it may be argued that in the *annus horribilis* that was 1947 the suddenness and ferocity of the violence took many—including possibly the perpetrators as we saw in Manto's 'Sharifan'—unawares, the same cannot be said for post-partition violence towards women in communally charged times. Much planning and strategising goes into the execution of these hate crimes not to mention copious amounts of sophistry, equivocation and whataboutery in their aftermath.

The 'retributive genocide' that Paul Brass* talked about in the context of partition acquires a much more sinister meaning and an altogether larger scale when hatred is aided and abetted by technology, not to mention power and privilege. Both history and literature hold out many lessons for us; if we don't pay any heed, if we feel no outrage, if we still say 'Let's not make this political!' or 'Why get religion into it? A rape is a rape!' we are wilfully missing the point. And in our wilfulness the list of Bilkis Banos, Bhanwari Devis, Asifas will go on and on...

---

*Paul Brass, 'The Partition of India and Retributive Genocide in the Punjab, 1946-47: Means, Methods and Purposes,' *Journal of Genocide Research*, 5:1, 71-101, DOI: 10.1080/14623520305657

18. We Shall See: Faiz and the Poetry of Witness

Sometimes, a poem, or one particular piece of writing casts a long shadow and comes to be seen as most representative of a writer's work. Such is the curious case of the rousing *Hum Dekheinge** (We Shall See) and Faiz Ahmad Faiz despite the fact that he enjoyed a fairly long innings and wrote on a range of subjects. What is more, poetry and politics ran as the warp and woof of his life creating a rich tapestry that glows with life to this day. Rising aeons above the lament of a lover for his beloved, Faiz's poetry is the agonised call of the conscience, of the seeing eye that sees and records or, to use a term coined by Carolyn Forche, the American poet and activist, the 'poetry of witness'.

Moving from an easy-going young man, shy with strangers but equipped with a ready wit in the company of friends, given to a liberal Left inclination, heavily influenced by classical

---

*Viewed as 'anti-Hindu', this poem caused widespread outrage in India especially during the ant-CAA protests. https://www.indiatvnews.com/fyi/explained-curious-case-faiz-ahmad-faiz-hum-dekhenge-iit-kanpur-link-575664

Persian traditions though he studied, and taught, English literature, Faiz evolved his own prosody and vocabulary that was at once contemporary yet exquisitely musical. Like his contemporary Majaz, Faiz too began to use the nazm for increasingly political, even revolutionary purposes. Unlike Majaz, however, Faiz had an academic bent of mind. Being a teacher, he retained a scholarly disposition which he brought to all subsequent vocations and callings.

Another useful comparison would be between Faiz and Iqbal. Both from the Punjab, they took to Urdu (not their mother tongue) as a bird takes to song. They wrote poetry that was at once passionate, direct, impetuous, that appealed with a startling near-prophetic call to the collective consciousness of their readers. Both used traditional poetic forms such as the elegy, the ode and the anthem and infused them with a fresh note of social consciousness. And, eventually, Faiz took the message of Marx where Iqbal had left it and carried it to a younger generation of Muslims who were, in the light of the growing importance of the literary grouping known as the Progressive Writers' Association (PWA), more receptive to its egalitarianism, concern for the poor and advocacy of change. Faiz remained a Marxist long after the decline of the Movement, but never an in doctrinaire one, nor was he ever a member of the Communist Party.

Faiz produced seven volumes of verse. His first collection, *Naqsh-e-Faryadi* (Imploring Imprints, published in 1941 while he was still in Amritsar, but written over a period of ten years) shows a strange intermingling of the romantic and revolutionary. It reflects the aches of a sensitive young man but also the sorrows of the world. The early poems have a haunting, dreamlike quality, such as 'Mere Nadeem' (My Friend), 'Husn aur Maut' (Beauty and Death), 'Aaj ki Raat' (Tonight). This trance was broken as he came in contact with Marxists and increasingly influenced by social realism. In 'Mujhse Pahli Si Muhabbat Mere Mahboob Na Mang' (My beloved, don't ask me to love you as I once did), for instance, the poet acknowledges the heart-tugging beauty of the beloved but talks of the other sorrows of the world which claim his attention. He juxtaposes the beloved's beauty against the miseries and ugliness of the world, a world which has hunger, disease and deprivation, a world that can never let him love her as he once did, for a love that is divorced from social reality is too individualistic, too meaningless:

Aur bhi dukh hain zamaane mein mohabbat ke siwa
Raahatein aur bhi hain wasl ki raahat ke siwa

There are other sorrows too apart from love
And other pleasures too apart from that of union

Another poem, 'Chand Roz Aur Meri Jaan' (A Few More Days, My Dearest), again has the poet addressing his beloved and comforting her that the days of cruelty, oppression and helplessness are about to end. The humiliations inflicted by strange hands (the British), he assures her, shall be short lived:

Zulm ki chhaon mein dum lene pe majbur hain hum
Aur kuchh der sitam sah lein tadap lein ro lein
Apne ajdad ki miras hai mazoor hain hum

We are constrained to breathe in the shade of tyranny
Bear it just a little longer, endure this oppression
This suffering that is our inheritance, and we are helpless...

Other poems from *Naqsh-e-Faryadi* that bear the stamp of progressivism are 'Raqeeb Se' (To the Rival), 'Tanhai' (Solitude), 'Bol Ke Lab Azaad Hain Tere' (Speak, For Your Lips are Free), 'Mauzoo-e-Sukhan' (Topic of Poetry), 'Hum Log' (We, the People). If in 'Bol', he is inciting his people to speak up and reminding them that they are free despite their fetters:

Bol, ki lab azaad hain tere
Bol zabaan ab tak teri hai
Tera sutvaan jism hai tera
Bol ki jaan ab tak teri hai

Speak, for your lips are free
Speak, for your tongue is still yours
Your supple body is still yours
Speak, for your life is still yours

In 'Hum Log', he seems to be chastising them for the fear, regret and sorrow that do not let them rise in revolt:

Dil ke aivan mein liye gul-shuda shammon ki qataar
Noor-e-ḳhurshid se sahme hue uktae hue
Husn-e-mahboob ke sayyal tasavvur ki tarah
Apni tareeki ko bheenche hue liptaae hue

Clasping a row of snuffed out candles in the niches of our hearts
Scared even of the light of the moon, wearied of all things
Like the remembrance of love's beauty now faded
Clutching our darkness, and being cloaked by it

In 'Mauzoo-e-Sukhan', he makes the most direct statement of what should concern a poet: should it just be the darkness of a beloved's tresses or the delicate tracery of henna on her pale hands or should it be all that has happened to the sons and daughters of Adam and Eve from time immemorial and all the tragedies and misfortunes that shall continue to happen? Should the poet not ask:

Inn damakte hue shahron ki faravan maḳhluq
Kyuu faqat marne ki hasrat mein jiya karti hai
Ye haseen khet phata padta hai jauban jin ka
Kis liye in mein faqat bhook uga karti hai

The countless souls who inhabit these glittering cities
Do they live simply with the desire to die one day?
These beautiful fields whose youth is bursting forth
Why does only hunger grow in them?

Faiz evolved a complex system of images, drawn from the classical Persian tradition that seemed on the face of it 'harmless' enough and could escape detection by hawk-eyed censors but had sharp political overtones. For instance, *aashiq* (lover) became patriot and revolutionary; *mashooq* (beloved) used for the country or people; *raqeeb* (rival) used interchangeably for imperialism, capitalism, tyranny, exploitation; *ishq* (love) became revolutionary zeal; *visaal* or *deedar* (union with the beloved) revolution or social change; *hijr* or *firaaq* (separation) oppression by the state; *rind* (libertine) rebel; *sharaab, maikhana, pyala, saqi* (wine, tavern, cup, cup-bearer) sources of social and political awareness; *haq* (truth) socialism; *khirad* (empirical knowledge) capitalism or the establishment; *zanjir* (chain) chain of slavery; *bulbul* (nightingale) nationalist poet; *gul* (rose) political ideal; *but* (idol) present-day rulers; and the *Kaaba*, any sacred space, even the country.

Faiz brought a new internationalism to Urdu poetry, for though the Urdu poet of the turn of the century had spoken of tremors in the Muslim world, it was only insofar as it concerned the Muslims of India. Faiz was saying it was as much his concern as anybody else's when someone somewhere oppressed the weak, or the mighty system crushed the lone voice of dissent. When Julius and Ethel Rosenberg were sent to the electric chair in 1953 on charges of being Soviet agents in America, Faiz wrote his hauntingly evocative 'Hum jo tareek raahon mein mare gaye' (We who were executed in the dark lanes). Similarly, his ode to Africa, written in 1955, 'Aa Jao Africa' (Come, Africa), is an ode to oppressed people everywhere; it was to show the way towards increasing internationalism in his range of interests.

In later years, Faiz would write with equal passion about Palestine, Namibia and Chile and justify it thus: '...as a writer or an artist, even though I run no state and command no power, I am entitled to feel that I am my brother's keeper, and my brother is the whole of mankind. And this is the relevance to me of peace, of freedom, of detente and the elimination of the nuclear menace. But out of this vast brotherhood, the nearest to me and dearest are the insulted and the humiliated, the homeless and the disinherited, the poor, the hungry and the sick at heart.'

It is precisely for these—the insulted and the humiliated—that the solemn, sonorous, eminently sing-able *Hum Dekheinge* is written. It contains a promise and a prophecy: one day the oppressed will occupy their rightful place when the tyrants will be vanquished and Truth shall prevail. Written in 1979 in response to General Zia ul Haq's repressive regime, it is as much a song for his own country reeling under a dictator as for people anywhere in the world fighting oppression at any time. And that is why it has found a life beyond its own time and circumstance, as good poetry invariably does. Perhaps there will be a time, in the none-too-distant future, when all things Pakistani will be anathema; cricket already is as are actors and singers from across the border. Those who cherished the shared heritage will be either dead and gone or woefully outnumbered. Perhaps poets and poetry from 'out there' too will be banned. Till then, *Hum Dekheinge...*

19. May Day: *Mazdoor Hain Hum, Majboor Hain Hum...*

1 May, known as Workers' Day or May Day, has been set aside as a day to mark the struggles and gains of the international labour movements. Halfway between the spring equinox and summer solstice, another and entirely unrelated May Day is also celebrated in some parts of the world; this has its roots in an ancient European tradition that celebrates the coming of summer with a May Queen, floral garlands and dancing around a May Pole. There is also the Mayday distress signal used in emergencies aboard a plane or ship (deriving from the phonetic equivalent of 'M'aidez', French for 'Help me'!) Instead, let us look at the May Day that derives its name from the workers uprising in Chicago on 1 May 1886 asking for an eight-hour work day and is still, a century and a half later, acknowledged as a day to commemorate workers' struggles worldwide. In many countries, the day is a public holiday.

As always in this volume, let us view the worker and labourer through the prism of Urdu poetry and see how the Urdu poet has viewed the *mazdoor* (labourer) and paid tribute to his unstinting and unacknowledged labour. A vast amount of poetry written on the 1st of May, traditionally, has the poet repeatedly identifying with the workers and making common cause with their oppression such as here in 'Mazdoor ki Bansuri' (The Labourer's Flute) by Jameel Mazhari:

Mazdoor hain hum, mazdoor hain hum, majboor thhe hum, majboor hain hum

We are labourers, we are labourers, we were oppressed, we are oppressed

A great deal of Urdu poetry contained a prophecy, that one day the *mazdoor* would arise from his centuries' old slumber and demand his rightful share, such as here in Majaz's 'Mazdooron ka Geet' (The Workers' Song):

Jis roz bag̊hawat kar denge
Duniya mein qayamat kar denge
Khwaabon ko haqiqat kar denge
Mazdoor hain hum mazdoor hain hum

The day we shall revolt
We shall bring catastrophe upon the world
We shall turn dreams into reality
We are the workers, we are the workers

In the years leading up to and immediately after independence, the writers' body known as the Progressive Writers' Association (PWA) became a self-appointed custodian of peasants' and workers' rights and vast amounts of poetry and fiction came to be written on the *dehqaan* (peasant) and *mazdoor*. Much was expected from the coming of independence, not least being the safeguarding of farmers' and workers' rights. While the abolition of *zamindari* and land reforms were put into effect almost immediately by the Nehru government, the rosy future predicted by some failed to materialize. In a poem entitled 'Kisaan' (Farmer), Kaifi Azmi talks of the toiling farmer, his back bent under the burden of debt, his state as wretched as ever, hungry, dressed in rags:

Cheer ke saal mein do baar zameen ka seena
Dafn ho jaata huun

Twice a year, I tear open the bosom of the earth
And bury myself

The film lyricists in the Bombay film industry, many of whom were either inspired by the Progressive Movement or were full-time members of the PWA, too were watchful of the interests of the farmers and agricultural labour. As late as the 1960s, when India found itself facing acute food shortages, mainstream *masala* movies of the Manoj 'Bharat' Kumar brand such as *Upkar* (Gift) interpreted Prime Minister Lal Bahadur Shastri's slogan of 'Jai Jawan Jai Kisan' (Hail the Soldier, Hail the Farmer) with songs such as *Mere desh ki dharti sona ugle ugle heere moti*...(The soil of my country yields gold and diamonds...)

The motif of the farmer and the labourer was taken up all through the 1980s in films such as *Mazdoor*:

Hum mehnatkash iss duniya se
Jab apna hissa mangengey
Ek baagh nahii ek khet nahii
Hum saari duniya mangengey

When labourers such as us
Ask for our share of the world
We will not ask for an orchard or a field
We will ask for the entire world

But possibly no one could have captured the irony of the labourers who build homes yet have no roof over their own head such as this by an unknown poet:

Shahr mein mazdoor jaisa dar-ba-dar koi nahin
Jis ne sab ke ghar banae us ka ghar koi nahin

There is no one as homeless as a labourer in a city
He who has made everyone's homes, has no home of his own

Apart from the generalised, somewhat rhetorical paeans in praise of the workers written at various times, there is specific poetry written on the day that celebrates workers, such as 'Yaum-e-Maii' (May Day) by Suroor Barabankwi:

Aaj Maii ka pahla din hai aaj ka din mazdoor ka din hai
Zulm-o-sitam ke madd-e-muqabil hausla-e-jamhoor ka din hai

Today is the first of May, today is the Day of the Worker
Faced with tyranny and oppression, today is the day of the
courage of democracy

Syed Mohammad Jafri in his 'Yakum Maii' (The First of May) notes sardonically:

Dekho har saal aaegi maah-e-Maii ki ye yakum
Sunte hain seedhi nahiin hotii kabhii kutte ki dum

See, this first of the month of May will come by every year
But we hear that a dog's crooked tail can never be set straight

Regrettably, even the Hindi film industry, ostensibly with its finger to the pulse of the nation, has stopped making films on the *mazdoor* and *kisaan*. There hasn't been anything along the lines of a blockbuster such as *Namak Haraam, Mazdoor, Kala Patthar,* or *Deevar* in recent times. Yes, there is a Kapil Sharma playing a food delivery man or a Ranbir Kapoor playing a salesman but given that the film industry accounts for 26% of India's GDP and employs 22% of the total workforce, why is the worker absent from the public consciousness? Is it because—despite all the talk of 'Make in India'—he is considered neither hip nor cool? Or because if he stands up and asks for his rights it would be seen as an unseemly blot on Shining India? Or because a restive workforce flies in the face of the narrative of development and progress?

20. Why Do We Love to Hate Iqbal, the Prophet of Change

That a school teacher in Pilibhit (Uttar Pradesh) should be suspended for 'making' his students sing Iqbal's *Lab pe aati hai dua*...(The prayer that springs to my lips...) should no longer surprise us.* That the song, entitled 'Bachhe ki Dua' was inspired by an English poem by Matilda B. Edwards (1836-1919) entitled 'A Child's Prayer' and is essentially a plea to be saved from any form of wrongdoing is a small detail that is often overlooked in the all-pervasive, ill-informed antipathy towards Iqbal. The vilification of Iqbal (1877-1938) as the father of the two-nation theory, as a passionate advocate of a Muslim Renaissance and a votary of pan-Islamism began soon after his death and once anointed as the 'national poet' of Pakistan, acquired the speed of a juggernaut in the years after partition for us in India. Now, given the deeply polarised times we live in, given our propensity to view the world in stark black or white, given our willing suspension of inquiry let alone

*https://indianexpress.com/article/india/vhp-complains-about-school-poem-headmaster-suspended-6070860/

curiosity in belief systems different from our own, the blind hatred towards Iqbal and all that he stands for seems inevitable.

But, given that the same Iqbal we love to hate also gave us *Saare jahan se achha Hindostan hamara* (This India of ours is the fairest country of all…which incidentally is adopted by not one but several military bands of different regiments of the Indian armed forces as their marching tune) as well as sweetly lyrical poems on Shri Ram (whom he called *Ram-e Hind* and *Imam-e Hind*), on Nanak (whom he called *mard-e kaamil* or the 'perfect man') as well as countless jewel-bright gems on the Himalayas and the Ganga, should make us pause to reflect. It might be worthwhile to look at his ouvre in its entirety to try and understand the movement in his poetic thought from the 'Tarana-e-Hind' (The Song of Hind) (written in 1904) to the 'Tarana-e-Milli' (The Song of a People) (in 1910) showing the progression from *Hindi hain hum watan hai Hindostan hamara* ('We are the people of Hind and Hindustan is our homeland') to *Muslim hain hum watan hai sara jahan hamara* ('We are Muslims and our homeland is the whole world'). Why did the romantic nationalism and the lyrical syncretism leach out to be replaced by a puritanical zeal? Why did the idea of living together no longer seem feasible, so lyrically expounded in poems such as:

Chishti ne jis zameen pe paigham-e haq sunaya
Nanak ne jis chaman mein wahdat ka geet gaya
Mera watan wahi hai, mera watan wahi hai

The country where Chishti propounded the message of truth
The country where Nanak sang the song of Oneness
That is my country, that is my country

One of the tallest figures in the Urdu literary arena in the first three decades of the 20th century, Iqbal moved from writing on specifically Indian subjects reflective of pluralism and multiculturalism to drawing upon world events to inspire, rouse and challenge the imagination of the Indian Muslims. He was among the earliest to introduce socialism and the socialist movement to young people in India through his rousing poetry. Iqbal was among the first to take note of the disquiet that was affecting the Indian Muslims and bring it within the ken of poetry. This disquiet found expression in different ways: there was the sorrow over the loss of freedom or power of any Islamic race, whether in the distant past or the present; concern about the future of the Islamic countries subject to European hegemony; and suspicion and distrust of western powers that had, in the first place, plotted and brought about the downfall of Muslim rule everywhere. In a rejoinder to his own famous 'Shikwa' (Complaint), 'Jawab-e-Shikwa' (Answer to the Complaint), Iqbal wrote:

Hai jo hangaama bapa yurish-e-bulġhari ka
Ghaafiloñ ke liye paiġham hai bedaari ka
Tu samajhta hai ye saamaan hai dil-aazaari ka
Imtihaan hai tire eesaar ka ḳhuddaari ka
Kyun hiraasaan hai sahil-e-faras-e-ada se
Noor-e-haq bujh na sakega nafas-e-ada se

The trouble that is raging in the Balkans
Is a message of awakening to the forgetful.
You may think it the means of vexing your heart.
But in reality it is a test of your self-sacrifice and self-reliance.
Why are you frightened at the neighing of the enemy's horse?
Truth's light can never be put out by the breath of the enemy.

The fate of fellow-Muslims in different parts of the colonized world seemed to carry a portent of worse things in store for them in India. When a feted and lionised poet such as Iqbal penned poems such as 'Masjid-e-Qartaba' (The Mosque at Cordoba) and 'O Ghafil Afghan'(O Heedless Afghan), it fed a growing paranoia of a terrible misfortune that was waiting to befall the Muslims of the sub-continent. The emotional tug of tradition, of memories of Islam's glorious past blurred Iqbal's vision of the future making it a bleak prospect. While on the one hand, he remembered the glorious civilisation that had produced the splendid mosque at Cordoba he was reminded also of the abject state of the Muslim in the present time. If one views Iqbal's vast and varied ouvre, one is struck with how often progressive, even socialist ideas are quickly negated by regressive, even reactionary ones. Standing before the mosque at Cordoba, he exclaims:

Aalam-e-nau hai abhi parda-e-taqdeer mein
Meri nigaahon mein hai us ki sahar be-hijaab
Parda utha duun agar chehra-e-afkaar se
Laa na sakega farang meri navaaon ki taab

Destiny's curtain till now muffles the world to be,
Yet, already, its dawn stands before me unveiled;
Were I to lift this mask hiding the face of my thoughts,
Europe could never endure songs as burning as mine!

In 'Farmaan-e-Khuda' (God's Command), Iqbal exhorts:

Uttho miri duniya ke ġharībon ko jaga do
Khaakh-e-umra ke dar-o-deewar hila do
Garmaao ġhulaamon ka lahu soz-e-yaqeen se
Kunjishk-e-faromaya ko shaaheen se lada do

Rise, and from their slumber wake the poor of my world
Shake the walls and windows of the mansions of the great
Kindle with the fire of faith the slow blood of the slaves
Make the fearful sparrow bold to meet the falcon's hate

In *Armaghan-i-Hejaz* (The Gift of Hejaz), in one of his last important works, 'Satan's Parliament' written in 1936, he puts these words in the mouth of Satan:

Dast-e-fitrat ne kiya hai jin garebaanon ko chaak
Mazdaki mantaq ki souzan se nahin hote rafoo
Kab dara sakte hain mujh ko ishtaraki koocha gard
Ye pareshan rozgar, ashufta maghaz, ashufta mu
Hai agar mujh ko khatar koi to uss ummat se hai
Jis ki khatstar mein hai ab tak shirar-e-arzu

...When Nature's hand
Has rent the sleeve, no needleworking logic
Of communism will put the stitches back.
I be afraid of socialists?—street-bawlers,
Ragged things, tortured brains, tormented souls!
No, if there is one monster in my path
It lurks within that people in whose ashes
Still glow the embers of an infinite hope

And, on the subject of women he is most inconclusive, in a small poem called 'Aurat' (Woman):

Main bhi mazloom-e-niswaan se hoon gham-naak bahut
Nahin mumkin magar uqda-e-mushkil ki kushood!

I too at the oppression of women am most sorrowful
But the problem is intricate, no solution do I find possible

Victor Kiernan, in an essay on Iqbal entitled 'The Prophet of Change' admits: 'Iqbal mirrored the confusions and contradictions of his highly complex environment, and there were to be moments when he could come near the brink of a narrow sectarianism.' Indeed, such is the duality of Iqbal's message—couched though it is in a language of a Muslim addressing fellow Muslims—that it can be read as the inspiration for both the Muslim nationalists and the seekers of pan-Islamism as well as by communists and socialists. While there is no denying the breadth and scope of Iqbal's ouvre, there is equally no denying his hold over the Muslim masses and his significance as the only major Muslim thinker of any stature during this time, it must also be said that, with hindsight, Iqbal offered the Indian Muslim a vision of the future that was confused, self-contradictory and profoundly reactionary.

The Age of Enlightenment in Europe had successfully brought together the spirit of modern, scientific enquiry and religion. In India, they remained mutually exclusive. Sir Syed's 'Aligarh Experiment' had not borne the desired result. The marriage of science and faith, progress and tradition failed to bear fruit. Why did this happen? What was the difference in the crucible of Upper India and Europe? Was it the presence of Islam that worked as a contraceptive? Or, was it the potent presence of the colonizer that emasculated? Be that as it may, Iqbal's misgivings about the future of Muslims in India stemmed from a very real fear.

It is easy, with hindsight, to look at a poet's shortcomings; but we would be guilty of a shortcoming of our own if we fail to at least acknowledge his fears. And, more importantly, if we fail to see him in the context of his time and age.

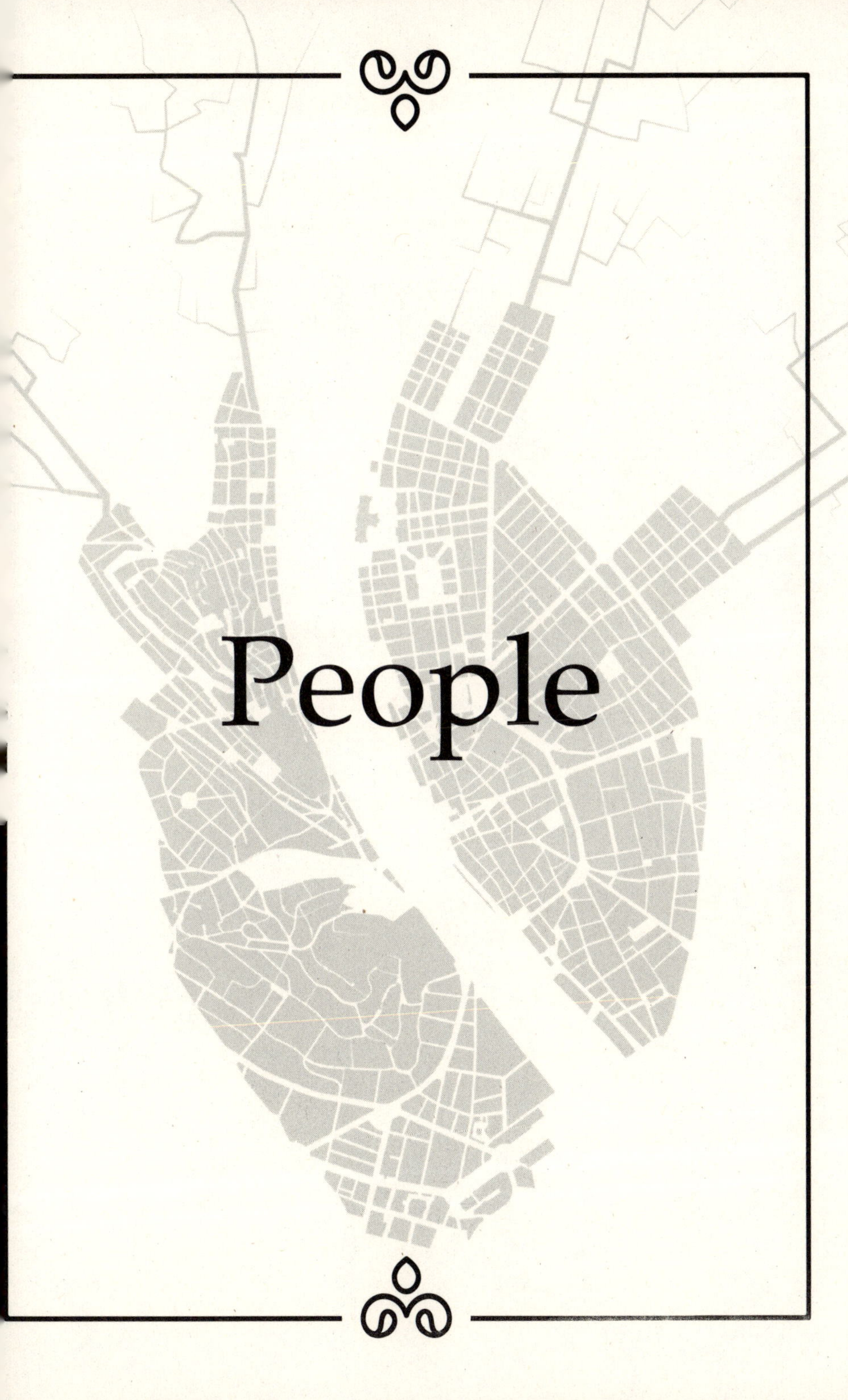

People

21. What Makes Gandhi Alive Today?

What makes a man, a national leader, stand out from others? Why does he continue to appeal to the modern mind? Why does the writer go back to revisit his life and work in search of new meanings? What is it about Gandhi—who was born over a 150 years ago in a world altogether different from ours, who died more than 70 years ago in a newly independent India, fresh from its 'tryst with destiny' moment, waiting to find its feet among the comity of nations—that still resonates with the Urdu poet of today? First, a sampling from some recent works and then a search for answers…

In a long, lyrical ghazal, Nushhur Wahidi speaks of Gandhi as a light that cannot be snuffed out, as a life force that will always show the way, as a treasure that can never be pillaged:

Woh hamesha ke liye chup hue magar ik jahan ko zabaan dii
Woh hamesha ke liye so gaye magar ik jahan ko jaga diya

He was silenced forever but he gave voice to a world
He went to sleep forever but he awakened a world

Writing especially on the occasion of Gandhi's birth, in a poem entitled 'Gandhi Jayanti', Kanval Dibaivi speaks with the pride of ownership, that a man such as Gandhi was 'ours':

Watan ke aasman par ek raḳhshanda sitare thhe
Hamein ye faḳhr hai ahl-e-jahaan Gandhi hamare thhe

He was a resplendent star in the country's firmament
We are proud that among all the people in the world, he was ours

Also writing on 2 October, Nazish Pratapgarhi seizes upon the occasion to exhort his country to remember all that Gandhi stood for: love for fellow beings, peace for all mankind, and above all the creed of *ahimsa* (non-violence). And forsaking all the bloodshed, hatred, violence, enmity and ill-will of past years, the poet is urging his people to take a pledge on this special day to replenish and renew:

Phir apne zehnon mein lahkao dosti ka chaman
Phir apni saanson se mahkao pyaar ka madhuban
Phir apne kaamon se chamkao sar-zameen-e-watan

Once again let the garden of friendship bloom in your mind
Once again let the forest of love become fragrant with your breath
Once again let the soil of your motherland burnish with your deeds

To the generations of Indian children who have seen the photograph of Gandhi hanging on a wall, for whom the 'Father of the Nation' is little more than a quaint, smiling, toothless figure in a loincloth, clutching a stick, here's Ataur Rehman Tariq writing about the nation's collective *maha pita* ('great father') in a poem entitled 'Bapu':

Bachcho tum ne Bapu ki tasveer to dekhi hogi
Eik nazar mein samjhoge tum un ko budha jogi

Children, you must have seen the picture of Bapu
At first glance you'd have taken him for an old ascetic

No talk of Gandhi's life is possible without a mention of his death, the manner in which he was killed, how and by whom. Here's Gulzar, a poet with a distinctly modern sensibility, presenting a harsh truth in a uniquely modern, straightforward way; without mincing words, and with great economy of expression, he is saying that just as Gandhi's legacy lives so does that other, opposing view that killed him:

Sawa gaz aasmaan odhe huwe sar pe
Badan par eik langoti lapete
Prarthana le liye nikla thha baahar

Kisi ne aagey badh kar
Tamancha rakh diya seene pe yeh keh ke
Tumhari raaye se sehmat nahi hoon main!

Tamancha chal raha hai—
Woh raaye marti nahi hai!

Wearing a yard-and-a-quarter of the sky on his head
A loincloth wrapped around his body
He had come out for prayer

Someone stepped forward and
Placing a pistol on his chest said:
I do not agree with your opinion!

That pistol is still firing—
That opinion does not die!

And now for a search for some answers as to why Gandhi remains relevant in a world that has changed dramatically, and not for the better, since he lived and worked. What is the reason for his enduring appeal? Charkh Chinoiti offers some clues:

Bapu ne har insan ko insan samjha
Bahbuudi-e-har-fard ko iman samjha

Injeel ko Quran ko aur Gita ko
Seene se lagaya unhein yaksaan samjha

Bapu treated every human being as a human
Regarded the welfare of every individual as his faith
Be it the Bible, or the Quran or the Gita
He embraced them to his bosom as equal

Abrar Kiratpuri, better known as a poet of the *hamd* and *naat* (poetry in praise of God), writes a lovely short poem telling us why we should remember this *rahbar*, guide/mentor, who showed us the way of *desh-bhakti*:

Dosti ka sabaq de gaya
Mar ke javed woh ho gaya

He has left a lesson of friendship
He has become undying after dying

That Gandhi is alive and well in the modern writer's imagination is evident from this short, very short, story by the Hindi writer Asghar Wajahat; so keen is its rapier-sharp insight, so deep the well of belief from which it springs that it gives you fresh reasons to hope:

The spirits come to Shah Alam Camp* after midnight. One night an old man's spirit comes along with all the other spirits. The old man's body is naked save for a skimpy loincloth. He wears chappals on his feet and holds a wooden staff in his hand. An old-fashioned fob watch peeps from the folds of his loincloth.

Someone asks the old man, "Are you too looking for a relative here in this camp?"

---

*Referring to a camp that was set up for the victims (all Muslims) in Ahmadabad after the Gujarat Riots of 2002. This is my translation from Asghar Wajahat's original written in Hindi.

The old man replies, “Yes, and no.”

The others leave him alone, taking him for a senile old man. The old man walks round and round the camp.

Someone again asks the old man, “Baba, whom are you looking for?”

The old man says, “I am looking for someone who can kill me.”

“Why?”

“I was killed fifty years ago by a bullet. Now I want the rioters to burn me alive.”

“But, why do you want that, Baba?”

“Simply to tell the world, that I was not killed by their bullet, nor will I die if they burn me alive.”

22. Nehru: What the Red Rose Said

My mother paints a vivid picture...of her father glued to the radio waiting for the daily despatches on Nehru's health. Like countless others across the country, her father would sit beside the radio and wait for news on the dearly beloved, ailing prime minister's health. The radio was playing *Mat ro mata, laal tere bahutere*...(Don't cry, Mother, you have many sons...) Suddenly, my mother tells me, he let out a wail and began to cry like a baby. The entire family joined in that collective outpouring of grief. A funerary gloom descended on the home. The cooking fire was not lit that day for no one could think of eating a morsel. It was as though a family elder had passed away. Such was the grief and the profound sense of loss.

In hindsight, the loss was indeed irreparable. Nehru's death on 27 May 1964 marked the end of an age of innocence—in life as in politics. Nehru's India lingered on, feeble and emaciated for a while but the man who had infused the idea with vim and vigour was gone. With the passing of years, wars were won, the country developed, the closed economy opened up, nuclear tests were successfully conducted but the secular spirit that Nehru embodied through thought and deed slowly began to leach out. The secular socialist republic that Nehru had helped fashion began to change colours.

Let us look at the spell Nehru cast over the writers and thinkers of his age and the effect he had on the Indian literary scene, especially the progressive writers' movement. Quick to align himself with the writers' fraternity—be it domestic or international—Nehru was known to extend a hand of solidarity to a good cause. As a gesture of camaraderie with the beleaguered people of Spain in their fight against fascist forces, Nehru joined the intellectual fraternity that had descended from different parts of the world. When Andre Malraux, Stephen Spender, W H Auden, Ernest Hemingway, and John Dos Passos leant their weight to the Spanish War, Nehru too visited the trenches of Spain.

In India, he was among the first to extend support to the fledgling All India Progressive Writers' Association in April 1936. In November 1937, he addressed the PWA session in Allahabad. In an informal but heart-felt speech, he stressed the role of the progressive writer in society. He also touched upon the Hindi-Urdu debate by saying an academic discussion was more likely to find a solution than politicians who can be relied upon to generate more heat and distrust rather than genuine debate! He urged the association to include only writers and not 'allow among yourself politicians like me' or else the creative and artistic side of their work would suffer, Nehru warned. Emphasising his point about keeping politicians at bay, he gave the example of European and American associations of progressive writers and writers like Voltaire whose writings influenced not just the French Revolution but the whole world for over a hundred years.

Under Nehru's personal directive, the central government set up the Sahitya Akademi with various state units under its umbrella, to look seriously into the question of translations from and into regional languages and truly make *bhasha* literatures intelligible to a national audience. The Sahitya Akademi was set up in 1954 with one of the staunchest Hindi progressives, Prabhakar Machwe, as its first Secretary.

The cinema of the late 1940s and all through the 1950s and the mid-60s continued to reflect the 'idea' of India that Nehru was at pains to imprint on the national consciousness. In this, the progressive lyricists did a yeoman's service in spreading this idea to the nooks and crannies of the popular imagination through hugely popular film songs. In B R Chopra's *Naya Daur* (New Era, 1957), Sahir Ludhianvi is exhorting his fellow countrymen and women to join hands, put their shoulder to the wheel and build a new and prosperous India:

Saathi haath badhana saathi re
Ek akela thak jayega, milkar bojh uthana

Come, my friend, extend your hand
One alone will tire, let us carry the burden together

And in 'Dhool ka Phool' (Flower of the Dust), Sahir is again urging people to put communal ill will aside and, in true Nehruvian style, become a liberal humanist:

Tu Hindu banega na Musalman banega
Insaan kii aulad hai insaan banega

You will be neither a Hindu nor a Muslim
Born of a human you will be a human

In 'Naunihal' (Young One), Kaifi Azmi celebrates the enduring legacy of Nehru whom he has long admired with this ode to Nehru's liberal humanism which he believes is a balm that a country scarred from a lingering post-partition ill-will desperately needs:

Meri awaaz suno, pyaar ka saaz suno
Kyun sajaii hai yeh chandan ki chita mere liye

Mai koi jism nahiin hoon ke jala dogey mujhey
Raakh ke saath bikhar jaaoonga mai duniya mein
Tum jahaan khaaoge thokar wahiin paogey mujhey

Hear my voice, hear the musical instrument of love
Why have you set up this pyre of sandalwood for me
I am not just a body that you can burn me
I will scatter in the wind with my ashes
Every time you stumble you will find me beside you

When Nehru dies, the shock and grief among the Urdu writers is near-palpable. They have already come to his defence when he found himself beleaguered after the debacle of the Indo-China war. Writing about the sick and ailing Nehru in 'Boorha Majhi' (The Old Boatman), Anand Narain Mulla makes a plea to the young and ruthless waiting to seize power:

Mujh ko dhaare se hataane ki yeh koshish na karo

Don't make this attempt to push me away from the current

When the terrible news comes of his death, a vast amount of poetry is written in a near-spontaneous outpouring of grief. Some among the progressives draw solace that Nehru's tired body may have given up, but his spirit will live on. Sahir writes:

Jism ki maut koi maut nahi hoti
Jism mitt jaane se insaan nahi mar jaate

The death of the body is not death
A person does not die with the body

In much the same vein, in 'Dil Tang Na Ho' (Don't Let Hearts Become Narrow), Ravish Siddiqui writes:

Wadi-e ishq se jab baad-e saba aayegi
Dil-e Nehru ke dhadakne ki sada aayegi

When the breeze blows in from the Valley of Love
It will bring the sound of Nehru's beating heart

But Makhdoom Mohiuddin knows the loss is irreplaceable for there may be many like him but there's only one Nehru:

Hazaar pairahan aaiyenge zamaane mein
Magar woh sandal-o gul ka ghubaar, musht-e bahaar...

A thousand raiments will come to this world
But that cloud of sandalwood and rose, that handful of spring...

In 'Khwabon ka Masiha' (The Prophet of Dreams), Aijaz Siddiqui too is lamenting the breaking of dreams that will never be dreamt again, just as Salaam Machlishehri in 'Surkh Gulabon ne Kaha' (The Red Roses Said) is invoking the metaphor of the garden for the country Nehru has single-handedly tended in the tumultuous years after independence. Rafat Sarosh, a young progressive at that time, holds out hope in his 'Jawahar Jyoti', of the 'light' of Nehru that will burn on:

Shola-e amn-o muhabbat hai Jawahar jyoti
Isski lau hai ke tabassum hai lab-e Nehru ka...

Jawahar's light is a spark of peace and love
Its flame is the smile on Nehru's lips...

23. Netaji Subhash Chandra Bose: *Eik Azaad Naghma*

Tum mujhe khoon do, main tumhe azaadi doonga (You give me blood, I will give you freedom). With this slogan Subhash Chandra Bose seized the popular imagination like few other leaders of his time. Popularly known as Netaji, this dashing well-dressed figure, whose daring exploits both on and off the political stage, made him a strikingly different person from the relatively staid political leaders of his time. Always immaculately dressed, fond of fast cars, unafraid of going against the grain and speaking of an armed struggle in which women were equal participants, he had little time for discussions and political parleys. Naturally, therefore, he soon caught the eye of the Urdu poets of his age who were not just verse smiths but also public intellectuals, polemicists and politically savvy pundits of their time. We find a fair amount of poetry written about Netaji, the hopes and expectations from his leadership and the grief and bewilderment when he disappeared from sight at the peak of his political career.

Razi Badayuni (1878-1939) from the medieval city of Badayun that has produced many a poet, wrote a panegyric entitled 'Babu Subhash Chandra Bose ke Naam' (To Babu Subhash Chandra Bose) extolling his exemplary bravery and courage, pleading with the Almighty to give him a long life so he may continue to do his extraordinary work, ending with this heart-felt wish:

Azad Hind Fauj ke aali commander
Babu Subhash Bose pe Bharat ko naaz hai
Azaadi-e-watan ke mujahid Khuda kare
Allah tujh ko ġhaib se taaqat ata kare

O Great Commander of the Azad Hind Army
Bharat is proud of Babu Subhash Bose
May this fighter for the country's freedom
Be granted strength from the Beyond by Allah

Tirlok Chand Mahroom, possibly the most prolific poet of his age who picked the smallest tremor in the political seismograph, was quick to take note of a giant-slayer such as Netaji. He too dwells on Bose's courage and strength, his willing embrace of *be-watani* (homelessness) for the sake of his homeland, and offers reasons why he made such an impact on the popular Indian imagination:

Kiya muztarab teri ghairat ne mujh ko
Na dekhi gayi tujh se zillat watan ki

Your self-respect has profoundly affected me
You couldn't bear to see the nation dishonoured

In a similar vein Darshan Singh Duggal speaks of the legacy of honour and self-respect Bose has bequeathed his country's women and men, a legacy he traces to Rana Pratap and Tipu Sultan:

Woh aashiq watan ka, woh dharti ka shaida
Woh Rana ka saani, woh Tipu ka paikar
Tashhaddud ke aagey bhala sir jhukata?

That lover of the nation, that mad devotee of the land
A match for Rana, made in the likeness of Tipu
Would he have bowed his head before aggression?

And goes on to end thus:

Watan ki hawaaon ka aazaad naghma
Zameen ka taraana sunaata rahega

A free song wafting in the nation's winds
He will keep humming the anthem of the soil

In 1943 Bose visited the grave of Bahadurshah Zafar, the last Mughal emperor, in Rangoon. Here, he gave his famous rallying cry of 'Dilli Chalo' (Go to Delhi) echoing the slogan of the mutineers of 1857 who had converged upon Delhi and made it a *markaz*, a centre, of their revolt when they hoisted the old and frail emperor on the throne of Delhi. Bose's Indian National Army held a parade near Zafar's burial spot with Bose describing Zafar as 'the man under whose sacred flag freedom-loving Hindus, Muslims and Sikhs fought side by side'. This moment is described in a long poem entitled 'Subhas Chandra Bose Bahadur Shah Zafar ke Mazaar Par' (Subhash Chandra Bose at the Grave of Bahadur Shah Zafar) by Jagan Nath Azad. Written in the first person, from Netaji's perspective, it is brimful with love for an exiled compatriot:

Aaj pahli baar teri qabr par aaya huun main
Be-nava huun nazr ko be-laus dil laaya huun main
Gardish-e-taqdeer ke haathon watan se duur huun
Ek bulbul huun magar sehn-e-chaman se duur huun

I have come to your grave for the first time
An indigent, all I have as offering is my unbiased heart
Misfortunes have caused me to be away from my homeland
I am a nightingale but far away from my country's courtyard

Going on to establish a bond with the last emperor who, like Bose, was *watan se duur* ('far away from the homeland'), he remembers the mutineers from Meerut, the valour of the Rani of Jhansi and vows to bring back Zafar's lost honour with the 'Tegh-i Hindi', the (metaphorical) sword he has unsheathed:

Teġh-e-Hindi jis ka loha manta hai ik jahan
Jis ki tezi ki gawaahi de raha hai aasman

The sword of Hind whose mettle is recognised by all
Whose sharpness is borne witness by the skies

As new facts emerge about Bose, he continues to be re-evaluated and re-imagined. A modern-day poet, Saeed Arfi, wrote a nazm entitled 'Woh Eik Sitara' (That Sole Star) on Netaji's centenary celebrations, describing Bose as a bright star that descended upon the earth to dispel the darkness of an enslaved nation, who shook Indians out of their lassitude, who lit the dark corners of our hearts with his rousing words, who wove dreams of courage and greatness for his people:

Woh zehn ki
Wusaton mein
Isss ummid ke saath
Azaaim ke beej bota raha
Ki
Aane waali nasl
Uss fasl ko
Kaamyaabi aur kaamrani se kaat sakey

In the vast expanses
Of the mind
He planted the seeds
Of determination
In the hope
That the coming generations
Would be able to harvest it
Successfully and profitably

24. Dilip Kumar's Enduring Love for Urdu

Like his colleague and childhood friend, Raj Kapoor, Dilip Kumar was born in the fabled Qissa Khwani Bazaar (the storytellers' marketplace) in Peshawar, and words were to remain his life-long friends. To be more precise, words and silences. Like the storytellers of yore, he knew how to modulate his voice (*lehje ka utaar-chadhaav*), how to drop to the lowest timbre, when to intersperse words with long pauses, how to use silences as much as words as an artiste's tool. In fact, it would not be an exaggeration to say that words, or dialogue delivery, would be Dilip Kumar's trademark as an actor in a career spanning over five decades.

In public life too, Dilip Kumar—born Muhammad Yusuf Khan to a Pathan fruit merchant's family—was known for his measured, immaculate use of words in the two languages he was most proficient in, namely, Urdu and English. Audiences thronged to hear him deliver the *sadaarati kalamaat* (the chair or chief guest's remarks) at many a mushaira both within the country and abroad among the Urdu-speaking diaspora. It was his immaculately enunciated, occasionally rhetorical and sometimes florid Urdu that won him more *wah wah* (applause) at such poetic soirees than many an established poet.

He was equally adept with words at non-literary gatherings. A friend who travelled with him across the small-towns of Uttar Pradesh as Dilip Kumar graciously lent his weight to electoral campaigns recalls a public meeting in Badaun that the thespian opened with the following remark: *Hum aur aap aksar andhere mein milte hain; aaj pehli baar roshni mein aap se mulaqaat ho rahi hai.* (You and I often meet in the dark; today for the first time we are meeting in the light.) These were simple words, simply said but so powerful. Needless to say, the crowd went wild.

Despite no formal education in Urdu, Dilip Kumar's love for the language was legendary and he chose to speak in his somewhat stylised Urdu whenever the opportunity arose. He was also known to host poets and writers for small, intimate soirees at his Mumbai home. Those who knew him, or had the occasion to hear him speak, remember his phenomenal recall of Urdu verses, of his wide and varied reading and his eclectic choice of Urdu poetry for the purpose of recitation. In his autobiography, for instance, he uses the following verse by way of dedicating the book to his parents:

Sukoon-e dil ke liye kuchh to ehtemaam karoon
Zara nazar jo miley phir unhein salaam karoon
Mujhe to hosh nahi aap mashwara dijiye
Kahaan se cheduun fasaana kahan tamaam karoon

I must make some preparations for my heart's peace
If I were to catch their gaze I will offer my salutation
I have no judgement; please give me advice
Where shall I begin my tale, where should I end it

In the same book, his wife Saira Bano writing in the Foreword reveals his great love for reading and how their house is adorned with many, many bookshelves containing books on a variety of subjects: 'Few among his countless followers know that Dilip Sahab has always been a voracious reader. Whether it is novels, plays or biographies, his love of classical literature has been foremost. The classics of Urdu, Persian and English literature adorn the bookshelves of our home. When he's done with the library bookshelves, we have to be ready to offer him a pick of the thousands of books tucked away carefully in our huge store rooms.' In his autobiography, Dilip Kumar credits his older brother, Ayub Khan, for inculcating a love for the Urdu language in him. Ayub Khan not only read widely but also wrote some short fiction in Urdu.

Among the modern poets, Dilip Kumar was known to recite, and occasionally hum the poetry of Faiz Ahmad Faiz. Among the older poets, Gulzar sahab reveals his penchant for reciting Nazeer Akbarabadi which Dilip Kumar seemed to have read extensively and could quote from memory. A story narration session with Dilip Kumar was a joy for a literary-minded film-maker and lyricist such as Gulzar sahab because apart from the film under discussion it invariably involved many impromptu poetic interludes. He recalls one such session in Bangalore when the thespian regaled Gulzar sahab by reciting the poetry of Nazeer Akbarabad. Listening to the poetry of this 18th century Agra-born poet recited by a Pathan from Peshawar whose Urdu, after decades in Mumbai, was still redolent with a *Peshori* inflection was a rare experience!

Gulzar sahab also narrates how Dilip Kumar would write out his own scenes, improvising when necessary according to his own acting styles, inserting the spoken words given by the screenplay writer with his characteristic pauses, arranging and re-arranging his dialogue to make it 'sit right' with his unique style of dialogue delivery. Often he would even write down his dialogue, in his immaculate Urdu script, in order to memorise it. Saira Bano too, refers to Dilip Kumar writing down his scenes and dialogues and working on the script till late in the night before the next's day's shooting.

Upon the actor's death in July 2021, Rehman Faris, a poet from Pakistan writes how impossible it is to imagine Dilip Kumar gone, how the late actor's eyes caused thousands of hearts to beat faster, how when his eyes have closed it seems the world has bid adieu to light, and how the dead actor, beloved of millions, will arise and address his admirers thus:

Gham nahin karna
Gulon ki zindagaani maut se kab ḳhatm hoti hai
Mohabbat ki kahaani maut se kab ḳhatm hoti hai

Don't grieve, for
The life of flowers is never cut short by death
The story of love is never cut short by death

Another poem written on his death by Irfan Shahood, a young poet also from Pakistan, 'Dilip Kumar ki Akhri Khwahish' (Dilip Kumar's Last Wish) imagines somewhat wistfully and—given the political climate on both sides of the border, almost hopelessly—of the dead actor's body being taken to the ancestral *haveli* in Mohalla Khuda Daad in Qissa Khwani Bazaar where he will once again see, smell, taste, hear the sights, scents, tastes and sounds of his beloved city of birth and, having had his fill, he might decide:

Fana ghaatiyon mein
Main yuun phail jaaoon ki waapas na aauun

So lose myself in the vales of mortality
That I might never return

Watching his old videos, one is struck by how deeply Dilip Kumar seemed to have drunk from the well of Urdu *zubaan* and *tehzeeb* (language and culture) and how deeply the *sheereeni* (sweetness) of Urdu *zubaan* had percolated into his own tone and tenor. Listening to the sheer joy with which he rolls the words around his tongue, as though savouring the *maza* (taste/savour) of each syllable, one wonders if there will ever again be another like him: *Aisa kahan se laoon ki tujh sa kahein jise*?

Postscript: A somewhat lesser-known fact about Dilip Kumar's otherwise well-documented love for the Urdu language is that he also wrote fiction in Urdu himself. I have been able to find two short stories so far: 'Eik Clerk ki Kahani' (The Story of a Clerk) and 'Zehn Eik Kashti Hai Mutallatum Lehron ke Darmiyan' (The Mind is a Boat Buffeted Amongst Turbulent Waves). I am looking for more which I hope to translate some day.

25. Lata Mangeshkar: *Shola Sa Lapak Jaae Hai Aawaaz To Dekho*

It must have been sometime in 1947 or 1948, when Hindi cinema's most iconic actor Dilip Kumar was still not so well-recognised as to get mobbed, and could easily travel to work in Bombay's trains. One day the music director Anil Biswas, Dilip Kumar and Lata Mangeshkar found themselves travelling in the same train compartment. Dilip Kumar asked Anil Biswas about the young girl, to which he said, she was a young singer who sang well. Dilip Kumar asked her name and where she was from. Biswas told him the name and that she was from Maharashtra. Dilip Kumar's response was: 'But their Urdu pronunciation isn't correct and in their singing you can smell *daal-bhaat* (lentils and rice).'

In today's India, reading about this encounter in the excellent book *Lata in Her Own Words...Conversations with Nasreen Munni Kabir* (Niyogi Books) I find Dilip Kumar's response incredible. That he could make such a statement and not worry about political correctness speaks of an India where people were possibly less uptight about regional identities and took statements such as this at face value without over-reading them or taking offence. It also speaks of an India where Urdu had not been demonised and knowing Urdu and speaking it correctly and well was a matter of pride not subversion.

However, what is most incredible is Lata Mangeshkar's response to Dilip Kumar's somewhat blithe statement. In her conversation with Nasreen Munni Kabir, she confesses to being terribly hurt at hearing such a thing. But, knowing how important it was to know Urdu as a singer in the Hindi film industry, she found merit in these harsh words and chose to do something about it. She knew the composer Mohammad Shafi who worked as an assistant to Anil Biswas and Naushad. She told him that she wanted to learn Urdu so she could pronounce it correctly. Shafi found her a *maulana*, a gentleman called Mehboob, who taught her Urdu for a short while. As Lata went on to say, 'When I speak, my Urdu isn't very good but when I sing I make sure there are no flaws in my diction.'

And so it was, that instead of being aggrieved or taking the high road of language chauvinism or parochialism, Lata strove to better herself. Whatever be her politics in the later years of her life, her devotion in the early years of her career to improve her Urdu remains laudable. The bell-like clarity of her voice may well have been a gift from God, honed by hours and hours of *riyaaz* (practice), but the immaculate pronunciation, the correct emphasis on the 'sound' of words were all her own doing. When singing in languages not her own, such as Urdu or Bangla or Tamil, she would first listen to someone who spoke the language who would read out the lyrics to her. She would then write the words phonetically in Hindi and proceed to sing it giving as much importance to words, as tunes, in her entire musical career.

Those who have worked with Lata vouch for the fact that she tried to understand the meanings of difficult Urdu words and expressions and not just mimic their correct pronunciation.

Possibly this understanding makes her sing Jan Nisar Akhtar's 'Ai Dil-e Nadaan' in *Razia Sultan* or 'Aap Yun Faaslon se Guzarte Rahey' for the little-known *Shankar Hussain* with such a wealth of feeling.

Then there are the many ghazals in the classical mould such as this by Sahir Ludhianvi for the film *Ghazal*, the ghazal which should be sung differently from a song given the compact brevity of the two-line sher that string it together are sung in a manner that the meaning of each sher should be understandable:

Naghma-o sher ki saughat kisey pesh karoon
Yeh chhalkatey huwey jazbaat kisey pesh karoon

To whom shall I offer this gift of song and verse
To whom shall I offer these brimful feelings

Or this by Majrooh Sultanpuri for the film *Dastak*:

Hum hain mataa-i koocha bazaar ki tarah
Utthti hai har nigaah kharidaar ki tarah

I am like the commodity in a marketplace
Every gaze that rises upon me like a buyer's

Or this by Naqsh Lyallpuri for *Dard*:

Ahl-e dil yuun hii nibha lete hain
Dard seene mein chhupa lete hain

People with a generous heart manage somehow
They manage to hide their pain in their breast

Then there is the tender ghazal by Makhdoom Mohiuddin she sang for *Bazaar*:

Phir chhirhi raat baat phoolon ki
Shaam phulon ki raat phoolon ki

Once again the talk turned to flowers
Of an evening of flowers, a night of flowers

A veritable treasure trove of non-film ghazals sung by Lata and Jagjit Singh is to be found in the album *Sajda* beginning with this gem by Qateel Shifai:

Dard se mera daaman bhar de Ya Allah
Phir chaahe diwaana kar de Ya Allah

Fill my hem with pain, O Allah
Later let me go mad, O Allah

No mention of Lata singing the Urdu ghazal can be complete without noting the ghazals she sang of Ghalib. Of the many to be found online, here is a particular favourite for the Saregama collection:

Phir mujhe deeda-e tar yaad aaya
Dil jigar tishna-e faryaad aaya

Once again I remember the tearful eyes
And the heart's thirst for supplication

Dilawar Figar, the poet from Pakistan best known for his humorous and satirical writings, was possibly writing only half in jest when he wrote in a poem entitled 'Mausiqui se Ilaaaj' (Cure by Music):

Jumla amraaz-e-ḳhabeesa ki dawa-e-kaargar
Naġhma-e-Sahir ba-aawaaz-e-Lata Mangeshkar

The most effective treatment for malevolent diseases of words
Are the songs of Sahir heard in the voice of Lata Mangeshkar

In India, Urdu poets too have paid tributes to Lata and her magical voice. In a long, loving ode to Lata, Akhtar Ansari calls hers a voice that:

Laakhon zehnon ko jo bakhshey eik khush-aaind soch
Eik pakeezah tahayyur, eik masoom anfaal

Grants lakhs of minds pleasing thoughts
A pure wonderment, an innocent treasure

Majrooh Sultanpuri, a poet and fine film lyricist who worked with Lata on songs such as *Aaja piya tohe pyaar doon, Toone O Rangeele kaisa jaadu kiya...* and *Bangley ke Peechhey...*, among others, wrote a poem entitled 'Lata Mangeshkar ke Naam' (To Lata Mageshkar) where he initially bemoans the state of the language in present times but goes on to say:

Mere lafzon ko jo chhuu leti hai aawaaz teri
Sarhadein torh ke urhh jaate hain ashaar mere

When your voice touches my words
My verses break their bounds and fly

If ever there can be an apt tribute for the Nightingale of India, it is this sher by Momin Khan Momin written centuries ago:

Uss ġhairat-e-naheed ki har taan hai deepak
Shola sa lapak jaae hai aawaaz to dekho

Every note of that modest beauty is lit
A flame leaps up: just see that voice!

26. *Brindaban ke Krishn Kanhaiya Allah Hu*

The child-god Krishna, his playfulness and his *leela* (a divine play of aesthetics), as also his *mohini* (ability to enchant) and the sage counsel he gives to a distressed warrior in his role as *parthasarthi*, the friendly charioteer of Arjuna, have been the subject of a great deal of Urdu poetry. While Maulana Hasrat Mohani is his most ardent and best-known admirer among the Urdu poets, of whom more later, there are numerous poems on different facets of Krishna's life and personality.

To begin with, let us look briefly at the long and lyrical poem on the birth of the blue god, entitled 'Janam Kanhaiya Ji' (The Birth of Kanhaiya ji) by Nazeer Akbarabadi. Redolent with the flavours of Braj, it tells the story of the birth of a baby boy to Devki and Vasudev at a time when they are imprisoned in their home by Devki's tyrannical brother, of Vasudev crossing the swollen Jamuna river to take the baby boy to safety in the home of Nand Baba, exchanging his infant daughter with Krishna:

> *...Ab Nand ke ghar ki baat suno waan eik achambha yeh thehra*

Jo raat ko janmi thhi ladki aur bhor ko dekha to ladka...
Sab naari aayin Gokul ki aur paas padosan aa baithiin
Kuchh dhol manjire laatii thhiin, kuchh geet jachha ke gaatiin thhiin...

And now listen to the miracle that happened in Nand's home
A girl had been born at night but by dawn it was a boy...
All the women of Gokul came, the ladies from the neighbourhood
Some brought drums and cymbals, some sang songs for a child's birth

In 'Har ki Tareef Mein' (In Praise of the Lord), Nazeer lists the many attributes of the beloved god:

Main kya kya dasaf kahuun yaaron uss shyaam baran auvtari ke
Sikshan, Kanhaiya, Murlidhar, Manmohan, Kunj Bihari ke
Gopal, Manohar, Saanwaliya, Ghanshyam, Atal Banwari ke
Nandlal Dulare, Sundar Chhab, Brij Chandr Mukut Chhalkari ke...

'Krishn Kanhaiyya' by Hafeez Jallundhari is yet another long love lyric, eminently sing-able in its melodious invocation of Krishna's beauty and the sheer magnetic pull of the flute-playing cowherd of Gokul:

Ai dekhne waalon
Iss husn ko dekho
Iss raaz ko samjho
Yeh naqsh-e-ḳhayaali
Yeh fikrat-e-aali
Yeh paikar-e-tanveer
Yeh Krishn ki tasveer

O ye who see
See this beauty
Understand this secret
This work of the imagination
This thought of the highest order
This embodiment of light
This picture of Krishna

'Sri Krishn' by Seemab Akbarabadi talks of the *preet ke geet* (the songs of love) and plays with the idea of cosmic 'play', of playing with the colourful spring of love:

Huwa tuloo sitaaron ki dilkashi le kar
Suroor aankh mein, nazron mein zindagi le kar

It rose with the loveliness of the stars
Bearing intoxication in the eyes, life in the gaze

Then there's Julius Naheef Dehelvi's 'Krishn Kanhaiya' brimful with adoration for Kanhaiya, which literally means a beautiful, adorable boy; interestingly, the poem stresses the all-inclusive love that Kanhaiya has for everyone, that makes no difference between *apne-paraye*:

Jo sun leta hai gosh-e-dil se afsaana Kanhaiya ka
Woh ho jaata hai sachche dil se diwaana Kanhaiya ka

He who listens attentively to the story of Krishna
Becomes a devotee of Krishna from the depths of his heart

Invoking Him by His many names—Gobind, Radha Kishan, Gopal, Radha Raman, Madhav Murari, Mukut Dhari Madan Gopal and so on—Munshi Banwari Lal Shola in 'Sri Krishn' talks of the combination of many qualities within one form and addresses him in words traditionally used in the *hamd* form of poetry for Allah:

Tu hii khaaliq hai kaun-o makaan ka
Tu hii razzaq hai har uns-o jaan ka

You are the creator of the universe
You are the provider of all love and life

Hailing the arrival of Krishna the messiah, Nihal Seoharvi employs the sort of metaphysical imagery one associates with Sufi mysticism in this nazm also entitled 'Sri Krishn':

Intizar-e jalwa-e haq me thha toor-e zindagi
Deen-e Aadam bhool baitha thha shaoor-e zindagi

The mountain of life was waiting for the light of truth
The faith of Adam had forgotten the discernment of life

Chandar Bhan Kaifi Dehelvi invokes Krishna's favouring of the poor and the humble over the rich and mighty here, in incidents related to his childhood friend Sudama and his choice of the home of Vidur when he visited Hastinapur instead of the palace of the Kauravas:

Khaa ke tandul kahin ezaaz Sudama ko diya
Saag ḳhush ho ke Vidur ji ka kiya nosh kahin

Where once he honoured Sudama by eating his rice
Another time he happily ate simple greens at Vidur ji's home

With its internal rhyme and alliterations, Nida Fazli's 'Brindaban ke Krishn Kanhaiya Allah Hu' (The Krishn Kanhaiya of Brindavan Allah, O Allah) makes Krishna a votary of inclusiveness, an all-embracing wholeness in which everything from the Ganga to the *gayya* (the cow), the *maulvi* and the *mazdoor* come together:

Maulviyon ka sajda pandit ki puja
Mazdooron ki haiyya haiyya Allah hu

The prostration of maulvis, the piety of pundits
The cries of the labourers, Allah O Allah

And, finally, no one can match the ardour of Maulana Hasrat Mohani, a practising Muslim, a *panch-waqta namazi* (one who prayed five times), one for whom worship of any deity is *kufr*, yet whose ardour for Hazrat Shri Krishna Alaihi Rahma (The Venerable Shri Krishna Blessed be His Name) knew no bounds. Of the vast amounts of poetry on his beloved Krishan ji maharaj, here's a verse on the worship of beauty:

Maslak-i ishq hai parastish-i husn
Hum nahin jaante aazab-o-sawaab

The path of love leads to the worship of beauty
I know neither (divine) reward nor punishment

Postscript: There are days, especially post 22 January 2024, when the cries to 'free' Mathura and Kashi rise to a shrill crescendo, one wonders if writing about any of this truly matters? One can go blue in the face invoking a Nida Fazli or a Hasrat Mohani but will the blind see, and the deaf hear? In the triumphal chest-thumping and a self-righteous rejoicing, are these voices even relevant?

27. *Mard-e-Kaamil Maryada Purushottam Ram*

Epics allow themselves to be read at multiple levels; the many stories contained within an epic can be 'broken down' and interpreted in different ways, to suit a variety of purposes while maintaining the over-arching, all-embracing integrity of the larger poetic story. In the case of the *Ramayana*, while it is primarily a religious text depicting the life of Ram, the Prince of the Kosalas, his 14-year exile, the various people—as also birds and beasts—he meets during his stay in the jungles, his journey to distant Lanka in pursuit of his wife who has been abducted by Raavan and his eventual, triumphant return to his home in Ayodhya, the story and the very persona of Ram are brimful with meaning and significance. As much a religious figure as an icon of morality, the character of Maryada Puroshattam Ram, the perfect man (*mard-e-kaamil*), the embodiment of goodness and manliness and everything that symbolises honour, chivalry and kindness has seized the imagination of the poet and creative writer from different Indian languages for millennia. His story has been told and retold in different ways in multiple languages and dialects.

The Urdu poet and writer is no exception. Of the many poems on the chief protagonist of the many *Ram Kathas* that have sprouted over the centuries, 'Ram' by Dr Muhammad Iqbal is remarkable. Brimming over with love and respect for *Ram-e Hind* whose very name is a badge of honour for the people of Hind, it lays claim to Ram in unequivocal terms, as someone that every Indian is proud of:

Labrez hai sharaab-e haqiqat se jaam-e Hind
Sab falsafi hain khitta-e maghrib ke Ram-e Hind

The goblet of Hind is brimful with the wine of Truth
All the philosophers acknowledge him as Ram of Hind

Similarly, Saghar Nizami's 'Ram' stakes his claim to honouring and loving the legacy of Ram making no distinction between the followers of Hinduism and the people of Hind who have the same reasons to love and respect him:

Zindagi ki rooh thha roohaniyat ki shaan thha
Woh mujassam roop mein insaan ke irfaan thha

He was the spirit of life, the pride of spirituality
He was knowledge incarnate in the form of a man

Then there's 'Sri Ram Chandar' by Zafar Ali Khan, a prolific poet now lost in the veils of time but in his time and age one who had his finger to the nation's pulse, who wrote on a range of subjects and was an influential editor of an Urdu newspaper. Here, in waxing eloquent on the many sterling qualities of Sri Ram Chandar and the message embodied in his life, he makes the telling point that the 'culture' of Hind is embodied in Sita, Lakshman and Ram:

Naqsh-e tehzeeb-e Hunood abhi numaya hai agar
To woh Sita se hai Lachman se hai aur Ram se hai

If the imprint of Indian civilization is still visible
Then it is due to Sita and Lakshman and Ram

'Ramayan ka Eik Scene' (A Scene from the Ramayan) by Brij Narain Chakbast is one of the best-loved and oft-quoted pieces of Urdu poetry. This long poem depicts Raja Ram Chandar taking leave from his parents, especially the poignant moment of leaving his mother, Kaushalya. Inspired as much by the soz (an elegy on the martyrdom of Husain, the grandson of prophet Muhammad) and marsiya (dirge) tradition that had flowered in the Awadh region as by the many retellings of the *Ram Katha* in the folk tradition, the poem is full of poetic imagery of a son, a much-loved ideal son, taking leave of his mother as he embarks on a journey of honour and commitment taking with him nothing from his princely home save his mother's blessings and the assurance that as long as he has the grace and favour of the Almighty even the wilderness can be as favourable as a mother's loving embrace:

Rukhsat huwa woh baap se lekar Khuda ka naam
Raah-e wafa ki manzil-e awaal huii tamaam

He took leave of his father taking the name of God
And so the first stage of the path of loyalty was crossed

Lakshman's unconditional love for Ram is described thus by Munshi Banwari Lal Shola:

Hain Ram Chandr maalik-e kaunain bahr-o bar
Sabki khabar jo lete hain kaun unki le khabar
Dukh unko naam maatr bhi mil sakta hii nahiin
Be-hukm jinke patta jo hil sakta hii nahiin

Ram Chandr is the master of both worlds
He who orders the world who can order him
He can not be given even an iota of grief
Not a leaf can stir without his order

Yet another poem, entitled 'Ram' by Rahbar Jaunpuri, while enumerating the many good qualities including his love for peace, harmony and truth, tells us why the land of Hindustan is proud of him. In walking the path of loyalty, Ram has become an enduring symbol of self-sacrifice just as Raavan has come to embody the *shar-pasand*, those who like evil:

Aaina-e-ḳhuloos-o-mohabbat yahan thhe Ram
Amn aur shanti ki zamaanat yahan thhe Ram

Ram was a mirror of love and affection
He was the surety of peace and tranquility

Occasionally, it's the 'smaller' stories of the lesser-known characters that seize the poetic imagination. Sita, who accompanied her husband and brother-in-law in exile forsaking the luxuries of the royal palace, is one of the principal dramatis personae but what of Urmila, the wife of Lakshman and younger sister of Sita? Like Sita, she too wanted to accompany her husband but Lakshman asked her to stay back and look after his ageing parents. She agreed, but at what cost? 'Urmila' by a contemporary poet, Tripurari, tells this unsung story and asks if Urmila's sacrifice was any less? Using a modern, everyday idiom and a natural, unaffected, enquiring tone he seems to be wondering how this flesh-and-blood young woman, prone to the body's human urges, would have coped in those barren 14 years of enforced separation from her husband?

Phuul se bhi sau guna nazuk
Jo Sita ki bahan thi

A hundred times more delicate than a flower
She who was Sita's sister

That epics can be read at multiple levels, including the political, is evident in the sorrowful, poignant, yet profoundly political

'Doosra Banwas' (The Second Exile) by Kaifi Azmi, as much an elegy to the death of an India that was, an India that always allowed differences to co-exist but one that was dealt a body blow on 6 December 1992. The nazm depicts Lord Ram, coming home from exile in the jungle, to find the *raqs-e-deewaangi* (the dance of madness) in the courtyard of his home in Ayodhya, the stains of blood on the banks of the Sarju river and his reaction to the demolition of the masjid that would, according to the poet, have been unequivocal. Ram would have felt as though he had been banished for a second time for such a city, filled with hate, could not have been his home:

Ram banbaas se jab lautke ghar mein aaye
Yaad jangal bahut aaya jo nagar mein aaye
Raqs-e-deewaangi aangan mein jo dekha hoga
Chhe December ko Shri Ram ne socha hoga
Itne deewaane kahan se mire ghar mein aaye

When Ram returned home from exile in the forest
He remembered the jungles when he came to the city
When he saw the dance of madness in his courtyard
On 6th December Shri Ram would have wondered
Where have all these madmen come from into my home

In the years to come, what will be the poetry about the triumphal celebrations beside the Saryu river on 22 January 2024? Only time will tell.

28. Shiv: The Drinker of Poison

The Urdu poets, forever ready to offer *aqeedat ke phool* (flowers of faith) to a pantheon of *mazhabi rahnuma* (religious figures who 'show the way'), have not been lacking in their love and affection for the Blue-Necked One. References abound to Shiv and his consort Parvati, to their marriage, to his drinking the *kalakuta* (poison) after the *samudra manthan* (churning of the oceans) which rendered his neck blue. Written by both Muslim poets and non-Muslims at a time when inclusion and pluralism was the norm rather than the exception, these need to be revived and re-read not merely for their evocations of communal harmony and goodwill, but also because much of it is simply good poetry.

Of the many *Shiv Puran* written and translated into Urdu, the most well regarded is the one by Munshi Shankar Dayal Farhat published by Naval Kishore Press in 1870. Each *adhyay* (chapter) begins with a prayer 'Sada Shivji ki nigah lutf idhar ho' (May Shivji's benevolent gaze be forever upon us) and goes on to describe in lyrical verse the essence of the original Sanskrit texts. The mythology of Shiv and Parvati as well as the essentials of *advaita* philosophy are made accessible in a homely manner such as the story of the hunter and the deer thus: *Eik hiran ka paani peena taalaab mein aur sayyad ka teer khenchna bel ke darakht se*...(The deer that drank water at a pond and the hunter that pulled an arrow from beneath the stone apple tree, the tree dedicated to Shiv...) An older version by an unknown author from Rai Bareilly, has a *Tamheed* (Preface) outlining the aims and objectives of the text followed by a *Dibacha* (Foreword) that, in keeping with the tradition of Urdu treatises of the times, begins with a *hamd* (in praise of Allah)! Today, its author would be hauled over coals for such a *ghor paap* (grave sin) but clearly those were kinder, gentler times.

Of the poems specifically on Shiv, here is Munawwar Lakhnawi writing 'Shivji ki Tareef Main' (In Praise of Shivji), listing the many attributes of 'Jagat Ishwar', 'Sansaar ke Swami' and concluding by describing him thus:

Rooh ko qaid-e tanasukh se rihaah karte hain
Hamatan lutf hain masroof-e karam rahte hain
Maghfirat Bakhsh jinhein ahl-e nazar kahte hain

He releases the soul from the prison of transmigration
He is entirely immersed in joy, engrossed in bounty
The discerning call him the Granter of Salvation

The poison that Shiv drank after the *samudra manthan* (churning of the ocean) becomes a metaphor for the poet. In a hauntingly lyrical poem entitled 'Kaash' (If Only), Sarwat Zehra wishes that the compromises a woman has to make all her life could be eaten like pieces of broken bangles that have been ground to a fine powder, or the 'poison of solitude' (*tanhai ka zahr)* drunk:

Shiv ke neel kanth ki tarah
Galey mein rakh kar jiya ja sakta

Like Shiv's blue-tinged neck
I too could live with it in my throat

In a long poem entitled 'Zindagi' (Life) by Kaifi Azmi, the ocean itself enters the poet's room and says:

Shiv ne ye bhejwaya hai lo piyo aur
Aaj Shiv ilm hai amrit hai amal

Shiv has sent this for you, here, drink it
Today Shiv is knowledge, nectar, action

The act of churning the dark waters which eventually yielded the ambrosial nectar is aspirational, emblematic, though eventually futile for mere mortals as in the poem 'Zahr ka Darya' (The River of Poison) by Qaleel Jhansvi:

Woh jis mein Shiv ko zahr peena na parhey
Woh kainat jo sab ko samaan karti ho

Where Shiv does not have to drink the poison
That universe which makes everyone equal

That the analogy of swallowing poison continues to impress generations of poets, especially women, is evident from this sher by Aziz Bano Darab Wafa:

Shiv to nahin hum phir bhi hum ne duniya bhar ke zahr piye
Itni kadwaahat hai munh mein kaise meethi baat karein

I am not Shiv yet I have drunk all the poisons of the world
Such is the bitterness in my mouth how can I talk sweetly

Then there was Nazeer Akbarabadi, one of the greatest chroniclers of the *longue duree* that was the 19th century, who has written on the humblest of subjects such as the *kakdi* (cucumber) seller in the bazaar of Agra and of a lived, multicultural, syncretic way of life where Holi was celebrated with as much vigour as Eid. In his ballad-like 'Mahadeoji ka

Byaah' (The Wedding of Mahadevji) with its opening lines redolent of piety and love, '*Pahle naam Ganesh ka lijiye sees nawaae*' (Begin with the name of Ganesh with your head bowed low), he goes on to say how the very re-telling of the incidents surrounding this wedding bring blessings upon the listeners:

Aur jis ne iss byaah ki mahima kahi banaaye
Uss ke bhi har haal mein Shivji rahein suhaaye

And whoever describes the glory of this match
Shivji will always keep them in good stead

An older poet, Munshi Dwarka Parshad Ufaq Lakhnawi, employs the traditional tropes and metaphors of classical Urdu *rubai* (a genre of poetry comprising four-line stanzas) in his 'Shankar Darshan' to describe the beauty of Shankar and Parvati:

Jism ka rang chamkte huwey neelam ki misaal
Chand ki rukh mein chamak chehrey pe suraj ka jalaal

The colour of his body like a glittering sapphire
The glow of the moon in his visage, the glory of the sun on his face

Long years ago, Iqbal, the poet we love to hate in New India, the India that is Bharat, wrote 'Naya Shivala' (A New Temple to Shiv) urging his fellow Indians thus:

Sooni parhi hui hai muddat se dil ki basti
Aa ik naya shivala is des mein bana dein
Duniya ke tirathon se ooncha ho apna tirath
Daaman-e-aasmaan se iss ka kalas mila dein

For too long the heart's dwelling has been desolate
Come, let us build a new temple to Shiv in this country
Of all the pilgrimage spots in the world let ours be the highest
Let us make its spire touch the hem of the skies

To come to present times, here's Ayush Charagh comparing Life to the river that's trapped in the matted, coiled tresses of the God:

Iss ka apni hii ravaani par nahiin hai ikhtiyaar
Zindagii Shiv ki jataaon mein hai Ganga ki tarah

It has no control over its own speed and swiftness
Like Ganga life is trapped in the matted hair of Shiv

And here's Ashutosh Rana, a television and film actor and also a fine poet, invoking Shiv's Ganga while writing of his own troubled, divisive times:

Shiv ki Ganga bhi paani hai
Aab-e zamzam bhi paani hai
Mulla bhi piye pandit bhi
Paani ka mazhab kya hoga?

The Ganga of Shiv is water
So is the water of the zamzam spring
The mulla drinks it so does the pandit
What will be the religion of water?

29. *Mehboob-e Ilahi* Nizamuddin Auliya

Referred to as *Mehboob-e Ilahi* (the Beloved of God), Hazrat Nizamuddin Auliya (1238-1325) belonged to the Sufi order known as the Chishtiya *silsila* (brotherhood), his predecessors being Fariduddin Ganjshakar, Qutbuddin Bakhtiyar Kaki and Moinuddin Chishti. His *dargah* (hospice) in Ghiyaspur, then a suburb of Delhi, now known as Basti Nizamuddin, drew all manner of folk from different faiths, young and old, illiterate and educated, rich and poor. In medieval India where power revolved around the twin axis of the sufis and the sultans, Hazrat Nizamuddin remained steadfast in maintaining his distance from the sultans and being close to the people who thronged his *jamaat-khana* (assembly house) for *zikr* (remembrance), *langar* (distribution of food and drink), and *sama* (listening). Experienced in dealing with different sorts of people and endowed as he was with deep insight into human nature, his discourses were brimful with *ilm-e ladunni* (inspired knowledge) that was revealed through *qissa* (incident) and *kahani* (stories), parables and allegories.

In the *Fawaidul Fuad*, a record of the Sufi master's conversations (known as *malfuzat* in the Sufi tradition) compiled by Amir Hasan Sijzi, Hazrat Nizamuddin is believed to have said that the first lesson about Sufism is neither about prayers nor organised rituals; instead it begins with mastery of the maxim: 'Whatever you do not like to be done to yourself, do not wish it to happen to others; wish for yourself what you wish others also.' Altruism, renunciation, distribution of food to the poor, and above all, forbearance and peaceful relations among people—these emerged as constant concerns in his conversations. Control over *nafs* (the baser instincts) was to be practiced for the *nafs* was the cause of all evil just as *qalb* (the human soul) produced peace, resignation and good will.

No mention of Hazrat Nizamuddin is complete without a reference to Amir Khusrau, his best-known poet-disciple. Intertwined for generations in popular memory, not least because of the many apocryphal stories associated with Khusrau's great love for the Hazrat, immortalised in the many qawwalis the poet taught the *qawwal-bacchas* (the families of those who were taught by Amir Khusrau himself) in the dargah of Hazrat Nizamuddin—compositions that are still sung by their descendents 700 years later—Khusrau's name crops up whenever there is talk of the Sufi master. Such was the intense love Khusrau had for his *pir* that he himself passed away shortly after his master's death and was buried close by. In fact, according to the Hazrat's own instructions, pilgrims first go to Khusrau's grave to offer *fateha* (funerary prayer) and only then to Nizamuddin Auliya's. Love for his *nijam* (as Khusrau lovingly addressed his master) flows like a coursing river through much of Khusrau's verses, as in:

Mujhe apne hi rang mein rang de rangeele
Tu to sahib mere mehboob-e ilahi

Colour me in your colours, O colourful one
You are my master, O beloved of God

And these lines composed when Khusrau heard of his Master's passing away when he was far away accompanying Sultan Ghiyasuddin on his Bengal expedition:

Gori sowey sej par mukh par daarey kes
Chal Khusrau ghar aapne saanjh bhaii chahu des

My beloved sleeps on the couch a lock of hair falling over her face
Come, Khusrau, it is time to go home as night falls all around

Here is Mirza Ghalib, 19th-century Delhi's pre-eminent poet who lies buried close beside Hazrat Nizamuddin Auliya's hospice, making a light-hearted reference to Khusrau's by-now legendary love for his master in referring to Sirajuddin Ahmad Khan of the Loharu family, who was his *shagird* (pupil) and took *islaah* (correction) from him:

Mile do murshidon ko qudrat-e-haq se hain do taalib
Nizamuddin ko Khusrau Siraajuddiin ko Ghalib

Two masters have found two students by the Power of Truth
Nizamuddin found Khusrau and Sirajuddin found Ghalib

Nizamuddin continued to exercise the imagination of the Urdu poet for centuries after his death. Here is Sir Muhammad Iqbal writing:

Farishtey padhtey hain jisko wo naam hai tera
Badi janaab teri, faiz-e aam hai tera

The name that angels recite, that name is yours
Your threshold is great, you work for the public good

That this 13th century Sufi continued to draw people of all faiths is evident from Darshan Singh Duggal who wrote a nazm entitled 'Mahbub-i Ilahi':

Har ik farq ki khaatir hai aastana tera
Sabhi ne dil ki muraadein yahan se payii hain

Your threshold is accessible to people of all kinds
Everyone has received their heart's desires from here

Even a contemporary poet such as Shahryar, with a thoroughly modern sensibility, has written an entire ghazal on Nizamuddin ji drawing attention to the *milli-juli sanskriti* (mixed culture) that is exemplified in Hazrat ji's life and legacy:

Nisbat rahe tum se sada Hazrat Nizamuddin ji
Maangun main kya iss ke siwa Hazrat Nizamuddin ji

Haathon se tum ne jo kiya raushan wafa ka ik diya
Aandhi ki zad mein wo jala Hazrat Nizamuddin ji

May I always remain close to you, Nizamuddin ji
What else can I ask for except this, Nizamuddin ji

The lamp of devotion that you lit with your hands
It remained lit in the eye of a storm, Nizamuddin ji

Pandit Anand Mohan Zutshi, better known by his pen name Gulzar Dehlvi, never missed a single *urs* (an occasion to mark the birth or death of a Sufi) at the dargah of Hazrat Nizamuddin till he died in 2020 aged 93. Of the many verses he wrote for his Khwaja, he was fond of reciting this one:

Jab se meri jabeen pe tere dar ki dhool hai
Kaante bhi raaste ke mere haq me phool hai

Ever since the dust of your door is on my forehead
Even the thorns in my path bloom like flowers for me

Hazrat Nizamuddin's own master, Shaikh Fariduddin Ganj-i Shakar also known as Baba Farid, had blessed him saying: 'You will be a tree under whose shadow the people will find rest…' Indeed, it came to be so and, in an increasingly divided world, his dargah in Basti Nizamuddin in tony South Delhi remains a rare oasis of harmony.

30. Mahavir: *Shanti ka Devta, Neki ka Autaar*

What is Indianness? The simplest answer is that indescribable quality of *being* Indian. It is that combination of the many living cultures that the Indian people embody and carry within themselves, their thoughts, their foods, smells, the sights and sounds around them in their everyday lived life that constitutes Indianness, *bhartiyata, Hindustaniyat.* Indianness is not the way mythology is interpreted or religion practiced; it is how daily life is perceived by the people. Yes, religion is a part of this life; in fact, a very important part considering we are a deeply religious and spiritual people. Religion adds flavour to life in our part of the Asian sub-continent just as salt or spices add flavour to our food but it doesn't define that Indianness or that quality that is native to us. The diverse sights and sounds, our history and geography, our messiahs and mass leaders, our languages and literary cultures come together to define our Indianness.

For long now, I have been drawn to the idea of how the Urdu poet has seen the 'other', in particular a religion vastly different from their own. While ALL religions talk of love and harmony, some are unique in their emphasis on certain aspects of Life. Jainism is one such example where the taking of a life, even the idea of causing harm to a sentient being is abhorrent. An ancient religion, possibly one of the oldest in the world, one of its cardinal beliefs is in reincarnation and that the cycle of birth, death and rebirth is determined by one's *karma* or actions. The spiritual goal of Jainism is to become liberated from the cycle of rebirth and achieve the state of *moksha* (liberation). The primary figures of Jainism are the 24 *Tirthankaras* (supreme preachers), the first being Rishabh and the most recent being Mahavir (599–527 BC)

Addressed variously as Vardhaman, Veer or Muni, Mahavir preached that *ahimsa* (non-violence) is the supreme moral virtue and spoke of *satya* (truth), *asteya* (not stealing or taking anything that has not been given), *brahmacharya* (abstinence) and *aparigraha* (non-attachment). For the Urdu poet, a man such as Mahavir Swamy is *mohabbat ka payami* (messenger of love), *shanti ka devta* (God of peace).

'Shraddha ke Phool: Bhagwan Mahavir ke Charno Mein' (Flowers of Devotion: At the Feet of Bhagwan Mahavir) by Darshan Singh Duggal is a poem that is brimful with love because it is addressed to a being whose beauty is such that it brings radiance to the heart (*dil chamak utthe hai teri husn-e-safa ki dhoop mein*) for he was a God who once walked the earth in a human form (*bhagwaan goya aadmi ke roop mein*). His *tyaag* (sacrifice) of not just his princely life but all worldly attachments made his soul *pakeeza*h (pure) causing his heart to seek pleasure from the fire of love for the Supreme Being (*dil ne lazzat lii magar ishq-e-Khuda ki aag se*). The poem ends with the poet beseeching:

Aman ke Ai Devta hai yeh gharhi aalaam ki
Chhaa gayi hai subh-e-aalam par siyahi shaam ki

De sadaaein rooh parwar ik nayi tanzeem ki
Phir zarurat hai zamaane ko teri taaleem ki

O God of peace, a time of adversities is upon us
The world's morning is stained by the dark of night
Soul stirring cries for a new world order can be heard
Once again the world needs your instruction

In a sweetly melodious poem entitled 'Mahadev Swamy' Unwan Chishti takes us back in time when a man such as Mahavir, son of Sidharth, walked this earth. Calling him *jagat ka sahara* (helper of the world), *ahinsa payami* (messenger of non-violence), *muhabbat ka haami* (assurer of love), the poet recalls the time of Mahavir's birth thus:

Likha hai ke jab aap tashreef laaye
Zameen hans parhi, aasmaan jagmagaye...
Ziarat ko khud Indr bhi jiske aaye
Woh thha husn-e-ishq mein maah-e-tamaami

It has been written that when you came to this world
The earth laughed and the sky was brilliantly lit...
The God Indra himself came to see him
In the beauty of his love he was like a full moon

In a long lyrical poem entitled 'Mahavir' Kiran Kashmiri refers to Mahvir as *Satya ahinsa ke paiğhambar* (prophet of truth and non-violence), *dukhiyon ke dildaar* (beloved of the poor), *neki ke autaar* (incarnation of goodness):

Tu ne jag ke dukh harne ko
Pal pal kasht sahe
Ghor tapasya aur faaqon se
Tan man saaf kiye...

To remove the sorrows of the world
You bore countless travails

With devout ascetism and starving
You cleansed your body and mind...

But then the poet goes on to ask somewhat earnestly:

Kya tere faaqon aur tap se
Pashu man shaant hua
Kyon ki teri hii dharti par
Aaj hain attyachaar
Dharti ambar ḳhoon mein doobey
Chaaron khoont dakait
Ab anaaj ki jagah ugaaye
Zinda laashein khet
Inn laashon ko
Inn kheton ko
Aakar phir do praan

But was the animal mind
Calmed by your meditation and starvation
Why is it that on your land
There are cruelties
The land and sky is drenched in blood
And dacoits reign all around
Fields produce living corpses
Instead of grain
To these corpses
And these fields
Give life again

Postscript: Gyan Chand Jain (1923-2007) is possibly the most prolific writer in Urdu from the Jain community. Born in Seohara, Uttar Pradesh, a scholar, thinker, literary critic and linguist, he has left behind scores of books, some being *Aam Lisaniyat* (General Linguistics), *Adabi Asnaaf* (Literary Genres), *Ghalib Shanaas Malik Ram* (Malik Ram the Knower of Ghalib), *Tafseer-e-Ghalib* (The Exegesis of Ghalib), *Rumooz-e-Ghalib* (Signs/Codes in Ghalib), *Tahqeeq ka Funn* (The Art of Research), *Tareekh-e-Adab-e-Urdu* (The History of Urdu Literature), among many others. His work on the Urdu masnawi tradition entitled *Urdu ki Nasri Daastaanein* (The Prose Epics in Urdu) is considered a seminal text on the subject published as it was in 1949 and established its author's reputation. However, his later work *Aik Bhasha: Do Likhaawat, Do Adab* (One Language: Two Scripts, Two Literatures) is considered controversial because it drives a wedge in the hearts of those who maintain that Urdu and Hindi are similar if not twin languages with a shared literary culture.

31. Gautam Buddha: *Mohabbat ka Payami, Reham ka Paighambar*

Over the years, as much of my work has been within the frame of reference of Urdu, I have been especially watchful of religion, how it colours perceptions, how it seeps into life—sometimes like an ambient light, sometimes like a torch with a blinding light. All along, in this journey of exploring religion, religiousness, religiosity, religious observances, *mazhabi rahnuma* or religious figures who 'show the way', have been of especial interest to me and I often find myself looking out for Urdu poetry that is either directly about them or alludes to them. While the direct poetry is often hagiographical, sometimes rhetorical, it is the seemingly stray references that almost never fail to delight me.

The name of Gautam Buddha is almost always invoked when the Urdu poet wishes to stress the antiquity of this ancient land. Seemab Akbarabadi begins his ode to Gautam with this exquisite invocation:

Husn jab afsurda phoolon ki tarah paamal thha
Jab mohabbat ka duniya mein ghalat istemaal thha

When beauty was downtrodden like crestfallen flowers
When Love was being wrongly used in this world

The poet goes on to describe how Gautam came into the world lighting the human heart with an otherworldly light:

Raushni jis ki na hogi maand woh mashaal hai tu
Sar-zameen-e-Hind ka irfaani-e-avval hai tu

You are that torch whose light shall never be dimmed
You are the first Enlightened One on the land of Hind

Maikash Akbarabadi relates the oft-told incidents from Gautam's life—his first sight of a dead body, of a sick person, a poor person—causing him to forsake his life of *aish-o-ishrat* (luxury and delight) and wander hither and thither (*phirte rahe tum ku-ba-ku*) till under the shade of a tree where:

Tum ko bil-aaḳhir sukoon-e-jaavedaanii mil gaya
Dafatan chamki haqeeqat ki tajalli saamne
Mehnat-e-paiham se raaz-e-zindagaani mil gaya

You at long last eventually found eternal peace
Suddenly the light of reality shone in front of you
You attained the secret of life through your constant toil

Calling him *mohabbat ke payami* (messenger of love), *reham ke paighambar* (prophet of mercy), Saaghar Nizami makes the interesting observation:

Teri taaqat se hua kum iqtidaar-e-birahman
Tukde tukde ho gaya husn-e-wiqaar-e-birahman

Your strength lessened the power of the Brahman
Shattering to pieces the beauty and prestige of the Brahman

And the poet goes on to beseech Gautam to come, once again, to this world that is enslaved and imprisoned by the *agyaar* (meaning enemies but referring here to the English):

Kar ghulami se rihaa hum ko phir armaan hai yahi
Aaj Hindustan mein mafhoom-e-nirvaan hai yahi

Free us once again from slavery: that's our only wish
That is the only known salvation in Hindustan today

In 'Tasweer-e-Haqiqat' (A Portrait of Reality), a poem directly written on the Buddha, Munawwar Lakhnawi poses a series of metaphysical questions ending with:

Farishtey dast-basta kiske gird-o-pesh hotey hain?
Yeh hasti kya hai woh sab jisko Gautam Budh kehte hain?

Who is this around whom the angels circumambulate with
folded hands?
Who is this being whom everyone calls Gautam Buddh?

Khalilur Rehman Azmi, a poet of the modernist trend, writes the soliloquy 'Main Gautam Nahin Hoon' (I am Not Gautam) saying how, while he is not Gautam, he too had left home in a bid to find himself, thinking he too would sit under the shade of a tree and wait for *gyan* (enlightenment) but the fire of the body, which he had carried with him from his home, kept smouldering and the strong winds outside his home fanned that fire and he met a fate that is very different from Gautam's:

Main aise sahra mein ab phir raha huun
Jahaan main hii main hoon
Jahaan mera saaya hai
Saaye ka saaya hai
Aur duur tak
Bas ḳhalaa hii ḳhalaa hai

I am now wandering about in a wilderness
Where there is only me
And my shadow
And my shadow's shadow

Till far, far away
There is only an emptiness

In a somewhat cryptic azaad nazm (a free poem in prose) entitled 'Budh', Adil Mansuri creates a very modern setting: of a man drawing long puffs on his pipe, filling the room with smoke and declaiming:

Gautam ke naam se yaad kiya jaaye
Aisa
Diwaaron par rengti
Chiyuntiyon se
Baar baar kah raha tha

I should be known by the name of Gautam
This
Is what he was repeatedly
Telling the ants
Crawling on the walls

And now for the stray references that never fail to delight and astonish as in this short poem entitled 'Naqsh-e-Jameel' (Beautiful Imprint); Akhtar Bastavi refers to the sheer beauty of a Buddha statue:

Ghir ke yuun nafrat mein bhi ulfat ka huun naqsh-e-jameel
Jaise Gautam Buddh ki moorat saaya-e-shamsheer mein

Despite being surrounded by hate, I am the beautiful imprint of love
Like the statue of Gautam Buddh in the shadow of the sword

Ali Sardar Jafri is asking:

Ram-o-Gautam ki zameen hurmat-e-insaan ki ameen
Baanjh ho jaaegii kya khoon ki barsaat ke baad

This land of Ram and Gautam, this trustee of the honour of man
Will it become barren after a rain of blood?

And elsewhere Jafri bemoans how in the modern age:

Ved Upnishad purze purze Gita Quran varaq varaq
Ram-o-Krishn-o-Gautam-o-Yazdan zaḳhm-rasida sab ke sab

Ved Upanishad torn to pieces, the Gita and Quran taken apart
Ram, Krishna, Gautam and Yazdan all are wounded

For every naysayer there is a yeasayer, for every pessimist an optimist. In a poem entitled 'Watan ka Raag' (The Song of the Nation) Afsar Meruthi is singing a song of shared living:

Krishn ki bansi ne phoonnkii hai rooh hamaari jaanon mein
Gautam ki aawaaz basii hai mahlon mein maidaanon mein

Krishna's lute has infused our lives with spirit
Gautam's voice lives in palaces and meadows

Finally, there's this by Anjum Irfani displaying a thoroughly modern interpretation to the detachment and forsaking of worldly desires that Gautam practiced:

Banaayaa hii nahin hum ne kabhi ye soch kar Anjum
Ki Gautam ki tarah ik din hamein ghar chhorh denaa thha

And so I, Anjum, never constructed a house
Thinking that one day, like Gautam, I would leave it

32. May You Know No Grief Save the Grief for Husain

Husain, son of Ali, grandson of the Prophet Muhammad, was a handsome, charismatic, fearless warrior and a loving family man. In the centuries since his death on 10 October 680 AD in the historic Battle of Karbala, he has become an enduring emblem of a brave man wronged, tragically felled by forces beyond his control yet choosing to fight till the bitter end despite a foreknowledge of the odds stacked against him. It is precisely this element of choice that makes Husain such a powerful symbol of martyrdom, one that transcends his time and circumstance. It is also the quality of unflinching, unyielding uprightness which could neither be silenced nor bought over, that makes Husain the ultimate 'alienated' hero. What adds to the poignancy of his situation is his aloneness at the hour of reckoning. Save for a handful of family members, no one came to his aid. The majority watched and listened but did nothing. This feeling of Husain's aloneness is captured in Mir Anees's much-recited marsiya:

Aaj Shabbir pe kya aalam-e-tanhai hai

What a world of solitude has descended upon Shabbir

A great deal of Urdu literature picks on motifs and dramatis personae from the Battle of Karbala, the 72 companions comprising family and friends who were martyred on the banks of the Euphrates river in present-day Iraq. There is, for instance, the recurring motif of thirst, of injustice, of besiegement. Then, there are the figures, each emblematic too: Husain for valour, Yazid for cruelty, Zainab for fortitude, and so on. Novelists such as Intizar Husain have woven the events of Karbala into their chronicles of life in the sub-continent but it is the poets who have time and again invoked Karbala as a metaphor as in this sher by Mohammad Alvi:

Dil hai pyaasa Husain ke maanind
Ye badan Karbala ka maidan hai

My heart is thirsty like Husain
This body is a field like Karbala

The universality of Husain's fight against unfairness and persecution is verbalised in this sher by Afzal Jinjhaanvi where thirst becomes a metaphor:

Husain ibn-e-Ali mujh ko yaad aate hain
Main jab bhi dekhtaa huun tishnagi kaa darvaza

I am reminded of Husain, son of Ali
Whenever I see the doorway of thirst

And this by Munawwar Rana:

Phir Karbala ke baad dikhaai nahin diya
Aisa koi bhi shaḳhs ki pyaasa kahein jise

After Karbala I have never ever again seen
Another such person whom I can call thirsty

That the story of Husain 'speaks' to a wide cross-section of society and not Muslims alone is evident from this sher by Gopal Mittal:

Kya shaan hai vallaah Husain-ibn-e-Ali ki
Sar kat gaya qad phir bhi hareefon se bada hai

By God, such is the glory of Husain, son of Ali
His head chopped, his stature is still taller than his rivals

That Husain fought the 'good fight' is picked by many poets and expressed in a myriad different ways, as here by Arshad Aziz:

Husain ibn-e-Ali ne ahal-e-maktab ko bataayaa hai
Sinaan ki nok par Quran-ḳhvani kis ko kahte hain

Husain, son of Ali, has shown the people of discernment
How to read the Quran that is balanced on the tips of swords

And here by Hasrat Mohani:

Thhe haq pe woh be-shak ki na hotey to na hotaa
Duniya mein bapaa maatam-e-Shabbir abhi tak

Indeed he was with the Truth or there wouldn't have been
This mourning for Shabbir for so long in this world

Husain's resistance to the tyranny of Yazid is emblematic of the suffering of all those who live under tyrannical regimes that seek to suppress the human spirit and snuff out resistance as verbalised in this sher by Shabnam Naqvi:

Phir Yazid-e-asr ke ab haath mein talvaar hai
Phir Husain-ibn-e-Ali ka tazkira karte raho

Once again the vile Yazid holds the sword in his hand
Once again just remind yourself of Husain, son of Ali

And in this by Ahmad Faraz:

Jab bhi zameer-o-zarf ka sauda ho doston
Qaaem raho Husain ke inkaar ki tarah

Whenever there is a trade of heart and conscience
Remain resolute like Husain's refusal

That every age produces its Yazid and Husain, every epoch sees a Karbala is borne out by this sher by Faiz Ahmad Faiz:

Har daur mein maluun shaqawat hai Shimar ki
Har ahd mein masood hai qurbani-e-Shabbir

Every era has the accursed villainy of (Yazid's general) Shimar
Every age is blessed by the martyrdom of Shabbir

In the lamentation and mourning over the King of Karbala, the Martyr of Martyrs, the Son of Ali, small, personal, localised griefs are subsumed in the grief for Husain (aka as Shabbir, the pet-name given by Prophet Muhammad) and his clansmen and women. North India, especially the *qasbahs* (a habitation that is larger than a village but smaller than a town in the Awadh region) of Awadh, has produced vast amounts of poetic literature commemorating the events surrounding the martyrdom of Husain. Urdu poets such as Mir Anees, Dabir, Gauhar Lukhnavi have written vast amounts of very poetic and hauntingly evocative elegies, all of which are recited in homes and *majlis khanas* (assembly rooms) during Muharram even today and recall the slaughter of innocents and infants. So, while profuse references to Husain are to be found buried in the many classical marsiyas, references to both Husain and to the events of Karbala continue to crop up in the writings of newer, contemporary poets as in this sher by young Lucky Farooqi Hasrat who sees Husain as an intercepter:

Dua-e-ḳhair ki phir kya kamii hai
Dua-go jab Husain ibn-e-Ali hai

There is no dearth of prayers for well being
When the well-wisher is Husain, son of Ali

And, finally, as Asad Rizvi says:

Agar ronaa hai to rone ki khaatir
Husain ibn-e-Ali ka gham bahut hai

If you must cry then for the sake of crying
The sorrow of Husain, son of Ali, is enough

Postscript: I am a Sunni Muslim by birth and practice. However, my mother has always been drawn to several aspects of the Shia faith and would take me along, from a young age, to *majlises* (assemblies to mourn the martyrs of Karbala) in the homes of friends and neighbours. We would listen intently and respectfully: sometimes simply taking in the sonorous beauty of the partly-known, partly not, words of the soz, nauha and marsiya, and sometimes remembering our own submerged griefs and sorrows. During the pandemic we learnt to join a *majlis* on zoom but we both feel there is nothing to match the experience of being in a room, listening to a marsiya or a *zikr* (narration) live. Neither my mother nor I join in the *maatam*, the rhythmic slapping of the left breast with the right hand that steadily becomes a pounding though we do find ourselves tapping our left shoulder with our right hand, ever so gently, and often in tune with the *salaam* that is being recited as the assembly gets to its feet.

33. Tipu Sultan, the Tiger of Mysore

A brave warrior till yesterday, today a cruel despot. A wise and far-sighted leader who resisted the expansion of the East India Company till recently, today a religious zealot. A hero for many, a bigot for some whose very name is anathema to the Hindu right—that is the fate of Tipu Sultan, the Tiger of Mysore, in New India. Parks named after him are vandalised, traffic circles renamed, litfests disturbed and history books rewritten.* But long before the controversies erupted and his legacy began to be contested with impunity for electoral gains, he was a national hero, an inventor of new weaponory such as the Mysore Rocket, a resistance fighter in the Anglo-Mysore wars. Naturally, therefore, a figure as charismatic, as heroic as Tipu could not have failed to catch the eye of the Urdu poet.

While several books have been written on Tipu and his exploits—both on and off the battlefield and Tipu was once a favourite pet-name for a boy in many households both north and south of the Vindhyas—it was the poet who took the

---

*https://economictimes.indiatimes.com/news/india/how-politics-reduced-tipu-sultan-from-a-national-hero-to-a-controversial-figure/articleshow/93822895.cms?from=mdr

legacy of *sher-dil Tipu* (Tipu the Braveheart) to the nooks and crannies of the popular imagination. There was a time when poets felt the need to inspire their readers they invoked a litany of names: Rani Lakshmi Bai, Tatya Tope and later Bhagat Singh, Subhash Chandra Bose, Maulana Mohamed Ali; Tipu Sultan's name invariably featured in that list. Ijtiba Rizvi, the poet from Chhapra in distant Bihar, takes his readers to the battleground where Tipu found martyrdom:

Hai tere baad tiri yaad iftiḳaar-e-watan
Tira mazaar hai sham-e-sar-e-mazaar-e-watan

After you your memory is this country's pride
Your grave is the lamp that casts its light over the country

On Tipu's 'never-say-die' spirit, his refusal to make compromises or negotiations, Iqbal writing in his 'Sultan Tipu ki Vasiyat' (The Testament of Tipu Sultan) reminds his readers the sage counsel the angel Gabriel once gave man: to never accept the heart of a man whose mind is enslaved and goes on to say:

Baatil dooyi pasand hai, haq laa-shareek hai
Shirkat mayana haqq-o-baatil na kar qubool

Falsehood conceals in masks but Truth is unique
There can be no mixing of truth and falsehood

Arsh Malsiyani locates Tipu in his time and place, in the land beside the Cauvery, in the battlefield of Seringapatam, where every speck of dust offers salutations to this lion of Deccan, this leader among the crusaders for freedom:

Woh awwalleen mujahid ki jis ne farmaaya
Rahega Hind naa hargiz firangiyon ka ġhulam
Padhaai ahl-e-watan ko namaaz-e-aazadi
Sikhaaye jis ne humein uss ke sab sujood-o-qayaam

He's the very first martyr who taught us that
Hind will not be a slave of the foreigner

Who showed his countrymen how to offer the namaaz of freedom
Who taught us all its prostrations and positions

Seemab Akbarabadi in his 'Sultan Shaheed' (Martyred Sultan) calls out:

Poochh Ai Maisore apne maazi-e zau-naak se
Barhana shamsheer ik chamkii thhii teri khaak se

O Mysore, ask your radiant past
A naked sword had once glimmered from your dust

Ale Ahmad Suroor, a teacher, a critic a fine prose stylist but also a poet with his finger to the pulse of the nation writes 'Tipu ki Awaaz' (The Voice of Tipu) that still courses across the land:

Mere lahu ki boondon mein ghaltaan thhiin bijliyaan
Khaak-e-Dakan ko maine sharar aashnaa kiya

Lightning was roiling in the drops of my blood
I made the dust of Deccan sparkle with desire

Speaking for the land that produced Tipu, Suroor goes on to say:

Maara hua huun go ḳhalish-e-intizaar ka
Mushtaaq aaj bhi huun payaam-e-bahaar ka

While I am a victim of the pain of waiting
I am still longing for the message of spring

But it was Sahir who seized the potential of a heroic figure, one who could be aspirational for young children in his 'Lori' (the lullaby a mother sings his child to sleep to) where a mother promises:

Kal subh jab main paas ke baazaar jaaungii
Siraj aur Tipu ki tasweer laauungii
Aur un ki zindagi ki kahaani sunaauungii
Tujh ko bhi waisi shaan se jeenaa sikhaauungii

Tomorrow morning when I go to the nearby market
I will bring photographs of (Nawab) Siraj (Uddaulah) and Tipu
And I will tell you the story of their lives
I will teach you to live a glorious life like them

That Tipu casts his spell over the present generation of poets is evident from this sher by Misdaque Azmi with its reference to the Nizam of Hyderabad who became an ally of the British in the final battle at Seringapatam where Tipu was killed:

Mar gaya Mizdaque bhi Sultan Tipu ki tarah
Dekh kar humraaz apna dushman-e-jaani ke saath

Like Tipu Sultan Mizdaque too died
Seeing his confidante with his sworn enemy

Another modern poet, Anas Nabeel wonders aloud why no Tipu has been born ever again:

Pilaati hain kise ab doodh maaen baa-vazu ho kar
Tabhi to hum mein ab Tipu koi paida nahin hota

Do cleansed mothers nurse their babies after ablutions
No wonder another Tipu has not been born amongst us

Imran Sani invokes Tipu's bravery thus for present-day readers:

Hausla jis ka jawaan hota hai Tipu ki tarah
Zulm ke saanp ka sar badh ke kuchal deta hai

He whose courage reaches its prime like Tipu's
He goes forth and crushes the serpent of tyranny

However, in the Battle of Perception where all information comes from the Font of All Knowledge, namely WhatsApp forwards, the Tiger of Mysore seems to be pitted in a binary with a certain Veer. The zealots among the Hindu Right who are busy painting Tipu as a traitor and oppressor, might do well to remember Arsh Malsiyani's poem: it was Tipu who taught the people of Hind the *Namaaz-e-Aazaadi*.

34. Rani Lakshmi Bai: *Hind Mata ki Ek Beti*

Two worlds—the decaying and the emergent—fused and merged in 1857. Pathos, confusion and conflict reigned supreme. Out of this disarray, a charismatic figure emerged: most unexpectedly she was a woman at a time when there were hardly any women in the public domain. She occupied a moment in time, briefly and luminously, a quivering, shimmering moment that was brimful with possibilities, possibilities that this woman from a modest family, though married into royalty, seized with great enterprise and aplomb. In the process, she became enshrined in the collective consciousness of the nation for decades to come. This was Lakshmibai of Jhansi, the widowed Rani of Maharaja Gangadhar Rao Newalkar, who chose the path of heroic resistance to the imperial juggernaut when all around her rulers and kingdoms were toppling like dominoes. When her husband's kingdom was annexed by Lord Dalhousie, Lakshmi Bai (born Manikarnika Tambe) chose to rise above being a victim of a grand colonial design and instead put up a good and brave, though ultimately doomed, fight to a force of cataclysmic change. In the process, she emerged as an icon of what is today regarded as the First War of Independence. Naturally, therefore, she has been neither overlooked nor forgotten by the Urdu poet.

Several full-length plays were written in Urdu on the life and tumultuous times of the Rani of Jhansi, one by Niyaz Fatehpuri in 1946 and another in the popular 'parsi theatre' style featuring the thespian Sohrab Modi as 'Raj Guru'. The latter had this rousing number:

Amar hai Jhansi ki Rani
Jiska raaj aur rajdhani
Jiska jeevan aur jawani
Thhi pehli qurbani...

May the Rani of Jhansi live for ever
Whose throne and kingdom
Whose life and youth
Was the first sacrifice...

Another Urdu drama, written in 1969 by Manju Qamar, had some robust poetic interjections by various dramatis personae such as this early warning:

Utth mujahid hosh me aa hosh se kuchh kaam le
Gir raha hai qaum ka parcham Khudara thaam le
Waqt Jhansi par parha hai waqt hai imdaad ka
Jaan-o-dil qurban kar apne watan ke naam par

Arise, O warrior, come to your senses and think sensibly
Your country's flag is falling; pick it for God's sake
Bad times have fallen upon Jhansi; it needs help
Sacrifice your life for the sake of your country

A popular pairing has been Lakshmi Bai of Jhansi and the medieval queen Raziya Sultan who ruled briefly from Delhi, both warrior queens who fell in battle after putting up a valiant fight, as in these lines from a nazm entitled 'Mera Watan' (My Country) by Rehbar Jaunpuri:

Jahaan paida huii Jhansi ki Rani
Hai Raziya jis ki azmat ki nishaani

(In the country) where the Rani of Jhansi was born
Of whose greatness Raziya is a symbol

Like the Rani of Jhansi, Begum Hazrat Mahal of Awadh too was similarly persecuted after her husband, Nawab Wajid Ali Shah was sent to exile and his kingdom usurped under the infamous 'Doctrine of Lapse'. Josh Malihabadi, in his iconic poem 'East India Company ke Farzandon Se' (To the Sons of the East India Company), remembers the unfair practices that the early colonialists employed in their haste to annex independent kingdoms:

Kya Awadh ki begamon ka bhi sataanaa yaad hai
Yaad hai Jhansi ki Rani ka zamaana yaad hai

Do remember how you tormented the begums of Awadh
Do you remember the time of the Rani of Jhansi

The Rani of Jhansi is invoked whenever the poet talks of the revolt of 1857 almost as though no mention of the mutiny is complete without a reference of the heroic queen and her martyrdom for a cause greater than merely the safeguarding of her own and her adopted son's interests. In a poem entitled 'Subhash Chandra Bose Bahadur Shah ke Mazar Par' (Subhash Chandra Bose at the Grave of Bahadur Shah Zafar, a poem alluded to earlier in this book) Jagan Nath Azad reminisces:

Meri nazron mein hai Merath aur Dehli ka zavaal
Jaanta huun main jo thaa Jhansi ki Rani ka ma.aal

I fully recall the state of decline of Meerut and Delhi
I know full well how (the matter of) the Rani of Jhansi ended

Incidentally, it must be remembered that the Rani of Jhansi Regiment was an all-female combat unit of the Indian National Army (INA), which was formed in 1943 by Indian nationalists in Southeast Asia during World War II.

Two extremely long poems, both directly on Lakshmi Bai, deserve our close attention. Makhmoor Jallundhari concludes his hagiographical poem thus:

Teri yalghaar teri azmat-e-dereena hai
Teri paikaar iss aadarsh ka aaina hai
Koi aurat jo nazakat mein kanwal hoti hai
Waqt aajaaye to dushman ki ajal hoti hai

Your assault is your long-cherished greatness
Your battle is the mirror of that principle
A woman who is like a lotus in her delicacy
Becomes the enemy's vanquisher when the time is nigh

In a poem running into all of ten and a half pages, Rahi Masoom Raza paints a chiaroscuro of the Rani's last fateful battle, contrasting her quietness with the din all around her. As sonorous as a marsiya and just as detailed in its descriptions of war and its re-imagined emotions of the dramatis personae, as climactic and as skillful in its gradual build-up of emotions as a nauha, and as fraught with emotions as a soz, the beleaguered Rani's battle near Gwalior is almost interchangeable with descriptions of the Battle of Karbala that Urdu elegists have long written about. In much the same way as a Mir Anees or Dabir, marsiya-writers of Awadh, had cried out at the fall of Husain, Raza (known to posterity as the script writer of the popular television series *Mahabharata* on Doordarshan) recreates the martyrdom of the slain Rani thus:

Ai zameen dekh teri simt ye kaun aata hai
Tujh mein ye kis ka lahu jazb hua jaata hai

O Earth, see who is coming in your direction
Whose blood is seeping and soaking into you

In a poem addressed to Sarojini Naidu, Kaifi Azmi alludes to Lakshmi Bai thus:

Woh khwaab Jhansi ki Rani ko jis ne chaunkaaya
Tira gihaad-e-musalsal usii ki hai taabeer

The dream that startled the Rani of Jhansi
Your constant crusade has been to turn it into reality

However, references to her crop up in surprising ways also when the context is neither historical nor factual. For instance, in a poem about the Urdu language and literature, the *zubaan-e-Urdu*, Bano Tahira Sayeed quite unexpectedly invokes the fallen queen thus:

Iss mein Jhansi ki rani ki lalkaar hai
Saaz-o-nagma ke hum-raah talwaar hai

It (Urdu) has the defiance of the queen of Jhansi
Along with the melody of the song it has the clash of the sword

In fact, Bano Tahira Sayeed seems so taken in by the heroic figure of the Rani that she has written an entire poem on her:

Hind mata ki ek beti
Naam thha jis ka Lakshmi Bai
Roop mein zan ke woh thhi ik shamsheer
Barq ki tarha kaundi lahraai

A daughter of Mother Hind
Her name was Lakshmi Bai
In the form of a woman she was a sword
That struck and slashed like lightning

The Rani of Jhansi lives on as embodiment of courage for the modern poet when all around him there is defeat and despair.

Invoking Rudyard Kipling who had (in)famously declared, 'The East is East, and the West is West, and never the twain shall meet,' Saleem Ahmed writes a nazm entitled 'Mashriq Haar Gaya' (The East has Lost) where he acknowledges this defeat thus:

Mashriq haar gaya hai!
Ye Buxar aur Plassey ki haar nahin hai
Tipu aur Jhansi ki Rani ki haar nahin hai
San-sattavan ki jang-e-aazadi ki haar nahin hai
Aisi haar to jeeti ja sakti hai (shaayad hum ne jeet bhi lii hai)
Lekin mashriq apni rooh ke andar haar gaya hai

The East has been defeated
It isn't the defeat of (the battles of) Buxar and Plassey
It isn't the defeat of Tipu or the Rani of Jhansi
It isn't the defeat in the War of Independence of 1857
It's a defeat that could have been won (perhaps we have even won it)
But the East has lost the battle of its soul

Postscript: In his book *A Begum and a Rani*, the historian Rudrangshu Mukerjee notes: 'Unwittingly or otherwise, writers on 1857 seem to have set up a hierarchy of heroes'. Setting out the curious case of the Rani of Jhansi and Begum Hazrat Mahal of Awadh, and their after-life, he notes how history has treated the two women so differently: one has been mythologised and eulogized, the other neglected and overlooked; the former has been kept alive in song and folk memory, the latter forgotten by bard and historian alike. Holding the early British historians and Indian writers such as Vinayak Damodar Savarkar equally responsible, Mukherjee notes: 'In a national movement that was largely male- and upper-caste dominated, it was "the natural order of things" to iconize Lakshmibai and not efface

Hazrat Mahal but relegate her. The quest for heroes in history creates its own problems of choice and discrimination.' Alas, remembrance and forgetting run like the warp and weft of our national narrative in the India that is Bharat.

35. Ghalib in a New World Order

Rakhiyo Ghalib mujhe iss talq-nawai pe maaf
Aaj kuchh dard mere dil mein siwa hota hai

If Ghalib sings in a bitter strain, forgive him
Today pain stabs more keenly at his heart

Mirza Asadullah Khan Ghalib (1797-1869), the pre-eminent poet of Delhi, lived through one of the most turbulent periods of recent Indian history and was a witness to the evanescent Mughal rule. Two worlds—the decaying and the emergent—were fusing and merging virtually before his eyes. Pathos, confusion and conflict reigned supreme as the Great Revolt of 1857 marked the end of an era and a new world order lay waiting to be unfurled. It would take several decades for the clouds of uncertainty to part and the debate on the Old Light versus the New to usher in the Lamp of New Learning, and an altogether new, modern sort of poetry.

Living in Delhi, Ghalib saw madness and mayhem descend upon the streets of his beloved city and witnessed the siege and slaughter of an entire way of life. While to some extent his response to the events of 1857 are contradictory since he was dependent on the pension he received from the British (he was, in his own words, a *namak-khwar-e-sarkar-e-angrez* or an 'eater of the salt of the British government' on account of his hereditary pension), there is much in his ouvre that is in the nature of a testimony to his times.

Ghalib did not live long enough to see the coming together of the writer and social reformer or the increasing social consciousness evident in Urdu literature nor indulge in any experiments with 'colonial modernity' as his immediate successors could such as Altaf Hussain Hali (1837-1914) or Muhammad Husain Azad (1830-1910). But in the long innings he enjoyed as a poet (having begun his poetic career as a lad of 11 in Agra before moving to Delhi), and the kinds of writings he did (apart from writing the ghazal, masnawi and qasida in both Urdu and Persian he was also a prolific and passionate letter writer), and the many different kinds of people he met and interacted with (from royal patrons to ordinary people in the bazaars not to mention the many *firangis* to be found in Delhi) coupled with the fact that in an age when travel was rare he travelled to Calcutta and the sights and sounds he saw along the way in a journey spanning four years (1825-1829)—all of this combined to create a worldview that can only be called catholic. The sheer range of his experiences possibly made him the man he was—liberal, humane, witty, proud, touchy, and sociable.

Ghalib found friends in almost all the cities he stopped in along the way to Calcutta, and back. He was new to each of these cities but never a stranger. This is proof of not only his stature and popularity as a poet but also how an informal network of contacts—in spite of the long distances and poor communication systems—has always existed and has always helped. Also, being a part of the feudal elite Ghalib took any help that came his way as his due and was never lacking in assurance and optimism. Ghalib also displayed every trait of a born traveler: he enjoyed the new and the different yet could distinguish between high and low, and had clear likes and dislikes.

Since travelling by boat was more expensive Ghalib initially set off on horseback, occasionally switching to a *lurhiya* or cart, with one or two servants when he could find them. When he fell ill in Kanpur, he crossed the Ganga in a hired palanquin and convalesced in Lucknow which seemed a most agreeable city to him. In a letter he called it the 'Baghdad of Hindustan', blissfully unapologetic that he had only heard of Baghdad and not seen it first-hand. What is more, he was hopeful of finding the patronage of the Nawab, Nasiruddin Haider, which would have alleviated his financial crisis somewhat. However, Ghalib being Ghalib laid down two conditions before a meeting could be arranged: one, that the Nawab must meet him with 'due honour'; and two, Ghalib be excused from presenting the customary *peshkash* (gift). Both requests were turned down and the promised meeting did not take place. For his part, Ghalib too had prepared only a prose encomium for the presentation and not a qasida (panegyric) as was expected. This incident serves to illustrate Ghalib's life-long tussle with those in authority, his seeming deference and yet his last-minute assertion of his own superiority no matter how constrained his circumstances and how desperately he might need that patronage. The incident in Lucknow mirrors several others in the Mughal court in Delhi and serves to illustrate Ghalib's own inflexible sense of his superiority—both as a poet and as a member of the nobility.

In Lucknow, Ghalib found himself at the centre of many literary debates on literature, culture and manners; the subject of language and its correct usage featured in most conversations between this guest from 'Dilli' and the Lucknow-wallahs. For instance, it was a subject of much merriment that the *qalam* (pen) is used with a masculine form in Lucknow and as a feminine in Delhi, as also *joota* (shoe). Ghalib held forth, amid much banter and witticism, on how language changes every 50 miles; he could say this with the assurance of a sophisticated traveler as he was among the few who had travelled thus far east from Delhi.

In Lucknow, Ghalib also found many young men who flocked to him for *islaah*, a customary practice when young or budding poets offer their work for correction or improvement to an *ustaad*, a senior or veteran poet. Whatever little they offered as *nazrana* funded his stay and his onward travel till Banda. In Banda (in the rough terrain of the Bundelkhand region) he stayed for six months as the guest of Nawab Zulfiqar Ali Bahadur. Ghalib's family had enjoyed a warm relationship with the Nawab's forefathers. Through the Nawab, Ghalib borrowed Rs 2,000 from one Amin Chand to fund his onward journey. By now, it had been nine months since he had left his home in Delhi.

While Allahabad made a poor impression upon him, Ghalib was entranced by Benares: the flat-bottomed boats on the wide Ganga, the bustle of the ghats offset by the serenity of the river, the sounds of ghungroos and thumris wafting from the houses of the famed courtesans of the city. He referred to Benares as the 'Kaaba of India'. He rented a haveli in the Naurangabad area, composed his famous ode to Benares, the masnavi with 108 verses titled 'Charagh-e Dair' (The Temple's Lamp). Incidentally, the number 108 has an especial significance in Hinduism and the Ganga river too has a 108 names.

Ghalib reached Calcutta in February 1927, a little over a year after leaving Delhi. Raja Sohan Lal helped him find comfortable living quarters in Mirza Ali Saudagar's haveli in Simla Bazar—at a rent of Rs 10 a month. Ghalib called on the

Chief Secretary, Andrew Sterling and on Simon Fraser, the Assistant Secretary. These meetings were cordial and Ghalib's case was taken up at the Governor-General's Council where it was decided that the matter should be taken up for decision through the British Agent in Delhi—as this was procedurally the correct channel. This suited Ghalib as the Agent in Delhi, Sir Edward Colebrook, was known to him. Ghalib went to the post office and at a cost of Rs 10 mailed a *mukhtarnama*, or power of attorney to his lawyer, Pandit Hira Lal in Delhi—with instructions to secure the appropriate recommendations. As he waited for a reply by return post, Ghalib lived the good life in Calcutta. The Nawab of Banda had sent him an additional loan; he had comfortable lodgings in a good locality, three servants, and one palanquin bearer. To supplement his resources, he sold off his horse for Rs 150 and fixed a budget of Rs 50 per month for himself.

A *mushaira* (poetic soiree) on the first Sunday of every solar month was the norm in Calcutta. Ghalib was invited to one where he recited two ghazals in Persian. Ghalib has left detailed accounts of his stay as well as the mushaira he attended; he estimated almost 5000 people were present when he recited his ghazals. Imagine his surprise when some among the audience criticised the construction of some of his Persian ghazals. Always touchy and temperamental, Ghalib was stung by what he thought was completely unwarranted criticism—that too of his command over Persian! An unseemly controversy ensued and cast a long shadow over his stay in Calcutta. Thirty years later, Ghalib would remember the controversy and spit fire at those who had the temerity to find faults in his 'mastery' over Persian. Ghalib was, however, advised to curtail the unspooling controversy. He wrote 'Baad-i Mukhalif' (An Adverse Wind)—ostensibly an apology, it still left no doubt as to who was right!

The late 1820s were witness to the changing ground realities as well as the altered relationship between the British and the feudal nobility. Ghalib found himself in the crosshairs of a paradigm shift when he set out on his long voyage in search of—what he considered—his rightful legacy in November 1825 and returned home four years later. He wasn't successful in his objective but he returned no doubt a wiser man, one who had seen the world and its ways—having travelled the long distance, variously, by horse, cart and boat. Ghalib returned to Delhi, angry, dejected and deeply bitter towards the British. Yet despite his disappointment, he continued a ceaseless barrage of correspondence and never quite gave up the hope that one day his pension would be enhanced. Despite his tenacity, Ghalib could never get a paisa more than the original amount.

Ghalib's share of the hereditary pension was Rs 62 and 50 paise per month. While adequate for a modest life style, the amount was never enough for his expenses: French wines, gambling, and the woman he maintained as his 'keep'. Money, or rather not having enough of it to spend, remained a lifelong preoccupation. He was forever borrowing and never in a position to repay. By 1825, his financial affairs had become critical as his creditors were losing patience, his debts were mounting and he had no way of returning even the interest forget the principal amounts he had borrowed from the city's major money-lenders—Mathura Das, Darbari Mal and Khub Chand—not to mention various small-time shop-keepers, grocers, and family members. Ghalib undertook the long journey to Calcutta as much to escape the clamour of the creditors as to find a lasting solution to what he knew was a chronic problem.

Ghalib pressed his case with the British authorities at every level: from the Resident at Delhi, the Lt-Governor at Agra, the Governor General in Council at Calcutta, the Court of Directors of the East India Company in London and finally Queen Victoria herself. And it was not as though he was short of patrons or did not know enough people of high rank from among the new elites of the British in India. Simon Fraser and Andrew Sterling—both Persian scholars and high officials—wrote letters of recommendation as did George Swinton, Chief Secretary to the Government. Despite these connections Ghalib got no reprieve because in the changing political climate, a new indifference had set in to the demands of the old feudal elite. When the case was taken up for hearing, the judgment went against Ghalib—not because his opponent was better connected or had a stronger case, but simply because people like Ghalib had little political currency for the great Imperial design. The new British attitude in the immediate aftermath of the Revolt was to deal firmly with what was perceived as a 'parasite class' and Ghalib and his ilk—with their pretensions of social/cultural superiority—were given short shrift.

In the aftermath of the Revolt, Ghalib had written:

Likhte rahe junoon ki hikaayat-e-khoon chakaan
Harchand ismain haath hamaare qalam huvey

We kept writing the blood drenched narratives of that madness
Although our hands were chopped off in the process.

Ghalib's hands were not chopped off. He lived another 12 years after the Revolt and witnessed the confusion and disarray that followed the loss of power and patronage. His pension was eventually restored in 1860 though never enhanced. I suspect it had less to do with Ghalib's tenacity and more to do with the conciliatory spirit of the British who could afford to show magnanimity to loyal subjects such as Ghalib. Or perhaps it had something to do with the intercession of Sir Syed Ahmad Khan and the Nawab of Rampur who had, to use a modern term, greater 'traction' and were, therefore, better suited to negotiate a colonised world.

36. Majaz: A Keats Was Born to Urdu...

On a cold December night in the year 1955, one of the best loved Urdu poets spent the entire night in a drunken stupor, on the terrace of a ramshackle working-class *sharab khana* (liquor shop), that he had named the Lorry's Top (*Laari ki Chhat*), in Lucknow's Lal Bagh. He died, aged 44, as a result of the chill he caught from lying in the open. He left behind a slender corpus but one that has earned him a place among the immortals of Urdu poetry. Like good poetry the world over, some of Majaz's poems transcend their time and place and can be read again and again by newer audiences. 'Awara' (Vagabond) is one of them. Written towards the end of the active phase of his life, in 1937, just before the demons of drink and despair pulled him down, it has all the brilliance of a lamp that will shortly be snuffed out:

Shehr ki raat aur main naashaad aur naakaara phiroon
Jagmgaati jaagti sadkon pe awara phiroon
Ghair ki basti hai kab tak dar-ba-dar mara phiroon
Ai gham-e-dil kya karoon, ai wahshat-e-dil kya karoon

A city night and I, I wander cheerless and worthless
Like a vagabond I wander these bright, awake streets

In this alien land how long can I wander without hearth or home
O my sorrowful heart what shall I do, O my frenzied heart what shall I do?

Born in Rudauli, a *qasbah* in Bara Banki district in the erstwhile United Provinces, on 19 October 1911, Asrarul Haq Majaz was the peoples' poet par excellence. He burst upon the Urdu literary firmament and caught the imagination of all those who had wearied of the Urdu poet's angst over the *shama-parwana* (lamp and moth motifs) and the *gul-o-bulbul* (popular tropes of the flower and the nightingale). He introduced a new sensibility and new literary concerns through startlingly fresh images and conceits, and above all a different sort of prosody—the nazm which resembled the ghazal in its close approximation of rhyme and metre but was free of the two-line constraint of the ghazal.

Majaz gained his early education in Lucknow, then went on to St John's College, Agra, and finally completed his BA at the Aligarh Muslim University in 1936. Those were the glory days of the Progressive Writers' Movement (PWM), and Majaz was swept along in the fervour of his times. After his graduation, he joined the All India Radio as sub-editor for a journal called *Awaaz* (Call), but his deep-rooted bohemianism and his unquenchable desire to live life on his own terms made him leave, in order to chart his own destiny as a poet. At the AIR he had differences with the legendary station director, Pitras Bukhari (with whom Saadat Hasan Manto too crossed swords) and chose to leave rather than submit to his demanding ways and authoritarianism. Swept up by the nation-wide wave of revolutionary fervour, along with progressive stalwarts like Ali Sardar Jafri and Syed Sibte Hasan, Majaz founded *Naya Adab* (New Literature), a magazine for the progressives in Lucknow. He was also associated with the journal *Adeeb*, brought out by the Hardinge Library in Delhi.

Ahang (Call), his first collection of poetry, was published in 1938. It established his reputation as the poet who sang sweetly of love and sorrow and social change, earning him the sobriquet of 'the Keats of Urdu poetry', and securing him a place of honour in the mushaira circuit, as well as making him an iconic figure among young men and women in campuses across northern India. He gave voice to the frustration and angst of a generation that was younger than him. His rejection of the world around him—whether it was in the angst-ridden 'Kyun?' (Why?) or the ballad-like geet he wrote for the workers of the world—reflect his deep longing for a better, more humane, more just world.

Majaz wrote of both love and revolution, of the need for social change, and the delights of an idealised beloved. Spurning the newly emerging azaad nazm that was gaining currency under the progressives, he wrote lilting, lyrical poetry which was full-bodied and flavoured with the vigour and radicalism of his time and age. It reflected, in ample measure, the currents of social change sweeping across India on the eve of Independence. At the same time, his nazms were as disciplined and immaculately constructed as his ghazals. Not for him the looseness of metre or the laxity of craft adopted—in the name of a Larger Cause with such devil-may-care abandon by some of his fellow poets. Majaz also wrote eminently rousing 'songs' such as 'Bol ari o dharti bol' (Speak, O Earth…) and the near-cultish 'Nazr-e-Aligarh' (To Aligarh) with its passionate, impetuous, foot-tapping beat that was adopted as the anthem by the Aligarh Muslim University, and for generations has brought Aligarians to their feet and close to tears. Its rousing, dramatic appeal to the young remains, to this day, unmatched, as does its call to rise for the nationalistic cause:

Jo abr yahan se uthega woh saare jahan pe barsega…

The clouds that arise from here shall rain upon the entire world…

Faiz Ahmad Faiz wrote the foreword to *Ahang* (Sound), praising Majaz's poetry for its wonderful mix of diverse qualities and appended one of Majaz's own verses as an epigraph:

Dekh shamsheer hai yeh, saaz hai yeh, jaam hai yeh
Tu jo shamsheer utha le to bada kaam hai yeh

Look, it is a sword, it is a musical instrument, a goblet of wine
If you raise the sword it shall become a mighty achievement

Other revolutionary poets beat their chests and make loud proclamations, Faiz said, but they cannot sing because they see only the horror of revolution, not its beauty. Majaz, on the other hand, could do precisely that: he could sing about the coming revolution because he saw it as a thing of beauty, a joy to behold and to rejoice in.

Then there is Majaz's address, *Naujawan Khatoon Se* (To a Young Woman) which has since been adopted as the slogan for the women's movement across South Asia:

Tere maathe pe yeh aanchal bahut hii khub hai lekin
Tu iss aanchal se ek parcham bana leti to achcha tha

The veil that covers your forehead looks lovely indeed
But it'd be better still if you turned your veil into a pennant

Majaz wrote compulsively, but much of what he wrote never got published, for it was written on wayward scraps of paper and indiscriminately handed over to admirers and friends. Therefore, his oeuvre is today established by little other than the slender collection entitled *Ahang*, which was re-published as *Shab-tab* (Brightly Shining) in 1945. Among his contemporaries were great poets like Makhdoom Mohiuddin, Majrooh Sultanpuri, Ali Sardar Jafri, Jan Nisar Akhtar, Kaifi Azmi and Sahir Ludhianvi, and two of his dear friends from his days at Agra, the poet Moin Ahsan Jazbi and the critic Ale

Ahmad Suroor who formed an inseparable trio during their days at St John's College, Agra, and later again at Aligarh.

Majaz fought a lifelong battle with chronic depression; he had three long spells of what can euphemistically be called mental ill health, in 1940, 1945 and 1952. The first time, he pulled himself from the maw of melancholia and self-destruction and moved to Delhi to stay with friends Shaukat Ansari and K M Ashraf. Majaz suffered his second nervous breakdown in 1945. Evidently, he could no more bear the terrible duality of his life: on the one hand, there were the Olympian heights of the mushaira where the skies would be rent by loud cries of wah wah when he stood up to recite his mesmeric poetry and, on the other hand, the ignominy of his clerical duties at the Hardinge Library. The third spell saw him, briefly, admitted in the Ranchi mental asylum. Little did he know that for all his straitened circumstances, in the eyes of those who knew him well, he was rich beyond measure. His heart broken, his spirit bruised, his body frail, his pockets empty, Majaz remained for his friends the epitome of *tehzeeb* and *sharafat*. Good opinions such as these, held by all those who knew Majaz remotely or well, could not save him. Like Manto, the demon of drink drove him to self-destruction.

Like Keats, Majaz died tragically young. He was buried in Lucknow, and the epitaph on his grave has a verse from one of his ghazals written in 1945:

Ab iske baad subh hai aur subh-e-nau Majaz
Hum par hai khatm shaam-e-gharibaan-e-Lukhnaw

And after this there is morn and the new morning Majaz
With me ends the eve of sorrows of Lucknow

And indeed, with Majaz gone, an entire way of life changed, the Lucknow of his days changed beyond all recognition, the Progressive Writers' Movement lost a strong ally, and Urdu lost its Keats.

37. The Satirical, Doubting Voice of Akbar Allahabadi

As the 19th century drew to a close, a new voice arose, the satirical doubting voice of Akbar Allahabadi (1846-1921) who could fully support neither the new nor the old, but did feel the need to admonish those who had forgotten the lessons of the Great Revolt of 1857. His barbs and arrows were directed both at the Muslim community and the colonial administration to which he belonged having worked as a judge. A man who contained many contraries, he has written ghazals in the high register of the classical ghazal-go and also tongue-in-cheek satires in an entirely new and altogether 'modern' way.

Some of his oft-quoted shers show his mastery over the haiku-like two-line verse that is the Urdu sher as here:

Hum aah bhi kahte hain to ho jaate hain badnaam
Woh qatl bhi kartein hain to charcha nahi hota

I am defamed if I so much as draw a sigh
And he can get away with murder without a word

And:

Duniya mein hoon duniya ka talabgaar nahin hoon
Baazaar se guzra hoon kharidaar nahin hoon

I live in this world but I am not desirous of the world
I am passing by the marketplace but I am not a buyer

Or this:

Log kahte hain badalta hai zamana sab ko
Mard woh hai jo zamaane ko badal de

People say the world changes everyone
But a man is one who can change the world

And this oft-quoted sher for lawyers:

Paida hua vakeel to shaitaan ne kaha
Lo aaj hum bhi saahib-e-aulaad ho gaye

When the first lawyer was born Satan said;
So, today I too have become Father to a Son

Employing the metaphor of *Buddhu Miyan* for the Indian Muslim (a confused, none-too-smart sort of Little Fellow) in some places and the *Shaikh* (a pompous, English stooge, occasionally a parody of Sir Syed Ahmad Khan, the somewhat anglicized founder of the new College at Aligarh) elsewhere, Akbar's poetry reflects all the contradictions of his age. About the new world order that is unfurling before him, he says:

Uloom unke, zubaan unki, press unke, lughaat unke

Science is theirs, as is the language, the press and the dictionaries

Writing directly on the marriage of empire and commerce, trade and British imperialism, Akbar says with his tongue firmly in his cheek:

Cheezein woh hain jo banein Europe mein
Baat woh hai jo Pioneer mein chhapey

Europe mein hai jo jung ki quwwat barhi huwi
Lekin fuzoon hai uss se tijarat barhi huwi
Mumkin nahin laga sakein woh tope har jagah
Dekho magar Pears ka hai soap har jagah

Real goods are those that are made in Europe
Real matter is that which is printed in The Pioneer
Though Europe has great capability to do war
Greater still is her power to do business
They cannot install a canon everywhere
But the soap made by Pears is everywhere

And of the power of the British merchants and traders with this characteristic play on words:

Boot Dawson ne banaayaa main ne ik mazmoon likha
Mulk mein mazmoon na phaila aur joota chal gaya

(The shoe company) Dawson made a boot while I wrote an article
My article didn't spread all over the country but the boot did and sold well

Of his great love for Gandhi he famously declared in his long poem, 'Gandhinama':

Madkhola government agar Akbar na hota
Usko bhi aap paate Gandhi ki gopiyon mein

Had Akbar not been a servant of the government
You would have found him too among Gandhi's gopis

Despite being home tutored, Akbar had a good command over the English language. This got him a job as a *naib tehsildar* (deputy magistrate) and he quickly rose to become first a lawyer and then, in quick succession, a *munsif* (a medium grade judge), a sessions judge, a district judge and finally a Khan Bahadur in 1894. Given his meteoric rise through the ranks of colonial India, his seeming opposition to progress, science, and the enlightened way of living and thinking seems odd, to say the least. But that is because Muslim intelligentsia in general and the Urdu writers in particular had massed themselves into two opposing and irreconcilable groups—those for Sir Syed Ahmad Khan and the 'Aligarh School' and those against. All those who stood for the Syed's views on education and the prospects for Muslims were automatically assumed to be liberal, progressive, forward-looking whereas those who opposed them, as Akbar did in biting verse, were taken to be regressive. Making fun of those who aped western ways, he says:

Public mein zara haath mila leejiye mujh se
Sahab mire imaan ki qeemat hai to ye hai

Please do shake my hand in public
If ever there's a price of my faith, sir, it is this

The Urdu critic, Ale Ahmad Suroor praises Akbar for unfailingly 'pointing to the feet of clay in the new god and the chink in the new armour, and particularly, the comic element in the earnestness of the new leaders of reform, their occasional naiveté and their enthusiasm.'

Qaum ke ġham mein dinner khaate hain hukkaam ke saath
Ranj leader ko bahut hai magar aaraam ke saath

In grief over the community they eat dinner with the rulers
The leader is indeed very sorrowful but in the best comfort

Suroor goes on to say: 'For forty years, Akbar acted like a spiritual seismograph, recording every shock and making it into poetry of a high order. Johnson said of Swift that "the rogue never hazards a metaphor". Akbar takes every risk, breaks all rules, takes sides, laments the failure of his mission, but does manage to check blind imitation of the west and help in a rediscovery of the east which marches towards progress with a new consciousness of its own heritage. He also sharpens our sensibility by making us aware of the false note in the new harmony which appeared to be perfect to us in the beginning.' Here is Akbar on the ills of modernity:

Tifl mein boo aaye kya maa baap ke atvaar ki
Doodh to dibbe ka hai taleem hai sarkaar ki

What sense of a mother and father will an infant have
(When) the milk comes from a jar and education from the government

And:

Hue iss qadar mohazzab kabhi ghar ka moonh na dekha
Kati umr hotalon mein mare aspataal jaa kar

So cultured did he become that he never stayed at home
Having spent his entire life in hotels he died in a hospital

Akbar's validation of Gandhi ji and everything he stood for is especially relevant for us—an angry, divided country—today:

Sun lo yeh bhed, mulk jo Gandhi ke saath hai
Tum kya ho, sirf peit ho, woh kya hai, haath hai

Listen to this secret: the country is with Gandhi
What are you: just a belly? What is he: he is the hand (that leads)

38. Maulana Hasrat Mohani: A Man of Many Parts

Born Syed Fazlul Hasan better known by his pen name, Hasrat Mohani (1875-1951), was a journalist and nationalist, freedom fighter and free thinker, poet and parliamentarian who wrote some of the most mystical ghazals such as 'Raushan jamaal-e-yaar se hai anjuman tamaam' (immortalised by Abida Parveen), was a founder-member of the powerful Progressive Writers Association (PWA) but never shy of crossing swords with it and plowing his own furrow, a member of the Communist Party of India (CPI) from its inception, he subsequently joined the Congress and after a brief dalliance with the Muslim League chose to stay on in free India as a Congressman, an active and vociferous member of the Constituent Assembly and a conscientious objector. As an ardent trade unionist, he is credited with first using, as a slogan, 'Inquilab Zindabad' at a labour rally in Calcutta in 1928.

Independent and liberal-minded, he was a practising Muslim who performed the Hajj all of 11 times yet liked to call himself a 'Sufi Muslim' and an *ishtiraki momin* (Communist

Muslim)! And to top it all, as though nothing was beyond the pale when it came to embracing seeming contraries, he was a devout Krishna bhakt who went to Mathura often to celebrate Janamshthami and also wrote the most lyrical ballads devoted to his 'Krishan ji Bhagwan'.

Hasrat's life and career begs the question: Is being a Muslim and a Marxist a contradiction in terms? Not really, it would seem. After all, both Islam and socialism preach equality and brotherhood and advocate an egalitarian society (there is much in Iqbal's early poetry that reflects a fascination for Marxism). Impressed by the Russian revolution, Hasrat carried its imprint on all his later writings. During his stint as member of the CPI, speaking as Chairman of the Reception Committee of a conference of several loosely-coalitioned kisan and workers' unions as well as communist-sympathiser groups held on 25 December 1925 at the same time as the Kanpur session of the Indian National Congress, he spoke thus:

> The movement of communism is the movement of peasants and workers. The people of India generally agree with the principles and aims and objects of this movement, but owing to certain misunderstandings some weak and nervous people fear the very name of communism…(our aims and objects are) to establish swaraj or complete independence by all fair means… some evilly-disposed persons incriminate communism as necessarily an anti-religious movement. The fact however is that in matters of religion we allow the largest possible latitude and toleration.

Hasrat's collected works, *Kulliyat-e-Hasrat Mohani*, reflects his wide and varied interests. Here, for instance, is Hasrat writing deeply romantic ghazals in the classical register:

Nahin aati to yaad un ki mahinon tak nahin aati
Magar jab yaad aate hain to aksar yaad aate hain

When I don't remember (her) I don't remember (her) for months
But when I do remember (her) then I remember (her) often

And more in the romantic strain:

Wafa tujh se ai bewafa chaahta huun
Miri saadgi dekh kya chaahta huun

O disloyal one I seek loyalty from you
Look at my simplicity, look what I seek

Writing prolifically in Urdu, he drew upon world events to inspire, rouse and challenge the imagination of the Indians. Be it international events such as the Balkan Wars, the Fall of Jerusalem, the breaking up of the Ottoman Empire or events abroad that had repercussions in India such as the two World Wars, or events specifically aimed at India such as the Rowlatt Act, we have a plethora of his poems, newspaper editorials and essays giving us a comprehensive idea of the disquiet that afflicted his generation. While writing in Urdu, he is not addressing Muslims alone; his range of interests is Catholic, all-embracing, inclusive. Here he is voicing his concerns on the Montagu Reforms of 1919 calling them paper flowers without any fragrance:

Kis darja fareib se hai mamlu
Tajwees reform-e Montagu
Mashhoor zamana hai mussalam
Dastoor ke hisb-e zeil pahlu
Qanoon pe ikhtiyar kaamil

How replete with deception it is
This scheme of reform by Montagu

In the whole wide world it is known
That these aspects of the Constitution spell
Complete control over legislation

On Bal Gangadhar Tilak who gave the call for Swaraj (self rule):

Ai Tilak, Ai iftikhar-e-jazba-e-hubb-e-watan
Haq shanaas wa haq pasand wa haq yaqeen wa haq sukhan

O Tilak, O glorious upholder of love for the nation, you were truly
One who knew your duty, loved it, believed in it, were eloquent about it

One of the earliest proponents of *mukammal azaadi* (complete freedom), long before Gandhi's call for *poorna swaaraj*, Hasrat has written at length about *hurriyat kaamil* (complete independence), as here:

Hurriyat kaamil ki qasam khaa ke uthhe hain
Ab saaya-e British ki taraf jaayenge hum kya

We who have taken the pledge of complete independence
We shall not even go near the shadow of the British

At the peak of Gandhi's first call to civil disobedience, he wrote of the cruelty and oppression that the colonial rulers imposed in the name of law and order:

Naam se qanoon ke howey kya kya sitam
Jabr ba zer-e-naqaab dekhiye kab tak rahe

Look at all that happens in the name of the law
Let's see how long this oppression remains masked

Imprisoned several times for his role in the national freedom struggle, he continued to write prolifically from behind the bars of his jail cell (*zindaan-e-firang* as he called it meaning the foreigner's prison); one of his oft-quoted shers being these lines from a long ghazal alluding to the long hours of hard physical labour political prisoners had to endure in colonial prisons such as grinding flour in stone grinders:

Hai mashq-e-suḳhan jaari chakki ki mashaqqat bhi
Ik turfa tamasha hai Hasrat ki tabiat bhi

My practice of poetry continues as does my labour at the grinding wheel
Hasrat's disposition is a strange and agreeable spectacle

Of the many odes he wrote to his favourite Krishan ji Maharaj, this is brimful with love and longing to 'see' his beloved in his Brajbhoomi:

Har zarra-e-sar-zameen-e-Gokul
Daara hai jamaal-e-dilbari ka

Every atom in the land of Gokul
Possesses the beauty of the beloved

Living in an India that now requires us to be resolutely one or the 'other', the Maulana's immense capacity to contain within himself many seemingly diverse ideologies and beliefs holds a lesson. It reminds us of William Blake who said: 'Without contraries there is no progression.' It makes a study of the life and career of this firebrand revolutionary, ethical dissenter, conscientious objector, poet-politician, freedom fighter, parliamentarian, important and timely.

Postscript: Such is my fascination for this remarkable man, that I am presently engaged in writing his full-length biography. I first encountered Hasrat during my PhD research on the Progressive Writers' Movement and was struck by his interventions in all the meetings of the progressives he attended starting from the very first in Lucknow on 9 April 1936. Over the years I read his poetry in dribs and drabs, and came across references to him in the memoirs of Urdu writers. Gradually, the fascination grew and with it the conviction that modern-day Indians need to know about this amazing personality, a contrarian and a maverick if ever there has been one in Indian politics but also, a patriot and true son of India.

39. *Shaheed-e-Aazam* Bhagat Singh

The sentencing of Bhagat Singh, along with his comrades, Shivaram Rajguru and Sukhdev Thapar, who were hanged to death on 23 March 1931 in the Lahore Jail, had a profound effect on the national imagination. Along with Chandra Shekhar Azad these young men were members of the Hindustan Socialist Republican Association, a grouping that was convinced that only an armed uprising could bring about freedom for the Indian people. Naturally therefore, these young freedom fighters, many felled in the prime of their youth, seized the popular imagination in a manner that many other tall poppies of the national freedom struggle did not. Hanged at 23, Bhagat Singh soon slipped from a flesh and blood person to a folk hero, a veritable symbol of the aspirations of the Indian people in the run up to Independence. In his autobiography, Khwaja Ahmad Abbas, for instance, paints a vivid scenario of his fellow students at the Aligarh Muslim University crying, with tears streaming down their face, when news of the hanging of Bhagat Singh reached them. Many Urdu poets, too, have written with vim and vigour of this *shaheed-e-aazam* (great martyr).

Aftab Rais Panipati in a poem entitled 'Chadha Diya Hai

Bhagat Singh ko Raat Phaansi Par' (Bhagat Singh was Hanged Last Night) talks of the feeling of lightning having struck the listener's heart when news reaches them of this cold-blooded and planned killing. Like daggers being struck in the bosom of Mother India, this news is received by a country that has been no stranger to tragedy from the gory days of the bloodbath in Jallianwala Bagh:

Gira ke hind mein koh-e-malaal jaatey hain
Watan ko chhod ke Bharat ke laal jaatey hain
Tadap rahey hain judaai mein be-qaraar-e-watan
Chaley hain aalam-e-baala ko jaan-nisaar-e-watan

Having dropped a mountain of regret on Hind they leave
These jewels of Bharat leave their country to go away
Their restless countrymen fretting in this separation
Having laid down their lives for their country they leave for the high heavens

Never one to disappoint, always ready with a poetic response to any major event in the country, virtually a 'first responder' in poetic terms, here is Tilok Chand Mahroom with not one but two dirge-like nauha on this great tragedy; here's the first one from 'Shaheed Bhagat Singh':

Zindaan mein shaheedon ka woh sardaar aaya
Shaidaa-e-watan paikar-e-eesaar aaya
Hai daar-o-rasan ki sarfaraazi ka din
Sardar Bhagat Singh sardar aaya

That commander of martyrs has come to the prison
That mad lover of his country, that epitome of sacrifice has come
It is the day of exaltation for the gallows and the cord
The commander, Sardar Bhagat Singh, has come

And the second entitled 'Dekh Ai Hilaal-e-Shaam: Bhagat Singh ki Phaansi' (See, O Evening Crescent: The Hanging of Bhagat Singh) is a ballad filled with anguish written as it is in 'real time', in 1931 itself, when the wound is still fresh, giving an eyewitness account of the scenario as Bhagat Singh and his comrades move towards the gallows inside the prison:

Ab aagey kya bataoon main nazuk hai yeh maqaam
Ai sunney waale ashk baha aur jigar ko thaam
Phandey galey mein daal ke takhtey nikaal ke
Jallad kar chukka hai jo karna thha uss ko kaam
Dekh ai hilaal-e-shaam!

How shall I narrate what follows, for this is a delicate stage
O listener, shed tears and hold your heart steady
With the noose around their neck and planks pulled away
The executioner has done what he had to do
See, O evening crescent, bear witness!

Josh Malihabadi's long poem 'East Indian Company ke Farzandon Se' (To the Sons of the East India Company), which comprises a long litany of names from Nawab Sirajuddaullah to Rani Lakshmi Bai of Jhansi (quoted previously in this volume) to Tipu Sultan and the deposed Wajid Ali Shah of Awadh—all of whom were victims of the avarice and lust of the English for power and wealth, mentions Bhagat Singh thus years after the young man's hanging:

Woh Bhagat Singh ab bhi jis ke ġham mein dil naashaad hai
Uss ki gardan mein jo daala thha woh phanda yaad hai

That Bhagat Singh whose memory still makes me unhappy
That noose that was placed on his neck, I still remember it

In a poem entitled 'Shaheed-e-Azaadi' (Martyr of Freedom), Jamal Bharti remembers Bhagat Singh thus:

Jo watan par nisaar hota hai
Rooh-o-dil mein maqaam paataa hai
Uss ko taareeḳh yaad karti hai
Misl-e-ḳhurshid jagmagata hai

He who lays down his life for the country
He finds a place in our soul and our heart
He is remembered by history
He shines like a sun

Several poems, while not specifically written on Bhagat Singh, nonetheless invoke his martyrdom when the subject is *wataniyat* (nationalism) or *watan-parasti* (loving one's nation) as in this nazm by Fazal Haq Azimabadi:

Tu Bhagat Singh ki aankhon ka tara bana

You became the light that gleamed in Bhagat Singh's eye

Or this by Ahmad Wasi:

Bhagat Singh aaj bhi zinda yahaan hai
Badaa pyaaraa mira Hindostan hai

Bhagat Singh is alive here to this day
How beautiful indeed is my Hindostan

The memory of Bhagat Singh is again invoked when the nation celebrates its freedom—a freedom that came at a great price—such as here in this poem entitled 'Amn ka Tyauhaar' (Festival of Peace) by Khayal Ansari:

Aaj woh din hai ki jis din ke liye thhe ḳhoon bahey
Chandra Shekhar aur Bhagat Singh aur phir Gandhi ke ḳhoon

Today is the day for which much blood was shed
The blood of Chandra Shekhar and Bhagat Singh and later Gandhi

Showing yet again how the shared bonds of history and culture shape us, Faheem Shanas Kazmi born in 1965 in Karachi writes with love and genuine admiration for a hero who is common to the two countries born from a tryst with destiny:

Kaheen jab sarfaroshi ki
Mohabbat istaqaamat ki
Shahaadat ki watan ki baat chalti hai
Mujhe tum yaad aate ho

I remember you
Whenever there's talk of bravery
Of a tenacious love for the country
Of laying down one's life

40. The Luminous Idealism of Anwar Jalalpuri

One of midnight's children who saw the sullying of many dreams yet retained a luminous idealism, a College-level teacher of English who wrote poetry in Urdu, a poet of some repute who enjoyed an extra-ordinary felicity, and dexterity, at performing the *nizamat* (the dexterous art of conducting a mushaira), a translator of texts as diverse as the *Shrimad Bhagwad Gita* and the poetry of Omar Khayyam and Rabindranath Tagore into Urdu—Anwar Jalalpuri was all this and more. Born in the *qasbah* of Jalalpur in Uttar Pradesh in 1947, Anwar Jalalpuri encapsulated within himself all that was best and brightest in Urdu *zuban* and *tehzeeb*. Perhaps it was this easy familiarity with the literary culture of Urdu that allowed him to hold sway over the often tempestuous world of mushairas for nearly four decades and made him a well-known name across much of the Urdu-speaking world.

The task of *nizamat*—of deciding the sequence of who reads when according to status and seniority as a poet, of maintaining the tempo and rhythm of a mushaira like a finely-strung instrument, of alternating the sombre moments with the light-hearted ones, of knowing exactly how to introduce each poet, of chivvying a reluctant audience to give the right amount of *daad* (praise through loud cries of *wah-wah*) and chastening them when they become rowdy or too boisterous—has been described in two ways. At its most graceful, *nizamat* can be likened to a maestro conducting an orchestra. On the other hand, given the rambunctious nature of many *mushairas*, the task of *nizamat* can be akin to weighing frogs in a weighing scale (*tarazu mein medhak tolna*, as someone once put it most memorably). However, Anwar Jalalpuri brought a rare elan to this task, as well as a gravitas. His last appearance in this role in India was at the venerable annual Shankar Shad Mushaira at Modern School in New Delhi on 16th December 2017.

As a poet, Anwar Jalalpuri will be remembered for a rich and varied corpus comprising the ghazal, nazm, naatiya shairi (devotional poetry). Steeped in tradition yet acutely aware of the world around him, he could rightly say:

Mera har sher haqiqat ki hai zinda tasveer
Apne ashaar mein qissa nahin likhkha main ne

Every verse of mine is the living portrait of reality
I haven't written a tale or a fantasy in my poetry

And elsewhere:

Main apne saath rakhta hoon sada akhlaq ka paaras
Issi patthar se mitti chhoo ke main sona banaata hoon

I always keep with me the alchemist's stone of good conduct
With this stone when I touch dust I can turn it into gold

The poet who wrote:

Khiraaj mujh ko diya aane wali sadiyon ne
Buland neze pe jab hi hua hai sar mera

The coming centuries have paid obeisance to me
Whenever my head has been raised aloft a spear

Also wrote:

Koi puchhega jis din waaqai ye zindagi kya hai
Zameen se ek mutthi khaak le kar hum uda denge

The day someone will ask what is life really
I will lift a fistful of earth and let it blow away

A prolific and eclectic writer, Jalalpuri was also a script-writer, essayist and literary critic with over 20 books to his credit in both Urdu and Devnagri. Of these, his *manzum* (verse) translation of the *Gita* deserves special mention. His *Urdu Shairi Mein Gita: Naghma-e Ilm-o Amal* (published in 2013) tries to tell the story of the human heart that transcends time and circumstance and addresses questions that have troubled mortals since time immemorial: Who is Man? What is the spirit? What is Life? What is Death? Does God exist? For this, Jalalpuri was awarded the Yash Bharti Award in Lucknow.

I had the occasion to read Jalalpuri's translation in some detail when I was looking at multiple translations of the *Gita* in Urdu over a century and a half. I liked the fact that he attempted to explain the meaning in simple language and thus expanded the 701 shlokas to 1761 couplets. Dedicated to the syncretic Ganga-Jamuni *tehzeeb* of India, and to all the *sharif* people who wish for peace the world over, it has a Foreword by the Hindi poet Gopaldas Neeraj and a Preface by Uday Prakash Singh so it covers a gamut of political shades and opinions. And yet, for all its political correctness (it was launched at a glittering ceremony by the then Chief Minister of Uttar Pradesh), I found it to be by far the most lyrical of the several versions I had studied (despite its short syntax, *chhoti behar)* because its translator was himself a fine poet. Every *adhyay* (chapter) began with a *saransh* (summary) that contained a key to understanding each chapter. Jalalpuri is successful in creating drama and urgency in the build-up to the point where Arjun's dialogue with Shri Krishan ji Maharaj begins:

Thhii tayyar Bhishm pitamah ki fauj
Garajdaar jaise samandar ki mauj

The army of Bhishm Pitamah was ready
Thundering like the waves of the ocean

As Arjun sits dejected in his chariot, his bow and arrow slipping from his hand, Krishna says:

Ai Arjun! hawaon ka rukh morh de
Yeh na-mardi aur buzdili chorh de...
Uthho jang ke waastey uthh parho
Le haath mein aslaah uthh parho...

Oh Arjun! Change the direction of the winds
Leave this unmanliness and cowardice...
Get up, get up for the sake of war
Get up, bearing your arms in your hand...

And then moving on through the mysteries of revelation...

Yeh ek gyan hai aur ek raaz bhi
Yeh mere batane ka andaz bhi

This is knowledge and a secret too
And so is the manner of my telling

And in the end Arjun responds:

Ai Aaqa! meri ab yeh aankhein khulin
Mujhe rehmatein barkatein ab miliin
Jo thhe mujh mein shak khatam sab ho gaye
Mere dil mein jalne lage ab diye

O master! my eyes have been opened
I have received mercy and blessings
All my misgivings have been removed
And my heart is lit up with lamps

Perhaps the best tribute to this crusader for communal harmony and shared living can be by paying heed to his words:

Na tera hai na mera hai yeh Hindostan sabka hai
Nahin samjhi gayi yeh baat to nuqsan sabka hai

Neither yours nor mine this Hindustan is everyone's
If this is not understood the loss will be everyone's

Passions

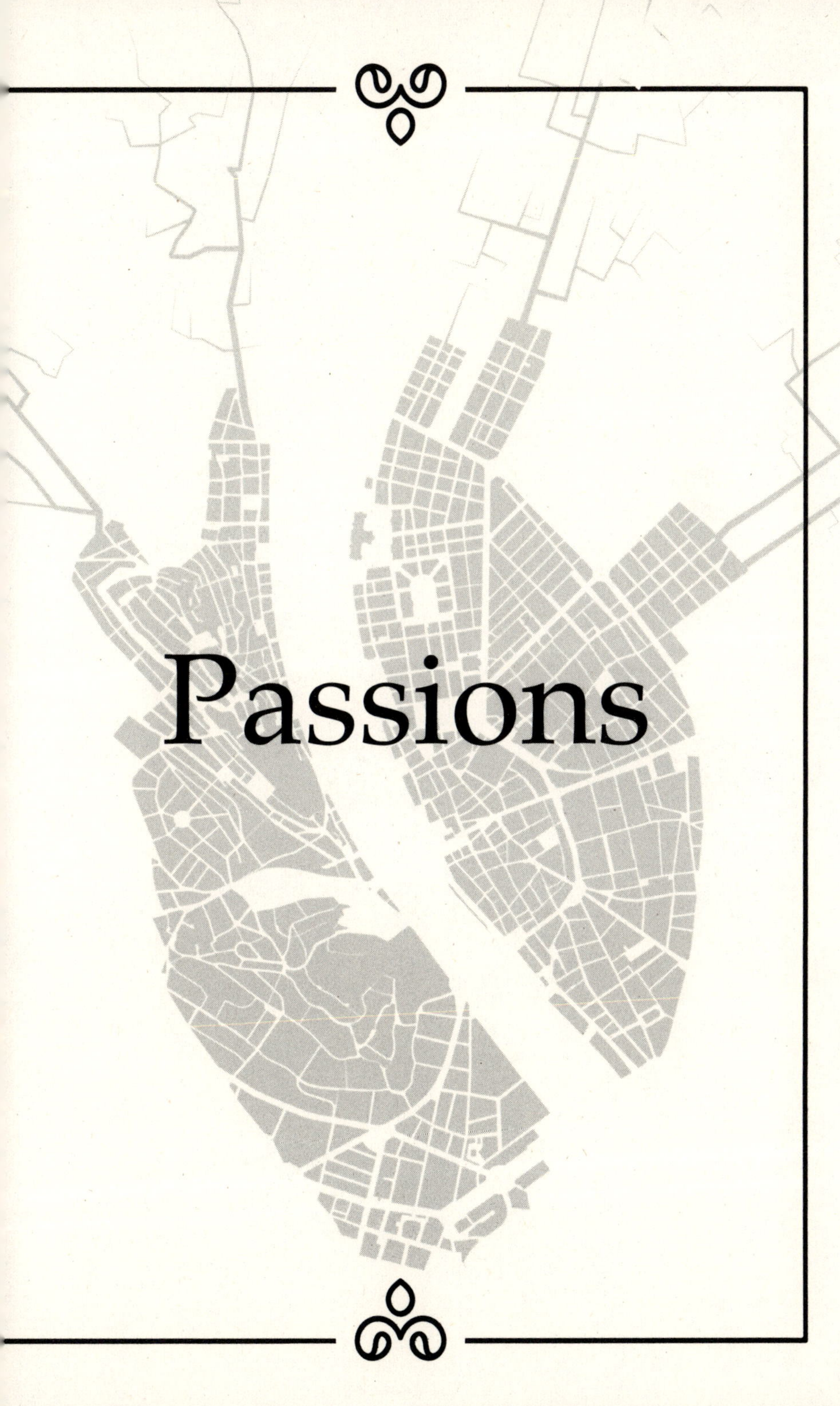

41. Of Passion, Poetry and Pandemic

Perhaps the most searing announcement of self-imposed social distancing, long before the term gained currency during the COVID-induced pandemic, is this ghazal by Delhi's pre-eminent poet, Mirza Ghalib:

Rahiye ab aisi jagah chal kar jahaan koi na ho
Hum-suḳhan koi na ho aur hum-zabaan koi na ho

Be-dar-o-diwaar sa ik ghar banaaya chaahiye
Koi hum-saaya na ho aur paasban koi na ho

Padiye gar bimaar to koi na ho timaardaar
Aur agar mar jaaiye to nauha-ḳhwaan koi na ho

Let us go and live somewhere where there is no one
No one who speaks to me in my language, no one to talk to

I will make something that is like a house
(But) There won't be any neighbours, nor anyone to guard it

Were I to fall ill, there will be no one to tend me
And when I die, no one to mourn me

Of course there was no Corona scare in Delhi then but in the immediate aftermath of the Revolt of 1857 many citizens of Delhi, who had chosen to stay back in their battle-scarred, besieged city, were house bound. With rations running low, plummeting morale and deteriorating civic conditions there was mounting news of the atrocities being unleashed by the British on hapless citizens. The three couplets above are said to have been written in response to the Nawab of Farrukhabad being picked up by the British for aiding the rebels, and abandoned on an island off the shore of Arabia. They reflect the hopelessness and escapism that afflicted many Indians of Ghalib's generation.

The words *bechaini*, *beqarari*, *dard*, especially *dard-e dil* (uneasiness, restlessness, pain, heartache, respectively) feature prominently in Urdu poetry, such as this sher by, again, Ghalib:

Ishq se tabiat ne zeest ka maza paaya
Dard ki dawaa paayi dard-e-be-dawa paaya

It's from love we learnt the savour of life
Found the cure for pain and the pain that has no cure

But if it is of sickness, ill health or malady (*bimaari*), in particular that we speak, there is Ghalib (again) with his oft-quoted:

Un ke dekhe se jo aa jaati hai munh par raunaq
Woh samajhte hain ki beemar ka haal achchha hai

The glow that comes to my face when they look at me
They think the patient is feeling better today

Of the others who have written on sickness, though almost always in the abstract, there is this by Mubarak Azimabadi:

Mehrbani chaaraasazon ki badhi
Jab badha darman to bimaari badhi

The kindness of my physicians increased
When the medicine increased so did the illness

And this by Khalilur Rehman Raz in much the same vein:

Kya sunaaein jan-ba-lab qaumon ki bimaari ka haal
Dard badhta hii gaya juun juun dawa karte rahe

What shall I tell you about the sickness of the nations at death's door
The pain increased as we increased the medicine

On *vaba* or epidemic in particular there is this by Hasan Naim:

Sab pareshan hain ki aaḳhir kis vaba mein woh mire
Jin ko ġhurbat ke alaava koi bimaari na thi

Everyone is worried about the epidemic that will ensnare
Them who have no illness save poverty

Seeing an old woman sleeping on the open ground at a time when death and disease are rampant in the country, Josh Malihabadi writes this in a long poem entitled 'Zaifa' (Old Woman):

Aur kis mausam mein jab taaun hai phaila hua
Zarra zarra hai vaba ke ḳhauf se simta hua

At this time when pestilence has spread
Every particle has shrunk with the fear of epidemic

The one time when fear of epidemic is very real and mortality often very high is during mass religious gatherings, such as the haj. While the haj has been studied from many perspectives—religious, sociological, cultural—it has seldom been viewed from the perspective of community health. Saurabh Mishra addresses this lacuna in his book *Pilgrimage, Politics, and Pestilence: The Haj from the Indian Subcontinent, 1860-1920* (OUP, 2011). He looks at the 'medicalisation' of Mecca as it reeled from one epidemic to another all through the late-19th century till it found some degree of stabilisation through the introduction of quarantine and other regularisations imposed by an increasingly threatened, and jittery, Europe. Running apace with this growing 'medicalisation' is what Mishra calls the increasing 'politicisation' as the Hejaz becomes a highly contested zone and the pilgrims a volatile, politically-driven lot than the meek, pious passengers of olden days.

Since the bulk of Haj pilgrims, in the period of Mishra's study, were from Asia and Africa where diseases, especially highly contagious ones such as cholera, small pox, typhoid, etc. were rampant, the colonial governments in these parts did their best to control the spread of epidemics at the source, that is, at the exit points for each country, usually the embarkation ports along the Indian Ocean. Since there was no rule in the Pilgrim Ships' Act regarding compulsory vaccination then, pilgrims could only be 'induced' to get themselves vaccinated by persuasion. Despite the best of intentions, disease and infection could not be entirely controlled. People continued to pour into Mecca either with forged certificates or without the knowledge that inoculations were for their own good.

Many even believed that being Allah's Guests, those who die in Mecca, considered the *Bait-ul Muqqaddas* or the Holiest of Homes, were assured a straight passage to heaven. They, therefore, not only made light of any inconveniences or misfortunes but even considered it a rare privilege to die and be buried in the soil of the holy sites. Among the pilgrims who have left behind travel accounts or *safarnamas*, the few who did note the abysmal lack of systems of sanitary intervention, chose to concentrate on the unsanitary conditions especially after the ritual sacrifice of an animal at Mina rather than the general state of affairs which bred disease and pestilence. Things reached such a pass in Mina that local authorities were often forced to raise a yellow flag on the mountain top to alert the incoming tide of pilgrims. The raising of the yellow flag struck terror among the devout, but did little to either douse their ardour or improve health and hygiene. Pilgrims continued to die of infectious diseases in the Hejaz like flies. In 1893 of the 200,000 pilgrims during haj, 33,000 perished.

Since the great majority of those who flocked to the holy cities were either poor or enfeebled by age, the health hazards of accumulating large numbers of people under unsanitary conditions increased manifold. Cholera, long a scourge in India, appeared in the Hejaz in 1831. From then on till the early-20th century, it continued to rage and claim thousands of pious victims. The Ottomans and later the Nejdis tried their best to contain it but by 1865 a major cholera epidemic was raging through the Hejaz. It is said to have originated in Java and was carried to Mecca by pilgrims, one-third of whom perished during the pilgrimage. By June the disease was raging in Alexandria. And later that same month it reached Marseilles and thence most of the cities of Europe. In November 1865 cholera was reported in New York City.

Once the threat of this annual epidemic ravaging western non-endemic, non-Islamic nations became very real, several international conferences were held. Quarantine stations were set up. Port authorities—both at the point of embarkation and disembarkation—were instructed to step up vigilance. Fumigation of pilgrims' luggage was made compulsory. The opening of the Suez Canal in 1869, lauded as a great victory for European hegemonic interests, was suddenly seen as a portal of death and destruction. For the first time in the history of the West's interaction with the Middle East, fear replaced greed. This fear was overlaid with self-preservation. The threat of devastating cholera epidemics invading Europe by way of the Hejaz succeeded in uniting rival European powers as the West realized it could not remain at the mercy of the pilgrimage to Mecca year after year. As a result of this fear, the haj became, according to Mishra:

> …not merely a subject of concern for European countries, it also *fashioned* medical practices and debates. It was the motive force behind the colonial government's stance on the subject of cholera and quarantines. It was also partly responsible for the lasting sway of the theory of non-contagiousness of cholera in India long after it had been thoroughly overturned in Europe.

The last of the great cholera epidemics in the Hejaz was reported in 1912 thus ending one chapter in the intertwined story of public health and politics as played out against the backdrop of pilgrimage. For the non-Muslim world, too, the focus of interest shifted from medical surveillance to a watchful mistrust of the increasing politicisation of the pilgrimage. The colonial governments, in particular, were alive to the changing perception of the haj itself—from trade and commerce, the focus shifted to politics and empire.

While outright intervention in the custodianship of the holy sites is still unimaginable, the politics of pilgrimage plays on in different guises in different parts of the world. In the case of India, there is the politics of assertiveness as in the case of the Kumbh Mela during the worst days of the COVID surge* and the Gangasagar Mela†.

---

*https://www.aljazeera.com/news/2021/4/12/india-thousands-join-hindu-festival-ritual-bath-as-covid-surges

†https://www.voanews.com/a/drones-spray-holy-water-at-india-hindu-festival-as-crowds-defy-covid-rules/6396692.html

42. *Saanson ki Mala...*

A prolonged bout of COVID—the dreaded Delta variant during the country-wide spike in April 2021—gave one ample time to dwell on the singular activity that, literally, makes the difference between life and death, namely breath. More specifically every single breath one draws. When life is measured not with coffee-spoons like Alfred J Prufrock was wont to do but in every lungful of air, when the tedium of the endless days and nights is broken by the hub-dub of the oxygen machine, puffs of steroids, frantic checks of the oximeter as well as endless steam inhalations, lying prone on one's belly in a position known as 'proning', breathing exercises and blowing up three tiny balls in a spirometer and feeling chuffed when even two balls manage to go up slightly, the very idea of breathing acquires a special, painful urgency. In the few moments of clarity, between all of the above, when enough oxygen is reaching your brain, you think fitfully of this whole business of *ukhdi hui saans, uljhi saansein, saanson ki mala, raahat ki saans* (harsh, tangled breath, a string of breaths and a sigh of relief respectively), and why the poet—long before the deadly pandemic struck an unsuspecting world—wrote so prolifically on the breath.

Every Urdu sher one had ever heard about breathing, be it laboured, faltering, stifled, ratchetty, tangled and so on—and yes, there's a gamut of breaths and the Urdu poet has managed to describe each one with an uncanny ability—acquires a special, poignant meaning in the light of one's own experiences, such as this by Mir Taqi Mir that many have quoted at some point without ever fully understanding its significance:

Le saans bhi ahista ki nazuk hai bahut kaam
Aafaq ki iss kaargah-e-shishagari ka

Draw breath gently for it is a delicate business
In this glass-making factory of the world

Or this by Makhdoom Mohiuddin, for all its romantic mooring nevertheless brimful with poignancy:

Saans rukti hai chhalakte hue paimaane mein
Koi leta thha tira naam-e-wafa aaḳhir-e-shab

Breath stops in goblets that are filled to the brim
When someone takes your name in the last watch

And this other also by Makhdoom that I have often recited to myself without ever realising what it would mean to my COVID-wracked body one day:

Raat bhar deeda-e-namnaak mein lahraate rahe
Saans ki tarah se aap aate rahe jaate rahe

You fluttered in my tearful eyes all night long
Like the breath that came and went all night long

Or this by Arshad Karim Ulfat that encapsulates the feeling of transience:

Saans chadhtii huii utartii huii
Zindagi toottii bikhartii huii

Breath that rises and falls
Life that breaks and scatters

And the keenness with which every breath cuts through your chest, like a sharp-edged knife, as described here by Saeed Shariq:

Saans ki dhaar zara ghusti zara kaatti hai
Kya daraanti hai ki ḳhud fasl-e-fana katti hai

The sharp edge of breath enters a bit and cuts a bit
What a sickle it is that cuts the harvest of mortality

Noman Shauque's sher acquires an especially macabre significance when news trickles in of friends and acquaintances dead and dying during the dreaded pandemic:

Aankh khul jae to ghar maatam-kada ban jaaegaa
Chal rahii hai saans jab tak chal rahaa hoon neend mein

If one were to wake suddenly the house would turn into a mourning chamber
Till I am drawing breath I am walking in my sleep

And this by Ghulam Murtaza Rahi that captures the surrealness of simply breathing in, breathing out:

Saanson ke aane jaane se lagtaa hai
Ik pal jeetaa hoon to ik pal martaa hoon

With the inhaling and exhaling of breaths
I get proof that I live for a moment, and die the next

Then there's Mustafa Zaidi who said:

Dil ke rishte ajeeb rishte hain
Saans leney se toot jaate hain

The ties of the heart are strange
They break when you breathe

And Sudarshan Fakir who could well have spoken up on behalf of countless COVID sufferers when he wrote of course in an altogether different context:

Mere rukte hii mirii saansein bhii ruk jaaengii
Faasle aur badhaa do ki main zinda hoon abhii

My breaths too will stop when I stop
Increase the distances for I am yet alive

When all of nature seems to be a reflection of one's own individual suffering as in this sher by Suroor Barabankvi:

Be-kasii barasti hai zindagi ke chehre se
Kaaenaat ki saansein dhal rahii hain aahon mein

Helplessness drips from the face of life
As though creation's breaths are turning to sighs

And finally, in the dark watches of endless nights and the half-gloom of interminable days when the body is wracked by fever and cough, the same breaths turn into a rosary, telling each breath as though a bead—in the raspy voice of the inimitable Nusrat Fateh Ali Khan singing the 16th-century Mira bhajan:

Saanson ki maala pe simrun main pee ka naam...

I shall recite the name of the Lord on the rosary of my breaths

In the final analysis, the one essential lesson one learnt during the COVID pandemic was that a disease as wretched as Corona needs equal doses of modern medicine and science as much as faith and prayer to see you through. Such was its randomness and such also its relentlessness that there was no easy answer as to why some were spared and some taken away, why some got off relatively lightly while others were put through the wringer.

43. *Ishq, Muhabbat, Pyaar*: And the Untranslatability of Love

If someone were to ask me to single out THE most romantic Urdu verse I would unhesitatingly pick out this jewel by Momin Khan Momin:

Tum mere paas hote ho goya
Jab koi doosra nahi hota

You are close beside me as if
No other person can be with me

The rest of the ghazal has several other, often-recited sher, too, such as:

Haal-e dil yaar se likhun kyunkar
Haath dil se juda nahin hota

How shall I describe my state to my beloved
I can not detach my hand from my heart

And:

Tum humare kissi tarah na huwe
Varna duniya mein kya nahin hota

You never ever became mine no matter what
Or else, what could I not have achieved in life

But poetry, like love, is subjective and deeply personal. And for me the one sher that stands out from Urdu's admittedly vast corpus of romantic poetry is this short, seemingly simple verse for reasons that are hard to describe. I like to, also, use this sher in lectures and translation workshops to demonstrate the futility and loss that lies at the heart of any translation. In Urdu, the entire *wazan* (weight) of the sher rests on the word *goya*, that almost untranslatable conjunction; as if, like, as though, apparently, etc. do not carry the same weight as *goya*. Momin's contemporary, Mirza Ghalib, is said to have declared his willingness to give away his entire *diwan* (set of literary works) for this one verse!

The same Momin, born as he was in an Age of Greats, both blessed and cursed to have contemporaries such as Ghalib and Zauq, living in an age when everyone—from the emperor Bahadurshah Zafar to the beggar on the streets of Delhi—was a *sahib-e kalaam* (a writer of verse) has also written:

Umr to saari kati ishq-e butaan mein Momin
Aakhri waqt mein kya khaak Musalman hongey

My entire life was spent in the worship of idols, Momin
Now in my last days why bother becoming a Muslim

As with much of Urdu poetry, the above sher can be read in a lay and a religious sense: the poet could be talking of the futility of turning religious in his old age or he could well be talking of turning his affections to a new lover! And then there is this—also by Momin—an exquisite jewel-like requiem to lost love:

Woh jo hum mein tum mein qarar thha tumhein yaad ho ke na yaad ho
Wohi yaani waada nibhah ka tumhein yaad ho ke na yaad ho

That love that you and I once had, wonder if you remember it or not
That same promise, that of constancy, wonder if you remember it or not

A bit like *goya* this poem has *yaani,* just as untranslatable and just as seemingly insignificant grammatically but serving much the same purpose, syntactically, as a keystone does in an arch architecturally.

In Ghalib, by far the most untranslatable word is *jigar*; literally and anatomically meaning liver but used for the heart, or the region thereabouts, in much of Urdu poetry:

Koi mere dil se poochhe tire teer-e-neem-kash ko
Ye khalish kahaan se hoti jo jigar ke paar hotaa

Someone should ask my heart about the pain of a half-drawn arrow
Would this pain have been there had it gone clean through the heart

Another of the 'greats', Mir Taqi Mir has written profusely on love and all matters of the heart leaving the matter of the beloved's gender vague and fluid. But there is nothing vague in this declaration that is virtually the 'rock edict' of romance in Urdu poetry:

Ishq ik Mir bhaari patthar hai
Kab ye tujh na-tavaan se uthhta hai

Love, Mir, is a heavy rock
How can one so feeble as you lift it

There is also another sher, wrongly attributed to Mir, but actually written by Taish Marairahvi that is still recited by forlorn lovers down the ages while the rest of Taish's no doubt excellent *kalaam* (poetic output) is lost from popular memory:

Woh aaye bazm mei itna to Taish ne dekha
Phir uske baad chiraghon mein roshni na rahi

He came to the assembly and that is all that Taish could see
For afterwards there was no light left in the lamps

Centuries later, how does the modern poet view love? With the nazm gaining greater currency and challenging the hegemony of the ghazal, Faiz Ahmad Faiz in 'Mujhse Pehli Si Muhabbat Mere Mahboob Na Mang' (My Beloved, Don't Ask Me To Love You As I Once Did) acknowledges the heart-tugging beauty of the beloved but talks of the other sorrows of the world which claim his attention. He juxtaposes the beloved's beauty against the miseries and ugliness of the world, a world which has hunger, disease and deprivation, a world that can never let him love her as he once did, for a love that is divorced from social reality is too individualistic, too meaningless:

Aur bhi dukh hain zamaane mein muhabbat ke siwa
Raahatein aur bhi hain vasl ki raahat ke siwa

There are other sorrows too apart from love
And other pleasures too apart from that of union

Of all the contemporary poets, perhaps the one who poses the greatest problem is Munawwar Rana who seems to have virtually replaced the beloved with the mother and the love we see time and again in his poetry spanning decades is a son's love for his mother in verses such as these:

Jab bhi kashti miri sailaab mein aa jaati hai
Ma dua karti hui ḳhwaab mein aa jaati hai

Whenever my boat reaches a flood
My mother, praying, appears in my dream

Then there is Shahryar, neither fully modernist nor a traditionalist, who sees the beloved as an enigma, who invents a new vocabulary of love, who asks questions such as:

Ya tere ilawa bhi kisi shai ki talab hai
Ya apni muhabbat pe bharosa nahin hum ko

Is it that I hanker for something apart from you
Or, is it that I do not trust my love for you

Much of Shahryar's poetry, especially his nazms, is concerned with matters of the body, with the relationship between men and women. He writes with naturalness and ease and none of the coy camouflage that some poets resort to, nor any of the overt, in-your-face sexuality that mars much of modern Urdu poetry. Instead there is an easy acceptance:

Raat tujhe sapne mein dekha
Tujhko chhoone ki khwahish ko
Kitni dushwari se taala

I saw you in a dream last night
And pushed away the desire to touch you
With such difficulty

To conclude, let us remember that love, be it romantic or bodily, is for the most part unattainable and, as for Shahryar, *goya ke*, as hard to find as a restful, dream-filled night's sleep!

44. *Naya Saal Mubarak*: Poetry on the New Year

It took the terrible years of the prolonged COVID-induced pandemic, with night curfews in place for two consecutive years, news of rising numbers of new cases and the threat of a looming 'third wave', to realise how much we took the festive season for granted. It began in October with the Durga Puja and Dussehra celebrations, running to Diwali and then Christmas with the New Year celebrations marking the finale of a season of good cheer that lasted almost three months. Shops and streets lit up, markets thronging with excited buyers, deals and offers on all manner of consumable goods. The COVID years brought in an altered reality.

Even at the best of times, the close of the old year and the dawn of the new one evokes mixed feelings in the human heart. When nights are bedecked like brides, there is chatter at parties and the tinkle of glasses and the laughter of strangers—the Urdu poet has noted all this and more. *Saal-e nau* or *naya saal*, the New Year, has been viewed with hope and hopelessness, anticipation and indifference, eagerness and apathy, enthusiasm and cynicism, optimism and pessimism, anger and joy, and everything in between. And this range of emotions has found ample expression in Urdu poetry down the ages. From a profusion of Urdu nazms, a great many bearing the same title of 'Naya Saal', here's a sampler…

Ali Sardar Jafri heralds the dawn of a new day that carries the promise of better days:

Purane saal ki thithuri hui parchhaaiyan simteen
Naye din ka naya suraj ufuq par uthta aata hai

The shivering shadows of the old year shrink
As the new sun of the new day rises on the horizon

Harking back to a time when people sent cards and called each other on landlines, Jafri writes:

Ye kis ne phone pe dii saal-e-nau ki tahniyat mujh ko
Tamanna raqs karti hai taḳhayyul gungunata hai

Who is it who has greeted me on the telephone for the New Year
Desire dances within me and my imagination hums with joy

An unknown poet strikes an optimistic note when he writes:

Naye saal mein pichhlii nafrat bhula dein
Chalo apni duniya ko jannat bana dein

Let us forget old hatreds in the New Year
Come, let us turn our world into paradise

Just as in 'Naya Calendar', Shabnam Rumani says:

Phir naye saal ka matlab humein samjhaati hai
Janwary sabz dupatte mein chali aati hai

Once again it explains the meaning of the New Year
January comes wearing a green dupatta

Turning the stereotype of newness and hope that the first month of the calendar signifies, Ameer Qazalbash says:

Yakum Janwary hai naya saal hai
December mein poochhunga kya haal hai

It is the 1st of January it is the New Year
I will ask you in December how you are

In a world that is unchanging in its misery and exploitation, the New Year steals upon us carrying promises it will never keep, declares Akhtar Payami:

Toot jaaenge mah-o-saal ke phaile huwe jaal
Phir naya saal dabe paanv chalaa aataa hai

The wide open nets of months and years will break
Once again the New Year comes soft footed upon us

With his tongue firmly in his cheek, Hasan Alvi writes:

Washington DC mein cherry ke darakhton par
Naye saal ke khwaab ugaaye jaaenge

On the cherry trees in Washington DC
The dreams of New Years will be grown

Parvin Shakir, the eternal romantic, wonders in this sher brimful with a delicate irony:

Kaun jaane ki naye saal mein tu kis ko padhe
Tera meaar badaltaa hai nisaabon ki tarah

Who knows who you will read in the New Year
Your standard changes like the syllabus of schools

Ibne Insha writes:

Ik saal gaya ik saal naya hai aane ko
Par waqt ka ab bhi hosh nahin diwaane ko

A year has gone past a new one is about to come
But the poor mad man has no sense of time still

Taking a quip at Mirza Ghalib who had declared that a Brahmin has prophesied that the coming year will be a good one, Ahmad Faraz says:

Na shab-o-roz hii badle hain na haal achchha hai
Kis barhaman ne kaha thha ki ye saal achchha hai
Neither the days and nights have changed nor is our situation better
Who is the Brahmin who had said that this would be a good year

Taking the high road of Marxism, Sahir Ludhianvi paints a grim picture of the dawn of a new day in the new year that is no different from any other for the poor in his nazm 'Subh-e Nau-roz' (Morning of the New Year). The gaiety and festivity of the urban rich is contrasted with the rural poor, with the daughter of a poor peasant in particular, and the poet seems to be almost shaming those who can bring themselves to partake of the festivities when there is such a stark dis-balance among the haves and the have-nots:

Phoot padeen mashriq se kirnein
Haal bana maazi ka fasana
Goonja mustaqbil ka tarana
Bheje hain ahbaab ne tohfe
Atey padey hain mez ke kone
Dulhan bani hui hain raahein
Jashn manaao sal-e-nau ke

The rays of the sun have burst from the east
The story of the past has become the present
The song of the future echoes

Friends have sent gifts
The tables are piled high with them
The roads are decorated like brides
Come, let us rejoice in celebrating the New Year

A similar sentiment is expressed by Aitbar Sajid who questions the futility of extending greetings in the New Year when the change of a calendar does not herald a change in one's fortunes:

Kisi ko saal-e-nau ki kya mubaarakbad dii jaaye
Calendar ke badalne se muqaddar kab badalta hai

Why offer congratulations for the New Year to any one
Destinies don't change with the change in calendars

Makhdoom Mohiuddin, the poet from Hyderabad and fiery progressive, too, is mocking the hollow gaiety of the New Year in his nazm entitled 'Naya Saal':

Karodon baras ki purani
Kuhan-sal duniya
Ye duniya bhi kya masḳhari hai
Naye saal ki shaal odhey
Ba-sad-tanz hum sab se ye kah rahi hai
Ki main to 'nayi' hoon
Hansi aa rahi hai

This ancient world
Old by crores of years
What a jester this world is
Wearing the shawl of a new year
With much irony it is telling us
I am 'new'
I want to laugh

Faiz Ludhianvi too is almost challenging the New Year in the following manner:

Tu naya hai to dikha subh nayi shaam nayi
Warna inn aankhon ne dekhe hain naye saal kai

If you are new show us a new morn and a new eve
Or else these eyes of mine have seen many a new year

There are others, however, who welcome the New Year, who see it as an occasion to mollify the angry and the hurt, forget old sorrows, such as Jauhar Rahmani is trying to do in this nazm:

Naye saal ki yuun ḳhushi hum manaaein
Ki roothe huon ko galey se lagaaein
Let us celebrate the New Year in such a way
That we embrace those who are angry with us

Speaking for myself, I draw solace from Faiz Ahmad Faiz in these bleak times that have consistently refused to yield *acche din* (good days) despite all promises:

Humne dil mein saja liye gulshan
Jab bahaaron ne berukhi ki hai
Zehar se dho liye hain honth apne
Lutf-e-saaqi ne jab kami ki hai

I have bedecked my heart with gardens
When the seasons of spring have shown indifference
I have rinsed my mouth with poison
When the kindness of the cup-bearer has been sparing

45. *Lo Phir Basant Aayi*

My mother recalls wearing something yellow on Basant as an undergraduate student at Aligarh Muslim University. So would all the girls and teachers at the Women's College. Some of the girls would cook something yellow, usually sweet yellow rice, to bring along and share with friends. The entire college would wear a festive look with yellow mustard and marigold flowers and the college garden would be ablaze with spring colours. Basant was as much a cultural event as it was a religious occasion but more importantly it was shared, common, *sanjha*.

Basant, also spelt as Vasant or Vasant Panchami or Sarswati Puja in honour of the goddess of knowledge and wisdom, marks the arrival of spring. Across much of India, this day falling on the fifth day of the month of *Maagh* according to the Hindu lunar calendar corresponds with roughly 40 days of pleasant weather immediately thereafter: the bitter cold of winter lessens and the harsh days of summer seem yet afar, the skies are clear, flowers bloom aplenty and the harvest is standing ready and tall in fields and farms.

The Urdu poet, with one finger to the pulse of the common people and the other busy writing paeans of togetherness and shared joy, has naturally therefore written copiously on Basant. In many instances conflating Basant with spring, there are references aplenty to Basant-Bahaar. For many, Basant is not so much a season or a moment in time as a state of mind, evocative of a mood of hope and happiness. But, equally, there are references to its moorings in an agrarian society and culture.

Fayyazuddin Ahmad Khan Fayyaz paints a vivid picture of the perceptible change in the weather with the coming of Basant with a noticeably balmy air, the gentleness of the sun:

Bahut khamosh aur pur-kaif tabdeeli hai Nature mein
Koi jis tarah kashti khhe raha hai prem sagar mein

There is a silent and intoxicating change in Nature
As though someone is rowing a boat in the Ocean of Love

Ufuq Lakhnavi invokes the traditional tropes of the wine and tavern to portray a picture of optimism and hope that poets down the ages have associated with the season of Basant:

Saaqi kuchh aaj tujh ko ḳhabar hai Basant ki
Har su bahaar pesh-e-nazar hai Basant ki

O cup-bearer, do you know that Basant is nigh
The spring of Basant is all around in full view

Insha Allah Khan Insha links the blaze of colours that herald the coming of spring with the fire (of hope/passion/desire) raging in one's breast thus:

Tu ne lagayi ab ki ye kya aag ai Basant
Jis se ki dil ki aag uthe jaag ai Basant

What a fire you have lit this time, O Basant
It has awakened the fire in my breast, O Basant

In a similar vein, Muneer Shikohabadi, the martyr of the Revolt of 1857 who was sentenced to imprisonment in the Cellular Jail in the Andamans, calls Basant the diligent gardener who brings myriad colours to the garden that is life:

Karta hai baǧh-e-dahr mein nairangiyan Basant
Aaya hai laakh rang se ai baǧhban Basant

Basant does many forms of strange magic in the Garden of Life
Basant, the gardener, has come in thousands of colours

With winter retreating and the coming of pleasant weather, Basant also marked fairs and festivals in many parts of rural India which were an eagerly awaited event in the cultural calendar of ordinary folk. Nazeer Akbarabadi paints a joyful picture of Basant replete with song and dance, as also food and drink amidst much revelry by men and women:

Dilbar galey lipat te hon sarson ka khet ho
Jab dekhiye Basant to kaisi Basant ho...

Lovers embracing in fields of mustard
Wherever you look, what a Basant it is...

Mahlaqa Chanda, the powerful courtesan from the Deccan often regarded as the first published woman poet in Urdu, has this to say about Basant thus indicating its pan-Indian reach and giving the lie to the notion that it is a largely North Indian festival:

Basant aai hai mauj-e-rang-e-gul hai josh-e-sahba hai
Khuda ke fazl se aish-o-tarab ki ab kami kya hai

With the coming of Basant there is a wave of colourful flowers and effervescence
By the Grace of God there is no shortage of pleasure and joy

With the coming of Basant, the koel that has been silent in the long dark winter months once again calls out from the mango trees which will shortly begin to bear fruit as Abru Shah Mubarak writes here with a play on the words *khaas-o-aam* meaning special and ordinary but also referring to *aam* (mangoes):

Koyal neen aa ke kook sunai Basant rut
Baurae ḳhas-o-aam ki aai Basant rut

The cry of the Koel heralds the coming of the season of Basant
The special and the ordinary bear fruit in the season of Basant

Listing the flowers that bloom during Basant—*tesu, geinda, sarson, kesar kusum* (flame of the forest, marigold, mustard, saffron, safflower)—Munshi Dwarka Prasad Ufaq Lakhnawi describes the temples and homes that are similarly bedecked with yellow flowers:

Hain isht devtaon ke mandir sajey huwey
Hain zard zard phoolon se kul dar sajey huwey

The temples of the favourite deities are decorated
As are the doorways festooned with yellow flowers

Linking the external with the internal, Bimal Krishan Ashk makes a statement that could be political or personal or both when he says:

Ab ke Basant aayi to aankhein ujad gaiin
Sarson ke khet mein koi patta hara na tha

This year when Basant came my eyes were laid barren
There wasn't a single green leaf in the field of mustard

In a similar vein M K Mahtab wrote a short story entitled 'Sarson ke Khet' (Fields of Mustard) invoking the terror and darkness of the dark days of insurgency in the Punjab when, as in the sher above, the golden fields of mustard fail to evoke joy in a plentiful harvest.

However, the last word on Basant comes from the pen of Hafeez Jalandhari in the form of the ballad-like 'Basanti Tarana' (The Song of Basant) immortalised by the mother-daughter duo of Mallika Pukhraj and Tahira Syed:

Lo phir Basant aayi
Phoolon pe rang laayi...
Aafat gai k̤hizaan ki
Qismat phiri jahaan ki...

Lo, Basant has come again
Bringing colour to the flowers...
The awful autumn has gone
The fate of the world changes...

46. *Bahaar* and the Idea of Spring

Given that the Indian climate is marked by a difference of temperature and rainfall more than anything else and falls under the category of 'tropical monsoon' with no clearly defined spring or autumn, the 'idea' of spring has an important place in our collective consciousness, and by extension our poetry. Just as there is copious amounts of poetry in Sanskrit on the six seasons as identified by the ancient Hindu calendar, namely, *vasant* (spring), *grishma* (summer), *varsha* (monsoon), *sharad* (autumn), *hemant* (early winter) and *shishir* (winter) and on *vasant* or spring in particular, so too there is a joyous celebration of *bahaar* in Urdu poetry.

Meaning beauty, glory, splendour, elegance, prime of life, bloom of youth, *bahaar* is used for spring, spring-time and verdure. But the Urdu poet, as is the poet's wont, infuses the word with a special agency to mean many things: exuberance, prosperity, a time of plenty, a promise of new beginnings as also beauty, fragility, impermanence. And, by extension, *bahaar* has also come to indicate the ecstasy of union and fruition as also the lament of the lover who is separated from his beloved and wants nothing more than to be united with her/him to enjoy the beauty and ephemeral splendor of this short-lived season.

At its simplest, here is Ahmad Faraz comparing spring at the peak of its glory with the beloved's face:

Bharii bahaar mein ik shaakh pe khilaa hai gulaab
Ki jaise tu ne hatheli pe gaal rakha hai

A rose has bloomed on a branch in the fullness of spring
Looking as though you have placed your face on your palm

And the classicist Jigar Moradabdi declaring the beloved's beauty that surpasses that of spring;

Sehn-e-chaman ko apni bahaaron pe naaz thha
Woh aa gaye to saari bahaaron pe chha gaye

The garden's courtyard prided itself on its springs
When she came, she held sway over all the springs

Fani Badayuni rues the frittering of the possibilities that spring offered:

Tinkon se khelte hi rahe aashiyan mein hum
Aaya bhi aur gaya bhi zamaana bahaar ka

We kept playing with twigs in our nests
The time of spring came and went away

The coming of spring is always most evocative for those who are in captivity—literal or metaphorical—for the bars of the cage—real or imaginary—enhance the sense of being deprived of all the abundance in nature's garden. This sense of deprivation is best captured by Sauda:

Kahiyo saba salaam humara bahaar se
Hum to chaman ko chhod ke soo-e-qafas chale

Convey my greetings to the spring, O breeze
I have left the garden and gone towards the cage

And Yagana Changezi:

Qafas-nasibon ko tadpa gaii hawa-e-bahar
Chhuri sii dil pe chali jab chali hawa-e-bahaar

Spring breezes trouble those destined for prison
Like a knife on the heart these breezes of spring

And in the same ghazal, the poet goes on to say:

Hawa mein aaj-kal ik dheemi dheemi wahshat hai
Isi zamaane se shayad hai ibtida-e-bahaar

There's a slight frenzy in the air these days
Perhaps the beginning of spring is in the world

With the rays of the sun becoming stronger and the coming of hot westerly winds, the colours begin to fade and the garden begins to look like a bride taking off her jewels. The image is beautifully captured in this sher by Ameer Minai:

Shaḳhon se barg-e-gul nahin jhadte hain baaġh mein
Zewar utar raha hai uroos-e-bahaar ka

It isn't the flower petals coming off the branches in the garden
It is the jewellery being taken off by the bride of spring

Used in conjunction with *khizaan* (autumn), *bahaar* reinforces the life principle as in this sher by Shakeel Badayuni:

Miri zindagi pe na muskura mujhe zindagi ka alam nahin
Jise tere ġham se ho waasta woh ḳhizaan bahaar se kum nahin

Don't smile at my life, I have no affliction in life
For him who has your grief autumn is no less than spring

Here's another version of the popular *bahaar-khizaan* trope with Arsh Malsiyani stressing the fickleness of both:

Nairangi-e-bahaar-o-khizaan dekhte rahey
Hairat se hum tilism-e-jahaan dekhte rahey

I watched the fickleness of spring and autumn
In amazement I beheld the illusion of the world

Faiz Ahmad Faiz has the last word on the possibilities *bahaar* offers and the terrible sadness that comes in the wake of a spring that is unlike any other:

Na gul khile hain na unse miley hain na mai pii hai
Ajeeb rang mein abke bahaar guzri hai

The flowers have not bloomed nor have we met her or drunk wine
This spring has passed by in an odd sort of way

47. *Dopahar ki Dhoop Mein...*

In my childhood, summers meant mangoes cooled in tubs of water, an abundance of fruit such as melons, jamun, phalsa, khinni, litchi, loquat, drinking cool water from clay *surahi* (pot) and *matka* that smelled of damp earth, afternoons in *khus* (vetiver)-scented rooms to escape from the sweltering *loo* winds, nights under starry skies redolent with the scent of *mogra*, *bela*, *chameli*, *raat ki raani* (all four being different types of jasmine). A rickety ceiling fan or even ricketier pedestal or table fan was usually enough. Coolers made an entrance as I stepped into my youth though ACs were still a far cry. The day-time heat was always intense, of course, but nights brought relief with the gentle *purvai* (east) breezes that carried with them the hint of *mehndi* (henna) leaves and myriad other scents.

Both the scorching summer days and the soothing nights find ample reflection in Urdu poetry. What follows is a sampler, though it also begs the question: what are we leaving for our future generations as we spend our days in the comfort of AC rooms and our nights huddled under AC quilts?

The summer afternoons that seemed endlessly long when

one had to perforce stay indoors to escape the sun's wrath is captured in this sher by Aitbar Sajid:

Phir wahi lambi dopahrein surmai hain phir wahi dil ki haalat hai
Baahar kitna sannata hai andar kitni vahshat hai

Again those long afternoons, again my grey heart
Such silence outside, such turbulence inside

And the wrath of the mid-day sun is likened to the terror of doomsday here by Nasir Kazmi:

Suraj sar pe aa pahuncha
Garmi hai ya roz-e-jaza

The sun has come directly overhead
The heat makes it seem like doomsday

The same Nasir Kazmi, in another sher, evokes the wonder of a summer night when a cool breeze blows and the harshness of the sun is momentarily forgotten:

Saara din tapte suraj ki garmi mein jalte rahe
Thandi thandi hawa phir chali so raho so raho

We burned in the scorching sun all day long
When the cooling breeze blew we slept, we slept

Khaleel Rampuri plays upon the idea of the *purvai*, the wind that that comes from the east and brings coolness though here it comes from the beloved's alley and brings blessed relief:

Garmi bahut hai aaj khula rakh makaan ko
Uss ki gali se raat ko purvai aaegi

Keep the house open in this heat
The *purvai* will blow from her alley tonight

Hasrat Mohani evokes the romance of the terraces and rooftops, transformed into magical spaces at night but deserted and scorching hot in the blistering summer sun in this gently romantic ghazal immortalised by Ghulam Ali:

Dopahar ki dhoop mein mere bulaane ke liye
Woh tira kothe pe nange paanv aana yaad hai

Coming to call me in the heat of the noon sun
I remember you coming barefoot to the rooftop

Rahat Indori too invokes the blistering power of the summer sun that scorches and blackens every vestige of spring:

Shahr kya dekhen ki har manzar mein jaale parh gaye
Aisi garmi hai ki peele phool kaale parh gaye

How can I see the city when everything is ruined
The heat is such that flowers have turned black

Meer Anees, the marsiya-go extraordinaire, too evokes the terrible scorching power of the sun:

Garmi se muztarib thha zamaana zameen par
Bhun jaata thha jo girta thha daana zameen par

The world was afflicted by such heat on this earth
As even a grain that fell to the ground was roasted

With his tongue firmly in his cheek, the irrepressible Nazeer Akbarabadi talks of the summer heat and that of the body's that makes it 'doubly hot':

Aate hii jo tum mere gale lag gaye wallah
Uss waqt to iss garmi ne sab maat ki garmi

You came and hugged me as soon as you came
And defeated the summer heat with your heat

Insha Allah Khan Insha plays upon a similar sentiment thus:

Garmi ne kuchh aag aur bhi seene mein lagaayi
Har taur ġharaz aap se milna hi kum achchha

The heat stoked yet another fire in my breast
It's better in every way to meet you less often

When others speak of the sun, Bashir Badr speaks of the shade, that too, the shade offered by the heavy, coiled tresses of the beloved:

Phir yaad bahut aayegi zulfon ki ghani shaam
Jab dhoop mein saaya koi sar par na milega

I will remember the dark evening of your tresses
When I find no shade from the sun over my head

Because in Urdu poetry for every idea there is a contrarian one too, here is Ahmad Mushtaq turning the same notion of sun and shade on its head thus:

Main bahut ḳhush thha karhi dhoop ke sannate mein
Kyuun tiri yaad ka baadal mire sar par aaya

I was happy in the silence of the scorching sun
Why did the cloud of your memory come overhead

48. Gulzar Sahab, *Baarish aur Hum*

Influenced by ancient and medieval texts and a vast and varied tradition of rain-related poetry, Urdu and Hindi writers continue to write of the magic of the rains. If Harivansh Rai Bachchan and Suryakant Tripathi Nirala speak of the drama of massed clouds and rumbling thunder, Intizar Husain evokes the tremulous beauty of freshly-bathed trees and a life that was once more attuned to the seasons: the songs and rituals, mostly among women, of cooking *pakwan* (special dishes), putting swings on trees, singing *kajri* and *saawani* (songs sung specially during the rains). However, for me nothing evokes the magic of the monsoon quite like Gulzar sahab in his uniquely individualistic manner. In the vast corpus of his non-film poetry, there is an astonishing variety of poems evoking the rains in their many moods and his contrarian view of it.

Here is one on the age-old relationship between rains and the anguished yearning for letters from the beloved in 'Baarish Hoti Hai Jab' (When it Rains):

Baarish hoti hai jab
To inn gaarey patthar ki deewaron par
Bheegey bheegey naqshe banne lagte hain

Hichki hichki baarish tab
Pehchaani sii ik likhaayi likhti hai
Baarish kuchh keh jaati hai

Damp designs are formed on
These brick and mortar walls
The hiccupping rain then writes
With a familiar hand
On these walls
The rain tells something!

The first chaste encounter of cool water and hot earth, grey sky and parched land, preceded by damp masses of moisture-laden clouds scudding across the skies, bringing darkness at noon and followed by days upon days of uninterrupted deluge have been described in myriad ways since time immemorial. Gulzar sahab describes his rain-drenched Mumbai thus:

Baarish aati hai to mere shahr ko kuchh ho jaata hai
Tin ki chhat, tirpaal ka chhajja, peepal, pattey, paneela
Sab bajne lagtey hain

Tang gali mein jaate jaate
Cycle ka pahiya paani ki kulliyan karta hai
Baarish mein kuchh lambe ho jaate hain qad bhi logon ke
Jitne ooper hain, utne hii pairon ke neeche paani mein
Ooper wala tairta hai to neeche wala doob ke chalta hai

Something happens to my city when the rain comes
Tin roofs, tarpaulin shades, peepal trees, leaves, gutters
Everything begins to sing!

Entering a narrow lane
The wheel of a cycle gargles and spouts water
Even people seem to become taller in the rain
They appear as much above the water as beneath it
When the upper part swims, the lower half paddles underwater...

Given the importance of rain in a primarily rain-fed agrarian system such as India's, it is little wonder that literature and popular culture have always dwelt extensively on the monsoon rain. The ancients called it *Varsha Ritu*, 'The Season of Rains'; Gulzar sahab calls it a 'Tree of Water'

Paani ka perh hai baarish jo pahaarhon pe uga karta hai
Shaakhein bahteen hain, umarhti hui, bal khaati hui
Barf ke beej gira karte hain
Jharne pakte hain to jhumkon ki tarah jhoolne lagte hain
Kohistaanon par
Belein girteen hain chhaton se
Mausmi perh hai, mausam mein uga karta hain

Rain is a tree of water that grows on mountains
Its branches flow, surging along, tossing and turning
When seeds of snow fall
Waterfalls ripen
And swing like ear-rings on mountain slopes
Vines droop from roofs
It's a seasonal plant; it only grows in its season

Not for Gulzar sahab the totemic images associated with the rains: dancing peacocks, croaking frogs, the fragrance of the *kadamba* (bur-flower tree) that classical texts have always evoked; instead there is this:

Ghurrata, chinghaarhta baadal
Aksar aisey loot ke le jaata hai basti
Jaisey Thakur ka koi gunda
Bad-masti karta nikle iss basti se

The growling, roaring cloud
Raids their habitation with the force
Of hired hoodlums of some Thakur
Rampaging drunkenly through a village

The *virahini* of the medieval baramasa ('Songs for the 12 Months of the Year') feels the pain of separation most keenly in the month of *saawan* (the fifth month of the lunar calendar) for it is during the rains that men traditionally stayed home or came back as business was slack possibly because roads became un-passable. Gulzar sahab's 'Sona' reacts differently to the rains:

Mujhe afsos hai, Sona...
Ke meri nazmon se hokar guzarte waqt baarish mein
Pareshaani hui tumko
Barhey be-waqt aatey hain ye saavan
Meri nazmon ki galiyaan yuun bhii aksar bheegi rahti hain
Kai gadhdhon mein paani jama rahta hai
Agar paanv parhey to monch aa jaane ka khatra hai

I am sorry, Sona...
That you were troubled as you
Passed through my poem in the rain
The month of *saavan* comes at a very inopportune time
With water filling the many potholes
The alleys of my poems are in any case often wet
And if you were to step in one you can even wrench your ankle

Tradition demanded that a young bride be called to her parents' home when her brother would be sent to fetch her at the beginning of the season; shortly after a token visit, she would return to her husband's home and resume her conjugal life. Gulzar sahab's lovers, refreshingly modern in their sensibility, react thus to the rains:

Deir tak baithe huwey donon ne baarish dekhi
Woh dikhaati thhi mujhe bijli ke taaron pe lataktii huii boondein
Jo ta.aqub mein thheen ek doosre ke
Aur ek doosre ko chhoote hii taaron se tapak jaati thheen

For a long time we sat and watched the rain
She showed me the droplets hanging from electric wires
In pursuit of each other
Falling off the wire as one touches the other…

The exuberance the rains cause, especially among the young, is captured with a turn of phrase that only Gulzar sahab possesses:

Baarish hoti hai to paani ko bhi lag jaate hain paanv
Dar-o-deewar se takra ke guzarta hai gali se
Aur uchhalta hai chhapaakon mein
Kisi match mein jeete huwe ladkon ki tarah

When it rains the water acquires feet of its own
Knocking off the doors and walls, it passes through the alley
And splashes about in puddles
Like boys who have won some match!

If the rains bring joy, they also cause sadness by their relentless, steady dripping:

Bus ek hii sur mein, eik hii lai mei subah se dekh
Kaise baras raha hai udaas paani

In the same tune, in the same rhythm
See how the sad rain has been falling all morning

To conclude, here is a sampling from his shers on the rains, a mere selection from a large number of rain-ghazals:

Raat ko jaaney kya hota hai hansne lagti hai
Tin ki chaadar par jab bajne lagti hai

God knows what happens to the night as it begins
To laugh when rain starts to ring out on the tin roof

❧

Andhere mein bheeni bheeni baarish baras rahi hai yoon
Deewar ki aarh mein jaise tum kooche se guzra karti theen

A soft muffled rain falls faintly in the darkness just so
Like you passing by the lane hugging the lee of the wall

Main chup karaata huun har shab umadti baarish ko
Magar ye roz gaii baat chhed deti hai

Every night I hush the surging rain
But it raises past subjects each day

Go barasti nahi sada aankhein
Abr to baarah maas hota hai

Though eyes don't rain always
They carry water all year round

And this one my personal favourite:

Perhon ko bhi kal to chaltey dekha thha
Paainche haath liye jal-thal ki baarish mein

I even saw trees walking about yesterday
Holding the hems of their trousers in the rain

49. *Haar-singhaar* and the Inexorable Tug of Nostalgia

Come December, the last of the *haar-singhaar* flowers are very nearly gone. From end-September and early October, they make their presence felt with their tremulous beauty and intoxicating fragrance across much of the Indian sub-continent. By mid-December the tree goes back to being a perfectly ordinary tree, neither too big nor especially handsome, its leaves a lackluster green and unremarkable, its bark a dull grey. But for the few months of its flowering from late September till end November, it becomes a thing of rare beauty and a joy to behold.

These white-petalled, orange-stemmed flowers open at dusk, release their fragrance all night long and are shed by dawn. When one wakes up in the morning, the ground beneath the tree is carpeted with these upturned white flowers with their bright orange stalks, their heady fragrance still permeating the air. Their appearance in late September marks the first winter chill, the onset of short days and long nights and the coming Durga puja celebrations (the flower happens to be the official flower of the state of West Bengal). Native to South

Asia, the flowering tree grows all over India and is known by many names: Night Flowering Jasmine, *Parijat*, *Sheuli*, *Shifali*. Sometimes also referred to as the Tree of Sorrows because its flowers fall and wilt with the first rays of the sun, it has great symbolic value too.

As *Parijat* it appears in several mythological and sacred texts. There are references to it having appeared from the *samudra manthan* (the churning of the ocean). It is said that Krishna's wife Satyabhama demanded the tree be planted in the backyard of her palace. And yet when the tree flowered, its flowers fell in the adjacent backyard of Rukmini, Krishna's favourite! Almost every part of the tree has medicinal value and is highly regarded in Ayurveda. Vastu too considers the Parijat an auspicious tree, a harbinger of prosperity and happiness. In earlier times, the vivid orange of its stalks were used to colour clothes; I sun-dry the stalks and use them to fleck my biryanis.

Given its many benefits, its symbolism and its own delicate beauty, how could the Urdu poet have remained immune to its charms? Indeed, it appears time and again as an embodiment of transience, a beauty that is destined to fade, a symbol of purity that is almost other-worldly.

Here is Iftikhar Arif, a pre-eminent modern poet, invoking the *haar-singhaar* flowers as witnesses to a love that is just as fleeting as the fragrance of these flowers in his nazm 'Hawain Anpadh Hain' (The Winds are Illiterate):

Ab ke baar phir
Mauj-e-bahaar ne
Farsh-e-sabz par
Saat-e-mahr mein
Haar-singhaar se
Hum donon ke naam likhe hain...

Once again
The ecstasy of spring

Has written both our names
In a moment of love
On the green ground
With haar-singhaar flowers

Azra Naqvi evokes the haar-singhaar as a symbol of a beauty that is so overwhelming that it cannot survive the harshness of reality in her nazm entitled 'Haar-singhaar'. She remembers the *haar-singhaar* tree from her childhood at the far end of her family home; the tree is gone, replaced by a high rise building:

Tum ne dekhe hain kabhi haar-singhaar
Woh dil-aavez se masoom se do-range phool
Raat ko shaḳh pe khilte thhe sitaaron ki tarah
Woh bhala din ki tamazat ke sitam kyun sahte
Iss liye aaḳhir-e-shab apne hii husn se be-ḳhud ho kar
Ose se bheege hue farsh pe kis pyaar se bichh jaate thhe

Have you ever seen the haar-singhaar
Those captivating, innocent, two-coloured flowers
Like stars, they would bloom on the branches at night
How could they tolerate the intense heat of the day
Enraptured by their own beauty in the last watch of the night
They would carpet the dew drenched ground with such love

Others too have commented on this night-blooming flower that withers at the first rays of the sun, such as in this sher by Bharatdeep Mathur Deep:

Unhein qubool nahin aaftab ki daawat
Jalega deep to phooleinge haar-singhaar ke phool

They cannot accept the invitation of the sun
The haar-singhaar will bloom when lamps are lit

In a long, beautiful poem entitled 'Aadhi Raat' (Midnight) Firaq Gorakhpuri recreates the sights, sounds, scents of a winter night when everything is covered by a blanket of sleep: the flowers have covered their faces and gone to sleep, the stars too seem dull and distant, nothing stirs; only the flower-laden *haar-singhaar* tree seems alive, releasing a heady burst of fragrance into the cool, still night air:

Kharha hai ose mein chup-chaap haar-singhaar ka perh
Dulhan ho jaise haya ki sugandh se bojhal

The haar-singhaar tree stands silent in the dewy night
Like a bride weighed down by the fragrance of modesty

At a time when high-end uber-luxe companies selling indie beauty products, build on the evocative power of words, the parijat and the *haar-singhaar* is being used as a 'brand' for body mists, after-bath oils, silkening body powders, et al in a bid to bottle this elusive fragrance. Called by different names, this white and orange flower is inextricably intertwined with nostalgia, with memories of a distant childhood, with homes that once had a *haar-singhaar* tree in their *sehn* (backyard). For those living in concrete jungles in cities, this flower-laden tree is a symbol of a lost age. It is only appropriate, therefore, that the *haar-singhaar* tree is often planted beside the grave of a loved one. Begum Akhtar's grave in Pasand Bagh, Lucknow, for instance, has a *haar-singhaar* tree that sheds its fragrant load over the Begum sleeping the eternal sleep.

50. Those Days of *Gulabi Jaade*

The way light fell, the angle of the sun's rays, the slight nip in the air, the strong, unmistakable scent of the *saptaparni* (alstonia or milkwood tree) flowers and the tremulous beauty of the *haar-singhaar* that would be found scattered on the dew-hardened ground, the call of the *dhunna* (cotton-wool carder) as he went home to home carding old cotton-wool to be filled in new covers, the early Nagpur oranges and crunchy water-chestnuts (*singharas*)—these were the signs of the onset of winter as days got shorter and nights steadily longer. For most of us in Upper India, till not so long ago, late October and early November were the most pleasurable days; called *gulabi jaada* (literally meaning 'pink winter'), these were days of mellow sunshine, blue skies, gentle breezes, golden afternoons.

These seem like a distant memory now; soon they will become an urban legend relegated to the same status as *qissa-kahanis* of kings and queens, fairies and elves. The terrible debilitating smog that chokes much of North India in its deadly grip has put paid to any talk of *gulabi jaada* given the surreal smog-infested gas chambers that our cities have now been reduced to, the *mai ki lazzat gulabi jaadon ki* (the wine-like intoxication of the pink winters) that Muztar Khairabadi alluded to will be reduced to mere nostalgia. Will there be another Ishrat Afreen who will write:

Yuunhi kisi ke dhyaan mein apne aap mein gaati dopahrein
Narm gulaabi jaadon wali baal sukhaati dopahrein

Afternoons that hum to themselves as they sit lost in someone's thoughts
Afternoons that dry their hair in the soft pink winter sunlight

Or a Gulzar who will paint these word pictures:

Dil dhoondhta hai phir wahi fursat ke raat din
Jaadon ki narm dhoop aur aangan mein leit kar
Aankhon pe kheenchkar tere aanchal ke saaye ko
Aundhe padey rahe kabhi karwat liye huwey

The heart searches again for those days of leisure
The soft winter sunlight as we lay in the courtyard
With the end of your aanchal pulled over our eyes
As we lay face down and sometimes on our side

Let us go back in the pages of Time to find a Nazeer Akbarabadi, the poet who has written on virtually every aspect of everyday life and has also waxed eloquent on the pleasures of winter: the months of *aghan* (corresponding with November-December) giving way to *poos* (corresponding with December-January), the days that run at a trot to welcome the long nights when teeth chatter with the cold, and the damp chill of winter rains (called *mahavat*) that leads to a 'cold wave':

Jab maah aghan ka dhalta ho tab dekh bahaarein jaadey ki
Aur hans hans poos sambhalta ho tab dekh baharein jaadey ki

When the month of *aghan* wanes witness the joys of winter
And the month of *poos* laughs and takes its place see the joys of winter

Nazeer Banarasi alludes to that sun that was once the only source for warmth for the poor who were otherwise destined to shiver through the winter cold when he writes: '*Seink detaa thaa jo jaade mein gareebon ke badan*', the sun that used to heat the body of the poor, the sun that now goes to hide behind a pall of smog and gloom.

Shakeeb Ayaaz evokes those days of early winter when the sunshine was once mellow and warm and inviting:

Naye jaade ki kachchi dhoop tanhaa
Mire ghar mein pasar kar so rahii hai

The tender sunshine of early winter
Is spread-eagled in my home fast asleep

In his nazm 'Yeh Jaade ke Din', Ameer Ahmad Khusro listed out almost all those things that we once associated with winter: sweaters, shawls (*doshala*), knitting, portable coal braziers called *angeethi*, the light *razais* (duvets) for early winters and the thick quilts called *lihaaf* for the long cold nights, the coarse woolen blankets called *kambal* (often bought from local weavers or from Khadi Gram Udyog outlets), and the hankering for piping hot meals:

Yeh jaadey ke din aur ye jaadon ki raatein
Lihaaf aur sutar ki har ghar mein baatein

These days and nights of winter
This talk of quilts and sweaters in every home

Then there were large numbers of verses—ranging from the playful to the indecorous—on the intimacy of snuggling beneath warm quilts in cold winter nights such as this sher by Insha Allah Khan:

Jaade mein kya maza ho woh to simat rahe hon
Aur khol kar razai hum bhi lipat rahe hon

It'd be such fun in winter if she were to be shrinking
And pulling back the quilt I too would be snuggling

Or this by Jan Nisar Akhtar, again with the play on *gulabi* but used here for the seductive allure of winter nights:

Kum nahiin nashe mein jaade ki gulaabi raatein
Aur agar teri jawaani bhi milaa di jaae

The rosy nights of winter are no less in their intoxication
Especially so if your youthfulness too is added to them

Given the steady degradation of nature, the havoc created by global warming, the desecration of the seasons created by our short-sighted greed, the spring that we have angered and driven away from our gardens, one is reminded of Faiz Ahmad Faiz who wrote:

Ravish-ravish hai wahi intizar ka mausam
Nahin hai koi bhi mausam bahaar ka mausam

Everywhere there is only the season of waiting
Nowhere is there any season that's the season of spring

Balbir Rathi may well have been speaking metaphorically, but every word rings true for the big cities we live in especially during the winter when it seems as though we are living in a gas chamber:

Phir fiza mein koi zahreela dhuan bhar jayega
Phir kisi din apne andar kuchh na kuchh mar jayega

Once again a toxic smoke will spread in the air
One again someday something will die inside us

Come November, this sher by Fahmi Badayuni says it all for those of us who hanker for the *gulabi jaade* we had once known:

Phir main zahreele kaar-ḳhaanon mein
Zinda rahne ka kaam karne laga

Once again, in these poisonous factories
I have begun to work at staying alive

51. An Ode to the Native and the Forgotten

It all started with the *khinni*...a meandering conversation with my sisters on a family chat led to a poignant lament about forgotten fruits and vegetables. Some whose taste we remembered well and clearly and some that were simply words for us but we had heard older relatives describe these native or regional species that either had a short shelf life or a peculiar taste liked only by a few. Some that are still available, such as the *jamun* (black plum) and *ber* (Indian jujube), are unrecognisable in their hybrid plumpness and complete lack of taste. So here's an ode to native fruits lost to the genie of hybridisation and market economics and, in the case of the *ganderi* and fresh sugarcane juice or the humble *singhara* (water chestnut) that grew in ditches, fallen victim to new ideas of health and hygiene.

Khinni (small, pale, elongated grape-shaped fruit with a slightly sour after taste), *falsa* (tart purple berries that could be eaten with *masala* or turned into a *sherbet*), *shahtoot* (mulberry fruit too fragile to be transported long distance and usually eaten straight from the trees), *kamrakh* (star fruit) and *jharberi ke ber* (small tart orange-red berries usually sold in combination with the *kamrakh* outside schools), *ganderi* (sugarcane stalks stripped and cut into bite-sized pieces stacked on slabs of ice with bright pink (*desi gulab*) rose petals scattered, rather scenically, on top by the vendors), *locquat* (that arrived for a few days in the peak of summer), *bael* (wood apple that most considered fit only to be consumed as a *sherbet* to beat the blistering loo winds and since it was known for its thirst-quenching properties was once often made during Ramzan till it was replaced with the ready-mixed Roohafza as the thirst-quencher of choice for most fasting folk), and some that we still find though seldom are the *chakotara* (pomelo) and *kakronda* (the plump pinkish-red berries that confectioners have been tricking us and passing off as cherries for decades).

Among the veggies there were the *desi tamatar* (pale orange and much smaller than the gigantic hybrid varieties now available) and reserved only for salads or the occasional *tamatar gosht* (a mutton preparation in a tomato-based curry), the *desi gaajar* (bright orangey and usually brought from the hills unlike the cold storage ones), *lasonde* (glue berries that I remember my grandmother pickling in vinegar), the famous *kachnaar ki kali* (buds that were transformed into a delicately spiced curried dish), and *phoot* (that seemed unable to make up its mind whether it was a cucumber or a melon). Of course, the list is endless with countless regional variations of forgotten or lost foods.

Since my frame of reference in this volume is Urdu poetry, alas there will be much that I will miss from a country as gastronomically rich and as culinarily diverse as ours but hopefully, this will serve to revive memories of once-dearly-beloved-but-now-forgotten foods for some and the discoveries of new delights that will make up for the lapses for others.

Let us begin with Nazeer Akbarabadi talking of the *qaliya* (mutton cooked in a variety of spices) with its thin, watery curry, once the beloved pairing with the mild *pulao* now overshadowed by the flamboyant *biryani-qorma*:

Nazeer yaar ki hum ne jo kal ziyaafat ki
Pakaaya qarz mangaa kar pulaav aur qaliya

I, Nazeer, arranged a banquet for my beloved
And took a loan to cook a pulao and qaliya

Here's more on the *qaliya*, the connoisseur's delight now virtually forgotten in favour of the heavier *qormas* (meat curries) that dominate restaurant menus and home-style cooking, in this sher by Hussain Meer Kashmiri:

Kya ḳhabar thhi inquilab asmaan ho jaaega
Qorma qaliya naseeb-e-ahmaqaan ho jaaega

Little did we know the Revolution would flee to the skies
And qormas and qaliyas destined only for the idiots

Majeed Lahori speaks of *bhune teetar* (roasted partridge) reduced to a distant memory in these politically correct times:

Murġhiyaan kofte machhli bhune teetar ande
Kis ke ghar jaega sailaab-e-ġhiza mere baad

Chickens, kofte, fish, roasted partridge, eggs
Whose house will this flood of foods be sent to after me

In her nazm, 'Woh Kaisi Auraten Thheen' (What Remarkable Women They Were), Asna Badr asks a rhetorical question but one that seems problematic to present-day feminists:

Jo sil par surkh mirchein pees kar saalan pakaatii thheen
Sahar se shaam tak masroof lekin muskuraatii thhiin

Grinding red chillies on a stone slab they would cook a curry

Busy from dawn till dusk, they would be working but always smiling

Perhaps nothing illustrates the way food and, by extension, our eating habits have changed over the years than this sher by Irfan Khalid:

Kaagaz ki paleton mein khaane ka taqaaza hai
Haalaat ke shaane pe culture ka janaaza hai

Food is expected to be eaten from paper plates
The bier of culture is carried on the shoulder of circumstances

Given how expensive mutton has become, one is reminded of these lines by the inimitable Saaghar Khayyami:

Eik maheena ho gaya band hai hum par mutton
Daawaton mein khaa rahein hain bhindiyan ahl-e sukhan

Khaa ke ghuinyyaan kya dikhlaaein shairi ka baankpan
Ho gaye palak ka patta naazuki se gulbadan

It has been a month since I have eaten mutton
Connoisseurs are eating ladies' fingers at feasts

What feats of poetry can one show after eating colocasia
The slender damsels have all turned into leaves of spinach

In an India where dress has become associated with religion, how can food be left behind? There was, for instance, a post from someone I went to school with demanding a posh, high-end online portal to explain if it was showing an 'ad for Eid'. Why? Because the two elegantly-dressed models are wearing green! It generated much humour among netizens: if the colour green is 'M', saffron is surely 'H'. As for food, the netizens hazarded many guesses based on half-baked historical knowledge or pure, undiluted bigotry: *samosa, jalebi, gulab jamun* are 'M' but *kheer/payasam* is 'H' while cake is surely

'C'. The droller ones maintained surely *palak* (spinach) is 'H' whereas a pumpkin cannot be anything but 'H'. As for flowers, roses are 'M' while 'lotuses' are 'H', and so on and so forth. Seeing no end in sight to this unsavoury—and completely unnecessary debate—let us draw solace from this sher by an unknown poet:

Maikhaana-e-hasti ka jab daur kharaab aayaa
Kullarh mein sharaab aai patte pe kabaab aayaa

When the bad days came in the tavern of Life
Wine came in a clay pot and kababs on a leaf

So much for *achche din*!

52. *Khaana-peena* in Urdu Poetry

Perhaps no other Urdu poet has written as much on food as Nazeer Akbarabadi, who we have encountered many times in these pages. In his vast and varied ouvre there are poems entitled 'Agre ki Kakdi' (The Cucumbers of Agra which he famously likened to Laila's ribs!) 'Tarbuz' (Watermelon), 'Kharbuze' (Melons), 'Santara' (Orange), 'Narangi' (Chinese Orange), 'Jalebiyan' (the swiggly, doodle-like syrupy sweets) but possibly the most recited are these lines on *roti* (flat bread) from 'Rotinama':

Jab aadmi ke peit mein aati hain rotiyaan
Phooli nahin badan mein samaati hain rotiyaan

When the rotis enter a man's stomach
They can barely suppress their gladness

Like Nazeer others have talked of seasonal foods, especially fruits. And rightly so. In a country with three well-demarcated seasons—winter, summer, rains—there are distinct foods that have been traditionally enjoyed according to the changing seasons. Of these, the king of summer fruits, mangoes, have received their fair share of attention from Urdu poets. Like

Ghalib, Akbar Allahabadi had no qualms about asking his friends to send him mangoes from their orchards: '*Iss fasl mein jo bhejiye bas aam bhejiye*' (The one thing you should send from this harvest are mangoes). Shaheen Iqbal Asar writes a qasida (panegyric) in praise of mangoes ending thus:

Ik faqat main hii nahin shaida Asar
Shaida hai aalam ka aalam aam ka

I am not the only one in love with mangoes
The entire universe is besotted with mangoes

Bashir Badr uses food as a metaphor for fruition, for reward, as in this sher:

Kuchh phal zaroor aainge roti ke perh mein
Jis din mira mutaalba manzoor ho gaya

Some fruits will surely appear on the tree of roti
On the day when my claims are accepted

As does Rahat Indori here:

Phal to sab mere darakhton ke pakey hain lekin
Itni kamzor hain shaakhein ki hilaa bhi na sakoon

All the fruits on my trees have ripened
But the branches are so weak I can't even shake them

This heart-felt prayer by Dilawar Figar acquires a new resonance now that meat has become so 'dear' for reasons of both politics and the pocket:

Ya rab mire naseeb mein akl-e-halaal ho
Khaane ko qorma ho khilaane ko daal ho

Dear Lord, let there be halal food for me
Enough qorma to eat, and daal to feed others

How camouflage—culinary or otherwise—doesn't always work is evident from this verse by Shauq Bahraichi:

Rahzan libaas-e-rahbari mein na chhup saka
Aalu ne laakh chaha par ghuiyaan na ho saka

The highway robber could not hide in the guise of a guide
Despite all efforts the potato couldn't turn into colocasia

Then there are the foods associated with festivals especially the *kabaab-sevaiyan-biryani* combination that is almost synonymous with the two Eids. Here is Murtaza Sahil Taslimi describing the *manzar* (scenario) in most Muslim households on Eid:

Theen sevaiyan qorma sheer aur biryani kabaab
Hum utthe khush-zaaeqa khaanon se ho kar faizyaab

There was sevaiyan, qorma, sheer, kabaab and biryani
We rose blessed from these delicious-tasting spreads

On a grimmer note, there are the foods that are offered to the poor, the neighbours and the extended family while offering *fateha* (funerary prayer) for the dead as described in this sher by the acerbic Akbar Allahabadi:

Bataauun aap ko marne ke baad kya hogaa
Pulao khaaenge ahbaab fateha hoga

Shall I tell you what will happen after you are dead?
Your friends will eat pulao after the *fateha* has been recited

While the food purists debate over the relative merits of a pulao versus biryani, the poet talks of both. Here is Dilawar Figaar talking of the pulao that will be served in a *waleeme ki daawat* (wedding reception):

Uss shokh ke waleeme mein khaa kar chikan pulao
Kankii ke chaawalon ka mazaa yaad aa gayaa

Eating chicken pulao at that lovely lady's wedding reception
I was reminded of the delicious taste of broken rice

The same Dilawar Figar speaks of the new-fangled trend of mini-mushairas in people's homes where poets are invited to recite their poetry followed by a lavish repast:

Qorma istu pasanda, kofta, shaami kabab
Jaane kya kya kha gaya yeh shair-e-maeda-ḳharaab

Qorma, stew, pasanda, kofta, shaami kabab
How much was eaten by this poet with bad digestion

There is also ample mention of the conjoined twins, sharaab-kabaab, in a great deal of Urdu poetry. Here is no less a person that Ibrahim Zauq, the last poet laureate of Mughal Delhi and *ustaad* (teacher) to the last Mughal emperor Bahadurshah Zafar, declaring:

Waiiza chhorh zikr-e-nemat-e-khuld
Kah sharaab-o-kabaab ki baatein

O Preacher stop these descriptions of the gifts from heaven
Let us talk instead of sharaab and kabaab

Every now and then the kabaab is used as a metaphor for burning with envy or sorrow as in this sher by Mir Taqi Mir:

Aatish-e-gham mein dil bhunaa shaayad
Deir se buu kabaab ki sii hai

The heart was roasted in the fire of sorrow
For long one can smell a kabaaab

Or this by Abdul Hamid Adam:

Kyaa zaruurat hai bahs karne kii
Kyuun kaleja kabaab karte ho

What's the need to argue?
Why turn your heart into a kabaab?

And this by Ameer Minai:

Kabaab-e-seekh hain hum karwatein har-suu badalte hain
Jal uthtaa hai jo ye pahluu to woh pahluu badalte hain

I am like a seekh kabaab turning this side and that
When one side begins to burn I turn the other side

In a similar vein, sherbet is often used as a metaphor as in this sher by Yagana Changezi:

Sherbat ka ghoont jaan ke peetaa hoon khoon-e-dil
Gham khaate khaate munh kaa maza tak bigarh gayaa

Knowingly I drink my heart's blood as though it is sherbat
The taste in my mouth has been ruined by all my sorrows

That food is inextricably intertwined with nostalgia and, by extension with one's warmest happiest memories is best illustrated by this sher by Nida Fazli redolent of a kitchen of yore with its everyday implements that would be unheard of by young people today:

Besan ki saundhi roti par khatti chatni jaisi maa
Yaad aati hai chaukaa baasan chimtaa phukni jaisi maa

Mother who was like the tart chutney on a chickpea flour roti
I remember her who was like the hearth, basin, tong, blowpipe

53. The Pervasive Presence of the *Paan*

Some of my earliest memories are of Abba, my grandfather, making *paan* (betel leaf) in his home in Aligarh. It was an elaborate ritual that required much advance planning. Of course the *paan* had to be bought by the *doli* (a woven cane platter, with *desi patta* being his favourite), washed, its stems and tips nipped with a small scissor kept in the *paandan* (an elaborate box for storing all the ingredients and implements that went into the making of a paan) for just this purpose, each *paan ka patta* folded neatly and precisely along its spine and torn into two equal halves, then carefully stored in a damp, cool, red piece of cloth (a pure somewhat coarse cotton called *tuul* not to be mistaken with the gauzy *tulle*). Then there was the making and folding of the *paan* itself: my grandfather, a professor and a poet, dreaming, pensive, thoughtful as he meticulously dabbed a bit of *kattha* (katechu paste) and the merest smear of *choona* (slaked lime), and folded it just so before carefully placing it in his *dibiya* (a small silver box that fitted in his pocket). The finely sliced *chhaliya* (areca nut) and a pinch of *tambaku* (tobacco) went into a *batua* (pouch), hand-stitched by my grandmother, Amma, from bits of silk and brocade; the *batua* accompanied the *dibiya* wherever Abba went: conferences, classrooms, talks, travel, walks.

Eating a *paan* and keeping a functioning *paandan* was once a way of life. Naturally, therefore, the *paan* was a cultural motif, cutting across religious divides, and speaking of a way of life that was leisurely, relaxed, unhurried, inclusive. From something one ate between meals or after meals, from an aid to digestion to a mouth freshener, occasionally laced with stimulants and even aphrodisiacs, it moved seamlessly to occupy a special place in popular culture. Offered as a mark of respect to honoured guests, strung across doorways to usher in good luck on auspicious occasions, offered to brides during wedding rituals, the humble *paan* leaf is truly pan-Indian in its reach across the length and breadth of India as well as spilling across the Indian sub-continent.

Given its presence in daily life—being sold from roadside kiosks to featuring on playing cards, embroidery motifs and jewellery—naturally therefore it appears in poetry, too. The Urdu poet has written reams and reams upon this not-quite-food, not-snack, yet ubiquitous leaf. The way it was traditionally made was a far cry from the bloated leaf we are accustomed to now seeing, bursting with all manner of candied fruit, flavoured betel nuts, over-sweet syrups and far too many contrasting tastes and textures. It was the subtle flavours that mixed with its red juices, that stained lips crimson, that caused some of the most popular and well-respected poets of their age to wax eloquent on its multifarious presence.

Zaheer Dehelvi talks of the ritual of 'sending' *paan*, of the women of the household making *paan* for guests and how offering *paan* was once a sign of hospitality, just as not sending *paan* was a slight and an offence:

Paan ban ban ke miri jaan kahaan jaate hain
Ye mire qatl ke saamaan kahaan jaate hain

Who are these paan being made and sent for?
Who are these instruments of my torture meant for?

Or this by Akbar Allahabadi on the coquetry that often accompanied the offering of a *gilauri* (a folded morsel of *paan* shaped like a triangle):

Lagaavat ki adaa se un ka kahnaa paan haazir hai
Qayaamat hai sitam hai dil fidaa hai jaan haazir hai

The affection with which she says: here is the paan
Wreaks havoc, inflicts cruelty, causes heartbreak

More on the *gilauri* by Asad Ali Khan Qalaq with its play on *honth chabana* (the act of biting one's lips, variously, to stay quiet or show regret or anger):

Honthon mein daab kar jo gilaurii di yaar ne
Kya daant peesey gairon ne kya kya chabaaye honth

When my beloved offered me a *gilauri* with one tucked behind her own lips
How others around us ground their teeth and how they bit their lips!

And this by Riaz Khairabadi:

Thha bahut un ko gilaurii kaa uthaanaa mushkil
Dast-e-naazuk se diyaa paan badii mushkil se

How difficult it was for her to raise a *gilauri* towards me
With such difficulty she offered me a *paan* with her delicate hand

The agony and ecstasy of love is brought forth in all its vividness in this sher by Mushafi Ghulam Hamdani:

Gar maza chaaho to katro dil sarotey se mira
Tum supaari ki dali rakhte ho naahaq paan mein

If you want real pleasure snip at my heart with a betel-slicer
Why do you needlessly place a betel nut in your betel leaf

Mir Taqi Mir speaks of the allure of the beloved speaking through a mouth full of *paan*:

Jab hum-kalaam hum se hota hai paan khaa kar
Kis rang se kare hai baatein chabaa chabaa kar

When he addresses me with his mouth full of *paan*
With such style he speaks to me as he chews on it

The red of the betel juice was routinely likened to fresh blood, blood from a lover's bleeding heart, as in this sher by Hatim:

Tere honton ke taiin paan se laal
Dekh kar ḳhoon-e-jigar khata hoon

Your lips stained crimson with *paan*
I look at them and eat the heart's blood

Nazeer Akbarabadi alludes to the use of the *paan* as a cosmetic to redden the lips:

Kaajal mehndi paan missi aur kanghi choti mein har aan
Kya kya rang banaavegi aur kya kya naqshe dhaalegi

Kohl henna lip-tint paan comb and braid each have such style
What artistry they have wrought and what impressions they will make

In our times, there's Gulzar who has written a great deal on the *paan*, such as this nazm:

Ki jaise paan mein mehngaa qimaam ghultaa hai
Ye kaisa ishq hai Urdu zabaan kaa...

Like expensive aromatic syrup that melts in the mouth with the *paan*
So does this love for the Urdu language

Then there were the limericks and tongue twisters and play on words and sounds (the wordplay is unmistakable in the Urdu original but lost, alas, in English) such as this untranslatable ditty:

Chha liya gham ne terey warna to main aisa katha
Mushkilein lakh aayein par main choo na kiya

Your sorrow enveloped me for I wasn't like this
Despite all the troubles that came my way I didn't squeak

Abba turning a page and leaving a faint red imprint from his paan-stained finger, Amma replenishing the *paandan* or chopping the *chhaliya* (betel-nut) with her *sarota* (betel-nut slicer), the rhythmic *khat-khat* as she sliced them with mathematical precision or cleaned the *quliyan* in the weekly over-haul (the small receptacles inside the *paandan*)—these are just memories now. But I draw solace from this sher by Bashir Badar:

Sunaa ke koi kahaani humein sulaati thhi
Duaaon jaisi badey paan-daan ki khushbu

It would put us to sleep by telling us a story
Like a blessing that fragrance of the big *paandan*

54. *Zahid Jo Apne Rozey Se Thoda Sawaab De*

Looking back, I am unable to pinpoint the exact age when Ramzan became Ramadan and Khuda Hafiz morphed into Allah Hafiz or, for that matter, when people began to greet each other with Ramadan Kareem. I suspect it may have gradually started with the growing Saudi influence and the robust petro-dollars sent back home by expatriate South Asians from the mid-80s onwards. Thirty years later, fuelled by social media and fanned by extravagant religiosity, we have a full-blown case of Ramzan/ Ramadan over-hype—be it through whatsapp greetings, special aisles in grocery stores the world over promoting iftaar staples such as Roohafza and dates, advertisement campaigns, special sales and offers leading up to Eid bonanzas.

Each year as the month of Ramzan approaches, I am reminded of the simplicity of the rozas of my childhood and the absence of religiosity from religion. The run-up to Ramzan began with the family gathering before the television set waiting for the 8 o'clock news bulletin. With any luck it would be the gorgeous Salma Sultan informing the nation, with a hint of a dimpled smile, that the moon had been sighted and the month of Ramzan would commence from the following day. And without further ado the special month would commence: alarms would be set, people would get up (or be woken up by harassed parents), eat a simple *sehri* (pre-dawn meal), go back to sleep and then proceed to their respective offices, schools and colleges. In the evenings, the family would gather for an extensive *iftaar* ('opening' not 'breaking' the fast at sunset) followed by an ample dinner where one or two family favourites would invariably be cooked.

However, everyone in the family went about their normal work days while fasting, making time for prayer and scripture but never at the cost of one or the other. Looking back, I am struck by the sheer normalcy of the Ramzans of my childhood and youth, of how our daily rhythms were modified but not radically altered. Food would be prepared and sent to the local mosque in large trays daily and at least once to neighbours; occasionally friends or neighbours were invited for an *iftaar* because the idea of sharing food with friends and family, as also the poor and the indigent, lies at the very heart of Ramzan. Quietly and discreetly packets of flour, pulses, rice would be made and sent to those in need. My mother has always had an especial knack of identifying those at the fringes of acute, urban poverty: the widow of our old sabziwala, an out-of-work driver, an ailing ayah, people who wouldn't beg despite living in dire straits. Through it all, the sheer normalcy with which Ramzan was treated year after year, without any hype or hoopla, certainly without excessive zeal or grand gestures of piety, seems remarkable today.

Perhaps that is why the poet and humourist too could write about the rigours of fasting in a lighter vein, something that seems unconscionable in our politically-charged, hyper-religious times. In this ghazal by Riyaz Khairabadi immortalised by Mallika Pukhraj, '*Jaagey tamaam raat, jagaayein tamaam raat*' (Staying awake all night, making others stay awake all night), there is a sher that cannot be written today:

Zahid jo apne rozey se thoda sawaab de
Mai-kash ussey sharaab pilaain tamaam raat

If the devout were to lend some blessings from his fast
The drinkers would ply him with wine all night long

Referring to the popular belief that Muslims had asked for a reduction in the five daily namaz, only to be awarded with compulsory fasting, Ahmad Husain Mail wrote at the turn of the last century:

Maangi najaat hijr se to maut aa gayi
Roze galey padey jo chhudaane gaye namaz

We asked for deliverance from separation and got Death instead
We went seeking exemption from namaz but got the rozas instead

On the importance of eating dates upon opening a fast, here is a classicist such as Mushafi Ghulam Hamdani with his tongue firmly in his cheek, or should one say on his lips, saying something that is, again, impossible to consider in these over-zealous times:

Ai Mushafi sad-shukr hua vasl mayassar
Iftaar kiya rozey mein uss lab ke rotab se

A hundred thanksgivings for this union, O Mushafi
I did an iftaar during my roza with the ripe date of her lips

Today, it requires courage from Tahzeeb Hafi, a young poet from Taunsa Sharif in Pakistan, to write with a similar play on '*kis munh se*':

Ye mera pahla Ramzan thha uss ke baġhair
Mat poochho kis munh se rozey kholey hain

This was my first Ramzan without her
Don't ask how I opened my fast

Another modern poet, Farhat Ehsas, has the temerity to suggest:

Phir soch ke ye sabr kiyaa ahl-e-hawas ne
Bas ek maheena hii to Ramzan rahegaa

The lust-filled people consoled themselves with the thought
After all, Ramzan will last only for a month

And here's a cheeky reference to the faithful who flock to the preachers during this month by Wazir Ali Saba Lakhnavi:

Hum rind-e-pareshan hain maah-e-Ramzan hai
Chamki hui in rozon mein vaaiz ki dukaan hai

We drinkers are a troubled lot in this month of Ramzan
While the preacher's shop is bustling during the days of fasting

For the Urdu poet, the conjoined roza-namaz was almost a trope or metaphor for the strait-jacket of organised religion. See this sher by Mir Taqi Mir:

Maanind-e-subha uqde na dil ke kabhu khule
Jii apna kyuun ki uchte na rozey namaz se

The knots of our heart did not open like the beads of the rosary
Why then should I not be disenchanted by roza and namaz

There was a time when a legendary scholar and teacher from Deoband, Shibli Nomani could write:

Tees din ke liye tark-e-mai-o-saqi kar luun
Vaaiz-e-sada ko rozon mein to raazi kar luun

For thirty days I'll relinquish wine and the bartender
I'll make the simple preacher happy at least during the fasts

Nazeer Akbarabadi summed the general sentiment on Eid day in most Muslim households, a sentiment applicable to this day, when he wrote:

Rozon ki sakhtiyon mein na hote gar aseer
To aisi Eid ki na khushi hoti dil pazeer

Had we not been captured by the severity of the roza
We would not have known the heart-warming joy of Eid

As does Abroo Shah Mubarak, another 18th century poet:

Gham ke peechho raast kahte hain ki shaadi hove hai
Hazrat-e-Ramzan gaye tashreef le ab Eid hai

After sorrow come the glad tidings of a wedding
After Mr Ramzan has taken his leave comes Eid

Fasting, prayer, reading the Holy Book, introspection, shoring up inner reserves of strength and stamina—this is what Ramzan was always meant to be about, not feasting and ostentatious displays of religiosity. Perhaps it took a calamity such as the pandemic that ravaged the world during much of 2020 to remind the 1.8 billion-strong Muslim population worldwide of the simplicity that lies at the heart of the roza.

55. On Eids Past and the Significance of Sacrifice

For those of us who live in cities the year round, the very idea of 'going home' for Eid is an evocative one mixing memory with desire, religion with culture, and *faraiz* (duties) with gastronomic delights. Airfares are known to spike on certain routes just before Eid given the sheer volume of those wanting to make it home even if it is no more than *dhaiyya chhoona* (reminiscent of a childhood game of touch-n-run).

Let me evoke for you a vignette from the past when I found myself celebrating Eid *en famile* in a small town in eastern Uttar Pradesh with my husband's extended family. It is the night before Eid; all around me sights, sounds and smells convey the excitement of the big day tomorrow. *Sewaiyan* (vermicelli) have been bought and cooked in vast quantities; this being the heart of the Gangetic plain, the syrupy version made out of an incredibly fine variety of *sewaiyan* popular in these parts has been made and stored ahead. Copious amounts of finely sliced onions have been fried to a nice crispy brown; they will be needed in the many meat preparations tomorrow. Stacks of crockery and cutlery have been washed in readiness for the visitors who will stream in all day long. New clothes have been stitched for young and old. The *chooriwali* (bangle-seller) has gone from home to home selling dozens of glittering glass bangles. The *mehndiwali* (the girl applying henna) has been instructed to show up late in the evening to apply intricate patterns on the palms of eagerly waiting young girls. And, of course, the goats have been bought and tethered in the compound; I can hear them bleating and see rows of little children solicitously offering them tender green leaves, for it is *sawaab* (pious act) to tend the sacrificial animals.

Unlike the other Eid, the Eid ul-Fitr that comes after the month-long fasting during Ramzan, this Eid, called the Eid ul-Zuha (also Eid al-Adha meaning the Feast of the Sacrifice) and popularly known as Bakreid in India, is a solemn occasion. While the word 'Eid' literally means festival and both occasions are festive, this is also a day of remembrance. It reminds Muslims the world over of Abraham's willingness to sacrifice the thing that was dearest to him—his first-born child Ishmael—to a command from Allah. It also marks the culmination of the annual Haj pilgrimage, which is not merely *farz* (obligatory) and one of the five pillars of Islam but also a matter of great pride and joy for Muslims the world over. And on any given Bakreid, every Muslim will know of some relative, friend, or neighbour who is away for Haj.

If Eid ul-Fitr gives the occasion to partake of the bounty that Allah has granted after a month of abstinence and introspection, this Eid reminds Muslims of the importance of *qurbani* (sacrifice) as well as patience and constancy—the hallmarks of a true Believer. While peace and salutations are offered to Abraham everyday as part of the daily *namaz*, on this day his obedience and willingness is commemorated by a token act of sacrificing an animal such as a goat or sheep.

The day begins with congregational prayers in an Eidgah; across South Asia women still do not normally go to the mosque to pray, preferring to offer their daily prayers as well as the special Eid ones at home. The Eid namaz is followed by a special *khutba* (sermon) by the imam who leads the congregation in prayer and then, after the customary Eid greeting of embracing three times, the men usually go to graveyards to offer *fateha* to dead and departed ancestors. The family graveyard, in my husband's hometown, is a charming spot surrounded by ancient mango trees and is located next to the Eidgah; it is cathartic to remember the dead in this serene space with towering trees and flowering bushes.

Back home, the sacrifice has to be performed at the earliest possible. Its meat is divided into three equal parts: one for the poor and needy, one for friends and neighbours and a third for one's self. No distinction is to be made who it goes to; for it must be sent to friends and neighbours regardless of religion or rank. And while the men and boys laze around, drink tea, go visiting soon after the *qurbani*, the women's work begins. Keeping a watchful eye on the proceedings, ensuring the butcher (who has taken over the job of cutting and cleaning from the men in the family) has cut the meat just so, dividing the meat with mathematical precision, wrapping the apportioned pieces in paper for distribution and then launching upon the humongous task of cooking the many delicacies that are Eid favourites—it is a long day for women.

The first of the many Eid dishes to tickle one's palate is always, always kaleji, goat's liver cooked in a pungent sauce redolent with the robust flavor of methi seeds. What follows is a day of relentless bingeing. Having had one's fill of whatever has been cooked in one's immediate family, one embarks on a gastronomic journey that has many known and unknown delights. The biryani at X Dadi's house is a cherished memory as are the kabab's at Y Chacha's home, not to mention the *akhra* (ribs) cooked by his widowed sister. The new daughter-in-law of Z Bhabhi, so one is told in tones of hushed awe, makes the most incredible *paye* (trotters). And then, of course, the *sheer* (milky sewaiyan) made by Z Bhabhi herself is the stuff that sweet dreams are made of. And so, going by past experience and new gossip on the family grapevine, one sets out on a house-hopping adventure. My daughters, being visitors, get more Eidi money than their resident cousins while the rest of us get to reconnect and replenish family bonds.

The years we cannot 'go home' for Eid, we find recourse in poetry, the sharper the better such as this by Meer Kallu Arsh:

Badle dumbe ke karein rind ussi ko qurban
Eid-e qurbaan mein jo sun paayein bayaan-e vaaiz

Instead of the sacrificial sheep the drinker sacrifices him
Who listens to the sermon of the preacher on the Eid of Sacrifice

Some poets have been brave enough to highlight the pop-up goat markets that sprout at this time and the exorbitant prices of goats and sheep that rise exponentially as Eid approaches. Writing an entire poem entitled 'Qurbani ke Bakrey', Syed Mohammad Jafri notes:

Chaurahon par khade hue bakron ke hain jo ġhol
Tu unn ke munh ko khol ke daanton ko mat tatol
Qeemat mein warna aaega fauran hii itna jhol
Soney ka jaise bakra ho aisa padega mol

The groups of goats standing at the crossroads
Don't pry open their mouth to examine their teeth
Or else there will be such a sudden change in their price
You will think you are buying a goat made of gold

The *qurbani ka bakra* (sacrificial goat though it can also be a lamb since both are offered by way of sacrifice and occasionally decorated with henna patterns or even garlands) becomes a metaphor for the lover as here by Zafar Iqbal:

Yun saja rakkha tha qurbani ka bakra shoḳh ne
Dil hamara dekhte hii dekhte bakri hua

She had displayed her sacrificial lamb so ostentatiously
That my heart immediately turned into a she-goat!

And on the recent phenomenon of e-qurbani, here is Khalid Irfan noting somewhat sardonically:

Khuda ke ghar mein Visa card ka system nahin hai
Credit card ke bakre ki qurbani se bachna

There's no system of Visa cards in God's house
Beware of the sacrifice of credit card goats

Since both Eids are an open house requiring no formal invitation thus affording plenty of opportunities to meet (and there seems a natural rhyme of Eid with *deed,* meaning 'to see'), there's a profusion of poetry on the social and cultural aspect of this festival:

Eid aai tum na aae kya maza hai Eid ka
Eid hii to naam hai ik doosre ki deed ka

Eid has come but you have not come
Eid is nothing but a name for seeing each other

56. Qawwali and the Coming Together of *Zamaan, Makaan, Ikhwaan*

I first heard Nusrat Fateh Ali Khan in a bar in Brussels sometime in the year 1994. I hadn't heard Nusrat's incredible voice with its amazing range and variations ever before; he was not such a hit in India at that point of time; though unbeknownst to me he was already big in the US and making inroads in Europe. This was a bar with a pocket-sized dancing floor; possibly a barn or a warehouse once, it had been converted into a very high end watering-hole in a hip part of Brussels. What I remember all these years later is that people around us were either tapping their feet or were up and dancing to the music; what is more, possibly they were people who did not understand a word of what Nusrat was saying and possibly the only two people in the room, my husband and I who could understand Nusrat, were neither dancing nor tapping our feet. Looking back, I see this as a moment of epiphany when I understood what qawwali means to people like us, those of us who are born and brought up in South Asia.

Qawwali is not background music against which you will carry on your conversation, nor is it something that you can get up and dance to. You might sway, yes, or beat your hands in unison with the qawwals, but it is something you sit and listen to. Qawwali, to my mind, no matter where it is being performed or heard, be it in a Sufi *khanqah* (hospice) or something you see on the screen or hear on a tape or, as in my case, hear in a bar, remains a devotional form of music. Of all the musical forms, the qawwali is the hardest to disengage from its moorings in Sufi Islam. The current that ripples through it is the mystical impulse of Islam.

There are three pre-requisites of qawwali, namely, *zamaan*, *makaan*, *ikhwan*, that is time, space and occasion. There is a designated time for it that does not clash with the times of the five daily namaz. The qawwali offered in the khanqah is usually between the Maghrib and Isha prayers in the late evening. The space must be clean, one that is conducive to leading to a state of *sama,* and *ikhwaan* refers to the gathering of like-minded people. The bar in Brussels failed on all three counts: it was neither the right time nor place, and certainly, the people gathered there had no commonality.

But what happens when all three conditions are met? Nothing short of pure magic! Let us look at how a qawwali proceeds and exactly what is being sung. There is, always, always, the hamd to begin with: the qawwal opens the proceedings with praise of Allah. The hamd is followed by the naat, a panegyric in praise of the Prophet Muhammad (Peace be Upon Him), moving seamlessly to the manqabat, in praise of Hazrat Ali or the Sufi saint in whose dargah a qawwali is being recited, such as Hazrat Nizamuddin.

Let us now look at the kalaam, the actual composition that is being sung. In several compositions, the words 'Allah' and 'Ali' merge and the qawwals sing them in such as way that the vowels fuse. The *tarana bol* are words that are generally meaningless but leaven the singing with a special alliterative energy, for instance:

Fa Ali-un maula
Man kunto maula
Dara dil-e dara dil-e dar-e daana
Hum tum tanaana nana, nana nana ray
Yalali yalali yala, yalayala ray
Man kunto maula...

(Whoever accepts me as a master,
Ali is his master too.)

The above is a Hadith, a saying of the Prophet Muhammad (PBH). The rest of the lines are *tarana bol* that are used for rhythmic chanting by Sufis.

Coming now to the secular or non-*khanqahi* qawwali popularised largely through Hindi cinema, some samples are: '*Nigaahein milaane ko jii chaahta hai*' (I feel like locking my gaze with yours), '*Humein to loot liya milke husn waalon ne*' (All these beautiful people have robbed me), '*Main idhar jaaoon yaa udhar jaaoon*' (Shall I go hither or thither). Most memorable is the iconic qawwali from *Mughal-e-Azam*—'*Teri mehfil mein qismat aazma kar hum bhi dekheinge*' (Today I too shall wager my fortune in your assembly, sung by Shamshad Begum with Lata Mangeshkar)—which is remembered even today for its archness and coquetry.

Hindi cinema also helped popularise another form of secular qawwali known as *Muqable ki Qawwali*, whereby two teams, usually comprising men and women, are pitted against each other as arch opponents, or even two teams of the same gender (as in *Mughal-e-Azam*). The 'filmy' qawwali has taken elements from diverse traditions such as the *mujra*, which, in turn, is inspired by the *bol batana* tradition of Kathak. Interestingly, filmy qawwalis such as '*Nigaahein milaane ko jii chaahta hai*' lend themselves both to a purely romantic or secular interpretation and also hark back to the mystic roots of the qawwali.

Filmy or non-filmy, *khanqahi* or non-*khanqahi*, the qawwali has two essential features: *takraar* which is repetitive, and a *gireh,* or a poetic knot. The *gireh* affords enormous flexibility and expansiveness to the qawwal, allowing him to travel seamlessly back and forth. It is the *gireh* that allows the qawwali to be free of the limitations of other poetic forms that lend themselves to singing, such as the ghazal. Perhaps it is the *gireh* that is also responsible for the longevity of the qawwali. The fact that it has remained alive for over 700 years is possibly because the *gireh* allows the qawwal to dip into his memory bag and pluck fragments of poetry across the ages. The qawwal can stud, almost like a master jeweller, seemingly random couplets by Bulleh Shah or Meera Bai or Kabir in a composition by Amir Khusrau. So, you can have a traditional composition by Amir Khusrau and you can have a *kalaam* by a contemporary Urdu poet all in the same qawwali. And, of course, Amir Khusrau himself would have a fragment in Farsi and another in Hindvi, as in:

Ze-hal-e-miskeen makun taġhaful duraie nainaan banaae batiyan
Ki taab-e-hijraan nadaram ai jaan na lehu kaahe lagaaye chhatiyan

Do not overlook my misery by blandishing your eyes and spinning tales
My patience brimmeth over, O my love, why do you not clasp me to your bosom

At the heart of the qawwali lies communication. It uses certain stock devices such as alternate voices, that is, two male performers and a backup, and within the lead performers too, there is an alteration. The stock device of more than one voice, that too, distinctly different voices, varies the tempo, but at the heart of it all, communication is the key. The word qawwali comes from the word *qaul* which means 'to speak'. Initially, it was used for the sayings of the Prophet but over the years, it has become absorbed in qawwali, thus reminding us of the essentially oral, vocal element of this art form.

In much of medieval Sufi poetry, there are some stock images such as *gori* (maiden), *panghat* (well), *matki kaa tutna* (the pitcher that breaks on its way to the well) or *kahe ko byahi bides* (images of girls married off and sent to live in an alien situation), and the dynamics between *saans aur bahu* (daughters-in-law and mothers-in-law). Borrowed from the folk, these elements allude to the hardships and obstacles in the path of true love, where the beloved is God, and how trials and tribulations, which are part of life, are a manifestation of the obstructions in the way of communion. Then, there are the many references to festivals. Amir Khusrau's compositions refer to Holi, Basant and various other festivals. So, you have lines like these addressed to the *suhaagan* (married woman):

Aaj basant manaale suhaagan, aaj Basant manaale
Anjan manjan ki piya mori, lambe neher lagayi
Naino se naina milaale suhaagan aaj Basant manaale

Rejoice, my love, rejoice, for spring is here, rejoice.
Bring out your lotions and potions, take long swings on the swings
Lock your gaze with mine, my love, celebrate spring with me

Also, the 'voice' in a qawwali is a predominantly feminine one; it deploys intensely feminine imagery, such as *piya, panghat, gori,* etc. But that voice has been deployed by the qawwals (mostly males) in a very manly, almost muscular fashion. There have been a handful of women qawwals in recent times such as Prabha Bharti, Chanchal Bharti, Shakila Bano Bhopali but, by and large, qawwali remains a male domain. Also qawwali continues to be written by modern poets. There is Kamil Kanpuri's 'Jo Ali Miley to Nabi Miley jo Nabi Miley to Khuda Milaa' (Finding Ali I Found the Prophet, Seeking the Prophet, I Sought the Almighty) and the qawwali written by Kaifi Azmi for the movie *Garam Hawa*—'Maula Saleem Chishti Aaqa Saleem Chishti' (O Master Saleem Chishti, O Lord Saleem Chishti).

There is historical evidence that the qawwali in some form or the other existed before Nizamuddin Aulia. However, the qawwali, as we understand it in its present form, emerged from the bylanes of Nayazpur, what we now call Basti Hazrat Nizamuddin, which is where Hazrat Nizamuddin set up his khanqah and which is where Hazrat Amir Khusrau would often come to spend some time. The bulk of the repertoire of the existing qawwals, regardless of their *silsila* (lineage traced to different Sufi masters), is actually composed by Amir Khusrau. There may be additions or alterations and an occasional new composition, but the bulk of the corpus has been written by Khusrau. Taken together, the actual sung words of the qawwals take us into a world of pluralism and multi-culturalism, where living together was very much a fact of life. For instance, here is Hazrat Nizamuddin declaring the following after witnessing a scene beside the bank of the Yamuna:

Har qaum raast raah-e deen va qibl gaahe
Sansar har ko pujey kul ko jagat sarahe

Every race has a direction in which they face to pray
The entire world worships something or the other

In response, Amir Khusrau wrote something that encapsulates not just the musicality but the whimsicality of the qawwali tradition, with its reliance on individuality and idiosyncrasy in mixing seeming contraries in its reference to the tilted cap of the beloved in the first line:

Man qibla raast kardam bar simt-e kaj kulahe
Mecce mein koi dhoondhe Kashi koi chaahe

I have turned my face towards the crooked cap (of Nizamuddin)
While some look for Him in Mecca others in Kashi

57. *Adab-e Atfaal*: Children's Literature in Urdu

Children's literature is more often than not didactic; it aims to educate and instruct, to teach the right moral values, to instill principles in young minds. Seldom does it also include pure and simple entertainment in its objectives. Written mostly by adults, equally seldom does it capture the child's eye for the small and the seemingly insignificant, the whimsical and the whacky. But in the few instances when it does include entertainment with instruction, it can be pure magic.

Known as *adab-e atfaal* (*atfaal* meaning children), children's literature in Urdu has had a rich and varied tradition. By far the most famous, and prolific, writer for children was Ismail Merathi (1844–1917) a schoolteacher and educationist. Some of his poems such as 'Naseehat' (Advice), 'Barsaat' (Rain), 'Humaari Gaaye' (Our Cow), 'Subah ki Aamad' (The Coming of Morning), 'Sach Kaho' (Speak the Truth), 'Baarish ka Pehla Qatra' (The First Drop of Rain), 'Pan Chakki' (Water Mill), 'Shafaq' (Twilight), found their way into school textbooks because of their edifying contents as in 'Naseehat' which warns children to guard against envy and greed, to apologise for one's mistakes, to forgive others when they express regret:

Bhalai karo to karo be-ġharaz
Gharaz ki bhalai to hai ik maraz

If you do good do so selflessly
Doing good for a reason is a disease

In these days of lynching by cow vigilantes, Ismail Merathi's nazm 'Hamari Gaaye' needs to be re-read for the love and veneration it teaches for the cow:

Rab ka shukr ada kar bhai
Jis ne hamari gaae banaai
Uss malik ko kyun na pukarein
Jis ne pilaain duudh ki dhaaren...
Subhan Allah duudh hai kaisa

Praise the lord, brother
Who has made our cow
Why should we not call out that Lord
Who has given us streams of milk to drink...
Praise Allah, how good is this milk

The much-derided Muhammad Iqbal who is the subject of periodic controversies and censure, has written some delightful nazms for children, such as 'Bachhe ki Dua' (A Child's Prayer) that got a school principal in Pilibhit fired and an FIR lodged against him in 2019 (see previous essay entitled 'Why Do We Love to Hate Iqbal, the Prophet of Change'). Written in 1902, it was inspired by an English poem by Matilda B. Edwards (1836-1919) titled 'A Child's Prayer'. Lyrically evocative, it is written from a child's perspective and is a sweetly poignant plea to be saved from any form of wrong doing. But this doesn't matter to those who find it offensive; what matters is the use of the words *Khudaya*, *Allah* and *Ya Rab* without thought for precisely what is being asked of this God:

Lab pe aati hai dua ban ke tamanna meri
Zindagi shama ki surat ho Khudaya meri
Duur duniya ka mire dam se andhera ho jaaye
Har jagah mere chamakne se ujala ho jaaye
Ho mire dum se yunhi mere watan ki zeenat
Jis tarah phool se hoti hai chaman ki zeenat

My wish rises to my lips like a prayer
O lord make my life like that of a candle
So I may remove darkness from the world
So I may spread light with my brightness
Let me add to the adornment of my country
Like a flower adds to the adornment of a garden

Other poems by Iqbal written for children are 'Pahaarh aur Gilheri' (The Mountain and the Squirrel), 'Eik Makra aur Makhi' (A Spider and Fly), 'Maa ka Khwaab' (A Mother's Dream), 'Hamdardi' (Sympathy) and the sweetly lyrical 'Tarana-e-Hind' (The Anthem of India) which I remember singing at school assemblies.

Several major Urdu poets have written poems for children, especially poems marking the *saalgirah* (birthday) of their own children where they spell out what they would want for their sons/daughters and, by extension, all children all over the world. There is Faiz Ahmad Faiz's 'Muneeza ki Saalgirah' (Muneeza's Birthday), Ale Ahmad Suroor's 'Meri Beti Jab Badi Ho Jaayegi' (When My Daughter Grows up), Sara Shagufta's 'Shaili Beti ke Naam' (To My Daughter Shaili), Gulzar's set of three poems for his daughter Meghna (aka Boski) and the most unusual 'Doraaha' (Crossroad) penned by Javed Akhtar for his daughter Zoya. Other memorable poetry for children are Kishwar Naheed's 'Chidiya aur Koyal' (The Bird and the Nightingale), Zehra Nigah's 'Mitthu Miyan' (Mitthu the Parrot), Syeda Farhat's 'Nayi Kahani' (New Story), Sufi Tabassum's 'Raja Rani ki Kahani' (The Story of the King and the Queen), Zubair Rizvi's 'Tabdeeli' (Change) on school-going children, among others.

Much of Urdu poetry has drawn children's attention to the marvels of nature such as this poem on the moon by Afsar Merathi that I distinctly remember from my own childhood:

Tum naddi par ja kar dekho
Jab naddi mein nahaaye chand
Kaisi lagaai dupki uss ne
Dar hai doob na jaaye chand

Go to the river and see
The moon when it bathes in the river
See how it dives into the water
I am scared it might drown

Then there's 'Machhliyon ke Masterji' (The Teacher of Fish) by Hafeez Jallundhari:

Nannhi ho tum bachchi ho tum
Sab aql ki kachchi ho tum
Aao miri batein suno

You are a child, just a lil girl
You are still of tender years
Come, listen to me

A fair amount of good poetry for children is to be found among film lyrics either sung by child artistes or by adults singing for children, such as this by Sahir Ludhianvi:

Bachchon tum taqdeer ho kal ke Hindostaan ki
Bapu ke vardaan ki Nehru ke armaan ki

Children you are the destiny of tomorrow's Hindustan
Of Bapu's gift and Nehru's aspirations

Coming to modern times, two names stand out for their whimsicality and quirkiness. Forsaking moralising and teaching, they write with joyful abandon. Here's the delightful Ibn-e Insha writing 'Billo ka Basta' (Billo's Schoolbag) that is stuffed full with all manner of things yet the quality of educaton being imparted to hapless Billo remains doubtful:

Urdu na jaano
English na jaano
Kahti ho ḳhud ko
Bilquis Bano

You don't know Urdu
You don't know English
And you call yourself
Bilquis Bano

And Gulzar who has kept alive the child in his heart with poems such as 'Lakdi ki Kathi' (The Wood of Wood), 'Sher aur Khargosh' (The Lion and the Rabbit) and the delightful 'Oot-Pataang' (Nonsense):

Kanon ki ik nagri dekhi jis mein saare kaane dekhe
Ek taraf se ahmaq saare ek taraf se siyaane thhe

I saw a city of one-eyed people where everyone had one eye
All the idiots on one side and the clever folk on the other

A fair amount of short fiction too has been written. Here again, Ismail Merathi has possibly written the lion's share. His stories, like his poetry, aim to instruct and educate in somewhat didactic stories such as 'Eik Gadha Sher Bana' (A Donkey Became a Tiger). Dr Zakir Husain, India's third President, wrote some delightful stories for children such as 'Abbu Khan ki Bakri' (Abbu Khan's Goat), 'Poori jo Kadhai se Bhaag Gayi' (The Puri that Ran Away from the Wok) at a time when a host of Urdu magazines were being published such as: *Khilona* (Toy), *Payaam-e-Taaliim* (The Message of Education), *Ghuncha* (Bud), *Phool* (Flower), *Bachhon ki Duniya* (Children's World). With Urdu publishing shrinking, it is left to a contemporary writer such as Zakia Mashhadi with her 'Kabootar ki Eid' (The Pigeon's Eid) or Gulzar in his 'Paaji Badal' (Naughty Cloud) or 'Narangi' (China Orange) to keep the glorious tradition of *adab-e atfaal* alive in India.

58. IPTA and Why Art Must Portray the Joys and Sorrows of the People

Something remarkable happened in a school hall in Bombay from 22-25 May 1943. The Fourth All-India Conference of the Progressive Writers' Association (PWA) took place in the Marwari Vidyalaya. Unlike the three previous all-India meetings of this influential literary grouping—the inaugural one being in Lucknow on 9 April 1936, followed by the second in Calcutta on 24-25 December 1938, and the third in Delhi in 1942—this one in Bombay was a grand affair. It was important also because on its concluding day, 25 of May, a remarkable institution came into being: this was the Indian People's Theatre Association (IPTA) with its motto of 'People's Theatre Stars the People'.

The Sri Lankan activist Anil de Silva was appointed its first General Secretary and N M Joshi, the trade union leader, its first President. While the initial impulse behind the formation of IPTA was the man-made Bengal Famine, and the Urdu poem by Wamiq Jaunpuri 'Bhooka Hai Bangaal' (Bengal is Hungry) became its rallying cry, soon almost all the big 'isms' of the time became grist to its mill: anti-colonialism, anti-fascism, anti-imperialism, feminism, land reform, rights of industrial workers, peasants and landless labour not to mention national unity, communal harmony, secularism, pluralism, multi-culturalism.

Gender justice and drawing attention to the plight of women remained at the heart of its endeavours irrespective of the medium. Virtually from its inception, the IPTA's influences remained astonishingly diverse: Kaifi Azmi's long poem 'Aurat' (The Woman), a play on the life of the Soviet heroine Tanya, the Kathakali dance of Kerala, the songs of Nazrul Islam and Rabindranath Tagore from Bengal, the list was eclectic combining traditional and modern styles and formats. Uday Shankar's troupe of dancers and musicians that included the sisters Zohra and Uzra among others, toured the country to collect donations for famine relief. Khwaja Ahmad Abbas's film *Dharti ke Laal* (Children of the Earth), written especially for IPTA by the progressive writer Krishan Chandar and Bijon Bhattacharya with lyrics by Sardar Jafri, Nemi Chandra Jain, Wamiq Jaunpuri and Prem Dhawan, was widely distributed in the USSR and received rave reviews.

Drawing inspiration from the strong Chinese Peoples' Theatre Movement and especially the innovative Living Newspaper format (where topical events or news was told in a dramatic form), IPTA sought to combine indigenous or folk elements in dance, drama and song from influences as diverse as Urdu poetry and Russian ballet. Groups of IPTA performers, initially called 'squads' (Bengal Squad, Punjab Squad, Central Squad, etc.) later called 'troupes' toured the length and breadth of the country, hiring several bogeys of a train, performing in small villages and hamlets before the humblest of audiences (such as women *beedi* [a cheap local cigarette made from tendu leaves] workers or manual scavengers), sleeping in the train and moving on to the next venue.

As the movement grew, and the IPTA spawned a host of cultural squads (separate ones for dance, drama, songs), even routine PWA meetings became lively, energetic occasions with songs and dances interspersed with academic discussions and poetry readings. The progressives wrote plays and songs which were shown to peasant and working-class as well as middle-class audiences in different parts of the country. For example, *Dhaani Baankein* (Green Bangles), a play on communal riots by the Urdu fiction writer Ismat Chughtai and *Yeh Kis ka Khoon Hai* (Whose Blood is This?) a play by Sardar Jafri set in Chittagong during the first Japanese bombing would be staged alongside films and documentaries from the Soviet Union.

While the plays, skits, ballets, shadow-plays dance-dramas and local forms such as the *tamasha* and *pawada* inspired by Marathi theatre, the *jhumur* from Assam and the *jatra* from Bengal were indeed popular, it was the songs that gained the troupes instant popularity. Salil Chowdhury, later to become a well-known film music composer, had spent his childhood among the tea plantations of Assam and knew at first-hand the plight and exploitation of the workers. He joined the 'Bharotiya Ganonatya Sangha' (as the IPTA was known in Bengal) and penned many a rousing song. While several songs from Salil Da's prodigious output all through the 1940s went unrecorded, some were collected in *Ganasangeet Sangraha* published and compiled by Subrata Rudra. These include: '*Uru taka taka taghina taghina*' (based on a folk song sung by Bengali peasants during sowing and harvesting), '*Aalor desh thekey aandhaar paar hoyee*' (about sacrifice and hard work for the nation), '*Dheu uthchhey karaa tutchhey*' (in support of the Naval Uprising) and later Hindi songs such as '*Aagey chalo, aagey chalo*' (Forward, move forward). Some Hindustani songs such as '*Suno Hind ke rehne walon suno suno*' (O ye people living in Hind, listen, listen) sung by Reba Roychoudhary, Shailendra's

'*Tu zinda hai to zindagi ke geet mein yaqeen kar*' (You are alive, have faith in the song of life), or *Jaane wale siphai se poochho* (Ask the departing soldier) written by Urdu poet Makdoom Mohiuddin became extremely popular with the masses.

Apart from popular songs, some written by well-known poets others by unknown poets, in Hindi, Urdu, Telugu, Malayalam existing folk songs and ballads that spoke of the workers and the peasants too were added to the repertoire of the IPTA performers. The tenure of P C Joshi as General Secretary of the CPI from 1935-1947 saw the fullest possible utilization of culture, literature and the performing arts. Joshi had, by this stage, already started the practice of gathering the country's prominent writers, journalists, artists, economists, historians, film and stage actors to rally around the party organ, *National Front*, and later *People's War* and *People's Age*. He commissioned Sunil Janah to take photographs of the Bengal Famine of 1943 and document people's movement elsewhere such as in Telangana. Joshi understood, and capitalised on, the need to use culture as a living tool and believed that the revival of folk traditions was vital if people of one language group were to know the folk tradition of other language groups.

Songs on Lenin, ballads on the defense of Stalingrad, heroism of the Red Army, translations into Urdu of the revolutionary Kazakh poet, Jambul Jabir who wrote 'Stalin Calls', the centuries-old ballads from the Punjab called the *Heer* were refashioned to weave in motifs of communal harmony—the idea being to revive and showcase India's rich, pluralistic heritage and at the same time draw attention to the plight of the toiling masses using images and ideas from revolutions in Russia, China, Spain as well as local, or home-grown movements such as Telangana or the Malabar Uprising. Contradictory though it may sound the IPTA and the PWA brought in a certain cosmopolitanism *and* a 'localism' or 'nativism', the idea being to make common cause and to bring the different voices against oppression on the same platform.

All through the 1940s and '50s, IPTA, PWA and the Bombay film industry existed like three interlinked circles, with overlapping memberships and a host of common concerns. Foremost among these common concerns was a socially transformative agenda that would fulfill the needs of a fledgling nation. For this they sought inspiration not only from Marxist tomes and ideologues but also from a Congress-inspired version of socialism and in post-Independence India an increasingly Nehruvian 'idea of India' that hailed schools, colleges, dams and factories as the 'temples of modern India'. Members of IPTA and PWA—some of whom worked in the film industry as actors, directors, scriptwriters, lyricists, technicians, etc. such as Prem Dhawan, Prithviraj Kapoor, Salil Chowdhury, Shailendra, A K Hangal, Balraj and Damyanti Sahni, Chetan and Uma Anand, Shaukat and Kaifi Azmi, Khwaja Ahmad Abbas, Ismat Chughtai and others—worked in tandem to produce a radically new set of images, metaphors, vocabulary, even aesthetics that influenced several generations of film-goers. Their most visible and immediate effect was the introduction of a non-sectarian ethos, one that rose above the narrow confines of caste, creed and religion and worked as a balm on a national psyche that had been traumatised by the communal outrages before, after and during the partition.

The glory days of the IPTA also spanned the most tumultuous period of modern Indian history—Gandhi's call to *satyagraha*, India's response to the rise of fascism, Nehru's Muslim Mass Contact Programme, Gandhi's second Civil Disobedience Movement, the Second World War and its impact on India, chronic food shortages, rise of trade union movements and *kisan sabhas* (peasant associations), strikes, lockouts, communal disturbances that scarred the nation in the years leading up to independence, partition and the immediate bloody aftermath that the Communist Party of India (CPI) dubbed 'false freedom'. Both the progressive writers and those within the IPTA faithfully reflected each of these momentous events that shaped the nation's destiny; at the same time, they drew the nation's attention to events outside the country such as the Rosenberg Trial, the decolonisation of Africa, the need for Afro-Asian unity, and the emergence of a new world order in which India must take its rightful place. In short, nothing was beyond the ken, no issue was too big or too small for the PWA and the IPTA as long as art was put to the service of humanity.

59. Nature in the Urdu Poet's Imagination

Descriptions of nature have been widespread in Urdu and Persian poetry. Vivid descriptions of Nature in general and spring, changes of seasons, clouds, breeze, morning and twilight in particular have been favourite subjects. It must also be said that there was a certain rhetorical quality to much of these subjects and an almost cosmetic beauty to these descriptions in the more stylised, classical tradition. It has also been argued that some of these much-favoured tropes such as *nargis* (narcissus flower), *sarv* (cyprus tree), *jurra* or *shahbaaz* (falcon), *gul-o-bubul* (the songbird that is supposed to cry its heart out for the rose) are not indigenous to India—neither geographically not culturally. With time, these images were 'nativised' in the Urdu that grew on Indian soil drawing from different languages and their literary traditions.

By the late 18th century when the ghazal reached its apex as a sophisticated and wholly Indian genre, there is nothing foreign or alien about the image of the rose and the bulbul. See, for example, this sher by Mir Taqi Mir:

Jis chaman zaar ka hai tu gul-e taar
Bulbul uss gulsitan ke hum bhi hain

The garden whose freshest dewy rose you are
We too are the bulbuls of that very garden

Or this sher by Atish:

Yeh arzu thhi tujhe gul ke ru ba ru kartey
Hum aur bulbul-e be-taab guftagu kartey

I longed to place you and the rose face to face
The restless bulbul and I could talk to each other

And, here, in Ghalib's rendering of time honoured images, the bulbul's lament becomes the anguished cry of the human heart as in:

Kehta hai kaun naala-e bulbul ko be-asar
Parde mein gul ke laakh jigar chaak ho gaye

Who can call the bulbul's lament to be of no use?
In the guise of a rose, a million hearts have been pierced

To go back in time, it would be worthwhile to mention a purely native literary tradition that has always celebrated nature. This is the *barahmasa* tradition. The *barahmasas* (meaning songs for the 12 months of the year, i.e. the year according to the Indian lunar calendar) are songs of separation—both mystic and secular—expressing love and longing for the beloved. The singer's mood changes with the seasons and thus allows the poet to draw in the local, seasonal and natural elements while essentially drawing upon a single theme: love, or rather meeting (*milna*) and its conjoined twin *bichhadna* (separation). Drawing upon its ancient roots in Prakrit, Sanskrit, Hindi and regional dialects, the *barahmasa* is almost entirely rural. It still survives in the form of *lok geet* or folk songs.

Sometime in the early 17th century (1636 or so) Afzal

Jhinjhanvi compiled the first *barahmasa* in Urdu, and called it *Bikat Kahani* (*bikat* meaning 'immense' or 'terrible'). Here's a sampling:

Ari jab kook koel ne sunayi
Tamami tan badan mein aag lahi
Andher rain, jugnu jagmagata
Oo ka jalti upar tais ka jalata?

Ah, when the cuckoo sounds her cooing
It sets my body aflame
The glow worm glows in the darkness of the night
Why does it burn one already on fire?

And, elsewhere:

Gayi barsaat rut nikhara falak sab
Nami danam ke sajan ghar phire kab
Piya bin aikal kaise rahoo ri
Sitam upar sitam kaise sahoon ri

The rains are gone, the skies are clear
But I don't know when my beloved will return
How will I live alone without my beloved?
How will I bear affliction upon affliction?

Drawing on the existing *barahmasa* tradition in Gujrati, Uzlat incorporated literary devices such as the *kah mukarni* (a kind of riddle played between women that peg around denial), *do arthi* (double meaning), *shesh arthi* (six meaning), *kabad, dohra, chhand, surtha,* and *jhoolna*. Here's a sample of *do arthi* couplet:

Papiha de namak ghaavon ko ke pee
Ghari sa har ghari doobe mera jee

The cuckoo pours salt over my wounds and tells me to drink it
While all the while my heart sinks from minute to minute

Coming to modern times, it is Iqbal who has written the most lyrical poetry on nature—on rivers, mountains, scenes of pastoral beauty. In the early part of his poetic career, we see shades of William Wordsworth and the Romantics in his description of rivers, skies, clouds, mountains.

On the stream that courses through the mountains in a nazm called 'Saqinama', Iqbal is unmatched in his musicality that mimics the untamed energy of a stream hurtling down a mountain:

Woh joo-e-kohistan uchakti hui
Atakti lachakti sarakti hui
Uchhalti phisalti sambhalti hui
Badey pech kha kar nikalti hui
Ruke jab to sil cheer deti hai ye
Pahaadon ke dil cheer deti hai ye

The rushing mountain stream
Stumbling, swaying, spurting
Jumping, sliding, gushing
Twisting, turning, coursing
Stabbing rocks when it stops
Piercing the heart of mountains

In a long lyrical poem on the humble glowworm, the 'Jugnu', he says:

Rangeen kiya sehar ko baanki dulhan ki soorat
Pehna ke laal jorha shabnam ki aarsi dii

It made the morning radiant like a beautiful bride
Clad in a red dress, gave the dew's mirror to see herself

And among the progressives, who saw a creative writer's primary impulse to be socially-engaged, purposive literature where depiction of the human condition takes primacy over depictions of nature, it is Sardar Jafri who is matchless in his depictions of nature. Here are some snatches from his *Mera Safar* (My Journey) which he begins with a line from Rumi 'Like Grass, I will sprout again and again' with echoes of Walt Whitman and his 'Leaves of Grass':

Lekin main yahaan phir aaungaa
Bachchon ke dahan se bolungaa
Chidiyon ki zabaan se gaaungaa
Jab beej hanseinge dharti mein
Aur konplein apni ungli se
Mitti ki tahon ko chhedeingi
Main patti patti kali kali
Apni aankhein phir kholungaa
Sarsabz hatheli par le kar
Shabnam ke qatre tolungaa

But I shall come here again
I shall speak from the mouth of babes
I shall sing in the tongue of birds
When seeds shall smile in the earth
And saplings tickle the layers
Of the soil with their fingers
With every bud and every leaf
I shall open my eyes yet again
Holding them in my green palms
I shall weigh the drops of dew

60. Poet-Fathers and Poet-Mothers Writing on Daughters

Much has been made of the Male Gaze in literature and the depiction of the woman in Urdu literature, and poetry in particular. But, what happens when the woman is not an object of desire but a subject of the purest, most tender love? When the woman is not a wife or beloved but a daughter, what then? Let us look at the depiction of the daughter, first from a poet-mother's pen then a poet-father's.

Sara Shagufta, the rebel poet who revolted against all norms of a patriarchal society in her brief but tumultuous life, who had declared 'My father was naked/ I took off my clothes and gave them to him', writes thus when it comes to having a daughter of her own in a heart-wrenching poem entitled 'Shaili Beti ke Naam':

Tujhe jab bhi koi dukh de
Iss dukh ka naam beti rakhna

Whenever someone gives you a hurt
Name that hurt Daughter

Writing an entire ghazal on the subject of what a daughter can do, Sameena Aslam Sameena writes:

Ye ladki kamzor si ladki Mariam bhi hai Zohra bhi
Rabiya Basri bani to phir waliyon se badh gai beti

This girl, this frail girl is a Mary and she is a Venus too
When she becomes a Rabia Basri, she is ahead of the saints

And here's Fatima Hasan in 'Meri Beti Chalna Seekh Gayi' (My Daughter Has Learnt to Walk) reaffirming her daughter's right to self-determination and control over her destiny:

Meri beti duniya ke naqshe mein
Apni marzi ke
Rangon ko bharna seekh gayi

In the map of the world, my daughter
Has learnt to fill out colours
According to her own wishes

Talking of what men, the most liberal and visionary of men, want for their daughters invariably reminds me of W B Yeats's 'A Prayer for My Daughter'. I first read it as a 20 year-old undergraduate student and while swayed by its lyrical intensity and evocative play upon words, was equally struck by the benign patriarchy that afflicts this Irish revolutionary as he looks down upon his infant daughter. Naturally enough, he wants to protect her from the storms of the world that await her but even the beauty he wishes for her when she grows up is not the fiery, tempestuous beauty of the women he knew and loved (a reference perhaps to Maud Gonne whom he immortalized in his early poems): 'May she be granted beauty and yet not/ Beauty to make a stranger's eye distraught.' He goes on to pray that she be blessed with courtesy and is not 'too opinionated' lest she end up 'an old bellows full of angry wind'! Clearly, what men want *from* their women and *for* their daughters are vastly different as is also evident from this *rubai* by Firaq Gorakhpuri:

Maan aur bahan bhi aur chaheti beti
Ghar ki rani bhi aur jeewan saathi
Phir bhi woh kamini sarasar devi
Aur sej pe besva woh ras ki putli

Mother and sister and beloved daughter too
She's Queen of the Household and fellow traveler too
And yet that loving woman is entirely a goddess
But on the bed she's a whore and a bundle of delight

Now, let us see what male Urdu poets have to say for their daughters. Faiz Ahmad Faiz, known as much for his rousing revolutionary poetry as for his romantic ghazals, is penning these sweet, loving thoughts for his 8-year-old daughter in 'Muneeza ki Saalgirah' (Muneeza's Birthday):

Hai Muneeza ki aaj saalgirah
Har taraf shor hai aaj mubarak ka
Chaand taarey duaein detey hain...

Today is Muneeza's birthday
There is a clamour of congratulations all around
The moon and the stars offer blessings...

There's often an assumption that daughters will fly away one day, that their stay in their father's home is, by its very nature, transitory, as in this sher by Jaan Kashmiri:

Jaan, phur kar ke kisi roz ye urh jaaengii
Betiyaan baap ke aangan mein hain chidiyon ki tarah

Jaan, they will fly away in the blink of an eye one day
Daughters are like birds in a father's courtyard

Here is the venerable Iftikhar Hussain Arif, a respected ghazal-go of the old school, reaffirming the bond between fathers and daughters, one that has more than a tinge of possessiveness:

Betiyan baap ki aankhon mein chhupe ḳhwaab ko pahchaanti hain
Aur koi doosra iss ḳhwaab ko padh le to bura maanti hain

Daughters recognize the dreams hidden in a father's eyes
And they don't like it when someone else reads those dreams

Gulzar has written three exquisite poems for his daughter, Meghna (aka Boski), one when she turned 18, the second when she was in labour and about to deliver her baby, and the third when she achieved professional acclaim as a film-maker in her own right. Here are the concluding lines from the third one, brimful with a father's pride and joy in his daughter's achievements and the affirmation that she has gone above and beyond his own accomplishments:

Badi ho kar meri beti ne khola aasman aur
Ungliyon se, naam apna likh ke raushan kar diya hai aasman mera
Kai barson se jo tah kar ke seene mein rakha hua thha

My daughter has grown up and opened the sky
And with her fingers, written her name and illuminated my sky
The sky that I had folded and kept away in my breast for many years

Javed Akhtar pens a most unusual poem for his daughter, Zoya, where he tells her that life is a crossroad: one road is easy, the other difficult. Entitled 'Doraha' (where two roads meet), he lists the twists and turns she will find in both and concludes with his wish that he would want her to take the difficult path:

Mujhe pata hai
Ye rasta asaan nahin hai
Lekin mujh ko ye ġham bhi hai
Tum ko ab tak
Kyuun apni pahchan nahin hai

I know
This path is not easy
But at the same time I am sad
That you still
Do not know yourself

My personal favourite, for entirely subjective reasons, is the poem my grandfather, Ale Ahmad Suroor, wrote for my mother, Mehjabeen; it is something I find myself repeating often for my own daughters:

Meri beti jab badi ho jayegi
Saare ghar mein chandni phailaigi
Maa ki aankhon mein jawaani aayegi
Baap ke dil ki kali khil jayegi...

When my daughter grows up
She will spread moonlight in the entire home
Youth will return to her mother's eyes
And her father's heart will bloom with joy

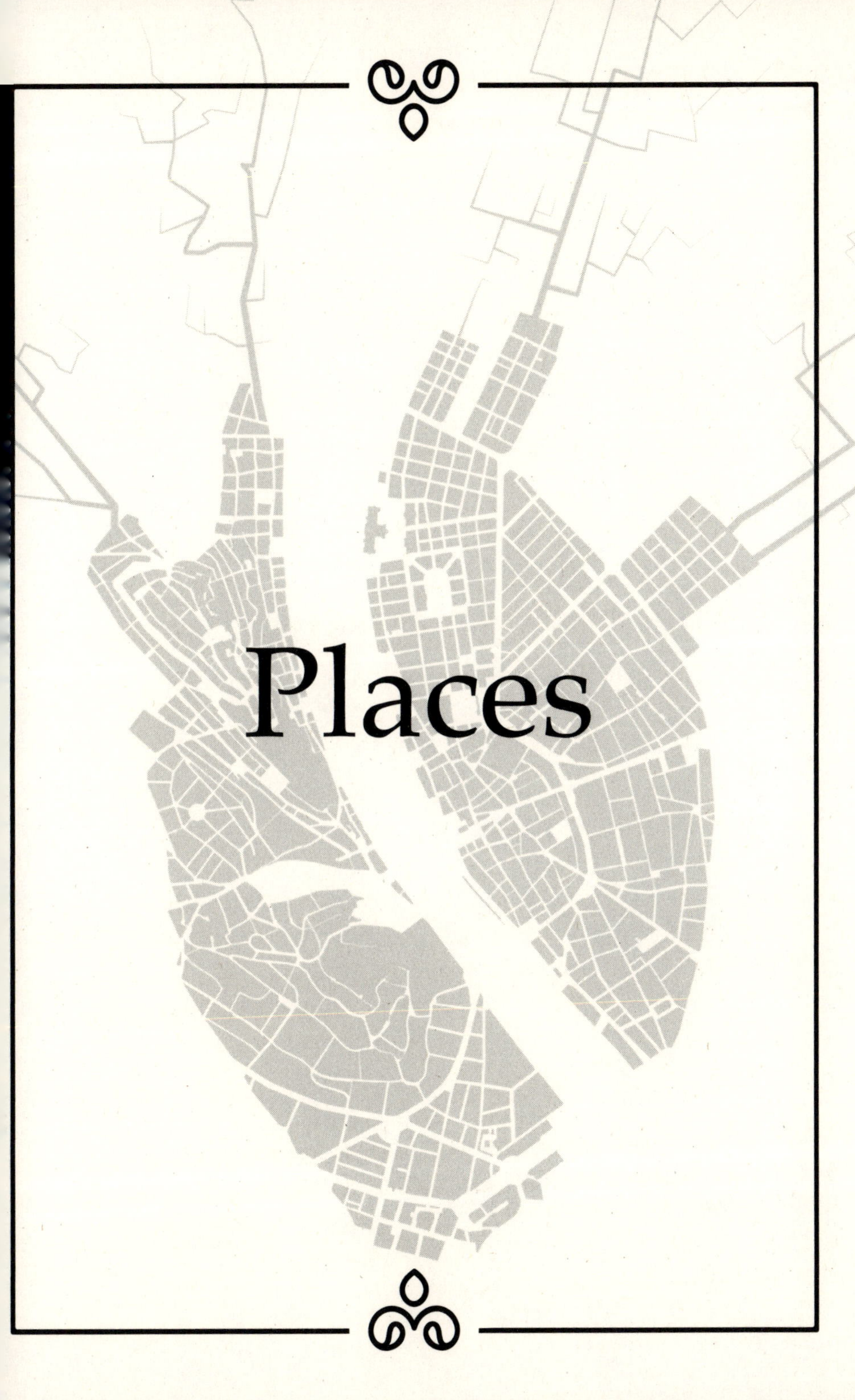

Places

61. Afghanistan: Heart of Asia, Cradle of Civilisations

My sole trip to Kabul was in the year 2008 when I had gone to attend a seminar on Khan Abdul Ghaffar Khan to mark his 20th death anniversary at the Kabul University. Till then, Kabul, and Afghanistan for that matter, was little more than an occasional literary motif: Tagore's short story 'Kabuliwalla' and Iqbal's hortatory poetry urging the Afghan people to awaken and arise, 'O Ghafil Afghan' (O Unmindful Afghan, that my grandfather had helped me memorise one long-ago summer holiday):

Rumi badle, Shaami badle, badla Hindustan
Tu bhi ai farzand-e Kohistan apni khudi pehchan
O ghafil Afghan, Apni khudi pehchan!

Rome has changed so has Syria and India
So must you, O dweller of the land of mountains
Know yourself, O unmindful Afghan, know yourself!

More than any other Urdu poet, Iqbal has written about the Afghan with empathy and admiration going so far as to dedicate his collection *Payaam-e Mashriq* to the King of

Afghanistan. Instead of the 'graveyard of empire' that western historians have generally seen Afghanistan as, for Iqbal it was the beating heart of Asia, the cradle of civilizations. In 1933, at the invitation of the Afghan government, Allama Iqbal had visited Afghanistan accompanied by Maulana Syed Sulaiman Nadvi (who later wrote a travelogue entitled *Sair-i- Afghanistan* detailing this trip) and Sir Ross Masood (the grandson of Sir Syed Ahmad Khan, the founder of the university at Aligarh who had accompanied Iqbal).

In more recent times, there have been poets such as Zehra Nigah writing about the fate of girls denied entry into schools under the Taliban in poems such as *Kahani Gul Zamina ki* (The Story of Gul Zamina):

Gul Zamina!
Suno
Toda-e-ḳhaak par
Apni konpal si ungli se
Kya likh rahi ho?

Gul Zamina ne sharbat bhari aankhein oopar uthaain aur kahne lagii:
'Kuchh hii din qabl
Ye toda-e-ḳhaak hii mera school thha
Main ne Allah ka naam
Ya Hafizo
Uss ki deewar par likh diya thha
Mere kaaġhaz, qalam aur kitabein
Mere kunbe ke humrah sab mit chuke hain

'Main yahan roz aati huun
Apni yaadon ke baste se
Pichhle sabaq dhundhti huun
Safha-e-ḳhaak par unn ko likhti huun
Aur laut jaati huun

Meri qismat mein padhna nahin hai
Na ho!
Mera amoḳhta
Mera likhna to jaari rahe'

Gul Zamina!
Listen
What are you writing
With your bud-like finger
On this heap of dirt?

Gul Zamina raised her hazel eyes
And said:
'Just a few days ago
This heap of dirt was my school
I had written the name of Allah
Ya Hafiz
On its wall
My books, pens and papers
Are all gone
Like my companions
From my clan

'I come here everyday
I search for past lessons
In the satchel of my memories
I write them on the pages of dirt
And go back
So what if I am not destined to read
Let it be so!
At least I can continue
To revise what I was taught'

Zehra Nigah has also written about the plight of child soldiers forced to bear arms as their world is systematically destroyed by surgical strikes of American remote-controlled drones in lyrical, pathos-driven yet politically astute poems such as 'Qissa Gul Badhshah ka' (The Story of Gul Badshah):

Log kahte hain ye amn ki jang hai
Amn ki jang mein hamla-aavar
Sirf bachchon ko be-dast-o-paa chhorhte hain
Unn ko bhooka nahin chhorhte
Aaḳhir insaaniyat bhi koi cheez hai

People say this is a War of Peace
And in a War of Peace the attackers
Simply leave the children without hands and feet
They don't leave them hungry
After all, there is such a thing as humanity

There have been other references to Afghans in Urdu poetry and popular culture, a sentiment best expressed in this humorous ditty by Hari Chand Akhtar:

Kaha Kabul chale jaen, kaha Kabul chale jaao
Kaha Afġhan ka dar hai, kaha Afġhan to hoga

I said: I will go to Kabul; he said: Yes, go to Kabul
I said: but I am scared of the Afghan; he said: Yes, the Afghan'll be there

In 2008, there were signs of a return to some sort of normalcy; an angered spring, bruised by the blight of the Mujahideen, could be coaxed to bud and blossom. Or, so it seemed then. Over a decade later, with the Taliban having grown in strength, one worries ever more. Once again, one is reminded of Iqbal, who for all his flawed political ideology, had warned:

Ashia yak paikar aab-o-gil ast
Millat Afghan dar aan paikar dil ast
Az fasaad aao fasaad Ashia
Az kushaad aao kushaad Ashia

The continent of Asia is an embodiment of water and clay
The Afghan nation is the heart in that body
Chaos in Afghanistan shall disturb all of Asia
Peace in Afghanistan shall guarantee peace in Asia

In a lighter vein, Kaleem Qaiser Balrampuri alludes to the devastation wrought upon poor benighted Afghanistan in this seemingly humorous verse but one that reflects the trampling of a land and its people for centuries:

Iss ko tum barbaad na karnaa
Dil Afghanistan nahiin hai

Do not destroy it
My heart is not Afghanistan

62. Iran and the Politics of Hijab Burning

Many years ago, on a visit to Tehran, I had chafed against the mandatory wearing of the head scarf and a long coat-like garment up to my knees; just as I did against the compulsory wearing of a head covering and a full-length abaya on subsequent visits to Saudi Arabia. I believe the wearing, or not wearing of one or both, neither adds nor detracts from my being a Muslim. I *know* I *am* one and save for Allah no one else has the right to judge me and find me wanting in my *imaan* (belief).

In India one has been vehemently opposed to the state stepping in and telling women what they cannot wear and, in the instance of the state of Karnataka, expressly forbidding girls from wearing hijab to school when they clearly wish to.* Yet, one finds oneself rejoicing at the defiant hijab burning and applauding the bravery of Iranian women in the face of a brutal, repressive state machinery. On the face of it, this duality is cause for some disquiet till one reaches the heart of the matter. As a practicing Muslim woman who does not

*https://www.scobserver.in/journal/karnataka-hijab-ban-timeline/

wear the hijab and who finds the all-enveloping version of it, such as the chaadar or burqa, deeply offensive as a tool of segregation and othering, the only way I can, in all honesty, explain my duality is by insisting on that bugbear of all peoples' protests: the right to freedom of personal choice. Essentially, what happened in Iran and the reaction of some of us in India to what happened in Karnataka are two sides of the same coin. What lies at the heart of both is men telling women what they can, or cannot,wear.

Seeing the protests in Iran as a challenge to religion would be as erroneous as seeing the protests against the banning of hijab in Karnataka as a challenge to the state. I believe both are protests against authoritarianism, toxic masculinity, and deeply ingrained patriarchy. In cutting off their hair or burning their hijab, Iranian women took on the might of an authoritarian state that has been telling them for nearly half a century not just to cover their head and wear loose, ill-fitting clothes but precisely how to do so. The Kurdish woman, Mahsa Amini, who allegedly died in police custody in September 2022, apparently died because she was wearing her head-scarf 'incorrectly' and needed to be taken, by force, to a 're-education centre' for lessons in modesty.*

In the nation-wide protests that followed over 30 people died and hundreds were injured in a brutal police crackdown across Iran. International observers viewed this, dubbed as 'Iran's George Floyd moment', being as much a women's movement as a civil rights protest insofar as 22-year old Amini's death becamea tipping point. The scale and extent of these protests, and the courage and defiance needed for public demonstrations in the face of severe suppression, indicate what may have started as protests against women-centric violence subsequently

---

*https://www.nbcnews.com/news/world/iran-blame-violence-killed-mahsa-amini-un-finds-rcna142504

turned into protests against a decades-old systemic abuse of human rights.

What we saw unfolding before our eyes were two scenarios: In Karnataka, a 'reformist' or 'secular' impulse of a 'progressive' state bent upon removing the outward symbols of backwardness from an already beleaguered minority that finds itself pushed into a corner by vigilante mobs. And in Iran an Islamic republic, bolstered by the might of state apparatus, bent upon enforcing what it considers its version of righteous conduct especially on women with all the brutality and power at its command. The impulse behind both was men controlling women. The mob of boys who heckled and bullied a lone hijab-clad girl in Karnataka were not propelled by a reformist zeal or compassion for an oppressed girl from a minority community who had been 'brainwashed' by her 'regressive' family; it was a muscular majoritarianism at its worst. By the same token, the moral police in Iran, with the poetic-sounding name *Gasht-e Ershad* literally meaning 'guidance patrols' were certainly not motivated by 'guidance'. Both were classic instances of over-reach and a blind, dogged refusal to take into account the concept of choice. The girls in the Dakshin Karnataka school want to wear a hijab. The protesting Iranian women don't. Ideally, it should be left to them but such is the politics and polemics of the hijab that everyone has a view. Let us see how the poet sees the hijab.

Literally meaning 'veil', 'curtain', 'modesty', 'bashfulness', the traditional Urdu poet used it alongside *husn* (beauty), *ishq* (love), *haya* (modesty) such as this sher by the last Mughal emperor Bahadurshah Zafar:

Kaii roz mein aaj woh mehr-liqa hua mere jo saamne jalva-numa
Mujhes abr-o-qaraar zara na raha ussey paas-e-hijab-o-hayana raha

After several days when my beloved appeared before me in all her splendour
I couldn't contain myself and she had no regard for modesty or coyness

Or this by Dagh Dehelvi:

Saath shokhii ke kuchh hijab bhi hai
Is ada ka kahiin jawaab bhi hai

There's coquetry with the hijab too
Can there be a match for such style

And this by Majaz:

Husn ko be-hijab hona thha
Shauq ko kaamyaab hona thha

Beauty had to be unveiled one day
Desire had to be successful one day

The hijab of the male Urdu poets' imagination is a far cry from the way many women see it: as an instrument of confinement, isolation, segregation and, by extension, discrimination. A feminist poet such as Fahmida Riaz views the hijab entirely differently from the traditional male Urdu poets in a poem entitled 'Chaadar aur Chaar Diwari' (The Veil and the Four Walls):

Huzoor main iss siyah chaadar ka kya karungi
Ye aap kyun mujh ko baḳhshte hain ba-sad inayat
Na sog mein hoon ki uss ko odhuun
Gham-o-alam ḳhalq ko dikhaoon
Na rog hoon main ki is ki tareekiyon mein ḳhiffat se doob jaoon
Na main gunahgar hoon na mujrim
Ki iss syahi ki mehr apni jabeen pe har haal mein lagaaoon…

Sir, what shall I do with this black chaadar
Why are you gifting it to me as a reward
I am not in mourning that I should wrap myself in it
To show my grief to the world
Nor am I suffering from a secret disease that I should drown in its darkness
I am neither a sinner nor a criminal;
That I must stamp my forehead with its blackness at all times

Coming back to Iran, many view the hijab as a legacy of the Shah's rapid (some feel too rapid) modernisation foisted upon a people not ready for it. On 8 January 1936, Reza Shah issued a decree known as 'Kashf-e Hijab' banning all forms of veilingsuch as the head scarf and chaadar. The ban was only enforced for a period of five years (1936-1941), however this piece of women's clothing remained as a fundamental problem of Iranian politics over the decades. Intrinsically linked to the hijab has been women's position in society, the ways in which the state defines and describes their place. After Ayatollah Khomeini made the hijab compulsory in the workplace in 1979, Iranian women took to the streets to protest and were violently attacked by pro-Revolution forces that would later morph into the notorious morality police that arrested Mahsa Amini in 2022.

Forugh Farrokhzad (1934-1967) is possibly the best known modern woman poet from Iran. Widely available through multiple translations in many languages, Farrokhzad's poetry—about desire, pain, courage, freedom—was banned in Iran after the Islamic Revolution; later, it was heavily censored, hidden, vilified but never went out of currency. Generations of Iranians continue to read her. Fragments from her poems pop up in placards during protest marches by Iranians in different parts of the world. The Pakistani poet Fahmida Riaz translated a selection of her poems from Farsi into Urdu in a collection entitled *Khule Dareeche Se* (Through the Open Window). Here is a fragment from 'Chaabi ki Gudiya' (The Wind-up Doll translated by Sholeh Wolpe in English and Fahmida Riaz in Urdu); even twice removed from the original Farsi it carries a scathing indictment of what men have done to women:

Sheeshe ki aankhon se iss duniya ko dekh sakti hai
Salaha eik makhmali dabbe mein
Kaahi-zada badan ke saath
Panniyon aur jhaalaron ke dher mein khwaabeedah rah sakti hai
Aur barzah dasti ki har chutki par
Be-sabab cheekh sakti hai
Aah, main bahut khush-qismat hoon

Like a wind-up doll one can look out
at the world through glass eyes,
spend years inside a felt box,
body stuffed with straw,
wrapped in layers of dainty lace.
With every salacious squeeze of one's hand,
for no reason one can cry:
Ah, how blessed, how happy I am!

Another Urdu poet from Pakistan, Parveen Shakir—known more for her feminine rather than overtly feminist poetry—wrote a poem entitled 'Forugh Farrokhzad ke Naam' (To Forugh Farrrokhzad) addressed to the powers-that-be who decide the fate of women with these blistering opening lines:

Musahib-e-shah se kaho ki
Faqih-e-aazam bhi aaj tasdeeq kar gaye hain
Ki fasl phir se gunahgaaron ki pak gayi hai...

Tell the emperor's favourite
That the religious scholars have today affirmed
That the crop of sinners is ripe for harvesting

The poem then goes to say that all the executioners in the land are ready and waiting, for one signal: when and where are hands and tongues to be chopped? Where are the doors to gainful employment to be closed? Where is the hunger for comforts to be killed? Where will men get a free license to wrongly accuse women of adultery? Where will they be stoned? Where will little girls be married off to men four times their age? All this must be indicated clearly but verbally, not in writing, or else it can create legal problems!

63. Bangladesh: When Spring Has Come to the Garden

Curled in the end lies a beginning and in every beginning lies the end of something old. Never is this truer than in the case of countries that are born after prolonged periods of parturition or when they are hived out of old nation states after much blood has been shed. The area that now constitutes Bangladesh has the unique distinction of having not one but three partums: the first in 1905 when Bengal was spliced into East and West Bengal, then in 1947 when fresh borders were drawn on the Indian sub-continent and the new wing of a new nation state called East Pakistan came into being, and the third in 1971 as Bangladesh was to be its final coming, an assertion of a proud new identity.

Since the frame of reference for this anthology is Urdu, that too specifically Urdu poetry, let us probe the intersection of literature and history to look at real historical events that led to the creation of Bangladesh, to probe the ways in which the Urdu poet attempted—sometimes partially, sometimes exhaustively—to capture the moments and memories of those days and months that led to the creation of Bangladesh. Our interest is, also, in those who attempt to look back with the benefit of hindsight and try to make sense of the madness and mayhem that took many by surprise. Some experienced it at first hand; others attempted to enter this great tragedy by way of empathy and imagination. All of these experiences and, by extension, their expression in creative writing are valid and worthy of our interest.

In the early years there was a small, almost minuscule, body of work in Urdu by Pakistani writers on the disintegration of Pakistan. Except for a handful of prose writers such as Intizar Husain and Masood Ashar, there was a tacit silence on the subject of what went wrong with the two-nation theory. The poet Faiz Ahmad Faiz was another exception to the rule that said since people from West Pakistan heard no evil, saw no evil, they could not, therefore, claim to bear witness to the evil that had been festering in the hearts of men who were once brothers. Written in 1974 Faiz's now-iconic poem 'Dhaka se Waapsi Par' (Upon Returning from Dhaka) is an acknowledgment of being a 'stranger amidst friends'; sung hauntingly by Nayyara Noor it is often disengaged from its essentially political mooring and, given its wording, often taken erroneously to be a purely romantic ghazal:

Hum ke thhehre ajnabi itni mudaraton ke baad
Phir banenge aashna kitni mulaqaton ke baad

We who have remained strangers after so many hospitalities
After how many meetings will we become acquaintances

Naushad Noori, an Urdu poet whose family had emigrated from India, wrote a poem entitled 'Mohenjodaro' (alluded to in the very first essay) urging people to hold on to their folk traditions. Written in 1952, this poem was published in *Afkaar* (Reflections) from Karachi and seems prescient, pointing towards the portents of disaster waiting to unfurl in the raging storm of language chauvinism:

Mere shehr ke rehne walon
Apni Pothi apni Gita
Apni lok kathain
Apni geeti mala
Apna apna harf-e-tahajji
Apni apni boli bhasha
Patte pathar post papyrus
Taambe lohe par likh rakhna
Wahi vaba phir phooti hai
Wahi bala phir tooti hai

O people of my city
Hold on to your Pothi and Gita
Your folk tales and fables
Your songs and ballads
Yours letters of the alphabet
Your languages and dialects
Inscribe them on copper and iron
And on leaves, stones, skin and papyrus

The creation of Bangladesh brought fresh perils for the Urdu-speakers who identified themselves as Bengali. Some found themselves living in ghettoes and camps, such as the notorious Geneva Camp in Dhaka, as refugees in their own land. Perceived as collaborators with the Pakistani state during the War of Liberation, shunned and despised by Bengalis who considered them traitors, many acquired an inferiority complex as a result of having to perforce live in a camp. Referred to disparagingly as 'Biharis' or 'stranded Pakistanis', their writings especially the Urdu poetry that came out of these camps, deserves to be studied for its complex skein of pragmatism and nostalgia, pathos and optimism, the pull of the past and the lure of the future.

Coming to poetry on the creation of Bangladesh, there's Zehra Nigah's 'Bhejo Nabi Ji Rehmatein' (Send Blessings Upon Us, O Prophet Ji), which begins with a moving depiction of a scene of pastoral domesticity that is rudely disrupted by an invasive presence, referring obliquely to the large-scale atrocities committed against women by the armed forces. Interestingly, the poem carries no specific reference either to the act of rape or the context and geographical location. Zehra Nigah has alluded to this in several conversations and interviews and thus the poem's context has been revealed:

Chadar jo sar se khinch gai
Quran ka chahra dhak gaya
Roti tawey per jal gayi
Handi ubal ker rah gayi
Bachchey ka jhoola gir parha
Tota pharhak kar cheekh utha
'Bhejo nabi ji rahmatein
Aal-e-nabi ka wasta'
Par koi aaya hi nahi!

The veil was ripped off her head
The face of the Quran was covered
The roti burnt on the pan
The pot on the fire boiled over
The baby fell from the hammock
The parrot cried out in agony:
'Send mercies upon us, O Prophet ji
I beseech you in the name of your kin!'
But no one came.

Afzal Ahmed Syed's traumatic experiences in 1971 limn his love for East Pakistan in 'Humey Bhool Jaana Chaiye' (We Should Forget). While it contains no explicit reference to the creation of Bangladesh, this poem, like much of Syed's poetry, circles back to his years in East Pakistan. Despite his sympathy for the Bangla speaking people and their right to a country of their own, he suffered terribly in the last years of his stay which included being labeled an 'internal sympathiser' causing him to flee the new country and make his home in Karachi:

Hamein bhool jaana chaahiye
Usss malbe se
Jis ka naam dil hai
Kisi ko zinda nikaala ja sakta hai
Hamein kuchh lafzon ko bilkul bhool jaana chaahiye
Maslan
Bani-nau-e-insaan

We should forget that debris
Whose name is Heart
From which no one can be pulled out alive
And there are some words that we should completely forget
Such as
Humanity

Naseer Turabi's dirge-like ghazal written immediately after the Fall of Dhaka has the knee-jerk Pakistani sorrow over a severed limb with no real acknowledgement of when and how the sepsis had set in. This ghazal was the definitive lament for Bangladesh long before it was used as the title track for a well-received Pakistani television drama series and gained immense popularity as sung by Qurratulain Baloch. Tarabi was in his office when he heard the news of the Fall of Dhaka on 16 December 1971 and wrote this ghazal with tears streaming down his face, as he has said in an online interview:

Woh humsafar thha magar uss se hum-navaaii na thhi
Ki dhoop chhaanv ka aalam raha judaaii na thhi

He was a fellow-traveler but he and I were never compatible
It was always sun and shade between us, never a severance

From India, there's Zia Sarhadi extending support while the war of independence is still raging, writing 'Bangladesh ki Kahani Bangaladesh ki Zubaani' (The Story of Bangladesh in Its Own Words):

Sisakti raat ka dhaancha badalne waala hai
Sahar qareeb hai sooraj nikalne wala hai

The skeleton of the sobbing night is about to change
The dawn is nigh the sun is about to come out

Jan Nisar Akhtar's poem 'Fateh Bangla' (The Bangla Victory) echoes all the popular Indian sentiments of solidarity, fellowship and a big-brotherly affection:

Arz-e Bangla tujhe kal aur haseen banna hai
Kitne taaron se sajegii teri gesu jaane
Kal tere baagh mein jhoomeingii bahaarein kya kya
Hum talak aaye na aaye teri khushbu jaane
Hum tujhe yaad rahein ya na rahein, tu jaane

Dear Bangla! You have to become yet more beautiful
Countless stars shall embellish your hair in the years ahead
Many, many springs shall come to dance in your garden
Who knows whether your fragrance will reach us or not
Whether you remember us or not, only you will know!

Here is Kaifi Azmi describing this new country thus:

Main koi mulk nahin hoon ke jala dogey mujhe
Koi deewar nahin hoon ke gira dogey mujhe
Koi sarhad bhi nahin hoon ke mita dogey mujhe

I am not a country that you can burn
I am not a wall that you can pull down
I am not a boundary that you can blur

And Maikash Akbarabadi welcoming the birth of a new nation:

Kya kiya khoon-e-shaheedaan-e-watan ka poocho
Fasl-e-gul baagh mein aayi huyi lagti hai mujhe

Ask what the blood of the martyrs has done for the country
The season of flowers seems to have arrived in the garden

64. The Great War and its Reflection in Urdu Poetry

❧

The First World War, or the Great War as it is also called, raged across Europe and several war arenas scattered across the world from 28 July 1914 to 11 November 1918. These four years saw the service of 1.3 million Indians, of whom 74,000 never made it back home. For their families, the war was something they couldn't quite understand. Given the large-scale Indian involvement in a war that the majority of Indians could not fully comprehend, we shall attempt to look at its reflection in the mirror of Indian literature to see how the poet, the publicist and the writer viewed the momentous years of the *Jang-e Azeem* as the Great War came to be called.

Several poets, lost in the veils of time and virtually unknown today, made interventions as did the more famous ones who continue to be well known though possibly not in the context of what they had to say about World War I. Presented below is a sampling of the socially-conscious, politically-aware message of the poets of the times. Not all of these poets are well-known today, nor is their poetry of a high caliber; yet fragments of their work have been included here simply to illustrate how the poet had his finger to the pulse of his age and circumstance.

Let us begin with Shibli Nomani and his wryly mocking 'Jang-e Europe aur Hindustani' (The War in Europe and Indians) which we shall quote from in its entirety:

Ek German ne mujh se kaha az rah-e ghuroor
'Asaan nahi hai fatah to dushwar bhi nahin
Bartania ki fauj hai dus lakh se bhi kum
Aur iss pe lutf yeh hai ke tayyar bhi nahin
Baquii raha France to woh rind-e lam yazal
Aain shanaas-e shewa-e paikaar bhi nahin'
Maine kaha ghalat hai tera dawa-e ghuroor
Diwana to nahi hai tu hoshiyar bhi nahin
Hum log ahl-e Hind hain German se dus guneh
Tujhko tameez-e andak-o bisiar bhi nahin
Sunta raha woh ghaur se mera kalaam aur
Phir woh kaha jo laiq-e izhaar bhi nahin
'Iss saadgi pe kaun na mar jaaye ai Khuda
Larhte hain aur haath mein talwar bhi nahin!'

Consumed with pride, a German said to me:
'Victory is not easy but it isn't impossible either
The army of Britannia is less than ten lakh
And not even prepared on top of that
As for France, they are a bunch of drunks
And not even familiar with the art of warfare'
I said your arrogant claim is all wrong
If not mad you are certainly not wise
We the people of Hind are ten times the Germans
Cleary you cannot tell big from small
He listened carefully to what I had to say
Then he said something that can't be described
'By God, anyone will lay down their life for such simplicity

You are willing to fight but without even a sword in your hand!'

That the Urdu poet was not content with mere high-flying rhetoric and was rooted—and aware—of immediate contemporary realities becomes evident when Brij Narain Chakbast declares in his 'Watan ka Raag' (The Song of the Homeland):

Zameen-e-Hind ki rutba mein arsh-e-aala hai
Yeh Home Rule ki ummeed ka ujala hai
Mrs Besant ne iss aarzu ko paala hai
Faqir qaum ke hain aur ye raag maala hai
Talab fuzool hai kante ki phool ke badle
Na lein bahisht bhi hum Home Rule ke badle

The land of Hind is higher in rank than the highest skies
All because of the light of hope brought forth by Home Rule
This hope has been nurtured by Mrs Besant
I am a mendicant of this land and this is my song
It's futile to wish for the thorn instead of the flower
We shall not accept even paradise instead of Home Rule

Similarly, Hasrat Mohani, in a poem titled 'Montagu Reforms', is scathing about the so-called reforms that were given as sops to gullible Indians during the war years, which were mere *kaagaz ke phool* (paper flowers) with no *khushboo* (fragrance) even for name's sake. The poem ends with a fervent plea that the people of Hind should not be taken in by the sorcery of the reforms:

Ai Hindi saada dil khabardar
Hargiz na chale tujh pe jadu
Kya paayega khaak phir jab inse
Iss waqt bhi kuchh na le saka tu

O simple people of Hind beware
Don't let this sorcery work on you
If you couldn't couldn't take anything from them now
You're not likely to get anything at all again

Josh Malihabadi, who acquired his moniker of the *shair-e-inquilab* or the 'revolutionary poet' during the war period, talks with vim and vigour of the revolution that is nigh, a revolution that will shake the foundations of the British empire in his 'Shikast-e Zindaan ka Khwaab' (The Dream of a Defeated Prison):

Kya Hind ka zindaan kaanp raha hai goonj rahi hain takbeerein
Uktaae hain shayad kuchh qaidi aur torh rahe hain zanjeerein
Deewaron ke neeche aa aa kar yuun jama hue hain zindaani

How the prison of Hind is trembling and the cries of God's greatness are echoing
Perhaps some prisoners have got fed up and are breaking their chains
The prisoners have gathered beneath the walls of the prisons

The great visionary poet Iqbal, who is at his most active, most powerful during these years, does not make direct references to actual events in the war arena; nevertheless, he is asking Indians to be careful, to heed the signs in 'Tasveer-e Dard' (A Picture of Pain):

Watan ki fikr kar naadaan musibat aane waali hai
Tiri barbaadiyon ke mashvare hain asmanon mein

Worry for your homeland, O innocents, trouble is brewing
The portents of disaster awaiting you are written in the skies

Adopting a fake admiring tone, Ahmaq Phaphoondvi seems to be praising the sharpness of the British brain in *Angrezi Zehn ki Tezi* (The Cleverness of the English Mind) when he's actually warning his readers of the perils of being divided while the British lord over them:

Kis tarah bapa hoon hangama aapas mein ho kyun kar khuna-rezi
Hai khatam unhein schemon main Angrezi zehn ki sab tezi
Ye qatl-o khoon ye jung-o jadal, ye zor-o sitam ye bajuz-o hasad
Baquii hii raheinge mulk mein sab, baqui hai agar raj Angrezi

Look at the turmoil and the bloodshed among our people
The cleverness of the English mind is used up in all such schemes
This murder 'n mayhem, wars 'n battles, cruelties 'n malice
All this will continue in the country if the rule of the English continues

Zafar Ali Khan sounds an early, and as it turns out in the face of the British going back on their promise of self-governance made during the war years, entirely premature bugle of freedom. While warning his fellow Indians to change with the changing winds that are blowing across the country as the war drags to an end, he's also pointing our attention to the 'Toadies', a dreaded word for the subservient Indians who will gladly accept any crumbs by way of reforms in his poem 'Azaadi ka Bigul' (The Bugle of Freedom):

Bartania ki meiz se kuchh reze gire hain
Ai toadiyon chunne tum innhe pet ke bal jao

Some crumbs have fallen from the table of Britannia
O Toadies, go crawling on your bellies to pick them

Finally, there's Agha Hashar Kashmiri who, in a sarcastic ode to Europe called 'Shukriya Europe', thanks it for turning the world into a *matamkhana* (mourning chamber), and for having successfully transformed the east into an example of hell.

Utth raha hai shor gham khakistar paamaal se
Keh raha hai Asia ro kar zabaan-e haal se
Bar mazaar-e ma gharibaan ne chiraghe ne gule
Ne pare parwane sozon ne sada-e bulbule

A shout is rising from the dust of the downtrodden
Asia is crying out and telling the world at large
On my poor grave there are neither lamps nor flowers
And not the wing of the moth or the sad song of the nightingale

65. Jallianwala Bagh: A Stain on Hindostan

Writers and poets have always taken note of history. Sometimes, when history is exceptionally brutal and bloody, the poet may fall silent but the prose writer is compelled to pick up his pen, and sometimes it is the other way round. Some events shake the conscience of thinking men and women the world over, send seismic tremors across the length and breadth of a nation, unspool events of unforeseen consequences and find reflection not only in the literature of their age but for generations to come. The cold-blooded massacre at Jallianwala Bagh on 13 April 1919 is one such incident. It marked a defining moment in the history of modern India. It is significant from a purely literary perspective too: the spurt in overtly political activities and a growing political consciousness that began to find reflection in Indian literature can be traced directly to it.

While a great deal of scholarly work has been done on the Jallianwala Bagh incident by professional historians, its reflection in Indian literature in the different *bhashas* (languages) and in Urdu in particular has been overlooked.

An incident that stirred the conscience of millions, one that had far-reaching implications for the national freedom struggle, that made British colonial interests in India morally untenable, found its way through pen and paper to reach the nooks and crannies of the popular imagination filtered through the mind of the creative writer. Let us see how.

To begin with, there is Saadat Hasan Manto who chronicled his age with all its darkness and imperfections and looked at people and events with a consciousness uncoloured by notions of nationalism, religion, morality, least of all sentimentality. Manto's take on contemporary politics in his short story '1919 ka Ek Din' (A Day in 1919) is a recasting of the terrible slaughter visited upon the poor benighted city of Amritsar (Manto, incidentally, was from this city) in the wake of the Jallianwala Bagh. Drawing upon popular accounts of the French Revolution which ascribe the first bullet fired in the Revolution hitting a prostitute, here Manto makes a 'hero' out of the good-for-nothing brother of the city's two most famous prostitutes. Remembering those days in this story written sometime in the late 1930s, he writes about real historical events with the deftness of a master storyteller:

> It is about those days in 1919, Brother, when agitations against the Rowlatt Act had sprung up all across the Punjab. I am talking about Amritsar. Sir Michael O'Dwyer had forbidden Mahatma Gandhi from entering the Punjab under the Defence of India Rules. Gandhi ji was on his way when he had been stopped near Palwal, arrested and sent back to Bombay. As far as I can understand, Brother, had the English not committed this grave mistake, the massacre at Jallianwala Bagh, which is the bloodiest chapter in the history of British rule in India, would never have occurred.

Abdullah Hussein's elegantly sprawling novel, *Udaas Naslein* (translated by the author himself as The Weary Generations) cuts a long swathe from the years 1913 till 1947; his protagonist Naim visits the Jallianwala Bagh as part of a citizens' inquiry committee and meets an old fisherman who tells him an incredible tale: it is he, the hunch-backed old fisherman, who inadvertently sets in motion a chain of events leading to the bloodbath. He also claims to have witnessed the murder of the Europeans on the city streets and the assault on the missionary woman (Marcella Sherwood); however, his testimony of a *gora* (white) officer in uniform who is hit by his fish and opens firing upon the crowd is a classic instance of magic realism, one that is all the more remarkable since it predates Salman Rushdie and his *Midnight's Children*!

An active member of the powerful literary grouping, the Progressive Writers' Association and a leading light among the 'Bombay Progressives', Khwaja Ahmad Abbas had a remarkable felicity for blending fact with fiction and writing stories based on real-life incidents. His *Inquilab*, with its sub-title 'First Great Novel about the Indian Revolution', is a semi-autobiographical novel of a young man's tryst with his destiny as he and his country move towards independence. Painting virtually a portrait gallery of the who's who of all the important political leaders of his age, Abbas recasts the story of the national freedom struggle through the eyes of Anwar, his alter-ego, and his friend Ratan.

Krishan Chandar's essay-like short story 'Amritsar: Before Independence, and After Independence' (*Amritsar: Azadi se Pehle, Azadi ke Baad*) contains moving accounts of two young men, not friends but neighbours: Siddiq and Om Prakash, who risk their lives for each other as bullets whizz past and death is as sudden as it is random. At moments such as this, bravery does not lie in either facing the bullets or surviving them; true bravery lies in facing death as the consequence of deliberate, wilful defiance. In Krishan Chandar's telling, the real heroes of the story are the valiant women of Amritsar: Begum, Zainab, Paro and Sham Kaur who defy General Dyer's completely illegal and humiliating 'crawling order' whereby anyone who wishes to walk down the alley where the Englishwoman, Marcella Sherwood, had been attacked by a mob, would have to crawl on their belly. All four women paid with their lives while resisting the order and became martyrs.

Dyer's infamous 'crawling order' is also the subject of Ghulam Abbas's short story 'Raingneywale' (Those Who Crawled). Born in Amritsar, Abbas would have been a mere lad of 10 ten years of age at the time of the incident but surely anyone with any links to the city would have carried the effect of that trauma in some way or to some degree. A hundred years later the humiliation that a depraved mind can heap upon those it considers inferior beings continues to horrify. At the same time, stories such as 'Those Who Crawled' need to be read and revisited so that we learn from the misdeeds of the past.

There was a time when poetry was considered the most suitable form for passing down history. Some of our greatest epics came to us in verse. There was a long lull when poetry was thought to be about the softer emotions of life, about love and romance and fantastical adventures in magical lands and realms of the imagination. With something as soul-stirring as the Jallianwala Bagh incident, the poets of the age were compelled to take note. In fact, 1919 marks a turning point in the literary history of India as poets in the different bhashas begin to take up newer, more immediate concerns like never before. No longer were the Urdu poets, in particular, content to sing of the *gul-o-bulbul* (the rose and the nightingale that were traditional motifs in conventional Urdu poetry) and *shama-parwana* (the moth and the candle as metaphors for love and the lover) or traipse around in the magic gardens of the *dastans* and *fasanas*.

This literary 'adventurism' required a new diction, and a new vocabulary. For these 'new age' poets language became a means, not an end of a creative exercise. No longer was it necessary to revive the debates on whether—or the extent to which—literature should reflect contemporary realities. Realism had crept into the poetry of even those who shied away from labels or chose not to belong to schools of thought.

While several poems were written in Urdu specifically on the massacre in Amritsar, some that deserve special mention are 'Jallianwala Bagh' by Muhammad Iqbal:

Har zair-e-chaman se kehti hai khaak-e-baagh
Ghafil naa reh jahan mein gadroon ki chaal se
Seencha gaya hai khoon-e-shaheedan se iska tukhm
Tu aansuon ka bukhl na kar iss nihaal se

The dust of this garden tells everyone who comes visiting
To not remain unmindful of the moving of the firmament
Its seed has been nourished with the blood of martyrs
Do not be miserly with your tears for this sapling

'Shikwa-e Saiyyad' (The Hunter's Complaint) by Tilok Chand Mahroom:

Naa tadapne ki ijazat hai naa faryaad kii hai
Ghut ke mar jaaoon ye marzi mere sayyad kii hai

Anguish is not permitted nor is protest allowed
My hunter has decreed that I should die quietly

'Mazalim-e Punjab' (The Tyrannies in the Punjab) by Zafar Ali Khan:

Maine Amritsar mein eik din apne khwaja se kaha
Pet ke bal reing leejiye bandaparwar aap bhi

One day I said to my Lord and master in Amritsar
You too begin to crawl on your belly, O benefactor

'East India Company ke Farzandon Se' (To the Children of the East Indian Company) by Josh Malihabad:

Zehn mein hoga ye taaza Hindiyon ka daaġh bhi?
Yaad to hoga tumhein Jallianwala Bagh bhi?

Surely you must recall that stain on Hindustan?
Surely you would remember Jallianwala Bagh?

And lastly 'Agar Seekhni ho Rehmat' (If You Wish to Learn Mercy) by Ahmaq Phaphoondvi. It gives a sense of the rising nationalistic consciousness that was a direct outcome of the barbaric action in the Punjab:

There is bloodshed in every direction and piles of corpses
Tyrants like Dyer and O'Dwyer rule in the manner of Changez
Shuddhi and Tableegh movements here, conch and calls there
Had these not been in our midst the British Rule would have been difficult

66. *Kaala Pani*: Across the Black Waters

The Andaman group of islands is a prized tourist destination today with lush greenery, the azure waters of the Bay of Bengal, beautiful vistas of sun and sand against a vanilla sky, and all the amenities of new age tourism. It seems hard to believe that a century ago this group of islands were referred to as Kaala Pani and for one to be sent across the 'black waters' was a fate worse than death for no one came here willingly, least of all on a pleasure trip. To be sentenced to imprisonment in the penal colony here, the furthest outpost of British India, was known to test the mettle of the sternest of souls causing many to do anything, even write mercy petitions to those very same powers-that-be that had, in the first place, ordered the exile.

Even a quick tour of the infamous Circular Jail in Port Blair is enough to give an inkling of the inhuman conditions of the poor souls who had been sent away to Kaala Pani. Though the prison complex we now know as the Cellular Jail was set up from 1896 to 1906, the Andaman Islands had been used to house criminals and political prisoners who had to be removed from civil society from the immediate aftermath of 1857, the First War of Independence. By the turn of the century more prisoners came to be deported here and soon a carefully calibrated system was in place: of control, capital punishment and calculated use of a captive workforce—be it for making ropes from coir fibre to pressing oil seeds to extract oil to hard physical labour for building the harbour, laying down roads and constructing the buildings of this bustling colonial outpost.

With the Independence struggle gaining momentum and large numbers of political activists being sent here, it was found that mere transportation across the seas and incarceration in a penal settlement on an island was not enough. Much thought went into the design of the solitary cells (hence the name 'cellular'), the spoke-like design of the long barracks converging at a central point with a watch tower, and the almost 'fine art' of torture and punishment. Public floggings at strategically-located lashing posts were routine as were hangings for the more recalcitrant among the prisoners. Such was the terror associated with its very name—*kaala pani* referring both to the religious injunction for staunch Hindus against travelling across the waters for it meant loss of caste and also as reference to the Sanskrit word *Kal* meaning Time/Death and used to mean the 'waters of death'—that soon it entered language and literature as myth and metaphor.

The Urdu poet alluded to it as a state of being marooned in unimaginably horrifying circumstances, as a living hell. That decades later the *saza* (punishment) of Kaala Pani continues to be used as a metaphor for being marooned on a hopeless island is evident from this sher by a modern poet such as Swapnil Tiwari:

Qaid huii hain aankhein khwaab jazeere par
Paa kar ek saza sii Kaale Pani ki

The eyes have been imprisoned on a dream island
Having been given a sentence like a Kaala Pani

And this somewhat simplistic one by Mukhtar Tonki:

Ranj-o-gham jitne hain un ko Kaala Pani bhej de
Ai Khudaa tu mere ghar mein shaadmaani bhej de

Send all manner of sorrows and despairs to Kaala Pani
O Lord, send nothing but happiness to my home

Here is Shad Lakhnawi playing with the tropes of punishment and exile, again, using the metaphor of the dreaded island penitentiary:

Zulf-e-siyah ke mujrim hain
Kaale paani bhijvaa do

I am a culprit of dark tresses
Have me sent to Kaala Pani

And Lala Madhav Ram Jauhar also picking on the idea of exile and banishment in this sher:

Iss balaa ko to Khuda jald kare shahr-badar
Kaale Pani ko ravaana shab-e-hijraan ho jaae

May God soon send this curse into banishment
May the night of our separation set off for Kaala Pani

But what of those who were actually sent to Kaala Pani and endured its debasements and indignities not to speak of its many tortures? Since the frame of reference for this volume is Urdu, we shall not mention the political prisoners who have left behind memoirs in other languages. Here we will only talk of the testimonies in Urdu. In prose there is the memoir of Maulana Mohammad Jafer Thanesari entitled *Kaala Pani: Tawareekh-e Ajeeb* (Kaala Pani: A Strange History). Sentenced in the Ambala Conspiracy Case of 1863, he spent 18 years in the Andamans. His account is remarkable for its descriptions of the living conditions, the interactions with other inmates, the complex system of punishment and 'reward'.

In poetry, there is the well-known instance of Maulana Fazl-e Haq Khairabadi (1797-1861). A poet, jurist, philosopher and theologian (also incidentally the great-great-grandfather of the Urdu poet and lyricist Javed Akhtar), he held the British guilty of unleashing terror upon the hapless Muslims after the Revolt of 1857. Having spent 22 months in captivity, he died in 1864 and is buried in Port Blair.

Like Maulana Fazl-e Haq Khairabadi, Munir Shikohabadi (1814-80), a poet too, was actively involved in the Uprising. Employed by the Nawab of Banda, he was arrested for his seditious activities and sent to the Andamans, where he wrote prolifically during his imprisonment in a long poem entitled 'Qaid se Najaat' (Liberation from Prison), he speaks of bidding farewell to his fellow-prisoners, his companions during the long incarceration and the hard labour, as he prepares to go back home where he will find a new life difficult to comprehend:

Bas-ki barson raha hoon zindaan mein
Bhooli qasr-e-sukhan ki memaari

Having lived in a prison for years
I have forgotten how to build the palace of poetry

And, finally, there is Vinayak Damodar Savarakar writing in Urdu in his prison diary, a copy of which is proudly displayed in the Cellular Jail museum; it is remarkable for its immaculate Urdu and its reference to Meraj, the journey the Prophet Muhammad (PBH) is said to have undertaken to the high heavens:

Abhi meraj ka kya zikr, yeh pehli hii manzil hai
Hazaaron manzilen karni hain tai hum ko kathin pehlay

Why talk of Meraj now, this is the first stage of the journey
We have to travel through thousands of difficult destinations

One doesn't know if this poem was written by him before, after or during his many mercy petitions to the English in which he described himself as a 'prodigal son' longing to return to the 'parental doors of the government'.

67. The Contrary, Comforting Space of the *Mai-Khana*

Given the puritanism and political correctness that has so overtaken the Urdu poet today, one looks back with a certain wistful nostalgia to the glorification of all manner of vices and sins and the abundant references to drinking, straying from the straight and narrow and the frequent slips into all forms of heresies and sacrilege. Questioning, probing, intent on investing new meanings into old, time-worn images and metaphors, the Urdu poet has traditionally enjoyed working within the time-honoured template of the ghazal and the compact brevity of the sher, reveling in the freedom of pouring new wine in old bottles. For instance, with each fresh catastrophe, the Urdu poet has evolved a vocabulary to express his angst, clothing his sorrow in a time-honoured repertoire of images and metaphors. Some favourite synonyms for the Beloved—*sitamgar, but, kafir, yaar*—began to be used mockingly for the British in the decades after 1857.

Of the many such time-worn images that can, with a bit of spit and polish, acquire new uses, my personal favourite has been the *mai-khana* or the *mai-kada*, meaning tavern, bar, inn or a place that serves *mai* or *sharaab* (wine) but used to mean many different things. It has remained the most enduring image of a forbidden space that is also, contrarily, welcoming and comforting. The contrariness or defiance of expectations, norms and rules of etiquette is best illustrated in this sher by Firakh Gorakhpuri:

Aaye thhe hanste khelte mai-khaane mein Firaaq
Jab pii chuke sharaab to sanjeeda ho gaye

We had come to the *mai-khana* in great spirits
Having drunk the wine we became somber

The *mai-kada*, literally meaning 'house of wine', can be a space where the pious and the good meet the impious who are, by extension, bad; the twain can meet in this volatile space that is brimful with possibilities. The *mai-khana* is also a place where one can meet a motley group of characters, people outside the safety net of friends and family and hence the colourful dramatis personae in a *mai-khana* also offer plenty of grist to the poet's mill. That the *mai-khana* is a cosmos outside the usual spaces of *shareef* (cultured) milieu is demonstrated in this sher by Bashir Badr:

Na tum hosh mein ho na hum hosh mein hain
Chalo mai-kade mein waheen baat hogi

Neither are you in your senses, nor am I
Let's go to the *mai-kada*; we will talk there

The *mai-khana* is also a place where subversive ideas are discussed, where rebellions are brewed, where plans are hatched, where dreams of revolts and uprisings dreamt, often at great cost. Kamal Siddiqui alludes to the heady potent brew that Life offers making the *mai-kada* not a physical space but a realm of ideas:

Zindagi naam isi mauj-e-mai-e-nab ka hai
Mai-kade se jo uthe daar-o-rasan tak pahunche

Life is the name of this pure, unmixed wine
That takes you from the bar to the gallows

The *mai-khana* comes with its own template of images such as the *saqi* (cup-bearer, or one who pours the wine), *rind* (drunkard or libertine), *mina* (decanter), *jaam*, *saaghar* or *paimana* (wine-goblet) in much the same way as the *masjid* (mosque) is a place associated with the *vaaiz* (preacher). Nobody presents this duality better than Ghalib, that old frequenter of the *mai-khana*:

Kahaan mai-ḳhane ka darwaza Ghalib aur kahaan vaaiz
Par itna jaante hain kal woh jaata thha ki hum nikle

There is the door to the tavern and then there is the preacher
But I do know that he was leaving as I was entering it yesterday

Look at the irreverence and a cocking of the snook in this sher by Sulaiman Ahmad Maani, one that we would be hard pressed to find in a contemporary poet constrained by the fear of outrage and hurt sensibilities:

Maani mai-khaane ko masjid se chale kahte huwe
Thodii tabdeeli ko ho aate hain sajda kar ke

Maani went towards the *mai-khana* from the mosque, saying
Let me go there for a prostration, for a change, and I'll be back

And the thankfulness that there is such a place as a tavern or else how long and tedious would be the journey of life for Abdul Hamid Adam:

Main mai-kade ki raah se ho kar nikal gaya
Warna safar hayat ka kaafi taveel thha

I took the route through the *mai-kada* and came out
Or else the journey of Life was quite a long one

This sher by Diwakar Rahi shows how the *mai-khana* can be a metaphor for anything one might want from life:

Ab to utni bhi mayassar nahin mai-ḳhane mein
Jitni hum chhorh diya karte thhe paimane mein

Now there isn't even enough to be found in a tavern
As much as we used to leave in the bottom of our goblet

As also this by Faiz Ahmad Faiz:

Mai-ḳhana salamat hai to hum surḳhi-e-mai se
Tazeen-e-dar-o-baam-e-haram karte raheinge

As long as the *mai-khana* is safe and secure we shall continue
To decorate the doors and walls of the mosque with the redness of wine

Like the *mai-khana* and its appropriation for multiple uses, there are several other words associated with *mai-noshi* (the enjoyment of wine), such as *bekhudi, suroor, khumar*, etc which have proudly been taken as *nom de plum* by generations of poets. Here Khumar Barabankvi plays on the binary of sin/repentance, indulgence/renunciation:

Guzre hain mai-kade se jo tauba ke baad hum
Kuchh duur aadatan bhi qadam dagmagae hain

When we went past the mai-kada after renunciation
Our steps faltered for a while out of sheer habit

Note the effrontery of Ibrahim Zauq, the poet laureate of Delhi and *ustaad* to the Mughal emperor Bahadur Shah Zafar, as he declares:

Zauq jo madrase ke bigde huwe hain mulla
Un ko mai-ḳhane mein le aao sanvar jaenge

Zauq bring all wayward mullahs from madrasas
To the *mai-khana*; they will all be reformed here

An effrontery that is also to be found in Kaleem Ajis, among the last of the greats in the modern generation:

Mai-kade ki taraf chala zahid
Subh ka bhula shaam ghar aaya

The devout went towards the mai-kada
Having lost his way in the morning he found it in the evening

But will there be another Qayem Chandpuri, a prominent 18th century poet and contemporary of Mir, who could say:

Koi din aage bhi zahid ajab zamana thha
Har ik mohalle ki masjid sharaab-ḳhana thha

Once, O devout, there used to be a strange time
Every mosque in every neighbourhood was a tavern

68. Badaun and the Curious Case of *Watan ki Mitti*

There was a time when the historic city of Badaun (also spelt as Budaun or pronounced Badayun), in the heart of the Rohilkhand region of Uttar Pradesh, was known for three things: *pirs*, poets and *peras*. The 13th-century Sufi saint Nizamuddin Auliya was born here and the two prominent dargahs known as Chhote Sarkar and Bade Sarkar drew thousands from far and wide. The *pera* made here—especially those at Mamman Khan Halwai's from sweetened milk that had been boiled till its golden brown, somewhat grainy residue could be compressed into discs and dusted with powdery sugar—drew its fair share of admirers in a '*pera* belt' girding the girth of western Uttar Pradesh. But it was the sufis, poets and men and women of letters, really, who had put this otherwise nondescript dusty little town on the map. It was once said, only partly in jest, that if you were to toss a pebble at a busy cross-section anywhere in this city, it would be sure to hit a poet—or two!

There was something about this little town beside the River Sot, a tributary of the Ganga that flows nearby, that sprouted *ilm-o adab* from its nooks and crannies. Ismat Chughtai, Jeelani Bano, Dilawar Figar, Ale Ahmad Suroor, Bekhud Badayuni, Ada Jafri, Fani Badayuni, Irfan Siddiqui, Shakeel Badayuni—the list of writers born here is long and illustrious. Far away from his *watan* (home), Irfan Siddiqui had lamented the loss of his ancestral city thus:

Badaun teri mitti se bichhad kar jee raha huun main
Nahin, ai jaan-e-man, bar-e-digar aisa nahin hoga

Separated from your soil, Badaun, I am living somehow
No, my dearest, this will not happen yet another time

Much like *adab* (literature), a syncretic culture too once blossomed in this soil nurtured by sufis and mystics. Just as Delhi came to be called *22 Khwaja ki Chaukhat* (The Threshold of the 22 Sufis), Badaun too had its many big and small shrines scattered across its many congested lanes earning it the moniker *Badaun Sharif* ('Noble Badaun') or even *Madina-e Auliya* ('the Madina of the Friends of God'). Mushafi Ghulam Hamadani was not being facetious when he said:

Qaatil tiri gali bhi Badaun se kam nahiin
Jis ke qadam qadam pe mazaar-e-shaheed hai

O my murderer, your alley is no less than a street of Badaun
On every step there is the shrine of a martyr

A continuously inhabited site, it was known as Vedamau in the *Mahabharata* and Buddhmau in Buddhist times which eventually got corrupted to Badayun. Captured by Qutb-ud-din Aibak in 1196, Badaun soon became an important outpost of the Delhi Sultanate. In 1223, Aibak's successor and son-in-law Shamsuddin Iltutmish built an imposing mosque crowned with a big central dome, now known as the Jama Masjid. Till Delhi's Jama Masjid was built, this was the largest congregational mosque in India. Iltutmish's son and heir Rukn-ud din Firuz and daughter Razia Sultan, who would go on to be the first woman to rule from Delhi, were both born in Badaun. By the 13th century, Badaun had emerged as an important centre of Islamic learning with sufis and students flocking to its many *madrassas* and *khanqahs*. Mystically inclined men from distant cities in Central Asia—from Farshor, Balkh, Sabzwar, Gilan, Hamadan—built their *aastana* (mystic's abode or hospice) here.

Delhi's best-loved Sufi, Hazrat Nizamuddin Auliya was born in Badaun in a modest home, his father Ahmad's father having migrated from Bukahra to Badaun. Hazrat Nizamuddin's father died when he was just five years old; his mother chose Badaun's most gifted teachers for her son's education. It was through a travelling musician who had been to both Multan and Ajodhan that the young Nizamuddn, then 12 years of age, heard of Baba Farid who was later to become his *pir* in the Chishti *silsila* going back to Khwaja Moinuddin Chishti. At 16 Nizamuddin travelled to Delhi with his mother and sister, making it his home; however, Badaun remained a revered city not just for his disciples but for all mystically inclined people. Hazrat Nizamuddin's best-known disciple, the poet-chronicler Amir Khusro declared the dust of Badaun to be better than the finest *surma* to cool the eyes.

The *Taj al-Maathir* (literally meaning 'a crown of glorious deeds', a history of the Delhi Sultanate) refers to Badaun as 'the mother of cities' and 'one of the important cities of the country of Hind'. By Balban's time, Badaun had emerged as an important garrison town with its Governor entrusted with the task of maintaining a large contingent of troops that could be easily, and quickly, sent to Delhi when the need arose. Badaun crops up repeatedly in *Baburnama* and *Akbarnama* as a city of eminence; in fact, several scholarly notes have been written in academic journals about the debate among translators over its correct spelling.

Today, Badaun's rich cultural history and Sufi past, as also its proximity to the power centre in Delhi, has been relegated to the ash-heap of history, rendered obsolete by the bugbear of electoral politics, worthy not even of a mention in oral histories and *qissa-kahani* of the garden variety. Muslims comprise 43.9% of the city's population, most being poor and disenfranchised, some working as mechanics, others involved in the *zari-zardozi* (embroidery with gold thread and tinsel) cottage industry with the writers, poets and mystics long having left its dusty alleys. Faring poorly in the BJP-SP-BSP tussle, Badaun's Muslims are inconsequential in the electoral math of modern India despite their size.

My mother's family hails from Badaun and much of my childhood was spent listening to fantastic stories about life in the two old neighbourhoods of Maulvi Tola and Sota Mohulla where the extended family had lived for generations. My grandparents, both true-blue Badayunis, had a fund of myths, legends, anecdotes to share—both thrilling and inspiring, in turns. Some were of the many *alims* and *maulvis* (learned men) in the family (hence the name Maulvi Tola) whose learning was so renowned that *jinns* (djinn or ethereal spirit) came to study with them in the guise of boys as well as the many *karamaat* (miracles) associated with the *buzurgs* and *auliyas* (respected elders and holy men) buried here. Some stories re-created for us city-bred children a lost world, a genteel Urdu-speaking milieu redolent with *tehzeeb*. Others recounted how a love for learning was virtually hard-wired in the DNA of Badaun-wallahs of yore: of mothers and aunts, many with no formal education, who could recite entire diwans (collected works of poetry), of the prodigious memory and voracious appetite for books and reading as though there was something in the very air of Badaun that made one fall in love with the literary arts.

I last visited Badaun for a family wedding when my

grandmother, Amma as we called her, was alive and well. Apart from the food and festivities, two incidents stand out clearly in my memory decades later: One, a visit to the family burial ground when Amma clung to the grave of a recently-departed aunt and wept. Watching her hugging that mound of moist earth (*kachchi matti*), I had a moment of epiphany: This is what *watan ki mitti* means! And second, when we went to look at the Jama Masjid and Amma, tired from all her exertions, happened to sit down at the *mimbar* (pulpit). A passing man, unused to seeing women in the mosque, attempted to reprimand her and Amma ticked him off roundly with her customary self-confidence: *Kahan likha hai ke hum yahan nahi baith saktey? Aur tum kaun ho*? ('Where does it say that I can't sit here? And who are you?') Calling out patriarchy seemed an admirable quality to my young impressionable mind, one I thought was eminently worth emulating. Equally strong was the impress of belonging: to a land that had been home to one's forebears for 800 years, to a soil that had taken generation after generation of one's *ajdaad* (ancestors) into its ample bosom to sleep the eternal sleep. As Badaun finds itself in the midst of a new controversy*, being billed an 'Ayodhya-in-the-making', I wonder what Amma would have made of the shrill cries to rewrite history.

---

*https://timesofindia.indiatimes.com/city/bareilly/hindu-outfit-claims-budaun-mosque-built-on-razed-temple/articleshow/93959423.cms

69. *Bangaal ka Jaadu*

That Bengal has long exercised a fascination for the collective Indian imagination is evident from several popular perceptions about the state that have found their way into literature and from there into everyday usage. In Urdu, especially in its poetry, there are numerous references to the magic of *Bangaal*, *Bangaal ka jaadu*, the fabled beauty of the women of *Bangaal* and their glorious long hair, *zulf-e-Bangaal* or *gesu-e-Bangaal* that is almost a metaphor for the typical Indian notion of beauty. Equally, there are references to the songs of Bengal—of Nazrul, Tagore and the nameless wandering Baul singers—from whom the Urdu poets claim they have learnt the warp and weft of weaving a poem.

Mirza Ghalib who set out on a journey from his home in Delhi to Calcutta, then the imperial capital, in an attempt to have his pension restored documented his experiences in letters to friends back home. While the pension was not restored, the four years that he took to travel to Calcutta and return to Delhi (November 1825-November 1829), were full of adventures and insights. Ghalib reached Calcutta in February 1927, a little over a year after leaving Delhi. Raja Sohan Lal helped him find comfortable living quarters in Mirza Ali Saudagar's haveli in Simla Bazar at a rent of Rs 10 a month. In the year-and-a-half that he lived in Calcutta, much of his time was taken up in meeting the colonial officials, attending mushairas, and taking in the sights and sounds of a city so different from his Dilli.

Ghalib was entranced by the printing press which was already quite popular and would come to Delhi only several years later. While in Calcutta Ghalib also benefitted from the translations of English classics being made freely and cheaply available through the recently established Fort William College. Being a port, a bigger city than Delhi and also the seat of the Empire, here Ghalib also had the occasion to observe several new innovations such as the wireless and the steam engine, each of which would leave a lasting impression upon him. In a letter, Ghalib went into raptures over the wines available in Calcutta, as well as the many succulent fruits, the lush greenery of the city, and the charms of the Bengali women. The mangoes of Bengal made an especial impression on the mango-loving poet; not all the fruits of *jannat* (heaven), he claimed, could erase the scent and flavour of the mangoes of Calcutta. And for Calcutta itself, this is what he has to say:

Kalkatte ka jo zikr kiya tu ne hum-nashin
Ik teer mere seene mein maara ki haaie haaie

When you mention Calcutta, my friend, it is as though
You pierce my breast with an arrow making me cry out

Not everyone was similarly enthused by this imperial city built beside the mighty Hooghly. Living in exile in straitened circumstances in Matiaburj, Nawab Wajid Ali Shah missed his beloved home in distant Lucknow beside the Gomti:

Yahi tashvish shab-o-roz hai Bangale mein
Lucknow phir kabhi dikhlaie muqaddar mera

Day and night, my only anxiety in Bengal is
Will Fate show me Lucknow ever again

Other poets too, many who had possibly never visited Bengal, have written about Bengal as a mythical, fabled land. Khan Janbaz declares:

Jii kartaa hai unn ko tirii tasviir dikhaa duun
Jo puuchhte hain mujh se ki Bangaal mein kyaa hai

I feel like showing your picture to those
Who ask me what is so special about Bengal

Alluding to the famous tresses of the women of Bengal Delhi-based Shuja Khawar writes:

Aaj merii arz par zulfein agar kholegaa woh
Kal hasad kii aag mein jal jaaegaa Bangaal bhar

If today she uncoils her hair upon my request
All of Bengal will be consumed in the fire of envy tomorrow

And here's more on the fabled hair in this sher by Syed Ahmad Shameem:

Misl-e-ḳhushbu-e-saba phaili hui hai har taraf
Gesu-e-Bangaal ki ḳhushbu hamaare shahr mein

Like a sweetly scented breeze that blows all about
The fragrance of the hair of Bengal blows in my city

However, there are numerous references, also, to the hunger that once stalked the land during the periodic, often man-made famines, especially the Great Bengal Famine of 1943 which shook the entire nation. The most famous of these is Wamiq Jaunpuri's 'Bhooka Hai Bangal' that became a rallying cry for the travelling drama groups of the newly created IPTA. Set to a rousing beat, it was carried to the nooks and crannies of undivided India as a song of solidarity and support with the people of Bengal:

Pyari-mata chinta mat kar hum hain aane waale
Kundan-ras kheton men teri gode basane waale

Beloved Mother, don't worry for we are coming
We shall pour gold in your fields and fill your lap with plenty

Extending similar support in a poem entitled 'Qahat-e Bangaal' (The Bengal Famine), Jigar Moradabadi writes of the awakening that he sees in Bengal, *bedaari-e ehsaas*, that comes to a people who have long chafed under injustice and oppression:

Bangal ki main sham-o-sahar dekh raha huun
Har chand ki huun duur magar dekh raha huun

I am watching the day and night unfurl in Bengal
Even though I am far away from it, I am seeing it

Hailing from Kakori, Furqat Kakorvi writes with immense empathy for the plight of 'his Bengal' as he alludes to the dance of death in the wake of the famine in 'Bangaal ki Raqqassa' (The Dancer of Bengal):

Nachiye nachiye paael ke baġhair
Jism uryan hi rahe
Shola-afshan hi rahe
Nachiye nachiye
Bhuuk aur maut ka raqs
Mere Bangaal ka raqs

Dance, dance without an anklet
While the bodies are naked
And the flames are dispersed
Dance, dance
The dance of hunger and death
The dance of my Bengal

There is also Sahir Ludhianvi's 'Bangaal' which talks of this land of plenty that has known such horrific wants because of the rapacity of its rulers. Sahir talks of the peasants in the fields and the workers in the factories, the glittering new roads and fertile lands and referring to the role played by Bengalis in the national freedom struggle and the natural propensity of the people of Bengal towards *ehtijaaj* (protest), goes on to ask:

Chaman ko iss liye maali ne ḳhuun se seencha thha
Ki uss ki apni nigahein bahaar ko tarsein

Was it for this day the gardener had watered the garden with his blood
That his own eyes should yearn for spring

And for Kalkatta (Calcutta and now Kolkata), the word *ehtijaaj* crops up again and again as in this sher by Ambar Shameem:

Khwab aansu ehtajaji zindagi
Puchhiye mat shahr-e-Kalkatta hai kya

Dreams, tears and a life of protest
Don't ask what is the city of Kolkata

While there is a great deal of poetry in Urdu on Bengali icons as diverse as M N Roy, C R Das, Subhash Chandra Bose, Rabindranath Tagore and Qazi Nazrul Islam, Hurmat-ul-Ikram sums up the city's *joi de-vivre* in his lyrical ode to Calcutta:

Bujhte huwe shararon ko jisne jaga diya
Phir eik baar dil ko dhadakna sikha diya

It taught the dying sparks to wake again
It taught the heart to beat once again

The results of the last state election in 2021 did, indeed, teach the heart to beat again and brought back to life the dying sparks and, once again, showed the way in Gopal Krishna Gokhale's memorable words: 'What Bengal thinks today, India thinks tomorrow.'

70. The Lament of Delhi: No Stranger to Tragedy

This Delhi, our present-day modern megapolis, is said to be the 11th Delhi built on the ruins of its past Delhis. Successive waves of Jats, Mongols, Afghans, Rohillas, Marathas, British attacks followed by the horrific communal violence in the years leading up to the partition, the outflow of the inhabitants of Shahjahanabad, the influx of 'refugees', the sprouting of refugee camps, the looting of evacuee properties—have time and again wreaked unimaginable havoc in the lives of ordinary citizens. Much of this carnage has found expression in Urdu poetry over the years, ranging from the morosely maudlin to the overtly political. So, if there is a Hakim Agha Jan Aish declaiming the fate of Delhi with a sweeping statement such as:

Nahiin haal-e-Dehli sunaane ke qaabil
Ye qissa hai aansuu bahaane ke qaabil

The state of Delhi is not worthy of recounting
This is a story fit only for the shedding of tears

There is also Dagh Dehelvi referring to the Purabiyas, the (uncouth) men from the East who unleashed mayhem upon the city on the orders of the British occupiers in the aftermath of the Revolt of 1857:

Ghazab mein aayi rayyat bala mein shehr aaya
Yeh Purabi nahi aaye khuda ka qahar aaya
Calamity has seized the populace, misfortune befallen the city
The coming of the Purabiyas has spelt God's doom for the city

In Urdu, there has existed a body of poetry known as shehr ashob, literally meaning 'misfortunes of the city' to express political and social decline and turmoil, written for the misfortunes that had beset great cities such as Lucknow and Delhi. While much of this genre of poetry was melodramatic, self-pitying and exaggerated with a great deal of rhetoric and play upon words in the best traditions of elegiac poetry such as nauha, marsiya and soz, shehr ashob also afforded ample opportunities for the poet to paint graphic word pictures of what he saw and experienced at first hand. Using the conventional imagery of the Persian-Arabic tradition, shehr ashob allowed the poet to speak of his personal sorrows and losses while, ostensibly, bemoaning a crumbling social order.

A collection of 40 poems called *Fughan-e-Dehli* (The Lament of Delhi) present a graphic picture of the havoc and destruction wrought first by the mutineers from Meerut and then the wrath unleashed by the British forces bent upon vengeance after the siege and sack of Delhi in 1857. Muhammad Sadruddun Khan Azurdah, a poet, scholar and magistrate, attacks the people of the Fort and holds them responsible for the calamity:

Aafat iss shehr mein quile ki badaulat aayi
Waan ke aamal se Dilli ki bhi shaamat aayi
Kaale Meerut se kya aaye ki shaamat aayi

Misfortune befell the city because of the fort
Due to their evil deeds retribution came upon Delhi
Calamity arrived with the black men from Meerut

On 20 September 1857, Delhi fell. British soldiers entered the Jama Masjid, desecrated it and set about unleashing the most terrible atrocities. In one week, 25,000 people were killed, the rebels and their sympathisers summarily executed, 1,60,000 inhabitants driven out of the city limits and forced to camp in the open countryside. Qazi Fazal Husain Afsurdah holds the soldiers and spies guilty for the madness that spirals out of control and catches both the 'guilty' and the 'innocent':

Fauj kya aayi qayamat aayi
Mukhbiron ne kar diye fitne barpa
Begunah aur baguna pakda gaya

Calamity came with the coming of the soldiers
The spies added fire to the fury
Both the guilty and the innocent were arrested

Ruing the slaughter of an age (*ek jahan qatl hua)* Zaheer Dehlvi writes:

People have been pulled out of their homes
Corpses line the road, layers upon layers
Neither grave, nor shroud, nor mourners are left

When the dust of the *Ghadar* settled, what remained was a city in ruins. As the 19th century drew to a close, Altaf Husain Hali, opened his 'Marsiya-e Dehlii' (An Elegy to Delhi) thus:

Tazkira Dehlii-e-marhuum ka ai dost na chhed
Na sunaa jaaegaa hum se ye fasaana hargiz

O friend, I beseech you, speak not of the Delhi that is no more
I shall not be able to hear this story at any cost

In prose, there is Shahid Ahmad Dehelvi's 'Dehli ki Bipda' (The Misfortune of Delhi) a bitter, first-hand account of a once-proud resident of the city who felt forced to flee his home and the madness and mayhem he witnessed during the partition years. There is also Ahmed Ali's iconic novel *Twilight in Delhi* that recounts the passing of an era and the enormous sense of loss for what is irretrievably gone.

In a city that has been no stranger to tragedy in recent memory, be it the 'Sikh' riots as they were dubbed in 1984, the North Delhi riots of 2020 brought on by the anti-CAA protests and the Covid spike of 2021 that left people gasping for breath in the face of an acute shortage of pumped oxygen, heaped pyres in make-shift cremation grounds, over-flowing graveyards, one is reminded of a particularly gory incident from the city's bloodied past. On 22 March 1739 when Nadir Shah ordered the massacre of Delhi's citizens, over 20,000 men, women and children were killed in cold blood in a few hours. The figure of the cruel invader watching blood flow like water in the streets of Delhi captured the imagination of generations of poets.

Kasey na maand ke deegar ba tegh e naaz kushi,
Chunee ke zinda kuni khalq ra wa baaz kushi

This is what Nadir Shah's lieutenant is believed to have said after the slaughter of Delhi. Roughly translated, it means 'You will have to revive them if you want to kill them again for you have all but decimated them.'

71. *Marsiya-e-Lakhnaw*: An Elegy to a Lost Past

Lucknow has long beckoned the poet and the pleasure-seeker, the dilettante and the craftsmen,the scholar and the connoisseur. Its literary and cultural landscape has been moulded by the different reigns it has witnessed: from the Delhi Sultanate to the Sharqi Sultanate, the Mughal Empire that gave way to the Nawabs of Awadh, the East India Company and finally the British Raj. However, it was during the reign of the Nawabs that Lucknow reached its apogee: music and dance flourished, poets and artists found patronage and several monuments were constructed such as the Bara Imambara, the Chhota Imambara, the Rumi Darwaza, etc. One of the enduring legacies of the roughly 150 years of nawabi rule was the culmination of a syncretic Hindu-Muslim culture that has come to be known as the Ganga-Jamuni Tehzeeb, mocked and derided in the New India that is Bharat but till quite recently the cause of much jubilation and celebration among votaries of pluralism and multi-culturalism.

With the fall and decline of Delhi after the Great Revolt of

1857, Lucknow emerged as the cultural capital of Upper India. Given its glorious mix of educational institutions, law courts, clubs, cinemas, coffeehouses not to mention the lingering whiff of Awadhi decadence mingling with the liberalism of a vibrant new class of educated Indians drawn from across the length and breadth of colonial India, it was a veritable smorgasbord of people, places and ideas. Its very air was a heady cocktail of the past and the present, and a future that lay coiled among its many aesthetically-designed buildings, parks and pavilions, waiting to unfurl.

Lucknow has produced its own 'school' of poetry—one that is distinct from the Delhi 'school' or the one in distant Deccan—and a large numbers of Urdu poets with many proudly bearing the city's name as their own, such as Arzoo Lakhnavi, Behzad Lakhnavi, Saqib Lakhnavi, Aziz Lakhnavi, Natiq Lakhnavi, Auj Lakhnavi, Munawwar Lakhnavi, Safi Lakhnavi to name just a few, and others who trace their roots to this city such as Daya Shankar Naseem, Ratan Nath Sarshar, Anand Narain Mullah, Insha Allah Khan, Anees, Dabeer, Aatish, Mushafi, Mir, Sauda, Nasikh, Jurat and in recent times Majaz, Malikzada Manzoor, Saaghar Khayyami, Mohsin Zaidi, Munawwar Rana, Javed Akhtar, etc. Naturally therefore, Lucknow and its *tehzeeb*, have found ample reflection in their poetry. Others, while not from Lucknow, too have written about the city.

Some poets have looked at Delhi and Lucknow as two centres of a great civilisation, the London and Paris of their milieu, both devastated and irretrievably destroyed by the forces of colonialism and modernity. Mirza Hadi Ruswa rues:

Dilli chhutii thhi pahle ab Lucknow bhii chhodein
Do shahar thhe ye apne donon tabaah nikle

First we left Delhi, now we must leave Lucknow
Both cities were ours, both have been destroyed

Comparing the devastation wrought upon the two cities that, in turn, destroyed an entire way of life Bismil Saeedi writes:

Kiya tabaah to Dilli ne bhi bahut Bismil
Magar Khuda ki qasam Lucknow ne loot liya

Delhi too devastated us indeed, Bismil
But, by God, Lucknow has looted us

Abdul Halim Sharar (1869-1926) an essayist and historian of Lucknow, wrote *Guzishta Lucknow* which was translated by E. S. Harcourt and Fakhir Hussain as *Lucknow: The Last Phase of an Oriental Culture.* Sharar paints a graphic picture of an Awadh that was at the peak of its glory between the reign of Nawab Asad-ud-daula and Wajid Ali Shah. His book is an extended celebration of the Lucknow form of Indo-Muslim culture and a city that was, in the words of the author, 'the Baghdad and Cordoba of India and the Nishapur and Bokhara of the east', where scholars flocked and artists were welcomed.

The plunder of Delhi by Nadir Shah in 1739 and the raids by Ahmad Shah Abdali in 1748 caused writers and poets to flock to Lucknow to seek their fortune in the courts of the Nawabs of Awadh. There too, however, the good life lasted a bare century and the dynastic rule established by Nawab Shuja-ud-daula in 1754 came to an ignominious end in 1856 with the annexation of Awadh by the British. Like Delhi, the plight of Lucknow—looted by rapacious rajahs and talukdars, besieged by famine and disease and bedeviled by a steady breakdown of law and order—too invited a copious outpouring of lament. A great deal of poetry in the shehr ashob tradition (alluded to in two previous essays) laments the destruction of an entire way of life such as these opening lines from 'Dehli Lakhnaw' by Hakim Agha Khan Aish:

Ho gaye weeraan Dehli-o-dayaar-e Lakhnaw
Ab kahaan woh lutf-e-Dehli-o-bahaar-e-Lakhnaw

The environs of Delhi and Lucknow are desolate
Gone are the delights of Delhi and the merriment of Lucknow

Sitting in Matiya Burj in distant Calcutta, the deposed Nawab Wajid Ali Shah wrote a largely self-pitying 'Huzn-e-Akhtar' (Sorrow of Akhtar, Akhtar being his nom de plum) with lines such as:

Awadh ka kabhi main bhi thha badshah
Mulazim mere thhe kabhi sau hazaar

Once I was the king of Awadh
I had a hundred thousand servants

And this as he was setting off on his fateful journey:

Dar-o-deewar pe hasrat se nazar karte hain
Khush raho ahl-e-watan hum to safar karte hain

I gaze longingly at these walls and doors
Stay well my countrymen for I set off on my journey

Mirza Muhammad Raza Barq, who had accompanied Wajid Ali Shah in exile, wrote the 'Marsiya-e-Lucknow' (Elegy to Lucknow), an elegy on the glory and richness of Lucknow's syncretic culture but one that unwittingly offered a critique of the excesses, indulgence and sheer hedonism of nawabi Awadh when precious *kewra* (sweet scenting extract, distilled from pandanus flowers) would be sprinkled on the streets for the debauched elite to walk upon. The refrain in Barq's marsiya was one of despair and hopelessness:

Dil mein taaqat naa rahi, aah mein taaseer nahin

The heart has no strength left, the sighs can no longer bear fruit

Akhtar Sheerani, while not from Lucknow, has written an entire poem entitled 'Lakhnaw' extolling its many virtues, its stately buildings, its beautiful gardens, everything that reminds him of its majestic past:

Mashriqui rang-e-tamaddun ki hai khaalis yaadgaar
Kyun naa ho har mashriqui dil se nisaar-e-Lakhnaw

It is a genuine memorial to the eastern way of living
Why then should every easterner not be a devotee of Lucknow

Turning the famed Lakhnawi *adaab* (etiquette) on its head, Munawwar Rana takes a jibe at his own city:

Badi mushkil se aate hain samajh mein Lucknow wale
Dilon mein faasle lab par magar aadaab rahtaa hai

It is very difficult to understand the people of Lucknow
Their hearts may be distant but there is always courtesy on their lips

Majaz, a true-blue Lakhnawi, writes an entire nazm titled 'Lucknow':

Firdaus-e-husn-o-ishq hai daamaan-e-Lucknow
Aankhon mein bas rahe hain ghazaalaan-e-Lucknow

The environs of Lucknow are a heaven of beauty and love
The doe-eyed beauties of Lucknow are imprinted in my gaze

And then there is Nazm Tabatabai who speaks for all those who have loved Lucknow:

Mujh ko samjho yaadgaar-e-raftagaan-e-Lucknow
Hoon qadd-e-aamdam Gubaar-e-kaarvaan-e-Lucknow

Consider me a memorial of the long gone Lucknow
While the size of a man I am the dust of the caravan of Lucknow

72. Taj Mahal: A Teardrop on the Cheek of Eternity

To those who claim the Taj Mahal was built by traitors and their very names must be excised from history, I will offer no plea on its tremulous beauty that caused Rabindranath Tagore to liken it to a 'teardrop on the cheek of eternity'. Nor will I draw attention to the obvious fact of it being a world heritage site drawing millions of tourists from India and abroad. These are facts and, like pearls, must not be cast before swine. Instead, let me present an alternative reading of the Taj, one presented by Urdu poets, especially the progressive poets; for, Urdu poetry can be relied upon to provide a contrarian, catholic view on almost anything on God's earth!

Deconstructing the image of the monument to love, Sahir Ludhianvi finds this showy exhibitionistic declaration of love an insult to the love of ordinary mortals who cannot afford an emperor's self indulgence. Sahir's nazm 'Taj Mahal' deserves to be quoted in fullto appreciate his scorn and derision for a love that is so ostentatious:

Taj tere liye ik mazhar-e-ulfat hii sahi
Tujhko is waadi-e-rangeen se aqeedat hii sahi

Meri mahboob kahin aur mila kar mujh se
Bazm-e-shahi mein ġharibon ka guzar kya maani
Sabt jis raah mein hon satwat-e-shahi ke nishan
Uss pe ulfat bhari ruhon ka safar kya maani
Meri mahbub pas-e-parda-e-tashheer-e-wafa
Tu ne satwat ke nishaanon ko to dekha hota
Murda-shahon ke maqabir se bahalne waali
Apne tareek makaanon ko to dekha hota
An-ginat logon ne duniya mein mohabbat kii hai
Kaun kahta hai ki saadiq na thhe jazbe un ke
Lekin un ke liye tashheer ka saaman nahin
Kyunki woh log bhi apni hii tarah muflis thhe
Yeh imarat-o-maqabir ye faseelein ye hisaar
Mutlaq-ul-hukm shahanshahon ki azmat ke sutoon
Sina-e-dahr ke nasoor hain kohna nasoor
Jazb hai un mein tire aur mire ajdaad ka ḳhoon
Meri mahboob unhein bhi to mohabbat hogi
Jinki sannai ne baḳhshi hai ussey shakl-e-jameel
Unn ke pyaron ke maqabir rahey benam-o-numood
Aaj tak un pe jalaii na kisi ne qandeel
Yeh chaman-zaar ye Jamuna ka kinara ye mahal
Yeh munaqqash dar-o-deewaar ye mehraab ye taaq
Ik shahanshah ne daulat ka sahara le kar
Hum ġharibon ki mohabbat ka udaya hai mazaaq
Meri mahboob kahin aur mila kar mujh se

For you the Taj may well be a mere manifestation of love
And you may perhaps be attached to this beautiful setting
But, my love, meet me somewhere else
For what place do the poor have in this assembly of royals
On paths that are engraved with the signs of power and royalty
What meaning can the passage of love-filled souls have on it?

My love, behind the curtains of professions of constancy
If only you had seen the signs of power and authority
O you who are pleased by the mausoleums of dead royals
If only you had seen the darkness of your own homes
Countless numbers of people have loved in this world
Who says that their emotions were not true?
But they did not have the provisions of publicity
Because those people were poor like you and me
This building, these graves, this enclosure, this fortress
These pillars bearing testimony to an emperor's unconditional supremacy
These are festering wounds on the chest of the world, ancient wounds
Mingled in them is the blood of our ancestors, yours and mine
My love, they too must have loved
Those whose craftsmanship has bestowed amazing beauty upon this edifice
The graves of their loved ones have remained unmarked, unlit
No one has placed so much as a paper lantern on their graves
This garden, this river bank beside the Jamuna, this palace
This sculpted door and wall, this archway, this niche,
An emperor has taken the assistance of all his wealth
And made fun of the love of poor people like us
My love, meet me somewhere else

And in much the same way, there is Kaifi Azmi, fellow member of the progressive writers' movement, urging his beloved whom he addresses as his 'friend' to come away from the Taj Mahal:

Dost! main dekh chuka Taj Mahal
...waapas chal

Marmari marmari phulon se ubalta hira
Chand kii aanch mein dahke hue seemin minar
Zehn-e-shair se yeh karta hua chashmak paiham
Ik malika ka ziya-posh-o faza-taab mazaar
Khud-ba-khud phir gae nazron mein ba-andaz-e-savaal
Woh jo raston pe padey rahtey hain lashon ki tarah
Khushk ho kar jo simat jaate hain be-rasaasab
Dhoop mein khopdiyan bajti hain tashon ki tarah
Dost main dekh chuka Taj Mahal
...waapas chal

My friend, I have seen the Taj Mahal
...let us go back
A diamond boiling over with alabaster flowers
Silvery minarets blazing in the fire of the moon
Winking continuously at the poet's mind
The grand and alluring mausoleum of an empress
Like a question, it flashed through the mind's eye
The thought of those who lie in the streets like corpses
Whose nerves and sinews shrink lifelessly
Whose skulls smash like cymbals in the heat
My friend, I have seen the Taj Mahal
...let us go back

Then, there are the more conventional responses to the spectacular beauty of the Taj, such as this by Mahshar Badayuni:

Allah main yeh Taj Mahal dekh raha huun
Ya pahlu-e-Jamuna mein kanval dekh raha huun

Dear God is it the Taj Mahal I am seeing
Or is it a lotus blooming beside the Yamuna

And this by Sikandar Ali Wajd:

Jadu nigah-e ishq ka patthar pe chal gaya
Ulfat ka khwaab qalib marmar pe dhal gaya

The magic of love's glance has worked on stone
The dream of adoration has been cast in marble

And by Waris Kirmani:

Jaane kis taazgii-e fikr ka izhaar kiya
Waqt ke husn gurezaan ko giraftaar kiya

Such freshness of the imagination it reflects
Capturing the fleeting beauty of Time

Waxing eloquent on its beauty, Unwaan Chishti concludes his ode to the exquisiteness of its alabaster perfection thus:

Husn-e-dil, husn-e-nazar, husn-e-tamanna hai yeh
Ishq ka baargah-e-husn mein sajda hai yeh

It is the beauty of the heart, beauty of the gaze, beauty of aspirations
It is the prostration of love in the palace of beauty

But the most fitting response to the hate mongers who have excised the very mention of the Taj from the Uttar Pradesh tourism booklet*, who are calling it a 'blot on Indian culture' rather than an enduring symbol of love, and are preparing to raze it to the ground in search of a temple called 'Tejo Mahalaya' housing a Shivling comes from the pen of Seemab Akbarabadi:

Kaash phir duniya aur eik Shahjahan paida karey
Kaash phir ho khaak se jism-e muhabbat jalwagar

If only the world were to produce another Shahjahan
If only another monument to love were to rise from this soil

---

*https://www.aljazeera.com/news/2017/10/9/taj-mahal-dropped-from-tourism-booklet-of-uttar-pradesh

73. Aligarh: *Ye Abr Hamesha Barsega...*

I was born in 1963 in Aligarh, the university town in Uttar Pradesh, India. My father was the Deputy Medical Officer, my mother worked in the Maulana Azad Library and my maternal grandfather was a Professor in the Department of Urdu—all at the Aligarh Muslim University. My parents lived in charming house provided by the university medical centre. However, I was born in my grandfather's house, One Shibli Road, a rambling old bungalow with a sprawling garden on the main University road. I lived in Aligarh till I was four years old when my parents moved to Delhi. But the link with Aligarh never snapped. We continued to travel several times a year—for the long summer vacations and several short trips whenever the opportunity arose.

The Aligarh of the late 1960s was a remarkable place. Having long since shed the 'taint' of its association with the Pakistan movement, the process of refashioning and re-inventing the University at Aligarh as the cradle of secularism had begun from the late 1940s itself. In his Convocation address of 20 February 1949, the venerable Maulana Abul Kalam Azad had expressed his happiness over the 'new awakening in the atmosphere of the university' and assured the students with the following words:

> 'You can expect in the secular and democratic set up that all the doors are open for you. With a sense of responsibility, I want to assure you that no door is closed for you. The only condition is that you have to work with dedication and devotion.'

In 1955, its Vice Chancellor Dr Zakir Husain had announced at the Annual Convocation: 'The way Aligarh works, the way Aligarh thinks, the contribution Aligarh makes to Indian life… will largely determine the place Mussalmans will occupy in the pattern of Indian life.' At pains to establish the secular and nationalist credentials of the University, Dr Zakir Husain sought out non-Muslim teachers from universities and colleges across the length and breadth of India and brought them to Aligarh. Under his active encouragement, far-seeing teachers got busy preparing a fresh crop of talented young men and women who would join Jawaharlal Nehru's nation-building project.

Colonel Bashir Husain Zaidi took over as Vice-Chancellor in 1956 from Dr Zakir Husain who departed, upon completion of his term, first to take up a position as a Member of the Rajya Sabha and then Governor of Bihar before going on to become the Vice-President and eventually the President of India. Zaidi, an able administrator who had supervised the bloodless accession of the princely state of Rampur to the Union of India, proved his mettle as not merely an efficient and diplomatic supervisor of this hallowed institution but also a master builder. Known to posterity as the 'Shahjahan of Aligarh', he launched upon an ambitious building project and added several fine specimens to Aligarh's sprawling and handsome campus. The sleek modern buildings built during his tenure such as the Kennedy House, the Maulana Azad Library, the University Polytechnic and the Engineering College showed that the University—having stabilised sufficiently during Dr Zakir Husain's tenure—was now poised for a new phase of growth and expansion. Zaidi and his successors—Badruddin Tyabji and Ali Yavar Jung—brought leading scholars from all over the country to come and teach at Aligarh.

By the early-1960s the University was bustling with some of the finest minds in different fields of the arts, humanities, social studies and natural sciences. The scene in the Departments of Urdu and Hindi was exceptionally lively. Ale Ahmad Suroor left his teaching job at the University of Lucknow and joined a Department that was teeming with some of the finest poets, fiction writers and critics: there was, of course, the venerable Rashid Ahmad Siddiqui, humourist, prose stylist and critic par excellence as well as Qazi Abdul Sattar, the novelist and short story writer, Khurshidul Islam, the poet and critic who had returned from a teaching stint at the School of Oriental and African Studies (SOAS) and brought with him a whiff of cosmopolitanism. Ralph Russell, who taught at SOAS, visited Aligarh and spent long hours honing his verbal skills with members of the Urdu Department and interacting with staff and students to fully understand the milieu of 'native' Urdu speakers. The famous Zaidi sisters, Sajida and Zahida, who taught in the Departments of Education and English respectively, were actively involved in the University's cultural life. The very air was redolent with cosmopolitanism and liberalism. And, yes, socialism and Marxism too! While Aligarh could not be called the stronghold of Communism in India, it certainly had its fair share of known and committed Communists and a generous number of those who could be called 'fellow travelers', that is, those who did not belong to any party or subscribe to any laid-down ideology but were nevertheless inclined towards a democratic, egalitarian and equitable world view.

It is this Aligarh that I wish to invoke here. Contrary to

popular perception, Aligarh was never the citadel of Islamic thought in India; it did indeed have thriving departments of Urdu, Arabic, Persian and Islamic Studies but then it also taught the natural sciences, mathematics, and soon enough, began to offer extremely popular—not to mention highly competitive courses—in medicine and engineering as well. While the majority of students and teachers were, indeed, Muslim, the campus ethos was neither 'Muslim' nor 'Islamic' per se. And while a great many people here, including my grandfather, Prof Ale Ahmad Suroor, had spent the bulk of their professional life in Aligarh there was nothing parochial about any of them. And, by extension, while Suroor was a teacher of Urdu and wrote in Urdu, there is nothing in his ouvre that made an explicit call to any one community. If ever there was a writer who can most effectively debunk the absurd misconception that Urdu is the language of Muslims or the cultural repository of Muslims alone, it is indeed people such as him. When his beloved Aligarh went through an intellectually lean phase, he wrote:

Khushk kheti hai magar us ko hari kahte hain
Kum-nigaahi ko bhi woh deeda-wari kahte hain

The fields are dry but they still call them green
Even short sightedness they deem sharp sightedness

A trenchant critic of Sir Syed Ahmad Khan, the founder of the school at Aligarh (initially called the MAO College before it evolved into AMU), Akbar Allahabadi (whom we have encountered previously in the pages of this volume) was severely critical of the 'Aligarh school'. Not one to mince words, he has written several bitingly satirical pieces of poetry on Aligarh such as:

Padhne ka na theek usool badhne ki na raah
Aur qibla koi nahin Aligarh ke siwa

No proper principle for learning, no path for progress
No *qibla* (to face while praying) except Aligarh

But there are others who have written paeans in praise of Aligarh and all that it symbolized. In a nostalgic ode to his alma mater, Shakeel Badayuni, the film lyricist, wrote 'Aligarh Chorhne ke Baad' (After Leaving Aligarh):

Woh tarane jo suna karta hoon tanhai mein
Unn taranon mein mujhe boo-e-wafa aati hai

The songs I hear in my solitude (since leaving Aligarh)
Those songs carry the scent of loyalty (towards Aligarh)

To be invited to speak at Aligarh, especially its fabled Students Union Hall was an invitation few would turn down. Luminaries from the world of literature, politics, public affairs have spoken from its hallowed portals. Josh Malihabadi addressed the university thus in a poem entitled 'Muslim University Aligarh se Khitaab':

Ai Aligarh ai jawan-qismat dabistan-e-kuhan
Aql ke fanoos se raushan hai teri anjuman

O Aligarh, O young of fortune, ancient school
Your assembly lit by the chandelier of knowledge

Many 'old boys' recall certain 'typical' motifs: the endless cups of tea consumed during their student days at Aligarh—some brewed in their hostel digs, some drunk at the many chai stalls dotted all over the campus, calling each other 'partner', wearing the trademark shervani and travelling across the campus on a bicycle. While the Aligarh 'biskut' with the tea might be optional, a great deal of debate and discussion about life, politics, gup and gossip was however compulsory. Abidullah Ghazi begins his 'Yaad-e-Aligarh' (In Memory of Aligarh) by invoking this best-loved memory:

Woh chai ki pyali pe yaron ke jalse
Woh sardi ki raatein woh zulfon ke qisse

Those meetings with friends over a cup of tea
Those winter nights, those anecdotes about tresses

In a long poem entitled 'Aligarh Tum To Waaqif Ho' (As You Know, Aligarh) Asna Badr lists all the things old boys and old girls recall with relish: of boys going to the Girls' College asking to meet their 'sisters', the popular tradition of 'hooting' at mushairas and public assemblies, the famous 'Aligarhi sense of humour' with *fiqra-kasna* (passing a funny, but apt, comment), attending the biggest event on the annual calendar, namely the *numaish* with its endless possibilities of eating, shopping, people gazing, the hostel rooms that were melting pots where students from the length and the breadth of the country got to know each other, the standard Aligarh breakfast of matri, jalebi, omelette, the 'see-off tea' at the railway station, and much else.

Given the number of writers Aligarh has produced, a great deal of excellent Urdu literature been written *in* Aligarh. Equally, a great deal has been written *about* Aligarh. Some of the greatest Urdu writers have studied at the Aligarh Muslim University such as Ismat Chughtai, Saadat Hasan Manto, Khwaja Ahmad Abbas, Qazi Abdus Sattar, Mushtaq Ahmad Yusufi. Among the poets there have been Ale Ahmad Suroor, Asrarul Haq Majaz, Moin Ahsan Jazbi, Shakeel Badayuni, Majrooh Sultanpuri, Akhtarul Iman, Jan Nisar Akhtar, Ali Sardar Jafri, Khalilur Rahman Azmi, Aashufta Changezi, Shahryar, Waheed Akhtar, Anwar Jalalpuri, Javed Akhtar and in recent times, Farhat Ehsas, Obaid Siddiqui, Hilal Fareed; the list is long and illustrious. However, the one poet who has more than paid his due to Aligarh, in fact several times over, is Majaz who penned the long, lyrical, tenderly loving yet rousing 'Nazr-e-Aligarh' (To Aligarh) in 1936. The university adopted it as its *tarana* (anthem) in 1954. It bears ample witness to the role Aligarh has always played in the life of the nation:

> *Ye abr hamesha barsa hai, ye abr hamesha barsega...*
>
> This cloud has always rained, this cloud will always rain...

74. The 'Bambayi' of the Progressives

Several Urdu writers came to Bombay all through the 1940s to look for work in the film industry—as script writers, lyricists, film journalists—and met with varying degrees of success. Josh Malihabadi, Akhtarul Iman, Krishan Chandar and Saghar Nizami were in Poona (where most of the film studios were initially located), but the lure of the silver screen drew them to the city that was fast becoming home to the biggest film industry in Asia. By the time the Second World War ended, some of the most dynamic writers of the age had flocked to Bombay from different parts of undivided India: among the Urdu writers there was Rajinder Singh Bedi, Hameed Akhtar, Sardar Jafri, Kaifi Azmi, Jan Nisar Akhtar, Majrooh Sultanpuri, Rifat Sarosh, Niyaz Haider, Hajra Mastoor and Khadija Mastoor, Saadat Hasan Manto, Miraji, Vishwamitra Adil, Ismat Chughtai and her husband Shahid Latif to name a few; Hindi writers included Upendranath Askh, Nemichandra Jain, Amritlal Nagar, Prem Dhawan; Marathi writers Mama Warerkar and Anna Bhau Sathe; and Gujarati writers Bakulesh Swapnath and Bhogilal Gandhi. They were all members of the Bombay branch of the Progressive Writers' Association (PWA) which was then the most active in the country.

The First All India Congress of the CPI took place in Bombay in May 1943. An equally important event occurred in its sidelines. The Fourth AIPWA met in the Marwari Vidyalaya and the Indian Peoples' Theatre Association (IPTA) was born. Also, the central office of the PWA moved from Lucknow to Bombay and the course and content of the movement increasingly began to come from a group known as the 'Bombay Progressives'. Also, Sajjad Zaheer, the powerful progressive ideologue, who had been in prison till 1942, moved to Bombay where he took charge of the PWA along with Sardar Jafri, Sibte Hasan, Kaifi Azmi and others. A host of Urdu journals, both film magazines as well as literary ones, and also the People's Publishing House, which gained an envious reputation of printing large copies of inexpensively priced high-quality books, soon put Bombay on the literary map.

It is to this Bombay—brimful with new ideas, a hub of the country's best minds, a melting pot of young people from different, far-flung regions, busy pouring new wine in new bottles—that Kaifi Azmi, a full-time member of the CPI, brought his Hyderabadi bride, Shaukat Azmi, to live in the commune in Andheri. Shaukat noted her first impressions thus in her autobiography *Kaifi & I:*

> 'We went to Kaifi's tiny room in which there was a loosely strung jute *charpai* with a *dhurrie*, a mattress, a sheet and a pillow. In one corner there was a chair and a small table on which there were some books, piles of newspapers, a mug and a glass. The simplicity of this room touched my heart…'

Shaukat describes Kaifi and his friends, who would become her fellow travelers, thus:

> 'They were enlightened and humane individuals who were struggling to create a new world for the poor, the

> destitute and the hungry. Although they were from different parts of India, these people were like one family where everyone was addressed as "Comrade", which at the time meant an evolved human being.'

Kaifi earned Rs 40 as monthly salary from the Party; from this he had to give Rs 30 towards his wife's boarding expense. To earn some extra money, he wrote a column for the Urdu daily, *Jamhuriat*. Partly to lighten the burden on Kaifi and partly in response to P C Joshi's command that 'the wife of a communist should never sit idle' Shaukat got drawn into the IPTA. Her first role was in Ismat Chughtai's *Dhani Bankein* (Green Bangles), a play on the Hindu-Muslim riots that were tearing the fabric of a newly independent India. Here, Shaukat became involved in the country's most vigorous cultural movement that had the likes of Zohra Segal, Uzra Butt, Bhishm Sahni, Prithviraj Kapoor, among its stalwarts.

Bombay became a melting pot where writers were writing rousing poetry asking the people of Asia and Africa to arise, to fight a common enemy and make common cause with a host of issues, be it anti-fascism, anti-colonialism, anti-imperialism as also nationalism, feminism, land reforms, widow remarriage, social inequalities, economic exploitation, and so on. There was something in the very air of Bombay that was redolent with the need for change and progress. Regardless of their sympathy for communism per se, there was no shortage of writers who saw the merit of purposive literature and were prepared to find common ground with the progressives despite their reservations about organised communism.

Among the Bombay progressives, the one person who gained the most name and fame not to mention top billing and a fortune was Sahir Ludhianvi. His lyrics in simple but chaste Hindustani, touched a chord with millions of Indians in films like *Pyasa* (Thirsty, 1957). Till the early 50s his reputation rested largely on his progressive poetry for the *mushaira* circuit since his first collection entitled *Talkhiyan* (Bitterness, 1943) had earned him instant recognition as the voice of an entire generation. In later years, he came to be regarded as a lyricist rather than poet and, like most progressives, learnt to make compromises by giving in to the demands of film-makers—a practice Kaifi once compared with digging a grave and then looking for a corpse to fit it given the fact that not only is the context pre-decided but so is the tune!

Members of the PWA were not living in a bubble; they were actively involved in the cultural life of the city and the political life of the nation. Khwaja Ahmad Abbas (1914-1987), for instance, was an active member of the Aligarh branch of the PWA during his student days who graduated effortlessly to becoming an integral part of the Bombay progressives' group during its glory days. Active in IPTA and the Bombay film industry as well as being a prolific novelist, short story writer and journalist, he made several important films like *Saat Hindustani* (Seven Indians, 1969) and *Do Boond Pani* (Two Drops of Water, 1972). *Neecha Nagar* (Lower City), based on a story by Hayatullah Ansari, won him the Palme d'Or at the Cannes Film festival in 1946 though it was 'Dharti ke Lal' (Jewels of the Earth), in the same year, his first directorial venture that saw a co-mingling of several talented progressive writers. Abbas had gained fame for writing the hugely popular column 'Last Page' in 1935 for the *Bombay Chronicle* and when it closed in 1947, he moved the column to *Blitz* where it continued till his death; it was known as *Azad Kalaam* (Free Pen) in the Urdu edition.

Like Abbas, Kaifi Azmi straddled the word of literary journals and films. In 1948 he wrote his first lyric for the film *Buzdil* (Coward), directed by Shahid Latif, the husband of his friend and fellow progressive, Ismat Chughtai and went on to write some of the most hauntingly evocative lyrics ever written for the Bombay film industry including the memorable '*Waqt ne kiya kya haseen sitam...*' (What a beautiful cruelty Time has inflicted...) An ardent member of the PWM and a major crowd puller at the peoples' *mushairas* organised by the progressives in industrial hubs such as Bhiwandi, Kaifi was equally active as a spokesperson for several workers' unions. A writer of tender lyrics and rousing anthems displaying an astonishing combination of passion and conviction, Azmi was the quintessential activist-poet. His three major poetry collections are entitled *Jhankar* (Tinking, 1943), *Akhir-e-Shab* (Small Hours of the Night, 1947) and *Awara Sijde* (Vagrant Prostrations, 1973).

Others who bridged the gap between literature and cinema were Kanhaiya Lal Kapoor, Ramanand Sagar, Kaifi Azmi, Akhtarul Iman. Not all, however, reached the heights scaled by Sahir. Majruh Sultanpuri, for instance, wrote his first lyrics for the film *Shah Jahan* in 1946 and then launched upon a highly lucrative career in Bombay. However, his leftist leanings did not leave him entirely and Morarji Desai's government put him in prison for writing anti-government film lyrics. Makhdoom Mohiuddin, fiery trade union leader and writer of romantic verse and fiercely political poetry, never wrote for films though several of his ghazals were used in films. The writers and lyricists occasionally also dabbled in making movies with mixed results. For instance, along with fellow progressive Vishwamitra Adil, the maverick writer Niyaz Haider wrote the lyrics for *Sarai ke Baahar* (Outside the Inn, 1947), the only film directed by prose stylist Krishan Chandar. Rajinder Singh Bedi (1915-1984), however, fared better than most. Beginning his professional life as a postal clerk, Bedi moved to Bombay as an established fiction writer and got involved with the film industry like many of his fellow progressives, but his diverse interests led him from writing the dialogue and screenplay of over 27 films to producing and directing memorable films such as *Garam Coat* (Warm Coat, 1955), *Dastak* (Tapping, 1970) and *Phagun* (the eleventh month of the Hindu calendar, 1958).

With time, while the Bombay progressives may have weakened as a literary grouping, their influence continued to be felt for a very long time in the work of the film lyricists.

In K A Abbas's *Saat Hindustani* (1969), we see Kaifi exhorting his fellow Indians to move forward and build a new and prosperous India:

> *Zulm hadd se badheyga to ghatt jayega*
> *Apni talwaar se aap cut jayega...*
>
> When tyranny crosses all limits it dies
> It gets slashed by its own sword

It is this kind of writings that bridges the gap between poetry and lyric, that blurs the distinction between 'high' and 'low' literature, and 'popular' and 'pedestrian', that limns wisdom with empathy that is the Bombay progressives' most valuable gift to Hindi cinema.

75. *Yeh Kya Jagah Hai Doston*: The City in the Poetry of Shahryar

Coming in the wake of the politically-engaged, socially-driven progressive writers' movement, Shahryar (1936-2012) represented the new poetic sensibility of the 1960s that could be fiercely individualistic yet profoundly humane. Having viewed, at first hand, the decline of progressivism and the commensurate rise of modernism or *jadidyat*, he was well placed to chart a poetic destiny that was closely intertwined with that of the new republic. And as Urdu became an increasingly cosmopolitan language, loosening its ties from rural India, the modern Urdu poet's landscape became increasingly city based. The Urdu poetry of the past 70 years exemplifies this shift towards the urban and possibly no one demonstrates this better than Shahryar. His poetry reflects the angst and the sense of alienation and dislocation that comes from living in a city where one has not fully been able to put down roots, where the walls of one's house are still new and alien, where nights are not always kind and merciful but long and harsh, where sleep is also not benevolent and merciful offering an escape or a haven but unyielding, withholding the possibility of escape and entirely without dreams.

From the first collection *Ism-e-Aazam* (The Great Name) itself, Shahryar began articulating a host of issues and finding 'common cause' with his readers: despondency over the social and political state of affairs, sense of dislocation that came as a natural corollary to urban life, bitterness over broken dreams and failed promises and yet an unfailing optimism that soared above the small sorrows and despairs and caused him to look at the future with hope. Given below are some scattered examples from *Ism-e-Aazam*:

Shahr phir shahr hai yaan jii to bahal jaata hai
Shahr se bhaag ke sahra ko na jaa, maan bhi jaa

The city is after all a city, it can distract the heart
Don't leave the city for the wilderness, listen to me

Laakh khurshid sar-e-baam agar hain to rahein
Hum koi mom nahin ke pighal jayenge

Let a thousand suns skim the top of my terrace
I am not made of wax that I will melt

Tujh se bichhde hain to ab kis se milati hai humein
Zindagi dekhiye kya rang dikhati hai hamein

Separated from you, who will we meet
Let us see what else life has to show us

Here's another sampling culled from later collections reflecting the many shades of a city dweller's life:

Ai junoon tujh se taqaza hai yahi dil ka mere
Shahr-e ummeed ke naqshe ko badalta dekhoon

O passion, this is the only demand my heart makes of you
That I may see the map of my city of dreams change

Ghar ki taameer tasawwur hii mein ho sakti hai
Apne naqshe ke mutabiq yeh zameen kuch kum hai

A home can be constructed only in one's imagination
This land is a bit less according to the map I have built

Tumhare shahr mein kuchh bhi huwa nahin hai kya?
Ki tumne cheekhon ko sachmuch suna nahin hai kya?

Has nothing happened in this city of yours?
Have you really not heard the screams?

And:

Main eik zamaane se hairaan hoon ke hakim-e shehr
Jo ho raha hai ussey dekhta naheen hai kya

For long I have wondered why the ruler of this city
Cannot see what is happening here

And in this nazm entitled 'Muzd-e Inquilab' (The Harbinger of Revolution):

Hawa banke jo qaid hai botalon ke badan mein
Woh sab dev hain
Khauf aur nafraton ke
Woh sab dev eik roze azaad hongey
Woh sab dev jis roze azaad hongey
To iss shahr ka eik-eik fard khud se pashemaan hoga
Tilism-e hawas toot jaane par hairaan hoga
Nigahein kabhi aasmanon ki jaanib uttheingii
Kabhi haath koi ishara kareingey

Kabhi hont kuchh bolne ka irada kareingey
Magar kuchh na hoga
Faqat jung hogii
Har eik simt se baarish-e sang hogii

Captured like air in the belly of bottles
They are all the genies of fear and hatred
One day these genies shall be released
On the day that these genies will be released
Every single person in this city will be ashamed of himself
And shocked at the breaking of the spell of lust
Eyes shall be raised towards the skies sometimes
Sometimes hands shall make some signs
And sometimes lips shall try to speak something
But nothing will happen
Only war will break out
And from every direction there will be a rain of stones

Of course, by far the best odes to the city that have emerged from Shahryar's pen are the ghazals that were adapted for two popular Hindi films, *Gaman* (1978) and *Umrao Jan* (1981), respectively. Incidentally, the near-iconic song picturised on Farooque Shaikh as he drives his taxi in the urban jungle that is Bombay in *Gaman*, '*Seene mein jalan, ankhon mein toofan sa kyun hai...*' (Why is there a heartburn in my chest, this storm in my eyes...), first appeared in *Ism-e-Aazam* in 1965; so did '*Yeh kya jageh hai doston, yeh kaun sa dayaar hai...*' (What is this place, friends, which is this land...) that was used to such poignant effect in *Umrao Jan*. Taken together, they best reflect the near-tilismic spell the city had cast on Shahryar the man and the poet causing the motif of the city to appear and reappear time and again in his ouvre:

Seene mein jalan aankhon mein toofan sa kyun hai
Iss shehr mein har shakhs pareshan sa kyun hai

Why this ache in my heart, why this storm in my eyes
Why is everyone in such turmoil in this city?

And

Yey kya jagah hai doston yeh kaun sa dayaar hai
Hadd-e nigah tak jahan ghubaar hii ghubaar hai

What is this place, which is this world
Till as far as the eye can see there is nothing but dust

76. Banaras: The Kaaba of Hindostan

~

The ancient temple town of Varanasi (popularly called Kashi or Banaras) is known for the holy Ganga River that flows through it, the historical and scenic ghats that line the river bank, the famous Ganga Aarti, the many ancient temples. It is also famous for its centuries-old tradition of weaving—both carpets and brocades. One of the oldest inhabited cities, it is supposed to be resting on Shiva's trident and is under the protective care of the Blue God. Such is the eternal charm of this ancient city by the river, that it beckons people of all faiths.

Mornings in Banaras are special; the sound of temple bells wafting over the river, smoke rising from the pyres on Manikarnika ghat, the eternal city gradually freeing itself from the cloak of sleep and the early morning aarti at the Assi ghat. For the modern-day traveler, Subh-e-Banaras is a government-sponsored tourist initiative that involves an early morning aarti, a boat ride, a dip in the Ganga and a 'surya namaskar'. But for the Urdu poet, *Subh-e-Banaras* (Morning in Banaras) predates this immersive experience of watching the sun rise over the river to the sound of mantras being chanted in a sing-song that is as old as Time. For the poet, it is a metaphor for new beginnings, of hope and renewal, of sublime beauty. Here is Lala Madhav Ram Jauhar using the metaphor to convey an abundance of good fortune:

Raat din chaiyn hum ai rashk-e-qamar rakhte hain
Shaam Awadh ki to Banaras ki sahar rakhte hain

O envy of the moon, I am content all day and night
I have evenings of Awadh and mornings of Banaras

Showing that no single community could celebrate the beauty of *Subh-e-Banaras*, Ajmal Sultanpuri writes in his lyrical ode to an India that is threatened by extinction in a poem entitled 'Kahan Hai Mera Hindostan' (Where is My India):

Jahaan ki subh Banaras dhaam
Jahaan bhagwaan karein ashnaan

Whose mornings are sacred as Banaras
Where the Gods come to bathe

When war clouds gathered over the sub-continent, the Jnanpith-award winning poet, Ali Sardar Jafri, spoke of peace in a poem entitled 'Dosti' (Friendship) urging the neighbours from across the hostile border thus:

Tum aao gulshan-e-Lahore se chaman-bardosh
Hum aaein subh-e-Banaras ki raushni le kar

You come from the garden of Lahore carrying spring on your shoulder
We will come bearing the light from the morning of Banaras

The popular trope of *Shaam-e-Awadh* (Evening in Awadh) and *Subh-e-Banaras* are further elaborated by Wahid Premi thus:

Hai shaam-e-Awadh gesu-e-dildaar ka partav
Aur subh-e-Banaras hai rukh-e-yaar ka partav

If evenings in Awadh are the reflection from the beloved's tresses
Mornings in Banaras are the light from the beloved's cheeks

And by Anwarul Hasan Anwar as:

Ye Awadh hai ki jahaan shaam kabhi khatm nahin
Woh Banaras hai jahaan roz sahar hoti hai

There's Awadh where evenings don't end
And Banaras where every day there's an evening

The city's best known Urdu poet was Nazeer Banarasi who has featured often in these pages. Immensely popular in his lifetime, he has written paeans to his beloved country's syncretic culture, its fairs and festivals, its *subh-o-shaam*, its scenic beauty, one such ode being 'Pyara Hindostan' (Beloved India):

Husn ki taskeen ishq ki dhaaras
Wah re apni subh-e-Banaras
Ghat ke patthar jaise paaras

Assuaging Beauty, comforting Love
Bravo my morning of Banaras
Where every stone on the river bank is the Alchemist's Stone

And now, for some poems devoted entirely to the city, each entitled simply 'Banaras'. Living in distant Lahore, Akhtar Shirani waxes eloquent about this city beside a sacred river with its many temples and temple bells, the devout bathing at the ghats, the boat rides on the river, the cool morning breezes and ending with this fervent plea:

Humare dil se nikalti hai ye dua Aḳhtar
Ki phir bhi shakl dikhaae Khuda Banaras ki

My earnest prayer is this, O Akhtar
That may god grant me another sight of Banaras

Safi Lakhnawi begins his long paean to the holy city with these lines that ought to shame the bigots who bay for the others' blood:

Dekh tera but-kada hai Kaaba-e-Hindostan

See, your temple is the Kaaba of Hindostan

Recreating the fabled morning, the *Subh-e-Banaras,* Raees Amrohvi, brings alive the spectacle of the sun rising from the folds of the night and spreading its light to reveal a magical sight:

Subha-e-Banaras dil ka sahara
Ganga ka manzar woh pyara pyara
Soney ki lehrein chaandi ki dhaara
Ho gar mayassar phir woh nazara
Morning in Banaras is uplifting
How lovely is the sight of the Ganga
Its waves like gold, its ripples like silver
If only I could see that sight again

Another poet from the city, Ravish Banarasi, writes with affection and a sense of ownership:

Ai mere achche Banaras, Kaaba ahl-e-hunood
Eik duniya ke liye teri zameen jaaye sujood

O my dear Banaras, you are the Kaaba for the Hindu
One part of the world bows in prostration on your ground

Then there is the masnavi entitled 'Charagh-e Dair' (The Temple's Lamp) by Ghalib (referred to earlier in the essay entitled 'Ghalib in a New World Order'). Translating from the original Persian, Maaz bin Bilal renders verses 46 and 47 as: 'This settlement is the seat/ of the idol-worshipping faithful,/ from beginning to end/ it is the pilgrimage of mystics./ The (supreme) place of worship for the conch-blowers,/ surely, (Banaras) is the Kaaba/ of Hindustan.'

Most remarkable, however, is a ghazal by Hatim Ali Mehr, a contemporary of Ghalib and an honorary magistrate at Agra. The ghazal has a qafiya of 'Banaras', that is, each sher ends with the word Banaras extolling some virtue of this city; one such sher being:

Meri ye wasiyyat hai ki mar jaoon agar main
To baad-e-saba ḳhaak ko pahunchaae Banaras

My will and testament is this that when I die
The morning breeze should carry my dust to Banaras

Postscript: One wouldn't be wrong in thinking that all of the above seems to belong to some enchanted past, far removed from the present. For, in the present we have witnessed posters sprouting on some ghats prohibiting the entry of non-Hindus. What is more, lest there be any doubt, the posters are explicit: 'This is a warning, not a request.'*

*https://thewire.in/communalism/hindu-right-groups-put-up-posters-at-varanasi-ghats-warning-non-hindus-not-to-visit

77. Kashmir: *Jannat-e-Rang-o-Bu*

❧

As a child, I remember listening—entranced—to my grandfather's stories about his 'walking holiday' in Kashmir in the summer of 1933, how as a young man he walked miles and miles with his friends, how he discovered and—in the process—fell in love with its hills and dales, valleys and high mountains, its gushing streams and its vast verdant meadows. Later, I read the many beautiful poems Abba (as we called our grandfather) wrote about his early love for this beautiful part of the country, poems that appeared in his very first collection of poetry entitled *Sal Sabeel.* About the rivers Jhelum and Lidder, the Sindh nullah in Kangan, the rolling meadows of Pahalgam, the pristine beauty of Sonmarg, the Shalimar and Nishat gardens, the one I liked most is about returning from Sonmarg that ends with the pledge:

> *Ai mauj-e-Sindh tera main naghma-khwaan rahoonga*
> *Tu bhi jawaan rahegi, main bhi jawaan rahunga*
>
> O rivulet of Sindh, I shall always sing your songs
> You shall remain ever youthful and so shall I

In much the same vein, Abba's friend and contemporary, Jagan Nath Azad whom we had the occasion to meet several times since he worked in Jammu and made frequent trips to the valley, wrote in his *Sair-e-Kashmir ka Eik Tassur* (An Impression of Travels in Kashmir). He spoke of the silence of the greens, the sound of the waterfalls, the vermillion of the autumnal leaves, the whiteness of the rocks:

Azad! zara dekh tu ye aalam-e-arzang
Mausam ke ye andaaz bahaaron ke ye nairang
Ye husn, ye tarteeb, ye tazeen, ye aahang

Azad! Just look at this incredible world
The coquetry of the seasons, the sorcery of spring
This beauty, this embellishment, this adornment, this orderliness

Years later, when Abba served as Director of the Iqbal Institute located in the scenic Kashmir University campus, my siblings and I spent 15 memorable summer vacations with him and Amma, our grandmother. On the very first day of the summer vacations we would board the Jhelum express from Delhi and spend the next 5-6 weeks being pampered by Abba and Amma, fed equal doses of love and laughter, good food and good poetry. Those 15 summers in Srinagar fostered a deep-seated love for this beautiful but scarred land.

In Urdu, some of the most lyrical descriptions of Kashmir and its spectacular beauty are found in the short stories of Krishan Chandar and Saadat Hasan Manto. Generations of poets too have written on this piece of heaven on earth with the most famous being this Persian verse attributed to Amir Khusro:

Gar firdaus bar-ru-e zameen ast
Hamin asto, hamin asto, hamin ast

If there is a heaven on earth
It is here, it is here, it is here

In his hymn to the motherland, 'Khaak-e-Hind' (The Dust of India) Brij Narain Chakbast too alludes to this perfectly natural pairing of Kashmir with the conception of paradise:

Kashmir se ayaan hai jannat ka rang ab tak

The colour of paradise is still manifested by Kashmir

Muhammad Rafi Sauda—one of the great 18th century poets and contemporary of Mir Taqi Mir—who is highly unlikely to have visited Kashmir, nevertheless refers to it showing the place it occupied in the popular Indian imagination:

Kashmir sii jagah mein naa-shukr naa rah zaahid
Jannat mein tu ai geedi maare hai ye kyun laatein

Don't be thankless in a place such as Kashmir, O hermit
Why do you kick about, you dolt, in this paradise

Even Ghalib, who like Sauda, had never visited Kashmir, nevertheless uses it as a metaphor for a place of fabled beauty whose gardens were said to resemble those of paradise:

Mir ke sher ka ahvaal kahun kya Ghalib
Jis ka divaan kum-az-gulshan-e-Kashmir nahin

O Ghalib, how shall I describe the poetry of Mir
Whose collected works are no less than the gardens of Kashmir

Kaifi Azmi, in his 'Jannat-e-Rang-o-Bu' (A Paradise of Colour and Fragrance) tells us why Indians have always reposed such pride in this cradle of the Himalayas:

Roz-e-azal se teri khaak taaj-e-zameen-e-Hind hai
Zewar-e-rang-o-bu tera zeb-e-jabeen-e-Hind hai

From the Day of Creation your soil is the crown in the land of Hind
Your ornaments of colour and fragrance adorn the forehead of Hind

Nazeer Banarasi's 'Pyara Hindostan' (Beloved Hindostan), from which we have quoted earlier, elaborates on the twinning of Kashmir and paradise thus:

Jannat ki tasveer ko dekho
Aao zaraa Kashmir ko dekho

See the picture of Paradise
Come, look at Kashmir

In a country whose weather is characterised as 'tropical monsoon', the snow-covered mountains of Kashmir crop up in the poet's imagination in unexpected ways, as in this sher by Saghar Azmi:

Kaashmir ki waadi mein be-parda jo nikle ho
Kya aag lagaaoge barfeeli chataanon mein

Having come out unveiled in the Kashmir valley
You will set these snow-covered rocks on fire

So much for the beauty and scenic splendor that Nature has lavished upon Kashmir. But what of its anguished soul, its battered, bruised spirit, its besieged, dehumanised population? What of the simmering discontent over decades of hostile central government policies emanating from New Delhi? It takes a young poet such as Varun Anand to allude to the stone pelting that had become the last resort of angry Kashmiris to express their angst against a brutal, repressive state machinery:

Tumhaari yaadein patthar baaziyaan karti hain seene mein
Humaare haal bhi ab hu-ba-hu Kashmir waale hain

Your memories pelt stones upon my breast
My state is the same as Kashmir's now

Abdus Sattar Danish points to the tectonic shift in the popular imagination that had hitherto viewed Kashmir as *jannat*; today, it is associated with *dahshat* (terror) due to forces beyond its control:

Naqsh hai har zulm jis ka waadi-e-Kashmir par
Uss ne dahshat-gard likkha amn ki tasveer par

He whose every cruelty is imprinted upon the Kashmir valley
He has written terrorist upon this picture of peace

Nida Fazli, who has enthralled us earlier with his 'Allah Hu' rhyme scheme, puts the spotlight on Kashmir in a ghazal with a qafiya of 'Ya Allah' that seems to be asking why Kashmir should only be viewed in a binary with war or terror:

Kargil aur Kashmir hii tere naam hon kyun
Bhai bahan mahbooba beti Ya Allah

Why should your name be just Kargil and Kashmir
Why can't it be brother, sister, beloved or daughter, O Allah

In a poem entitled 'Kashmir' Akhtar Payami is asking uncomfortable questions, throwing light on issues that are often hidden behind polemics, and upturning the much-trotted metaphor of *jannat* to show its dark under belly:

Surḳh phoolon se lahu phoot raha hai shayad
Aaj jannat mein jahannum ke nazaare dekho

Perhaps it's blood that's bursting from red flowers
Look at these tableaux of hell in heaven today

Postscript: I returned to Kashmir 35 years after those halcyon summer days; this time, I was accompanied by my daughter. We took a skiing holiday in the winter wonderland that is Gulmarg. While the mountain resort was a safe haven bustling with tourists from different parts of India, the capital city was eerily silent and subdued, almost stupefied under a blanket of heavy security and a bitterly cold winter. We came away numbed and chilled to the bone by the sandbags and the security cordons, the barbed wires and the all-pervasive armed personnel and, above all, the immense silence that held Srinagar in its grip. All the while, in my head, Abba's voice was whispering words he had recited to me a lifetime ago:

> *Tuk dekh liya, dil shaad kiya, khush-waqt huwe, aur chal nikle...*
>
> I saw it for a while, gladdened my heart, had a good time, and I have moved on...

The irony was gall bitter as, coming away from Kashmir this time, my heart was not *shaad* but *naa-shaad* (unhappy, not happy).

78. *Ganga Maiya Tohre Piyari Chadhaibo*

Perhaps it is entirely in keeping with the spirit that propels this volume that we should begin this soliloquy on India's holiest river, the sacred Ganga, with these words from the one Urdu poet who is most hated in the New India that is Bharat. Writing his 'Tarana-e-Hind' (The Song of India) in 1904 as a patriotic song for children that went on to become one of the most popular songs for school choruses till its political baggage was discovered and it was promptly discarded, Iqbal begins with '*Saare jahan se achha Hindostan hamara*' (Our India is the fairest in the entire world) and contains these memorable lines:

Ai aabrood-e-Ganga woh din hai yaad tujh ko
Utra tire kinaare jab kaarvaan hamara

O waters of the Ganga do you remember that day
When our caravan had halted beside your banks

Waves upon waves of people came over the centuries and settled down in the fertile lands watered by this mighty river. Flowing for a distance of 2,525 km, all the way from the mountains to the sea, it has fostered an entire civilisation and a way of life. In a long poem entitled 'Ganga', Suroor Barabankvi addresses the river thus:

Ai aabrood-e-Ganga uff rii tiri safaai
Ye tera husn dil-kash ye tarz-o-dil-rubaai

O waters of the Ganga, such is your purity
Your beauty is so heart-tugging it steals my heart

The last of the great classical Mughal poets, Dagh Dehlvi, speaks naturally, effortlessly, organically of bathing in the Ganga in this sher:

Gham se kahiin najaat miley chaiyn paaen hum
Dil khoon mein nahaaye to Ganga nahaaen hum

If we were to escape sorrow and find some peace
Our heart would bathe in blood and we bathe in the Ganga

That the Ganga is a synonym for purity is found in a poem about Urdu written by Sardar Jafri:

Haseen dilkash jawaan Urdu
Zabaan woh dhul ke jis ko Ganga ke jal se paakeezgi mili hai

Beautiful, alluring, youthful Urdu
A language that has been washed in the waters of the Ganga
to attain purity

Waseem Barelvi likens his city to the river in this nazm:

Shahr mera udaas Ganga sa
Koi bhi aaye aur apne paap
Kho ke jaata hai dho ke jaata hai

My city is like the sad Ganga
Whoever comes here with his sins
Loses them by washing in the river

The boat on the river image is re-imagined thus by Ibn Safi:

Husn banaa jab bahti Ganga
Ishq hua kaaghaz ki naav

When beauty turned into a flowing Ganga
Love became a paper boat

That the Ganga is loved equally by all is evident from this whimsical sher by Nida Fazli from a ghazal that has been referred to earlier ('Brindaban ke Krishn Kanhaiya Allah Hu'):

Jaisa jis ka bartan waisa us ka tan
Ghat-ti badh-ti Ganga maiya Allah hu

A person's body is akin to the size of his utensil
Mother Ganga rises and falls, Allah, O Allah

In a lyrically tender poem entitled 'Tere Khushbu Mein Basey Khat' (Letters Drenched in Your Fragrance) Rajinder Nath Rahbar writes about surrendering his most treasured possessions in the safekeeping of the river:

Umr-bhar ki jo kamaaii thhi ganvaa aayaa hoon
Tere khat aaj main Ganga mein bahaa aayaa hoon

I have thrown away whatever was my lifelong earning
Today I have floated away your letters in the Ganga

Two modern Hindi poets writing the ghazal in Hindi have written about the Ganga thus. First Gopaldas Neeraj:

Aag bahtii hai yahaan Ganga mein Jhelum mein bhi
Koi batlaaye kahaan jaa ke nahaayaa jaaye

Fire flows in the Ganga and in the Jhelum too
Someone should tell me where I should go to bathe

And Dushyant Kumar:

Ho gayii hai peer parvat sii pighalnii chaahiye
Iss Himaale se koi Ganga nikalnii chaahiye

The pain is so immense that the mountain should melt
A Ganga should emerge from this Himalaya

Then there are the countless film songs that celebrate the Ganga, such as '*Ganga aaye kahan se, Ganga jaaye kahan re...*' from the film *Kabuliwala*, '*Tu ganga ki mauj main Jamuna ka dhaara...*' from *Baiju Bawra*, '*Hum uss desh ke waasi hain...*' from *Jis Desh Mein Ganga Bahti Hai*, '*Mere man ki Ganga aur tere man ki Jamuna...*' from *Sangam*, '*Ganga maiyya mein jab tak ke paani rahe...*' from *Suhaag Raat*, '*Ganga tera paani amrit*' from the eponymous film. Each, in their own way, reinforced the image in the nooks and crannies of the popular imagination that had been fostered by the Urdu poet for a long, long time.

Postscript: My husband's family is from eastern Uttar Pradesh. The river Varna flows close beside his home; the Varna is a tributary of the Ganga and together with Assi it creates the name of India's holiest city beside the mighty Ganga, Varanasi. On my first visit as a new bride to my in-laws home, I remember my husband proudly introducing me to the river that flows past his ancestral lands with a fragment of this song: '*Ganga maiya tohre piyari chadhaibo...*' (O Mother Ganga, I offer this yellow dhoti to you...) A wealth of love, and pride, lay hidden in these simple words. On each subsequent visit, over the years, I have whispered these words to the river upon first catching sight of it as it glimmers beside the road or flows beneath a bridge.

79. *Ai Himala Ai Faseel-e-Kishwar-e-Hindustan*

Like the Ganga, much has been written in Urdu poetry about the Himalayas (written as, and pronounced, 'Himala'). In fact, the two often come together and rightly so for the river has her home in the mighty mountains that bound India in the north. While the Ganga is both a living, breathing national treasure and a metaphor for *pakeezgi* (purity) for the Urdu poet, the Himala stands for *pukhtagi* (strength and solidness) and *paasbani* (protection). And, as for the Ganga, the most-reviled poet of our times, Allama Iqbal, has written some of the most beautiful lines on the Himala too:

Ai Himala ai faseel-e-kishwar-e-Hindustan
Choomta hai teri peshaani ko jhuk kar aasman

O Himala, O border of the country that is India
The sky bends down to kiss you on your forehead

Showing how the Ganga and Himala are intertwined in the popular imagination, Sahir Ludhianvi celebrates India's independence with these words:

Ab koi gulshan na ujde ab watan azad hai
Rooh Ganga ki Himala ka badan azad hai

Let no garden be desolate now the country is free
The spirit of Ganga the body of Himala is free

In much the same way, Moin Ehsan Jazbi writing on 15 August 1947 celebrates the dawn of a new freedom thus:

Badey naaz se aaj ubhra hai suraj
Himala ke oonche kalas jagmagae
Pahadon ke chashmon ko sona banaya

The sun has arisen with an immense pride today
The high domes of the Himalayas are radiant
The streams gushing from mountains molten gold

Nazeer Banarasi, who has appeared in the pages of this volume bearing gifts of deeply patriotic poetry, has this to say about the mountain range that has guarded the country with its arms spread wide:

Kalaon ka mandir adab ka shivala
Pavan ka purana nigahban Himala
Yeh Bharat ka mastak hai Bharat ka mastak
Kisi ke jhukaaiye nahi jhukne wala
Himalaya ki chattan ban kar ladeinge
Hum eik-eik chappe ki khaatir ladeinge

A temple of the arts, a sanctuary of learning
An old custodian of the winds
It's the forehead of India
It's not one to bow at anyone's command
Like a rock of the Himala we shall fight
We shall fight for every inch of our space

Written during the Indo-China war of 1963, the poem concludes with urging fellow Indians to do everything in their might to save the Himala:

Bache jis tarah bhi Himala bachao
Bachao watan ka shivala bachao!

No matter how: Save the Himala
Save the country's sanctuary, save it!

Nazeer Banarasi alludes to the Himala often in jewel-like references such as this studded in longer poems about the beauty that is India, '*Hansta parbat hansmukh jharna*' (the laughing mountain, the cheerful waterfalls) or when he urges Indians to come together to save the country:

Lahu mein Gang-o-Jaman dono ki ravaani hai
Tumhara dil nahi Bharat ki rajdhani hai
Himala ki tarah apna sar utha kar chalo
Dil aaj dil se, qadam se qadam mila kar chalo

The swiftness of Ganga and Jamuna in our blood
It isn't your heart, it is the capital of Bharat
Walk with your head held high like the Himala
Walk, with your heart beating in step with each other

Elsewhere he admonishes the poet who has, for far too long, been content to write of love and romance in his ghazals:

Iss waqt ghazal ki baat na kar
Santaan hanse to kaise hanse
Iss waqt hai mata khatre mein
Sansaar ke parvat ka raja
Hai apna Himala khatre mein
Hai saamna kitne khatron ka
Hai desh ki seema khatre mein
Ai dost watan se ghaat na kar
Iss waqt ghazal ki baat na kar

Don't talk of the ghazal at a time like this
How can a child laugh at a time like this

When the mother is in danger at a time like this
The king of all the mountains of the world
Our very own Himala is in danger
It is facing so many threats and risks
The country's borders are in peril
O friend, don't deceive the country
Don't talk of the ghazal at a time like this

That there was a time when the poets took note of what was happening at the frontier and wrote in white heat about China's aggression and India's military debacle in the Indo-China war seems untenable today. Latter day Chinese excursions into Indian territory come and gone with nary a poetic response.

Film lyricists have penned some beautiful patriotic songs which invariably featured the mighty mountain as an invincible protector. Kavi Pradeep, whose pen has produced many a memorable song, wrote this in 1943 for the film *Qismat* (Destiny); it was set to music by Anil Biswas and sung by Khan Mastana and Amirbai Karnataki. Regrettably it has been appropriated by a militant, muscular nationalism that sees machismo in its *lalkaar* (call of defiance, rebuke):

Aaj Himalay ki choti se phir humne lalkara hai
Duur hato ai duniya walon Hindostan hamara hai

Again we have called out from the top of the Himalaya
Stay away, O rest of the world, India is ours

Also from Kavi Pradeep's pen is '*Ai Mere Watan ke Logon…*' (O people of my country…) sung by Lata Mangeshkar with these lines portraying the immense hurt of the Indian people when the Himalaya is attacked:

Jab ghaayal hua Himalaya
Khatre mein padi azaadi

When the Himalaya was wounded
When freedom was in peril

That the Himala also appears as a metaphor for immensity is evident from this sher by Ahmad Alvi:

Banaane ko Himala nafraton ke
Galat-fahmii ki ik raai bahut hai

To make a Himalaya of hatreds
A misunderstanding the size of a rye seed is enough

Postscript: Sorely lacking even a smidgeon of musical talent, I was never chosen to sing in the school choir despite multiple auditions; however, nothing could stop me from memorizing the lyrics of the songs that were routinely sung by the choir during morning assembly. From a hoary past when Iqbal's 'Saare Jahan Se Achha' was considered perfectly kosher for school assemblies, I have a luminous memory of singing lustily, and entirely out of tune, about a *parbat* that was a *paasban*, a benign presence that allowed rivers to play in his lap:

Parbat woh sabse uncha, humsaya asman ka
Woh santari hamara, woh paasban hamara

Godi mein khelti hain, uski hazaron nadiyan
Gulshan hai jinke dam se rashk-e-jinan hamara

That highest mountain, that companion of the skies
He is our sentry, he is our protector

A thousand rivers play in his lap because of whom
Our garden is the envy of paradise

80. *Kahan Hai Mera Hindostan?*

From its earliest days Urdu poetry has been a living testament to shared living, a co-mingling of cultures. Ram and Rahim appeared as two sides of the same coin, the coin being *Hindustaniyat*, that ineffable state of Being Indian. Some of the most lyrical, most tender, most moving poetry has been written in Urdu on India and its *azmat* (greatness), *shohrat* (fame), on why the poet loves it unconditionally and what is the basis of the *wataniyat* (nationalist feelings) that so permeates much of Urdu poetry. In this final essay let us revisit some of the spectacular poetry written on Hindustan and, in the process, also ask ourselves some uncomfortable questions.

I must desist from quoting Iqbal—though it must be stated that he has indeed written some marvelous poetry on Hindustan—lest I be accused of holding a subversive brief for him. Let me instead quote from poets who have been inexplicably overlooked in recent times. Let us begin with Brij Narain Chakbast's 'Khaak-e Hind' (The Dust of Hind) that invokes Gautam and Sarmad, Akbar and Rana Pratap, Kashmir and Ganga and ends with the fervent plea:

Gard-o-ġhubar yaan ka ḳhilat hai apne tan ko
Mar kar bhi chahte hain ḳhaak-e-watan kafan ko

The dust of this land is a robe of honour for our body
Even after death we want the dust of our land as our shroud

Extolling the virtues of his fellow countrymen Maharaj Bahadur Barq Dehelvi in his 'Ahl-e-Hind' (People of Hind) notes how the ancient civilisations of Rome and Greece, Syria and Central Asia disappeared, only the Indian civilisation has lasted. Brimful with *hubb-e-watani* (love for the homeland), the poem ends with the assertion that it was the essential goodness and humanity of the people of Hind that is the reason for the longevity of this civilisation:

Apne mooh se kya batayein hum ke kya woh log thhe
Nafs-kash neki ke putle thhe, mujassam yog thhe

How can I sing the praises of those people with my own mouth
They were icons of goodness, yogis incarnate, evolved beings

In 'Gulzar-e-Watan' (The Country's Garden) Durga Sahay Suroor Jahanabadi paints an idealised picture of a garden where the bulbul has no fear of the hunter, the flowers unafraid of autumn:

Phoolon ka kunj-e-dilkash Bharat mein ik banayein
Hubb-e-watan ke paudey issme naye lagaayein

Let us make a pleasing nook of flowers in Bharat
Let us plant new flowers of love for the nation

Then there's Firaq Gorakhpuri who wrote the following sher referring to the waves upon waves of people who came to India over the centuries making it their home, carrying bits and pieces of their cultures and their DNA to create a unique Indian identity:

Sar-zamin-e-hind par aqvaam-e-aalam ke Firaq
Qaafile baste gaye Hindostan banta gaya

O Firaq nations of the world kept coming to the land of Hind
Caravans upon caravans settled here and Hindostan was created

Gopal Mittal paints a picture of harmony among people of different faiths who live with mutual respect in 'Ai Watan' (O Nation):

Salaam ho teri galiyon pe ai watan ke jahan
Yeh rasm aam hai jo chhahe sar uttha ke jiye

Salutations to your lanes, O my country, where
It is the norm to walk with one's head held high

Zafar Ali Khan, newspaper editor, political activist, freedom fighter and a popular poet in his lifetime, talks of a pure, sublime love for his homeland that transcends religion, caste and creed:

Naquus se ġharaz hai na matlab azaan se hai
Mujh ko agar hai ishq to Hindostan se hai

I wish to have nothing to do with the conch or the azaan
If there is anything I love 'tis only Hindostan

So when did it all begin to unravel? When did the poet begin to notice—and point—towards those misgivings that were nibbling away at the joy of a new found freedom? The years immediately after independence were marked by serious introspection. By the time of the first Republic Day, Sahir Ludhianvi's disenchantment with the new republic is already palpable. In a poem titled 'Chhabees Janwary' (26 January), Sahir invokes the beautiful dreams the nation had dreamt, and asks all Indians to collectively pose some difficult questions:

Aao ki aaj ġhaur karein iss sawaal par
Dekhe thhe hum ne jo woh haseen ḳhwaab kya huwe

Come, let us ponder over this question
What happened to those beautiful dreams we had dreamt

Josh Malihabadi in a poem called 'Maatam-e Azadi' (The Lament for Freedom) strikes a somber note as early as 1948; its reverberations can be heard 75 years later:

Ai ham nafas! Fasana e Hindustan naa pooch
Apna gala kharosh-e tarranum se phat gaya
Talwar se bacha, to rag-e gul se kat gaya

O friend, don't ask me for the tale of Hindustan
Our throats were torn by the scratching of our songs
When we escaped the sword, we were beheaded by the veins of the rose

In the same vein as Faiz Ahmad Faiz's famous lament at the disappointments of freedom, here is Ibadat Barelwi warning of the worse that lies in store, a warning that seems prophetic today:

Haan talkhi-e-ayam abhi aur badhegi
Haan ahl-e-sitam mashq-e-sitam karte raheinge

Yes, the bitterness among the people will increase, still more
Yes, the perpetrators of cruelty will keep practicing cruelty

Nazeer Banarsi, the old optimist keeps alive the garden in his heart and alludes to the co-existence of the thorns and the buds:

Kantey hon chahe phool hon fasl-e-bahar ke
Paale hain donon ek hii parvardigar ke
Hum Bhartiya shikaar hain apne hi waar ke

Be it thorns or flowers in the harvest of spring
Both are raised by the same Almighty God
We Indians are the victims of our own arrows

Perhaps the greatest lesson is to be learnt from this verse by a traditionalist such as Jigar Moradabadi, who was seldom known to take up a political position yet here he is—refusing to shy away from voicing his disappointment with an independent but truncated India where the heedless gardeners have done nothing to bring back the angered spring:

Naya zamana banane chale thhey deewaaney
Nai zameen naya aasman banaa na sakey

The foolish folk had set out to make a new world
But they could not make a new earth and a new sky

And finally there is this sweetly naïve poem by Ajmal Sultanpuri who is in search of the India of his childhood:

Musalmaan aur Hindu ki jaan
Kahaan hai mera Hindostan
Main uss ko dhoodh raha hoon

The life of Muslims and Hindus
Where is my India?
I am searching for it

It would be a sad day if the poet could only fret and fume, bemoan and decry. For every lament there is a rejoicing, for every despair a ray of hope, for every old hurt a new resolve. I, for one, take heart from these lines from 'Lahu ka Teeka' (a mark on the forehead made with blood) by Anand Narain Mulla:

Watan phir tujh to paimana-e-wafa dene ka waqt aaya
Tere namoos par sab kuchh luta dene ka waqt aaya

O country, the time to offer you the goblet of constancy has come again
To give up everything to preserve your fair name has come again

Acknowledgements

Several of these essays were first published in online portals such as *Quint*, *Scroll*, *The Wire*, etc as well as newspapers such as the *Indian Express*, *Times of India*, etc. All have been substantially reworked and, in many cases, elaborated. I am grateful to the editors who encouraged me to write these pieces in the first instance and, in some cases, helped me develop my ideas.

I am deeply grateful to Himanjali Sankar, my editor at Simon & Schuster India, who commissioned this book and helped in its gestation. She has been an ardent and close reader offering suggestions that have helped give clarity to my occasionally impetuous and impassioned thoughts. All along, she has stayed true to the golden rule of editing: Avoid over-editing and don't change the author's voice or meaning. I thank her for believing in this book. I must also thank Megha Mukherjee and Sayantan Ghosh who took the baton from Himanjali after the editing and saw this volume through its final stages.

Finally, I must acknowledge the debt I owe to the two-volume set of Urdu poetry entitled *Hindustan Humara*, edited by the poet Jan Nisar Akhtar. For the past several years these two books have never been far from my writing space, becoming somewhat ragged in the process (the spine of one has disintegrated through constant use and the other is showing much wear and tear). Immaculately arranged under broad but concise headings, these twin volumes contain within their pages a wealth of poetry on subjects as diverse as political landmarks—be it the decline of Lucknow and Delhi, the revolt of 1857, milestones in the journey towards freedom such as the massacre at Jallianwala Bagh or the Montague Reforms, the First and Second World War, India's tryst with destiny, the years immediately after independence, the wars with China and Pakistan, the creation of Bangladesh and so on—as well as the *azmat* (greatness) of India and *hubb-e-watani* (love for the nation) among Indians. There are also poems on fairs, festivals, religious figures, political leaders, seasons, foods, cities, art, architecture, and much else. This book, in its present form, could not have been possible were it not for *Hindustan Humara*; for, the two volumes have proved to be not merely a valuable resource, an easy and handy reference but a guiding light and an inspiration.

R.J.

Jammu and Kashmir

Past Tense, Present Imperfect and Future Indefinite

जम्मू कश्मीर की दलदल पूर्ण समस्या का साकार रूप

भूत व्यग्र, वर्तमान विकृत एवं भविष्य संदिग्ध तथा अनिश्चित्

Jammu and Kashmir

Past Tense, Present Imperfect and Future Indefinite

जम्मू कश्मीर की दलदल पूर्ण समस्या का साकार रूप

भूत व्यग्र, वर्तमान विकृत एवं भविष्य संदिग्ध तथा अनिश्चित्

Professor Dr. K.L. Bhatia
B.A. (Hons.); LL.M., Ph.D. (Pune)
DAAD and Max Planck Fellow and Alumni
Emeritus Professor of Law,
College of Legal Studies
University of Petroleum and Energy Studies
V&PO Bidholi, via Premnagar, Dehradun. Uttrakhand
[Former Head & Dean, Faculty of Law, and Director
The Law School, University of Jammu and Director, Amity Law School]

DEEP & DEEP PUBLICATIONS PVT. LTD.
F-159, Rajouri Garden, New Delhi - 110027

JAMMU AND KASHMIR
Past Tense, Present Imperfect and Future Indefinite

ISBN 978-81-8450-387-6

Typeset by THE LASER PRINTERS
8/15, 3rd Floor, Subhash Nagar, New Delhi-110027

Printed in India at MAYUR ENTERPRISES, WZ Plot No. 3, Gujjar Market, Tihar Village, New Delhi - 110 018

Published by DEEP & DEEP PUBLICATIONS PVT. LTD.
F-159, Rajouri Garden, New Delhi-110027.
Phones: 25435369, 25440916
Sales Showroom: 2/13, Ansari Road, Daryaganj, New Delhi-110002
Phone/Fax: 23245122

Contents

Preface

Being a conscientious citizen of India, I have tried, with diffidence, modesty and humility, to analyze the open or veiled game plans that not only throw a new light on certain aspects of the Jammu-Kashmir issue, but also unfold the contrived plans of those who have made a 'no-problem Jammu-Kashmir' a 'problem Jammu-Kashmir'. It has become a new challenge in the context of an internal as well as external security problem. The subject-matter of Jammu-Kashmir has been close to my heart. After an in depth study of different game plans being projected at different levels the world over, I thought it as my duty to make a critique analysis of the issues with the sole objective in mind let "We the People of India" know the reality of veiled and contrived fictions. In this tiny bilingual write up I have made a modest analysis of such contrived fictions with the sole object as to how to come out of this cobweb. Jammu-Kashmir is an integral and irrevocable part of Indian "Sovereign, Socialist, Secular, Democratic, Republic". My sole modest endeavor has been to present that the State of Jammu-Kashmir ought not to have been a contending issue because she has immutably and imperishably been a part of Indian Nation historically, morally, ethically, legally, socially, constitutionally and internationally. However, it has been confounded and complicated by those actors whose contrived plots that are full of tragedies, have been striving hard to reverse this historical truth and trying to make us believe globally the truth of their lies. Such actors' open or veiled efforts have speciously succeeded to make the "no-dispute" a "dispute", and making honest nationalists the victims of situational crisis. This monograph shows the games of such planners replacing "simple Kashmir" into "Kashmir imbroglio". It also narrates the saga of events, which have not only embittered

Indo-Pakistan relations, but also converted "communal harmony" into "communal disharmony". My only object through this succinct write up has been "save Jammu-Kashmir" from the hands of those actors whose only approach has been to disintegrate Jammu-Kashmir from Union of India that is *Bharat*.

I express my sincere tributes to all my warm and dear friends who have sharpened my analysis-visions with their wise suggestions.

PROFESSOR DR. K.L BHATIA
Professor Emeritus

प्रस्तावना

जम्मू–कश्मीर का विषम विषय मेरा मार्मिक हार्दिक विषय है। भारत का एक जागरुक नागरिक होने के नाते विषय का सही दिशा में विश्लेषण करना मैं अपना कर्तव्य समझता हूं। जम्मू–कश्मीर समस्या ना होकर भी एक जटिल समस्या है। यह जटिल समस्या कई विकृत प्रवृत्तियों का परिणाम है। अतैव आन्तरिक और बाह्य सुरक्षा का अहम विषय है।

जम्मू–कश्मीर विकृत प्रवृत्तियों के हाथों अनेकानेक प्रकार के प्रयोगों के अध्यन का विषय बन गया है एवं अंततोगत्वा यह अनेकानेक खिलाड़ियों के हाथों कठपुतली है। मैने इन सबका भारतीयता एवं भारतीय दृष्टि के माध्यम से विश्लेषण करने का विनम्र प्रयास किया है। यह विनम्र प्रयास विकृत प्रवृत्तियों की विचारधाराओं को चेतना हेतु है कि जम्मू–कश्मीर भारत गणराज्य का अभिन्न एवं अटूट अंग है।

मैं उन सर्व बन्धुओं एवं मित्रगण का आभार प्रकट करता हूं जिन्होंने मेरे इस विनम्र प्रयास में सहयोग दिया है।

प्रो० डॉ० के०एल० भाटिया

Introduction

The internal as well as external political complications and complexities that have beset Jammu and Kashmir are matters of common knowledge the world over. I do not cherish any intention to covering them. However, the modest approach in this write up is purely as well as exclusively that of a student of law.

Is Jammu and Kashmir a problem? If there is problem, it is a problem of unrealistic contrived contrivances of contrived plots that are full of tragedies. Jammu and Kashmir State is a problem of contrived history of modern era. The conviviality begins with the accession of Jammu and Kashmir with the Union of India as her integral part on 26th and 27th October 1947, and since then the State has been a contentious issue internally as well as externally. It, thus, is conceived of social, economic, political, national and international dimensions. Besides, it seems that Jammu and Kashmir problem is the consequence of obstinate approach by some people at different times. It has been confounded and complicated unconscientiously by those who have had varying and inconsistent behaviour pattern. In this quicksand is it easy to find out a solution satisfying the audacity of all? Besides the political gimmicks, it has been off the line notoriety in the hands of those who have aspired and loved to remain out of the main streamline of the Nation. It has been a bone of contention between the integrationists and disintegrationists. Fairly speaking, the State of Jammu and Kashmir ought not to have been a contending issue because she has immutably been a part of Indian Nation historically, religiously, morally, ethically, legally, constitutionally, and internationally [The State of J&K along with other States of India has had *de jure* recognition by international community on the declaration of India's independence and State's accession]. The disintegrationists have been striving hard to reverse this historical truth, and trying to make us all believe globally the truth of their million dollars lies. It has been an abode of *Devatas, Saints, Sages, Seers, Faqirs, and Peers* and that precisely seems to be the reason that is heaven on the earth. It is a place of *Shrines* of all faiths and beliefs symbolizing the communal harmony of the region. It is also a place of *Shiva Shrines* located in the serene and picturesque cascading environ that unequivocally indicates the emergence, growth and existence of a widespread cult of *Shiva*. Be that as it may, the malign charter starts with the launch of mischievous movements with multi-dimensional consequences. The State of Jammu and Kashmir has been presented only with one gloss of school of thought and that school of thought was so much of one sided that it adopted those soft strategies to resolve the unknotted J&K problem that virtually made J&K knotty. In the backdrop of this, it may be no exageration to submit that J&K is a riddle wrapped in mystery inside an enigma. How to come out of this riddle there has to be a roadmap with new strategies, advanced visions, and farsighted perceptions. In the making of a roadmap, it may be appropriate to have a deep peep into the conduct of those who have been responsible to quagmire a quark.

Backgrounder

The quagmire started with the launch of movements against the ruler of the State [Maharaja Hari Singh] by those who had dreamt to be in the shoes of the ruler by overthrowing him out of power. The Maharaja had maintained opposition to such conscriptions, because the opponents were behaving against the ruler, as he seemed to be a foreigner ruler on the Indian soil. And, the attempts to equate such movements with the Indian freedom movement seem to be unnatural, specious, fictitious, factious and anti-national. Besides, varying and inconsistent statements of stands of 1931, 1942, 1947, 1949, 1950, 1953 by those who aspired to be loyal with Pakistan treating the Valley of Kashmir as their *affaire de Coeur*.

The voluminous literature on Kashmir shows sordid intrigue and treachery that has battered relations between India and Pakistan on the one hand, and India and Kashmiri psyche on the other hand. It also unfolds the endeavours, open or veiled, by Super Powers to make the no-dispute a dispute to serve the ends of the power block. It also makes the revelations of the haplessness and helplessness of Sardar Patel, Gopalaswami Ayyanger, Hari Singh, M.C. Mahajan, and host of others who were victims of situational crisis. It shows the replacement of "simple Kashmir" into "Kashmir Imbroglio". It narrates the saga of events that "a vehement exponent of accession to India seems to have been converted to 'independent Kashmir'." It also reflects the impetus on certain aspects of the Kashmir issue, which have not only embittered perpetually India-Pakistan relations, but also converted "communal harmony" into "communal disharmony". In the backdrop of it, it shall be appropriate to mention about the sequence of events that throw a new light on certain aspects of the Kashmir issue.

The State of J&K, covering an area of 86,024 square miles (222,236 square km), has a strategic importance as its territory [the Valley of Kashmir, Jammu, Ladakh, Balitstan, Gilgit, Hunza and Nagar] shares borders with Pakistan in the west, Afghanistan in the north, China in the north and east. Besides, it is close to the Soviet border in the North-West, and is the old trade route to Central Asia.

The modern history is testimony to the fact that a new era in the history of the State of J&K had begun with the enthronement of Maharajah Hari Singh in September 1925 who succeeded the royal power and sovereignty status as a linear descendent of the Dogra Maharajah Gulab Singh who created the State of Jammu and Kashmir under the treaty of Amritsar in March 1846 by paying rupees 75 lakhs as war indemnity to the British colonial government after the demise of Maharajah Ranjit Singh in 1839. [C. Joseph Chacko: India's Contribution to the Field of International Law Concepts, 1958]. The movement known as "Kashmir for Kashmiris" launched under the leadership of Shankarlal Koul could be conceded a black lung chapter in the history of J&K as it induced Hari Singh to enact the "State Subject Law, 1927" imposing restrictions on the entry of non-Kashmiris in Government jobs and on the sale of immovable property to them. [Premnath Bazaz: Kashmir in Crucible]. Reading Room Party organization founded in 1930 in Srinagar by a few Muslim graduates of which Sheikh Mohammed Abdullah was also a member seems to be the foundation stone of the feeling of alienation mainly not only from the government of Hari Singh, but also the rest of the non-Muslim population. This gave birth to isolation and escapism. This was furthered by the foundation of the Muslim Conference under the chairmanship of Sheikh Abdullah who began the fight for democratic rights for Muslims alone. It led to tension between Hindus and Muslims and to communal riots in Srinagar in June 1931. Hindus suffered heavily. Why Sheikh Abdullah did not raise his voice and concern for non-Muslims who, too, were the significant components of the population? Communal disturbances sowed the seeds of communal disharmony. In August 1945, Sheikh Abdullah, as Chairman of National Conference, spelt out his program for building a new Kashmir. Why did he not spell out his module for the entire State? Another phase of opposition to the Hari Singh

Government was the launch of "Quit Kashmir" agitation speciously equating it with the "Quit India" movement. The Indian Independence Act, 1947 provided for transfer of power to two newly created Dominions from one Indian Continent, viz., India and Pakistan. Vide that law; a plan/roadmap for Indian Princely States was defined by which the Princely States were to accede to either Dominion by 15th August 1947. Paramountcy lapsed on 15th August 1947. All but three Princely States had acceded to either India or Pakistan. Incidents of belated accession of Princely States of Hyderabad and Junagad are meaningfully well placed in history, and, perhaps, that indecisiveness had been the root cause of unpleasantness. Be that as it may, *Afridis*/ tribesmen, soldiers in plain clothes, and desperadoes with modern weapons, from North-West-Frontier Province of West Pakistan, with the connivance and active support of Pakistan's Government invaded Kashmir on 22nd October 1947 as a consequence to coerce Hari Singh to accede to Pakistan. This crisis made Hari Singh to listen to the advice of several Indian leaders of different shades and ideology to accede to India and seek Indian Government's help to uproot the invaders/aggressors from Kashmir. Under these special circumstances, the sovereign Hari Singh like other sovereigns of about 560 Indian Princely States acceded to India by signing the unconditional Instrument of Accession on 26th October 1947 and accepted by the Governor-General Mountbatten on 27th October 1947. In the backdrop of this, a reference to sections of Maharajah Hari Singh's letter as the independent sovereign ruler of his State to Lord Mountbatten is significant: "My dear Lord Mountbatten, I have to inform Your Excellency that a grave emergency has arisen in my State and request immediate assistance of your Government. . . . Your Government was aware that the State of Jammu and Kashmir has not acceded to either the Dominion of India or to Pakistan. I wanted to take time to decide to which Dominion I should accede, whether it is not in the best interest of both the dominions and my State to stand independent, of course with friendly and cordial relations with both. Though my State had a 'Standstill Agreement' with the Pakistan Government, that Government permitted steady and increasing strangulation of supplies like food, salt and petrol to my State. . . . Afridis, soldiers in plain clothes, and desperadoes with modern weapons had been allowed to infiltrate into my

State. These enemies . . . were engaged in the wanton destruction of life and property and were marching on with the aim of capturing Srinagar, the summer capital of my Government, as a first step to over-running the whole State. . . . The mass infiltration of tribesmen . . . in motor trucks . . . and fully armed with up-to-date weapons cannot possibly be done without the knowledge of the Provincial Government of the Northwest Frontier Province and the Government of Pakistan. . . . [With such conditions prevailing in my State], I have no option but to ask for help from the Indian Dominion. Naturally they [the Indian Dominion] cannot send the help asked for by me without my State acceding to the Dominion of India. I have accordingly decided to do so and I attach the Instrument of Accession for acceptance by your Government". [C. Joseph Chacko, *Ibid.*].

Lord Mountbatten, the last British Governor-General and the first Governor-General of free Independent India, promptly accepted the Instrument of Accession and replied vide his letter dated 27th October 1947: "In the special circumstances mentioned by Your Highness, my Government have decided to accept the accession of Kashmir State to the Dominion of India. . . . It is my Government's wish that, as soon as law and order have been restored in Kashmir and her soil cleared of the invaders, the question of the State's accession should be settled by a reference to the people". [C. Joseph Chacko, *Ibid.*].

The Maharajah Hari Singh of Jammu and Kashmir State acceded to India on 26th October 1947; the accession was accepted by the Government of India on 27th October 1947; and, on 28th October 1947 the Prime Minister of India Pandit Jawaharlal Nehru wired to the Prime Minister of Pakistan informing him that "action Government of India has taken has been forced upon them by circumstances and imminent and grave danger to Srinagar. . . . In regard to accession also it has been made clear that this is subject to reference to people of State and their decision. Government of India has no desire to impose any decision and will abide by people's wishes. But these cannot be ascertained till peace and law and order prevail . . ." [C. Joseph Chacko, *Ibid.*].

Jammu and Kashmir's accession to India is final and irrevocable and in conformity with International Law. The Maharajah of the State of Jammu and Kashmir was an independent sovereign as per Indian Independence Act, 1947.

Oppenheim, an international jurist, appears to submit the tests: "In every monarchy the monarch appears as the representative of the sovereignty of the State, and thereby becomes a sovereign himself; and this fact is recognized in international law . . . International law recognizes all monarchs as equally sovereign . . ." [Oppenheim, *International Law*, Vol. I, p. 758]. Hence, all such sovereigns represent their States and they are International Persons or subjects of International Law.

Professor Philip C. Jessup, an outstanding jurist of International Law of Columbia University, has recognized the marks of statehood: (a) a permanent population; (b) a defined territory; (c) a government; and (d) capacity to enter into relations with other States. [U.N. Security Council Records, 383rd meeting, December 2, 1948, p. 9.].

In the backdrop of these tests, it may be conclusively submitted that the Maharajah of Jammu and Kashmir representing his State had all the requisite attributes of an International Person/ Subject in International Law on and after August 15, 1947.

In this context, a reference to the decision of J&K High Court rendered by Justice Shamiri in *Magher Singh* v. *Principal Secretary, Jammu and Kashmir* [A.I.R. 1953, J&K 25] may be made that unequivocally neatly discusses the status of Maharajah of Jammu and Kashmir prior and subsequent to the Indian Independence Act, 1947:

> "Previous to the partition of British India into two Dominions of Pakistan and India there was no doubt that the Ruler of Jammu and Kashmir was under the suzerainty of the British Crown inasmuch as foreign relations were under the exclusive control of the Crown Representative. But insofar as the internal sovereignty of the ruler was concerned it was absolutely unlimited and there were no fetters on it. In this connection it would be relevant to reproduce sections 4 and 5 of the Jammu and Kashmir Constitution Act . . . as they stood amended in November, 1951.
>
> 'Section 4: The territories for the time being vested in H.H. are governed by and in the name of H.H. and all rights, authorities and jurisdiction which appertain or are incidental to the government of such territories are exercisable by H.H.'

'Section 5: Notwithstanding anything contained in this or any other Act all powers, legislative, executive and judicial in relation to the State and its government are hereby declared to be and to have always been inherent in and possessed and retained by His Highness and nothing contained in this or any other Act shall affect or be deemed to have affected the right, or prerogative of His Highness to make laws, and issue proclamations, orders and ordinances by virtue of his inherent authority'."

The High Court, thus, decreed that (1) so far as the internal sovereignty of the State was concerned, the powers of the ruler were similar to those of the British Parliament; (2) with the passage of section 7 of the Indian Independence Act of 1947 the State of Jammu and Kashmir "became an independent and sovereign State in the full sense of international law"; (3) consequently, "His Highness became an uncontrolled and absolute sovereign"; (4) the signature and submission of the Instrument of Accession to the Government of India was "subject always to the terms thereof", and for no other purpose, and that therefore; (5) the proclamation of His Highness transferring and entrusting his powers to "Shree Yuvraj [Yuvaraj Karan Singh] was perfectly valid and constitutional".

In the backdrop of the above, it unequivocally seems that the action of Maharajah Hari Singh as an independent and absolute Monarch of an independent State of Jammu and Kashmir is beyond any doubt thoroughly, legally, politically, socially, ethically, and morally compatible with all points of international law, and is not open to challenge from the standpoint of the international law governing sovereign entities at any international forum. In my humble opinion the accession of Jammu and Kashmir, therefore, to the Indian Union in terms of Instrument of Accession was an act of legal plenitude. If this act of accession is questioned on the grounds of its possible illegality, unconstitutionality, then all accessions whether to India or Pakistan would be open to similar objections that may consequently lead to disintegration inviting a Pandora box of intrigues as well as incongruities. It may also be pertinent to deal with the oft-hackneyed offer of plebiscite which India is alleged to have made with a view of finding a solution to a dispute between India and Pakistan with reference to Kashmir. The acceding Monarch Maharajah Hari Singh had never used the term plebiscite or any other condition in his Instrument of Accession to the Government of India.

However, the contentious point that needs in depth probing seems to be pondered, viz., but for unilateral cease-fire, the Indian soldiers of Indian defense forces when were in winning position could have uprooted the tribesmen from the Indian soil of Kashmir, and, further, could not have been the soaring cause for the creation of POK. Nehru-Mountbatten duo personal promises to finalize the accession through the will of the people, that is, plebiscite, [Durga Das: Sardar Patel's Correspondence: 1971: pp. 73, 81, 257, 341] was incompatible legally, constitutionally, politically, ethically, socially, and morally, and as such self-created difficulties by unnecessarily volunteering for "in accordance with the wishes of the people" or "question of accession should be settled by a reference to the people", mischievously and speciously construed as plebiscite, has been responsible for muddling and making Kashmir a highly intricate problem as well as playing for high stakes. Under Mountbatten's encouragement Jawaharlal Nehru taking the Kashmir case to UNO further made a local/ National issue an International one and opened a floodgate for the intervention of UK, USA, Russia, China, Muslim countries, Militants as well as terrorist groups, Terrorist Training Centers in POK, and Pakistan, Jamat-e-Islami, a Hard Core Pro-Pak group, Hurriyyat, a conglomeration of some Militant groups, to wean India and seems to be inclined to bleed India to the last drop; UN Resolutions, Tashkent Agreement, Simla Agreement, Lahore Declaration, Islamabad Declaration have yielded no results except the prize we are fighting for is the Valley of Kashmir. The cumulative impetus is fraught with both danger and disaster, and there has been a debit balance throughout so far as achievements are concerned with *coup de grace* results.

Propositions: Internal and External

What type of an action is needed to finally end that has been getting worse, a number of methods have been presented locally, nationally, and internationally to jettison the conditions so that the coming events may not further weaken the situation.

LOCAL GAME PLAN

The most regrettable happening of the past presented by Sheikh Abdullah and his National Conference has been the New Kashmir Module whereby Jammu Region could have three districts of Jammu, Udhampur and Kathua and leaving the rest of the territory of J&K to a Muslim republic like Pakistan. [Durga Das: *Id.* at p. 128]. This module presents the mindset of those people who have had narrower vision to resolve the Kashmir issue. Neo New Kashmir modules have been in the framework of Pre-1953, autonomy—greater autonomy and regional autonomy. Pre-1953 and autonomy are the two sides of the same coin. They are like mistress at their home without any checks and balances. In the autonomy reports it has *a multo fortiori* been recommended to have Pre-1953 position, viz., what was the political, legal and constitutional status of J&K before the detention of Sheikh Abdullah that should be restored. The provisions of the Indian Constitution were extended to the State of J&K vide Constitutional (Application to the State of J&K) Order 1954 that superseded the Constitutional (Application to the State of J&K) Order 1950. By 1950 Constitutional Order the provisions of Articles 1 and 370 of the Constitution of India were extended to the State of J&K with the adoption and enforcement of the Constitution of India. Subsequently, the Constituent Assembly of

J&K in 1956 in *proprio vigore* ratified the accession of J&K with the Union of India as one of her integral federal unit and also adopted as well as enforced Constitution of J&K. [C. Joseph Chacko, *Ibid*]. Besides, over 370 Central Laws have been extended to the State of J&K so that the people of J&K, too, have the equal fruits of those laws by that the citizens of India have the profits. Pre-1953 proposition is fraught with dangerous consequences. First, it shall be step forward to the rescinding of the provisions of the Constitution of India as well as the Constitution of J&K that shall leap backward to the Constitutional status of 1933. Once this happens it shall automatically mean J&K ceasing to be an integral part of India as per Article 1 and Schedules I and IV of the Constitution of India, and Section 3 of the Constitution of J&K. Second, the permanent residents of J&K shall cease to be the citizens of India thus depriving them the benefits of the rights, the Basic rights, and the Fundamental rights of the citizenry. Third, it shall amount to an invitation for resettlement of those who left the country voluntarily to settle in other sovereign State by giving up Indian citizenship and permanent residence of J&K for their loyalty to Pakistan. Such people have fought 1947, 1965, 1971 wars against India and fighting proxy war against India as Militants, terrorists, secessionists, wagers of war, infiltrators, incinerators inciting, instigating and coercing the people of the State of J&K to join hands with them for the perpetuation of their unholy acts of omissions and commission with pernicious effects. This proposition is incompatible with all social, political, legal, constitutional, and international norms, namely, what is not constitutionally permissible to do directly that is not permitted to do indirectly. Fourth, it shall deprive the people of J&K the national integration profits enjoined under the Constitution of India such as Supreme Court jurisdiction (original, appellate, and PIL), over 370 Central Laws, Comptroller and Auditor General, Election Commission, and a host of others. Fifth, it shall lead to the superimposition of another fiefdom and serfdom.

The propagators of 'self-rule' seem to be ignorant about the in depth meaning of the phrase they have coined as a solution to the naughty knotty J&K problem. Self-rule was a movement launched by *Swarajists* (freedom fighters) against the British rulers in India for the restoration of self-rule by democratic means by the Indians, for the Indians, and of the Indians. In J&K, her people have been exercising their enfranchisements since 1957 by democratic means for the self-rule by them, for them and of them. What more does self-rule mean? It is nothing but a mischievious propagation to misguide the people. Similarly, healing touch proposition has yielded negative results as it encouraged militants/terrorists and secessionists to squeeze maximum benefits from government chest at the cost of nationalists. The State Governments have failed to provide meaningful healing touch to the West Pak refugees and internally displaced persons who have been living as strangers in their own home. Article 370 is adopted version of the draft Article 306-A. It was adopted by the Constituent Assembly unanimously and without a single dissentient voice and without a speech from anybody raising any note of criticism including the four representatives from J&K in the Constituent Assembly, viz., Sheikh Mohammed Abdullah, Mirza Afzal Beig, Moulana Masoodi, and M.R. Baigra who were signatories (24th January 1950) to the adopted text of the Constitution of India on 26th November 1949. [CAD, Vols. X-XII, 1989 Ed., pp. 421-29]. Article 370 was enjoined in the Constitution of India as a temporary measure to eventually meet the special situations created by special unforeseen circumstances with the sole objective that it should rescind with the ceasing of the special hostile situations and never making it as an entrenched one. But working with the provisions of Article 370, it seems, has generated the feeling of alienation. Its language ought to have been similar to the language of Article 371, viz., as a special measure for the development of non-developed/under developed spatial areas of the Indian territory so that such areas, too, get an equal opportunity to come up in the streamline of the Indian Nation with the feeling of equalization. Alienation has permeated an attitude of secessionism, separatism, militancy and terrorism. This also is responsible for an idea of an independent Kashmir mooted by those who have perhaps proved to be one of the greatest betrayals in history of modern India. [Durga Das, *op. cit.* at pp. 266-68]. Their hurting and injurious language is "Accession to either side cannot bring peace. We want to live in friendship with both Dominions. Perhaps a middle path between them, with economic co-operation with each, will be the only way of doing it. But Britain, the United States and other members of the United Nations must guarantee not only by India and Pakistan but an independent Kashmir also. . . ." [Vide Sheikh Abdullah in an interview with Michael Davidson, quoted in Durga Das, *Ibid.*] Besides, it is difficult to define what ordinary Kashmiris want/aspire/desire. Many express that they want/aspire to be masters of their own will or destiny without any checks and balances. Many express the view that they only want to be left alone but do not define what would that entail. Be that as it may, no one should be misled by this hotch potch. This seems to be the real mindset of all those who are perpetuating the suspected plan in the garb of hard-core and soft-core conglomerates. And, Article 370 is responsible for the permeation of this type of behaviour pattern. Erasing of it has become non-practical because it has been allowed to oscillate between political will and legal viability. To me, it seems that the retention of Article 370 and alienation perpetuity has been due to those who may have desired to evaporate it but could not do so because when the flesh is weak, the spirit however willing cannot execute.

What has been the impetus of all the above-mentioned movements/proposals/propositions? What results have they yielded so far? The experiments have yielded no meaningful results for the only reason that the propositions have been presented insincerely, unconscientiously, and superciliously.

PAKISTAN GAME PLAN

Pakistan has only one game plan to have Kashmir within her fold by any foul play that is visible in the incidents of aggression caused by Pakistan in 1947, 1965, 1971, Kargil invasion 1999, and Proxy war occasioned by the ticklish tactics of militancy, terrorism, terrorists training camps on her soil, Jihad, and her militants' or terrorists' attack in Mumbai on 26.11.2008. Pakistan aspires to destabilize India with her supercilious approach and as such has dishonoured all peace rapprochements of UN Resolutions, Tashkent Agreement, Simla Agreement, Lahore Declaration, etc. However, it has come to be sensitive to Confidence Building Measures after Islamabad Declaration that is the reiteration of Lahore Declaration. Besides, political pronouncements "putting the Kashmir problem in hibernation for the generation next", and "conflict management and simultaneous creation of trading bloc in South Asia as part of efforts to settle outstanding issues with

India like the Kashmir problem" are inasmuch as unclear as that of deficiency of sound mind.

INTERNATIONAL GAME PLAN

International Game Plan emanates from the thesis of Postcolonial perceptions having base on the carving out of artificial boundaries through European conquests and settlements establishing the destabilizing legacy in the Third World whereby the boundaries of the State and those of the ethnic nation did not coincide. Kashmir problem, perhaps, may have to be perceived as an example of such British legacy worked out by Mountbatten by encouraging Jawaharlal Nehru to declare unilateral ceasefire that culminated into the artificial creation of POK. This unequivocally seems to have opened floodgate of international interventionists in Kashmir affairs like a harlot, the Kashmir problem is at the disposal of everyone. International modules, thus, are based on "Strategic Interdependence" perceptions. "Strategic Interdependence" relates to international security issues that primarily involve the defense capabilities and deterrence postures adopted by States against threats from each other under conditions of strategic interdependence. "Strategic Interdependence" denotes the relative power distributions among States, although the constitution and measurement of power remain subject to debate. [Raju, G.C. Thomas, "What is Third World Security?" *Annual Review of Political Science*, 6(1) 2003, 205-32]. Measurement of power refers to existing military capabilities and mobilization potential based on a State's economic and technological capacities and capabilities. Be that as it may, military capability and potential as a measurement of power was complicated by the "advent of nuclear weapons" that made "traditional" "measurement of power" of "absolute capabilities" as irrelevancy and the psychology and motivation to deter an attack became the more important factor in the calculus of power. [*Ibid.*]. This new model has permeated "Strategic Interdependence", which has come up as India started perceiving some utility in acquiring or preserving a nuclear deterrent capability in case of interventionists intervention in Kashmir affairs that affect India's internal, external or regional security interests. [*Ibid.*].

In the backdrop of this, it is imperative to have perceptions of international modules directed to resolve Kashmir issue as "Back Channel Diplomacy" or "Quiet Diplomacy". The authors of "Kashmir: The Road to Peace" argue that the "modules can be useful to all those who want to replace violençe with diplomacy and bring peace to the people of Kashmir". [Public International Law Policy Group]. The module is debatable from Indian perspective because that raises many debatable issues. However, the proposed module presents "model language" of the "proposed agreements" between *Kashmir* v. *India* v. *Pakistan* to be incorporated in a "Constitutional Framework" as follows:

Abbreviation	*Official Name of Agreement*
1. Burundi Agreement	Arusha Peace and Reconciliation Agreement for Burundi, August 20, 2000.
2. Dayton Accords	The General Framework Agreement for Peace in Bosnia and Herzegovina (initiated in Dayton on 21 November 1995 and signed in Paris on 14 December 1995.
3. East Timor Agreement	Agreement between the Republic of Indonesia and the Portuguese Republic on the Question of East Timor, 5 May 1999.
4. El Salvador Agreement	El Salvador Peace Agreement 16 January 1992.
5. Guatemala Agreement	Guatemala Agreement on Identity and Rights of Indigenous Peoples, March 31, 1995.
6. KFOR Agreement	Military Technical Agreement between the International Security Force (KFOR) and the Governments of Federal Republic of Yugoslavia and the Republic of Serbia, June 9, 1999.
7. Kosovo Interim Agreement	The Interim Agreement for Peace and Self-Government in Kosovo, February 23, 1999.
8. Lahore Declaration	Lahore Declaration by the Prime Ministers of the Republic of India and the Islamic Republic of Pakistan, February 21, 1999.
9. Northern Ireland Agreement	The Northern Ireland Peace Agreement: The Agreement Reached in the multi-party Negotiations, October 4, 1998.

10. Papua New Guinea Agreement	Bougainvillea Peace Agreement, August 30, 2001.
11. Sierra Leone Agreement	Peace Agreement between the Government of Sierra Leone and the Revolutionary United Front of Sierra Leone, Lome', Togo, May 25 to July 7, 1999.
12. Simla Agreement	Simla Agreement on Bilateral Relations between India and Pakistan signed by Prime Minister of India Mrs. Indira Gandhi and President of Pakistan Z.A. Bhutto, July 3, 1972.
13. South African Constitution	Constitution of the Republic of South Africa, May 8, 1996.
14. Sudan Protocol	Sudan's Machakos Protocol, July 20, 2002.
15. Tashkent Declaration	Tashkent Declaration, January 10, 1996.
16. Angola Ceasefire	Angola-Unita Ceasefire Agreement, April 2002.
17. Lusaka Protocol	Angola-Lusaka Protocol, Lusaka, Zambia, November 15, 1994.
18. Somalia Ceasefire	Somalia Agreement on Implementing the ceasefire and on modalities of disarmament (Supplement to the General Agreement signed in Addis Ababa, on January 8, 1993.

THE GIST OF THE ABOVE MODULE

A. Constitutional Status of Article 370

1. Article 370 of the Constitution of India shall be made permanent. Deleting the term "temporary" from the Article as well as references to Article 370 and replacing it with the word "special" shall accomplish this.
2. All Presidential Orders restricting the scope of Article 370 shall be rescinded. There shall be no further acts by the Indian Government to create ambiguity as to the Status of Kashmir.
3. The rights created herein for the self-governance of the semi-autonomous region of Kashmir are non-derogable.

B. Governance Retained by India

All powers not delegated to India by this Agreement are reserved to Kashmir, respectively, or to its people.

(a) Defense

1. The Indian Government will continue to exercise competence over the external defense of Kashmir. The State of Kashmir continues to be a part of India and as such India still maintains control over its defense. Indian military presence in Kashmir. shall be reactionary only.
2. Kashmir shall closely supervise any Indian defense force in Kashmir to prevent abuses by the Indian force. If such abuses, as those prescribed in this Agreement's section on human rights, do take place, the Kashmir legislature shall have the authority to submit the issue to the Human Rights Committee for adjudication.

(b) Foreign Affairs

1. The Indian Government will continue to exercise control over the foreign affairs of the region.
2. The Indian Government shall consult with the Kashmir legislature regarding any foreign affairs decisions affecting the region. The Kashmir legislature shall approve any decisions of India that relate specifically and singularly to the foreign affairs of Kashmir but to no other region.

(c) Fiscal Policy

1. Kashmir will still require continued support from the Central Government and as such the Indian Government should continue to exercise control over monetary policy of the region.
2. India shall also retain control over national taxation. The government of Kashmir shall control regional taxation for Kashmir.
3. The Indian Government shall ensure the full economic development of Kashmir. This shall entail increased investment in the region and the strengthening of economic growth programs through education and

monetary support. India shall also continue to govern Kashmiri participation in the Indian common market, with the objective to continue active participation.

C. Status of Kashmir Borders

(a) The border of Kashmir shall not change as a result of this agreement. The Line of Control (LOC) will be the official border, as defined by the 1972 Simla Agreement that separates Azad Kashmir from Kashmir. The northern, southern, and eastern borders shall not vary from what they are at the time of the signature of the agreement.

(b) Azad Kashmir shall not be considered a part of the new special autonomous region. If the populous of Azad Kashmir expresses an interest in joining the special autonomous region of Kashmir, Kashmir shall support a referendum and give credence to its outcome.

D. Kashmiri Participation in Central Government

(a) Kashmir shall continue to participate in the structure of the Indian Government so far as those structures affect Kashmir. This determination shall be based on those powers retained by the Indian Government as detailed in this Agreement.

(b) Selection of Kashmiri representatives shall not change from the existing methods.

(c) The government of Kashmir shall be consulted by the Government of India for the purpose of taking Kashmiri views into account on issues within the Indian Government of particular relevance to the Kashmir.

E. Determination of Kashmiri Citizenship and Symbols of Identity

1. All the people living in Kashmir for a minimum of 7 years at the time of signing of the Agreement shall be considered citizens of Kashmir.
2. All people living in Kashmir for less than 7 years at the time of the signing of the Agreement shall be granted Kashmiri citizenship after fulfilling 7 year residency requirement.

3. There shall be no denial of citizenship based on the race, religion or sex of an individual. The Kashmiri legislature shall ensure the grant of citizenship to all those requesting it.
4. Accusations of discrimination for citizenship shall be adjudicated as a type of discrimination before the International Criminal Court.
5. The Constitutional Congress or new Kashmiri government will set the regulations for issuance of identity documents such as passport.
6. There shall be no denial of identity documents based on race, religion or sex.
7. The Constitutional Congress, or new Kashmiri government, shall determine the symbols of national identity such as flag and coat of arms. The Indian flag shall continue to fly at national ceremonies and other legally required events.

F. Mechanism for Enforcement of Special Autonomy Status

Upon an allegation by either Kashmir or Pakistan that the principles for heightened autonomy provided for in this section are being abused, a committee appointed by the United Nations Secretary General, comprised of internationals, will investigate the allegation. If the appoint committee determines that there is a violation, the Human Rights Committee of Kashmir will attempt to resolve the situation. If the Committee determines that it is beyond its capabilities to remedy the situation, the United Nations High Commissioner for Human Rights will bring the issue to the United Nations Security Council for immediate resolution.

G. Constitutional Status of Kashmir

The Kashmir government shall be granted full competence over all matters not controlled by the Central Government as specified above. This will mean full, meaningful and exclusive control over all matters concerning the establishment of all legal, political, social, cultural and educational policies in Kashmir.

H. Legislation

The Kashmir government shall be granted complete competence over the enactment, repeal and reform of laws in the region in conformity with its Constitution. This power shall not be fettered in any way by the Indian Government except in its spheres of influence as specified above. Any legislation passed must, however, not be contrary to the spirit of the Indian Constitution.

I. Financial Matters

The Kashmir government shall be granted control over local taxation and shall be responsible for the manner in which State funds are allocated. The exercise of this power must be done in an equitable manner and with no prejudice to members of minority groups.

J. Policy-making

The government of Kashmir shall be accorded authority for formulating and implementing measures concerning all aspects of the region's social, cultural, educational and scientific policy.

K. Corruption

The government of Kashmir is called upon to address the problem of corruption through the enforcement of anti-corruption measures, including prompt and impartial investigation and prosecution of offenders.

L. Elections

(a) Both parties shall ensure that the conditions exist for the conduct of free and fair elections in the region. This will include ensuring an open and free political environment for all citizens, a safe and secure environment that ensures freedom of assembly, association and expression, the access to all available resources to all candidates without prejudice. Both parties must also ensure free exercise of media for campaigning candidates.

(b) The Indian Government shall accept the presence of an

international election observer body to monitor the conduct of the elections and to certify that the elections have been free and fair.

(c) This international body must be accorded full access to all aspects of the electoral process including voter registration, access to polling centers and dissemination of ballots following the election.

(d) The body shall work in conjunction with Electoral Commission of India to ensure that secure and transparent voting procedures are followed.

(e) Any allegations of violation of procedures must be investigated and any parties found to be guilty shall have penalties imposed on them including removing the candidate from the party list.

M. Candidates

A person's past political associations or activities shall not be a bar to holding office. All candidates must, however, renounce all use of violence.

N. Human Rights

1. Kashmir agrees to promote and protect human rights in the region. To this end, it will give full force and effect to the international human rights treaties to which it is bound through the ratification of the treaties by the Government of India, namely, Universal Declaration of Human Rights; International Covenants on Civil and Political Rights, and Economic, Social and Cultural Rights; Convention on the Elimination of All Forms of Discrimination against Women; Convention on the Rights of the Child.
2. In addition to the international treaties listed above, other Conventions that India has not acceded to will be adopted by the Kashmiri government, namely, Convention against torture and other Cruel, Inhuman or Degrading Treatment or Punishment; declaration on the Elimination of all Forms of Intolerance and of Discrimination Based on Religion or Belief.
3. Fundamental Rights of All Kashmiri People:

(i) The rights and duties proclaimed and guaranteed inter alia by the Universal Declaration of Human Rights, the International Covenants on Human Rights, the Convention on the Elimination of All Forms of Discrimination against Women and the Convention on the Rights of the Child shall form an integral part of the Constitution of Kashmir as a Bill of Rights that receives the same pre-eminence in judicial matters as the Constitution itself. These fundamental rights, both in the treaties named above and the provisions specifically enumerated below, shall not be limited or derogated from, except in justifiable circumstances acceptable in international law and set forth in the Constitution.

(ii) All citizens shall have rights and obligations.

(iii) Human dignity shall be respected and protected.

(iv) All women and men shall be equal. No one may be discriminated against, *inter alia*, on grounds of origin, race, ethnicity, gender, color, language, social situation, or religious, philosophical or political convictions, or by reason of a physical or mental handicap. All citizens shall enjoy equal protection of the law, as well as equal treatment under the law.

(v) The State or its organs shall arbitrarily deal with no person.

(vi) All women and men shall have the right to life.

(vii) All women and men shall have the right to personal freedom, including to physical and mental integrity, and to freedom of movement. Torture and any other kind of cruel, inhuman, degrading treatment or punishment shall be prohibited. Everyone shall have the right to be free from violence from either public or private sources.

(viii) The State shall to the extent possible ensure that all citizens have the means to lead an existence consistent with human dignity.

(ix) All women and men shall have the right to respect for their private and family life, residence and personal communications.

(x) Freedom of expression and of the media shall be

guaranteed. The State shall respect freedom of religion, belief, conscience and opinion.

(xi) No one shall be arbitrarily deprived of her/his nationality or denied the right to change it.

(xii) No one may be denied access to basic education. The State shall organize public education, and shall develop and promote access to secondary and post-secondary education.

(xiii) All citizens shall have the right to move and settle freely anywhere in the regional territory, as well as to leave it and return to it.

(xiv) Everyone shall have the right, in judicial or administrative proceedings, for her/his case to be dealt with equitably and decided within a reasonable time limit. Everyone shall have the right to due process and fair trial.

(xv) No one may be deprived of her/his liberty other than in conformity with the law.

(xvi) Each individual shall have the duty to respect and show consideration for her/his fellow citizens without any discrimination.

(xvii) Any restriction of a fundamental right must have a legal basis; it must be justified by the public interest or by the protection of another person's fundamental right; it must be proportional to the objective pursued.

(xviii) Fundamental rights must be respected throughout the legal, administrative and institutional order. The Constitution shall be the supreme law and must be upheld by the Legislature, the Executive and the Judiciary. Any law that is not in conformity with the Constitution shall be invalid.

O. Religious Minority: Freedom of Religion

1. Every person shall have the right to freedom of conscience, religion, thought, belief, and opinion.
2. No one shall be subject to coercion, which would impair his or her freedom to have a religion or belief of his choice.
3. Freedom to manifest one's religion or belief may be

subject only to such limitations as are prescribed by law and are necessary to protect public safety, order, health or morals or the fundamental rights and freedoms of others.

4. Without derogating from the generality of sub-section (1), religious observances may be conducted at State or State-aided institutions under rules established by an appropriate authority for that purpose, provided that such religious observances are conducted on an equitable basis and attendance at them is free and voluntary.
5. Nothing in this Article shall preclude legislation recognizing:
   - a system of personal and family law adhered to by persons professing a particular religion; and
   - the validity of marriages concluded under a system of religious law subject to specified procedures.
6. The right to freedom of thought, conscience, religion or belief shall include, *inter alia*, the following freedoms:
   - To worship or assemble in connection with a religion or belief, and to establish and maintain places for these purposes;
   - To establish and maintain appropriate charitable or humanitarian institutions;
   - To make, acquire and use to an adequate extent the necessary articles and materials related to the rites or customs of a religion or belief;
   - To write, issue and disseminate relevant publications in these areas;
   - To teach a religion or belief in places suitable for these purposes;
   - To solicit and receive voluntary financial and other contributions from individuals and institutions;
   - To train, appoint, elect or designate by succession appropriate leaders called for by the requirements and standards of any religion or belief;
   - To observe days or rest and to celebrate holidays and ceremonies in accordance with the precepts of one's religion or belief; and
   - To establish and maintain communications with

individuals and communities in matters of religion and belief at the national and international levels.

7. Religion may be considered in hiring practices to the extent that under-represented groups are promoted to achieve proper representation within the economic community.
8. Any written or verbal incitement, through media or otherwise, of ethnic or religious hostility or hatred shall be prohibited and, if communicated, promptly suppressed with perpetrators subjected to prison term that shall be incorporated into the criminal laws of Kashmir.

P. Women's Rights

It is recognized that women are practically vulnerable, being confronted with discrimination as women, and also having to deal with a social situation characterized by intense poverty, exploitation, and violence. The government undertakes to take the following measures to ensure the protection of women's human rights.

(a) Governmental

(i) Establish a Division of Women's Rights within the Department of Human Rights, with the participation of such women, including legal advice services and social services, to ensure the right of women to full and equal participation in political, civil, economic, social, and cultural life.

(ii) Ensure that the Division of Women's Rights is afforded the opportunity to integrate gender concerns into all levels of the government bureaucracy.

(iii) Promote the dissemination and faithful implementation of the Convention on the Elimination of All Forms of Discrimination against Women.

(b) Legal

(i) Review and update the penalties imposed by current legislation for sexual crimes, harassment against women, and intra-family violence, and prosecute these crimes.

(ii) The equal status of the human rights of men and women shall be guaranteed.

(iii) Enable women to participate freely and willingly in any gender empowering legal measures directly affecting their society and rights as human beings under the Geneva Conventions.

(iv) As the health and safety of women and children are fundamental in the sustainability of the Kashmiri people, the rights of women should be honored and respected in Kashmiri society. As such, any treaty concerning the general rights of the Kashmiri people shall be included and represented in any future decision about the legal statutes of Kashmir.

(c) Political

(i) Ensure that social and political organizations adopt specific policies to enhance and promote the role of women in the process of strengthening civilian power.

(ii) Ensure that at all times in the exercise of power, women, whether organized or not, are provided with and guaranteed opportunities to participate.

(iii) Women shall enjoy representation in any governmental body that rules Kashmir through the visible and elected representation of female leaders.

(iv) Women shall be given significant representation in both governmental and civil bodies.

(v) The role of women in civil society and community life shall not be undermined or silences.

(vi) Women shall equally participate in democratic institutions.

(d) Civil

(i) Women not participating in combat shall be respected as civilians. As such, they are outside of the conflict and shall not be engaged by combatants. Women and children shall not be utilized as shields in war.

(ii) Guarantee women and girls participation at all levels of public life by ensuring their fundamental rights to education, work, health care, political participation, freedom of movement, and equitable treatment under the law.

(iii) Education for women is of paramount importance to the future generations of Kashmiris. Women and girls shall not be denied access to education based on gender.

Q. Chlidren's Rights

(i) Every child has an inherent right to life, and to the fundamental freedoms enumerated above, to the extent practicable in accordance with the age and maturity of the child.

(ii) Every child shall have his or her rights upheld, without discrimination of any kind, as set forth in the UN Convention on the Rights of the Child.

(iii) Every child shall have the right to special measures to protect or promote her/his care, welfare, health and physical security, and to be protected from maltreatment, abuse or exploitation.

(iv) Young people should be employed in public service projects as well as income-generating projects that provide social assistance to youth in certain difficult circumstances such as orphans, street children, and abandoned.

(v) A child shall not be separated from his or her parents against their will, except when competent authorities subject to judicial review determine, in accordance with applicable law and procedures, that such separation is necessary for the best interests of the child. Such determination may be necessary in a particular case such as one involving abuse or neglect of the child by parents, or one where the parents are living separately and a decision must be made as to the child's place of residence.

(vi) Measures shall be taken to combat the illicit transfer and non-return of children abroad.

R. Education

(i) Illiteracy shall be eradicated among youth through compulsory education for the first nine years of schooling (Basic Education) and the government shall endeavor to provide free schooling for a further three years.

(ii) Peace shall be taught as a facet of other disciplines throughout elementary school, and taught as a separate subject in the secondary school level, with a mandatory minimum one-class requirement for graduation.

(iii) The government shall offer vocational and technical training to those youth over 9 that do not attend school that will allow them carry out projects that will contribute to their personal development and to the economic and social development of Kashmir.

(iv) A region-wise campaign will be conducted via the Education Division to help the various groups in the population live together again in peace. The campaign shall endeavor to raise awareness of the issues involved with peaceful co-existence and the capability, through various forms of non-violent action, to fulfil that promise.

(v) Political and administrative leaders and economic agents shall receive additional training in the peaceful settlement of disputes.

S. Refugees

(i) All Kashmiri refugees and displaced persons, located outside Kashmir, shall have the right to return and live in safety, and dignity, free from intimidation or coercion of any kind.

(ii) Individuals who left Kashmir prior to 1990 shall receive financial compensation for the loss of their property and are welcome to resettle within Kashmir.

(iii) Individuals who left Kashmir after 1990 may also receive financial compensation for the lost property, but may file claims to receive the property itself if they choose.

(iv) The claims of refugees shall be investigated and confirmed through the Refugee Division. Any financial compensation that will be granted shall be processed via the Refugee Division.

(v) The Refugee Division shall help returnees recover their

property and bank accounts whose existence has been duly proven that were left in Kashmir before their exile.

T. Department of Human Rights

The government of Kashmir shall add a new Department of Human Rights to the existing government structure. In furtherance of the goal of an effective and functioning human rights body, technical and material assistance may be sought from the United Nations Special Commission on Human Rights, the United Nations Center for Human Rights, and other relevant international organizations.

1. Powers and Responsibilities of the Department: The Department of Human Rights shall:

   (i) receive, consider and follow-up with complaints regarding possible human rights violations;
   (ii) carry out the necessary investigations autonomously, effectively and in accordance with the political constitution of the Jammu and Kashmir State and international norms regarding human rights;
   (iii) determine whether or not a violation of human rights has occurred on the basis of all the information it is able to obtain in the exercise of the powers referred to herein, taking into consideration any investigations that the competent constitutional institutions may carry out; and
   (iv) the Department shall be empowered to establish itself and move freely throughout Kashmir; interview any person or group of persons freely and privately for the proper performance of its functions; collect whatever information may be relevant for the implementation of its mandate; disseminate information relating to its functions and activities to the Kashmiri public through the mass media.

2. In the performance of its functions the Department shall take into account the situation of the most vulnerable groups of society and to the population directly affected

by the armed confrontation (including displaced persona, refugees and returnees).

3. In verifying the observance of human rights, the Department shall pay particular attention to rights to life, integrity and security of person, liberty, due process, freedom of expression, freedom of movement, freedom of association, and political rights.
4. The Department shall conduct its activities on a permanent and ongoing basis. With the exception of the activities of the Indian soldiers and police force during the years prior to the signing of the Agreement, which will be investigated by the Division of Religious Minorities, all human rights violations occurring prior to the signature are investigated through the Reconciliation Divisions and not through the permanent or other *ad-hoc* Divisions of the Department.
5. A Kashmiri native agreed upon by both the Kashmir Legislative Council and Kashmir Legislative Assembly shall head the Department. The individual should be selected based on the strength of his or her reputation for fairness, integrity, quality of work, and knowledge/background in the human rights field. The individual shall be an eminent person of high moral standing who possesses a demonstrated commitment to human rights and the rights of members of regional communities. His or her term shall last for six years, with the possibility of one re-appointment.
6. The Department shall have its own offices, adequate communication facilities and secretarial support staff. The Department shall be housed in the summertime in Srinagar, and during wintertime reside in Jammu. Support staff for the Department can be hired through the regular civil servant hiring process, while ensuring that the staff comprises a representative selection of the population including women, members of both religious majorities and any minority groups in the region.
7. The Department will include Divisions responsible for Fundamental Human Rights, Religious Minority, Women, Children, Refugees, Education, and Reconciliation.

8. A consortium of local human rights and civil society groups in Kashmir shall be encouraged to help monitor human rights observance. This group will have the authority to investigate claims and allegations regarding the performance of the Department, and verify that the hiring goals are met.

A succinct glance at the abovementioned proposed module shows that it has hidden agenda that encourages secessionism. And, for that reason alone, the proposed module can't be conceded as peace module but encouraging secessionism/seceding module, interventionist module interfering with the sovereignty of the country, an interventionist foreign Constituent Assembly dictating changes in the Indian Constitutional Framework that itself is against the Basic Structure of the Constitution of India, and it should not be encouraged for several reasons. First, the proposed solution-module encourages heightened autonomy, which has since been rejected by the Parliament of India as the State of J&K enjoys maximum autonomy enjoined under Article 370, with the possibility of independence in the near future. Second, it shall open the re-examination and re-determination of accession. The authors of the proposed module should remember that the Instrument of Accession were matter of past history, and past history is a dead history, and any endeavors to revive it should be fraught with dangerous consequences by giving fuel to the fire. This shall lead to the revival of all the documents of accession did the successors of about 560 Indian Princely States so desire. God forbids that this does not happen because that may lead to bloodbath. Third, Kashmir and Kashmiris are unable to defend itself from nationalists and integrationists interested in the unity and integrity of India, its territory, and its people. Fourth, the proposed module is Kashmir as well as Kashmiri centric. It nowhere represents the concern of Ladakh and Ladakhiat, and Jammu and Jammuiat. It shall only escalate alienation amidst three regions—*Kashmir Valley* v. *Jammu* v. *Ladakh like Kashmir* v. *India* v. *Pakistan*. Fifth, seceding is incompatible with constitutional permissibility, because the integration is so well neatly woven in the language of Article 1 of the Constitution of India "India that is Bharat shall be the Union of States" that makes seceding and secession impossible, non-workable and impractical. (C.A.D., Vol. VII, p. 43; *In re Berubari*, A.I.R. 1960 S.C. 845; *Maganbhai* v. *Union of India*, A.I.R. 1969 S.C. 783; *Union of India* v. *Sukumar Sen Gupta*, A.I.R. 1990 S.C. 1692). Sixth, secession is rarely recognized in the international community under the aegis of International Law. Secession will *a fortiori* cause a grant secessionist movement in India that would escalate militancy, terrorism, and violence in the country.

NATIONAL GAME PLAN

India faces challenges to her integrity, sovereignty, security both internal and external, and defense from the propagators/perpetrators/authors of the abovementioned Local, Pakistan, and International Game Plans. Besides, India has successfully been combating as well as quelling the ticklish game plans thrust by militant/terrorist groups like Jammu & Kashmir Liberation Front (JKLF 1977), All Parties Hurriyyat Conference: 1993: a coalition and conglomeration of 26 guerilla and political groups (some claim that it is actually a creation of the United States Institution of Peace—a Washington-based think tank), Muttahida Jihad Council, Hizb-ul-Mujahidin, Jaish-e-Mohammed, Lashkkar-e-Tayyiba, through Armed Forces, Politically, Diplomatically, and strategically by caring the respect for the observance of human rights to human dignity of those who are not the propagators or perpetrators or vouchers of secessionism, separatism, terrorism, and militancy. Another challenge that India faces is Pakistan's contempt for Accords/Agreements be that UN Resolutions of 1948, 1949, Tashkent Declaration 1966, Simla Agreement 1972, Lahore Declaration 1999. These Accords were meant to ease the tension between India and Pakistan over Kashmir. These Accords were to be a milestone in the development of synergic relationship. Had those Accords been honored there ought to have, it is assumed, developed a model SAARC like model European Union and EURO.

It may be argued that Pakistan signed the Accords/Agreements with the least intention to adhere to them. [Brahama Chellaney, Why The Agreements Failed, *The Hindustan Times*, Sep. 8, 1999]. The contemptuous behavior of Pakistan was visible of planning the Kargil invasion while it signed the Lahore

Declaration (*Ibid.*). It has unequivocally *a multo fortiori* been opined that Pakistan has been the ultimate hypocrite by continuing to swear by the 1948 and 1949 UN Resolutions while at the same time violating them by refusing to withdraw from J&K (*Ibid.*). It may, however, be expressed that the only Accords/Agreements Pakistan have enforced that placed the onus of compliance on India for reasons not far to seek.

Encountered by these challenges, Islamabad Declaration reiterating Lahore Declaration, India and Pakistan initiated Confidence Building Measures to restore peace and normalcy in the region by initiating several measures in this perspective such as people to people contact through Muzfarabad Kaman Amman Setu route, Wagha route, Khokhara route, road and railway routes, exchange of journalists, cultural troops, etc. through the aegis of Social Sciences Study Center and other agencies.

Besides, India initiated internal CBM by holding First Jammu and Kashmir Round Table Conference in Delhi in February 2006, and Second Jammu and Kashmir Round Table Conference in Srinagar on 24th and 25th May 2006. The Prime Minister of India, Dr. Manmohan Singh, declared the strategic policy plan by identifying five issues for an in-depth examination by five Committees, namely,

Group I: Confidence Building Measures Across Segments of Society in the State: Headed by Mr. Mohd. Ansari

The Group will evolve:

- Measures to improve the condition of people affected by militancy.
- Schemes to rehabilitate all orphans and widows affected by militancy.
- Issues relating to the relaxation of conditions for persons who have foresworn militancy.
- An effective rehabilitation policy, including employment, for Kashmiri Pandit migrants.
- An approach considering issues relating to return of Kashmiri youth from areas controlled by Pakistan.
- Measures to protect and preserve the unique cultural and religious heritage of the State.

Group II: Strengthening Relations Across the Line of Control: Headed by Mr. M.K. Rasgotra

To recommend measures to:

- Simplify procedures to facilitate travel across the Line of Control.
- Increase goods traffic.
- Expand people-to-people contact.
- Open up new routes such as Kargil, Skardu, etc.

Group III: Economic Development: Headed by Dr. C. Rangarajan

To evolve strategy that ensures:

- Balanced economic development and employment generation.
- Balanced regional and sub-regional development within the State.

Group IV: Ensuring Good Governance: Headed by Mr. N.C. Saxena

To consider effective measures to:

- Increase responsiveness, accountability and transparency of the administration.
- Strengthen local self-government.
- Effectively monitor development programs.
- Institute zero tolerance for human rights violations.
- Strengthen the Right to Information.
- Provide adequate security to all segments of society, particularly the minority communities.

Group V: Strengthening Relations between the State and the Centre: Headed by Justice Sageer Ahmad

To deliberate on:

- Matters relating to the special status of Jammu and Kashmir within the Indian Union.
- Methods of strengthening democracy, secularism and the rule of law in the State.
- Deliberate on effective devolution of powers among

different regions to meet regional, sub-regional and ethnic aspirations.

Representation of almost all political parties has been taken care of, but the Report (Annexures 1-5) ignores the consensus of views of all the representatives. It is a "Quiet Diplomacy" to "quietus of genesis of Centre-State issues." It was consisted of 21 member. The Group had only met for the first and the last time on 2-3 September, 2007 with a consensus opinion to meet again to deliberate upon the issues. Suddenly and surprisingly, Justice Sageer Ahmad submitted the "Summary of Recommendations" without the signatures of the Chairman of the Group Justice Sageer Ahmad as well as 21 members. This is disrespect to the members. A Justice has done injustice to the issues. The recommendations show a "de-strengthening approach" in place of "strengthening Relations between the State and the Centre." With all diffidence, modesty and humility, it is submitted that the report is 'judicially mockery, political gimmicks and socio-ethic joke'. It is devoid of all cannons of socio-judicious ethics. Justice Sageer Ahmad's report sounds bad because it proposes bad reforms and, therefore, not beautiful. Its recommendations are bad for the country and worse for the State. The reasons are not far to seek. The working of Centre-State relations does not depend on the independence approach, but on the "functional reciprocal dependence" approach that shall culminate into the success of strengthening of Centre-State relations within Constitutional scheme, Constitutional values, Constitutional culture, and Constitutional morality.

Critical Observations and Concluding Summations

Indian Game Plan seems to be of new strategy to come out of the cobweb of Local, Pakistan and International Game Plans, which are Kashmir Valley centric with least concern for the nationalist feelings of Jammu and Ladakh populace. The above tripartite approach is coupled with blow hot and blow cold behavior pattern. Be that as it may, the most important issue is that the Indian Game Plan ought not to fall prey of the abovementioned tripartite Game plans. India has to be tactics in her synergic strategy planning lest it becomes the victim in the trapping of tripartite deceptive Game Plans. India's Game Plan ought to be modeled in safeguarding her boundaries, sovereignty, integrity, internal and external security, and defense. She has to evolve new strategies to combat the challenges that are threats to her internal as well as external security. The security threats are multifaceted nature that spring from the problems of Postcolonial world, namely, interethnic, racial, quasi-racial, ideological, strategic, economic, social, and neo-political alignments. These Groups, four out of five, seem to have addressed themselves certain penetrating questions to plug loopholes in the system and suggested remedial measures in improving the system. This appears may not have been an easy task. It seems a Herculean task, because in the restoration of the confidence of all, including the politicians, have to be conscientious, sincere and above politicking in their behavior pattern. Whether their recommendations are another docket for the cupboards as well as the spiders to weave enchanting deceptive fabric, the time would only speak. However, in my opinion, these Groups have not addressed minutely the basic question why, how and under what circumstances did confidence loose? Who is in the garb of whom? In the answer of these million dollar questions alone lay the perpetual confidence building strategy. Militancy, terrorism and proxy war thrust on India from across the borders are responsible to give rise to matters of internal as well as external contentions and are responsible obstacles in confidence building measures. Successive State governments have not been considering State of J&K as one composite unit, but in three different units, and as such a contributory factor in simmering the confidence. Lack of good governance, accountability, and transparency are equally responsible for the loss of confidence of the populace in the functioning of the system, and, hence, obstacles in sustainable governance. The regressive corruption is on the ascendancy and progressive corruption on the decay, and 'care me not' responsive as well as responsible attitudes having been developing resentment, dissatisfaction and belying faith. Emergence, perpetuation, and continuation of fundamentalism are another factor for simmering the confidence. Exodus of Hindus in majority from the Valley has not only changed the demography but also has been responsible for the loss of confidence and faith of the said populace, designated as internally displaced persons, in the governments and their style of functioning. Exodus of Hindus, due to the impetus of terrorism, from other parts of the State and her apathy/impassiveness for such internally displaced persons seems another cause of loss of confidence. Maligning the security forces in the pretext of human rights as well as International Humanitarian Laws violations sloganeering gives boost to the militants, terrorists, propagators of proxy war to escalate in their nefarious activities, and demoralization of security forces as well as nationalists. This aspect as required to be addressed has not gained that sort of intensity as was expected, and as such leaves a wide void to be filled in when seems to be a futuristic strategy. There is no uniform rehabilitation or resettlement policy for internally displaced persons, displaced persons and refugees from West Pakistan of 1947, and, naturally, lack of confidence as well as faith. The Working Group on

Confidence Building Measures in its Report of January 2007 has, *inter alia*, recommended that "the rehabilitation problems of refugees of 1947 who came over from adjoining areas of Pakistan across International border need to be examined and settled once for all. These persons are not eligible for being permanent residents of the State". The status of such refugee-persons has been addressed with deceptive as well as contemptuous *lingua fauna*. The status of such refugee-persons continues to be that of homeless persons; non-domicile persons, and speaks volumes about their fate. The Working Group on the Confidence Building Measures has evaporated the soup and sauce of the confidence of such refugee-persona. We aspire for External Confidence Building Measures, but give least to the Internal Confidence Building Measures, seem to be a big paradox. We appear to have missed the opportunity once again by loosing the confidence of such persona who have confidence in us in the long cherished hope that they would cease to be homeless as well as non-domiciliary. The Vth Working Group on Centre-State Relations on the subject matter has failed to address the problem in the right perspectives; rather its language seems to be of artificiality and contrived paradigms because of its minimal insights into the mutual coordination of Law and Morality. The Working Group appears to have made this law and morality knot a riddle wrapped in mystery inside an enigma. Its recommendation seems to be lost of farsightedness, because it permeates the Othello's Sword to hang on the heads of such refugee-persona. Its maximalists' perception appears to leave the problem unresolved in the hands of those who failed to resolve it. This seems, in my opinion, the matter in the hands of those who though may have the desire to contribute but could not do so because when the flesh is weak, the spirit however willing cannot execute. Self-rule and autonomy are political ideologies of two different political parties, which do not carry majority support from all the regions of the State. Self-rule and autonomy stand rejected by Parliament of India, and as such cannot be conceded as viable solutions to the confidence building. Jammu and Ladakh regions represent nationalist and integrationist behavior pattern to remain in coordination as well as cooperation with the Union of India, whereas Valley presents otherwise. What a paradox in confidence building measures! Coordination between delimitation and communalization has belied confidence-building hopes of straightening demographic imbalances. Inclusion of Article 370 in the text of the Constitution of India has never been the aspiration of "We the people of J&K and India", and as such its continuation belies hopes of confidence building. Working with the Constitution and democracy have been examined as well as re-examined with reiterations by Sarkaria Commission and Venkatachallia Commission that any interference with the working of the Constitution and democracy will offend the Basic Structure of the Constitutional culture. The endeavors of the Working Group have to be to strengthen coordinative as well as cooperative federal culture and that alone will bring strength in the Unity and Integrity of the Indian Nation. And, the only efforts that are required in this direction are to not to belittle the present working of Center-State relations' confidence. Equitable Developments and financial allocations on the basis of equalization in the three regions of the State shall develop faith and confidence in the whole populace of the State. Eco-tourism (economic and ecological) shall be the focus for the whole State. Promotion of pilgrimages like Shardapeeth will yield confidence. Confidence building on *ad hoc* basis amidst one section of the populace shall be at the cost of entire populace that shall not yield meaningful results. Groups like Hurriyyat, JKLF, etc. that do not represent the voice of the entire population of the State must not be encouraged, otherwise that shall cost heavily in confidence building measures. Any political mileage if given to any political party shall be disastrous; the only mileage that has to be worked out will be for the Unity and Integrity of the Indian Nation, and nothing less, nothing more. To enhance confidence, there have to be no compromise—internally and externally. The "Havana Joint Mechanism to Terrorism Statement" of September 2006 both by Prime Minister of India Dr. Manmohan Singh and President of Pakistan General Pervez Musharraff seems to be susceptible and has many hidden compromises, and as such has to be perceived as well as pursued with utmost caution. It is quintessential to submit that proposed local, Pakistan and international modules are not short of quagmire because those modules encourage self-determination, self-rule, autonomy, independence, secessionism, ceding on the basis of 'Back Channel Diplomacy' conceived in four comprehensive formulae, namely, Northern Ireland, Kosovo, East Timor, American Think Tank. It may be niche to submit that India has to some time pursue hard-state policies as well as strategies in place of soft-state policies through dialogue in order to resolve inconclusive dispute with synergic strategies lest it becomes indefinite. Synergic strategy and comity in the South Asia region [SAARC] to developing trade, commerce, culture relationship, academia exchange, may yield positive results, this synergic comity shall only strengthen South Asia region and may be an envious harbinger for the others to emulate. This needs courageous strategies to work out perpetual peace solutions for the good of human beings, for the happiness of human beings, for the prosperous development of human beings. This is the only synergic strategy to keep the history in the past and march progressively like pilgrimage progress for everlasting peace and prosperity. This is the only human right module that may have to be worked out with synergic strategy. We must keep before our eyes the wise saying. "Eternal vigilance is the price of liberty". We must behave in such a manner that it might not ever be said in repentance of us that:

> *"Khola Kafas To Taqate Parwaz Hi Nahin*
> *Bulbul Tere Nasib Ko Sayyad Kya Kare".*

REFERENCES

1. Durga Das, Sardar Patel's Correspondence New Light on Kashmir, 1945-1950, Vol. I, 1971.
2. Collier's Encyclopedia: http://www.mtholyoke.edu/acad/interl/colkash.htm
3. K.L. Bhatia, Jammu and Kashmir Article 370 of the Constitution of India, 1997.
4. htt://www.criisweb.org/showreport.cfm?reportid; Somini Sen Gupta, The India-Pakistan Tension: The Background; Struggle for Kashmir is Fueled by Clashing, *New York Times*, January 13, 2002.
5. U.N. Documents on the Kashmir Issue can be procured at the UN Website www.un.org

6. C. Joseph Chacko, India's Contribution to International Law, Kashmir and International Law, Rescueil Des Cours, 1958.
7. South Asia Terrorism Portal Statement: htt://www.satp.org/satporgtp/countries/India/states/jandk/terrorist outfits/Hurriyat.htm
8. John Gershman, Crisis Watch Profile: Kashmir at http://www.selfdetermine.org/conflicts/kashmir/html
9. Howard B. Schaffer, Reconsidering the US Role, *The Washington Quarterly*, Spring (2001).
10. International Crisis Group, Kashmir: Confrontation and Miscalculation, Asia Report No: 35 (2002).
11. Somini Sengupta, The India-Pakistan Tension, *op. cit.*
12. Brahma Chellenay, Pakistan's Contempt for Accords, *The Hindustan Times*, September 8, 1999, www.jammu-kashmir.com/archives/archives1999/99september08.html
13. Ajay Singh and Anthony Davis, *Asia Week*, Unaligned Line of Control: Why India and Pakistan Differ over the Border, www.asiaweek.com/news/990709/nat3.html
14. Kuldip Nayar, Pak May Challenge Siachen Control, www.rediff.com/news/1999/jul/16nayar.htm
15. John Gerhman, Overview of Self-Determination Issues, Self-Determination on Forcus, http://www.selfdetermine.org/conflicts/Kashmir body.html
16. Strobe Talbot, Talbot on Self-Determination in an Interdependent World, Foreign Policy, Spring 2000, http://www.usembassy.
17. EU Report on Kashmir backs India's Stand, 2007.
18. Jammu and Kashmir: Self-Determination. Demands for a Plebiscite and Secession: Examining the Contradictions, http://www.members.tripod.com
19. Eric Kolodner, The Future of the Right to Self-Determination, 10 *Conn. J. Int'l. L.*, 153 (1994).
20. Yves Beigbeder, International Monitoring of Plebiscite, Referenda and National Elections: Self-Determination and Transition to Democracy, 1994.
21. Irrma Foley, Karen Heymann, Susan Kagondu, Catherine Kihara and Lynne Madnick, Kashmir: The Road to Peace, Public International Law and Policy Group, www.publicinternationallaw.org
22. Jammu and Kashmir Government and Administration, http://www.jammukashmir.nic.in/govt/welcome.html
23. Article 370: Law and Politics, *Frontline*, Volume 17, September 2000, http://www.flonnet.com
24. Arvind Lavakare, The Indeterminate Life of Article 370, II, June 2002.
25. J&K Autonomy Committee Report, Vols. I and II, 2000, http://www.indiainfo.com/news/2000/06/20/constitution.html

26. Election Commission of India: Background Information on Jammu and Kashmir, http://www.eci.gov.in
27. Raju G.C. Thomas, What is Third World Security?, Department of Political Science, Marquette University, Milwaukee, Wisconsin, *Annual Review of Political Science,* Vol. 6: 205-32, 2003, http://www.arjournals.annualreviews.org
28. Prem Nath Bazaz, Kashmir in Crucible.
29. C.A.D., Vol. VII, p. 43.
30. C.A.D., Vols. X-XII, 1989 Ed., Reprint, pp. 421-29.
31. *Magher Singh* v. *Principal Secretary, Jammu and Kashmir,* A.I.R. 1953, J&K 25.
32. *In re Berubari,* A.I.R. 1960 S.C. 845.
33. *Maganbhai* v. *Union of India,* A.I.R. 1969, S.C. 783.
34. *Union of India* v. *Sukumar Sen Gupta,* A.I.R. 1990, S.C. 1629.

The Constitution of Jammu & Kashmir : The Genesis of Crisis—Past Tense, Present Imperfect and Future Indefinite

I feel honoured to be fortunate enough to present the views in the august gathering in the presence of respected Lt. Gen. (Rtd.) Shri S.K. Sinha, the former Governor of J&K State, and Shri Arun Jaitely, the Honourable Member of Parliament and the Leader of Opposition in the Rajya Sabha, on the most unfortunate topic of the day, which is of contrived nature.

THE DISTURBING QUESTIONS

- Why a special Constitutional treatment to only one Federal Unit of the Indian Federation that is Union of States?
- Why a separate Constitution of J&K within the federal structure of the Constitution of India when all the States of Union of India work within the Constitutional scheme of India?

THE GENESIS OF THE CONSTITUTION OF J&K

The Genesis of the Constitution of J&K is Article 370 of the Constitution of India moved by Shri Gopalaswamy Ayyanger as Article 306-A in the Constituent Assembly of India on Monday, 17 October, 1949.

Article 306-A was not originally a part of the "Draft Constitution" prepared by the Drafting Committee headed by

Dr. B.R. Ambedkar and presented in the Constituent Assembly of India under the Chairmanship of Dr. Rajendra Prasad.

At the outset; it may be submitted that the four representatives of J&K in the Constituent Assembly, namely, Mr. Sheikh Mohd. Abdullaha, Mr. Afzal Beg, Mr. Maulana Masoodi, and Mr. M.R. Baigra, did not overtly and covertly utter a single word on the extent and language of Article 306-A irrespective of the fact that they were present physically in the Constituent Assembly on the day of its presentation in the Constituent Assembly. [They were the signatories to the final adopted Constitution of India]

It is also a matter of historical fact that there was no word from Dr. B.R. Ambedkar, because he was not in favour of a separate and special constitutional status to J&K. He reportedly happened to convey: "You want India to defend Kashmir, give Kashmiris equal rights all over India, but you want to deny India and Indians all rights in Kashmir. I am Law Minister of India. I can't be a party to such a betrayal of National interest".

It is also a matter of history that except Mr. Gopalaswamy Ayyanger and Mr. Maulana Hasrat Mohani, no other Member of the Constituent assembly did participate in the debate on the extent and content of Article 306-A.

A SEPARATE CONSTITUTION OF J&K A BY PRODUCT OF ARTICLE 370!

- It is a known fact that the separate Constitution of J&K is the by product of Article 370.
- It creates a sovereignty within a sovereign [Indian] permeating the feelings of a separate country as well as separatism.
- It is against the basic structure of the Constitution of India and, hence, legally and constitutionally incompatible, and not permissible.

WHAT DOES ARTICLE 370 ENJOIN?

The language of Article 370 (original 306-A) is inasmuch as deceitful as the beautiful language of Constitution of J&K is deceitful and the root cause of separatism.

1. Article 238 shall not apply in relation to the State of J&K. [Paradox: Article 238 originally related to Part B States in the original constitutional language, which was repealed from the Constitution of India by Seventh Amendment Act, 1956 as a consequence of States Reorganization Act, 1956 doing away with Part A,B,C states. Unfortunately, this Article continues to occupy a place in the language of Article 370)!
2. The power of Parliament to make laws for the State of J&K shall be limited to
   (i) those matters in the Union List and Concurrent List which, in consultation with the Government of the State, are declared by the President to correspond to matters specified in the Instrument of Accession governing the accession of the State to India, i.e., Defence, Foreign Affairs, and Communication.
   (ii) such other matters in the said List as, with the concurrence of the Government of the State, the President may by order specify, i.e., Central Laws in terms of matters enumerated in the Union List and Concurrent List shall not extend to the State of J&K without the concurrence of the State Government.
3. The provisions of Article 1 of Constitution of India shall apply in relation to the State of J&K. [Article 1 states India that is BHARAT shall be the Union of States — Schedule I and Schedule IV. Article 1 became operative on the date of the adoption of the Constitution of India, i.e., 26 November, 1949; Accession on 26/27 October, 1947, J&K like other Native/Princely States part of Indian Federal Democratic Republic on the date of adoption of the Constitution of India, i.e., 26 November, 1949].
4. Such of the other provisions of the Indian Constitution and subject to such exceptions and modifications shall apply in relation to the State of J&K as the President may by Order specify. (Constitutional Application Order, 1950: Articles 1 and 5-11, i.e., Citizenship of India — All permanent residents of J&K became citizens of India

under it; Constitution Application Orders 1954,1962, 1966 and 1985—extended provisions of the Indian Constitution from time to time with certain modifications; Article 35-A added as fundamental right for J&K giving special privileges to the permanent residents of J&K].

Pre-1953 or Pre-1947 or autonomy or Azadi demands amount to the cessation of Article 1 (J&K no more federal unit of Indian federation) and withdrawal of Citizenship right to the people of J&K.

5. The President may, by public notification, declare that this Article shall cease to be operative or shall be operative only with such exceptions and modifications and from such date as he may specify: *Provided that the recommendations of the Constituent Assembly of the State shall be necessary before the President issues such notification.*
   - This is the root for the establishment of the Constituent Assembly for the making of J&K Constitution.
   - This Article can be abrogated by the State Assembly as it enjoys constituent making power by amending J&K Constitution. (Section 147 of J&K Constitution). The Governor of the State during first six months' governor's rule under J&K Constitution can recommend for its deletion [as legislative and executive powers are vested in the Governor]. The Governor during the operation of President's rule under Article 356 of the Constitution of India can recommend for its deletion or abrogation and the Parliament of India can play such role.
   - It facilitates the growth of secessionism, terrorism, militancy, subversion and demand for independence *Azadi*, self rule, pre-1953, pre-1947, autonomy and internal autonomy.
   - It also facilitates the growth and continuation of corrupt oligarchies, and personal aberrations.
   - It puts false and fictitious notions and hopes in the minds of the youth.

- It gives rise to regional tensions and conflicts [three regions of the State: Jammu, Kashmir and Ladakh].
- It makes the nationalists and integrationists of Jammu and Ladakh regions people to suffer.
- It makes an inroad for autonomy assumed to be available just on the stroke of pen pushing, which is otherwise incompatible and not attainable in practice under the constitutional provisions, constitutional practices and conventions.

WHAT DOES AUTONOMY OR PRE-1953 OR PRE-1947 OR SELF RULE POSITION IMPLY?

- It amounts to deprivation of right of Indian citizenship to the permanent residents of J&K, thus depriving them the fruits of fundamental rights.
- It shall amount to the deprivation of the status of J&K State within the framework of the Constitution of India, which declares India that is Bharat shall be the Union of State.
- It shall amount to the propagators of Azadi or autonomy or pre-1953 or pre-1947 to say: "You will send and I will spend without accountability; you will have no say even if I build a corrupt and callous oligarchy and cause a situation in which Damocles sword of secession, subversion, militancy, terrorism, self rule, loyalties across the border, pre-1953, pre-1947 could be kept hanging permanently on your head".

HOW FAR J&K CONSTITUTION THE ROOT CAUSE FOR SUBVERSIVE, SECESSIONIST, TERRORIST, MILITANCY ACTIVITIES

See the Preamble language of the Indian Constitution and J&K Constitution:

- Indian Constitution: "We the People of India ..."
- J&K Constitution: "We the People of J&K..."
- How people of J&K are different from the people of India? This language gives the impression as people of J&K are different from the people of India. This seems to be the root cause of subversion, secessionism,

separatism, terrorism, militancy, pre-1953 or pre-1947 or self rule or autonomy.

- Sections 6-9 of he J&K Constitution are also the root cause of secessionism, subversion, etc. The language of these sections could have been summed up in one Section, viz., the permanent residents of J&K shall be the permanent citizens of India. This could have facilitated all citizens of India to integrate culminating into the complete integration of J&K to India, and there ought not have been the direct consequences of subversion, secessionism, separatism, militancy, terrorism, and across border loyalties.
- In the backdrop of this, the Instrument of Accession became a thing of the past, and a dead past could not have been the bone of contention every now and then. Hence, it can't be reopened.
- Besides, a specious or fictitious impression has been created that all princely States except the State of J&K agreed to integrate themselves to India by accepting the Constitution of India that would come. I quote Hari Singh's announcement of 15 July, 194 as mentioned in Durga Dass, Sardar Patel's Correspondence, Vol. I, pp. 66-68 and 13-15:
- "... Naturally we are interested in the progress of India as a whole. *My views on the subject are well known and on more than one occasion I have Riven expression to them. They are briefly that we look forward to taking our due place in the new constitutional structure of India*, whereby we hope that India will be able to take its proper place as a great nation, one of the brotherhood of nations, and to wield great influence in the affairs of the world, thus adding to human civilization those aspects of our great culture which will help to solve the problems of mankind".
- *Had this announcement of Hari Singh taken conscientiously and seriously, there ought not have born Article 370 and a separate Constitution of J&K breeding secessionism, subversion, pre-1953, pre-1947, autonomy, terrorism, self rule, militancy, and across border loyalties.*

ARTICLE 370 AND J&K CONSTITUTION *MOGNA CORTO OF DISCRIMINATION*

Mr. Maulana Hasrat Mohani asked in the Constituent Assembly—Why this discrimination? To which Mr. Gopalaswamy Ayyengar replied—may be speciously relevant then but not now—that Kashmir's conditions were special and required special treatment. Special conditions were:

1. War was going on within the limits of J&K.
2. There was cease fire agreed; but the conditions in the State were unusual. Normalcy was to be restored.
3. Part of the State was in the hands of rebels and enemies [(POK): Azadi, self rule, autonomy could have been liberation of POK and its complete integration to India in terms of Instrument of Accession since POK happened to be the integral geographical and territorial part of J&K sending unequivocal signals to the rulers across the border].
4. We were engaged with U.N. in regard to J&K. Freedom from entanglement was possible when the Kashmir problem was satisfactorily settled [J&K disputant reference to U.N. now is redundant].
5. Government of India had committed themselves to the people of Kashmir to ascertain whether they will remain with the Republic of India or wish to go out of it. Government of India committed to the will of the people by means of plebiscite provided that peaceful and normal conditions were restored and the impartiality of the plebiscite could be guaranteed [This is the price We the People of India are paying].
6. Praja Sabha was dead.
7. We had also agreed that the will of the people, through the instrument of a Constituent Assembly, will determine the Constitution of the state as well as the sphere of Union jurisdiction over the State [This speaks bankruptcy of farsightedness by conceiving a separate Constitution for the State with the disastrous consequences like Azadi or self rule or autonomy or pre-

1953 or pre-1947 or subversive activities or secessionism or militancy or terrorism or loyalties across the border, and the price We the People of India are paying the Valley of Kashmir].

8. It was inevitable to establish an interim system and Article 306-A (370) was an attempt to establish interim system. It could have come to an end as soon as normalcy was restored, peace was established, and Constituent Assembly accepted the Instrument of Accession. [This had already happened. The Constituent Assembly of J&K had already accepted in unequivocal language the Instrument of Accession, and the Constitution of J&K by its Preamble language: " We the people of J&K having solemnly resolved, in pursuance of accession of this State to India which took place on 26th day of October, 1947, to further define the existing relationship of the State with the Union of India as an integral part thereof, ... and assuring the Unity of the Nation". Hereafter, it ought to have mentioned, by a reference to the contents of the letter of Maharaja Hari Singh as mentioned above, to further define the existing relationship of the State of J&K with the Union of India as its integral federal Unit within the framework of the Constitution of India that shall apply and extend to the State of J&K as it applies and extends to other UNION OF STATES of India that is BHARAT. Here, we lost the golden opportunity and thus paying the price of our past follies the Valley of Kashmir at the sufferance of the citizens of Jammu and Ladakh who have no links with secessionism or separatism or azadi or autonomy or pre-1953 or pre-1947 or self rule or militancy or terrorism or loyalties across the border taking instructions from them for subversive activities or notorious proxy war activities].

SUBMISSIONS

1. Political will lacked farsightedness and committed a mistake by moving and adopting Article 306-A (370).

2. It was unwise to recommend and propose a separate Constituent Assembly for J&K, which gave a separate Constitution of J&K, thus, sowing the seeds for generating separate feelings of secessionism or subversion or pre-1953 or pre-1947 or azadi or autonomy or self-rule.

3. How there could be two sovereign bodies (Constituent Assemblies—one for India and another for J&K) within one federal democratic republic India that is BHARAT. Hence, against the basic structure of the Constitutional spirit.

4. It disturbs to assure the Unity and Integrity of One Nation in the maintenance of uniformity.

5. Remodel the language of Article 370 by replacing its language empowering the Governor of the State to take steps to develop those areas of the State which have thus far been neglected to bringing them in the mainstream as provided in the constitutional language of Articles 371 and 371A-371I [temporary and special provisions for the States of Maharashtra and Gujarat, Nagaland, Assam, Manipur, Andhra Pradesh, Sikkim, Mizoram, Arunachal Pradesh, Goa].

6. To bring full moon integration, to recommend to scrap a separate Constitution of J&K to do away with the psyches of separatism or secessionism or subversion or pre-1953 or pre-1947 or autonomy or azadi or self rule or across border loyalties.

7. To achieve, let us solemnly resolve to generate public opinion in the country lest:

"Khola Kafas To Taqote Porwoz Hi Nahin
Bulbul Tere Nasib Ko Sayyad Kya Kare"

प्रस्तावना

जम्मू और कश्मीर को घेरने वाली आंतरिक और बाह्य राजनीतिक उलझनों और जटिलताओं से विश्व परिचित है। मेरा अभिप्रायः इन्हें ढकने का नहीं है। यह आलेख विशुद्ध रूप से और मात्र रूप से एक विधि विद्यार्थी ज्ञाता के नाते एक विनम्र प्रयास है ताकि पाठक इससे परिचित हो सकें।

क्या जम्मू कश्मीर एक समस्या है? यदि यह समस्या है तो यह समस्या कृत्रिम विकारयुक्त काल्पनिक नीतियों का सामूहिक परिणाम है। वास्तव में जम्मू कश्मीर समस्या आधुनिक इतिहास के विकृत तथ्यों का स्वरूप प्रस्तुत करता है। 26–27 अक्तूबर 1947 को इस विकृति का प्रारंभ जम्मू कश्मीर का भारत गणराज्य के साथ विलय होने पर आरंभ हुआ जब यह राज्य भारत का अटूट अंग बना। तबसे लेकर यह विषय आंतरिक और बाह्य दृष्टि के अनेकानेक उलझनों का शिकार होता गया। इसके अतिरिक्त यह लगता है कि अलग–अलग समय पर कुछ लोगों की हठधर्मी के कारण जम्मू कश्मीर की यह समस्या विकट से विकटतम् होती गई। यह परिस्थिति उन सत्ता आसीन लोगों के कारण बन गई जिनका व्यवहार हमेशा अस्थिर एवं काल्पनिक बना रहा। ऐसे लोग जो भारत की मुख्य धारा से बाहर रहना चाहते थे, उन लोगों के षड्यंत्रों का शिकार बन गया। कश्मीर समस्या विलयवादी और अलगाववादी शक्तियों के बीच के संघर्ष का परिणाम है। जम्मू कश्मीर का विलय विवाद का विषय नहीं बनना चाहिए था क्योंकि यह ऐतिहासिक, धार्मिक, नैतिक, संवैधानिक और कानूनी दृष्टि से भारत का अभिन्न अंग बन चुका था। अलगाववादी भरसक प्रयास कर रहे थे कि इस ऐतिहासिक सत्य के अपने झूठे प्रचार से विश्व को भ्रम में डाल सकें। इसमें कोई संदेह नहीं कि कश्मीर समस्या का आधार झूठ, निरंतर झूठ और कोरे झूठ से उत्पन्न हुआ है। ग्रेटर कश्मीर, नया कश्मीर, जनमत संग्रह, स्वशासन, स्वाययत्ता और पुनर्वास की घोषणाओं ने इसको और उलझा कर रख दिया है। कश्मीर देवी–देवताओं, संतों, ऋषियों, फकीरों और पीरों की पूज्य स्थली रही है और इसलिए इसको

धरती पर स्वर्ग कहा जाता है। जहां पर भिन्न मतों और आस्था रखने वालों के अपने–अपने श्रद्धा स्थल रहे हैं। जिसके कारण यहां सदैव धार्मिक सद्भावना बनी रही है। यह क्षेत्र भगवान शिव के पवित्र स्थानों से भरा है, इसलिए इस धरती पर 'शैवमत' का प्रादुर्भाव हुआ और यह मत फल फूलकर भारत के एक महान दर्शन के रूप में प्रस्थापित हुआ है। जम्मू कश्मीर की तथाकथित समस्या एक पक्षीय विचार से उपजी और इसके समाधान के लिए ऐसी नरम नीतियां अपनाई गई जिसके कारण यह समस्या सुलझने की बजाए और अधिक उलझ गई। यह कहना गलत न होगा कि हमारे नीति निर्धारकों ने स्वयं ही इस सीधे सादे प्रश्न को एक ऐसी पहेली बना दिया कि जिससे बाहर निकल पाना आसान नहीं रहा। इस वक्त यह उपयुक्त होगा कि जिन लोगों ने इस साधारण समस्या को उलझा दिया है उनके विचार और व्यवहार का विश्लेषण किया जाए। 1931, 1942, 1947, 1949, 1950, 1953 में जिन सांप्रदायिक और अलगाववादी मुस्लिम कश्मीरी नेताओं और उनके समर्थकों ने इस राज्य को पाकिस्तान में मिलाने, जनमत संग्रह करवाने तथा जम्मू कश्मीर पर भारत की प्रभुसत्ता को कम करने के लिए षड्यंत्र रचे, उनके प्रति हमारी नीतियां कभी भी सुदृढ़ एवं निर्णायक नहीं रही। कश्मीर के अंदर ऐसा विषैला साहित्य छपता और बहता रहा जिसके कारण कई भारत विरोधी षड्यंत्र बनते रहे और परिणाम स्वरूप भारत और पाकिस्तान की दूरियां बढ़ती रहीं। दूसरी ओर, कश्मीर की मानसिकता विकृत होती रही। महा शक्तियों की प्रत्यक्ष और गुप्त नीतियां भी इस परिस्थिति को अधिक भयावह बनाने के लिए अपना योगदान देती रहीं। इन घटनाओं से कुछेक ऐसे तथ्यों का भी उद्घाटन होता है जिसके कारण सरदार पटेल, गोपालास्वामी अईअंगर, महाराजा हरीसिंह, मेहरचंद महाजन और इन सरीखों अनेकानेक दूसरे महत्वपूर्ण लोग भी परिस्थितियों का शिकार बनते रहे हैं। एक साधारण कश्मीर विषय को उलझा हुआ जटिल कश्मीर विषय बना दिया। यह चीज भी सामने आ जाती है कि इन परिस्थितियों के कारण जम्मू कश्मीर के भारत के साथ विलय के कट्टर समर्थक भी एक स्वतंत्र कश्मीर की बात सोचने लग पड़े। एक सीधा एवं सरल कश्मीर ऐसा विकृत हुआ जिसने भारत और पाकिस्तान के संबंधों को सदा के लिए कड़वाहट से भर दिया और दूसरी ओर परस्पर धार्मिक सद्भावना के स्थान पर धार्मिक संघर्ष का वातावरण बना दिया। इन तथ्यों की पृष्ठभूमि में यह युक्तियुक्त होगा कि उन घटनाओं की श्रृंखला का उल्लेख किया जाए जो कश्मीर समस्या के कई पक्षों पर प्रकाश डालने वाले हैं।

घटनाओं की पृष्ठभूमि

जम्मू कश्मीर राज्य का क्षेत्रफल 86024 वर्ग मील है (2,22,236 स्क. कि. मी.)। यह राज्य कश्मीर घाटी, जम्मू, लद्दाख, बालितस्तान, गिलगित, हूजां और नगर क्षेत्रों को मिलाकर बना है। इस क्षेत्र का सामरिक महत्व है। इसकी सीमाएं पश्चिम में पाकिस्तान और उत्तर में अफगानिस्तान, उत्तर–पूर्व में चीन के साथ मिलती हैं। इसके अतिरिक्त यह रूस के बहुत निकट पड़ता है। मध्य एशिया को जाने वाला मार्ग इसी क्षेत्र से गुजरता है। आधुनिक इतिहास इस बात का साक्षी है कि सितंबर 1925 में महाराजा हरीसिंह के सत्तारूढ़ होने पर जम्मू कश्मीर राज्य में एक नए युग का प्रारंभ हुआ। 'कश्मीर कश्मीरियों के लिए' का आंदोलन जो शंकरलाल कौल की अध्यक्षता में आरंभ किया गया वह जम्मू कश्मीर के इतिहास के ऊपर एक काला धब्बा है। महाराजा हरीसिंह ने 1927 में स्टेट सब्जेक्ट कानून लागू करके कश्मीर से बाहर लोगों के लिए सरकारी नौकरियों और अचल संपत्ति खरीदने पर पाबंदी लगा दी थी। (प्रेमनाथ बजाज : कश्मीर इन करूसीबल)

1930 में श्रीनगर के कुछ मुस्लिम स्नातकों ने जिसमें शेख मुहम्मद अब्दुल्ला भी शामिल थे, एक रीडिंग रूम नाम की पार्टी का गठन किया। रीडिंग रूम पार्टी का गठन ही कश्मीर के मुसलमानों को महाराजा हरीसिंह के राज्य से दूर करने और मुस्लिम जनसंख्या से दूर रखने का कारण बन गया। इस घटना ने कश्मीरी मुसलमानों को सबसे अलग–थलग रहने का भाव पैदा कर दिया। शेख मुहम्मद अब्दुल्ला द्वारा 'मुस्लिम कान्फ्रेंस के गठन के कारण यह अलगाववाद की धारणा और सुदृढ़ हुई और शेख अब्दुल्ला ने महाराजा हरीसिंह के विरुद्ध मुसलमानों के प्रजातांत्रिक अधिकारों का संघर्ष शुरु कर दिया। इसके कारण हिंदू और मुसलमानों में मनमुटाव शुरु हो गया। जून 1931 में कश्मीर के अंदर सांप्रदायिक दंगे प्रारंभ हो गए। इन सांप्रदायिक दंगों में हिंदूओं

की बड़ी हानि हुई। तब हिंदू जनसंख्या के हित हेतु शेख मुहम्मद अब्दुल्ला ने कोई आवाज़ क्यों नहीं उठाई ? वह केवल मुस्लिम जनसंख्या के हित हेतु ही अपनी आवाज़ पुरज़ोर उठाते रहे। क्यों ? क्या इससे उनकी मानसिकता स्पष्ट नहीं होती है। इन दंगों ने राज्य में सांप्रदायिक संघर्ष का बीज बो दिया। अगस्त 1945 में जब शेख अब्दुल्ला नेशनल कान्फ्रेंस के अध्यक्ष थे, ने 'नया कश्मीर' की रूपरेखा बनाना आरंभ कर दिया। उसने समस्त जम्मू कश्मीर राज्य के लिए कोई रूपरेखा क्यों तैयार नहीं की ? शेख मुहम्मद अब्दुल्ला ने महाराजा हरीसिंह का विरोध करने के लिए ''भारत छोड़ो'' की तर्ज़ पर ''कश्मीर छोड़ो'' आंदोलन शुरू कर दिया। इंडियन इन्डिपेंडेंट एक्ट 1947 के माध्यम से ब्रिटिश पारलियामेंट ने हिंदूस्तान और पाकिस्तान को सत्ता हस्तांतरण का कानून बनाया। उसमें राजाओं द्वारा शासित राज्यों के लिए यह प्रावधान रखा गया कि वह भारत अन्यथा पाकिस्तान में से किसी के साथ अपने राज्य का विलय कर सकते हैं। 15 अगस्त 1947 को अंग्रेज़ों की प्रभुसत्ता समाप्त हो गई। तीन रियासतों को छोड़कर बाकी सब रियासतों का विलय हिंदूस्तान या पाकिस्तान के साथ हो गया। हैदराबाद और जूनागढ़ की रियासतों का विलय अनेक कारणों से विलंब से हुआ। परंतु आज तक इस बारे में कोई झगड़ा अथवा प्रश्नचिह्न नहीं हुआ है। जम्मू कश्मीर के महाराजा हरीसिंह भी समय पर निर्णय नहीं कर पा रहे थे। संभवता यही विलंब निर्णय बाद के संघर्ष का कारण बना। 22 अक्तूबर 1947 को उत्तर पश्चिम सीमा प्रान्त के कबालियों ने पाकिस्तान की सक्रिय सहायता और सांठ–गांठ से कश्मीर घाटी पर आक्रमण किया ताकि महाराजा हरीसिंह को पाकिस्तान के साथ अपने राज्य का विलय करने के लिए मजबूर कर दिया जाए। इस विकट परिस्थिति ने महाराजा हरीसिंह को मजबूर कर दिया कि वह भारत के अनेक नेताओं की बात माने और कश्मीर के आक्रमणकारियों को उखाड़ फेंकने के लिए भारत सरकार की सहायता ले। इन विशेष परिस्थितियों में महाराजा हरीसिंह ने अन्य लगभग 560 स्वतंत्र राज्यों की तरह बिना शर्त विलय पत्र पर हस्ताक्षर करके 26 अक्तूबर 1947 को भारत के साथ विलय किया जिसको 27 अक्तूबर 1947 को गवर्नर जनरल माउंटबेटन ने स्वीकार कर लिया। (सी० जोसेफ चेको, भारत का अन्तर्राष्ट्रीय विधि विचार–विनिमय में योगदान, 1958)

28 अक्तूबर 1947 को भारत के प्रधानमंत्री पंडित जवाहरलाल नेहरु ने पाकिस्तान के प्रधानमंत्री को तार करके सूचना दी कि, ''भारतीय सरकार ने

जो कार्यवाही की है, वह श्रीनगर पर आने वाले संकट की परिस्थितियों को देखते हुए उन पर थोपा गया है। राज्यारोहण के संदर्भ में यह भी स्पष्ट कर दिया गया है कि यह सब राज्य के लोगों के निर्णय और उनके संदर्भ के अधीन है। भारतीय सरकार उन पर अपना निर्णय थोपने की कोई इच्छा नहीं रखती और लोगों की इच्छाओं को स्वीकार करेगी। पर यह सब तब तक संभव नहीं है जब तक शांति और कानून की व्यवस्था लागू न हो जाए।" (सी० जोसेफ चेको, भारत का अन्तर्राष्ट्रीय विधि विचार–विनिमय में योगदान, 1958)

जम्मू और कश्मीर का राज्यारोहण भारत में अंतिम और अटल है। अन्य कोई विकल्प नहीं है; यह अन्तर्राष्ट्रीय विधि को दृढ़ करता है। भारतीय स्वाधीनता अधिनियम, 1947 के अनुसार जम्मू और कश्मीर राज्य के महाराजा एक स्वतंत्र राजा हैं। अन्तर्राष्ट्रीय विधिशास्त्री ओप्पेंहेइम ने कहा, हर राज्य का राजा अपने राज्य के अधिपति के रूप में होता है और स्वयं प्रशासक बन जाता है। (ओप्पेंहेइम, अन्तर्राष्ट्रीय विधि, खंड एक, पृ० 758) यह तथ्य अतर्राष्ट्रीय विधि में अभिज्ञात हैं कि सभी शासक एक समान हैं और प्रभुसत्ता के प्रतिनिधि के रूप में प्रतीत होते हैं। वे अन्तर्राष्ट्रीय व्यक्ति हैं और अन्तर्राष्ट्रीय विधि का विषय हैं। कोलम्बिया विश्वविद्यालय के अन्तर्राष्ट्रीय विधि के उत्कृष्ट विधिशास्त्री आचार्य फिलप सी. जेस्सुप ने राज्य के अधिराजे को कुछ चिह्न देकर प्रमाणित किया है :

1. स्थायी जनसंख्या।
2. परिभाषित राज्यक्षेत्र।
3. सरकार ; और
4. अन्य राज्यों के साथ रिश्ता बनाने की क्षमता।

(यू.एन. सुरक्षा परिषद्, काउंसिल रिकार्ड्स्, 383 बैठक, दिसंबर 2, 1948, पृ० 9)

इन सबकी पृष्ठभूमि में यह निश्चय के साथ कहा जा सकता है कि जम्मू और कश्मीर के महाराजा अपने राज्य का नेतृत्व करते थे, 15 अगस्त 1947 से पहले भी तथा बाद में भी उनके पास अन्तर्राष्ट्रीय विधि का अन्तर्राष्ट्रीय विषय–चिह्न बनने के सारे गुण थे। इस विषय में जम्मू और कश्मीर उच्च न्यायालय के न्यायधीश शामीरी द्वारा दिए निर्णय "मघेर सिंह बनाम प्रिंसिपल सेक्रेटरी जम्मू–कश्मीर" (ए०आई०आर० 1953, जम्मू–कश्मीर 25) का संदर्भ दिया जा सकता है : "निस्संदेह जम्मू–कश्मीर के महाराजा की स्थिति भारतीय

स्वाधीनता अधिनियम से पूर्व और बाद में स्वच्छता की परिचर्चा करती है। ब्रिटिश भारत के दो राज्यों भारत–पाकिस्तान के विभाजन से पहले कोई शक नहीं था कि जम्मू–कश्मीर का शासक ब्रिटिश राज की सूजरेनिटी के उतना ही अंदर था, जितना कि उसके अंदर विदेशी रिश्ते थे। लेकिन अब तक आंतरिक राजा का राज्य बिल्कुल सीमाहीन था। उस पर कोई बंधन नहीं था। इस संदर्भ में सैक्शन 4 और सैक्शन 5 जम्मू–कश्मीर संविधान अधिनियम को बनाना सही था जो नवंबर 1951 में संशोधित हुआ।''

''सैक्शन 4 : इस समय जो राज्य एच०एच० में हैं, वो उनके द्वारा और उन्हीं के नाम पर नियंत्रित हैं। सारे आकस्मिक अधिकार कुछ ऐसे राज्यों की तरफ हैं, जिन पर एच०एच० काम कर सकता है।''

''सैक्शन 5 : सैक्शन 5 या किसी अन्य अधिनियम का साथ यदि हम न दे तो राज्य और उसकी सरकार से संदर्भित सारे अधिकार जो व्यवस्थापक, निर्वाहक और न्यायिक हैं, स्वाभाविक होने के कारण हमेशा से महामहिम के द्वारा अपनाए गए हैं और रखे गए हैं। इस सैक्शन या किसी भी अन्य अधिनियम ने महामहिम के परम अधिकार को विधि बनाने के लिए, घोषणा करने और आज्ञा देने के लिए तथा नियुक्ति करने और उनके स्वाभाविक प्राधिकार की हैसियत से प्रभावित नहीं किया है और न ही करेंगे।''

इसलिए उच्च न्यायालय ने यह आदेश दिया कि :

''1. जहां तक आंतरिक राज्य के प्रभुत्व की बात है, शासक के अधिकार ब्रिटिश संसद के समान थे।''

''2. भारतीय स्वाधीनता अधिनियम 1947 के सैक्शन 7 के अंश के साथ जम्मू और कश्मीर राज्य अन्तर्राष्ट्रीय विधि की संपूर्णता में एक स्वतंत्र और प्रधान राज्य बन गया।''

''3. इस संपूर्णता में महत्वपूर्ण बन गए लोग अनियंत्रित हो गए।''

''4. हस्ताक्षर और राज्यारोहण की आज्ञा भारतीय सरकार की स्थिति पर आधारित थी और किसी और लक्ष्य के लिए थी।''

''5. महत्वपूर्ण बन गए लोग ने विश्वास के साथ स्थानांतरण की घोषणा की। उनके द्वारा अपना अधिकार युवराज कर्णसिंह को देना संवैधानिक दृष्टि से बिल्कुल सही था।''

यदि एकतरफा युद्धबंदी का फैसला न लिया होता तो भारत की सुरक्षा सेनाएं जो कश्मीर की धरती से कबालियों को उखाड़ कर बाहर फेंकने में

सक्षम थीं, सफल होतीं और बाद में विवादास्पद पाक अधिकृत क्षेत्र (पी०ओ०के०) न बन पाता। पंडित जवाहरलाल नेहरु और माउंटबेटन दोनों के "लोगों की इच्छा जानकर" विलय को अंतिम रूप देने के वायदे "जनमतसंग्रह" की मांग के रूप में सामने आए (दुर्गादास, सरदार पटेल का पत्रकला : 1971, पृ० 73, 81, 257, 341)। "जनमत संग्रह" की बात कानूनी एवं संवैधानिक रूप से राज्य के और भारत के संविधान के साथ मेल नहीं खाती। इस तरह हमने स्वयंमेव जनमत संग्रह की बात करके एक मुफ्त का सिरदर्द अपने लिए पैदा कर लिया जिसके कारण यह समस्या उलझनों से भर गई और अनेक बड़े खतरे पैदा हो गए। माउंटबेटन के उकसाने पर पंडित जवाहरलाल नेहरु कश्मीर का मामला यू०एन०ओ० में ले गए और हमने एक राष्ट्रीय विवाद को अन्ततोगत्वा एक अन्तर्राष्ट्रीय विषय बना दिया और इंग्लैंड, अमेरीका, रूस, चीन और मुस्लिम देशों द्वारा हस्तक्षेप के दरवाज़े खोल दिए। विवादास्पद पाक अधिकृत क्षेत्र में आतंकवादियों के प्रशिक्षण शिविर और पाकिस्तान जमाते इस्लामी के कट्टरवाद पाक समर्थक गुट और अनेक अलगाववादी संगठनों का झुंड जिसे हुर्रियत के नाम से जाना जाता है, कश्मीर को भारत से अलग करने और भारत के खून का आखिरी कतरा तक निकालने के लिए संघर्षरत हैं। यू०एन०ओ० का प्रस्ताव, ताशकंद समझौता, शिमला समझौता, लाहौर और इस्लामाबाद की घोषणाएं सब निश्फल साबित हुए और इनका कोई परिणाम नहीं निकला। इसका एक मुख्य कारण पाकिस्तान की हठधर्मी और 'मैं न मानूं' विकृत। परिणामस्वरूप हम आज भी कश्मीर घाटी के लिए लड़ रहे हैं। इन सब बातों का सामूहिक परिणाम हमारे लिए घाटा ही घाटा है। इनके अतिरिक्त अन्य अनेकानेक भयानक तथा भयावह परिस्थितियां पैदा हो चुकी हैं।

आंतरिक और बाह्य समस्याएं

अंततोगत्वा विचार करने की बात यह है कि जो परिस्थितियां बिगड़ चुकी हैं, उनका हल क्या निकाला जाए। स्थानीय, राष्ट्रीय और अन्तर्राष्ट्रीय स्तर पर ऐसे हल प्रस्तुत किए जा रहे हैं जिससे बिगड़ती हुई परिस्थिति को और अधिक न बिगड़ने दिया जाए। उपर्युक्त तीन पक्षीय हलों का आलोचनात्मक विश्लेषण इस प्रकार है।

इसका आकलन करना अनिवार्य है ताकि भारत की संप्रभुता एवं अखंडता बनी रहे। इन खेलों/योजनाओं की भीतरी सच्चाईयों का सही अवलोकन अनिवार्य है।

स्थानीय प्रतिरूपक

भूतकाल में शेख मुहम्मद अब्दुल्ला और उनकी नेशनल कान्फ्रेंस ने प्रतिरूपक प्रस्तुत किया था जिसके अन्तर्गत जम्मू क्षेत्र के पास जम्मू, उधमपुर, कठुआ के तीन जिले रहे और बाकी राज्य का समस्त क्षेत्र पाकिस्तान की तरह मुस्लिम गणराज्य के लिए छोड़ दिया जाए (दुर्गादास, पृ० 128)। यह प्रतिरूपक उन लोगों की तंग मानसिकता को प्रस्तुत करता है जो कश्मीर समस्या को एक प्रकार से हल करना चाहते हैं। नयी कश्मीर प्रतिरूपक, 1953 के पूर्व की स्थिति अटानमी अथवा स्वाययत्ता की कल्पना है – बृहत्त स्वाययत्ता और क्षेत्रीय स्वाययत्ता।1953 के पूर्व की स्थिति अथवा स्वाययत्ता दोनों ही स्थिति के दो पहलू हैं। यह कल्पना अपने घर में पूरा ऐसा मालिक बनकर बैठने की है जिसमें कोई जबावदेही, पूछताछ, पारदर्शिता और संतुलन न हो। दूसरे शब्दों में 1953 से पूर्व की मांग राज्य में राजनैतिक, कानूनी और संवैधानिक उस स्थिति को बहाल करने की इंगित है जो शेख मुहममद अब्दुल्ला की नज़रबंदी से पहले की स्थिति थी। भारत के संविधान के कुछ अंश जम्मू कश्मीर

पर लागू किए गए थे (1954 का संविधान आर्डर जिसके अन्तर्गत संविधान घोषणा 1950 की संवैधानिक व्यवस्था को निरस्त कर दिया था)। 1950 के संवैधानिक आर्डर के द्वारा भारतीय संविधान की धारा एक और धारा 370 को जम्मू कश्मीर में लागू कर दिया था जिस समय भारत के संविधान को संपूर्ण देश में लागू किया गया था। तदुपरांत जम्मू कश्मीर की संविधान सभा ने जम्मू कश्मीर के भारत गणराज्य संघ के साथ स्थाई विलय पर अपनी मोहर लगाई थी और जम्मू कश्मीर भारतीय संघ की एक स्थाई इकाई बन गई। जम्मू कश्मीर का संविधान भी धारा 3 के अन्तर्गत इसकी पुष्टि करता है। भारतीय संविधान की धारा 370 की व्यवस्था अनुसार केंद्र के लगभग 370 के अधिक कानून जम्मू कश्मीर में भी लागू हुए ताकि जम्मू कश्मीर के लोग भी भारत गणराज्य संघ की मुख्य धारा में प्रवाहित होकर वह सारे लाभ उठा सकें जो समस्त भारत के नागरिक लाभ उठा रहे हैं। 1953 के पूर्व की स्थिति मांग को लागू करने पर कई अनेकानेक भयंकर परिणाम हो सकते हैं जिनकी कल्पना मात्र से ही सिहरन होती है। यह एक ऐसा कदम होगा जो भारत के संविधान के लागू अंशों को राज्य से हटाने की बात होगी और अन्ततोगत्वा उसे 1933 के संविधान की स्थिति में लाने की बात होगी। अगर यह एक बार कर दिया गया, जम्मू कश्मीर धीरे–धीरे भारत का एक अभिन्न अटूट अंग बनने की बजाए इससे अलग होने की स्थिति में आ जाएगा जिसका उल्लेख भारतीय संविधान की धारा 1 और शड्यूल 1 और 4 में दिया गया है। इसी तरह से जम्मू कश्मीर संविधान की धारा 3 भी प्रभावित होगी। दूसरी बात यह है कि जम्मू कश्मीर के स्थाई नागरिक भारत के नागरिक होना बंद हो जाएंगे। तीसरी बात यह है कि यह कदम उन लोगों को दुबारा आकर बसने का निमंत्रण हो जाएगा जिन्होंने अपनी इच्छा से यह देश छोड़ दिया था और दूसरे देश जाकर आबाद हो गए थे क्योंकि वह पाकिस्तान के वफादार थे। इन्हीं लोगों ने 1947, 1965, 1971 में भारत के खिलाफ युद्ध लड़े थे और आज भी छद्म युद्ध कर रहे हैं। इन लोगों के लिए आतंकवादी, उग्रवादी, अलगाववादी और युद्ध पिपासे घुसपैठिए शब्द–संज्ञा इस्तेमाल किए गए हैं। यह तत्व जम्मू कश्मीर के लोगों को अपनी गतिविधियों से मज़बूर कर दें कि वह पाकिस्तान के साथ हाथ मिलाएं और देशद्रोह की गतिविधियों में संलग्न होएं। अन्तर्राष्ट्रीय कानून और संविधान से खिलवाड़ करके अलगाववादी और पाकिस्तान के द्वारा आतंकवाद, आतंकवादी एवं घुसपैठियों को निरंतर प्रोत्साहित करने के हथकंडे अपनाए जा रहे हैं।

चौथी बात यह है कि यदि इन व्यवस्थाओं को मान लिया जाए तो जम्मू कश्मीर भारत के संविधान के सब लाभों से वंचित हो जाएगा जिसको बाकी देश के लोग उठा रहे हैं जैसे भारत का उच्चतम न्यायालय और उसकी मौलिक एपीलेट और पी०आई०एल० ऑथोरिटी और ऐसे 370 के लगभग केंद्रीय कानून, नियंत्रक ऑडिटर, जनरल, चुनाव आयोग और भारतीय संविधान की अनेक धाराएं। यह तत्व जम्मू कश्मीर के लोगों को अपनी गतिविधियों से मज़बूर कर दे कि वह पाकिस्तान के साथ हाथ मिलाए और देशद्रोह की गतिविधियों में संलग्न होए। अन्तर्राष्ट्रीय कानून और संविधान की धज्जियां उड़ा करके अलगाववादी और पाकिस्तान के द्वारा यह हथकंडे हथियाए जा रहे हैं। पांचवी बात यह है कि जम्मू कश्मीर के ऊपर एक ओर नबावशाही या सुलतानशाही लाद दी जाएगी। स्वशासन के ढिंढोलची इस बात से पूर्णतया अनभिज्ञ हैं कि स्वशासन का अर्थ क्या है और स्वशासन ही जम्मू कश्मीर की समस्या का हल कैसे ? स्वराज्य का आंदोलन स्वराज्यवादियों ने ब्रिटिश हुकुमरानों के विरुद्ध शुरु किया था और मांग की थी कि भारत के ऊपर भारतीयों का राज्य भारतीयों के द्वारा भारतीयों के वास्ते ही हो। परंतु जम्मू कश्मीर के अंदर लोग पहले से ही अपने मतों का उपयोग करके अपनी चुनी हुई सरकारें बना रहे हैं। 1957 से वह अपने मतों का इस्तेमाल करके अपने लिए अपनी सरकार चुन रहे हैं। इससे अधिक स्वशासन और क्या हो सकता है ! यह लोगों को भ्रम में डालने के लिए एक शरारतपूर्ण प्रचार है। दूसरी तरफ हीलिंग टच के नारे ने भी लोगों को भ्रमित किया है। राज्य सरकार पश्चिमी पंजाब के शरणार्थियों और राज्य के अंदर के ही बेघर हुए लोगों को हीलिंग टच देने में असफल हुई है और वह लोग आज भी अपने घरों में बेगानों की तरह रह रहे हैं। धारा 370 ड्राफ्ट धारा 306 ए का अंतिम रूप है जिसको संविधान सभा ने बिना किसी आपत्ति के मत से पारित किया। किसी ने भी इसकी आलोचना नहीं की और न ही कोई अन्य आपत्ति उठाई। भारत की संविधान सभा ने शेख मुहम्मद अब्दुल्ला, मिर्जा अफज़ल बेग, मौलाना मासूदी और मोती राम बैगरा चार सदस्य बैठे हुए थे। इन्होंने 26 नवंबर 1949 को संविधान को अपनाया तथा अन्य समस्त सदस्यों के साथ संविधान की मूल प्रति पर 24.01.1950 अपने हस्ताक्षर किए। धारा 370 को भारत के संविधान में एक अस्थाई प्रावधान के रूप में रखा गया ताकि समय–समय पर उत्पन्न होने वाली विशेष परिस्थितियों में उसका उपयोग किया जा सके और इस बात का आश्वासन दिया गया कि विशेष विकट

परिस्थितियां समाप्त होने पर इसे समाप्त कर दिया जाएगा। परंतु दुर्भाग्य से धारा 370 के कारण देश से अलग होने की भावना ही प्रबल हुई। धारा 370 की भाषा वास्तव धारा 371 की तरह होनी चाहिए थी। इसको इस रूप में प्रस्तुत किया जाना चाहिए था कि यह विशेष कदम अविकसित तथा अर्धविकसित क्षेत्रों के पूर्ण विकास हेतु उठा सके ताकि उन क्षेत्रों के निवासी भी जीवन में अपना विकास करने के लिए समान अवसर प्राप्त कर सकें और बाकी समाज के साथ बराबरी की सतह पर आ सकें। परंतु दुःख का विषय है कि इस धारा 370 के कारण देश से अलग होने आतंकवाद और अलगाववाद का भाव ही पनपा है। स्वतंत्र कश्मीर की मांग भी इसी के कारण बड़ी है। यह भारत के आधुनिक इतिहास का सबसे बड़ा विश्वासघात है। उनकी भाषा बड़ी घातक और दुःख पहुंचाने वाली है। "दोनों में से किसी देश के साथ विलय शांति नहीं ला सकता। हम दोनों कंधों के साथ दोस्त बनकर रहना चाहते हैं। शायद उनके दिमाग में यह एक बीच का रास्ता है जिसके अन्तर्गत परस्पर आर्थिक सहयोग ही एक रास्ता होगा ऐसी व्यवस्था बनाने का। स्वतंत्र कश्मीर की गारंटी केवल भारत और पाकिस्तान ही नहीं, अपितु अमेरीका, ब्रिटेन और संयुक्त राष्ट्र संघ के अन्य सदस्य भी दें।" (द्वारा शेख अब्दुल्ला : दुर्गादास में प्रस्तुत)। इसके अतिरिक्त यह कहना कठिन है कि सर्वसाधारण कश्मीरी की क्या इच्छा है और वह क्या चाहता है। एक विचार तो यह है कि कश्मीरी स्वयं ही अपने भाग्य का विधाता बनना चाहता है और उसके ऊपर कोई भी नियंत्रण उसे संतुलित रखने के लिए न हो। कुछ लोगों का मत है कि कश्मीरी बिल्कुल अलग रहना चाहता है यह जाने बगैर कि यह स्थिति उसे कहां पहुंचाएगी। परंतु यह अनेक उलझन भरे सुझाव गलत रास्ते पर डालने वाले हैं। ऐसा प्रतीत होता है कि कुछ लोग इस विषय में नर्मदल के हैं और कुछ गर्मदल के हैं। इन सब परिस्थितियों के लिए धारा 370 जिम्मेदार है। इस धारा को भारत के संविधान से पूर्णतया निरस्त करना ही देश और राज्य के हित में है और जम्मू कश्मीर की समस्या के समाधान में लाभकारी है। परंतु इसका निरस्तीकरण राजनैतिक इच्छा और कानूनी व्यवस्था के बीच त्रिशंकु की तरह लटक रहा है।

उपरोक्त सब सुझावों का क्या परिणाम हुआ है, यह देखने की और चिंतन की बात है। अभी तक जितने प्रयोग हुए हैं, उनका कोई परिणाम नहीं निकला है। इसका कारण यह है कि इन सभी सुझावों के पीछे कोई प्रामाणिकता नहीं है।

पाकिस्तान रणनीति (गेम प्लान)

पाकिस्तान तो चाहता है कि कश्मीर किसी तरह भी उसके अधिकार क्षेत्र में आ जाए। पाकिस्तान की यह इच्छा 1947, 1965, 1971 और 1999 के कारगिल पर किए गए आक्रमण से सिद्ध होती है। पाकिस्तान ने कश्मीर पर अधिकार प्राप्त करने के लिए आतंकवाद और जेहाद का रास्ता चुना है जिसके द्वारा वह अपनी भूमि पर आतंकवादियों के प्रशिक्षण शिविर चलाकर कश्मीर में बल्कि देश भर में राजनैतिक अस्थिरता पैदा करने में लगा हुआ है। पाकिस्तान ने आज तक हिन्दूस्तान के साथ किसी भी समझौते की कदर नहीं की वह चाहे यू०एन० का प्रस्ताव (संयुक्त राष्ट्र संकल्प) हो, ताशकंद या शिमला समझौता हो अथवा लाहौर की घोषणा। आज तक हिंदूस्तान और पाकिस्तान के बीच विश्वास का सेतु निर्माण करने के लिए पाकिस्तान ने बड़ी बेशर्मी से उनको तोड़ा।

अन्तर्राष्ट्रीय रणनीति (गेम प्लान)

द्वितीय महायुद्ध के बाद अनेक यूरोपीय देशों को जो विदित क्षेत्र मजबूरन छोड़ने पड़े, वहां उन्होंने स्वतंत्र होने वाले अनेक देशों की सीमा निर्धारण करने का काम अपने ढंग से शुरु किया। कश्मीर की समस्या ब्रिटिश सरकार की इस नीति का ही परिणाम है जिसका नक्शा लार्ड माउंटबेटन ने नेहरु को प्रोत्साहन देकर तैयार किया। इसी कारण एक तरफा युद्ध विराम की घोषणा हुई और एक बनावटी पी०ओ०के० की स्थापना हुई। इसी नीति के कारण कश्मीर में अन्तर्राष्ट्रीय शक्तियों द्वारा दखल देने के कारण दरवाजे खुल गए और उन्होंने कश्मीर समस्या के हल के लिए कई विदेशी मॉड्यूल प्रस्तुत करने प्रारंभ कर दिए। सबसे पहले इस समस्या के समाधान के लिए स्ट्रेटेजिक इंडीपेंडेंस मॉड्यूल का सुझाव प्रस्तुत किया। इस सुरक्षा का संबंध अन्तर्राष्ट्रीय सुरक्षा के साथ है। बुनियादी तौर पर एक राज्य की अपनी सुरक्षा और दूसरे राज्य के द्वारा आक्रमण की स्थिति में उनको निरस्त करने की क्षमता का प्रावधान है जिसे स्ट्रेटेजिक इंडीपेंडेंस का नाम दिया गया है। स्ट्रेटेजिक इंडीपेंडेंस स्टेट्स राज्यों के बीच (मध्य) शक्तियों के विभाजन की व्यवस्था करता है जबकि इसका संविधान और परस्पर शक्तियों का विभाजन एक विवाद का विषय है (राजू जी०सी० थामस : व्हॉट इज थर्ड वर्ल्ड सिक्योरिटी)।

तीसरी विश्व सुरक्षा

शक्तियों का माप सैनिक क्षमताओं से संबंधित है और उसका आधार राज्य की आर्थिक और तकनीकी क्षमताओं पर निर्भर करता है। चाहे वह सैनिक क्षमता हो या अन्य प्रकार की क्षमता हो, परंतु आणविक हत्यारों के सामने आ जाने के बाद सैनिक शक्ति को परंपरागत ढंग से मापने का सारा सिलसिला ही बदल गया है। सैन्य शक्ति को मापने का पुराना तरीका बिल्कुल बेकार हो गया है और अब इसी आणविक आक्रमण को रोकने की मानसिकता निर्माण करना ज़्यादा आवश्यक हो गया है। अब स्ट्रेटेजिक इंडीपेंडेंस इस नए मॉड्यूल की कल्पना से भारत की सैन्य शक्ति न्यूकलियर क्षमता प्राप्त करने के बाद बदल गई है और इसके बीच में दखल देने वाली शक्तियों को भारत के आंतरिक, बाह्य और क्षेत्रीय सुरक्षात्मक समस्याओं का भी विचार करना है। इन नई परिस्थितियों में कभी कश्मीर समस्या के समाधान के लिए ''बैक चैनल डिप्लोमेसी'' का भी प्रारंभ हुआ है। 'कश्मीर रोड टू पीस' के लेखक–निर्माता तर्क देते हैं कि ''बैक चैनल डिप्लोमेसी'' उन सब के लिए लाभदायक हो सकती है जो शक्ति प्रयोग के स्थान पर कूटनीति को कश्मीर के शान्ति स्थापन करने के लिए प्रयोग में लाना चाहते हैं। भारत की दृष्टि से एक मॉड्यूल के ऊपर बहस हो सकती है क्योंकि इससे अनेक विवाद योग्य विषय निकल सकते हैं। इस तरह से जो मॉड्यूल प्रस्तुत किया गया है और जिस तरह के कश्मीर भारत पाकिस्तान के बीच में समझौते हुए हैं, उनको एक संवैधानिक ढांचे में इस प्रकार से रखा जा सकता है।

ढांचे का स्वरूप	समझौते का आधिकारिक नाम
1. बुरुंडी एग्रीमेंट	अरुषा पीस एंड रीकॉनसाईलेशन एग्रीमेंट फॉर बुरुंडी, अगस्त 20, 2000.
2. डेटोन एकोर्ड्स	द जनरल फ्रेमवर्क एग्रीमेंट फॉर पीस इन बोसनिया एंड हरज़ीगोविना (इनीशिएटिड इन डेटोन ऑन 21 नवंबर 1995 एंड साइंड इन पैरिस ऑन 14 दिसंबर 1995।)
3. ईस्ट टाईमोर एग्रीमेंट	एग्रीमेंट बिटविन द रिपब्लिक ऑफ इनडोनेशिया एंड द पोरच्यूग्यूईस रिपब्लिक ऑन द क्यूशचन ऑफ ईस्ट टाईमोर, 5 मई 1999.
4. इल सल्वेडोर एग्रीमेंट	इल सल्वेडोर पीस एग्रीमेंट, 16 जनवरी 1992.

5. ग्यूएटमाला एग्रीमेंट	ग्यूएटमाला एग्रीमेंट ऑन आइडेंटिटी एंड राईट्स ऑफ इनडीजीनियस पिपील्स मार्च 31, 1995.
6. केफौर एग्रीमेंट	मीलिटरी टेक्नीकल एग्रीमेंट बिटविन द इंटरनेशनल सिक्योरिटी फोर्स (केफौर) एंड द गवर्नमेंट्स ऑफ फीडरल रिपब्लिक ऑफ यूगोस्लाविया एंड द रिपब्लिक ऑफ सरबिया, जून 9, 1999.
7. कोसोवो इनटीरिम एग्रीमेंट	द इनटीरिम एग्रीमेंट फॉर पीस एंड सैल्फ गवर्नमेंट इन कोसोवो, फरवरी 23, 1999.
8. लाहौर डेकलेरेशन	लाहौर डेकलेरेशन बाय द प्राइमीनिस्टर्स ऑफ द रिपब्लिक ऑफ इंडिया एंड द इस्लामिक रिपब्लिक ऑफ पाकिस्तान, फरवरी 21, 1999.
9. नॉरदन आईरलैंड एग्रीमेंट	द नॉरदन आईरलैंड पीस एग्रीमेंट : द एग्रीमेंट रीचड् इन द मल्टी–पार्टी नीगोशिएशन्स, अक्तूबर 4, 1998.
10. पपूआ न्यू गूईनिया एग्रीमेंट	बोउगेनविलिया पीस एग्रीमेंट अगस्त 30, 2001.
11. साईर्रा लीओनी एग्रीमेंट	पीस एग्रीमेंट बिटवीन द गवर्नमेंट ऑफ साईर्रा लीओनी एंड द रीवोल्यूशनरी यूनाईटेड फ्रंट ऑफ साईर्रा लीओनी, लोम, टोगो, मई 25 टू जुलाई 7, 1999.
12. शिमला एग्रीमेंट	शिमला एग्रीमेंट ऑन बीलेटरल रीलेशन्स बिटवीन इंडिया एंड पाकिस्तान साइंड बाई प्राईमीनिस्टर ऑफ इंडिया मिसेस इंदिरा गांधी एंड प्रेसीडेंट ऑफ पाकिस्तान जेड०ए० भुट्टो, जुलाई 3, 1972.
13. साउथ अफ्रीकन कॉन्सटीट्यूशन	कॉन्सटीट्यूशन ऑफ द रिपब्लिक ऑफ साउथ अफ्रीका, मई 8, 1996.
14. सूडन प्रोटोकोल	सूडन्स मेकहेकोस प्रोटोकोल, जुलाई 20, 2002.
15. तशकेंट डेकलेरेशन	तशकेंट डेकलेरेशन, जनवरी 10, 1996.
16. एंगोला, सीज़फायर	एंगोला–उनीता सीज़फायर एग्रीमेंट, अप्रैल 2002.
17. लूसाका प्रोटोकोल	एंगोला–लूसाका प्रोटोकोल, लूसाका, जंबिया, नवंबर 15, 1994.

18. सोमालिया सीज़फायर — सोमालिया एग्रीमेंट ऑन इंप्लीमेंटिंग द सीज़फायर एंड ऑन मोडेलिटीस ऑफ डीसारमेमेंट (सप्लीमेंट टू द जनरल एग्रीमेंट साइंड इन एडडिस एबाबा, ऑन जनवरी 8, 1993)

उपरोक्त मॉड्यूल का सार

(क) धारा 370 का संवैधानिक स्वरूप

भारत के संविधान की धारा 370 को स्थाई प्रावधान बनाया जाए और इस धारा से अस्थाई शब्द को निकाल दिया जाए। और इसमें एक शब्द "विशेष" या स्पेशल जोड़ दिया जाए। धारा 370 की क्षमताओं को कम करने वाले सारे प्रेसीडेंशियल नार्म्स को निरस्त किया जाए। आगे भारत सरकार की ओर से कश्मीर के संवैधानिक स्टेटस को साथ छेड़–छाड़ करके किसी प्रकार की एमबीगूयिटी न पैदा की जाए। इस तरह से जो कश्मीर को स्वाययत्ता के अधिकार मिले, उनके बीच में कभी भी कोई दखलअंदाजी न की जाए।

(ख) भारत द्वारा कायम किया गया शासन

इस समझौते के अन्तर्गत जो अधिकार भारत को न मिले हों, वह कश्मीर और यहां के लोगों के लिए सुरक्षित रखे जाएं।

(1) सुरक्षा

कश्मीर की बाह्य सुरक्षा के लिए सब शक्तियां पहले की तरह भारत सरकार के हाथ में रही। जम्मू कश्मीर राज्य भारत का अंग है इसलिए कश्मीर की सुरक्षा के ऊपर भारत का ही आधिपत्य रहे। कश्मीर में भारतीय सेना की उपस्थिति केवल आवश्यकता तक ही सीमित रहे। कश्मीर बड़े ध्यान से भारत की सुरक्षा सेना के ऊपर नज़र रखे ताकि सेना शक्ति का दुरुपयोग न कर पाए। अगर इस तरह का दुरुपयोग होता है तो समझौते के अन्तर्गत का नवाधिकार रक्षा के प्रावधान के अन्तर्गत कश्मीर विधानसभा को अधिकार हो कि वह यह मामला फैसला करने के लिए मानवाधिकार (ह्यूमन राइट्स) कमेटी के सामने रख सके।

(2) विदेशी मामलात

भारत सरकार इस क्षेत्र के विदेशी मामलात पर अपना नियंत्रण जारी रखेगी।

भारत सरकार किसी भी विदेशी मामले के साथ विषय पर जिसका असर इस क्षेत्र को प्रभावित करता है, कश्मीर विधानसभा के साथ परामर्श करेगी। कश्मीर की विधानसभा भारत के किसी फैसले को स्वीकार करेगी जिसका संबंध केवल विशेष रूप से एकमेव कश्मीर के विदेशी मामले के साथ होगा और भारत की ओर किसी परदेश के साथ नहीं होगा।

(3) आर्थिक नीति

1. कश्मीर को अभी भी केन्द्रीय सरकार के समर्थन की जरूरत पड़ेगी और ऐसे ही भारतीय सरकार को भी राज्य की आर्थिक नीति पर नियंत्रण रखना जारी रखना चाहिए।
2. भारत को राष्ट्रीय कर निर्धारण पर भी नियंत्रण रखना चाहिए। कश्मीर सरकार को कश्मीर के लिए राज्य कर निर्धारण पर संयम रखना चाहिए।
3. भारतीय सरकार को कश्मीर के पूरे आर्थिक विकास को आश्वस्त करना चाहिए। यह राज्य के बढ़ते हुए निवेश को स्थिर करेगा और ज्ञान तथा आर्थिक सहारे से आर्थिक विकास कार्यक्रम को प्रबल करेगा। कश्मीर का भारत के सामान्य बाज़ार में भाग लेने पर भारत इस उद्देश्य के साथ शासन करना जारी रखेगा कि कश्मीर का सक्रिय सहयोग मिलता रहे।

(ग) कश्मीर बार्डर की वस्तुस्थिति

1. इस करार की वजह से कश्मीर की सीमा बदलनी नहीं चाहिए। लाइन ऑफ कन्ट्रोल (LOC) इसकी व्यावहारिक सीमा होगी। जिस तरह 1972 शिमला करार में कहा गया है, जो आज़ाद कश्मीर को कश्मीर से अलग करता है। उत्तर, पूर्व और दक्षिणी सीमाएं तबसे हैं, जबसे इस करार पर हस्ताक्षर हुए हैं ; उन्हें बदलना नहीं चाहिए।
2. आजाद कश्मीर को नए विशेष स्वतंत्र राज्य का भाग नहीं मानना चाहिए। अगर स्वतंत्र कश्मीर की आबादी कश्मीर के विशेष स्वतंत्र राज्य से जुड़ने की अपनी रुचि दिखाती है, तो कश्मीर की जनता की सम्मति लेनी चाहिए (refrendum) और उसके परिणाम पर विश्वास रखना चाहिए।

(घ) केन्द्रीय सरकार द्वारा कश्मीर विभाजन

1. कश्मीर को भारतीय सरकार द्वारा बनाए ढांचे में भाग लेना चाहिए जब तक कि वह कश्मीर को प्रभावित करे। इस करार के अनुसार, यह दृढ़ता भारतीय सरकार द्वारा कायम शक्तियों पर आधारित होनी चाहिए।
2. कश्मीरी प्रतिनिधि का चुनाव अब भी तकनीकों से बदलना नहीं चाहिए।
3. भारतीय सरकार को कश्मीरी दृष्टिकोण के संदर्भ में कश्मीर सरकार की सम्मति लेनी चाहिए।

(ड.) कश्मीरी नागरिकता की पहचान और पहचान चिह्न

1. सभी लोग जो कश्मीर में करार के हस्ताक्षर के समय कम से कम 7 वर्षों से रह रहे हैं, उन्हें कश्मीर का नागरिक मानना चाहिए।
2. सभी लोग जो कश्मीर में करार के हस्ताक्षर के समय 7 वर्षों से कम रहे हैं, उन्हें 7 साल में नागरिक जरूरतों के बाद कश्मीरी नागरिकता मिलनी चाहिए।
3. कौम, धर्म और लिंग के आधार पर किसी भी तरह की नागरिकता की मनाही नहीं होनी चाहिए। कश्मीरी विधानसभा को उन सभी को आश्वस्त करना चाहिए जो नागरिकता की मांग कर रहे हैं।
4. नागरिकता के लिए भेदभाव के आरोप पर अन्तर्राष्ट्रीय अपराधी न्यायालय के सामने निर्णयादेश देना चाहिए।
5. संवैधानिक कांग्रेस या नयी कश्मीरी सरकार ही पहचान–पत्र कायदे बनाएगी जैसे पासपोर्ट के प्रकाशन पर !
6. किसी तरह की मनाही पहचान–पत्र के लिए कौम, धर्म या लिंग के आधार पर नहीं होनी चाहिए।
7. संवैधानिक कांग्रेस या नयी कश्मीरी सरकार को राष्ट्रीय पहचान के चिह्न बनाने चाहिए जैसे ध्वज और हाथों की परत। भारतीय ध्वज को राष्ट्रीय तथा दूसरे विधिक समारोह पर फहराते रहना चाहिए।

(च) स्वायतता अन्यथा स्वतंत्रता की विशिष्ट वस्तुस्थिति लागू होने की प्रक्रिया

कश्मीर या पाकिस्तान द्वारा बढ़ते हुए स्वयंसिद्धांतों अथवा स्वायतता अन्यथा स्वतंत्रता का आरोप, जो इस भाग में दिए गए हैं, को आरोपित अपशब्द

कहे गए हैं, यूनाइटेड नेशन सेक्रेटरी जनरल द्वारा बनाई गई अन्तर्राष्ट्रीय समिति ऐसे आरोप की जांच करेगी। अगर बनाई गई समिति खंडन को दृढ़ करती है, तो मानव अधिकार समिति इस स्थिति को हल करने की कोशिश करेगी। अगर समिति की सामर्थ्य इस स्थिति को हल करने की क्षमताओं से परे है, तो यूनाइटेड नेशन हाई कमीशन मानव अधिकार हेतु इस विषय को जल्दी से जल्दी हल करने के लिए यूनाइटेड नेशन सिक्योरिटी काउंसिल के सामने लाएगी।

(छ) कश्मीर की संवैधानिक वस्तुस्थिति

कश्मीर सरकार को उन विषयों के लिए पूरे अधिकार मिलने चाहिए जो केन्द्रीय सरकार के नियंत्रण में नहीं हैं। मतलब, कश्मीर स्थापना को लेकर सभी विषयों पर पूरा, अर्थपूर्ण और स्वतंत्र नियंत्रण जो विधि, राजनीतिक, सामाजिक, सांस्कृतिक और शैक्षिक राजनीति से संबद्ध होंगे।

(ज) व्यवस्थापना

कश्मीर सरकार को राज्य में संविधान की सहमति के साथ विधिक अधिनियम, खंडन और उन्नति की ओर उन्मुख करने का पूरा अधिकार मिलना चाहिए। भारतीय सरकार द्वारा उसके प्रभावित होने वाले क्षेत्र के अतिरिक्त इस शक्ति पर किसी प्रकार का बंधन नहीं होना चाहिए। वस्तुतः कोई भी विधान सभा कोई भी विधि–विधान विधान द्वारा पारित भारतीय संविधान की मुख्य धारा के विपरीत नहीं होना चाहिए।

(झ) आर्थिक विषय

कश्मीर सरकार को स्थानीय कर निर्धारण का नियंत्रण मिलना चाहिए और उसे राज्य की निधि का बंटवारा होने के लिए जिम्मेदार होना चाहिए। इस शक्ति का अभ्यास अल्पसंख्यक लोगों के साथ निष्पक्ष रूप से होना चाहिए।

(ञ) नीति निर्माण

कश्मीर सरकार को उन मापदंडों तथा रणनीति को बनाने और अमल में लाने के लिए अधिकार मिलना चाहिए जो राज्य की सामाजिक, शैक्षिक, सांस्कृतिक और वैज्ञानिक नीतियों से संबंध रखता है।

(ट) भ्रष्टाचार

कश्मीर सरकार भ्रष्टाचार विरुद्ध मापदंडों को अपनाए और अपराधियों का तत्पर और निष्पक्ष अनुसरण करे एवं उसे भ्रष्टाचार की समस्या को उपयुक्त दिशा निर्धारित करने हेतु सम्बोधित करने का प्रयास करना चाहिए।

(ठ) चुनाव

1. दोनों दलों को यह आश्वस्त करना चाहिए कि राज्य में मुक्त और स्वच्छ चुनाव की स्थिति कायम रहे। इसमें खुला और मुक्त राजनीतिक वातावरण बनाना नागरिकों के लिए आश्वासन होगा। एक सुरक्षित वातावरण जिसमें सभी उम्मीदवारों को बिना किसी हस्तक्षेप के मौजूद साधनों के आंतरिक सम्मेलन, सभा और उक्ति की आजादी होगी। दोनों दलों को मीडिया का अभ्यास कराना आंदोलनकारी उम्मीदवार के लिए निश्चित करना चाहिए।
2. भारतीय सरकार को अन्तर्राष्ट्रीय चुनावी प्रेक्षक समिति की उपस्थिति को स्वीकार करना चाहिए जो चुनाव के संचालन पर निगरानी रखेगी और यह प्रमाणित करेगी कि चुनाव मुक्त और स्वच्छ धरातल पर हो।
3. चयन केंद्र में प्रवेश और मतदान का प्रसार चुनाव होने के बाद हो। इस अन्तर्राष्ट्रीय समिति को चुनावी प्रक्रिया के सभी विभागों में वोटर के पंजीकरण को मिलाकर पूरा स्वागत मिलना चाहिए।
4. इस समिति को यह आश्वस्त करने के लिए इलेक्शन कमीशन ऑफ इंडिया के साथ_संयोजित होकर काम करना चाहिए कि चुनावी प्रक्रिया सुरक्षित और पारदर्शी है।

(ड) उम्मीदवार

किसी व्यक्ति का पुराना राजनीतिक संबंध या गतिविधियां अधिकारित कार्यालय में बाधा नहीं होनी चाहिए। हलांकि सभी उम्मीदवारों को हिंसा को अस्वीकार एवं तज्य/त्याग करना चाहिए।

(ण) मानवाधिकार

1. कश्मीर मानव अधिकारों को प्रोत्साहित और सुरक्षा करने के लिए सहमत है। अंततः यह भारत सरकार द्वारा संधि की संपुष्टि से अन्तर्राष्ट्रीय मानव

संधि को बल और परिणाम प्रदान करेगा तथा मानवीय अधिकारों की सार्वभौमिक घोषणा, मानवीय अधिकारों पर अन्तर्राष्ट्रीय प्रसंविदाएं, महिलाओं पर से सभी प्रकार के भेद–भाव को हटाने का प्रयास तथा बच्चों के अधिकार आदि विषयों पर अधिकार और दायित्व की घोषणा करेगा।

2. कश्मीर सरकार द्वारा अन्तर्राष्ट्रीय मानवाधिकार उन सभी संधि के साथ ही दूसरी प्रथाएं प्रताड़ना, क्रूरता, अमानवीय या क्षति करने वाला व्यवहार, सभी प्रकार की सजा या धर्म और विश्वास के आधार पर भेदभाव आदि भी अपनाई जाएंगी जिसे भारत ने अभी तक नहीं अपनाया है।

सभी कश्मीरी लोगों के मूलभूत अधिकार

1. मानवीय अधिकारों की सार्वभौमिक घोषणा, मानवीय अधिकारों पर अन्तर्राष्ट्रीय प्रसंविदाएं, महिलाओं पर से सभी प्रकार के भेद–भाव को हटाने का प्रयास तथा बच्चों के अधिकार आदि विषयों पर अधिकार और दायित्व की घोषणा तथा गारंटी कश्मीर के संविधान का एक संपूर्ण पात्र है। जिसे अधिकारों के अनुरूप उसी प्रकार की श्रेष्ठता मिली है जिस तरह संविधान को मिली है। अन्तर्राष्ट्रीय विधि के तहत अपनाई गई क्षमा करने योग्य घटनाएं जिन्हें संविधान में आगे रखा गया है, के अतिरिक्त ऊपर दिए गए संधि–पत्र का मूलभूत व्यवहार और नीचे दी गई व्यवस्था सीमित या अप्रतिष्ठित नहीं होनी चाहिए।
2. सभी नागरिकों के अधिकार और दायित्व होने चाहिए।
3. मानवीय गौरव की गरिमा का मान और सुरक्षा होनी चाहिए।
4. सभी महिलाएं और पुरुष एक समान होने चाहिए। जन्म, परंपरा, जाति, लिंग, रंग, भाषा, सामाजिक स्थिति, दर्शन, धार्मिक या राजनैतिक धारणा अथवा शारीरिक या मानसिक असहायता की वजह से किसी के विरुद्ध भी भेदभाव नहीं होना चाहिए। कानून के अनुसार, सभी नागरिकों को समान सुरक्षा और समान व्यवहार का लाभ उठाना चाहिए।
5. राज्य या उसके अंग को मनमाने ढंग से किसी से बात नहीं करना चाहिए।
6. सभी महिलाओं और पुरुषों को जीवन जीने का अधिकार होना चाहिए।
7. सभी महिलाओं और पुरुषों को व्यक्तिगत आजादी का व्यवहार होना चाहिए। जिसमें शारीरिक और मानसिक अखंडता और कुछ करने का

अधिकार भी सम्मिलित है। किसी भी प्रकार की क्रूर, अमानवीय, अपमानजनक व्यवहार, सज़ा और यातना वर्णित होनी चाहिए। हर किसी के पास यह अधिकार होना चाहिए कि वह सामाजिक या व्यक्तिगत हिंसा से मुक्त हो।

8. राज्य को एक सीमा तक यह आश्वासन होना चाहिए कि सभी नागरिकों के पास साधन हों जिससे वे मानवीय गौरव के अनुकूल रह सकें।
9. सभी महिलाओं और पुरुषों को अपने निजी और पारिवारिक जीवन, निवास और व्यक्तिगत वार्तालाप का आदर करने का अधिकार है।
10. अभिव्यक्ति और संचार की स्वतंत्रता का आश्वासन दिया जाना चाहिए। राज्य को धर्म, विश्वास, विवेक और विचारों का सम्मान करना चाहिए।
11. किसी को भी मनमाने ढंग से उसकी राष्ट्रीयता से वंचित करने या उसे बदलने के अधिकार से मनाही नहीं होनी चाहिए।
12. किसी को भी मूल शिक्षा प्राप्त करने की मनाही नहीं होनी चाहिए। राज्य को आम जनता की शिक्षा का प्रबंध करना चाहिए तथा माध्यमिक और उत्तर माध्यमिक शिक्षा का विकास और प्रोत्साहन होना चाहिए।
13. सभी नागरिकों को यह अधिकार होना चाहिए कि वे राज्य के क्षेत्र में मुक्त होकर कहीं भी घूम सकें, उसे छोड़ सकें या वापस आ सकें।
14. न्यायसंबंधी प्रशासनिक प्रक्रिया में सभी को यह अधिकार है कि उनका केस निष्पक्ष और निर्धारित समय सीमा में हो।
15. नियमों के समर्थन के अतिरिक्त कोई भी अपनी आजादी से वंचित नहीं रहना चाहिए।
16. सभी लोगों का यह कर्तव्य है कि वे अपने सहनागरिकों का आदर करें और बिना किसी भेदभाव के अपने सहनागरिकों पर ध्यान दें।
17. मूलभूत अधिकारों के लिए किसी भी प्रकार की पाबंदी पर एक न्यायिक धरातल होना चाहिए। यह जनता के हित के लिए या दूसरे व्यक्ति के मूलभूत अधिकारों की रक्षा के लिए होना चाहिए। लक्ष्य का अनुसरण इसके अनुरूप होना चाहिए।
18. न्यायिक, प्रशासनिक और संस्थानिक आदेश के तहत मूलभूत अधिकारों का सम्मान होना चाहिए। संविधान ही परम कानून होना चाहिए तथा विधानसभा, प्रबंधकर्ता और न्याय के धरातल पर इसकी पुष्टि होनी चाहिए।

(त) धार्मिक अल्पसंख्यक : स्वतंत्रता और धर्म

1. हर व्यक्ति को अपने विवेक, धर्म, सोच, विश्वास और विचार की स्वतंत्रता का अधिकार होना चाहिए।
2. किसी पर भी बलप्रयोग नहीं होना चाहिए कि धर्म या विश्वास का पालन की उसकी स्वतंत्रता को नष्ट कर दे।
3. अपने धर्म या विश्वास को व्यक्त करने की स्वतंत्रता कानून के बताए अनुसार सीमित रहनी चाहिए जो जनता की सुरक्षा, आदेश, स्वास्थ्य, सिद्धांतों, मूलभूत अधिकार और दूसरों की स्वतंत्रता के लिए आवश्यक है।
4. राज्य या राज्य के संस्थानों में उन नियमों के अनुसार सबसैक्शन (1) की जैनरेलिटी को अप्रतिष्ठित किए बिना धार्मिक अनुसरण किए जा सकते हैं जो इसी के लिए उचित समिति द्वारा बनाए गए हैं। पर इन धार्मिक अनुसरण को एक समान धरातल पर किया जाना चाहिए और उसमें भाग लेने के लिए मुक्त और स्वतंत्रता होनी चाहिए।
5. इस धारा में कुछ भी विधानसभा को वंचित न करें, जो कि सामने लाती हैं :–
   (अ) व्यक्तिगत और पारिवारिक न्याय जिससे एक विशिष्ट धर्म का अनुसरण करने वाले लोग जुड़े हुए हैं।
   (ब) विवाह की मान्यता को बताए गए व्यवहार (प्रोसीड्यूर) की तरह ही काम करना चाहिए। इसका निष्कर्ष धार्मिक कानून के सिस्टम के अन्तर्गत निकाला गया है।
6. चिंतन, धर्म और विश्वास की स्वतंत्रता के अधिकार को सम्मिलित करना चाहिए जिसे अनेक विषयों की स्वतंत्रता है : –
   (क) धर्म या विश्वास के संदर्भ में संगठित होना तथा इन चीजों के लिए जगह बनाना और उसे संभाले रखना।
   (ख) आवश्यक धमार्थ और मानवीय संस्थानों को बनाना और देखभाल करना।
   (ग) आवश्यक चीजों और बातों को बनाना, अपनाना और उपयोग करना जो किसी धर्म या विश्वास के सिद्धांतों से संबंध रखते हैं।
   (घ) इन क्षेत्रों में आवश्यक पत्र लिखना, विवाद करना, और विस्तार करना।

(ड) उपयुक्त स्थानों पर धर्म या विश्वास के बारे में सिखाना।

(च) याचना करना और अपनी इच्छा से व्यक्ति और संस्थानों से आर्थिक या किसी और प्रकार की सहायता लेना।

(छ) धर्म और विश्वास की जरूरत के लिए बुलाए गए नेता को सिखाना, चुनना और पदनामित करना।

(ज) प्रत्येक धर्म और विश्वास के अनुसार आराम करना, छुट्यिों, समारोह को मनाना।

(झ) धर्म और विश्वास के संदर्भ में राष्ट्रीय और अन्तर्राष्ट्रीय स्तरों पर व्यक्ति और समाज से वार्तालाप करना और उसे संभाले रखना।

7. किराए पर दिए जाने के अभ्यास में धर्म अर्थात पंथ को उस हद तक सहमत करना जब तक कि अप्रस्तुत ग्रुप को प्रोत्साहन मिले ताकि वह आर्थिक समूह में अच्छी प्रस्तुति पा सके।

8. परंपरावादी, धार्मिक विरोध या नफरत को संचार या किसी भी अन्य माध्यम द्वारा लिखित या मौलिक रूप से उकसाना प्रतिबन्धित होना चाहिए। कश्मीर के आपराधिक नियमों में ऐसे अपराधों के लिए जेल अथवा सज़ा का प्रावधान अनिवार्य हो।

(त) स्त्रियों के अधिकार

यह प्रमाणित है कि महिलाएं व्यवहार में अतिसंवेदनशील होती हैं और महिला होने के कारण भेदभाव का सामना करना तथा गरीबी, शोषण, हिंसा आदि सामाजिक स्थिति का सामना भी वे करती हैं। सरकार निम्न बातों का संकल्प ले जिससे महिलाओं के मानवीय अधिकारों की सुरक्षा निश्चित हो जाए:

(अ) सरकारी

1. मानवीय अधिकार विभाग के तहत कानूनी सलाह, सेवा और समाज सेवा में रत महिलाओं के सहयोग से महिलाओं के अधिकारों को निश्चित करना जिससे उन्हें समान सहयोग मिले तथा राजनैतिक, असैनिक, आर्थिक, सामाजिक और सांस्कृतिक जीवन का अंग बनें।

2. यह निश्चित हो कि महिलाओं के अधिकारों को यह अवसर मिले कि वह सरकारी तंत्र की सभी सीमाओं तक लिंग संबंधी बातों का अनुकलन करें।

3. महिलाओं के विरुद्ध होने वाले भेदभाव को हटाने के समझौते को विश्वसनीय माना जाए तथा उसके विस्तार को प्रोत्साहित किया जाए।

(आ) न्यायिक

1. सेक्सुअल अपराध, महिलाओं के विरुद्ध छेड़छाड़, पारिवारिक हिंसा आदि अपराधों पर विधानसभा द्वारा लगाए गए दंड को दुबारा देखना और अपडेट करना चाहिए।
2. महिलाओं और पुरुषों के मानवीय अधिकारों को समान ओहदा मिलना चाहिए।
3. महिलाओं को काबिल बनाना जिससे वह किसी भी लिंग शक्ति निधि माप में मुक्त होकर अपनी इच्छा से सहयोग दे। जनेवा समझोते के अन्तर्गत जो समाज और अधिकारों को प्रभावित कर रहा हो।
4. महिलाओं और बच्चों का स्वास्थ्य और सुरक्षा कश्मीरी लोगों के चिरस्थाई होने के लिए मूलभूत है। कश्मीरी समाज में महिलाओं के अधिकारों को प्रतिष्ठा और सम्मान मिलना चाहिए। भविष्य के किसी भी निर्णय में कश्मीर की विधिक अवस्था को देखते हुए कश्मीरी लोगों के आम अधिकारों से संबंध रखने वाला कोई भी संधि–पत्र सम्मिलित और प्रस्तुत होना चाहिए।

(इ) राजनैतिक

1. प्रशासनिक शक्ति को मज़बूत करने की प्रक्रिया में महिलाओं की भूमिका को बढ़ावा देने हेतु यह निश्चित हो कि सामाजिक और राजनीतिक संस्थाएं विशेष नीतियां अपनाएं।
2. यह निश्चित हो कि शक्ति के अभ्यास में महिलाएं व्यवस्थित हों या न हो, उन्हें भाग लेने का अवसर और अधिकार मिलने चाहिए।
3. कश्मीर पर शासन कर रहे किसी भी सरकारी तंत्र में स्वयं को प्रस्तुत करने का लाभ महिलाओं को उठाना चाहिए।
4. सरकारी और प्रशासनिक तंत्र में भी महिलाओं को प्रस्तुति का अधिकार मिलना चाहिए।
5. सभ्य समाज और वर्ग में महिलाओं की भूमिका को दबाना और शांत नहीं करना चाहिए।
6. लोकतांत्रिक संस्थाओं में महिलाओं को समान सहयोग देना चाहिए।

(ई) सभ्यता

1. युद्ध में भाग न लेने वाली महिलाओं का प्रशासनिक तौर पर सामाजिक सम्मान होना चाहिए। वैसे ही वह लड़ाई से बांहर है। विरोध करने वालों द्वारा वह बांधी नहीं जानी चाहिए। महिलाओं और बच्चों को युद्ध में ढाल की तरह प्रयोग नहीं करना चाहिए।
2. कानून के अन्तर्गत महिलाओं और लड़कियों को शिक्षा, नौकरी, मूलभूत अधिकार, स्वास्थ्य रक्षा, राजनीतिक सहयोग, काम करने की स्वतंत्रता आदि सामाजिक जीवन के हर धरातल पर सहयोग देना चाहिए।
3. कश्मीरीयों की भावी पीढ़ी के लिए महिला शिक्षा का महत्व प्रधानतम है। लिंग भेद के आधार पर महिलाओं और लड़कियों को शिक्षा से वंचित नहीं करना चाहिए।

(थ) बच्चों के अधिकार

1. बच्चे की अवस्था और परिपक्वता के हिसाब से हर बच्चे को जीने का और मूलभूत स्वतंत्रता प्राप्त करने का स्वाभाविक अधिकार है।
2. बिना किसी प्रकार के भेद–भाव के हर बच्चे के अधिकार की पुष्टि होनी चाहिए। जैसे यू०एन०ओ० समझौता बच्चे के अधिकारों के लिए दिया गया है।
3. सभी बच्चों को विशेष प्रबंधों को प्राप्त करने का अधिकार होना चाहिए जो दुर्व्यवहार, अपमान और शोषण से मुक्त कर उनकी देखभाल, स्वास्थ्य रक्षा और शारीरिक सुरक्षा को बढ़ावा दे।
4. अनाथ, सड़क पर छोड़े हुए बच्चों आदि मुश्किल परिस्थितियां झेल रहे युवाओं को सामाजिक सहयोग देने के लिए जनता सेवा योजना तथा जनसंख्या की आय से संबंधित योजना में नौकरी देनी चाहिए।
5. किसी बच्चे को उसकी इच्छा के विरुद्ध उसके मां–बाप से अलग नहीं करना चाहिए। इसके अतिरिक्त योग्य अधिकारी न्यायिक तौर पर देखकर उपर्युक्त नियम व कानून के अनुसार यह दृढ़ करें कि बच्चे के हित के लिए अलगाव जरूरी है या नहीं। मां–बाप द्वारा अपमान या अनदेखा करने जैसी विशिष्ट परिस्थिति में या मां–बाप के अलग होने पर बच्चे के रहने की जगह का निर्णय लेना हो, तब ऐसी दृढ़ता जरूरी है।

(द) शिक्षा

1. अनिवार्य शिक्षा के द्वारा युवाओं के बीच अशिक्षा को समाप्त कर देना चाहिए। प्राथमिक शिक्षा के पहले नौ सालों के दौरान् सरकार की कोशिश होनी चाहिए कि आगे के तीन सालों के लिए मुफ्त शिक्षा दे।
2. प्राथमिक शिक्षा के दौरान् दूसरे अनुशासन का पहलू शांति हो। स्नातक के लिए एक क्लास जरूरत के लिए माध्यमिक शिक्षा को एक अलग विषय की तरह पढ़ाना चाहिए।
3. नौ वर्ष से ज्यादा अवस्था के बच्चों को जो स्कूल नहीं जाते, सरकार को व्यावसायिक और तकनीति शिक्षा देनी चाहिए। यह उन्हें अपना व्यक्तिगत विकास करने के लिए उस तरह के प्रोजेक्ट को करने के प्रति प्रेरित करेगा जो कश्मीर के आर्थिक और सामाजिक विकास में मदद करेगा।
4. शिक्षा विभाग द्वारा एक क्षेत्रीय आंदोलन किया जाएगा जो आबादी के अलग–अलग समूहों को एक साथ रहने में मदद करेगा। इस तरह का आंदोलन अलग–अलग प्रकार की अहिंसक गतिविधियों द्वारा शांतिपूर्वक रहने के साथ–साथ क्षमताओं के बारे में जागरूकता पैदा करने की कोशिश करेगा।
5. युद्ध को शांतिपूर्वक स्थिरता में बदलने के लिए राजनैतिक और प्रशासनिक नेताओं और आर्थिकतावादियों को अतिरिक्त शिक्षा देनी चाहिए।

(ध) शरणार्थी

1. कश्मीर से बाहर स्थित सभी कश्मीरी शरणार्थियों और स्थानांतरित लोगों को लौटने का सभी धमकियों और जबरदस्ती से मुक्त होकर तथा सुरक्षा और गौरव के साथ जीने का अधिकार होना चाहिए।
2. 1990 से पहले कश्मीर छोड़ने वाले सभी उनकी खोई हुई संपत्ति के लिए तथा कश्मीर में फिर से स्थापित होने के लिए आर्थिक सहारा मिलना चाहिए तथा उनका स्वागत होना चाहिए।
3. 1990 के बाद कश्मीर छोड़ने वाले सभी लोगों को अपनी खोई हुई संपत्ति के लिए तथा उस संपत्ति को वापस पाने के लिए आर्थिक प्रतिफल मिलना चाहिए।
4. शरणार्थी विभाग द्वारा शरणार्थियों के दावों की तहकीकात होना निश्चित

होना चाहिए। किसी भी प्रकार के आर्थिक प्रतिफल पर शरणार्थी विभाग द्वारा काम किया जाना चाहिए।

5. जिन शरणार्थियों की संपत्ति को मान्यता प्रमाणित की गई है वह कश्मीर में रह गई है, शरणार्थी विभाग को वापस आने वालों की संपत्ति और बैंक खाते वसूलने में उनकी मदद करनी चाहिए।

(न) मानवाधिकार विभाग

उपयोगी और कार्यशील मानवीय अधिकार विभाग के लक्ष्य को बढ़ाते हुए कश्मीर सरकार को सरकारी ढांचे में मानवीय अधिकारों के लिए एक नया विभाग जोड़ना चाहिए। इसके लिए मानव अधिकार पर संयुक्त राष्ट्र का विशेष अधिकार तथा मानव अधिकार का संयुक्त राष्ट्र केंद्र आदि अन्तर्राष्ट्रीय संस्थानों से तकनीकी और भौतिक सहयोग लिया जा सकता है।

(क) मानव अधिकार विभाग की शक्तियां और दायित्व

1. मानवीय अधिकारों के उल्लंघन से संबंधित शिकायतों पर ध्यान देना चाहिए और काम करना चाहिए।
2. मानवाधिकारों के बारे में अन्तर्राष्ट्रीय मापांक के राजनैतिक संविधान के अनुसार प्रभाव और स्वतंत्रता के साथ जरूरी तहकीकात करना चाहिए।
3. शक्ति के अभ्यास के दौरान् उचित संवैधानिक संस्थाओं द्वारा जानकारी के आधार पर इस तहकीकात को ध्यान में रखना चाहिए कि निर्दिष्ट मानवाधिकारों का उल्लंघन हुआ है कि नही।
4. कश्मीरी जनता के बीच संचार द्वारा किसी भी व्यक्ति और समूह का उन्मुक्त और व्यावहारिक साक्षात्कार करना, अपने कार्यों की अच्छी प्रस्तुति और आदेश के अमल के लिए उचित जानकारी इकट्ठी करना, अपने कार्यों और गतिविधियों से संबंधित जानकारी फैलाना आदि को ध्यान में रख विभाग को खुद को स्थापित करने और कश्मीर में मुक्त होकर घूमने का अधिकार होना चाहिए।
5. अपने कार्यों की प्रस्तुति में विभाग को सबसे संवेदनशील समूह की स्थिति का तथा सेना से प्रभावित हो रही आबादी (स्थानांतरित, शरणार्थी और वापस लौटने वाले) का ध्यान रखना चाहिए।
6. मानवीय अधिकारों के अनुसरण को स्थापित करने में विभाग को व्यक्ति

के जीवन, अखंडता, सुरक्षा, स्वतंत्रता, अभिव्यक्ति, घूमने और संगठित होने की स्वतंत्रता और राजनैतिक अधिकारों पर विशिष्ट ध्यान देना चाहिए।

7. भारतीय सैनिक और सुरक्षा बल की गतिविधियां जो करार पर हस्ताक्षर करने के पूर्व हुई, वे धार्मिक अल्पसंख्यक विभाग द्वारा जांची जाएंगी। सभी मानवीय अधिकारों का उल्लंघन जो हस्ताक्षर से पहले हुआ, उसे मैत्री विभाग द्वारा पुनः जांचा जाएगा। विभाग को अपनी गतिविधियां स्थाई आधार पर तीव्र गति से करना चाहिए।
8. कश्मीर विधान परिषद् और कश्मीर विधानसभा संगठन द्वारा सहमति दिए गए कश्मीर मूल निवासी को ही विभाग का नेतृत्व करना चाहिए। उसकी प्रतिष्ठा की ताकत, निष्पक्षता, अखंडता, काम की विशिष्टता, ज्ञान की पृष्ठभूमि आदि मानवाधिकारों के आधार पर होना चाहिए। उस व्यक्ति को श्रेष्ठ होना चाहिए जिसके सिद्धांत ऊचे हों, जिसकी प्रतिबद्धता क्षेत्रीय समाज के सदस्यों तथा मानवाधिकारों की तरफ हो। उसकी अवधि दुबारा नियुक्ति के आश्वासन के साथ 6 साल की हो।
9. विभाग के पास अपने कार्यालय, संचार–साधन और लिपीकीय सहायक अधिकारी होने चाहिए। विभाग का स्थायित्व ग्रीष्म ऋतु में श्रीनगर में और शरद ऋतु में जम्मू में होना चाहिए। सिविलियन सेवक को किराए पर लेने की प्रक्रिया से सहायक अधिकारी को विभाग के लिए लिया जा सकता है इस निश्चितता के साथ कि आबादी (जिसमें महिलाएं, धार्मिक बहुमत के सदस्य आर किसी भी क्षेत्र का अल्पसंख्यक समूह) सहायक अधिकारी की प्रस्तुति के चुनाव में सम्मिलित है।
10. विभाग उन परिमाणों का ध्यान रखेगा जो मूलभूत मानवाधिकारों, धार्मिक अल्पसंख्यक, महिलाओं, बच्चों, शरणार्थी, शिक्षा और पुनः मैत्री आदि के लिए जिम्मेदार होगा।
11. स्थानीय मानवाधिकारों के संघ और असैनिक समाज समूह को कश्मीर में बढ़ावा मिलना चाहिए जो मानवाधिकारों के अनुसरण पर दृष्टि रखें। इस समूह का अधिकार विभाग की प्रस्तुति के संदर्भ में दावों और आरोपों की जांच करना और यह पुष्ट करना होगा कि सभी लक्ष्य पूरे हों।

ऊपर दिए गए मापांक पर एक संक्षिप्त एवं विहंगम दृष्टि डालें तो इसमें निहित कार्यक्रम सिर्फ इस कारण से फूट की भावना को बढ़ावा देगा। और

इस वजह से दिए गए मापदंड को शांति मापदंड नहीं माना जा सकता बल्कि इसे हस्तक्षेप मापदंड माना जा सकता है जो देश की सत्ता में दखल दे रहा है। हस्तक्षेप करने वाला विदेशी संवैधानिक संगठन जो भारतीय संवैधानिक ढांचे को बदलने की कोशिश कर रहा है और भारतीय संविधान के प्राथमिक ढांचे के खिलाफ है, उसे अनेक कारणों से बढ़ावा नहीं मिलना चाहिए। पहला, मापदंड का प्रस्तुत किया गया समाधान बढ़ती स्वायतता एवं स्वतंत्रता को बढ़ावा देता है जो भारत के संसद द्वारा त्याग दिया गया है। धारा 370 के निर्देशानुसार, जम्मू–कश्मीर का राज्य भविष्य में विशेष तौर पर अधिकतम स्वायतता के आसार के साथ अधिकतम स्वतंत्रता का आनंद लेता है। दूसरा, इसे (instrument of accession) स्वीकृति के निरीक्षण और पुनः निरीक्षण को दुबारा नहीं खोलना चाहिए। प्रस्तुत किए गए मापांक में लेखक उन सभी नकारात्मक खिलाड़ियों को यह याद दिलाना चाहता है कि स्वीकृति का यंत्र ऐतिहासिक अतीत का विषय है। ऐतिहासिक अतीत एक निर्जीव इतिहास है और कोई भी कोशिश उसे आग में घी डालने के समान खतरनाक परिणामों से पुनर्जीवित करने के लिए पर्याप्त होगी। स्वीकृति के सभी दास्तावेजों को पुनर्जीवित करने का भयावह दुष्परिणाम लगभग 560 भारतीय राजसी राज्यों के उत्तराधिकारियों को सुप्त शेर को जगाने के समान है। भगवान की कृपा से यह नहीं हुआ क्योंकि ऐसी दुर्घटना खून की होली एवं खून की नदी बहाव को जन्म देता। तीसरा, कश्मीर और कश्मीरी खुद को राष्ट्रीय तौर पर जोड़ने वाले लोगों, जो भारत और भारतीयों की एकता और अखंडता में रुचि रखते हैं, से खुद को बचाने में असहाय हैं। चौथा, प्रस्तुत मापदंड कश्मीर और कश्मीरियों पर आधारित है। यह कहीं भी लद्दाख और लद्दाखियों तथा जम्मू और जम्मूवासियों के विषय को नहीं दिखाता। यह सिर्फ तीन क्षेत्रों के बीच विराग को बढ़ावा देता है – कश्मीर घाटी बनाम जम्मू बनाम लद्दाख जैसे कि कश्मीर बनाम भारत बनाम पाकिस्तान। पांचवा, संवैधानिक अनुमति के अनुसार अलग होना अयोग्यता है क्योंकि जोड़ने की प्रक्रिया को इतने अच्छे से बुना गया है। भारतीय संविधान के धारा 1 की भाषा में, "भारत के राज्यों का संगठन होना चाहिए," जो अलग होने को नामुमकिन, अक्रियान्वन और अव्यावहारिक है। (सी०ए०डी० वोल्यूम, VII, p. 43 ; इन री बैरूबरी, ए०आई०आर० 1960, एस०सी० 845 ; मगनभाई, ए०आई०आर० 1990, एस०सी० 1692)

छठा, अन्तर्राष्ट्रीय कानून के संरक्षण के अन्तर्गत अलग होना अन्तर्राष्ट्रीय समाज में मुश्किल से माना जाता है। अलग होना पूरे भारत में अलगाववाद की भावना पैदा करेगा जो देश में उग्रवाद, आतंकवाद और हिंसा को बढ़ावा देगा।

राष्ट्रीय रणनीति

भारत अपनी अखंडता, स्वतंत्रता, प्रभुसत्ता, आंतरिक और बाहरी सुरक्षा, स्थानीय, पाकिस्तान, अन्तर्राष्ट्रीय लेखकीय सुरक्षा और रणनीति के अपराधकर्ताओं को सह रहा है और इन सबसे जूझ रहा है। इसके अलावा भारत कामयाबी से विरोध कर रहा है और अस्थिर रणनीतियों का मुकाबला कर रहा है और आतंकवाद तथा उग्रवाद को समाप्त करने का भरसक प्रयास कर रहा है जो कि आतंकवादी समूहों जैसे जम्मू और कश्मीर मुक्ति फ्रंट है (जे०के०एल०एफ० 1977)। हुर्रियत सम्मेलन 1993 अनेक समूहों का गठजोड़ जिसमें अनेक संगठनीकरण 26 गोरिल्ला और राजनीतिक समूहों का गढ़ है {कुछ लोग दावा करते हैं कि यह वास्तव में यूनाइटेड स्टेट्स के शांति संस्थान (वांशिंगटन में स्थापित शांति संस्था) का आविष्कार है।}, मुत्ताहिदा जिहाद सभा, हिज्ब–उल–मुजाहिदिन, जैशै–ए–मुहम्मद, लश्कर–ए–तोईबा आदि का अस्तित्व, सशक्त सेनाओं द्वारा राजनैतिक व्यवहार कुशलता और कूटनीति द्वारा मानवीय अधिकारों के अनुसरण के विरुद्ध एवं विरोध में है। पाकिस्तान के अवमानना समझौते की चुनौती को भी भारत सह रहा है। भारत और पाकिस्तान के बीच के तनाव को शांत करने के लिए कश्मीर को लेकर यू०एन० रीजोल्यूशन 1948–49, ताशकेंट डकलेरेशन, शिमला एग्रीमेंट 1972, लेहोर डेक्लेरेशन 1999 बना था। समन्वित रिश्तेदारी के विकास में यह समझौते एक मील के पत्थर साबित होने थे। अगर यह समझौते मान्य होते तो यूरोपियन संगठन मॉडल और यूरो की तरह सर्च मॉडल बनता। यह तर्क किया जा सकता है कि पाकिस्तान ने करार पर हस्ताक्षर किए यह सोचकर कि वह उनके साथ कदापि नहीं रहेगा (ब्रहामा चीलैनी, द हिंदुसतान टाईम्स, सितंबर 8. 1999)। पाकिस्तान ने जब लाहौर घोषणा पर हस्ताक्षर किए तो उसका घृणायुक्त व्यवहार कारगिल आक्रमण की योजना को दिखाता था। निसंदेह यह कहा जा सकता है कि 1948 और 1949 रीजोल्यूशन की शपथ को लेते समय पाकिस्तान आखिर तक पाखंड को अपनाए रहा ; जम्मू–कश्मीर को न छोड़कर उस समय वह उसका उल्लंघन भी कर रहा था। हलांकि यह जताया जा

सकता है कि वह करार जिन्हें पाकिस्तान ने लागू किया है जिनको प्रमाणित करने का भार भारत पर ही रहा है। उन वजहों को ढूंढने में अधिक मुश्किल भी नहीं है।

इन चुनौतियों से जूझने के बाद, इस्लामाबाद घोषणा लाहौर घोषणा को दोहराती है। भारत–पाकिस्तान ने राज्य में शांति और सामान्य स्थिति वापस लाने के लिए व्यक्ति से व्यक्ति का संपर्क, मुजफराबाद कमान आमान सेतु मार्ग, वागहा मार्ग, खोखारा मार्ग, सड़क और रेलवे मार्ग, पत्रकारों का आदान–प्रदान, सांस्कृतिक दल, सामाजिक विज्ञान, शिक्षा केंन्द्र, दूसरे कार्यालयों के संरक्षण इत्यादि द्वारा आत्मविश्वास बनाए रखने वाले बहुत से उपाय अपनाने आरंभ किए। इसके अलावा भारत ने आंतरिक सी०बी०एम, पहली जम्मू–कश्मीर राउंड टेबल सम्मेलन, दिल्ली में फरवरी 2006 और श्रीनगर में 24 व 25 मई 2006 जम्मू–कश्मीर राउंड टेबल सम्मेलन आरंभ किया। भारत के प्रधानमंत्री डॉ० मनमोहन सिंह ने पंच कमेटी द्वारा उन्हें अंदरूनी जांच के लिए भेजा और कूटनीति योजना की घोषणा की।

समूह 1

राज्य में, समाज के अलग–अलग भागों में आत्मविश्वास बढ़ाने वाले उपायः श्री मोहम्मद अंसारी के नेतृत्व मेंः–

1. सेना द्वारा प्रभावित लोगों की स्थिति सुधारने के उपाय।
2. सेना द्वारा प्रभावित विधवाओं और अनाथों को पूर्व अवस्था में लाने की योजनाएं।
3. उन लोगों की स्थिति में शिथिलता जिन्होंने सैनिक बनने की सौगन्ध ली है।
4. पूर्व अवस्था में एक असरदार प्रभाव लाने की नीति जिसमें स्थानांतरित कश्मीरी पंडित के लिए रोजगारी सम्मिलित हो।
5. एक सिफारिश उन कश्मीरी युवाओं के लिए जो पाकिस्तान के अधीन क्षेत्रों से संबंध रखते हैं।
6. राज्य की अद्‌भुत सांस्कृतिक और धार्मिक परंपरा को सुरक्षित रखने के उपाय।

समूह 2

एल०ओ०सी० के आर–पार के रिश्तों को मज़बूत करना : श्री एम०के० रस्गोत्रा के नेतृत्व में उपायों का सुझाव देना :

1. उस प्रक्रिया को सरल करना जो एल०ओ०सी० के आर–पार यात्रा करने को सहज बनाएं।
2. समानों के व्यापार को बढ़ाना।
3. व्यक्ति से व्यक्ति का संपर्क बढ़ाना।
4. नए रास्तों को खोलना जैसे कि कारगिल, शकरदू आदि।

समूह 3

डॉ० सी० रंगराजन के नेतृत्व में आर्थिक विकास :

1. उन नीतियों को उभारना जो संतुलित आर्थिक प्रादुर्भाव और रोजगार को आश्वस्त करें।
2. नियंत्रित आर्थिक विकास और रोजगार पैदा करना।
3. राज्य में नियंत्रित क्षेत्रीय और उप–क्षेत्रीय विकास।

समूह 4

श्री एन०सी० सक्सेना के नेतृत्व में अच्छे अधिकारों को आश्वासन देना :

प्रभावशाली उपायों को ध्यान में रखना जिससे :–

1. प्रशासन की जवाबदारी, उत्तरदायित्व और पारदर्शिता बढ़े।
2. स्थानीय स्व–सरकार को मज़बूत करना।
3. विकासशील कार्यक्रमों को प्रभावशाली ढंग से देखना।
4. मानवाधिकारों का उल्लंघन करने वालों के लिए सहनशक्ति को शून्य मनस्कता का बनाना।
5. जानकारी के आधार को मज़बूत करना।
6. समाज के सभी वर्गों, विशेष रूप से अल्पसंख्यक को उपयुक्त सुरक्षा प्रदान करना।

समूह 5

केंद्र और राज्य के रिश्तों को मज़बूत करना :

सावधानी रखना :

1. जो विषय जम्मू–कश्मीर के विशिष्ट पद से भारतीय संघ के अन्तर्गत संबंध रखते हैं।
2. विधियां, जो लोकतंत्र, सांप्रदायिकता और कानून के क्षेत्र को मज़बूत करती हैं।
3. विभिन्न राज्यों के मध्य, क्षेत्रीय, उपक्षेत्रीय और पौराणिक इच्छाओं इच्छाओं को पाने के लिए शक्ति के प्रभावशाली आक्रमण के प्रति सावधान होना। सभी राजनैतिक दलों के प्रस्तुतिकरण पर ध्यान रखा गया है।

आलोचनात्मक विश्लेषण और निष्कर्ष का सार

स्थानीय, पाकिस्तान और अन्तर्राष्ट्रीय रणनीति के जाल से बाहर आने के लिए भारतीय रणनीति एक नई कूटनीति अपना रहा है जो कश्मीर घाटी के आस–पास सीमित है और जम्मू और लद्दाख के जनसाधारण से बहुत कम ताल्लुक रखते हैं। यह त्रिभागी पहुंच बहुत गरम और बहुंत ठंडे व्यवहार प्रतिरूप के साथ आती है। सबसे महत्वपूर्ण बात यह है कि भारतीय रणनीति कहीं इस त्रिभागी रणनीति का शिकार न हो जाए। भारत को अपनी समन्वित व्यूह रचना की योजना में चालाक होना पड़ेगा वरना शायद वह त्रिभागीय कपटी राजनीति के जाल का शिकार बन जाएगा। भारतीय रणनीति का ऐसा प्रतिरूप होना चाहिए जो उसकी सीमाओं, प्रभुत्व, अखंडता, अंदर और बाहर की सुरक्षा और रक्षा की सुरक्षा करे। उसको उन चुनौतियों से जूझने के लिए नई योजनाएं बनानी पड़ेंगी जो उसकी अंदर और बाहर की सुरक्षा के लिए खतरा है। यह सुरक्षा का खतरा बहुआयामी व्यवहार है जो पोस्ट–संघजीवी दुनिया की परेशानियों से पैदा होता है। जैसे – पारंपरिक जाति संबंधी, प्रायः जाति–संबंधी, विचार पद्धति, कूटनीति, आर्थिक, सामाजिक और नव–राजनैतिक पंक्तियां। इस समूह में पांच में से चार ने अपने–आप को पहचान दी है, कुछ प्रश्नों को समझाया है और सिस्टम को सुधारने के सुखदायक उपाय दिए जिससे वह सिस्टम के छिद्रों को बंद कर सके। यह एक आसान कार्य नहीं रहा होगा। यह एक अतिकठिन काम लगता है क्योंकि नेताओं सहित सभी के आत्मविश्वास को वापस लाने के लिए अपने निष्कपट व्यवहार और सद्विवेक से राजनीति से ऊपर उठना होगा। उनके सुझाव दूसरे अफसरों की अलमारी के लिए चिट्ठी है। यह मकड़ी के मनोहर धोखा देने वाले वस्त्रों की तरह होंगे या नहीं, यह समय ही बताएगा। इन समूहों ने बारीकी से यह मूल प्रश्न नहीं उठाया कि कैसे, क्यों और किन स्थितियों में आत्मविश्वास खत्म हुआ ! कौन किसके वश

में है ! अगर निरंतर आत्मविश्वास पैदा करें तो इन बहुमूल्य प्रश्नों के जबाव अकेले ही दिए जा सकते हैं। उग्रवाद, आतंकवाद और छद्‌मयुद्ध लड़ाई सीमापार से भारत पर प्रहार कर रही है। यह अंदर और बाहर के विवाद के विषयों को पैदा करने के लिए जिम्मेदार है और आत्मविश्वास पैदा करने के उपायों में विध्न डालने के लिए जिम्मेदार हैं। अलग–अलग राज्य सरकारें जम्मू और कश्मीर को पृथक विभागों से निर्मित एक भाग नहीं मान रहीं बल्कि तीन भागों में मान रही हैं और यह आत्मविश्वास को कम करने में सहायक है। अच्छा शासन, उत्तरदायित्व और पारदर्शिता की कमी भी जनसामान्य के आत्मविश्वास के खोने में समान रूप से जिम्मेदार है। और इसीलिए जीवन धारण करने योग्य अधिकार में बाधा है। जो हमें पीछे ले जाए, वो भ्रष्टाचार बढ़ रहा है और आगे बढ़ाने वाला रुख कम हो रहा है। क्रोध, असंतोष में लिपटा हुआ सच 'मेरी चिंता छोड़ो' जैसा जबाव और जिम्मेदारी भरा भाव पैदा कर रहे हैं। जल्दी, स्थिरता और प्रधानता को आगे बढ़ाना आत्मविश्वास को घटाने के दूसरे फैक्टर हैं। घाटी से हिंदू जनसंख्या की विदाई ने न सिर्फ सामाजिक स्थिति बदल दी है बल्कि लोगों के आत्मविश्वास और विश्वास के खोने के लिए भी जिम्मेदार है। सरकार और उसके काम करने की शैली में अंदर से हटाए लोगों का ब्यौरा दिया गया है। बढ़ते आतंकवाद को देखते हुए राज्यों के भागों से हिंदुओं का विदा होना, सरकार की अचेतना और उदासीनता आदि स्थितियां उनका आत्मविश्वास घटने का एक कारण है। मानवीय अधिकारों के बहाने अन्तर्राष्ट्रीय मानवीय कानून का उल्लंघन हुआ है और इससे सुरक्षा दलों की बदनामी हुई है। इसने आतंकवाद और प्रतिनिधि युद्ध को बढ़ावा दिया है जिससे वह अपनी उच्छृंखल गतिविधियों, सुरक्षा बलों और राष्ट्रवादियों के उत्साह भंग में आगे बढ़ सके। यह पक्ष जिस तरह से रखा जाना चाहिए था, उतनी तीव्रता से रखा नहीं गया। इससे यह एक ऐसा बड़ा सा रिक्त स्थान छोड़ गया जिसे भरना भविष्य संबंधी नीति है। कश्मीर घाटी तथा प्रदेश के अन्य भागों से घर से बेघर (शरणार्थियों) और 1947 के पश्चिमी पाकिस्तान के शरणार्थियों के आत्मविश्वास की कमी कों दूर करने के लिए कोई भी पुनः सुधार या पुनरुद्धार नीति नहीं है। आत्मविश्वास बढ़ाने के उपायों पर कार्यरत समूह ने जनवरी 2007 की अपनी रिपोर्ट में यह सुझाव दिया कि, "पाकिस्तान का जो निकटस्थ क्षेत्र है, उसके पार की अन्तर्राष्ट्रीय सीमा से आए शरणार्थियों की पुनरुद्धार समस्या का निरीक्षण होना चाहिए तथा उसका निर्णय हो जाना

चाहिए। ये लोग राज्य के स्थायी नागरिक बनने के योग्य नहीं हैं। ऐसे शरणार्थियों की वस्तुस्थिति को कपट तथा अपमानजनक ढंग से प्रस्तुत किया गया है। इनकी स्थिति जो अब भी बेघर और अस्थानीय लोगों की है, उनके भविष्य के बारे में बताती है। आत्मविश्वास बढ़ाने के उपायों पर कार्यरत समूहों ने ऐसे शरणार्थियों के आत्मविश्वास को समाप्त कर दिया है। हम बाह्य आत्मविश्वास बढ़ाने का उपाय चाहते हैं और आंतरिक आत्मविश्वास को बढ़ाने पर कम ध्यान देते हैं। उनके मन में संजोई आशा थी और हम पर विश्वास था कि अब वे बेघर और अस्थानीय नहीं रहेंगे। उनके आत्मविश्वास को खोकर हमने एक बार फिर उनके विश्वास को प्राप्त करने का मौका खो दिया है। इस विषय को सही दृष्टि से सामने रखने में कार्यरत समूह असफल हो गया। उनकी भाषा बनावटी लगती है क्योंकि वह कानून और सद्भावना के आपसी संगठन का न्यूनतम निरीक्षण कर पाया। कार्यरत समूह ने कानून और पुण्यशीलता के इस संबंध को एक ऐसी पहेली बना दिया जो रहस्मयी तरीके से प्रहेलिका में लिपटी है। उसके सुझाव दूरदर्शिता को ध्यान में रखकर नहीं दिए गए क्योंकि यह ओथेलो की तलवार की तरह शणार्थियों के सिर पर लटकने के लिए सहमति दे रही है। उसके विप्लववादी ज्ञान ने समस्या को सुलझाए बिना ही उन लोगों के हाथ में छोड़ दिया जो इसे सुलझा नहीं सके। मेरे विचार से यह विषय उन लोगों के हाथ में है जो योगदान देना चाहते थे पर नहीं दे पाए क्योंकि जब शरीर कमज़ोर होता है तो आत्मा चाह कर भी काम नहीं कर सकती। स्वराज्य और स्वतंत्रता दो अलग–अलग राजनैतिक दलों के राजनैतिक आदर्श हैं जिन्हें राज्य के किसी भी क्षेत्र से लोगों का सहयोग नहीं मिला। स्व–राज्य और स्वतंत्रता अन्यथा स्वायतता भारत के संसद द्वारा नकार एवं ठुकरा दिए गए हैं। जम्मू और लद्दाख क्षेत्र खुद को राष्ट्रवादी, अखंडता और एकता से पूर्ण दिखाते हैं जो भारत के संगठन के साथ संबंध और सहयोग बनाए हुए हैं। कश्मीर घाटी इसको अलग ढंग से प्रस्तुत करती है कि आत्मविश्वास पैदा करने वाले उपायों से असत्याभास झलकता है।

सीमांकन और सामुदायिकता के बीच का संबंध परस्पर जुड़ा हुआ है। इसने आत्मविश्वास बनाए रखने की आशा को अनियंत्रित, कठोर सामाजिक स्थिति से जोड़ दिया है। धारा 370 को सम्मिलित करना भारतीय संविधान के लेख में कभी भी 'भारत और जम्मू कश्मीर के नागरिकों की इच्छा' नहीं रही। आत्मविश्वास बढ़ाने के लिए आगे बढ़ने की उनकी इच्छा उन्हें अपने साथ

जोड़ लेती है। सरकारिया कमीशन ने, वेंकटाचेलिया कमीशन ने संविधान और लोकतंत्र के साथ काम करने का निरीक्षण और पुनःनिरीक्षण किया है। और माना है कि संविधान और लोकतंत्र के काम में दखल देना संवैधानिक संस्कृति के मूल ढांचे का उल्लंघन करेगा। कार्यरत समूह को उद्यमी होना चाहिए जिससे समकक्ष और सहायक संघीय संस्कृति मज़बूत हो। यह अकेले ही भारतीय राष्ट्र की एकता और अखंडता में मज़बूती लाएगी। इस दिशा में सिर्फ इतना प्रयास करना है कि केन्द्रीय राज्य संबंधी आत्मविश्वास को बनाए रखने के लिए किए जा रहे वर्तमान कार्यों का अनादर न हो। एक समान विकास और आर्थिक बंटवारे को, जो राज्य के तीनों क्षेत्रों में निष्पक्षता के आधार पर हुआ है, राज्य के सामान्यजन में विश्वास और आत्मविश्वास पैदा करना चाहिए। पूरे राज्य का ध्यान पर्यावरण–पर्यटन (आर्थिक और अर्थशास्त्री) पर होना चाहिए। शारदापीठ जैसी तीर्थयात्रा को बढ़ावा देना आत्मविश्वास से भरेगा। किंतु इसका परिणाम स्वार्थ से भरा नहीं होना चाहिए। हुर्रियत और जे०के०एल०एफ० जैसे समूह को बढ़ावा नहीं मिलना चाहिए जो राज्य की पूरी जनसंख्या की आवाज़ को संबोधित नहीं करते हैं। इस बात को बढ़ावा मिला तो यह आत्मविश्वास बढ़ाने के उपायों को प्रभावित करेगा। किसी भी राजनैतिक दल को राजनैतिक भत्ते का मिलना हानिकारक होगा। सिर्फ ऐसे भत्ते पर काम होना चाहिए जो भारतीय राष्ट्र की एकता और अखंडता के लिए हो। इसमें आंतरिक और बाह्य स्तर पर कोई समझौता नहीं होना चाहिए। सितंबर 2006 का 'हवाना ज्वाइंट मैकेनिज़्म टू टूरिस्ट स्टेटमेंट' भारत के प्रधानमंत्री डॉ० मनमोहन सिंह तथा पाकिस्तान के राष्ट्रपति जनरल मुशर्रफ द्वारा ग्रहणीय है और बहुत से छुपे हुए समझौतों से युक्त है। अधिकाधिक सावधानी के साथ इसे ऐसे ही देखा जाना चाहिए और अनुसरण किया जाना चाहिए जैसे Quiet Diplomacy को। यह बताना सर्वोत्कृष्ट है कि प्रस्तुत स्थानीय, पाकिस्तान और अन्तर्राष्ट्रीय मापदंड दलदल से कम नहीं है क्योंकि यह सुदृढ़ता, स्वराज्य, स्वतंत्रता, स्वायतता, आज़ादी और उग्रवाद एवं अलगाववाद को बढ़ावा देता है। यह बैक चैनल डिप्लोमेसी के रूप में ग्रहण किया गया है जो चार विस्तृत फार्मूलों – 'नॉरदन आईरलैंड, कोसोवो, ईस्ट टाइमोर, अमेरिकन थिंक टैंक' में है। यह बताना ताक पर रखने के समान होगा कि भारत को कभी–कभी सरल राजनीतियों की जगह कठिन राजनैतिक

और कूटनीतिक पद्धतियां अपनानी चाहिए जिससे समन्वित नीतियों के साथ बिना किसी परिणाम के विवाद सुलझ सके। अन्यथा यह अनियमित हो जाएगा। साउथ एशिया में समन्वित नीति और शिष्टाचार, व्यापार, क्रय–विक्रय, सांस्कृतिक रिश्ता और शैक्षिक आदान–प्रदान का बढ़ना अच्छे परिणाम देगा। यह समन्वित शिष्टाचार सिर्फ साउथ एशिया क्षेत्र को मज़बूत करेगा। दूसरों की बराबरी करेगा इसलिए कि एवं सद्भावना द्वेष फैलाने वाला अग्रदूत होगा। मानव की खुशी, उसकी सफलता और विकास के लिए, शांति परिणामों पर निरंतर काम करने के लिए इसे साहसी नीतियां चाहिए। इतिहास को भूतकाल में रखने के लिए और तीर्थयात्री की तरह आगे बढ़ने के लिए, हमेशा की शांति और समृद्धि के लिए सिर्फ यही एक समन्वित नीति, एक मानव अधिकार मापदंड है। हमें अपने सामने यह उक्ति रखनी चाहिए कि, ''अनंत सावधानी स्वतंत्रता का मोल होता है।'' हमें इस तरह व्यवहार करना चाहिए कि हमारे लिए यह कभी दुबारा न कहा जाए कि ––

''खोला कफ़स तो ताकते परवाज़ ही नहीं,
बुलबुल तेरे नसीब को सैयाद क्या करे !!''

APPENDICES

Appendix I

Summary of Reports of Five Working Groups on Jammu and Kashmir

SUMMARY OF REPORT OF WORKING GROUP-I ON CONFIDENCE BUILDING MEASURES ACROSS SEGMENTS OF SOCIETY IN THE STATE

The Working group on confidence building measures across segments of society in the State was chaired by Shri Mohammad Hamid Ansari and comprised of 17 other members (list attached) drawn from across the political spectrum and other spheres of life. The Working Group held three meetings on 27.07.2006, 15.09.2006 and 24.11.2006.

2. The Group had the following agenda:

- Measures to improve the condition of people affected by militancy.
- Schemes to rehabilitate all orphans and widows affected by militancy.
- Issues relating to the relaxation of conditions for persons who have forsworn militancy.
- An effective rehabilitation policy, including employment, for Kashmiri Pandit migrants.
- An approach considering issues relating to return of Kashmiri youth from areas controlled by Pakistan.

3. After consolidating all the view points and identifying the items of convergence the recommendations were finalized after thorough discussions.

4. The Group expressed serious concern over the incidents of human rights violations in Jammu and Kashmir. The necessity of curbing human rights violations are considered to be one of the most important measures to be taken so that the innocent persons do not become victims of counter-insurgency measures. It was also felt that this would also help to enhance India's International image. The Group therefore recommended strengthening of the State Human Rights Commission along the lines of the NHRC, revitalization of its functioning and setting up of an Empowered Committee for monitoring the Action Taken Report on its recommendations.

5. The Working Group recommended administering the relief to the victims of militancy prescribing an order of priority for the victims to receive relief assistance. Considering the limitation on the numbers of Government jobs available it is necessary to prioritize normative conditions in the provision for jobs to victims' families. The Working Group was of the view that wherever it is not possible to provide Government jobs, a one-time compensation of Rs. 5.00 lacs be given. A rehabilitation package for the injured victims and relief/compensation for victims of the Kargil War was also suggested.

6. The Group recommended review and revocation of laws that impinge on fundamental rights of common citizen, such as Armed Forces Special Powers Act. Law and order was to be maintained through normal laws to the maximum extent.

7. The Group deliberated on the conditions of widows and orphans of those killed in militancy-related violence. It was considered necessary to set-up a special cell to get complete data including wives and children of persons missing or presumed dead for making effective rehabilitation schemes. They should complete the work within 3 months. The widow relief of Rs. 500 at present should be revised and orphans provided scholarships to cover cost of education and their livelihood concern by a suitable scheme. Orphans of killed militants with no other source of income should be included as a goodwill gesture. Relief measures should be monitored regularly and malpractices curbed effectively.

8. The Group felt that there is a need to create conditions for persons who have forsworn the path of militancy to avoid reversion back to militancy and to provide them a definite policy/

package for their rehabilitation. They should be treated in a dignified manner. The Group has recommended that the security forces should be instructed to keep a check on fake encounters and fake recovery of arms. Cases of all persons in jails should be reviewed and those who are under trial for minor offences should be given general amnesty.

9. The Group also recommended devising an effective rehabilitation policy including employment for Kashmiri Pandit migrants. Further, it has been recommended that the rights of Kashmiri Pandit migrants to return to the places of their original residence should be recognized and a comprehensive package devised in consultation with their representatives. This should be based on comprehensive collection of database. It should include other militancy affected migrants of Jammu region. Jobs for Kashmiri Pandits should be identified in Police and other Civil Service vacancies besides Government of India offices located in J&K. Relief to NoKs who could not be provided jobs as prescribed under SRO-43 should be increased from Rs. 1 lakh to Rs. 5 lakhs. An inventory of their properties should be prepared to examine illegal occupation. Adequate compensation/rent should be provided to the properties of migrants occupied by SFs. All camp migrants should be provided living conditions and accommodation. Kashmiri Pandits living in the Valley should also be provided opportunities of education and employment. It is also necessary to start a dialogue with the representatives of Kashmiri Pandit migrants with a view to design a package for their return and rehabilitation within next three years. The Working Group also recommended setting up of a Minority Commission for J&K.

10. The Working Group recommended to categorize youth into those who joined militancy for misguided ideological reasons, monetary considerations and forced circumstances. It suggested consideration of a policy within a framework of CBM enunciated in the RTC and after verifying the identity of persons returning from the other side within a time frame to be decided. Such persons should be given a rehabilitation package and treated with dignity to join the mainstream similar to para 8 above.

11. The recommendations of the Group included preparation of a comprehensive policy to preserve monuments, sites, building structures, objects and landscapes that are significant in indigenous history, architecture, archaeology, engineering and

traditional art forms by a body of experts through an autonomous institution.

12. The Group recommended that problems being faced by the refugees who came from West Pakistan in 1947 such as State Subject Status should be settled once for all. The Working Group expressed concern and need for further relief and rehabilitation of refugees of 1965 and 1971 wars who have not been fully rehabilitated living mostly in Jammu Division.

13. The Working Group touched upon balanced regional development, economic development of certain communities and the need for more power projects.

14. The Group also suggested the following steps to stop migration:

(i) Centre and State Government to consider application of internationally accepted policy in consultation with experts.

(ii) To start unconditional dialogue process with militant groups for finding sustainable solutions to the problems of militancy.

(iii) To examine the role of media in generating an image of the people of the State so as to lessen the indignity and suspicion that the people face outside the State.

Composition of Working Group-I

1. Shri Mohammad Hamid Ansari, Chairperson, National Commission of Minorities — Chairman
2. Shri Ali Mohammad Sagar, MLA (Ex-Minister J&K) National Conference — Member
3. Shri Molvi Iftikhar Ansari, Ex-Minister, J&K People's Democratic Party — Member
4. Peerzada Mohammad Sayeed, Minister for School Education, IT, Science & Technology, Haj & Auqaf President, J&K PCC — Member
5. Prof. Chaman Lal Gupta, Ex-MoS, Govt. of India, BJP — Member
6. Shri Omkar Nath Trisal, Advocate, CPI (M) — Member
7. Shri Hakeem Mohd. Yaseen, Minister of Transport, J&K, PDF — Member

8.	Shri Yashpal Kundal, MLA, Panthers Party	Member
9.	Shri Tsering Dorjee, Chairman, LAHDC, Leh	Member
10.	Shri Asgar Hussain Karbalai, Chairman, LAHDC, Kargil	Member
11.	Dr. Agni Shekhar, Panun Kashmir Movement	Member
12.	Shri Taj Mohi-ud-Din, Minister for Consumer Affairs, J&K	Member
13.	Shri Shabir Khan, Vice Chairman, State Pahari Board	Member
14.	Sardar T.S. Wazir, President, Shiromani Gurudwara Prabandhak Committee, Jammu	Member
15.	Shri R.S. Chib, Ex-Minister, J&K	Member
16.	Shri Gh. Nabi Khayal, Journalist	Member
17.	Master Tassaduq Hussain, Ex-MLC	Member
18.	Sheikh Abdul Rehman, Ex-MP & Ex-MLA	Member

SUMMARY OF RECOMMENDATIONS OF WORKING GROUP-II ON STRENGTHENING RELATIONS ACROSS THE LINE OF CONTROL (LOC): JAMMU AND KASHMIR

The Working Group submitted the report in January 2007 on the following agenda taken up for deliberation:

1. 'Measures to simplify procedures to facilitate travel across the Line of Control'.
2. 'Measures to increase goods traffic'.
3. 'Measures to expand people-to-people contacts, including promotion of pilgrimage and group tourism'.
4. 'Measures to open up new routes such as Kargil-Skardu'.

Methodology and Guiding Principles Adopted by the Group

The Group recognized and was motivated in their efforts on the importance of people-to-people contacts and free travel facilities for the purpose of persons residing on two sides of the LoC thereby resulting in promotion of friendly and beneficial cooperation and the strengthening of peace in the region. The Working Group was guided by the belief that the opening of routes for trade and commerce would help in not only improving the economic conditions on both sides but also it would be an important step towards normalization of the situation.

The Working Group has made the following important recommendations on the issues concerned in pursuance to agenda:

1 (a) Expand Eligibility for Travel and Visit Across LoC

The Working Group recommended that the category of persons eligible to travel across the LoC from among divided families be not restricted to relations only, but to expand and cover persons who want to visit places of religious interest, tourism, and those requiring medical aid. However, tourism was to be allowed in groups only.

1 (b) Simplify and Speed up Procedure for Travel Across the LoC

All residents of Jammu and Kashmir may be required to obtain Permanent Resident Certificate (PRC). The PRC should be taken as the basic document on the strength of which travel permit is issued and Security clearance completed within a maximum period of two months. Traders should be issued multiple entry/exit permit valid for a minimum period of one year. Priority for clearance should be given for Emergency cases like serious illness, death or marriage in the family. Applications for travel permit should be accepted and disposed of in more number of places beginning Anantnag, Baramullah, Poonch and Rajouri besides Jammu and Srinagar and relations permitted to go upto the border.

2. Measures to Increase Trade and Commerce between Two Sides

The Working Group recommended the Provision of a Joint Consultative Machinery of officials and representative of trade and commerce from both sides to resolve difficulties. The eligible list of items for export should include handicrafts, fruits and other items manufactured by SSIs in J&K, and similar list finalized for imports from the other side. The hazardous goods should be allowed to be transported in a special vehicle and authorized to travel across LoC direct to the destination or earmarked transport depots at the LoC. Provision should be made for effective and quick mechanism for unloading, checking, etc. Concerted efforts may be taken to improve infrastructure support for goods and passengers traffic. The Working Group also suggested reciprocal waiver of customs duties for 3 years, promotion of trade fairs, Common Free Trade Area and reasonable levy of state Tax on goods traded.

3. Measures to expand people-to-people contact, including promotion of pilgrimage and group tourism

The Working Group recommendations suggested Exchange visits between students and faculty members of the Universities on two sides of the LoC; Organized visit of school students; Short-term courses in certain specific subjects; Consideration for the grant of admission to PoK students in J&K Universities; Exchange visits of groups of journalists, academicians, lawyers, etc. Cultural trips in the fields of music, dance, etc. After due consideration of security aspects the landline and mobile communication should also be permitted.

4. Measures to Open up New Routes Across the LoC

The Working Group recommended opening up of additional routes viz., Kargil-Skardu; Jammu-Sialkote; Turtuk-Khapulu, Chhamb-Jorian to Mirpur; Gurez-Astroor-Gilgit; Titwal-Chilhan; Jhangar (Nowshera)-Mirpur and Kotli. Additional contact points need to be established and in the Ladakh region Hundurman and any suitable point in Turtuk-Khapulu route was suggested. The Initiative to open new routes, should be taken unilaterally, integrated check post set-up to facilitate trade. Persons holding passport and visas should be allowed to travel on Jammu- Sialkote route for which appropriate mechanism are to be created.

5. Additional Recommendations on other Issues

The Working Group recommended constitution of a Joint Consultative Group of 10 numbers of the legislatures on both sides and to exchange views periodically on social, economic, cultural and trade-related matters of mutual interest. The Working Group recommended consultation, as necessary, for the provision of disaster and relief measures, exchange visits of groups of professionals for horticulture, tourism promotion etc., programme for the removal of land mines for better utilization of agricultural and grazing lands, consideration for opening of Leh-Xinjiang route across LOC with China and Leh to be promoted as an alternative for the Kailash-Mansarovar yatra.

The Working Group also noted that it understands and appreciates that in implementing its recommendations the Central and the State Governments will have to take into account the prevailing security situation.

Composition of Working Group-II

1.	Shri M. Rasgotra	Chairman
2.	Choudhary Mian Aitaf, MLA (Ex. Minister), National Conference	Member
3.	Shri Tariq Hamid Qara, Minister for Finance, J&K, People's Democratic Party	Member
4.	Shri Abdul Gani Vakil, MLC, Senior Vice-President, J&K PCC Congress	Member
5.	Shri Ashok Khajuria, State President, Bhartiya Janta Party, J&K	Member
6.	Shri Ghulam Nabi Malik, CPI(M)	Member
7.	Prof. Bhim Singh, MLC, President, Panthers Party	Member
8.	Shri Haji Nissar Ali, Minister for Social Welfare, J&K	Member
9.	Prof Ashok Aima	Member
10.	Qazi Mehboob Illahi	Member
11.	Shri Mohd. Yousuf Bhat, CPI	Member

SUMMARY OF REPORT OF WORKING GROUP-III ON ECONOMIC DEVELOPMENT OF JAMMU & KASHMIR

The Working Group on Economic Development was chaired by Dr. C. Rangrajan and comprised of 11 other Members drawn from across the political spectrum. The composition of the Working Group is given in the annexure. The Working Group held three meetings and identified sectors which will have the maximum impact on growth and employment generation. The specific focus is on inclusive growth and balanced economic development of three regions. The Working Group was of the view that the development challenges of J&K can be identified by the following six objectives:

(i) Reconstruction and maintenance of existing physical assets.
(ii) Investment in physical infrastructure particularly power and roads.
(iii) Investment in social infrastructure.
(iv) Creating a conducive climate for private investment.
(v) Balanced regional development.
(vi) Comprehensive fiscal adjustment.

2. The Working Group accordingly, came up with a number of recommendations for achievement of the above mentioned objectives. To achieve the first objective of Reconstruction and maintenance of existing physical assets, the working group has felt that what needs to be done is to have three sub-plans within the state plan. The first sub-plan will focus on completing ongoing projects, the second sub-plan to bring all existing assets to working order, and the third sub-plan focused on capacity creation in the infrastructure sector.

3. To achieve the second objective of investment in physical infrastructure particularly power and roads, the working group has made recommendations relating to augmenting capacity and efficient management of power sector, improvement in road connectivity including rural roads to facilitate movement of goods to major markets. The recommendations relate to solving the power shortage problem in the short-term (transfer of Dulhasti HEP) and in the long-term (transfer of Bursar HEP), strengthening of infrastructure and power sector reforms. In power sector, the working group has recommended transfer of 390 MW Dulhasti HEP to State Government (financial implication Rs. 4933 crore) and transfer of 1020 MW Bursar Project for execution by the State Government instead of NHPC. The group has also made recommendations relating to enhancement of states share of free power in Central Projects, simplification of procedures for various clearances, acquiring stake in thermal projects and exploiting Geo-Thermal and Micro-Hydel Projects to reduce dependency on Hydel Power. The group has also made recommendations relating

to power sector reforms such as functioning of State Electricity Regulatory Commission reducing transmission and distribution losses and rationalization of tariff, establishing distribution regions/circles, improving Accelerated Power Development and Reform Programme fund utilization.

4. The group made the following recommendations regarding development of Communications, Rural Roads and Telecom. The recommendations include according high priority to four-laning and repairing National Highways, early completion of the railway project on extending the railhead from Udhampur to Katra and from there to Kashmir Valley early, improving rural connectivity and redress the imbalance in rural road density across districts, revising unit cost norms of road construction per km length, specifically taking into account the hilly terrain of J&K, including the cost of land acquisition as a part of the project in the road construction schemes of the Government of India, land acquisition law to be modified such that the owners get a fair value for their land, implementing reduction in stamp duty to encourage sellers and buyers to indicate the correct value of transactions, revising the subsidy policy of Government of India for rural telephony, reducing entry tax on telecom equipment and sorting out inter-connection impasse by Department of Telecommunication.

5. To achieve the third objective of investment in social infrastructure, the working group made the following recommendations relating to Health, Employment and Education. The recommendations pertaining to health are implementation of the National Rural Health Mission without further delay by completing all preparatory work, setting up Mobile Diagnostic and Primary Clinics at the block level, setting up advanced mobile units with emergency care facilities for dealing with injuries from IED blasts, grenade explosions and other such militancy-related emergencies, creating a telemedicine network, designing and implementing an appropriate health insurance scheme for BPL families.

6. The recommendations relating to Employment and Education are upgrading existing vocational and technical training institutions and making them fully functional by providing them with building, equipment and trained faculty, expeditiously establishing 13 new ITIs, creating an incentive structure for encouraging the private sector to open IT training institutes in the

state, delivering the adult literacy programme through "literacy volunteers" drawn from the ranks of the educated unemployed in the state and appointing agricultural graduates in all the 2700 Panchayats in the state for agricultural extension effort.

7. To achieve the fourth objective of creating conducive climate for private investment, the working group made recommendations relating to industrial development and commerce. The recommendations include creation of Special Investment Zone with world class infrastructure, captive power generation and distribution, high quality services and utilities, dedicated infrastructure facilities, fast track and single window clearances, and liberalized labour laws, leveraging the special concession package announced by the Centre to attract investments to the state, Special package for revival of sick industrial units both in the public sector and the private sector, constructing and air cargo complex and a container depot (which could possibly be located in Jammu), revitalizing handicraft sector through targeted investment and skill upgradation of artisans, exploring the potential for trade across the border and scope for co-operation on subjects of common interest, upgradation and rehabilitation of industrial estates and creation of an Asset Reconstruction Company. The financial implication of the major proposals amount to Rs. 475 crore.

8. To achieve the fifth objective of balanced regional development of three regions of the State, the Working Group felt that the three regions of the state have different comparative advantages and the development strategies for each region has to be consistent with these the advantages. The Group recommended that resources should be deployed in such a way that no region feels aggrieved or left behind. The recommendations include adopting the participative and inclusive process inherent in the State Finance Commission to give fillip to balanced regional development, making District Development Boards more inclusive by including elected representatives and prominent person from among the backward communities, carrying out functions like minor roads, lanes, drainage, local level water supply schemes, primary education, rural health through the local bodies, involving public representatives in the process of allocations from the State Plan, examining establishment of a separate Directorate for Gujjars and Bakkerwals.

9. To achieve the sixth objective of comprehensive fiscal adjustment, the Working Group has recommended re-structuring public finances of the state to generate resources for development by pruning the unproductive expenditure, and redesigning the flow of central assistance to finance development expenditure rather than filling non-plan revenue gap.

10. The Working Group also made recommendations relating to development of other sectors of economy. The recommendations relating to Tourism are preparation of tourism vision document and a master plan based on sustainable tourism, exploiting state's rich cultural heritage and developing modern allurements like shopping, food courts, multiplexes, music festivals and sports events. The recommendations relating to Agriculture, Irrigation and Forest are diversifying production and adopting market-oriented products, encouraging new avenues like floriculture, aromatic and medicinal plant cultivation, completing on going irrigation projects, tapping the main rivers per minor irrigation projects, reforestation of degraded forests and using fallow land for fast growing trees. The Group also made recommendations relating to Horticulture such as market development schemes for fruit and fruit processing, better sorting, grading, packaging, and cold chain storage facilities to improve price realization.

11. Apart from the above, The Working Group also made recommendations on the other issues such as restoring properties occupied by the Army and Central paramilitary forces to owners or paying compensation, giving attention to internal roads in areas of tourist importance like Patnitop, Katra, Sonmarg, Yusmarg, etc. and expediting the work on Mughal Road, development of lakes and ponds for fisheries development by Panchayats, exploring an alternate route through Ladakh for the Kailash-Mansarovar pilgrimage, giving a special package for better drinking water facilities in *Kandi* areas, exploring possibility of relocation of business activities in Srinagar to other places in view of the congestion, conducting survey of mineral resources and relaxing eligibility norms for police and para military forces for aspirants from the state.

12. Finally, the Working Group recommended setting of a small monitoring authority for implementation of these recommendations. The financial implication of the major

recommendations of the Working Group amount to Rs. 7947 crore.

Composition of Working Group-III

1.	**Dr. C. Rangarajan, Chairman, Prime Minister's Economic Advisory Council**	**Chairman**
2.	Shri Omar Abdullah, M.P., President, National Conference	Member
3.	Shri Muzaffar Hussain Baig, MLA, Ex. Deputy Chief Minister, Peoples Democratic Party (PDP)	Member
4.	Shri Gulchain Singh Charak, MLC, Minister for Public Works Deptt., J&K Congress (INC) (Representing Dogra Sadar Sabha)	Member
5.	Shri Nirmal Singh, Ex. State President BJP, J&K	Member
6.	Shri Shyam Prasad Kesar, Member, State Committee CPI (M)	Member
7.	Shri Ghulam Mohd. Sheikh, CPI	Member
8.	Shri Balwant Singh Mankotia, MLA, Panthers Party	Member
9.	Shri Nawang Rigzin Jora, Minister for Power, Representing Ladakh	Member
10.	Thakur Puran Singh, MLA, Ex MoS(J), Representing Paharis	Member
11.	Shri Nizam-ud-din Khatana, Representing Gujjars & Bakkerwals	Member
12.	Shri Mohd. Sharief Niaz, Ex. Minister	Member

SUMMARY OF RECOMMENDATIONS OF WORKING GROUP-IV ON ENSURING GOOD GOVERNANCE IN J&K

The Working Group on ensuring good governance submitted the report in March 2007.

The Working Group held its meetings on 8.8.2006, 20.11.2006 and 10.02.2007 at Srinagar, Jammu.

(1) The Working Group recommended the appointment of the Chief Information Commissioner of the State, the

Appellate Authorities and the Departmental Information Officers for effective implementation of the Right to Information Act.

(2) The Working Group recommended the introduction of e-governance in the State for the purposes of computerization of the functioning of government departments and public services such as Land records; Sub-Registrars Offices; Treasury operations; Electoral rolls; issue of Certificates, etc. The capacity of Information Technology department must be built to serve such purpose. The Working Group laid stress on introducing Information Kiosks at key service delivery institutions and to introduce Single Window Payment system for utilities like water, electricity, telephone, etc. Websites and on-line redressal methods should be incorporated in all government departments.

(3) The Working Group recommended Review of laws and Simplification of rules and procedures in departments which have a large public interface, e.g. Land Acquisition Act, land use changes, etc. Levy of fees should be more for commercial and industrial use in land use; digitized photographs of buyers and sellers be made compulsory; making Stakeholder benefits a reality in project rehabilitation are among the other suggestions of the Working Group. The Working Group suggested measures to promote entrepreneurship; formatting and standardization of forms and certificates; adoption of Single File system to bring about transparency in Government.

(4) The Working Group recommended independent Committees to assess performance of Police, Municipalities and Revenue departments once in 3 years.

(5) The Working Group recommended a 3 year tenure for officials, bringing down the weightage to interview in recruitments of teachers, review of qualifications in tune with higher specialization, fixing of responsibility and accountability, merit based promotions, etc. The Working Group recommended dual signing of Government orders to eliminate fake orders.

(6) The Working Group prescribed formulation of Citizens Charter and their review of implementation besides a system of public hearings at the District and State levels for increasing government visibility and people participation.

(7) The Working Group also recommended self-assessment of department by presenting a Report card by the Ministers and performance review of outcomes and expenditure, public perception surveys, institutional strengthening, public-private partnership, social audit and fiscal reform, etc. The budget cycle should be 2 years and a roll over facility followed for the unspent balances at the end of 1 year.

(8) The Working Group recommended implementation of Panchayati Raj Act in letter and spirit giving them appropriate devolution as per advice of State Finance Commission. J&K Government should examine extending of the 73rd Amendment. Capacity building of functionaries, mobilization of community leadership as partners and effective transfer of funds and functions are among the important suggestions in this regard.

(9) Programme implementation should be made more transparent by the use of Information Technology, e.g. tendering process could be made on-line. For proper monitoring the Working Group suggested elimination of overlapping jurisdictions, measurement of outcomes, and timely receipt of funds by the departments, etc.

(10) The Working Group considered measures to institute Zero-tolerance of Human Rights violations. For this purpose the Working Group recommended strengthening of the State Human Rights Commission (SHRC) for speedy redressal of complaints. There should also be comprehensive training for law enforcement Agencies on the subject. Political and civil society members should be part of a High Powered Committee to enforce Human rights, ensure accountability and implementation of laws. The State Government should act on all the

recommendations of SHRC and there should be a speaking order for non-acceptance on any account.

(11) The Working Group recommended that there should be sensitization of the RTI Act, biannual review of the application filed to bring about transparency in Government.

(12) The Working Group recommended Security Forces to adopt a Citizen Friendly approach; Safeguarding the life and property of innocents; Offering Special protection to minority residential areas; Activating local bodies to have a system of community watch on elements who pose a threat and isolating them besides setting up of a Minority Commission to look into their problems.

(13) A High Level State Committee reporting to the Highest authority should oversee the implementation of the recommendations was suggested by the Working Group and also the setting up of an Special Purpose Vehicle for their delivery.

Composition of Working Group-IV

1.	**Shri N.C. Saxena**	**Chairman**
2.	Shri Ajay Sadhotra, MLA, (Ex-Minister, J&K), National Conference	Member
3.	Sardar Rangil Singh, Ex-Minister, J&K People's Democratic Party	Member
4.	Pandit Mangat Ram Sharma, Minister for Health & Labour, J&K Congress (INC)	Member
5.	Prof. Hari Om, State Vice-President, BJP, J&K	Member
6.	Shri Abdul Gani Hafiz, State Committee, CPI(M)	Member
7.	Prof. K.S. Jamwal, Panthers Party	Member
8.	Shri P. Namgyal, MLC (Ex-Minister, GoI)	Member
9.	Shri Amar Nath, Kashmiri Pandit Samiti, Vaishnavi	Member
10.	Mohd. Shafi Pandit, Chairman, State Public Service Commission	Member
11.	Shri Nizam-ud-Din, MLC, J&K	Member
12.	Shri Bashir Ahmad Dar, Ex-Secretary, Board of School Education	Member

JAMMU AND KASHMIR
CONFIDENCE BUILDING MEASURES ACROSS SEGMENTS OF SOCIETY IN THE STATE
Report of the Working Group
January 2007

CONTENTS

THE WORKING GROUP

	Name	Designation	Role
1.	Shri Mohammad Hamid Ansari	Chairperson, National Commission for Minorities.	Chairman
2.	Shri Ali Mohammad Sagar	ML A, (Ex-Minister, J&K) National Conference	Member
3.	Shri Molvi Iftikhar Ansari	Ex-Minister, J&K People's Democratic Party	Member
4.	Peerzada Mohammad Sayeed	Minister for School Education, IT, Science & Technology, Haj & Auqaf President, J&K PCC	Member
5.	Prof. Chaman Lal Gupta	Ex-MoS, Govt. of India, BJP	Member
6.	Shri Omkar Nath Trisal	Advocate, CPI(M)	Member
7.	Shri Hakeem Mohammad Yaseen	Minister for Transport J&K, PDF	Member
8.	Shri Yashpal Kundal	MLA, Panthers Party	Member
9.	Shri Tsering, Dorjee	Chairman, Ladakh Autonomous Hill Development Council, Leh	Member
10.	Shri Asgar Hussain Karbalai	Chairman, Ladakh Autonomous Hill Development Council, Kargil	Member
11.	Dr. Agni Shekhar	Panun Kashmir Movement	Member

12.	Shri Taj Mohi-ud-Din	Minister for Consumer Affairs, J&K	Member
13.	Shri Shabir Khan	Vice-Chairman, State Pahari Board	Member
14.	Sardar T.S. Wazir	President, Shiromani Gurudwara Prabandhak Committee, Jammu	Member
15.	Shri R.S. Chib	Ex-Minister, J&K	Member
16.	Shri Gh. Nabi Khayal	Journalist	Member
17.	Master Tassaduq Hussain	Ex-MLC	Member
18.	Sheikh Abdul Rehman	Ex-MP & Ex-MLA	Member

The Working Group was constituted after an announcement was made by Dr. Manmohan Singh, the Hon'ble Prime Minister of India in the Round Table Conference held at Srinagar on 24th and 25th May, 2006.

The Group had the following Agenda before it:

1. Measures to improve the condition of people affected by militancy.
2. Schemes to rehabilitate all orphans and widows affected by militancy.
3. Issues relating to the relaxation of conditions for persons who have foresworn militancy.
4. An effective rehabilitation policy, including employment, for Kashmiri Pandit migrants.
5. An approach considering issues relating to return of Kashmiri youth from areas controlled by Pakistan.
6. Measures to protect and preserve the unique cultural and religious heritage of the State.

Methodology Adopted by the Group

The Working Group in the 1st meeting decided that there will be a consensus approach to the issues placed before the Group and that the Group members should try to find a solution in public interest and above party considerations. Accordingly, the remarks and comments from each member were obtained on different issues. Thereafter, the suggestions made by the members were classified with reference to the agenda items and placed before the Group for further considerations.

The Chairman had extensive discussions with senior representatives of National and State political parties as also journalists and other opinion makers. After consolidating all view points and identifying the items of convergence, a set of draft recommendations were prepared and placed before the Working Group for consideration and final approval. The recommendations were finalized after thorough discussions and are now presented in the form of this report.

The Chairman also made field visits to migrant camps to examine the situation on ground for an appropriate consideration and appreciation of the Working Group in its deliberations.

Some other issues were raised by the members which are not strictly within the purview of the Working Group but recommendations about them have also been made. It was decided that some of the issues would be referred to other Working Groups for detailed examination and their recommendations.

Meetings

The Working Group held three meetings on the dates and places mentioned against each:

I. 27.07.2006 Srinagar. Sher-i-Kashmir International Convention Complex
II. 15. 09.2006 Jammu. Govt. Guest House, Canal Road.
III. 24.11.2006 Jammu. Govt. Guest House, Canal Road.

Background of the Issues

Issue No. 1—Measures to improve the conditions of people affected by militancy

The State has been facing the problem of militancy from 1989 onwards which has continued to date. During this period a large number of militants crafted over from across the border who included foreign Nationals mainly from Pakistan and Afghanistan, youth who have gone from the State and received extensive training in the use of arms and ammunition across the line of control and certain other persons who provided local assistance to the militants. The militants and their acts caused extensive damage to the infrastructure in the State and damaged a large number of public and private buildings, Government schools and colleges, hospitals, bridges, besides causing damage to a large number of religious and historically important monuments.

A large number of persons belonging to all communities were killed by being deliberately targeted or in cross fire and the situation lead to the migration of more than 90% of Kashmiri Pandits from Kashmir valley as also some Kashmiri Muslims and Sikhs.

Logically the entire population of Jammu and Kashmir can be termed to have been affected by militancy in one way or the other, but *for the purpose of this issue the Working Group has considered only those who have been directly affected*. The Working Group concerns itself only with the rehabilitation and improvement of conditions of the militancy victims and did not go deeper into the causes or the genesis of the militancy in the State.

Issue No. 2—Schemes to rehabilitate all orphans and widows affected by militancy

As a direct result of militancy a large number of persons were killed due to various reasons based on community and political affiliations and also such persons termed as being Government informers or mixed up with security force. Another important category is that of the security persons both from within the State and outside who fell victim in directly fighting the militants or sometimes being targeted specifically. This has resulted into a number of widows and orphans requiring rehabilitation measures in the State. The number of such persons is, however, not exactly available and the Working Group has recommended that full information should be collected.

Issue No. 3—Issues relating to relaxation of conditions for persons who have forsworn militancy

During the years of militancy a large number of persons are reported to have come across the line of control who were of Nationalities other than Indian. But a large number of local youth also got involved in militancy by getting training across the border or remaining within the State. As a result of peace process some of them have now forsworn militancy and surrendered before the political leaders or the security forces. The Working Group has examined their special problems of rehabilitation, and their joining the mainstream.

Issue No. 4—An effective rehabilitation policy, including employment for Kashmiri Pandit migrants.

With the start of militancy in 1989 there was a large scale migration of Kashmiri Pandits from Kashmir valley. This process had started towards the end of 1989 and continued for the next one and half years in full force. Thereafter, the migration continued but the number was not as large as initially. It is estimated that a total number of more than three lakh persons migrated, who now are mainly based in Jammu, Kathua and Udhampur districts in Jammu division and New Delhi outside the State. Some of the families migrated to other places also but their number is comparatively not very large.

While migrating, the Kashmiri Pandits carried their belongings wherewithal and also some moveable assets. The houses and buildings remained unattended, which were locked at the lime of migration.

After 1995-96 a trend started when the property in Kashmir valley was disposed off initially, which can be termed as a distress sale, but in later years a fair price was obtained. As the transactions took place individually, figures in detail are not available, but most of the transactions are legally valid.

The migrants started getting relief, which included cash, and free rations for which different types of scales were sanctioned from time to time. At present the migrants who are living in camps in Jammu are getting the cash assistance and other facilities as follows:

Cash Relief	Rs. 750 per head (Maximum ceiling Rs. 3000 per family)
Ration	9 Kg rice per person per month
	2 Kg Atta per person per month
	1 Kg sugar per ration ticket/card

The total number of families registered as migrants by the office of the Relief Commissioner, Jammu amounts to 34,131 that include 5,889 living in camps in Jammu and 28,242 as non-camp migrants. Of these 30,206 families are Hindus, 2,170 are Muslims, 1,749 are Sikhs and 06 families are registered as others.

Whereas it cannot be denied that Kashmiri Pandits have a right to go back to their places but rehabilitation, avenues of employment and other facilities are required which have been examined by the Working Group.

It is estimated that the total population of Kashmiri Pandits in the Valley before migration was about 3.50 lakh. While the majority migrated, about 18,000 persons still remained as in 1997.

Issue No. 5—An approach considering issues relating to return of Kashmiri Youth from areas controlled by Pakistan

It has been expressed in a number of quarters that Kashmiri youth who went across the line of control for getting training and creating acts of militancy came back during the last many years, but a number of them are still remaining in areas under the control of Pakistan. Some visitors who went across have reported that many of the youth who were earlier disillusioned are now keen to return back to their native places and lead a normal life. Although this issue has international dimensions, the Working Group has examined whether a peaceful return and rehabilitation would be feasible.

The number of such persons is not known but their existence is substantiated by various reports.

Issue No. 6—Measures to protect and preserve the unique cultural and religious heritage of the State

Jammu and Kashmir presents the unique picture of a land where unity transcends the innumerable varieties and diversities of race, religions, language: and culture.

The grand past of the state is exemplified by the presence of several temples, shrines. Gompas of Ladakh, the Buddhist Viharas, for example, the remains of prehistoric settlements in Burzahom in Kashmir: the architectural ruins of Avantipura temples on the right bank of the Jhelum; the ruins of Martand temple, dedicated to the sun-god, situated four miles from Anantnag; and the temple ruins of Pandrethan, Paraspur and that of Pari Mahal. The Makdum Shah Shrine, the Chrar-I-Sharief Shrine and the Shah Hamdan mosque are one of the richest illustrations of the all-pervasive religious and architectural sense in the State. Besides, the spread of Budhism in the North-Western part of the subcontinent in evident from the 3rd great Buddhist council that was held in Kashmir during the time of King Kanishka.

Kashmir hits inherited a rich cultural and literary legacy, with one of its greatest pieces as *Raj Tarangini* or 'the River of Kings' by Kalhana and *Tarikh-Wagai-Kashmiri by* Mulla Ahmad Kashmiri. The Kashmiris speak 13 different languages and dialects, the chief amongst these being Dogri, Kashmiri. Pahari, Ladakhi and Dardi.

The rich music tradition of Kashmir includes classical and folk music, as well as the vocal and instrumental. Kashmiri classical music is usually called *'Soofiana Kalam'*, meaning 'mystical poetry', the wording being usually in Persian. The Ladakhis are mainly Buddhists; their monastries play an important part in their cultural and artistic activities. Then there is Pahari music of the plains. There are unique folk-dances of Kud, Bhaderwah, etc. *'Chakri'* a kind of folk-music and folk-dance combined together is the most popular and most widely played-music of the people of Kashmir.

Besides, the exquisite workmanship of the Kashimiri shawl and the elegant and graceful miniature art in the form of Basohli paintings representing the Pahari School of paintings render even more colour and richness to the culture and art of the State.

The State boasts of elaborate wood-carving in walnut, the art of Paper-machic, the silver-ware, the Kashmiri carpets and rugs; the silk and silk embroidery, that are world famous.

Needless to say, the great forest wealth, abundance of limestone and presence of gold and precious stones in the State simply add to its invaluable possessions.

With such a rich cultural and religious heritage, there is all the more necessity for its preservation as one of the best illustrations of composite culture in the world.

Recommendations of the Working Group

Issue No. 1. "Measures to improve the conditions of people affected by militancy"

The necessity of curbing human rights violations was stressed by most members of the Working Group. Emphasis was placed on Prime Minister's assurance of 'zero tolerance' for human rights violations, as on India's international commitments and international image. It was considered imperative to develop a mechanism in which responsibility for specific human rights violations can be fixed and derelict officials identified and proceeded against.

In this context, the need for strengthening the Human Rights Commission of J&K, and revitalizing it's functioning, was repeatedly stressed.

Recommendation No. 1.1

Human rights awareness should be inculcated in all civil and military government functionaries, and in the public. The State Human Rights Commission should be strengthened, along the lines of the NHRC, to enable it to ensure that innocent persons do not become victims of counter-insurgency measures. The following specific measures be taken:

(a) Investigative machinery, independent of the regular police, be provided to the Commission.
(b) Implementation of the recommendations of the Commission be made obligatory. In case a recommendation cannot be accepted, a Speaking Order should indicate reasons thereof.
(c) An Empowered Committee be appointed to report regularly on the action taken by the Government on the recommendations of the Commission.

Recommendation No. 1.2

While all victims of militancy stand in need of relief and assistance, the actual administration of relief/provision of jobs may be undertaken in the following order:

(a) Next of kin of persons—political workers/personalities, Government functionaries, police and para-military personnel—who were specifically targeted by the militants.
(b) Next of kin of those who were not involved in militancy and who lost their lives due to being caught in crossfire in counter-insurgency operation.
(c) Innocent persons who suffered injury due to acts of militancy.
(d) Persons rendered invalid due to mine blasts.

(e) Persons having suffered loss of livelihood due to agricultural land being taken over by the security forces/army, or in border fencing and laying of land mines.

(f) Criteria for the above-mentioned categories are prescribed in SRO-43. However, limitations on the number of available government jobs necessitate prescribing of priorities. The following norms should be considered for this purpose:
   - For families having no source of income, the beneficiary should be a direct dependent and an immediate family member of the deceased;
   - The beneficiary should be totally unemployed, Self-employed persons should not be considered eligible for this purpose;
   - In those cases, where employment cannot be provided as per the above criteria, a one time compensation of Rs. 5 lakhs be given and the case closed; and
   - Government may provide for 30% reservation for SRO-43 cases for vacancies in Class IV, Junior Assistant or equivalent. Wherever a technical qualification is necessary, the beneficiary should possess it.

(g) Persons injured due to militant action should be provided full rehabilitation package for treatment. They should also be assisted in rehabilitating the business/economic activity they were engaged in prior to getting injured.

(h) Relief/compensation as per established, precedents, mid-procedures, should be extended to victims of the Kargil War, including persons rendered invalid due to cross-firing and mine blast; and those who suffered loss of crops due to army taking over agricultural land or border fencing and land mines.

Recommendation No. 1.3

Certain laws made operational during the period of militancy (e.g. Armed Forces Special Powers Act, Disturbed Areas Act) impinge on fundamental rights of citizens and adversely affect the public. They should be reviewed and revoked. Law and order matters should be dealt with, to the maximum extent possible, through normal laws.

Issue No. 2—"Schemes to rehabilitate all orphans and widows affected by militancy"

Recommendation No. 2.1

Complete data of widows and orphans; affected by militancy, should be collected for making effective schemes for their rehabilitation. The data should also include wives and children of persons missing or presumed dead. Setting up of a special cell for their identification and rehabilitation should be considered. This cell will complete the collection of this data within a period of three months.

Recommendation No. 2.2

(i) The widows and orphans who are covered under the provisions of SRO-43 should be provided relief as in the case of victims of militancy under issue No. 1.

(ii) Relief to certain widows, which presently amounts to only Rs. 500 is inadequate and should be raised to a realistic level.

(iii) A suitable scheme of providing scholarship to orphans who are of school going age may be prepared. The scholarship should cover to the cost of education as also the financial requirements of the orphan.

(iv) The State Government, as a matter of policy, may consider extending the scheme of scholarship mentioned above to orphans of killed militants whose family has no other source of income. This would only be a good will gesture.

Recommendation No. 2.3

Administrative delays/malpractices in reaching relief to the concerned should be curbed. All Additional Deputy Commissioners or any other officer designated at the district level be empowered to ensure that relief measures are monitored regularly. Any person entitled to relief should be able to approach this officer.

Issue No. 3.—"Issues relating to relaxation of conditions for persons who have forsworn militancy"

Recommendation No. 3.1

The following may be considered by the State Government:

(i) A definite policy/package for rehabilitation is required so as to discourage any reverting back to militancy.

(ii) Persons who have forsworn militancy and wish to join the mainstream should be treated with dignity and a conscious effort made to prevent undignified treatment being accorded to them.

(iii) Security Forces should be instructed to keep a check on fake encounters and fake recovery of arms.

(iv) Cases of all persons in jail should be reviewed, and general amnesty given to those under-trial for minor offences or who are innocent.

Issue No. 4.—An effective rehabilitation policy, including employment for Kashmiri Pandit migrants"

Recommendation No. 4.1

(i) The rights of Kashmiri Pandit migrants to return to the places of their original residence should be recognized without any ambiguity and made a part of the State policy.

(ii) A comprehensive package should be prepared for rehabilitation of migrants in consultation with their representatives. Apart from Kashmiri migrants, militancy-affected migrants within Jammu region, namely in Rajouri, Poonch and Doda also need to be rehabilitated. However, collection of complete data on these migrants is a pre-requisite for devising of any rehabilitation package.

Recommendation No. 4.2

The following specific notions may be considered:

(A) Job Opportunities

(i) Jobs to the Kashmiri Pandit migrants may be provided against retirement vacancies for which certain organizations can be earmarked including Police, and offices of HODs and Civil Secretariat which have in built security arrangements.

(ii) The job opportunities in the State being limited, the GoI may, in their offices located in J&K, accommodate SRO-43 candidates of the State belonging to Kashmiri Pandits.

(iii) Relief in SRO-43 cases should be increased from Rs. 1 lakh to Rs. 5 lakh as one-time compensation so as to enable the jobless migrants to engage in self-employment. [As also recommended at No. 1.2 (f)].

(B) Migrants' Properties

(a) An inventory of properties, including orchards of migrants, should be generated and examined for illegal occupation, if any, and full compensation of the properties be given once regaining of ownership is ruled out and the property is appropriately valued for.

(b) The property of migrants in Kashmir valley, which is presently under the occupation of security forces, should make the owners eligible to receive adequate rent or compensation for the use of such properties including lands and buildings.

(C) Other Matters

(a) All Camp migrants should be provided living conditions and accommodation in accordance with the package already approved by the Hon'ble Prime Minister. A number of residential buildings on that account are being constructed at Jammu. The same pattern should be followed for all camp migrants.

(b) While the State Government may take all the measures as recommended for rehabilitation and improving living conditions of migrants it must not ignore the fact that a small number continue to live in Kashmir Valley and did not leave their places of residence. It would be necessary to ensure that they may continue to live in peace and have ample opportunities of employment and education. Special problems faced by them regarding safeguard of their property or other assets should be looked into.

(c) Setting up of Minorities Commission for Jammu & Kashmir should be considered.

Recommendation No. 4.3

The following may be considered for arriving at a long/medium-term policy:

(i) A dialogue should be started with the representatives of Kashmiri Pandit migrants for a detailed scheme regarding the future of rehabilitation aid and assistance to camp migrants and those who are receiving cash/kind relief/grants.

(ii) A dialogue should also be started with representatives of migrant community for designing a package for return and rehabilitation of migrants including identification of such categories who will return in the next three years.

Issue No. 5.—An approach considering issues relating to return of Kashmiri youth from areas controlled by Pakistan"

The youth who have gone into militancy have to be considered under the following categories:

(a) Youth who joined militancy for misguided ideological reasons;

(b) Youth who have gone for monetary considerations; and

(c) Youth who have been forced into militancy.

A careful assessment of their number is necessary in the first instance for taking a view on a long-term basis.

Recommendation No. 5.1

A policy on this question be made keeping in view the following:

(a) It be within the framework of the Confidence-Building Measures enunciated by Hon'ble Prime Minister in the Round Table Conference.
(b) An effective method be adopted for proper verification of the identity of the persons who returns from the other side.
(c) Once a person is allowed to return, he should be extended the benefit of recommendation 3.1(i) and 3.1 (ii) above.
(d) The offer to permit return should within a time frame to be determined politically to maximize its impact.

Issue No. 6.—"Measures to Protect and preserve the unique cultural and religious heritage of the State"

Recommendation No. 6.1

(a) Cultural and religious heritage include monuments, sites, building structures, objects and landscapes that are significant in indigenous history, architecture, archeology, engineering and culture. Historically, architecturally, and culturally, they make a major contribution to the society and should, therefore, be preserved.
(b) A comprehensive policy on preservation of cultural and religious heritage of the State is required and the work of preservation should be assigned to some autonomous institution
(c) Steps should be taken to preserve and continue traditional art forms like sufiana music, miniature paintings, folk dances, etc. A comprehensive plan should be got prepared by a body of expects in the field which could include those who have served with the Academy

of Art and Culture and persons who have sufficient local knowledge in this behalf.

Other Issues

The main issues on the agenda of the Working Group have been covered broadly as above. Certain other issues were also raised by members which the Working Group regards as worth considering at the level of the Government of India and the State Government. These issues and the recommendation of the Working Group are as below:

Issue No. 7.—The rehabilitation problems of refugees of 1947 who came over from adjoining areas of Pakistan across International border need to be examined and settled once for all. These persons are not eligible for being permanent residents of the state.

Issue No. 8.—There are certain refugees who have not been provided full rehabilitation after the wars with Pakistan in 1965 and 1971. They are mostly concentrated in the Jammu division and their status as also requirements of further relief or rehabilitation should be addressed to.

Issue No. 9.—For balanced development and redress of the feeling that there is discrimination against certain region or sub-regions within the State, it was suggested that the systems of Regional or Sub-regional Councils be examined. Since this issue also falls in the purview of Working Group No. III on "Economic Development", the same has been posed to that Working Group with the suggestion that this Working Group considers that the settlement of this issue is of prime importance.

Issue No. 10.—Another important item of the requirement of accelerated economic development of certain communities which have been deprived for a long time like Gujjars, Bakkerwals and the Pahari-speaking people. This issue has also been referred to the Working Group No. III on "Economic Development".

Issue No. 11.—An important issue related to all sections of the society is availability of power, which is very vital for industrial development as also for a decent living in all households. All possibilities for setting up of new power projects within the framework of Indus Water Treaty should be considered.

Issue No. 12.—The State has been facing problems relating to migration in which the Working Group has proposed case specific recommendations of immediate nature. In addition, it may be necessary to examine in detail the reasons and the problems related to migration and steps that any recurrence should not take place.

The following may therefore be considered:

(a) It has to be recognized that the problem of militancy and alienation of some sections of the society has to be tackled in a very broad framework in this behalf. Central and State Governments may consider application of internationally accepted policies; in consultation with experts.

(b) An unconditional dialogue process should be started with militant groups for finding a sustainable solution to the problem of militancy in the State.

(c) The probable role of media should be examined in generating an image of the people of the State so as to lessen the indignity and suspicion that the people, especially youth face outside the State.

Acknowledgements

The Chairman was assisted in convening the Working Group meetings, recording the proceedings, making all other arrangements for Group's work including the preparation of the records of various meetings and Group's final report by a team of officers headed by Shri Ajit Kumar, IAS, Financial Commissioner (Coordination) and including officers and staff of the office of the Resident Commissioner, New Delhi, Commissioner/Secy. General Administration Department and the Hospitality and Protocol Department of the State Govt.

(MOHAMMAD HAMID ANSARI)

New Delhi
Dated January 10, 2007

ECONOMIC DEVELOPMENT OF JAMMU AND KASHMIR

Report of Working Group No. III

March 2007

Working Group No. III on "Economic Development" of Jammu and Kashmir

1.	Dr. C. Rangarajan, Chairman, Prime Minister's Economic Advisory Council	Chairman
2.	Shri Omar Abdullah, MP President National Conference	Member
3.	Shri Muzaffar Hussain Baig, MLA Ex. Deputy Chief Minister People's Democratic Party (PDP)	Member
4.	Shri Gulchain Singh Charak, MLC Minister for Public Works Dept., J&K Congress (INC) (Representing Dogra Sadar Sabha)	Member
5.	Shri Nirrnal Singh Ex. State President BJP, J&K, BJP	Member
6.	Shri Shyam Prasad Kesar Member State Committee CPI(M)	Member
7.	Shri Ghulam Mohd. Sheikh, CPI	Member
8.	Shri Balwant Singh Mankotia, MLA, Panthers Party	Member
9.	Shri Nawang Rigzin Jora, Minister for Power Representing Ladakh	Member
10.	Thakur Puran Singh, MLA, Ex MoS, Representing Paharis	Member
11.	Shri Nizam-ud-din Khatana Representing Gujjars & Bakkerwals	Member
12.	Shri Mohd. Sharief Niaz, Ex. Minister	Member

The Working Group was constituted following an announcement made by the Prime Minister in the Round Table

Conference at Srinagar on 24th and 28th May, 2006. The Working Group held three meetings in all between Aug. 2006 to Feb. 2007 (Schedule of meetings at Appendix 3). It also held consultations with the Chief Minister of J&K at Srinagar on Aug. 29, 2006. The Working Group wishes to thank the (officers of Government of Jammu and Kashmir for their advice and the officers of Economic Advisory Council to PM for assistance throughout this task.

CONTENTS

6. **Irrigation**
   Animal Husbandry and Pasture Development
   Forest and Environment
   Issues and Status
   Initiatives

7. **Industrial Development and Commerce**
   Special Industrial Zone
   Special Concession Package
   Other Initiatives
   Revitalising Handicrafts
   Trade across the border
   Small Scale Industry

8. **Health**
   Issues and Status
   Ongoing initiatives
   Way Forward

9. **Education and Employment**
   Context
   Training
   Adult Literacy Volunteers
   Agricultural Extension Workers

10. **Regional Development**
    Context
    Institutional Arrangements
    Backward Communities

11. **Other Issues and Recommendations**

12. **Implementation and Monitoring**

Appendices

Appendix 1 Working Group Recommendations—Summary
Appendix 2 Financial Package
Appendix 3 Schedule of Meeting of the Working Group

INTRODUCTION AND OVERVIEW

Approach of the Working Group

1.1 The State Plan provides the platform for Jammu and Kashmir (J&K) to pursue its development. Besides, there is the large initiative through the Prime Minister's Reconstruction Plan, with an outlay of Rs. 24000 crores, aimed at three basic thrust areas: (i) expanding economic infrastructure; (ii) expanding the provision of basic services; and (iii) employment and income generation.

1.2 In another important initiative, the Prime Minister had constituted a Task Force under the chairmanship of Dr. C. Rangarajan on the 'Development of Jammu and Kashmir'. The Task Force, whose report was submitted to the Prime Minister in December 2006, made comprehensive recommendations on growth generating initiatives for the state focusing on important sectors like power, rural roads, telecom, tourism, horticulture and food processing, health as also some quick yielding projects. The Working Group has studied the report of the Task Force and supports the recommendations made therein.

1.3 Rapid and sustained economic development of J&K is the common agenda of both the Working Group and the Task Force; hence some overlap in recommendations is inevitable, and perhaps also desirable. However, the mandate of the Working Group extends beyond that of the Task Force especially with respect to the thrust on balanced regional and sub-regional development and employment generation. Accordingly, the Working Group has identified sectors which will have the maximum impact on growth and employment generation in Jammu and Kashmir. The specific focus of the recommendations is on inclusive growth and on balanced economic development.

Development Challenge

1.4 Long-term development of Jammu and Kashmir (J&K) is a formidable challenge in many ways. The state has to reconstruct an economy ravaged by two decades of militancy and terrorism and at the same time deliver quickly on growth and poverty reduction which, in the ultimate analysis, is the most sustainable solution to restoring peace and order. J&K has some unique economic disadvantages arising out of remoteness and poor connectivity, hilly and often inhospitable terrain, vulnerability to natural disasters, a weak resource base, poor infrastructure, sparse population density, shallow markets and most importantly a law and order situation threatened by militancy. Taken together, all these factors have resulted in a classic "backwardness trap" of low economic activity, low employment and low-income generation.

1.5 The economic disadvantage indicated above has substantial implications for the size and nature of the development problem and for the approach to be adopted. First, the internal market is too small to take advantage of scale economies in production. The alternative of scaling up production to viable levels by exporting to markets outside the state is infeasible because of poor connectivity. Second, unit costs of service delivery are high because of high costs of inputs as also low population densities. Third, the private sector, which should be the engine of growth, has not taken off in part because of low supply and demand linkages and in part because of inhibition of the private sector on account of security concerns. Consequently, the burden of generating economic activity has had to be borne almost exclusively by the public sector. Fourth, the virtual absence of the private sector has meant a low tax base. Fifth, the beneficial impact of public expenditure has been lost to some extent. Such benefits have tended to spill over beyond the state as much of the contractors' payments are transferred and purchases are made beyond the state—a phenomenon referred to as the 'missing multiplier'. Finally, excessive and prolonged dependence on central assistance has led to a complacent attitude towards resource generation, fiscal responsibility and accountability for results.

1.6 The above analysis suggests that the approach to long-term development of J&K should focus on generating economic activity within the state and on mainstreaming the state into the national and the global economy. The most efficient way of doing this is to focus on sectors and projects that yield quick results while at the same time laying the foundation for long-term growth. The immediate priority in this regard is repair and reconstruction of assets damaged by militancy and terrorism. Next, long-term development requires investment in physical and social infrastructure. This does not mean only creation of new assets but it also means operation and maintenance (O&M) of existing assets. Experience shows that O&M of existing assets yields a much higher return for every rupee spent than creation of new assets. In practical terms this means repair and maintenance of existing roads, irrigation and drinking water works as well as staffing and equipping schools and health centers.

1.7 Inclusive growth means ensuring that the benefits of growth translate into poverty reduction. In other words, growth should be such that the poor contribute to growth and the poor benefit from growth. This requires better education and health. The Government has a critical responsibility in improving the reach and quality of education and health. Investment in social infrastructure therefore assumes significance in this context.

1.8 Low level of employment opportunities is a dominant and vocal concern in J&K. This results in the common argument that there should be a frontal thrust on explicit employment generation programmes. Experience of the last 50 years has however shown that the most effective way of generating sustainable employment is through accelerating growth; special employment programmes through incentives and subsidies have been both costly and ineffective. While heightened economic activity creates the demand for jobs, state intervention will be required to improve the employability of the job-seekers so as to match the emerging demand with appropriate supply.

1.9 Like most large states, J&K too faces the problem of regional imbalances which are not only inimical to growth but also engender political tensions. Balanced regional development of the three regions of the state—Jammu, Kashmir and Ladakh should also receive priority attention.

Agenda—Six Objectives

1.10 Accordingly, the development challenges of J&K can be defined by six objectives:

(i) Reconstruction and maintenance of existing physical assets

1.11 There is an urgent need to change the methodology of the plan. Currently there is too much focus on creation of new assets at the expense of maintaining existing assets although the latter yield better value for money. In the case of J&K what needs to be done is to have three sub-plans within the state plan. The first sub-plan will focus on completing ongoing projects. Like in every state the tendency in J&K too has been to shut new projects every year without completing the ongoing ones. The result has been a large work programme, thin spreading of available resources and consequent inefficiencies in public resource allocation. The problem has been compounded in J&K because of the law and order situation over the last several years. Efficiency demands that the ongoing works have the first charge on available resources. The Working Group has been informed that the Government is already working on this sub-plan. The second is a "comprehensive maintenance" sub-plan to bring all capital assets to working order. The third is a "new capital sub-plan" focused on capacity creation in the infrastructure sector.

(ii) Investment in physical infrastructure—power and roads

1.12 Power is by far the most crucial infrastructure sector for J&K. Almost every other development initiative of the Government is linked in some way to improving the power situation in the state. In fact, if expenditure on power purchase and receipts are netted out of the revenue account of the Government, the state will not only balance the revenue account but also will in fact generate a surplus for capital spending. The key priorities in the power sector are augmenting capacity and more efficient management of the sector.

1.13 Improvement in road connectivity is another infrastructure priority. The road density in the state is among the lowest in the country and what roads exist are in poor shape. Improving and expanding the highway corridors is important. Equally important is connecting the villages and towns to the main corridors through an internal road network so as to facilitate movement of goods from the farms and firms to the major markets and also to redress the imbalances in road density across the state.

1.14 In terms of expenditure allocations, it is best for the state to use the funds under centrally sponsored schemes, in particular Bharat Nirman, to create the road infrastructure. Both the PM's Reconstruction Programme and the ADB assistance have components for roads. The state plan should therefore, focus on filling gaps in areas outside of these programmes, particularly to balance the road density across the state.

(iii) Investment in social infrastructure

1.15 Investment in education and health is a priority across the country, but it has greater urgency in a state like J&K where the delivery systems have atrophied on account of the law and order problems. Education and health are not only important for human resource development but also for restoring the faith of the people in the institutions of governance.

(iv) Conducive climate for private investment

1.16 No matter how successful the fiscal adjustment, public resources will be limited. The Government should use its scarce resources in areas where it alone can operate such as in providing public goods and merit goods and leave the rest of economic space to the private sector. For the private sector to respond to this initiative by stepping up investment, the state needs to create a policy and physical environment conducive to private sector development. This will be the route to sustainable development of the state.

1.17 Even as the India growth story is the global toast, much of the positive benefits of this are bypassing J&K. The most important reason is the negative investor perception about the security situation in the state. Second, competition, among the states for attracting both domestic and foreign investment is very fierce and J&K is handicapped in joining this competition because of its poor infrastructure situation and remoteness from markets. The third reason is the land ownership issue which prohibits non-Kashmiris from owning property in the state.

1.18 J&K is trying to overcome many of these problems. The perception on the security situation can only improve over time as positive information percolates. What J&K needs are a couple of demonstrable successes. For this purpose, the state needs to attract some large and medium industrial houses to invest in the state. Second, some of the geographical handicaps of J&K are sought to be neutralized by the tax incentive package announced by the Center. However, J&K has not benefited as much from this package as have some other states, which too have a similar package such as Himachal Pradesh and Uttaranchal. Here again, improving perceptions will help. Third, the state government has relaxed some of the regulations relating to land lease like extending the lease period to 90 years. It will help if the government launches a vigorous promotion drive to disseminate information and correct the misperceptions. Finally, the state government should review all economic legislation on the statute book and weed out all legislation that is no longer relevant.

(v) Balanced regional development

1.19 Balanced regional development is important for every state but particularly so for J&K. It is far easier to restore law and order and give a sense of security when every region feels 'included' in the process of growth. The three regions of the state —Jammu, Kashmir Valley and Ladakh—have different comparative advantages and the development strategy for each region has to be consistent with these differences. Importantly, resources should also be deployed in such a way that no region feels aggrieved or left behind.

(vi) Comprehensive fiscal adjustment

1.20 The nature and size of the development problem cast a significant fiscal burden on the state. Fiscal adjustment in the state has to proceed at two levels. The first is to restructure public finances to generate resources for development. This requires generating own revenues, pruning unproductive expenditure and redirecting expenditures to productive uses. While investments in new physical and social infrastructure is necessary, it is equally important to spend on maintaining existing assets as that will provide good value for money.

1.21 The second level of adjustment is to redesign the flow of central assistance. Although; J&K has been receiving a fair measure of central assistance, much of it has gone to fill the non-plan revenue gap of the state rather than finance development expenditure. This is not advisable. The state government should have the undivided responsibility of managing its non-plan gap. Central assistance should be devoted entirely to development where the end use can be monitored and where the outcomes can be more concretely defined.

POWER SECTOR

Current Scenario

2.1 The rich water resources of Jammu and Kashmir offer immense potential for commercial hydropower generation of as much as 14,000 MW. Only 10% of this has been exploited so far.

2.2 The power sector of the state is characterized by huge revenue losses, vast supply-demand gaps, weak infrastructure and very high T & D losses. The T&D losses are in the range of 68% among the highest in the country. As of March 2006, the state faced peak deficit of 418 MW (26%) and energy deficit of 352 MU (35%) in power supply.

2.3 J&K has 14 hydroelectric projects with a total capacity of 1474 MW (304 in the state sector and 1101 MW in the central sector). Two hydroelectric projects, namely, Dulhasti (390 MW) and Baglihar (450 MW), are under construction. 7 more Hydroelectric Projects with an installed capacity of 2839 MW have been handed over to NHPC for implementation.

Initiatives

2.4 The recommendation of the Task Force on the transfer of Dulhasti HE project, presently in the central sector, to J&K is a welcome step. While this will provide some comfort on the generation side, there will still be pressing need to augment capacity further. To meet this need, it will be imperative to take up new power projects under the Prime Minister's 50,000 MW hydro initiative. The projects that can be taken up immediately are the following:

(i)	Sawalkote	600 MW
(ii)	Kiru	430 MW
(iii)	Kawar	320 MW
(iv)	Ralte	560 MW
(v)	Shamnot	370 MW

2.5 The pre-feasibility reports for these projects are available and follow-up action for implementation of these projects needs to be initiated urgently. These would be in addition to the seven projects with NHPC, out of which one of the projects, i.e. Bursar

Storage Scheme (1020 MW) (under the PMs Reconstruction Plan) has been recommended by the Task Force for transfer to J&K for execution in the state sector. The Working Group supports this recommendation, as it will mean that the full benefit of the allocation under the Prime Minister's Reconstruction Plan will accrue to the state as opposed to just 12% share in the power, that would be the case if the project is implemented in the central sector. Transfer of Dulhasti and Bursar will neutralize to some extent the disadvantages the state faces in developing its hydro potential. Nonetheless, there is a strong case for additional support. One option is to slightly enhance J&K's share in central hydro projects based on the state's rivers beyond the current norm of 12%.

2.6 The long delays in execution of power projects are a major concern. NHPC and the state power sector must expeditiously complete these projects and an immediate step would be simplification of procedures for various clearances like forest, pollution control, etc.

Thermal, Geothermal and Micro Hydel Projects

2.7 J&K is currently excessively dependent on hydropower. Correcting this imbalance is important for managing the demand-supply imbalances. It will therefore be advisable for J&K to acquire a stake in a few thermal projects including IPPs outside the state. This will ensure supply of thermal power on a long-term and assured basis. To go forward with this proposal, the state can seek the help of a power trading company.

2.8 Studies show that J&K has potential geothermal energy contained in its underground reservoirs of steam/water and hot dry rocks. Its uses include power generation, direct use of heat for space heating, agriculture, aquaculture, industrial processes, balneology, tourism, etc. Geothermal energy is particularly useful in hilly and remote areas in J&K where cost of conventional energy is high. In the state, geothermal resources have been identified in Puga-Chhumathang in Ladakh. Commercial potential for a 50 MW geothermal plant was identified but the project is yet to take off. Implementation of this pilot project can provide a platform for mainstreaming geothermal source of energy during the 11th Plan period.

2.9 J&K should exploit its significant micro, mini and small hydel potential for local supply which will reduce the dependence on grid supply. These decentralized plants will be more economical in remote hilly areas.

Reforms

2.10 Augmenting power generation capacity is necessary but not sufficient. There cannot be sustainable results unless efforts to increase generation capacity are accompanied by reforms in transmission and distribution. The State Electricity Regulatory Commission needs to be made fully functional. There is a need to establish a Transmission Utility for reduction of T&D losses and efficient management of power supply. A long-term plan will be necessary which would include establishment of distribution regions/circles and energy audit.

2.11 Under the Accelerated Power Development and Reform Programme (APDRP), the state has an allocation of Rs. 1100 crores. The schemes sanctioned should be implemented quickly and progress monitored on a regular basis.

2.12 The state should ensure rationalization of tariff, time bound loss reduction and close monitoring for stoppage of power misutilization and theft.

2.13 Besides high T&D losses, the gap in revenue recovered affects the overall finances of the state. Moreover, the new generation projects will entail additional debt servicing obligations. These obligations cannot be met unless the financial position of the power sector is strengthened. This requires fiduciary controls by way of fully accounting for all the power that is generated, diligently billing and collecting the dues.

COMMUNICATION, RURAL ROADS AND TELECOM

Context

3.1 The problem of connectivity in Jammu and Kashmir operates at two levels: the problem of road connectivity to J&K—the state is connected to the rest of the country through just one highway; and the problem of road connectivity within J&K—there is a huge disparity in the road density across districts in the state especially the rural roads sector.

3.2 To address the first problem, a high priority has to be accorded to four laning the National Highway, which extends from Jalandhar to Jammu and further to Srinagar. High priority must also be accorded to undertaking repairs on the highway especially at Panthal arid Ramban where frequent landslides lead to closure of the highway for extended periods. The feasibility of constructing by-passes for these stretches can be examined. The National Highway is already a part of the North-South corridor and work on four-laning this needs to be accelerated. The other thrust area would be the early completion of the railway project of extending the railhead from Udhampur to Katra and from thereon to the Kashmir Valley for which the schedule is already laid down.

3.3 Regarding the second problem of road connectivity within J&K, the Working Group is of the view that rural roads should be the focus area for the state and all efforts must be made to leverage the funds available under the Bharat Nirman scheme of the centre. Some equalization of road density will come about through the Rural Road Connectivity Scheme of Bharat Nirman which aims at connecting every habitation with a population of 1000 in the plains and population of 500 in the hilly areas. There is need to revise these norms downwards for J&K keeping in view its terrain and the highly scattered population.

Rural Roads

3.4 At 13% the road density (road length per 100 sq kms) in J&K is amongst the lowest in the country. Moreover, there are huge inter-district variations in road density ranging from a high of 81.8% in Budgam to a low of 5% in Doda. Bringing places like Rajouri and Doda to state level average let alone the national-level average requires great effort and sizeable investment. Using the ballpark norm that it takes Rs. 2.43 crore per unit "index of road", the investment needed to equalize the road density across the state will be of the order of Rs. 1750 crores.

3.5 While estimating the requirement for investment, it is essential that the norms for unit cost of road for km length, as estimated for the rest of the country, be revised specifically taking into account the hilly terrain of J&K. Suitable modifications may also need to be made for difficult terrain within the state.

3.6 A major constraint in implementing road projects is land acquisition. Due to the hilly terrain, the land acquisition requirement is comparatively higher. Since land holdings are small and the rural populace is heavily dependent on subsistence farming, there is great resistance to parting with the land for road construction. The problem is further exacerbated by theiow price at which the land is acquired by the state authorities who fix the price based on the sale deeds in the area. There is a tendency to understate the value of the land to avoid the heavy stamp duty.

3.7 Owing to these constraints, and inadequate budgets, the state government is unable to make land available on time for central projects and the road construction programme suffers. A two-pronged strategy is required to resolve the problem. Firstly, the Government of India road construction schemes must include the cost of land acquisition as a part of the project. Secondly, the land acquisition law must be modified such that the owners get a fair value for their land. An important parameter in fixing the fair price would be the fact that whenever an area is opened up for road construction, the cost of adjoining lands increases manifold but the person who sacrifices the land for road construction seldom benefits from this beneficiation. Thus 'fair value' must be based on the prospective (post-project) value of land rather than past sale transactions. The recent decision of the state government to reduce stamp duty from 20% to 10% in rural areas and 14% to 7% in urban areas is a welcome step. This will encourage land transactions to disclose the correct transaction value on the sale deeds and hence aid the determination of a 'fair value'. However, the implementation of this reduction has been hampered by the non-completion of 'zoning' which must be expedited.

Telecom

3.8 Development of the telecom infrastructure holds out considerable promise for the development of J&K not only because of the economic benefits it will bring but also because it will deepen J&K's integration with the rest of the country thereby strengthening social and emotional ties.

3.9 With mobile services launched only in August 2003, J&K has been a late entrant into the telecom sector. Even so the state has caught up with the rest of the country—the teledensity of J&K as of June 2006 at 11.0 was only marginally short of the national average of 13.7. Disaggregated figures however show that telecom penetration has been uneven across the urban and rural segments with the latter performing substantially below the national average. Growth in Internet connections and quality of connectivity is poor. Similarly, Broadband services, a crucial infrastructure for a knowledge economy and for IT enabled services have been recently launched only in two major cities, i.e. Jammu and Srinagar. As against a total of 1.32 million connections in the country (March 2006), only 4612 connections are working in the state. There is need to actively promote Broadband since this has the potential to trigger the IT-BPO sector which is employment intensive.

3.10 The main constraint to telecom growth in J&K emanates from the supply side, namely high rollout costs, lack of adequate connectivity between the operators, security concerns, high entry cost burden and bureaucratic delays. To overcome these, first the subsidy policy of GoI for rural telephony must be revised for J&K in view of the difficult terrain and the security situation. Second, the high entry tax on telecom equipment should be reduced to incentivize investments in the state. Third, the state government must streamline the issue of clearances (like forest, municipal and local bodies) to minimize the transaction costs for the service providers. Finally, the Department of Telecom must sort out the issue of interconnect between operators to improve the quality of service and drive down costs.

TOURISM

Issues and Status

4.1 J&K was a mainstream tourist destination long before tourism in the modern form emerged as a growth industry. The state's scenic beauty, its temples and shrines and its rugged terrain offered broad-based attraction for tourists across the entire spectrum, and tourism had for long remained the backbone of J&K economy. This healthy growth got derailed in the wake of the insurgency of the 1990s. Over the last two years, tourism has begun to recover, but it is still a far way-off from becoming the preeminent engine of growth that it once was. This is an opportune time for J&K to aggressively reposition itself as a tourist destination riding on the back of the economic buoyancy around the world and at home in India. The state needs to market itself in three distinct niches—leisure tourism in the valley, religious tourism in Jammu and adventure tourism in Ladakh.

4.2 The Valley attracted 7 lakh tourists in 1988/89, averaging a growth rate of 10+%. This healthy progress was jolted by the insurgency in the 90s and tourism went on a decline. There were early signs of recovery in 2003 when tourist arrivals touched 1.9 lakhs. The recovery accelerated in the following two years with tourist arrivals of 3.8 lakhs in 2004 and 6.1 lakhs in 2005: Sporadic incidents of violence through 2006 have dampened the growth in 2006 with arrivals of 3.8 lakhs up to August 2006. Security is after all a pre-requisite for tourism to flourish.

4.3 If there were no insurgency, tourism would have maintained its growth track and it is estimated that annual tourist arrivals today would have been in the range of 15-18 lakhs. Tourism's share of the state's GSDP, which was 10% in 1988/89; would have gone up to 5%-20% if not higher.

4.4 As per available figures available, in the Valley there are 18,000 beds in hotels and houseboats but most of them require upgrading and proper maintenance. The valley needs another 6,000 beds by 2010 and 3,000 more thereafter up to 2015.

4.5 The present accommodation in Jammu and Katra is 15,000 beds, but the bulk of them are below required standard and inadequate to meet the need. In the next 10 years, 10,000 additional beds will be needed.

4.6 In Ladakh, 5,400 beds are available which are inadequate and there is an urgent requirement of 2,000 beds.

Creating Infrastructure

4.7 For upgradation of infrastructure including hotel rooms, the state has to find resources under the State Plan and also help the industry in getting appropriate loans from the banking sector. To accelerate renovations and new constructions of houseboats, hotels, and shikaras, a sum of Rs. 30 crore may be allocated for immediate disbursement as soft loans with an appropriate monitoring mechanism.

4.8 Even with finance in place, development of permanent infrastructure will take time. Development of paying guest accommodation should be explored as an interim measure. Across the world and now also in India, paying guest accommodation for domestic and international tourists at important tourist centers is helping to supplement the existing accommodation. The concept offers visiting tourists an opportunity to stay with a local family, experience the local way of life and to discover local culture and cuisine. A three-stage approach would be required to exploit this opportunity in the state. First, eligibility norms for categorizing an existing facility as 'paying guest' accommodation must be evolved. Though there are some norms established by the tourism ministry, these may need to be customized for J&K. Second, the process of registration of paying guest accommodation must commence. Third, soft loans must be extended to the house owners to enable them to refurbish the facilities as per the norms. This initiative will, apart from providing affordable accommodation, also involve the local people and generate employment opportunities.

Initiatives

4.9 To achieve the tourism targets, the state needs (a) Vision Document; and (b) a Master Plan based on research by a reputed organization. Support can be obtained from international agencies. This would be very necessary in view of environmental considerations.

4.10 Tourism is also related to better road connectivity which has to be addressed on a priority basis.

4.11 The facilities and check points at airports, railway stations and bus stands need to be tourist-friendly.

4.12 Effort will need to be made to attract entrepreneurs from the rest of the country with incentives like single window clearance and easy availability of land for projects in and around Srinagar and other places of tourist interest. Wherever possible, land should be made available on long-term lease. Should that not be possible, government should join as partner in the venture with land as its equity contribution while the private partner brings in the investment and management expertise.

4.13 The State needs to spend more on tourism promotion

and develop facilities for golf, convention centers and heli-skiing to attract tourists in high-income brackets.

4.14 Although J&K's natural beauty and religious shrines are large tourist draws, they need to be supplemented by facilities also for entertainment and recreation. It will be necessary to create facilities like shopping complexes, food courts, and multiplex music festivals and sports events. The issue of heritage tourism needs to be examined in a larger context especially in the Ladakh area which could prove attractive for tourists from South East Asia.

4.15 Many beautiful spots in the state with tourism potential are outside the tourist circuit because of lack of connectivity and infrastructure. It will be necessary to identify such places located in all three regions of the state—Jammu, Kashmir and Ladakh—and connect them with good roads and build hotels and lodges to attract tourists.

AGRICULTURE, IRRIGATION AND FOREST

Context

5.1 Agriculture, engaging 65% of the population, is an important contributor to the state economy. However, heavy dependence on cereals, small peasant holdings and subsistence farming have all created a sub-optimal cycle of low productivity and low investment, which is reflected by the low contribution of this sector (27%) to the GSDP.

5.2 The productivity of most crops is below the national average, and the state has a deficit in food crops, oilseeds and vegetables. Over 80% of the net sown area is under food crops and only 42% of the area is under irrigation.

Improving Productivity

5.3 The state has three main agro-climatic zones and various micro agro-climatic zones. There is an immediate need to evolve sub-regional strategies for investment and growth. Diversification of production and adoption of market-oriented products are natural corollaries of the sub-regional strategy.

5.4 In addition, improving availability of inputs like seeds, fertilizer, pesticides and most importantly micro-credit are other important initiatives which are important for raising agricultural production.

5.5 Another important strategy would be to actively encourage new avenues like floriculture, aromatic and medicinal plant cultivation, especially those with low volume and high values as these have the potential to enhance economic activity and increase incomes. Horticulture is particularly suitable for hilly areas which are anyway unsuitable for traditional agriculture.

Irrigation

5.6 Intensive agriculture will depend on availability of assured irrigation, which is a precondition for improvements in agricultural production and productivity. With less than half the cultivable area under irrigation, there is need to complete the ongoing irrigation projects expeditiously. The state should explore the options for claiming the full share of water from Thein Dam in the Ravi Canal Project.

5.7 Despite the restrictive nature of the Indus Water Treaty, it is possible to exploit tributaries of main rivers to increase the area under irrigation. The main rivers like Ujh, Tawi, Ante (Rajouri), Basantar and streams in Doda district can be tapped for local minor irrigation projects. This will enable herbal farming in the Shivalik region. Another initiative in the region of Shiwalik Hill (Udhampur and Kathua) would be to explore rainwater harvesting in tanks and ponds for both irrigation as also domestic use.

Animal Husbandry and Pasture Development

5.8 A large number of people in the state, especially Gujjars and Bakkerwals are dependent on cattle rearing and sheep breeding. However, the productivity in the sector is low and the state still depends on imports for animal products. Despite a high ratio of 900 animals per 1000 persons, only 4% of the gross cropped area is under fodder cultivation. Pasture development, especially in the hilly areas, and cultivation of high yield grasses are two immediate initiatives that would boost growth in the sector.

5.9 A significant concern of the pastoralists who depend on rearing of livestock, is the need for protection mechanism against loss of animals due to death. Currently, there is a Livestock Insurance Scheme under the 10th FYP which is being implemented on a pilot basis; in Jammu and Pulwama.[1] Under the scheme, Government gives a 50% subsidy on the insurance premium for crossbred and high yielding cattle and buffaloes. The scheme will be extended to the whole country and more species of livestock in the 11th FYP, depending on its performance during the pilot period (2005-06 and 2006-07). The state must urgency expedite the implementation of the Scheme and set-up district committees to review and suggest appropriate modifications to enable the scheme to be implemented in the whole state.

5.10 Since the closure of Himalayan Wool Combers, there are no facilities for processing of wool in the state. The producers are unable to get a fair price, hence an important initiative would be to encourage investments in production and local value addition by way of primary processing of wool especially for the high value 'pashmina'.

Forests and Environment

5.11 Forests are a lifeline of the state be it for tourism, hydropower generation or for refurbishing the ground water table. In addition, they contribute to creating a dust-free Switzerland-like climate in the state beyond Patnitop, which may be conducive for setting up 'footloose industries' like electronics which are employment intensive.

5.12 Up to the 1980s, the forests were a revenue-generating sector. This position changed subsequently due to heavy felling of trees, degradation of the forests and encroachment into forest area. Returns became non-commensurate with investment. To reverse the situation and to meet the demand for timber and minor forest produce like 'kattha' and charcoal, reforestation of the degraded forests, strengthening the forest demarcation division and using fallow land for fast growing trees are three important strategies. The last strategy was implemented in the form of the 'social forestry' project. Under this plan scheme a number of plantations and village wood lots were raised by using fast growing species having timber value. The project was successful

1. The scheme is being implemented on a pilot basis in 100 selected districts all over the country.

in the initial implementation and did succeed in greening fallow land. However, the panchayats and the local communities were unable to maintain the plantations once the project was handed over. The project has a lot of potential and can be revived on a pilot basis in some identified areas. However, community training and handholding for some period after completion of the project may yield better results.

HORTICULTURE

Issues and Status

6.1 Horticulture and food processing have tremendous potential of being growth engines. An estimated 25 lakh persons are connected directly or indirectly with the horticulture sector. Fruit production expanded from 0.93 million tons in 1999/2000 to 1.4 million tons by 2005/06. Productivity, however, remains low compared to international levels: for apples, the main horticulture commodity, productivity has been hovering at 10 tons/hectare compared to 26 tons in USA, Australia and New Zealand. The sector as a whole is locked in a sub-optimal cycle of low productivity and low investment.

6.2 The problems that horticulture sector faces are locational disadvantage, the poor condition of National Highway, the presence of many layers of intermediation in the distribution and virtual absence of post-harvest infrastructure.

Initiatives

6.3 About 30% of apple production in the state is low-grade fruit, which requires processing rather than direct sale. The capacity for the food processing has therefore to increase from the present 65,000 tons to 3 lakh tons in a short time. An immediate initiative would be a market development scheme for processing horticulture produce, which should cover apple pulp, jams, jellies, squashes, juices, etc. This should ideally be done in public-private partnership or through joint ventures with grower's participation.

6.4 Certain minor fruit products can be encouraged in wasteland areas, which are not otherwise suitable for high value fruit crops, commonly known as Kandi area in the Jammu Division.

6.5 For better pricing of fruit, it is necessary to have better sorting, grading and packaging, which automatically increases price advantage. Besides a plan for establishment of cold chain storage has to be quickly formulated and implemented.

6.6 It is necessary to train farmers to increase capacity in high value products like aromatic and medicinal plants, organic vegetables and better quality fruit, in addition to traditional horticultural produce.

INDUSTRIAL DEVELOPMENT AND COMMERCE

Special Industrial Zone

7.1 Creating employment opportunities is one of the biggest challenges for J&K. Although agriculture will need focus, bulk of the employment generation for the educated youth will have to emanate from the industrial sector.

7.2 What J&K needs is a big banner initiative—one that will raise the profile of the state among potential investors. The best option in this regard is an SEZ. However, the viability of an SEZ is doubtful given the state's land locked geography, infrastructure deficit and distance from the ports. Instead what J&K should attempt is a Special Industrial Zone (SIZ). The SIZ will mimic all the physical attributes and governance structures of SEZs but not necessarily their fiscal and statutory dimensions. Like SEZs, the SIZ top will be a large area with world class infrastructure, captive power generation and distribution, high quality services and utilities, dedicated infrastructure facilities, fast track and single window clearances, and to the extent possible liberalized labour laws, Units in an SIZ however will have neither tax concessions nor export obligations. They will be free to sell in the country or export. The main effort should be to provide a hassle free environment where entrepreneurs are free of all the disadvantages that cripple their productivity and efficiency and are enabled to compete at the global level from a level playing field.

7.3 The most compelling argument for an SIZ is that it is by far the most efficient way for J&K to spend its limited resources to attract investment. Ideally, the Government should improve infrastructure across board but given its fiscal pressures, that is hardly possible. On the other hand, spreading the available resources too thin is sub-optimal. What will be optimal will be for the Government to concentrate its resources in one focal area.

7.4 The SIZ is a model that other states too can adopt. But it is particularly appropriate! for J&K as the SIZ will make it possible to ring fence the zone in a physical sense to protect against security threats. The Working Group recommends Rs. 200 crore outlay by the Centre for this.

Special Concession Package

7.5 In order to encourage investment, in 2002 the Centre announced a special concession package for industries set-up in J&K. However, the impact of the package as measured by fresh investment has been limited as compared to a similar incentive package for investment in the neighbouring state of Uttaranchal. In a welcome measure, the 2007-08 budget extended the income tax and central excise exemptions for investments in J&K up to 2012. What this means is that there will be a window of time between 2010 and 2012 when central excise exemption would be available exclusively in J&K (not in the other two states).

7.6 The other concessions available for investments in J&K are the 3% interest subsidy on working capital, insurance cover on capital investment and the income tax exemptions of 100% for 10 years.[2] The state government must launch a vigorous promotion drive to disseminate information about the concession package, specially emphasizing the additional benefits. The other complementary measures that the state must initiate are review of the existing land policy, offering matching concessions for priority sectors by way of reduction in state taxes and development of industrial estates by leveraging the funds under the PM's Reconstruction Plan. Another priority would be review and reform in the procedure for various clearances which go a long way in reducing the transaction costs for the investors. Most importantly the state must actively woo large industrial houses, as even a couple of successes will have a large demonstration effect.

2. The income tax exemption for Himachal and Uttaranchal was 100% for the first five years and thereafter 30% for companies and 25% for other than companies for the next five years

Other Initiatives

7.7 J&K also needs a special package for revival of sick industrial units both in the public sector (e.g. ITI and HMT) and the private sector.

7.8 Inadequate access is a major constraint to industrial growth. J&K immediately needs an air cargo complex and a container depot which could possibly be located in Jammu.

7.9 Non-availability of credit is a major bottleneck for local entrepreneurs. The public sector banks and the J&K Bank Ltd. should be encouraged to take a lead in this regard.

Revitalizing Handicrafts

7.10 J&K, once famous for its handicrafts, has lost its niche in this segment owing to neglect and lack of an organized effort to keep up with the changing market dynamics. Revival of the handicrafts through an artisan development programme is potentially an important avenue for improving the livelihood of a sizable segment of the rural population. This requires interventions across the entire chain—skill upgradation, organization of production, finance and marketing.

7.11 The Confederation of Indian Industry (CII) had recently undertaken a project by forming Kiran, a self-help group with 45 women in the 18-25 age group. The project was supported through a tripartite agreement between CII, Dastkar and Sadbhavana Trust. An internal assessment by CII found that the project had lost its momentum in the second year itself primarily due to two factors—design and marketing. Other constraints identified were inadequate government initiatives, lack of facilities for skill upgradation (which affected both quality and consistency) and limited number of NGOs which could assist in capacity building and commercial development.

7.12 The CII experience suggests that the two key challenges to be addressed for moving forward are: (i) reestablishing the niche for J&K handicrafts in both domestic and external Markets; and (ii) improving the skill endowment. This calls for a two-stage approach.

7.13 The first stage effort which can yield quick wins is to find markets for what is already being produced. The focus is on market development by working with the Directorate of

Handicrafts; Export Promotion Council (the key player in the Moradabad brassware success story) and adequately stocking and refurbishing the J&K State emporia across the country.

7.14 The second stage approach with a medium-term focus will be to identify consumer demand in domestic and external markets so as to reorient supply to match this demand. This would ideally start with a market survey followed by creating an enabling infrastructure in the state to have international buying houses to visit the production facilities in the state. The key priorities from the supply side will be capacity building aimed at improving the skill endowment, raising productivity, and enhancing quality followed by finance and marketing support. This is an initiative ideally done in a PPP mode. The state government should identify a high profile corporate house which will invest in the soft and hard infrastructure with an eye on long-term sustainable profits.

Trade Across the Border

7.15 The peace initiative between Pakistan and India and the opening of bus routes across the LOC are welcome developments. If trading is permitted across the border, it will open up immense opportunities not only with PoK but also with Pakistan and other Central Asian countries. There is great potential for trade in handicrafts, horticulture products, shawls, garments, carpets and dry fruits. The other potentially profitable items of trade are export of construction material and medicines. It would be useful to identify items that can be imported from PoK and also explore scope for co-operation on subjects of common interest like environment protection, water management, natural disaster management and forestry. To convert this opportunity, a major initiative on construction and refurbishing of border roads will have to be undertaken. Some potential candidate routes are Jammu-Suchetgarh-Sialkot, Kargil-Skardu, Nowshera-Mirpur and Tangdhar across the Neelam valley.

Small Scale Industry

7.16 Despite internal problems, the SSI sector of J&K has witnessed rapid growth. The total of around 73,000 SSI units in the state, out of which 67% are located in rural areas, provide employment to a lakh and half people. The small scale industries cover traditional areas like carpet weaving, handlooms, handicrafts as also new areas like food processing, bulk drugs, metallic and non-metallic products, etc.

7.17 The Units are not evenly distributed across the state. They are largely concentrated in Jammu, Srinagar and Kathua followed by Baramullah, Anantnag and Pulwama. With only a few units, Ladakh lags way behind in SSI development.

7.18 The operations of the small scale sector have however been hampered by a host of factors such as poor infrastructure like power, roads and transport, shortage of industrial sheds and plots, lack of adequate credit, non-availability of skilled manpower and the law and order situation. The state government has attempted to correct the situation by refurbishing infrastructure and setting up industrial estates, a 'growth centre', and an export promotion industrial park. In addition, the state government offers a host of incentives to the SSI sector like exemption of GST on purchase of raw material and sale of finished goods, price preference in government procurement and toll tax exemption.

7.19 Reviving the SSI sector has a high development payoff because of its employment intensity and export potential. While the above incentives by the state government help, they are by no means adequate to revive the SSI sector. They need to be supplemented by at least one major initiative by the Centre.

7.20 One possible initiative is to help revive the industrial estates in the state. Many of them need immediate comprehensive maintenance and upgradation by way of repair of roads, drainage systems, creation of landfils for disposal of hazardous waste, water and power supply. The existing Industrial Infrastructure Scheme (IIUS) of Government of India provides for upgradation and rehabilitation of industrial estates at a total cost of up to Rs. 50 crore per estate provided the concerned SSI units within the estate and the state government make matching contribution to the extent of 15% and 10% respectively. In other words, GoI will provide up to Rs. 37.50 crore per estate provided the state government and the estate together contribute Rs. 12.50 crore. Currently, J&K is unable to take advantage of the scheme as neither the state government nor the SSI units are in a position to mobilize their required contributions. The Working Group recommends that the Center waive the requirement of counterpart contribution and help revive the industrial estates. This can be tried on a pilot basis for six estates well distributed across the state. The additional contribution from GoI will be Rs. 75 crore at the rate of Rs. 12.50 crore per estate.

7.21 Industrial sickness is rampant, and as per a recent report, as many as 22,000 SSI units have closed down. This sickness, in turn, has corrupted the balance sheets of the financial institutions (FIs). Providing a way out for the FIs to clean up their balance sheets is therefore a necessary precondition for revival of sick units. Most of the FIs in J&K were working well till 1989. The J&K State Financial Corporation (JKSFC) which was the lead financial institution for term lending to industry was earning cash profits till 1989. However, the viability of JKSFC was severely dented by the militancy in the valley. A large number of small-scale units closed down and consequently defaulted on their loan repayments which in turn eroded the financial viability of JKSFC. Between 1990 and 1997, the non-performing asset (NPA) portfolio of JKSFC increased by a whopping 645%. The track record of SIDCO, the State Industrial Development Corporation was similar. Its NPA accounts rose from 8 in 1990 to 68 in 1997 with the infected assets accounting for Rs. 198 crores. The only financial institution operating at full capacity presently is the J&K Bank. With the collapse of the public sector FIs, most of the financing for trade and some minimal production activity is coming from the informal sector which is both limited and costly.

7.22 As recommended by the Task Force on Development of J&K, revival of the financial sector of the state calls for the setting up of an Asset Reconstruction Company. The ARC will take over the infected assets of the state level FIs. This will clean up the balance sheets of the FIs, restore their viability and make them eligible for drawing refinance from central institutions. It is proposed that the initial corpus of the ARC can be Rs. 300 crores with a contribution of Rs. 200 crores from the Center and a contribution of Rs. 100 crores from the FIs in J&K.

HEALTH

Issues and Status

8.1 Human capital, as characterized by good education and good health, is an important determinant of economic growth. In

J&K, health care delivery is important not only for human resource development but also for restoring the faith of the people in the institutions of governance.

8.2 As compared to the national average, the aggregate health indicators like birth rate, death rate, infant mortality rate and maternal health indicators present a satisfactory picture but practically on every parameter, J&K lags behind the best performing state in the country. The main reason for this is that the public health care delivery system of the state has atrophied over the years of militancy forcing people to buy health care from the private sector. There is an immediate need for revitalizing health delivery particularly targeted at poorer segments of the population who cannot afford private health care.

8.3 The health infrastructure in J&K at all levels (primary, secondary and tertiary) suffers from shortages that are both qualitative and quantitative in nature which is made worse by the acute manpower shortage of paramedics, doctors and specialists. The non-availability is more acute in rural areas.

On-going Initiatives

8.4 The on-going initiatives in the state include the Prime Minister's Reconstruction Plan which has schemes for setting up of Anganwadi centers, increased outlay under National Rural Health Mission, construction of Rural Health Centre buildings and two prestigious projects of upgrading the Jammu Medical College and Srinagar Medical College with allocations of Rs. 120 crore each.

Way Forward

8.5 The NRHM with its focus on quality health care and community-based approach needs to be implemented to ensure achievement of clearly defined and measurable targets. The Scheme should be monitored for completion in time.

8.6 It would be necessary to take up, as a short-term measure, setting up of mobile clinics, which should have Doctors and paramedics and other facilities like X-ray, ECG and Ultra Sound. These could have specific route and schedule that is pre-determined to ensure availability of services to uncovered population. It would be desirable to have one such unit for each block, i.e. 107 such units for the state as a whole. These units would not only improve access and coverage but also optimize utilization of healthcare services. At an estimated capital cost of Rs. 30 lakhs per unit, each consisting of one vehicle for the staff and one for the equipment, the total capital cost for 100 units will be Rs. 30 crore. The operating cost will be Rs. 23 lakhs per unit or a total of Rs. 23 crores for 100 units[3].

8.7 We recommend an allocation of Rs. 30 crore for this scheme to cover the capital cost phased over three years. The release should be linked to progress under NRHM as measured by predetermined and agreed criteria and should also be subject to the state government making the corresponding allocation in the budget for the recurring costs.

8.8 In addition to the above it is extremely important to set-up advanced mobile units with emergency care facilities for dealing with injuries from IED blasts, grenade explosions and other such militancy-related emergencies. These mobile units must be stationed at strategic locations and be capable of rushing to site of militant attack on an emergence drill protocol similar to that of fire tenders. These units will not only provide physical relief to the victims but also enable the State to score a psychological win over the militants.

8.9 Other important initiatives in improving healthcare would be encouraging PPP for setting up (secondary and tertiary healthcare facilities, establishing a telemedicine network and health insurance for covering medical expenses for BPL families.

EDUCATION AND EMPLOYMENT CONTEXT

9.1 Low level of employment opportunities is a dominant and vocal concern in J&K. The long years of militancy have eroded the industrial base completely. Most PSUs are closed down and private investment shied away due to the disturbed law and order conditions. In addition, there is no reliable data on employment which makes it difficult to design appropriate interventions.

9.2 The most effective way of generating sustainable employment is through accelerating economic growth, which has been the dominant concern of this Working Group. While heightened economic activity creates the demand for jobs, state intervention

3. Figures taken from the NRHM document.

will be required to improve the employability of the job-seekers so as to match the emerging demand with appropriate supply.

Training

9.3 To improve employability both in the public and private sectors, training and skill upgradation are essential. The existing institutions lack essential infrastructure including the most crucial one—qualified teachers. While it is important to build new institutes, it is equally important to upgrade the existing vocational and technical training institutions and make them fully functional by providing them with building, equipment and trained faculty. In this regard, the expeditious establishment of the 13 ITIs which have been in the pipeline forlong is important.

9.4 The BPO revolution in the country has leveraged the IT skills of young people. However, the youth of Jammu and Kashmir have been unable to share this uptrend due to lack of adequate IT training facilities in the state. This vital gap needs to be bridged at the earliest through active intervention by the state to make it attractive for institutes like NUT, WIPRO and others to open training centers in the state.

Adult Literacy Volunteers

9.5 Adult Literacy is an important instrument in economic development as also for curbing militancy. It not only improves the livelihood of the poor but also gives them a stake in societal progress. One way of delivering the programme is through literacy volunteers' drawn from the ranks of the educated unemployed in the state.

9.6 At the rate one for 30 adults, the requirement will be for 85000 literacy volunteers. At a consolidated stipend of Rs. 2000 per month, the total bill will be of the order of Rs. 17 crores per month or Rs. 200 crores per year. If necessary the programme could be started on a pilot basis in 2-3 districts and rolled out in phases after building in the lessons of experience.

9.7 The programme can be linked to skill upgradation in five sectors, which are employment intensive—tourism, horticulture/floriculture, handicrafts, food processing and environment. The programme structured this way will deliver several benefits. It will improve adult literacy, it will improve the income earning capacity of the poor, and it will mitigate the problem of educated unemployment.

9.8 The Employment of these literacy volunteers' will be limited to two years whereafter the programme will be gradually wound down. By then other employment avenues should open up to provide alternate avenues to the disbanded volunteers. This literacy volunteer programme will go a long way to meet the foremost concern of the state—that of providing employment avenues to the educated unemployed.

Agricultural Extension Workers

9.9 Agricultural extension effort in J&K has suffered over the last 20 years in part because of the pressures of militancy and in part for want of adequate staff. This is a vital gap that needs to be filled on a priority basis. One cost effective way of doing this is to appoint an agricultural graduate in each of the 2700 panchayats in the state. Their main responsibility will be to set-up an agri-clinic in the respective panchayat for disseminating improved agricultural technologies and practices. They would also be responsible for supplying seeds, fertilizers and pesticides. We recommend an allocation of Rs. 250 crores for this phased over three years.

REGIONAL DEVELOPMENT

Context

10.1 Like every other state in the country, J&K too suffers from regional imbalances. The root cause of such imbalances is the inequitable distribution of natural resources and economic opportunities, and they tend to get aggravated over time unless corrective action is taken to redress them. Regional imbalances are not unique to India; they exist in all large countries and have been the source of a lot of political strife and discontent. Redressing regional imbalances has all along been a central aim of our development effort, but the success has not been uniform nor the results always sustained. Demonstrable striving to redress regional imbalances is particularly important in a state like J&K not only for the economic benefits it offers but also for the positive externalities it will have by way of restoring law and order and inspiring the trust and confidence of people.

10.2 During its meetings, the Working Group noted that

there is a widespread feeling amongst the three regions—Kashmir, Jammu and Ladakh, that the fruits of economic development have not been shared equally. (This feeling is more pronounced in the case of the latter two). At the sub-regional level, there are numerous backward areas. Some of them which found mention during deliberations were Chenab valley, parts of Doda district, Rajouri, Poonch and certain areas of Udhampur and Kathua districts like Gulabgarh and Basholi in Jammu, districts of Kupwara, Tangdhar and Gurez in Kashmir and practically the whole of Ladakh.

10.3 For balanced regional development, it is important that the development initiatives identified in this report are implemented effectively and quickly. Beyond that it is also necessary to put in place institutional arrangements that give a sense of involvement and participation to the people in the development process.

Institutional Arrangements

10.4 An important initiative in establishing institutional arrangements is the passing of the J&K State Finance Commission Act which mandates and authorizes the Government to establish a State Finance Commission. The terms of reference of the proposed SFC are far more extensive than those of other state SFCs and give special emphasis to identifying backward districts and assessing the extent of backwardness and suggesting remedial measures. The analysis and recommendations of the SFC should provide a platform not only for financial devolution to the municipalities and panchayats but also for administrative and functional decentralization. The participatory and inclusive processes inherent therein will give a fillip to balanced regional development.

10.5 The District Development Boards (DDBs), functioning in the state since 1978, are an important arrangement and already have people's representatives taking stock of development requirements and the progress achieved by various programmes in the district. To make the DDBs more inclusive, it may be useful to include elected representatives from Panchayati Raj Institutions and local bodies in the DDB's. In areas where Panchayats are not functional, prominent persons from the local communities may be taken on board the DDB. In the case of backward communities like Gujjars, Bakkerwals and Gaddis, wherever their population is sizeable, prominent persons from their community must be inducted as members of the respective DDB.

10.6 To improve community participation in development, local bodies like Panchayats, City Corporations and Municipalities should be strengthened. A number of functions like minor roads, lanes, drainage, local level water supply schemes, primary education and rural health care should be carried out through the local bodies. These local bodies can also be centers of economic activity promotion.

10.7 Panchayati Raj institutions in J&K are being revived after two decades. Much of the institutional and physical infrastructure has crumbled or been destroyed. It is difficult to revive panchayats without providing some basic infrastructure and facilities. We recommend a grant of Rs. 100,000 for each panchayat to build basic facilities and provide some minimal administrative infrastructure. The total cost for the 2700 panchayats of the state will work out to Rs. 27 crores.

10.8 Presently, state plan allocations are divided into state and district components in the ratio of 60:40. There was a suggestion in the Working Group that districts should be provided larger funding and that this ratio should be revised to 50:50. The state plan provides for relatively large infrastructure projects whose benefits typically extend beyond the borders of a single district, oftentimes encompassing the entire state. A District Plan, on the other hand, provides for schemes with localized benefits. There is an obvious trade-off here. The state government may consider this suggestion of the Working Group along with all its implications.

Backward Communities

10.9 There was a unanimous view in the Working Group that the development process bypasses some communities and groups despite a lot of pronouncements and indeed good intentions for Improving their lot. They remain trapped in backwardness because of locational disadvantage, traditional occupation patterns or sheer lack of opportunities. Particularly mentioned in this regard were the Gujjars, Bakkerwals[4], Gaddis, Panaris and people

4. Chairman visited a colony of Doodhi Gujjars and noted their lack of access to basic amenities.

living in hilly areas and Kandi belts. There was a view that the mandate to improve the lot of these extremely backward groups gets diluted as it gets clubbed; with development of backward classes and tribes. A dominant suggestion was that there must be a separate Directorate for development of Gujjars and Bakkerwals with separate funding and that this Directorate must be housed in the Planning Department. The Government may examine this suggestion.

OTHER ISSUES AND RECOMMENDATIONS

11.1 The recommendations made in the previous sections address the core sectors that have a multiplier effect on the economy. In addition, the following stand alone recommendations made by members of the Working Group warrant urgent consideration—

(a) Army and paramilitary forces have reportedly occupied land, orchards, houses and other buildings like schools and public health facilities in militancy infested areas. This has deprived the owners of a source of income, and in some cases of a source of livelihood. It is important to restore the properties to the owners by providing alternate accommodation for the security forces. If that is not possible, at least payment of rent on a regular basis must be ensured.

(b) Internal roads in areas of tourist importance like Patni Top, Katra, Sonmarg, Yusmarg, etc. must be given attention. Needing high priority are the roads in the upper reaches, including the ones with the Border Roads Organization. The four laning of the national highway must be extended up to Baramullah. This will be important if the trade route from Baramullah-Uri-Muzzafarabad is opened.

(c) The 'Mughal Road', a proposed alternative to the national highway, which will go from Jammu to Rajouri, Poonch and to Kashmir Valley should be completed as quickly as possible.

(d) The state has a number of local lakes and ponds, which could be developed by Panchayats for Fisheries

Development. They would also add to better environment protection and ground water recharge.

(e) An alternate route for the Kailash Mansarovar Pilgrimage through Ladakh should be explored. Because of the large multiplier effect of tourism, this will give a fillip to economic development of Ladakh.

(f) There are about 70,000 families of 1947 refugees from west Pakistan who do not enjoy the status of permanent residents of the state. This issue needs resolution. It is understood that this is being examined by two other Working Groups.

(g) A special package for better drinking water facilities in Kandi areas should be prepared.

(h) Over the last several years, the cities of Srinagar and Jammu have become highly congested. A decongestion plan aimed at shifting businesses and offices that do not have public dealing on a regular basis must be designed and implemented.

(i) The state has a very large area under forests and cold desert in Ladakh. An extensive survey of mineral resources can be made for exploitation of the economic mineral belt.

(j) Many aspirants from the state are unable to join the police and paramilitary forces because they do not meet the eligibility criteria by way of education. However, giving access to local people in security enforcement can have a demonstrably benign effect on the security situation. The Center must examine a way of providing recruitment access to these people by relaxing the eligibility norms.

IMPLEMENTATION AND MONITORING

12.1 The Working Group urges the Government to set-up a Monitoring Committee to oversee the translation of its recommendations into concreter schemes, their approval with appropriate financing and the effective utilization of funds. The Monitoring Committee will report periodically to the Chief Minister.

APPENDIX I—1

Working Group Recommendations—Summary

1. Power Sector

- Transfer of 390 MW Dulhasti Hydel Power Project from NHPC to J&K (para 2.4)
- Projects to be undertaken on priority—Sawalkot (600 MW), Kiru (430 MW), Kawar (320 MW), Ralte (560 MW) and Shamnot (370 MW) (para 2.4)
- Transfer of 1020 MW Bursar Storage Scheme from NHPC to J&K for execution in the state sector (para 2.5)
- Slightly enhance J&K share of free power in central hydel projects (para 2.5)
- Simplification of procedures for various clearances, like forest and pollution control (para 2.6)
- Acquire stake in thermal projects and exploit geothermal potential in the state (para 2.7 and 2.8)
- Exploit micro, mini and small hydro potential (para 2.9)
- The States Electricity Regulatory Commission to be made fully functional (para 2.10)
- Establish a Transmission Utility for reduction of T&D losses and efficient management of power supply (para 2.10)
- Establish distribution regions/circles (para 2.10)
- Improve Accelerated Power Development and Reform Programme fund utilization (para 2.11)
- Rationalization of tariff, time bound loss reduction and close monitoring for stoppage of power misutilization and theft (para 2.12)

2. Communication, Rural Roads and Telecom

- High priority to be accorded to four laning and repairing the National Highway (para 3.2)
- Early completion of the railway project of extending the railhead from Udhampur to Katra and thereon to Kashmir Valley (para 3.2)
- Improve rural connectivity and redress the imbalance in rural road density across districts of the state (para 3.4)

- Norms for unit cost of road for km length, as estimated for the rest of the country, be revised and specifically take into account the hilly terrain of J&K (para 3.5)
- Government of India road construction schemes to include the cost of land acquisition as a part of the project (para 3.7)
- Land acquisition law to be modified such that the owners get a fair value for their land (para 3.7)
- Implement the reduction in stamp duty to encourage the sellers and buyers to indicate the correct transaction value (para 3.7)
- Revise subsidy policy of the Government of India for rural telephony (para 3.11)
- Reduce entry tax on telecom equipment (para 3.11)
- DoT to sort out the interconnection impasse (para 3.11)

3. Tourism Sector

- Renovations and new constructions of house boats, hotels, and shikaras (para 4.7)
- Develop 'paying guest' accommodation (para 4.8)
- Prepare a tourism vision document and a master plan based on sustainable tourism (para 4.9)
- Improve road connectivity (para 4.10)
- Tourist friendly facilities and check points at airports, railway stations and bus stands (para 4.11)
- Attract entrepreneurs with easy availability of land and single window clearance (para 4.12)
- Need to increase expenditure on promotions (para 4.13)
- Exploit state's rich cultural heritage and develop modern allurements like shopping, food courts, multiplexes, music festivals and sports events (para 4.14)
- Harness heritage tourism (para 4.14)

4. Agriculture, Irrigation and Forest

- Evolve sub-regional strategies for investment and growth (para 5.3)
- Diversify production and adopt market-oriented products (para 5.3)
- Improve availability of inputs like seeds, fertilizer, pesticides and micro-credit (para 5.4)

- Encourage new avenues like floriculture, aromatic and medicinal plant cultivation (para 5.5)
- Complete the ongoing irrigation projects expeditiously (para 5.6)
- Explore the options for claiming the full share of water from Thein Dam in the Ravi Canal Project (para 5.6)
- Tap the main rivers for minor irrigation projects (para 5.7)
- Pasture development, especially in the hilly areas and cultivation of high yield grasses (para 5.8)
- Expedite implementation of Livestock Insurance Scheme (para 5.9)
- Set-up a processing center for wool (para 5.10)
- Need for reforestation of the degraded forests and using fallow land for fast growing trees (para 5.12)

5. Horticulture

- Market development scheme for fruit and fruit processing (para 6.3)
- Encourage minor fruit products in wasteland areas (para 6.4)
- Better sorting and grading, packaging and cold chain storage facilities to improve price realization (para 6.5)
- Train farmers to increase capacity in high value products (para 6.6)

6. Industrial Development and Commerce

- Create a Special Investment Zone with world class infrastructure, captive power generation and distribution, high quality services and utilities, dedicated infrastructure facilities, fast track and single window clearances, and liberalized labour laws (para 7.2)
- Leverage the special concession package announced by the Centre, to attract investments within the state (para 7.6)
- Special package for revival of sick industrial units both in the public sector and the private sector (para 7.7)
- An air cargo complex and a container depot which could possibly be located in Jammu (para 7.8)
- Revitalize handicraft sector through targeted investment and skill upgradation of artisans (para 7.12)
- Explore the potential for trade across the border and scope for

co-operation on subjects of common interest (para 7.15)
- Upgradation and rehabilitation of industrial estates (para 7.20)
- Setting up an Asset Reconstruction Company (para 7.22)

7. Health Sector

- Get implementation of National Rural Health Mission started without further delay by completing all preparatory work (para 8.5)
- Set-up Mobile Diagnostic and Primary Clinics at block level (para 8.6)
- Set-up advanced mobile units with emergency care facilities for dealing with injuries from IED blasts, grenade explosions and other such militancy-related emergencies (para 8.8)
- Create a telemedicine network (para 8.9)
- Design and implement an appropriate health insurance scheme for BPL families (para 8.9)

8. Employment and Education

- Upgrade the existing vocational and technical training institutions and make them fully functional by providing them with building, equipment and trained faculty (para 9.3)
- Expeditious establishment of 13 ITI's (para 9.3)
- Create an incentive structure for encouraging private sector to open IT training institutes in the state (para 9.4)
- Deliver the adult literacy programme through 'literacy volunteers' drawn from the ranks of the educated unemployed in the state (para 9.5)
- Appoint agricultural graduates in the 2700 Panchayats in the state for agricultural extension effort (para 9.9)

9. Regional Development

- The participative and inclusive process inherent in the State Finance Commission to give fillip to balanced regional development (para 10.4)
- Male the District Development Boards more inclusive by including elected representatives and prominent people from backward communities (para 10.5)
- Functions like minor roads, lanes, drainage, local level water supply schemes, primary education, rural health care to be

carried out through the local bodies (para 10.6)
- Involve public representatives in the process of allocations under the state plan (para 10.8)
- Examine the establishment of a separate Directorate for Gujjars and Bakkerwals (para 10.9)

10. Other Issues and Recommendations (para 11.1)

- Properties occupied by army and paramilitary forces to be restored to owners or compensation paid
- Internal roads in areas of tourist importance like Patni Top, Katra, Sonmarg, Yusmarg, etc. be given attention and work on Mughal road be expedited
- Panchayats to develop local lakes and ponds, for Fisheries Development
- Explore an alternate route through Ladakh for the Kailash Mansarovar Pilgrimage
- Special package for better drinking water facilities in Kandi areas
- In view of the congestion in Srinagar and Jammu explore possibility of relocation of business activity at other places
- Survey of mineral resources to be undertaken
- Relax eligibility norms for police and paramilitary forces for aspirants from the state.

11. Implementation and Monitoring

- Set-up a small monitoring authority for implementation of these recommendations and translating the same into financial terms (para 12.1)

APPENDIX I—2

Financial Package Implicit in Working Group Recommendations

(Rupees crore)

1.	Transfer of Dulhasti Hydel Power Project (para 2.4)	4933 *
2.	Rural Roads Improvement (para 3.4)	1750
3.	Renovation and new construction of houseboats, hotels and shikara's (para 4.7)	30
4.	Market Development Scheme (Fruit and fruit processing) (para 6.3)	50
5.	Industrial Development	
	(i) Development of SIZ (para 7.4)	200
	(ii) Revival of Industrial Estates (para 7.20)	75
	(iii) Asset Reconstruction Company (para 7.22)	200
6.	Health	
	(i) Mobile Clinics (para 8.6)	30
	(ii) Telemedicine (para 8.9)	2
7.	Adult Literacy and creating Urban Employment (para 9.6) @ Rs. 200 p.a	400
8.	Agricultural extension workers (para 9.9)	250
9.	Strengthening of Panchayati Raj Institutions by making 2700 Panchayat offices functional (para 10.7)	27
	Total	7947

* The net present value (at 7% discount rate) of GoI's liability is Rs. 4933 crore and would involve a cash outflow of Rs. 984 crores in the first year tapering off to Rs. 321 crores in the 10th year).

APPENDIX I—3

Meetings of the Working Group

1st Meeting	Srinagar	29 August 2006
2nd Meeting	Jammu	1 December 2006
3rd Meeting	Jammu	23 February 2007

WORKING GROUP ON ENSURING GOOD GOVERNANCE IN JAMMU AND KASHMIR

Final Report
March 2007

REPORT OF THE WORKING GROUP ON GOOD GOVERNANCE

Table of Contents

List of Tables and Diagrams

List of Boxes

The Working Group

1. Shri N.C. Saxena	Chairman	
2. Shri Ajay Sadhotra	MLA, (Ex-Minister, J&K) National Conference	Member
3. Sardar Rangil Singh	Ex-Minister, J&K People's Democratic Party	Member
4. Pandit Mangat Ram Sharma	Minister for Health & Labour, J&K Congress (INC)	Member
5. Prof. Hari Om	State Vice-President, BJP, J&K	Member
6. Shri Abdul Gani Hafiz	Member, State Committee, CPI (M)	Member
7. Prof. K.S. Jamwal	Panthers Party	Member
8. Shri P. Namgyal	MLC, (Ex-Minister, GoI)	Member
9. Shri Amar Nath Vaishnavi	Kashmiri Pandit Samiti	Member
10. Mohd. Shafi Pandit	Chairman State Public Service Commission	Member
11. Shri Nizam-ud-Din	MLC, J&K	Member
12. Shri Bashir Ahmad Dar	Ex-Secretary, Board of School Education	Member

The Working Group was constituted in implementation of the decision concerning the establishment of five working groups announced by the Prime Minister of India at the Round Table Conference held at Srinagar on 24th and 25th May, 2006.

The Group had the following Agenda before it:

To consider effective measures to:

1. Increase responsiveness, accountability and transparency of the administration
2. Strengthen local self-government

3. Effectively monitor development programmes
4. Institute zero-tolerance for human rights violations
5. Strengthen the Right to Information
6. Provide adequate security to all segments of society, particularly the minority communities

Meetings

I	8. 8.2006	Srinagar	Sher-i-Kashmir International Convention Complex
II	20.11.2006	Jammu	State Guest House, Canal Road
III	10.02.2007	Jammu	State Guest House, Canal Road

Summary of the Recommendations

Issue No. 1—To consider effective measures to increase responsiveness, accountability and transparency of the administration

Recommendation No. 1

Appointment of **Chief Information Commissioner** of the State, the Appellate Authorities and the Departmental Information Officers for effective implementation of the Right to Information.

Encouraging people to make use of the Right to Information Act by creating awareness. For this purpose, an awareness campaign should be launched through print and electronic media for which budget provision should also be made.

Recommendation No. 2

Introduction of **e-governance** in the State may be attempted in the following areas:

(a) Building up the capacity of the Information Technology Department by instituting a Directorate and field organisations.
(b) Land records may be computerized and placed on a web site to enable landholders to got the information without the need to approach Government officials.
(c) Sub-Registrar's offices should be computerized and brought under the control of the Revenue Department

and merging it ultimately with the Tehsil office.

(d) Treasury operations should also be fully computerized.

(e) Computerization of service delivery procedures should be undertaken for issue of certificates. Electoral rolls in Urdu for all 87 Assembly constituencies have been computerized by the NIC, J&K. This data-base could be used for speedy disbursal of certificates.

(f) Setting up of Information Kiosks at key service delivery institution such as Revenue offices, Registration offices and Police Stations will facilitate giving basic information on procedures to be followed for availing services in the respective Departments.

(g) Mass training in the use of computers should be given to the Government functionaries who would actually be operating the system. Thereafter, they should not be frequently transferred.

(h) The Government may introduce IT enabled single window payment systems for utilities like water, electricity rents and telephones etc.

(i) The process of developing web sites for each of the Government departments should be speeded up and an on-line grievance redressal mechanism should be incorporated to make administration more visible.

(j) An attempt towards introducing e-governance in Police procedures for filing FIRs and for getting police verification done for passport, etc. can be considered to be made.

Recommendation No. 3

Simplification of Rules and Procedures

Review of laws should be attempted in Departments, which have a large public interface (such as revenue laws) so that procedures can be simplified. For example, the Land acquisition and some other laws could be simplified on the following lines:

(a) The present Land Acquisition Act is unfair to the people, as it does not give a fair value and hence creates resistance to the acquisition for public purposes among the owners. The following amendments to the J&K Land Acquisition Act need to be brought into force at the earliest:

I. Consent award could be the primary mode of settling the amount of compensation, which should not be less than the value calculated on the basis of the principle enunciated in the main text.

II. Whenever land acquired for a public purpose is transferred to an individual or a company for a consideration, 25 per cent of the difference between such consideration and the compensation will be given to the original land owners.

III. The rate of solatium should be increased from the present 15% of the market value to 30% as is prevalent in the rest of the country.

IV. A time limit of maximum of 18 months to be fixed for the completion of the acquisition proceedings from the date of notification of the Act under Section 4 of the Act. Presently there is no such time limit except 2 year's time limit from the date of publication of declaration under Section 6 of the Act.

V. Whenever the quantum of land being procured exceeds a certain limit/percentage of land of the owner/tiller then there should be adequate measures for proper rehabilitation of the persons affected by the project by way of employment, skill-upgradation, sharing stakes in the benefits of the project, e.g. the person whose land is being acquired for irrigation purposes should be provided an alternative piece of land in the command area of the irrigation project.

VI. Presently there is no fee charged by the Government for the conversion of agriculture land for non-agriculture purposes as is done in the rest of the country. Conversion of agriculture land puts premium on the society as the Government will be obliged to ensure food security despite reduction in the area under cultivation and thus cost will ultimately fall on the society through taxation. It is, therefore, desirable that reasonable amount of conversion fee should be levied for conversion of agriculture land to non-agriculture purposes. The levy should be more for the land put to commercial or industrial use.

VII. The Ministry of Rural Development, GoI is likely to come up with a revised draft of the Land Acquisition Act, as well as a Rehabilitation Policy. J&K government should study the draft and model its policy on the GOI pattern.

VIII. It should be compulsory to put digitized photographs of the buyers and the sellers on the Sale/ Purchase Deeds relating to immovable property. This practice is being followed now in Haryana and Delhi.

IX. Instead of acquiring land sometimes it may be more convenient, for both the farmers and government, to take land on a long-term lease by the government from the owners by paying two times the gross value of current annual production.

(b) A Committee should be set-up to identify specific laws and rules that hamper entrepreneurship. A systematic review needs to be undertaken for areas from where Government must withdraw, in a phased manner, its role and also define the Departments, which do not now serve any public purpose, which need to be wound up. A study in respect of Public Sector Undertakings would also be necessary.

(c) Formats for various certificates must be standardized and simplified. The already existing data for BPL census, electoral rolls may be used for computerization of the data.

(d) **Pe-regulation** has made almost no impact at the state level. The systems of buying and selling land, getting a ration card of security back, and Rent Control Acts, all need a thorough revision. One can set-up an industry worth billions of Rupees in India without any license today, but a farmer can neither set-up a brick kiln unit, nor a rice shelling plant, and not even cut a tree standing on his own private field without bribing several officials. It is a sad commentary on our laws that the informal sector, which provides maximum employment, is mostly declared as illegal and subject to the whims of law enforcing agencies. A Committee should be set-up to identify specific laws and rules, which hamper entrepreneurship.

(e) **File movement**—More emphasis need to be placed on a system like that of the 'Desk Officer' where the operating level concerned is responsible for the maintenance of record. This would lead to an increase in result-orientation, the possibility of flatter organisations and a reduction in dependence on lower levels. Up to Special Secretaries to the State Government, officers should be encouraged to keep the most important files in their personal cupboard, so as to expedite the process of decision-making, increase transparency, and reduce the chances of corruption by the lower functionaries. A single filing system should be followed in dealing with proposals from Head of the Department. This will also encourage transparency within government.

Recommendation No. 4

Departments such as the Police and Revenue, which have more public dealing, should be assessed in terms of their policies and performance once in three years by an independent Committee consisting of professionals, stakeholders in the relevant fields and prominent citizens.

Recommendation No. 5

(a) A new Transfer Policy should be formulated stressing that the officials are in place for at least three years and the Policy is adhered to strictly. The Transfer policy should have the following objectives:
  - The need to curb the overall incidence of premature/ untimely transfers.
  - Eliminate transfer industry and transfers resulting from political interference.

- The policy should be seen as fair, objective, and leading to career development.
- The aptitude and experience of officers should be kept in view while giving a posting.
- Non-cadre persons should not be allowed to occupy cadre posts beyond a fixed time of six months or one year.

(b) In the recruitment by the Public Service Commission the amount of discretion can be brought down, for example, by reducing the weightage given to the interview for recruitment of teachers. The prescribed qualifications for various posts should be reviewed from time to time keeping with the rising trend of specialization and higher qualifications.

(c) (i) For the sake of fixing responsibility and accountability, it should be mentioned in each Government order the level at which the decision has been taken. The reason for disallowing a petition should be fully mentioned and the reasons for delay in disposal of the petitions should be fully explained. There may be a system of clear Job Descriptions in every department for every post to increase accountability levels.

(ii) To eliminate fake orders, every Government order must be signed by two officers of the Department.

(d) All promotions shall be merit based, seniority alone should not be the criteria. There should be an effective system of writing APRs (Confidential Reports), which should be regularly maintained and not written up only at the time of promotion.

Recommendation No. 6

(a) Every Department should prepare and publish a Citizens' Charter in a time-bound manner. Periodic review of the Departments adherence to the Citizens Charters may be undertaken by the GAD, but preferably through independent agencies. The guidelines for formulating Citizens Charters may be prepared by GAD and disseminated. An ideal charter should have the following components:

1. Clear responsibility—who will provide the service?
2. What does the citizen need to do—application, fee, information, etc.
3. What is the time frame in which the service shall be delivered.
4. What is the compensation for delay.
5. What is the redressal mechanism.

(b) A system of **public hearings** both at the district level as well as State level would be useful in strengthening accountability, increasing government visibility and ensuring people's participation.

(c) **Self-Assessment:** At the end of the Financial year, the concerned Ministers may present a complete Report Card or self-assessment giving various details, which could, *inter-alia,* include the performance of the Department including expenditure incurred, the outcomes obtained, details of performance; including underachievement, austerity measure or resource savings and the innovations introduced.

(d) **Surveys:** Government departments should also mount surveys of the perceptions and experiences of the ordinary people and civil society in sectors which have a public interface. These surveys will both measure public perception and experience of the integrity of staff interacting with the public and overall performance in the delivery of services.

(e) **Institutional strengthening:** As a part of the capacity building, periodic training programmes may be made mandatory for all Government officials on subjects such as service delivery improvement, leadership, change management and performance management. Before this, the basic infrastructure crucial to service delivery must be in place. Redeployment and right sizing of staff would assist in good governance.

(f) **People's participation:** The basic building block of good governance is the people's participation. The

Government could go in for using governance-reform tools like building public-private partnerships, social audit and citizens' score card. Government could identify and select a few dedicated NGOs based on pre-determined criteria to partner in strengthening public service delivery.

(g) **Performance Management:** Each Department, in consultation with various stakeholders, should set 3 to 5 outcomes that it would like to achieve in the next 2 to 3 years and work towards achieving those. In this process each Department should prepare a Status Paper of services it offers to citizens, plan for improving services and then set the outcomes to achieve.

(h) **Fiscal Management:** Fiscal reform is a critical component of good governance. The State of J&K has its specific problems of budget cycles and utilization of finances. There should be some mechanism to monitor whether the current year's expenditure is more or less over the past few years. The budget cycle is too short for full utilization of funds for capital works. Expenditure budget should be valid for two years, so that capital expenditure can be completed without surrender of funds. The practice of releasing large amounts of funds at the end of financial year, resulting in many irregularities in booking the expenditure, should be done away with. A "Roll-over" facility may be followed with the unspent of one year being carried over to the next without having to go through the elaborate annual plan and budgeting process, thereby preventing waste of time that is spent on replanning during the first few months of the following year.

Issue No. 2.—To consider effective measures to strengthen local self-government

Recommendation No. 7

The Panchayati Raj Act needs to be implemented in letter and spirit and for this purpose the Panchayats and the Block Panchayat Boards, etc. should be given appropriate devolution of the State revenue, as per the advice of the State Finance Commission. Some of the assets of the Government and local institutions like primary and middle schools, water supply schemes should also be transferred to the local Panchayats for management on sustainable basis.

The Godbole Committee Report had suggested that J&K should consider extending the provisions of the 73rd Amendment of the Indian Constitution, this should be examined. For reviving the institutions of local Self-Government, some of the suggestions could be as follows:

- A comprehensive capacity assessment exercise followed by a capacity building.
- Effective transfer of funds, functions and functionaries to the Panchayats would have to be taken up on priority.
- Activity Mapping exercise being followed in other States and rationalization of schemes to be implemented by PRIs.
- Capacity building of Panchayat members may also be undertaken simultaneously by organizing training courses.
- Mobilization of community to be partners in local governance has to be taken up through local leadership.

Issue No. 3.—To consider measures to effectively monitor development programmes.

Recommendation No. 8

The State and district administration should be streamlined by way of sincere attempts in clarifying roles and responsibilities, and eliminating overlapping jurisdictions to strengthen the capacity to clearly pinpoint responsibility. Efforts should be made to ensure linkages between activities undertaken and actually delivered to the common man. The outcome should be more regularly measured and their determinants analyzed. Initially, measurement of outcomes may just be for information, and the sake of openness. Over time, such measures could be used to hold districts and departments accountable for improvements.

Information should not only be collected and submitted but should also be used for taking corrective and remedial action.

As regards utilization of funds received from Government of India review should be made every month whether the entitled funds are being received in the State by the concerned Departments.

District level programme implementation could be made more transparent by the use of Information Technology. For instance, the tendering process for carrying out works and procurement could be made on line.

Issue No. 4.—To consider effective measures to institute zero-tolerance for human rights violations.

Recommendation No. 9

(a) The State Human Rights Commission requires to be strengthened as the body enforcing respect for human rights. The press and civil society organization can act as watchdogs and help ensure speedy redressal of complaints of human rights violations. Also comprehensive training must be imparted to the law enforcing agencies on what comprises human rights and its violations.

(b) There should be a high-powered Committee (including political representatives and civil society members) for enforcing human rights and emphasis on rule of law, accountability and proper implementation of laws.

(c) All recommendations should be acted upon by the State Government and in case any recommendation is not accepted, reasons for the same should be given through a speaking order.

Issue No. 5.—To consider effective measures to strengthen the Right to Information

Recommendation No. 10

With the introduction of the Right to Information Act, it is necessary that officers belonging to State Government and Local Self-Government Institutions (LSGIs) be suitably sensitized and trained in this respect.

Further dissemination of the contents of the Right to Information Act and biannual review or the applications filed under RTI and the status thereof should also find place in the efforts to improve transparency in administration.

This issue has also been examined and recommendation made at Issue No. 1: Recommendation No. 1.

Issue No. 6.—To consider effective measures to provide adequate security to all segments of society, particularly the minority communities.

Recommendation No. 11

(a) The security forces have to adopt a citizen-friendly approach and ensure that while militancy and law and order are adequately tackled, innocent persons should not be harmed and their life and property adequately protected.

(b) The areas having residence of minorities or others who have a threat should be identified and provided with special protection. Help of para military forces should also be taken in this regard and their units located in vulnerable areas.

(c) Local Panchayats and other bodies should be asked to have a system of community watch to ensure that elements who pose a threat are identified in advance and are unable to get any local support.

(d) Setting up of a Minorities Commission to regularly look into the problems of Minorities should be examined.

Implementation

The recommendations of the Working Group have been arrived at after careful thought to examine in depth the issues placed before it. For translating the recommendations in focused action it would be necessary to appoint a Committee (reporting directly to the highest authority in the State) to oversee the implementation of the recommendations. The strategy would include sequencing of reform, a definitive administrative set-up for implementation, getting the Departments on board for undertaking reform, comprehensive, mass training on good governance and the monitoring of the implementation processes itself. What would be required would be a Special Purpose Vehicle for delivery of reforms.

CHAPTER I

Introduction

The Working Group on Ensuring Good Governance is part of the five groups set-up as an outcome of the second Round Table Conference of the Prime Minister on Jammu and Kashmir (May 2006). The mandate of the Working Group is to consider effective measures to increase responsiveness, accountability and transparency of the administration, strengthen local self-government, monitor development programmes, strengthen the right to information, institute zero tolerance for human rights violations and provide adequate security to all segments of society.

Keeping in mind the mandate of the Group, the present report outlines a good governance agenda for J&K. The suggestions presented in this document are the outcome of a series of deliberations undertaken by the Group members on the status of governance and administrative systems in the State. The focus of reform and the end outcome, it was discussed, would be improved services to the citizens—this would be brought about by instituting measures to make administration more effective and empower citizens with information and knowledge.

Background

Reforms in governance of the State of J&K are coming at an opportune time. As it is, the state is in the best of times and worst of times. It is in the worst of times as in the last few years citizens have been complaining about the state of administration, there has been a sense of unease over the trend that public service provision has been taking, leading to a pessimistic view of the future. Citizen's apathy towards the government has grown, fuelled by the instability caused by the militancy situation. The government's position has been unenviable as it has battled with this instability and the citizens' perceptions of the absence of any "visible" improvement in government services. However, the brighter side belongs to the beginnings of recognition of the need for reform and some major steps undertaken towards revitalizing administration by the State government. If the latter trend is supported there is every reason to believe that the current pessimism will be short-lived and J&K will be well on its way into treating a model in governance-focused on citizen-centric administration.

A brief overview of the development indicators of the state are in order. Despite the fact that the proportion of people below the poverty line in J&K is least of all the states in India, the State has not done well in terms of many other socio-economic indicators. Nearly 80% of the population lives in rural areas and 70% is employed in the agricultural sector.[1] The industrial and infrastructural base of the state is also unsatisfactory with coverage of roads and railways being amongst the lowest in the country.

The comparative picture for J&K and India as a whole on some indicators is shown in the following tables:

TABLE 1

Literacy Rates—All India and J&K (1951-2001)

(per cent)

Sl. No.	*Year*	*All India*	*J&K*
1.	1951	16.67	—
2.	1961	24.02	11.03
3.	1971	29.45	—
4.	1981	36.03	32.68
5.	1991	52.21	—
6.	2001	65.38	54.46

In literacy, J&K ranks third from the bottom compared to other states and the only states with lower literacy rates are Bihar and Jharkhand.

In health, too, its achievements have been modest. Basic indicators such as birth and death rates show that much remains to be done to bring the state at par with higher ranking states in the country. The crude birth rate per 1000 was 13.27% during 1999-2000 and the crude death rate was 3.03% during the same period. The state-wise Infant Mortality Rate is shown below:

1. *Source:* Directorate of Economics and Statistic , Government of J&K.

Box 1: IMR in 2004

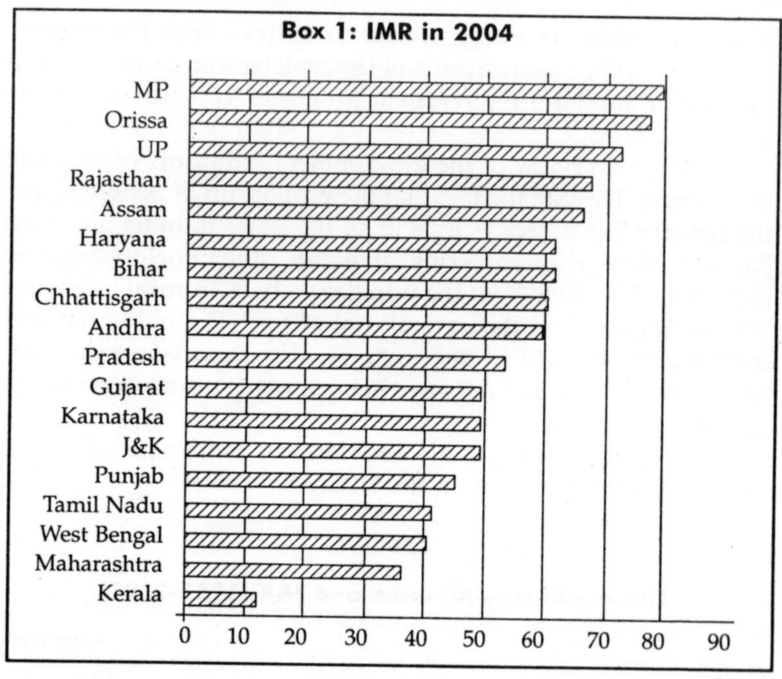

The change in percentage of malnourished children below three years between 1998 and 2006 is shown below, based on NFHS II and NFHS III findings (Box 2).

The Table 2 depicts, in brief, the comparative standing of J&K amongst the various states of India in terms of development indicators:

As shown in Table 2, although the overall achievement rating for J&K is 'B', the achievements in other indicators are inadequate, with social well-being ranking at 'E'. It can be seen that in almost every aspect of the human development indices J&K is nearer the bottom than the top in both the ranks and the ratings.

The inadequacy of social development is also evident from the trend in development spending. It is apparent that the expenditure on establishment, maintenance and services has been on the increase in the state, while less emphasis has been placed on investments and growth-oriented development expenditure. This trend is reflected in the Budget for 2005-06 as well where capital expenditure is placed at Rs. 3828 crores as against revenue

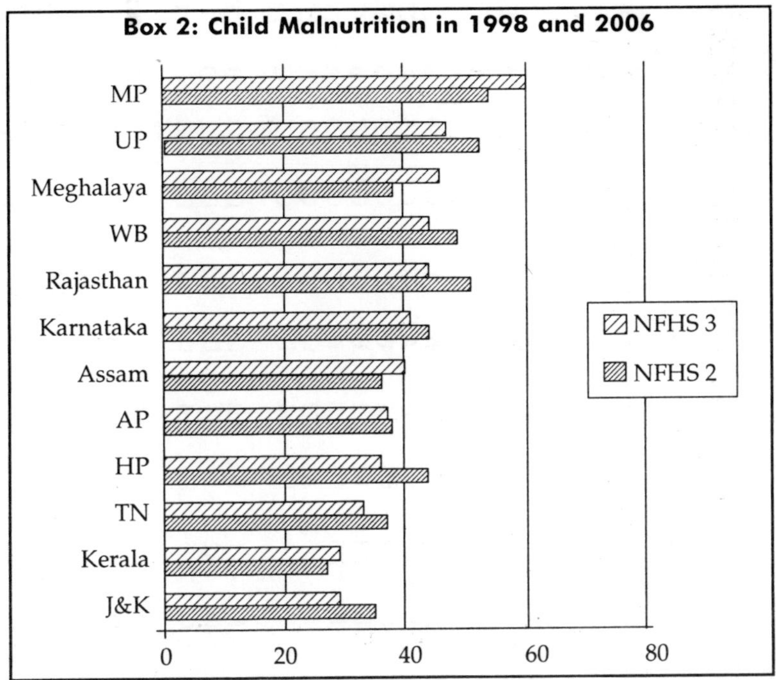

expenditure of Rs. 9117 crores.[2] Development spending clearly has taken a back seat. This fact, however, has not escaped the concern of the Government which has put in process initiatives to check mounting revenue expenditure (such as restructuring PSUs) and improve revenue receipts (such as promoting tourism).

The Process of Governance Reform

Reforms Already Initiated

There is a keen focus on governance reform already present in the state. Many initiatives to enhance efficiency of government procedures and development programmes have been put in place[3]. This is a heartening development and the initiatives are listed below:

1. Work Culture in government offices: a circular has been

2. Govt. of J&K, Budget at a Glance, 2005-06.
3. *Source:* General Administration Department, Government of J&K.

TABLE 2

Ranking and Rating for Major 20 States in India based on the Performance in some Development Indicators

States	Infrastructure Reservation										High Value Agriculture		Personal Finance				General	
1	2	3	4	5	6	7	8	9	10	11	12	13	14	15	16	17	18	19
Kerala	A	2.5	A	1.5	A	4	A	3.1	B	2.5	A	1.4	A	2.7	A	2.8	A	2.7
Himachal Pradesh	B	1.6	A	1.8	B	3	B	2.2	B	2.4	A	1.5	B	2.2	A	2.5	C	1.7
Punjab	A	2.5	C	0.7	B	2.4	D	0.2	B	2.3	C	0.2	A	2.9	A	2.3	A	2.7
Haryana	B	2	C	0.8	C	2.3	B	1.6	C	1.4	C	0.7	B	2.1	B	2.3	A	2.9
Jammu & Kashmir	C	1.5	B	1.2	E	2.2	C	1.3	C	1.4	A	1.5	B	2	C	1.9	B	2.3
Maharashtra	A	2.8	B	1	A	2	B	1.2	B	2.5	B	1	A	2.6	C	1.5	A	2.5
Uttarakhand	B	2	B	3	B	2.6	C	1.3	C	1.9	C	0.7	B	2.1	C	1.8	B	2.1
Karnataka	A	2.4	C	0.5	C	2.3	B	2	B	2.3	B	1.2	B	1.9	C	1.7	B	2.5
Gujarat	A	2.3	B	1.1	C	2.4	B	2.3	B	2.5	C	0.8	B	2.1	C	1.3	A	2.6
Tamil Nadu	A	2.6	A	1.4	B	2.4	B	2.5	B	2.6	A	1.3	C	1.8	C	1.8	A	2.7
Rajasthan	C	1.3	D	0.4	D	1.3	B	2.2	C	1.6	D	2.4	D	1.2	C	1.5	C	1.4
Andhra Pradesh	B	2.1	C	0.9	D	1.6	C	1.4	B	2.1	B	1.2	D	1.4	D	1.3	B	2.3
Uttar Pradesh	C	1	D	0.4	D	1.2	D	0.9	D	1.2	E	0.4	D	1.2	D	1.2	D	1
West Bengal	B	2	D	0.3	C	2.4	C	1.3	C	1.5	D	0.4	C	1.6	D	1.1	C	1.6
Madhya Pradesh	C	1.2	C	0.8	D	1.3	B	2.3	D	1.1	C	0.5	B	1.1	D	0.3	C	1.4
Jharkhand	D	0.6	C	0.4	E	0.3	D	0.9	D	1	C	0.8	D	1.3	D	0.5	D	0.7
Orissa	D	0.5	D	0.4	D	1.3	B	2.1	D	0.5	C	0.7	D	0.6	E	0.5	D	0.3
Chandigarh	C	1.1	C	0.3	D	2	B	2.2	D	1	C	0.7	D	0.8	E	0.4	C	1.1
Assam	C	1.1	C	0.5	D	1.2	D	0.4	D	0.5	C	0.6	D	1	E	0.3	C	1.3
Bihar	E	0	E	0	E	0	D	0.3	D	0.1	E	0.2	D	0.2	E	0	E	0

issued regarding punctuality in government offices, redressal of public grievances, checking of wasteful expenditure, checking corruption, monitoring of development works in quantifiable terms and against physical and financial targets, touring by officials in districts and outlying areas for inspection and redressal of problems.

2. The Right to Information Act has been passed and Accountability Commission set up.
3. Monitoring system for development schemes is being institutionalized by placing Additional District Development Commissioners in each district.
4. Internal vigilance has been strengthened by nomination of Departmental Vigilance Officers.
5. The process of introduction of computers in government offices has begun; efforts are on to computerize treasuries for better financial management.
6. Departments have been asked to notify Citizens Charters.
7. Chief Minister's Gold Medal is being awarded to officials with high integrity.
8. Declared policy of Zero Tolerance for Human Rights Violations

Ensuring Good Governance—Improving Public Services

It is recognized universally that good governance entails improving services by the government to the public through efficient administrative systems, timeliness, reducing corruption and effective implementation of development programmes. The role of the state in efficient provision of basic services is crucial, more so in a developing nation. The need for government's interest and involvement in the social development is captured by this quote from the *World Development Report—2004*.

"Services—A Public Responsibility

By financing, providing, or regulating the services that contribute to health and education outcomes, governments around the world demonstrate a responsibility for the health and education of their people. Why? First, these services are replete with market failures—with externalities, as when an infected child spreads the disease to playmates, or a farmer benefits from a neighbour's ability to read. So the private sector, left to its devices, will not achieve the level of health and education that society desires. Second, basic health and basic education are considered fundamental human rights. The Universal Declaration of Human Rights asserts an individual's right to "a standard of living adequate for the health and well-being of himself and of his family, inducing...medical care...[and a right to education that is] . . . free, at least in the elementary and fundamental stages." No matter how daunting the problems of delivery maybe. Therefore, the public sector cannot walk away from health and education. The challenge is to see how the government, in collaboration with the private sector, communities and outside partners, can meet this fundamental responsibility."

The Working Group on Good Governance has been instituted at an opportune time, when the process of governance reform is already in its incipient stage. The mandate of the Group clarifies the path that the reform process must naturally take and the themes of accountability, transparency, responsiveness in administration fit neatly into the vision of the State Government, while the focus on strengthening local self-government, strengthening the right to information and instituting zero tolerance for human rights violations underscore the citizen-centric approach to governance. What follows is a description of the proposals for good governance worked out by the Group. The ensuing chapters are organized around the following themes:

- Proposals for Good Governance in Jammu and Kashmir
- Implementation Arrangements.

CHAPTER 2
Proposals for Good Governance in Jammu & Kashmir

One of democracy's key roles is to deliver essential public services effectively. These services or public goods mostly relate to the rights of citizens viz. shelter, food, health and education and security. Translated into specific services these include housing and property rights, public distribution of essential food items, free and compulsory education upto secondary level, provision of basic health services including drinking water and sanitation facilities and maintenance of law and order.

These services are provided by various departments like Revenue, Registration, Education, Health, Rural development and police. As part of the reforms in governance many of these services are also supposed to be delivered under the aegis of rural and urban local governments. The local governments in India, generally, and in J&K specifically have not yet taken sufficient roots. While it is agreed generally that the transfer of the 3 Fs—funds, functions and functionaries are essential, there is neither complete agreement nor blueprints available for a quick and efficient transfer of the same.

Not only do public services need to be delivered efficiently in a democracy, they also have to be done so in a manner that is transparent and accountable to the citizens. The aspect of transparency has been strengthened by the legislation on Right to Information. Some features of this legislation are of immense value to civil society in monitoring not only the progress of various schemes and plans but also in understanding how decisions have been arrived at. The positive aspect of this for the government itself is that decision-makers will become more introspective when demand for information comes from below.

This introspection should ideally lead to a review of relevance of policies, procedures and practices arising in a particular context to a different one. While most of the procedures and practices are dictated by, for instance, a paper-based society; the current society itself lies in an era of sweeping technological changes that warrant reforms.

The mandate of the Group covers all these aspects of governance. Therefore, this chapter outlines a set of reforms covering the following areas:

(1) e-governance, simplification of rules and procedures (Mandate: responsiveness and efficiency in administration).
(2) Transparency and accountability in administration, Institutional strengthening, performance ; management (Mandate: accountability, transparency, responsiveness).

(3) Fiscal Management.
(4) Programme monitoring and implementation.
(5) Enforcing zero tolerance; for human rights violations and security to all sections of society.
(6) Strengthening local self-government.

The reforms being suggested by the Group are accompanied by examples of similar initiatives in other states."[4]

I. E-governance

Introduction of computers in various service delivery procedures and in functioning of government departments has been attempted successfully in many states (including Andhra Pradesh, Kerala, Karnataka, Uttar Pradesh and Madhya Pradesh). These initiatives have not only enhanced efficiency but reduced the direct contact of the public with the government machinery to the benefit of both. Some of the ways in which it may be applied to J&K follow.

Building up the capacity of the Information Technology Department.—At present the IT Department is functioning without a Directorate and field organizations. This lack of capacity has stalled the implementation of the few projects taken up by the Department for automation of administrative processes. Consequently, funds allocated under various schemes by the State Government and the GoI are going unspent. For instance, an amount of Rs. 5.92 crores under ACA in the outlay for 2005-06 was surrendered, as it could not be spent.

Computerization of land records.—Land records may be computerized and placed on a dedicated website so that they are available to the citizens at the click of a button, without approaching government officials. At present, the Survey Settlement operation is in progress in four tehsils of Kashmir. The data is stored in flash memory cards and brought to Srinagar for integration into special software. The process of computerization requires being undertaken on a wide scale and connectivity built up so that land records are accessible easily.

Computerization of Sub-Registrar's Office, and then bringing it

4. A set of best practices from across Indian states may be viewed in Annexure I.

under the control of the Revenue Department (sequencing is important here; one should not attempt changing the department unless all records have been computerized and placed on website), and merging it ultimately with the Tahsil Office. At present, the Registration Department is under the judicial wing, which creates anomalies in administration.

Computerization of service delivery procedures such as issue of certificates—Entry of father's name in the electoral roll and a copy of land records downloaded from the website should be sufficient proof of a person's native status, and he/she should be given a certificate accordingly without any further enquiry. Electoral Rolls in Urdu for all 87 Assembly constituencies have been computerized by the NIC J&K; this database could be used for speedy disbursal of certificates.

Setting up Information Kiosks at key service delivery institutions such as Revenue offices, Registration offices and Police Stations. This will facilitate giving basic information on procedures to be followed for availing services in the respective departments. Apart from reducing the workload on officials, this step would make information easily accessible to citizens. At present, Community Information Centres have been set-up at 60 Blocks in J&K (in Phase 1). The need is to focus on the specific service delivery points such as in the above-mentioned Departments so that common services are easily accessible to citizens.

Outsourcing some of the functions, such as data entry, to reduce burden on service delivery officials.

Mass training to government functionaries on the use of computers as in the states of Kerala, Tamil Nadu, Andhra Pradesh, Karnataka and Gujarat.

IT-enabled single window payment systems for utilities like water, electricity, telephones (on the lines of e-Seva in Andhra Pradesh and FRIENDS in Kerala).

Websites for each of the government departments with an online grievance redressal mechanism to make administration more visible and bring it closer to the citizens (This has been attempted under the Lokvani project in Sitapur District in Uttar Pradesh and Bangalore City Corporation). Another method of grievance-redressal could be the use of media for public interface (such as CM Online of Gujarat and Sutharyakerala of the Kerala government). At present the J&K government Departments are in the process of developing websites, this effort should be speeded up.

By introducing e-governance in Police procedures for filing FIRs, or for getting police verification done for passport, etc. may be simplified. For instance, if the list of those who have been convicted or prosecuted for serious offences is computerized it may be possible to do away with field verification of a person's reputation through constables for the purpose of issue of a passport, and verification formalities could be completed centrally on the basis of the computerized database. Similarly, it may be examined if FIRs could be accepted through fax, or through e-mail. The objective should be to reduce personal contact with the Police personnel to the extent possible. A system of on-line receipt of such applications could be introduced for which the petitioner needs to go only to a kiosk, and send his/her application by e-mail. Even copies of documents can be scanned and sent along with the application. The applicant should immediately within seconds get an acknowledgement with a particular number so that he could trace the movement of his application on the computer itself.

Treasury operations must also be computerized in order to save on time and reduce cumbersome procedures.

Box 3

Friends Project: Kerala

The FRIENDS project has been implemented by the Information Technology Department, Government of Kerala in collaboration with various departments like the Kerala State Electricity Board, Kerala Water Authority, BSNL, Revenue Department, Civil Supplies Department, Motor Vehicles Department, Universities and the Local Bodies of the State. It is a "Single Window Scheme" giving the citizens the option of paying for the common services rendered to them under a single roof. FRIENDS is a multiple agency bill collection system. The FRIENDS project envisages facilitating the collection of various payments pertaining to payees within specified area limits like corporation, municipality, etc. at a single centre.

FRIENDS is an example of improving access, timeliness, reduction in the channels of citizen-government interface—all through the effective use of Information Technology.

II. Simplification of Rules and Procedures

Rules and procedures governing various administrative procedures must be reviewed in order to increase timeliness in service delivery. Some of the suggestions in this regard are:

Review of laws in departments with public interface (such as Revenue Laws) so that procedures can be simplified. For instance, the problem in land acquisition for schemes such as Bharat Nirman is due to complicated rules. One solution could be that instead of acquiring land it may be taken on a long-term lease by the government from the owners by paying two times the gross value of current annual production. Other simplifications in the Land Acquisition Law could be as follows:

1. For determining the market value of land the Collector could take recourse to three different modes of assessment. Firstly, on the basis of existing sale deeds as has been done in most cases so far. Secondly, the Collector may take into account the scheduled rates for that category of land fixed under the Indian Stamps Act for registration of sale deeds. Thirdly, the Collector may calculate the gross annual production from each plot and fix the compensation as 20 times the gross value of annual production. The final market value for assessment will be the highest among the three amounts arrived at by these three methods.
2. Consent award could be the primary mode of settling the amount of compensation, which should not be less than the value calculated on the basis of the principle enunciated above.
3. Whenever land acquired for a public purpose is transferred to an individual or a company for a consideration, 25 per cent of the difference between such consideration and the compensation will be given to the original land owners.
4. The rate of solatium should be increased from the present 15% of the market value to 30% as is prevalent in the rest of the country.
5. A time limit of maximum of 18 months to be fixed for the completion of the acquisition proceedings from the

date of notification of the Act under Section 4 of the Act. Presently, there is no such time limit except 2 years' time limit from the date of publication of declaration under Section 6 of the Act.

6. Whenever the quantum of land being procured exceeds a certain limit/percentage of land of the owner/tiller then there should be adequate measures for proper rehabilitation of the persons affected by the project by way of employment, skill-upgradation, sharing stakes in the benefits of the project e.g. the person whose land is being acquired for irrigation purposes should be provided an alternative piece of land in the command area of the irrigation project.
7. Presently there is no fee charged by the Government for the conversion of agriculture land for non-agriculture purposes as is done in the rest of the country. Conversion of agriculture land puts premium on the society as the Government will be obliged to ensure food security despite reduction in the area under cultivation and thus cost will ultimately fall on the society through taxation. It is, therefore, desirable that reasonable amount of conversion fee should be levied for conversion of agriculture land to non-agriculture purposes. The levy should be more for the land put to commercial or industrial use.

The Ministry of Rural Development, GOI is likely to come up with a revised draft of the Land Acquisition Act, as well as a Rehabilitation Policy. J&K government should study the draft and model its policy on the GOI pattern.

De-regulation has made almost no impact at the state level. The systems of buying and selling land, getting a ration card or security back, and Rent Control Acts, all need a thorough revision. One can set-up an industry worth billions of Rupees in India without any license today, but a farmer can neither set-up a brick kiln unit, nor a rice shelling plant, and not even cut a tree standing on his own private field without bribing several officials. It is a sad commentary on our laws that the informal sector which provides maximum employment is mostly declared as illegal and subject to the whims of law enforcing agencies. A Committee should be set-up to identify specific laws and rules which hamper entrepreneurship. A systematic review needs to be undertaken to review the areas in which government must withdraw, albeit in a phased manner, and departments which need to be wound up should be defined.

Formats for various certificates must be standardized and simplified—Such certificates are needed for Ration Card, caste, backward area, income, etc. Computerizing the data for all families will sort out the problem once for all. The already existing data for BPL census may be used. Help of village panchayat and electoral rolls may also be taken in compiling the data.

File movement—More emphasis needs to be placed on a system like that of the 'Desk Officer' where the operating level concerned is responsible for the maintenance of record. This would lead to an increase in result-orientation, the possibility of flatter organisations and a reduction in dependence on lower levels. Up to Special Secretaries to the State Government, officers should be encouraged to keep the most important files in their personal cupboard, so as to expedite the process of decision-making, increase transparency, and reduce the chances of corruption by the lower functionaries. A single filing system should be followed in dealing with proposals from Head of the Department. This will also encourage transparency within government.

Orders under the Essential Commodities Act—There are a large number of licenses and permits to be obtained from the authorities under the EC Act. Apart from this a large number of registers are to be maintained and returns filed periodically. Inspections are carried out regularly to ensure adherences to the licenses obtained. These have increased bureaucratic rents and the operational costs of supply of essential commodities. The controls and restrictions, imposed by the State Government under the EC Act, are dis-incentives to production and distribution of essential commodities. A committee should be set-up to examine this so as to reduce corruption by curtailing the influence of various inspectors and their discretionary activities.

III. Transparency and Accountability in Administration

Corruption = Monopoly + Discretion – Transparency (in governance)

Accountability is essential for greater responsiveness to the needs of the public and thus to improve service quality—whether it is the individual civil servant who is directly accountable, or the department as a whole. Priorities for enhancing both internal and external civil service accountability should include: improved information systems and accountability for inputs; better audit; face-to-face meetings with consumers and user groups; publishing budget summaries in a form accessible to the public; a stronger performance evaluation system; scrutiny and active use of quarterly and annual reports; and selective use of contractual appointments.

Departmental Assessments—Departments such as the Police and Revenue, which have more dealings with the people, should be assessed once in three years by an Independent Committee, consisting of professionals such as journalists, retired judges or members of the armed forces, academicians, activists, NGOs, and even retired government servants. These should look at their policies and performance, and suggest constructive steps for their improvement. At present the systems of internal inspection are elaborate (although fallen into disuse) but often preclude the possibility of a 'fresh look' as they are totally governmental and rigid. The system should be made more; open so that the civil service can gain from the expertise of outsiders in the mode of donor agency evaluations of projects. The teams would undertake surveys of quality of service delivery in key areas; scrutinize policies, programs and delivery mechanisms. The civil servant's views on work constraints and reporting fraud and corruption should be elicited. The reviews conducted should also form the basis of time bound changes and improvements which should be monitored.

Review of Transfer Policy—There is immense pressure for transfers in most departments such as Education, Revenue and Health. The Transfer Policy must be reviewed so that officials are in place for at least three years and the Policy adhered to strictly. A system of Cadre Management Authorities as set-up by the Karnataka government and a blanket ban on general transfers is an example. A good transfer policy should have several objectives, such as:

- the need to curb the overall incidence of transfers,
- eliminate 'transfer industry' and politicized transfers,
- the policy should be seen as fair, objective, and leading to career development,
- the aptitude and experience of officers should be kept in view while giving a posting, and
- non-cadre persons should not be allowed to occupy cadre posts beyond a fixed time of six months or one year.

To begin with, GAD should calculate the average tenure of Principal Secretaries, Secretaries and Deputy Commissioners/ Superintendent of Police every quarter, and publicize this fact, so that political consensus is built up on the need for longer tenures.

There should be adequate publicity about who can transfer officials at various levels in government. This will ensure that government does not meddle with the transfers of low level officials. Powers of transfers of all Class II officers should be with the HOD, and not government.

Stability index should be calculated for important posts, such as Secretaries, Deputy Commissioners, and District Superintendent of Police. An average of at least two years for each group should be fixed, so that although government would be free to transfer an officer before two years without calling for explanation, the average must be maintained above two years.

At least for higher ranks of the civil services, e.g. Chief Secretary and DGP, postings may be made contractual for a fixed period of at least two years, and officers be monetarily compensated if removed before the period of the contract without their consent or explanation.

The recent Supreme Court order on Police Reforms should be strictly implemented in letter and in spirit.

At the same time it must be recognized that some posts would have more attraction for the employees than others. These may be due to better location where good schools or cheap government housing is available, more challenges, the pull of private practice for doctors, or simply more opportunities to make money. Except for the Indian Foreign Service no other service categorises posts according to its demand so as to ensure that everyone gets a fair chance to serve on both important and difficult (such as in remote and disturbed areas) assignments. Posts should be categorised in each department according to the nature of duties and geographical location into A, B and C posts, and the kind of mix that should dictate the average officer's span of career should be charted out. It should be possible to know through websites that total transparency is being observed and whether some 'well connected' officials have not been able to get 'plum' postings and avoid difficult areas. It is noteworthy that the region of Ladakh already has its transfer policy which had an incentive system for postings in difficult areas.

Box 4

Review of Transfer Policy in Karnataka

The critical problem of frequent transfers has plagued many state governments by hampering the efficiency and effectiveness of public services. The problem had reached gigantic proportions in Karnataka during 2000-01 and the Departments accounting for most transfers were crucial ones such as Police, PWD and frontline officials in departments such as Health and Education. After imposing a blanket ban on transfers in 2001-02, the government decided to create a committee system to address requests for transfers at all levels. The innovation in this scheme was that Cadre Management Authorities were created for A, B, C, and D category posts. The new transfer rules raised minimum tenures across groups and certain cadres were exempt from transfers altogether. These measures reduced political interference to a large extent by creating a system of rules and increasing transparency by creating a database to track transfers over time.

Recruitments: In recruitments by the Public Service Commission the amount of discretion can be brought down. For instance, as against the 20% marks set aside for the interview for recruitment of teachers, the weightage may be brought down to 10% first, and then ultimately to zero. Also the list of selected candidates along with the aggregate marks secured by them may be published twice—once before the interview and again after, so that transparency of the process is increased as also the satisfaction level of the applicants.

In order to tackle the large number of writs and cases filed with respect to government appointments, contractual employees may be hired with the specific purpose of following up and getting such cases disposed. Simultaneously, Service Rules may also be revised.

There should be a survey of all government servants, which should be computerized and put on a website. This will help in eliminating various people who are still drawing salaries from government, though their age is more than 60, or they were recruited as cooks or orderlies for officers who have retired. High wages with little accountability for actual service delivery has made public sector agencies and bodies an obvious target for patronage hiring, which results in massive over-staffing. It appears that Government is committed to public service providers, but not to public service provision.

At present a large number of *adhoc* appointments have been made in gross violation of Service Rules. Non-cadre people are occupying cadre posts. There are instances in J&K where Chief Engineers retire, but their substantive post is only as Assistant Engineer, because regular appointments are not made. Therefore, a department-wise drive should be organized to regularize appointments. This will also need simplification of PSC procedures. The state government will recruit a large number of teachers, AWWs, ANMs, and other medical staff in the coming years. Some states are able to complete recruitment with minimum complaints or litigation, because they follow a fair and transparent procedure. If appointment is for a particular post (and not to the cadre), postings to remote and difficult places does not pose a problem. To eliminate take orders, every Government order must be signed by two officers of the Department

Fixing responsibility and accountability: The control that the politicians exercise on the civil servants often amounts to backseat driving. In the present system it is difficult to fix responsibility for decisions, or for not taking decisions. The term public interest is most abused today, as it is used to cover hidden and malafide motives knowing fully well that the public is not in a position to challenge the bonafides of decision-makers. It is here that a fundamental change is required in the Rules of Business. It should be mentioned in each government order the level at which decision has been taken.

- The reasons for disallowing a petition should be fully mentioned, that is, it should be a speaking order, and the reasons for delay in disposal of petitions should be fully explained.

There may be a system of clear Job Descriptions in every department for every post. This would increase accountability levels.

There should be an effective system of writing APRs (Confidential Reports), which should be regularly maintained and not written up only at the time of promotion.

Reducing corruption: In particular, property and tax returns of all senior officers should be available for scrutiny by the public. These could be put on a 'home page' of the government on the Internet, so that anyone having access to Internet could access such information and get in touch with government if the stated facts are contrary to his knowledge.

Annual awards for whistle-blowers—Governments should in each department institute annual awards for recognition of the contribution made by such persons in exposing wrong-doings in the government.

Citizens Charter: Every Department should prepare and publish a Citizens' Charter in a time-bound manner. Periodic review of the Departments adherence to Citizens' Charters may be undertaken by GAD, preferably through independent agencies. The guidelines for formulating Citizens' Charters may be prepared by GAD and disseminated. An ideal charter should have the following components:

1. Clear responsibility—who will provide the service?
2. What does the citizen need to do—application, fee, information, etc.
3. What is the time frame in which the service shall be delivered.
4. What is the compensation for delay.
5. What is the redressal mechanism.

During introduction of citizens' charters, it should be noted that merely notifying citizen's charters should not be an end in itself. Each department should organise large-scale capacity building programmes to bring in attitudinal change in their employees. Officials should interface with public on at least one fixed day in addition to routine interaction, so that a system is devised for ensuring a speedy disposal of grievances at all levels of governance. At present, there is no institutionalized system in J&K for monitoring the progress on redressal of grievances (how many complaints received, how many disposed-off to the satisfaction of the complainant, how many pending, etc.), although J&K officers are very open to public and receive their applications without grudge.

Proactive publication and display of information by various Departments on services delivered and pending is a must, so as to reduce the number of applications for grievance redressal.

Face to face meetings of officials with citizens: A system of public hearings both at the District level as well as Departmental level would be useful in strengthening accountability, increasing government visibility and increasing peoples' participation. The experience of Nationalized Banks could be a pointer in this direction.

Report Cards: At the end of the Financial year, the concerned Ministers ought to present a complete Report Card or self-assessment giving various details, which could, *inter-alia,* include their performance including expenditure incurred, the outcomes obtained, details of performance, including under-achievement, austerity measure or resource savings, if any and innovations introduced. This should be telecast live on all TV channels and also have representative Sarpanches of Gram Panchayats, randomly selected to be present and give their assessment or appraisal.

Strengthening the Right to Information: With the introduction of the Right to Information Act, it is necessary that officers belonging to State Government and Local Self-Government Institutions (LSGIs) be suitably sensitized and trained in this respect. With a view to bringing in transparency and accountability, such capacity building programmes can be held by the Training Division or the GAD. Similarly, using e-Governance, most of the information pertaining to each office can be published on the web. This will make the process of responding to requests from citizens for information easier and faster. The aim of the Department should be to publish information that meets the three Rs: *reliable, relevant* and *regular.*

Appointment of Chief Information Commissioner of the State, the Appellate Authorities and the Departmental Information Officers for effective implementation of the Right to Information may also be done.

Also people should be encouraged to make use of the Right to Information Act by creating awareness. For this purpose, an awareness campaign should be launched through print and electronic media for which budget provision should also be made.

In the context of development works enforcing the rule that all muster rolls and bills are regularly read out and explained to the people in the village, and put on the web (at least in some places on a pilot basis) would provide the necessary (empowering) information to the public. To do this, no radical change in official rules is required. On the contrary, existing rules already provide for such sharing of vital relevant information with the public and village panchayats. However, such rules are mostly observed in the breach, because it suits the bureaucracy to conceal such information to enable its arbitrary and nepotistic exercise of power.

Further dissemination of the contents of the Right to Information Act and biannual review of the applications filed under RTI and the status thereof should also find place in the efforts to improve transparency in administration.

Surveys: Government departments should also mount surveys of the perceptions and experiences of the ordinary people and civil society in sectors that have a public interface. These surveys will both measure public perception and experience of the integrity of staff interacting with the public and overall performance in the delivery of services. Surveys should be carried out by an independent institute/survey body of recognized survey experience and integrity, and the results be published in a time bound manner. Implementation of the recommendations of these surveys should be ensured. Similarly, publication of reports of state-sponsored commissions and key policy papers should be compulsory. It is not enough that the J&K government departments and the state governments use professional and academic organisations to undertake impact studies from time to time. Their findings must be publicised and discussed with key stakeholders so that improvements in design and delivery can be effected at the earliest. Government should also put on its website findings of the impact studies, and distribute these in the workshops it organizes. Dissemination of results is critical for use. Results that are not widely disseminated, through mechanisms tailored to different groups in civil society, will not be used, and the resources that were spent in getting such results will be wasted.

Exit polls: There should be periodical exit polls of all government offices which have large interlace with public. Some of the questions could be: How long did it take to have a citizen's work attended to? Did he/she receive courteous and helpful treatment? Was he/she asked to pay any bribe? These would help in assessing satisfaction levels of citizens and would serve as important outcome indicators.

IV. Institutional Strengthening

To carry out reforms leading to good governance, it is essential that the required capacities in knowledge, skills and aptitude be developed amongst government functionaries through a well designed and sustained strengthening of institutions and individuals.

Capacity building: Periodic Training programmes may be made mandatory for all government officials on subjects such as design of programmes and monitoring, results-based management, service delivery improvement, leadership, change management and performance management. The capacity of State-based training institutions may be enhanced and Faculty may be called from other Institutions in the country to impart training.

Infrastructure: Many of the frontline service delivery Institutions lack adequate infrastructure for effective citizen-centric service delivery. Basic infrastructure, adequate space, provision of computers and other items crucial to service delivery must be in place even before an attempt is made to bring about attitudinal change in government functionaries for good governance.

Human Resources: There is a widespread belief that government institutions are overstaffed and downsizing is the order of the day. While in many instances government departments are overstaffed as Clerks, peons and drivers, at the same time service departments are woefully understaffed at the frontline level, for instance, as teachers, doctors and para-medical staff. A study of the frontline service delivery institutions is necessary in order to assess the situation at the ground level. Redeployment and 'rightsizing' would assist in good governance. J&K has a specific problem in this regard as employees are unwilling to serve in areas that are prone to militancy with the result that primary health centres, primary schools and other frontline service delivery institutions fall short of staff. For doctors, practice in rural areas as a first posting may be made mandatory with increased remuneration. In addition setting up of paid clinics in Government Hospitals with sharing of fees by doctors and hospitals may be considered as an option for ensuring attendance.

V. Peoples' Participation

Peoples' participation is the basic building block of good governance and is now widely recognized as a crucial ingredient in governance reform. Some of the ways of enhancing peoples' participation could be:

Building public-private partnerships: Government could identify and select a few dedicated NGOs based on pre-determined criteria to partner in strengthening public service delivery. These could be particularly useful in the social sector—for instance in motivating girl children to attend school, in disseminating information on health programmes and in IEC for sanitation programmes. The Education Department has already got the Hole in the Wall initiative of NIIT working in some schools. Other NGOs and private sector organizations could be identified with specific areas of work to augment the State's activities and programme implementation.

Social Audit: At the State level social audit of the Government could be conducted by accredited panels of eminent citizens of unimpeachable integrity and social commitment and be identified jointly by all political parties, ruling and opposition. They may be empowered to co-opt experts. The reports of the Audit should be made public.

Citizens' Scorecard: Monitoring of government provision of services may be undertaken in the form of a Citizens' Scorecard (as done in the case of Bangalore Municipal Corporation) and community scorecards. In Bangalore the satisfaction from public hospitals improved from 25 to 34 percent between 1994-99, but jumped to 78 per cent in 2003. This highlights the importance of regular information flows in ensuring standards of public service delivery. A similar initiative could be undertaken on a pilot basis for selected government institutions in J&K.

Box 5

Kudumbasree—An Example of Peoples' Participation

Kudumbasree is a poverty eradication project launched by the Government of Kerala with the active support of the Centre and NABARD with the aim of wiping out absolute poverty from the State within 10 years.

The project is implemented by the State Poverty Eradication Mission of the State government through local self-governing bodies. In this model, nine non-economic indicators are used to identify the beneficiary 'at risk' families -possession of a *kutcha* house, no access to safe drinking water and sanitation, presence of illiterate adults in the family with not more than one earning member, family barely getting two meals a day or less, presence of children below the age of five, presence of an alcoholic or drug addict member in the family and persons belonging to the Scheduled Caste or Scheduled Tribe. In 1994 the Community Based Nutrition Programme and Poverty Alleviation Project (CBNP & PAP) started functioning with UNICEF assistance and participation of the local community in the area of Malappuram, considered the most backward district of Kerala. Over 4000 neighbourhood self-help groups were formed under this project. These SHGs started mobilising savings and were linked to various commercial banks under the Linkage Banking Programme of NABARD. The implementation of various government-sponsored programmes for improving health and sanitation in Malappuram District was channelled through these SHGs. Besides empowering women through community organisation, Kudumbasree encourages and guides them in starting small livelihood earning enterprises. Products manufactured by such enterprises are sold through the rural marketing network.

The Kudumbasree network has expanded in Kerala and has been a model for community mobilization and self-help initiatives all over the State. It is also an example of active peoples' participation, women's empowerment and constructive linkages between the government and citizens.

VI. Performance Management

Each Department, in consultation with various stakeholders, should set 3 to 5 outcomes that it would like to achieve in the next 2 to 3 years and work towards achieving those. For instance, these could be reducing absenteeism of doctors and teachers in remote areas, completing all engineering works on which 50% work has already been done, increasing the utilization of budget for centrally sponsored schemes to 95% or more, measuring and improving the satisfaction level from public services (such as PDS, tahsils, etc.) to at least 50%. In this process each Department should prepare a Status Paper of services it offers to citizens (which should be freely available), plan for improving services and then set the outcomes to achieve.

Each Department may be given the option of volunteering for a "Charter Mark" Certification in achieving standards in service delivery. (This has been an initiative of the GoI in many States) Charter Mark is a quality standard which encourages and rewards improvements in public service with reference to the commitments and standards notified in the Citizens' Charter. Those agencies which are implementing their Charters exemplarily and are providing an excellent standard of service receive certification/recognition in the form of a 'Charter Mark' after an independent assessment. The Kerala government has over the last two years got a few of the Departments to work towards the Charter mark

The promotion system must reward performance and penalize (and correct) under-performance.

Each Department may also be encouraged to produce the best website in the State for which an award may be instituted by the Government.

VII. Fiscal Management

Fiscal reform is another critical component of good governance. This is especially important for J&K given its specific problems of budget cycles and utilization of finances.

There is no tradition in J&K of monitoring social sector expenditure, and find out whether the current year's expenditure is more or less (as % of total expenditure, or as % of NSDP) as compared to previous years. For instance, the Reserve Bank data given below shows that expenditure on Education and Health did not increase in J&K (this was also the pattern in most Indian states) over the past few years. However, during our interviews we got the impression that senior officers were not aware of such a trend.

Changes in Expenditure on Education and Health as % of Total Expenditure (J&K and all states)

Box 6

Year	*Education*		*Health*	
	J&K	*All States*	*J&K*	*All States*
2000-01	11.1	17.4	4.9	4.7
2001-02	11.6	16.1	5.5	4.4
2002-03	10.9	15	5.2	4.1
2003-04	8.9	12.6	4.4	3.6
2004-05	8.9	13.4	4.5	3.8

Budget: Release of budget is neither certain nor timely. The budget cycle is too short for full utilisation of funds for capital works. Expenditure budget should be valid for two years, so that capital expenditure can be completed without surrender of funds. Similarly for centrally sponsored schemes, approval of the state legislature should not be necessary for using central funds that are transferred to the state consolidated fund.

Funds allocated to the departments in the state budgets are not released during the year in an orderly manner and that far too many references have to be made to the Finance Department (FD) for prior approval for release of funds on ways and means considerations. The same is found to be true in respect of release of funds to District Boards Large funds are released at the end of the financial year resulting in many irregularities in booking the expenditure. Government of J&K should publicise for each department the percentage of funds spent each year in the last month, week, and last day of the year.

The delay in release of central funds to departments is because of fiscal stress and consequently funds being used for purposes other than intended, mainly to meet state's other exigencies. This is reflected by the fairly large backlog in audit certificates, to be submitted by the state for CSS. As J&K follows a cash basis of accounting, releases to implementing units are treated as expenditure and reported back to the GoI, which is not conducive to good management. This accounting policy has in-built incentive for the state to 'spend' the budget for fear of lapse of budgets, without sufficient focus on utilisation of the funds. This is evidenced by the large fund releases in the last quarter of the financial year. It also creates conditions for transfer of funds to lower level implementing units and often results in funds lying idle at various levels with little oversight. There is no pressure on the state to obtain expenditures reports, utilization certificates and audit assurance on the actual utilization of funds.

Roll-over Plans: Annual Plans, Budgets and Allocations have the disadvantage of the process starting all over again the following year with a few more months spent on re-planning. A "Roll-over" facility may be followed with the unspent budget of one year being carried over to the next without having to go through the elaborate annual plan and budgeting process. The GoI may be requested to try out a few pilot projects based on this concept. This concept is used very often in the corporate sector.

Transparency: Again, as in other administrative functions, transparency in financial management requires: (i) publication of program performance reports, and (ii) feedback mechanisms to elicit client feedback on the quality of services provided.

VIII. Programme Monitoring and Implementation

Officials at all levels spend a great deal of time in collecting and submitting information, but these are not used for taking corrective and remedial action or for analysis, but only for forwarding it to a higher level, or for answering Assembly Questions. Field staff reports only on activities, it is not involved in impact assessment, or in qualitative monitoring. The concept of stakeholder monitoring is unknown. No indicators exist for assessing public participation or their awareness.

Emphasis is laid only on the initial or current expenses. After five years, little is done or monitored. Secondly, when money has been allocated for a particular activity in a particular area, it is assumed that the work in question has been done, and that it was sufficient. This ignores the fact that either of the above assumptions could be wrong. The primary monitoring activities have to do with fiscal accountability. While it is necessary, it should not be allowed to overshadow the need for technical and resource monitoring and planning work accordingly. At present, there is great pressure on the field staff as a whole to account for funds utilized, but not in terms of longer-term results, because those are not monitored. Thus financial planning is divorced from physical planning.

In some cases academic institutions are asked to review the schemes. Their approach emphasizes rigour, but often its completion requires years and policy-makers lose their patience with their work. There are also reports by professional consulting organisations, especially on centrally sponsored schemes. However, the Departments look upon giving of funds to consulting organisations as a patronage activity. Little interest is taken in ensuring the quality of the report, or in following up on their recommendations.

Therefore, it is not enough that the government departments use professional and academic organisations to undertake impact studies from time to time. Their findings must be publicised and discussed with key stakeholders so that improvements in design and delivery can be effected at the earliest. Governments should also put on its website findings of the impact studies, and distribute these in the workshops it organizes. Dissemination of results is critical for use. Results that are not widely disseminated, through mechanisms tailored to different groups in civil society, will not be used, and the resources that were spent in getting such results will be wasted.

To sum up, weaknesses in public expenditure management —both budget programming and budget execution—have reduced the effectiveness of public spending. Expenditure programming has been approached as an accounting exercise, rather than as a tool for achieving policy objectives. The focus has been on inputs rather than outputs and outcomes, with departments asked to explain where they would spend money, but not held to account for delivery against performance indicators. On the other hand, the nature and extent of risk of fraud, waste and abuse of public funds is growing.

Streamlining State and District Administration: A recent report on decentralization in Karnataka reveals the astounding fact that there are over 400 'plan' schemes in each of the state's 27 districts, many of which constitute only small trickles of money but enough to justify the continuation of posts and salaries to administer such 'programs'. In total, there are about 658 budget heads in the average Karnataka district budget operated by the district authorities directly, and another 1,000 heads operated by the state government in the district.[5] The confusion in districts across much of India generated by the proliferation of schemes, budget heads, and related establishments costs is compounded by overlapping and poorly defined functions involving a plethora of line departments, elected councils, and planning authorities. There could be similarly a large number of schemes in J&K. Without a serious attempt at streamlining state and district administration, clarifying roles and responsibilities, and eliminating overlapping jurisdictions, confusion, and an accompanying loss of the capacity to clearly pinpoint responsibility, will become near permanent features of governance in India. Disentangling this maze, particularly developing clearer and shorter paths for the flow of funds as well as for taking decisions among center, state, and local government, is thus an important factor in enforcing accountability across the system.

Programme monitoring: Monitoring of programmes is critical to ensure proper fund utilization and measure outcomes. The recent J&K government initiative of introducing Additional District Development Commissioners in the Districts as independent programme monitoring agencies is a welcome move. Further efforts for ensuring linkages between activities undertaken and actually delivered would strengthen programme monitoring to a great extent.

Outcome Measurement: Apart from generating and disseminating information regarding services and their progress (as discussed in the section on Transparency above), providers and policy-makers should know (and be constantly learning) about what works,. This requires outcomes to be more regularly measured and their determinants analyzed. One critical role of the state government, when districts and departments have the primary responsibility for the delivery of publicly-funded services,

5. Government of Karnataka, Department of Rural Development and Panchayat Raj, Report of the Working Group on Decentralisation, (Bangalore: Department of Rural Development and Panchayat Raj, 2002), p. 101.

is to be an independent source for this measurement. Initially, measurement of outcomes may just be for information and the sake of openness. Over time, such measures could be used to hold districts and departments accountable for improvements—perhaps to the extent of conditioning fiscal transfers to District Boards based on progress. It is in the experimentation that such flexibility allows that solutions to the problem of implementation can be found. Lessons learned will help all districts and departments improve their performance.

Documentation and dissemination: Being able to document what actually happens is absolutely critical to an outcome orientation. Without good information on what has happened, a focus on results is impossible. And for good information, one requires monitoring or tracking of progress in accordance with objectives and indicators, along with evaluation that can look at broader considerations.

Capture district-wise data to fix accountability: Often data on performance reaches late, or is not available district-wise, with the result that accountability cannot be fixed. On the other hand, state governments do not discourage reporting of inflated figures from the districts, which again renders monitoring ineffective. For instance, the Rapid Household Survey, conducted in 1998-99 and repeated in 2002-03 indicates a fall in full immunisations across the country from 54.2 per cent in 1998-99 to 48.2 per cent in 2002-03, with rapid decline in the poorer states, as shown in Table 3. Similarly, delivery at public institutions has declined from 24% to 18.5%, and ANM making home visit within two weeks from 14.1 to 12.7% during the same period.

TABLE 3

Full Immunisation under Universal Immunisation Programme

(per cent)

	1998-99	*2002-03*
Uttar Pradesh	43.7	29.8
Andhra Pradesh	74.5	61.6
Assam	46.7	27.6
Haryana	66	57.9
Madhya Pradesh	48.4	34

(MTA X Plan)

Had this data been available timely and for each district, it would be easy to fix responsibility and help in outcome monitoring. On the other hand, as data is often not verified or collected through independent sources, no action is taken against officers indulgirig in bogus reporting. Similarly, district-wise data on IMR needs to be made available for every year in J&K.

According to an article in Indian Pediatrics (August 17, 2005), results of a survey in district Kargil showed that only 65% of infants received full primary immunization, with rural areas fairing worse (62%) than the urban areas (72%). Coverage rates were similar in boys and girls. Antigen-wise, the highest coverage (92.5%) was seen for BCG, and the poorest (65%) for measles vaccine. The attrition from the first to third dose of DPT and OPV (from 89% to 83%) was remarkable; drop-out rates from the 3rd priming dose (83%) to booster (31%) at 16-24 months were far steeper. Some 7.5% of the infants remained completely un-immunized, while 28.5% were only partially primed. However, since the results of such honest surveys are not known to district authorities, no action is taken to improve the situation.

Fund utilization: The Chief Secretary should review every month whether the entitled funds from GoI are being received in the state by the concerned departments. Information on SGRY for 2005-06 (Table 4) shows that as against an allocation of 26 crores, districts could receive only 15 crores, presumably because of delay in submission in UCs. The data for SGSY reveals a similar picture (Table 5). Similarly, gross underutilization has also been reported. For instance in SGSY, as against the total availability of funds to the tune of Rs. 72 crore during 2005-06, expenditure was only Rs. 36 crore. As for the Total Sanitation Campaign, as against the availability of Rs. 130 crores, expenditure was nil.[6] In fact J&K has the dubious distinction of recording poorest performance in construction of household toilets, as shown below:

Transparency in programme implementation: District-level programme implementation could be made more transparent by the use of Information Technology. For instance, the tendering process for carrying out works and procurement could be made online. Many States in India have experimented with this initiative. Punjab has for example implemented electronic

6. Rural Development Department, Government of J&K.

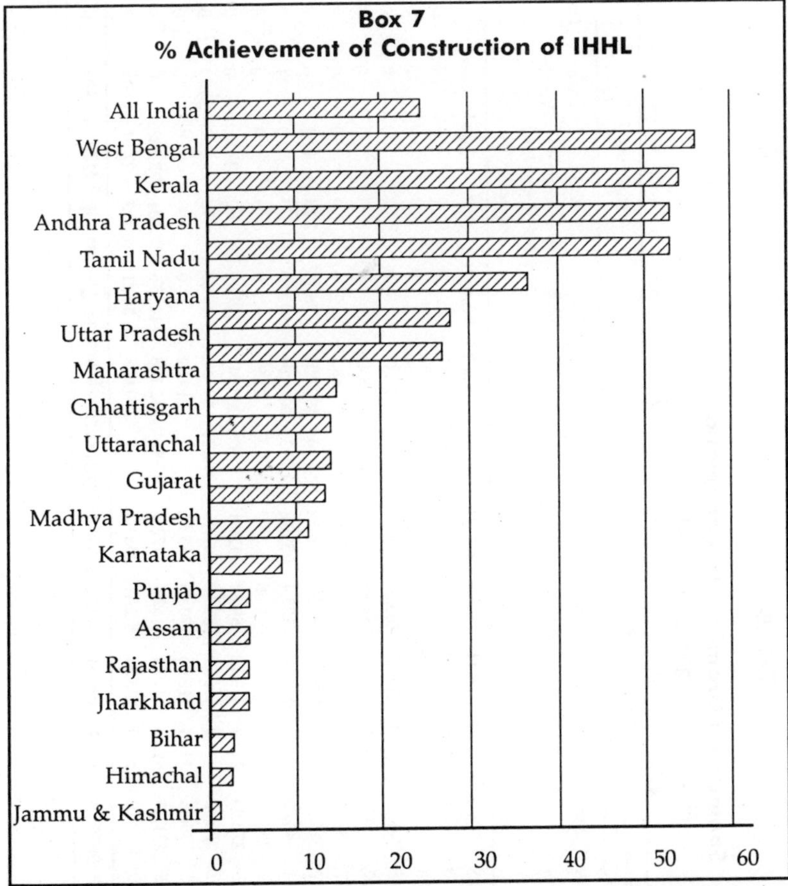

tendering or e-tendering, whereby traditional tendering processes are carried but using the internet. The scheme covers the full cycle of purchasing from indent to receipt of goods and connects buyers and suppliers through electronic exchange of information. Such processes would ensure greater transparency in administration and reduce the opportunities for siphoning funds by various actors in the process.

IX. Enforcing zero tolerance for human rights violations and security to all sections of society

Policy decision: A recent *India Today* Survey on the State of the

TABLE 4

Sampoorna Grameen Rozgar Yojana
Financial Progress, Year 2005-06

S. No.	District	Till Month	Opening Balance	Allocation			Central RIs	Releases			Misc. Receipt	Total Availability	Utilization				
				Centre	State	Total	Last Yr. red. this Year	Centre	State	Total			Gen. Works	SC/ST		Maintenance	Train
														Ind. Beneficiaries	Habi.		
1.	Anantnag	March	32.49	390.7	138.5	529.2	0	356.44	138.5	494.94	1.77	520.2	385.652	0	82.44	6.83	0
2.	Badgam	March	0	0	0	0	0	0	0	0	0	0	0	0	0	0	0
3.	Baramulla	March	0	0	0	0	0	0	0	0	0	0	0	0	0	0	0
4.	Doda	June	0	259.96	86.65	346.61	0	114.38	105.09	219.47	0	219.47	0	0	0	0	0
5.	Jammu	June	14.26	321	107	428	26.79	0	81.88	81.88	0.48	123.41	0	0	0	0	0
6.	Kargil	Nov.	74.26	163.74	100.7	338.7	0	163.74	100.7	264.44	0	338.7	119.76	0	0	0	0
7.	Kathua	Dec.	0.634	227.89	82.42	310.31	0	136.73	61.79	196.52	0	199.154	78.13	2.28	51.33	0	0
8.	Kupwara	March	44.901	219.63	123.4	343.03	0	131.78	123.4	255.18	1.213	301.294	260.883	0	0	11	0
9.	Leh	June	23.99	193.79	64.6	258.39	0	0	0	0	0	23.99	0	0	0	0	0
10.	Pulwama	Feb.	2.015	199.13	79.5	278.63	24.93	119.48	59.62	179.1	0	206.045	117.49	3.2	37.85	0	0
11.	Punch	Dec.	6.11	193.81	68.22	262.03	0	116.29	51.16	167.45	24.27	197.83	48.07	0	0	50.13	0
12.	Rajouri	June	0.17	263.1	87.7	350.8	32.94	115.76	70.15	185.91	0	219.02	0	0	0	0	0
13.	Srinagar	Mar.	3.322	168.93	62.5	231.43	61.58	110.4	62.5	172.9	4.386	242.188	144.576	12.104	72.888	0	0
14.	Udhampur	Nov.	3.658	0	0	0	0	133.54	102.41	235.95	0	239.608	34.21	14.113	27.51	1.934	0
	Total		205.81	2601.68	1001.19	3677.13	146.24	1498.54	957.2	2455.74	32.119	2839.909	1188.771	31.697	272.018	69.894	0

TABLE 5

Swarnajayanti Gram Swarozgar Yojana
Financial Progress, Year 2005-06

S. No.	District	Till Month	Opening Balance	Allocation			Releases		Misc. Receipts				Total funds Available	Utilization of Funds
				Centre	State	Total	Central (%)	State	Interest incurred	Return of subsidy	Others	Total		
1	2	3	4	5	6	7	8	9	10	11	12	13	14	15
1.	Anantnag	03	32.46	73.31	24.437	96.31	35.11 (47.89)	23	1.5	2.53	0	4.03	94.6	56.56
2.	Baramulla	03	40.82	77	25.667	121.85	56.9 (73.9)	0	0	0	0	0	97.72	75.57
3.	Badgam	03	32.65	48.41	16.137	69.26	26.34 (54.41)	20.85	0	0	0	0	79.84	50.58
4.	Doda	03	17.53	133.8	44.6	178.4	30.74 (22.97)	44.6	1.39	2.025	0	3.415	96.285	76.8
5.	Jammu	03	9.01	51.68	17.227	81.48	24.75 (47.89)	29.81	3.02	1.85	0	4.87	68.44	58.83
6.	Kargil	03	4.48	7.11	2.37	7.11	4.8 (67.51)	7	0.09	0.77	0	0.86	17.14	15.85

(Contd.)

TABLE 5 (*Contd.*)

1	2	3	4	5	6	7	8	9	10	11	12	13	14	15
7.	Kathua	03	3.38	28.44	9.48	43.19	13.62 (47.89)	14.75	1.27	0	0	1.27	33.02	32.56
8.	Kupwara	03	10	38.86	12.953	60.76	33.26 (85.59)	21.9	0.34	0	0	0.34	65.5	41.6
9.	Leh	03	1.89	6.34	2.113	6.34	8.22 (129.65)	2.74	0.02	1.71	0	1.73	14.58	14.16
10.	Punch	03	4.59	33.86	11.287	53.51	16.23 (47.93)	19.65	0.13	0.25	0	0.38	40.85	36.64
11.	Pulwama	03	5.59	30.41	10.137	46.26	30.41 (100)	15.85	0.21	0	0	0.21	52.06	36.03
12.	Rajouri	03	0.05	50.36	16.787	73.76	51.41 (102.08)	23.4	0.43	0.08	0	0.51	75.37	65.98
13.	Srinagar	03	5.72	22.89	7.63	34.44	10.96 (47.88)	8.66	0.45	1.81	0	2.26	27.6	27.43
14.	Udhampur	03	11.93	68.07	22.69	68.07	65.67 (96.47)	30	0.008	10.742	0	10.75	118.35	152.5
	Total		180.1	670.54	223.515	940.74	408.42 (60.91)	262.21	8.858	21.767	0	30.625	881.355	740.7

States[7] shows that among all the States, J&K has the largest police force relative to its population: 3,740 policemen per million people. In the same survey, J&K is ranked 17 out of 20 big Indian States. J&K has continuously been in the limelight for human rights violations by its security forces (including armed forces and police). Recently a Human Rights Watch Report alleged that the State's failure to end widespread human rights abuses by security forces and militants was responsible for fuelling the cycle of violence in the State. Clearly human rights violations have been a major issue of concern in the State and the declared (by the State government) policy of 'zero tolerance for human rights violations' comes at an appropriate time.

Capacity Building: The State Human Rights Commission requires strengthening as the body enforcing respect for human rights. That awareness about the Commission has grown is evident by the increase in the number of complaints it has received —from 395 in 2001 to 474 in 2002. However, it suffers from resource constraints and requires more teeth to carry out its tasks. Applications should be disposed in a time-bound manner. All recommendations should be acted upon by the State Government and in case any recommendation is not accepted, reasons for the same should be given through a speaking order. There should be a high-powered Committee (including political representatives and civil society members) for enforcing human rights and emphasis on rule of law, accountability and proper implementation of laws.

Awareness generation: The Press and civil society organizations can be brought into the picture for awareness generation activities and positive reporting on human rights issues. These agencies can act as watchdogs and help ensure speedy redressal of complaints of human rights violations. Also comprehensive training must be imparted to the law enforcing agencies on what comprises human rights and its violations.

X. Strengthening Local Self-Government

State Finance Commission: J&K has set-up a State Finance

7. *India Today*, Special Issue, 'State of the States', September 11, 2006.
8. Entitled 'Everyone Lives in Fear: Patterns of Impunity in Jammu and Kashmir'.

Commission and this is a move towards analyzing the problems in Panchayats and redressing them. The Godbole Committee Report had suggested that J&K should consider extending the provisions of the 73rd Amendment of the Indian Constitution to the State for reviving these institutions.

Status: The following tables show the status of Panchayati Raj in the State after the 2001 elections. (Table 6)

The Table 6 show that in Kashmir Division more than 50% of the seats for Panches are lying vacant. The panchayats in the States are not functioning as instruments of vigorous local self-government. This is evidenced by the following facts:

1. Halqa Panchayats have very limited powers of taxation. They also do not have the necessary apparatus for decentralized planning—neither functions nor functionaries.
2. Halqa Panchayats have limited activities under their jurisdiction. Many areas considered important to be governed at the local level, such as primary education, are in limited purview of the Hatqa Panchayats.
3. There is no independent Election Commission in the State.
4. Members of District Development Boards are not directly elected.
5. There are no Block Development Councils.

In this situation a reconsideration of the State PR Act is required. Some of the suggestions for strengthening local self-government could be:

(i) A comprehensive capacity assessment exercise followed by a capacity building one.
(ii) Effective transfer of funds, functions and functionaries to the Panchayats would have to be taken up on priority.
(iii) Activity Mapping exercise on the lines of that which is being carried out in other states and rationalization of schemes to be implemented by PRIs.
(iv) Training for capacity building of Panchayat members may also be undertaken simultaneously.

TABLE 6

Information Regarding Panchayat Election, J&K, 2001[9]

District	No. of Blocks	No. of Panches	No. of Sarpanches elected	No. of Sarpanches vacancies	Total No. of Panches to be elected	No. of Panches elected	No. of vacancies of Panches	No. of Pyts. Notified by Govt.	No. of Pyts. yet to be notified
A. Kashmir Division									
Kupwara	9	224	168	58	1471	915	556	95	129
Baramulla	14	276	162	114	2148	902	1246	93	178
Leh	6	68	68	—	448	448	—	67	1
Kargil	7	65	65	—	453	453	—	65	—
Budgam	8	199	61	138	1444	315	1129	25	174
Srinagar	4	93	67	2(3	666	247	419	21	72
Anantnag	10	309	251	58	2242	1191	1051	121	188
Pulwama	6	236	202	34	1586	684	902	26	210
Total	64	1470	1042	428	10458	5155	5303	518	952
B. Jammu Division									
Jammu	11	295	294	01	2448	2443	05	295	0
Kathua	08	183	182	01	1394	1391	03	182	1
Poonch	05	115	115	—	1028	1026	02	114	1
Udhampur	12	21	212	03	1840	1792	48	210	5
Doda	14	262	216	29	2004	1698	306	216	46
Rajouri	07	160	160	—	1376	1364	12	160	0
Total	57	12 30	1196	34	10090	9714	376	1177	53

Source: Reconstructed from the information received from Directorate of Rural Development, Srinagar/Jammu.

9. State Development Report, Planning Commission, GoI.

(v) Mobilization of community to be partners in local governance.

XI. Measures to Provide Adequate Security to all Segments of Society, Particularly the Minority Communities

(1) The security forces have to adopt a citizen-friendly approach and ensure that while militancy and law and order are adequately tackled, innocent persons should not be harmed and their life and property adequately protected.

(2) The areas having residence of minorities or others who have a threat should be identified and provided with special protection. Help of para military forces should also be taken in this regard and their units located in vulnerable areas.

(3) Local Panchayats and other bodies should be asked to have a system of community watch to ensure that elements who pose a threat are identified in advance and are unable to get any local support.

(4) Setting up of a Minorities Commission to regularly look into the problems of Minorities should be examined.

Conclusion

The above-mentioned proposals have been made keeping in mind the specific task given to the Working Group. In addition, the Group also observed that reform of legislature and judiciary is also important apart from that of administration. However, implementation is the key to success of good governance initiatives. Full implementation of these suggestions is what would make for good governance. Therefore; the Group felt that it is necessary that a set of guiding principles and steps to be followed for implementation are listed out separately. The next chapter sets out these guidelines and action steps for J&K state.

CHAPTER 3

Implementation of the Good Governance Initiatives

The initiatives suggested by the Working Group would require strategic changes at the line department level and at the level of the frontline service delivery institutions. It is imperative that staff actually get to know and practice good governance principles. The Government of J&K's good governance planning process should have as its basic premise and as a *sine qua non* that all efforts should be aimed at providing quality services to the citizens, especially the poor and the marginalized. The following may be viewed as the key ingredients for success of good governance initiatives:

- That all government departments and institutions have the capacity to carry out the implementation of the initiatives.
- That the concept of citizen-centric service delivery is firmly engrained as the basic premise on which institutions base their working.
- That standards are set for each department and institution so that improvement in service delivery becomes clearly measurable, and
- That good governance is sustained over time.

Strategy Outline

The initiatives suggested by the Working Group may be implemented in a structured manner. Not only is it essential that the sequencing of reform be undertaken, implementation may be undertaken in comprehensive manner to ensure service delivery improvement, administrative efficiency and sustainability of reform. The strategy would include a definitive administrative set-up for implementation, getting the Departments on board for undertaking reform, comprehensive, mass training on good governance and citizen-centric service delivery and the monitoring of the implementation processes itself (through external means and by the state government itself). What would be required would be a Special Purpose Vehicle for delivery of reforms, support systems for implementation and purposive training. At a later stage in the process, standards could be ensured through a baseline survey, a citizens' survey and a social audit. Monitoring and impact evaluation for the reforms may be in the form of a Social Audit, post-implementation as a longer term vision. All these steps would need to be preceded by policy change adopting good governance as the stated policy. Some of these arrangements and requirements are discussed in some detail below. Diagram 1 depicts the strategy for reform (please refer page 38)

A Special Purpose Vehicle for Good Governance Implementation

The Government of J&K may think of establishing a "Special Purpose Vehicle" (SPV) on good governance management on the lines of a 'Centre for Modernizing Government'. This could be an independent training-*cum*-implementation Centre or may be part of GAD. If independent, the SPV could have wider participation from the community on its governing structure and should have as its main goal enabling the government to ensure it delivers on the basic issues of governance and services. One wing of the Centre could be responsible for undertaking IT-related administrative reforms and implementing them and the other could be devoted to Training of officials for capacity building. A High level Committee chaired by the Chief Secretary should monitor the progress periodically. The Centre may be responsible for developing a Results-Based Management strategy for implementing the reforms suggested.

In addition, for the concept of good governance to be ingrained across board, the strategy could be to use extensive training in a "mass instruction" mode. The instruction material may include tailor-made mass-communication-based modules on good governance and service delivery management that could be beamed through television, sent as compact disks, could be transmitted as streaming videos through the Internet, delivered through personal contact sessions by paid and volunteer instructors to the government institutions. In addition, the Government of J&K would have to ensure one very important feature: that is, all instruction materials relate to the local conditions and features.

This SPV should also be able to conceptualize and carry forward the utilization of the mass instruction mentioned above by providing grassroots support in implementation of initiatives. It is evident from the case of other states, that the current thinking and capacity of State Institutes of Administration are not adequately geared to address these tasks. The need for a new approach may be stated here, and it may be suggested that this area could be one where a Public-Private Partnership could bear fruits.

Support Systems for Implementation

Software for tracking implementation: A part of the implementation arrangements may be the development of software for tracking progress of the initiatives. What is required, especially considering the need for sustainability is an IT tool that would not only show progress but also give analytical inputs to a decision-maker. What could be thought of as the implementation progresses is custom-made software going beyond standard ERP for business enterprises. It should have at least the following features: on-line data capture, 'user-friendly rules for decision-making, real-time data on infrastructure, human resource, finances, procedures and processes, analytical information—including easy features for aggregation and dis-aggregation on various parameters—that would aid managerial decision-making, a platform for sharing information across departments and institutions, quick-search facility, successful case studies, unique features that need to be factored in for exceptional cases, etc. The depth and breadth of data and information requirements would vary according to where in the hierarchy of government a user fits in, and hence; the design would have to be multi-layered.

Programme Support Executives: At the level of the department or the district, implementation could be undertaken by a separate cadre of people posted in each of the districts. This could be in the nature of Support Executives—a cadre of young trained and qualified men and women who have basic managerial skills and qualifications. This would serve the dual purpose of implementing the initiatives and providing employment to qualified youth in the state. The Support Executives may be hired by the SPV (suggested above) and could be stationed in the District headquarters or in the selected departments to carry out implementation and report progress to the implementing agency.

Reform Champions: No service can be reconstructed without the support of a champion who is usually an experienced manager. For champions to succeed, they usually need political support to insulate themselves from pressures to reverse changes that reduce rent-seeking opportunities for politicians, employees, and, in some cases, consumers as well. Strong support from the Chief Minister in the case of both Andhra Pradesh and Karnataka in the past has made it possible for IT initiatives to succeed without major employee resistance. It is also hard to imagine the innovations introduced to control transfers in Karnataka, especially mass transfers, without the support of the Chief Minister. In Maharashtra, the reform of the Stamps and Registration Department, which generates substantial annual revenues, was overseen by a dedicated manager who had the support of the Cabinet, which approved his restructuring package, including turning over core functions in the Department to the private sector. Managerial champions thus require well-honed political skills to convince politicians to take risks, while reform-minded politicians require good managers to implement their larger goals.

Annual Index of Good Governance: The concept of good governance needs to be translated into a quantifiable annual index, and measured for each district, on the basis of certain agreed indicators such as infant mortality rate, extent of immunisation, literacy rate for women, availability of safe drinking water supply, electrification of rural households, extent of power dues recovered, rural and urban unemployment, percentage of girls married below 18 years, percentage of villages not connected by all weather roads, number of class I government officials prosecuted and convicted for corruption, and so on. Some universally accepted criteria for good budgetary practices may also be included in the index. Once these figures are publicized, districts may get into a competitive mode towards improving their score. Financial transfers to the districts should be linked to such an index.

Political and Administrative Will: Needless to say that such comprehensive reforms need for their sustenance strong political and administrative will from the top. In its absence, reforms remain only on paper.

Sequencing of reform: Government of J&K should decide the sequencing of the suggestions given in this report. Not all reforms can be undertaken simultaneously. Government should take up those where the negative side-effects are minimal. These are like the low hanging fruits where benefits far outweigh the costs.

A good civil service is necessary but not sufficient for good governance; a bad civil service is sufficient but not necessary for bad governance. Hence the paramount necessity of improving the performance of the civil service, without which services will never reach the 'Aam Admi'.

DIAGRAM 1

Implementation Arrangements

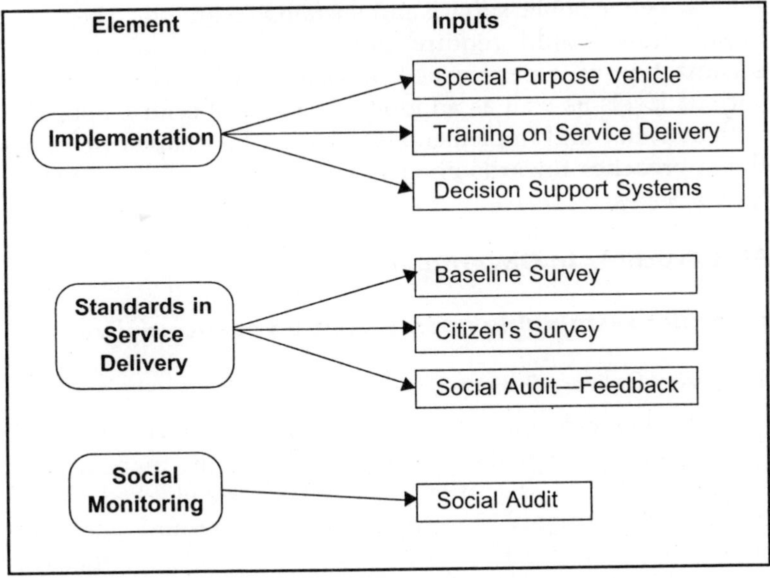

APPENDIX I—4

Best Practices in Governance Across Indian States

Introduction

Achieving good governance implies that the operational arms of the government or government institutions that directly interface with the citizens will plan and act in such a way as to achieve better public service and sustainable growth. These two broad aims would require interventions in the realm of organization of the concerned departments and institutions at various levels as well as adoption of a citizen-centric approach both at policy and implementation level. This chapter describes the approaches towards good governance adopted in various Indian States.

Best Practices in Governance

I. Kerala: sustainable people-centred service delivery

1. Service Delivery Project

The Government of Kerala identified service delivery improvement, particularly to the poor and the marginalized sections of society as a priority. In 2003-04 it embarked upon a major Service delivery improvement programme and within this context developed a now policy for service delivery that was capable of application to all public services provided by state and local self-governments. The Service Delivery Project (SDP) became one of the action-research fast track projects designed to test out the ground level realities in putting into action the superstructure of results-based management system through the Service Delivery Policy. The SDP seeks to create 2585 model institutions in 8 departments and 22 categories of Institutions. The key focus areas in SDP have been setting standards, implementation, relating resource allocation to services provided and social monitoring. The project involves the preparation of service delivery (improvement plans by frontline officials in the selected institutions, and implementation of those plans on a fast track basis through an intense process of identifying existing and new services through consultation, assessing requirements and budgeting for improvements - all at the frontline service delivery level. This has been the first effort of its kind in India for a State government to attempt sustainability of its public services on such a large scale through participatory planning. The process of mapping services across departments and planning for improvement on this large scale may be a model for other States to follow.

2. *DC Suite*

The District of Palakkad in Kerala became in 2002-03 the first IT enabled district headquarters in India. The district collectorate underwent total computerization, which was part of the Modernizing of Government Programme (MGP) of the Kerala Government. The objective of the exercise was to make the services of the collectorate more citizen-friendly. DC Suite is a web enabled centralized and integrated service delivery system consisting of a set of applications covering 21 functional areas of work in the Collectorate. These include an electronic file management system, revenue recovery management and public grievance monitoring system. It enables the public to retrieve information through multi-channel service delivery access points like touch screen kiosks, interactive voice response system, SMS, service counters, e-mail, internet kiosks. It has the scope of interconnectivity with other IT enabled development projects in the State, thus taking services to the grassroots level, improving access and promoting transparency in administrative systems.

3. *Kudumbasree*

Kudumbdsree is a poverty eradication project launched by the Government of Kerala with the active support of the Centre and NABARD with the aim of wiping out absolute poverty from the State within 10 years.

The project is implemented by the State Poverty Eradication Mission of the State government through local self-governing bodies. In this model, nine non-economic indicators are used to identify the beneficiary 'at risk' families—possession of a *kutcha* house, no access to safe drinking water and sanitation, presence of illiterate adults in the family with not more than one earning member, family barely getting two meals a day or less, presence of children below the age of five, presence of an alcoholic or drug addict member in the family and persons belonging to the Scheduled Caste or Scheduled Tribe. In 1994 the Community Based Nutrition Programme and Poverty Alleviation Project (CBNP & PAP) started functioning with UNICEF assistance and participation of the local community in the area of Malappuram, considered the most backward district of-Kerala. Over 4000 neighbourhood self-help groups were formed under this project. These SHGs started mobilising savings and were linked to various commercial banks under the Linkage Banking Programme of NABARD. The implementation of various government-sponsored programmes for improving health and sanitation in Malappuram District was channelled through these SHGs. Besides empowering women through community organisation, Kudumbasree encourages and guides them in starting small livelihood earning enterprises. Products manufactured by such enterprises are sold through the rural marketing network.

The Kudumbasree network has expanded in Kerala and has been a model for community mobilization and self-help initiatives all over the State. It is also an example of active peoples' participation, women's empowerment and constructive linkages between the government and citizens.

4. FRIENDS

The FRIENDS project has been implemented by the Information Technology Department, Government of Kerala in collaboration with various departments like the Kerala State Electricity Board, Kerala Water Authority, BSNL Revenue Department, Civil Supplies Department, Motor Vehicles Department, Universities and the Local Bodies of the State. It is a "Single Window Scheme" giving the citizens the option of paying for the common services rendered to them under a single roof. FRIENDS is a multiple agency bill collection system. The FRIENDS project envisages facilitating the collection of various payments pertaining to payees within specified area limits like corporation municipality etc. at a single centre.

FRIENDS is an example of improving access, timeliness, reduction in the channel of citizen-government interface—all through the effective use of Information Technology.

II. Experiences from Andhra Pradesh

I. The Indira Kranti Pratham Project

The extremely poor groups in Andhra Pradesh were organized under the Velugu scheme in 2000 (recently renamed Indira Kranti Pratham). It is another example of successfully organizing communities (especially women members) into self-help groups to enhance their resource management capacities. To date approximately 6 million rural poor women have been organized into self-help groups and village organizations at the village level, Mandal Samakhyas at the block level, and Zilla Samakhyas at the district level. According to a recent World Bank Report (2006) Velugu has significantly increased the access of self-help groups to commercial credit. Total annual credit to poor households and their groups has increased twelve-fold from Rs. 2.3 crore in 2000 to Rs. 27.6 crore in 2005. The total credit flow from commercial banks to these groups since 2000 has grown to Rs. 63.1 crore and is expected to reach 100 crore by the time the project closes. As in the case of Kudumbasree of Kerala, Velugu has been used extensively for the implementation of development projects at the district level.

2. e-Seva

e-Seva is an e-governance tool built on the public-private partnership model. It provides citizens with a transparent, efficient and effective administrative system and is a one-stop shop for a range of citizen-friendly services. The services include those of the State, Local, Central government and private business. Connection with all departments online enables transactions at an e-Seva centre to be simultaneously updated in the servers of participating departments

III. Maharashtra: Examples of Good Governance

1. SETHU

This project implemented in the Thane Collectorate has involved delegation of certificate issuing powers from the Collector to the Deputy Collector, SDM and Tahsildar for the entire district. This system has been a good example of simplification of government procedure in favour of the citizens availing the services. It has significantly reduced transaction time and made the procedure transparent since the initial processing of applications is done on a computer through a cooperative society. The citizen is able to correct mistakes in data entry on the spot and the decision on his/her application is made within 24 hours.

The SETHU project is an example of private-public partnership with the involvement of civil society actors in processing applications and in initial funding of the set-up. It is also yet another instance of IT leading to improvement in service delivery by cutting time and reducing the margin for errors.

2. Upgradation of Stamps and Registration Department

Modernization of sub-registries in the State has been brought about through extensive employee consultation. Subsequently, office maintenance was given out to private contractors for maintenance for five years. The element of discretion involved in the acceptance of applications by the sub-registrar has been done away with and documents are required to be automatically accepted and returned within a set standard time. The Ready Reckoner manual for determining property values has been computerized reducing the time taking in generating stamp values. This effort has made the standardization of service delivery possible across all sub-registries simultaneously. Facilities have been put in place for online interaction of the citizens with the department, thus taking services closer to the people.

IV. Reform in Karnataka

1. Rules for transfers of civil servants

The critical problem of frequent transfers has plagued many state governments by hampering the efficiency and effectiveness of public services. The problem had reached gigantic proportions in Karnataka during 2000-01 and the Departments accounting for most transfers were crucial ones such as Police, PWD and frontline officials in departments such as Health and Education. After imposing a blanket ban on transfers in 2001-02, the government decided to create a committee system to address requests for transfers at all levels. The innovation in this scheme was that Cadre Management Authorities were created for A, B, C, and D category posts. The new transfer rules raised minimum tenures across groups and certain cadres were exempt from transfers altogether. These measures reduced political interference to a large extent by creating a system of rules and increasing transparency by creating a database to track transfers over time.

2. The Learning Guarantee Programme

The Learning Guarantee Programme (LGP) is an example of public-private partnership in the education sector. An initiative of the Azim Premji Foundation from 2003-05, the aim of the project was to improve the quality of primary education by focusing on learning outcomes. The foundation worked with the State government in north-east Karnataka to support experimentation with innovative approaches on a large scale so that the lessons learnt could be successfully integrated into the large educational system. The difference in this programme was that it went beyond the issues of access to education to focus on pedagogical approaches and ultimately on the learning levels of cognitive and non-cognitive competencies. The focus was thus on the effectively assessing outcomes of learning in an area where high drop out rates and grade repetition rates had almost become a norm. The programme was also an innovation where it went beyond emphasizing inputs to analyzing outcomes.

The LGP used an incentive-based approach to optimize the ability of schools to achieve the objectives of universal enrolment, retention and enhanced learning levels. The success factors wore communicated from one school to all participating schools to motivate teachers, students and community members to strive for learning guarantee.

V. One Day Governance in Gujarat

The Gujarat government has initiated a number of e-governance schemes including e-grama and SWAGAT (State-wide attention of grievances by application of Technology) in recent times. One initiative that has won acclaim in the State has been the 'One Day Governance' scheme. The Scheme has entailed setting up of civic facilitation centres (Nagarik Seva Kendras) in Municipalities, Municipal Corporations, Taluka Offices and Collectorates. These centres are like the one-stop counters adopted by other states (like Maharashtra, Andhra Pradesh mentioned already). Wherein citizens can apply for various certificates like income, caste, domicile certificates, file affidavits, apply for Arms License Renewal, and many other documents and expect to get their documents within a few hours. This has resulted in cutting delays, reducing arbitrariness in service delivery and greater efficiency through the use of Information Technology.

VI. Tamil Nadu Good Governance

Public-private partnership in health care in Tamil Nadu

This good governance initiative in Tamil Nadu came about in 1997 by a realization by the government that resources were simply not enough for adequate upkeep and upgradation of health care institutions. The government therefore initiated a programme of industrial participation for maintenance of government health care facilities. Gaps in the public health system were identified and institutions requiring immediate attention identified. Industrialists were requested to volunteer to 'adopt' institutions and contribute to the infrastructure of that facility. The other models were of 'partial adoption', each differing from the other in terms of capital investment.

Apart from attracting investment in healthcare facilities, the programme resulted in facilitating local ownership and supervision and in developing important inter-sectoral linkages. It also created the much-needed asset base for medical facilities in the State.

VII. Examples from Madhya Pradesh

1. Gyandoot

Gyandoot is the Stockholm Challenge IT Award (2000) winning e-governance initiative of the Government of Madhya Pradesh. Initiated in the Dhar district—a tribal dominated district —the programme installed computer networks in the district connecting 31 village centres. The project provided online services including land revenue transactions, public grievance redressal, a matrimonial site, employment news and free e-mail facility on social issues. This helped improve interface between citizens and government and enabled knowledge access in a region populated by the marginalized tribal peoples.

2. *Rogi Kalyan Samiti*

The Rogi Kalyan Samiti project began in 1994 and involved management of public hospitals through community participation. Conceived as a response to local problems to improve the availability and quality of hospital infrastructure and services, a Samiti is set-up as a registered society but with active participation of the State government. It can use the premises and assets of the hospital it has been set-up for, raise additional resources and spend them in running the hospital and improving its services. Additional resources are usually raised through donations from the community and by levying user charges graded by peoples' ability to pay. The network of Rogi Kalyan Samiti has expanded significantly in Madhya Pradesh and has shown that even the poor are willing to pay user charges for better quality health care. It is also an example of community empowerment and participation in development. The project won the Global Development Network Award for the most innovative development project in 2001.

VIII. The Uttar Pradesh Example: Lokvani

Lokvani is an e-governance project one of the first of its kind in the State of Uttar Pradesh. The project, launched in Sitapur District of U.P. provides various e-governance services to the citizens. What is noteworthy in the project is that it provides an online grievance redressal mechanism in the form of online submission, monitoring and disposal of complaints. The system has been easy to access and operate a fact underscored by the popularity of the online public grievances redressal which received 11,000 complaints by March 2005 (it was launched in 2004). Lokvani also provides details of various government schemes, government prescribed forms, details of developmental work in the district, lists of old age pensioners, lists of scholarship beneficiaries, Funds allotted in various government schemes, allotment of foodgrains to kotedars, allotments of funds to gram panchayats, etc. The project has benefited citizens in a big way as it has enabled access to services at the Block, tehsil and town level, so citizens no longer have to travel all the way to the District office.

IX. Private Sector Initiatives to Improve Rural Livelihood[10]

1. ICICI banking services for the poor

To address the rural poor's unequal access to finance, ICICI Bank has led multiple initiatives to provide banking services at an affordable cost to the poor. ICICI has partnered with others to co-locate automatic teller machines with rural Internet kiosks and explore SmartCard technology to provide secure, low-cost transactions and loan management. More important, ICICI Bank has created a network of 8,000 self-help groups, covering about 160,000 women, to serve as the vehicle for creating successful, micro-financed businesses. In the process, ICICI Bank has given these women the means to transform their social and economic lives, their families, and their villages.

2. ITC e-Choupal

ITC e-Choupal illustrates how improvements in technology and communications infrastructure can be good for both equity and efficiency in product markets. ITC e-Choupal today reaches out to and empowers over 3.5 million farmers in 31,000 villages by enabling them to readily access crop-specific, customized, and comprehensive information in their local language. Vernacular websites provide real-time information to even the smallest marginal farmers on the prevailing Indian and international prices and price trends for their crop, expert knowledge on best farming practices, and micro-level weather forecast. This significantly improves the farmers' decision-making ability, thereby helping them better align their agricultural produce to market demand and ensure better quality, productivity, and price discovery. The ITC e-Choupal model has been specifically designed to tackle the challenges posed by the unique features of Indian agriculture, which is characterized by fragmented farms, weak infrastructure, information asymmetry, and numerous intermediaries. Over the next decade, the ITC e-Choupal network aims to cover more than 100,000 Indian villages, representing a sixth of rural India, and to create more than 10 million e-farmers.

[10] From the World Bank Development Policy Review, 2006.

ACKNOWLEDGEMENT

The Working Group on Good Governance was set-up by the Hon. Prime Minister as an outcome of the Second Round Table Conference on Jammu & Kashmir (J&K). The constitution of the Group and the terms of reference were detailed by the Hon. Chief Minister, Shri Ghulam Nabi Azad. The Group was charged with the mandate of considering effective measures to improve accountability, responsiveness and transparency in administration, enforce the Right to Information, improving monitoring and implementation of development programmes, strengthen local self-government and institute zero tolerance for human rights violations in the state.

Accordingly, the Group held a preliminary meeting in August 2006 at Srinagar to chalk out a plan of action and identify the important issues in governance of the state. Preliminary data collection including examples of good governance from other states was completed prior to consultations with the members of the Group. Subsequently, a series of meetings were held with senior officials of the Government of J&K to discuss the various policies, programmes and schemes of crucial sectors such as health, education, rural development, finance, etc. Based on these deliberations, a draft of the suggestions for good governance was prepared and presented at the second meeting of the Group in Jammu in November 2006. The present report is based on consensus that was developed during this meeting.

This report would not have been possible but for the keen interest shown by the Hon. Chief Minister Shri Ghulam Nabi Azad in the development of the state of Jammu & Kashmir. We are grateful to him for all the support and even more so for the wonderful hospitality we received in J&K.

Thanks are due to all the members of the Working Group on Good Governance who actively participated in the various meetings and also provided us their written comments and suggestions.

We were fortunate to have had senior officials from various departments sharing their analysis and insights about the outstanding issues in J&K with us. I am indebted to them for this. For reasons of space I am not individually naming them here.

A work of this nature required close coordination, which was ably provided by Shri Ajit Kumar, Financial Commissioner (Coordination), ably supported by Ms. Shally Ranjan, OSD. We are thankful to them for this as also for managing our logistics.

I am thankful to Ms. Tina Mathur, Consultant to the Group, for providing various intellectual inputs as also the initial drafts of the presentations and the report.

Above all, I would like to thank the people of J&K for the warmth that they showed us and I do hope that we have suggested measures for good governance in this report which will ultimately benefit them.

NARESH CHANDRA SAXENA
Chairman

APPENDIX I—5

Working Group V

SUMMARY OF RECOMMENDATIONS

1. Article 370 of the Constitution of India

It is for the people of the State of Jammu and Kashmir to decide how long to continue Article 370 in its present form and when to make it permanent of abrogate. The matter being 60 years old, should be settled once for all.

2. Demand of Autonomy by National Conference

The question of "Autonomy" and its demand can be examined in the light of the 'Kashmir Accord' or in some other manner or on the basis of some other formula as the present Prime Minister may deem fit and appropriate so as to restore the 'Autonomy[1] to the extent possible.

The question of appointment of the Governor and dismissal of the popular Government by the Governor may be considered and resolved.

3. Demand of Self Rule

Mr. M.H. Beg on behalf of PDP explained orally the concept of "Self Rule" but the 'Self Rule' as proposed by the PDP could not be considered in all its detail as the document containing the various aspects of the 'Self Rule' were not provided to the Working Group as promised by POP during the course of the proceedings.

Basically it appears to relate to 'Autonomy' in a wider context, which requires to be considered by the Central Government if and when approached with documents containing specific proposals of the "Self Rule". This document should be on record.

4. Term of Legislative Assembly of the State

Any change in the term of the Assembly will require political consensus among the various political parties in the State and it can be effected only through a Constitutional Amendment.

5. Representation/Reservation for Scheduled Tribe and Women in the Assembly

On this issue, the national pattern may be a good guide subject to political consensus.

6. Abolition of State Legislative Council

The present position may be maintained.

7. Increase in the number of Assembly seats and De-limitation Commission

Since the Constitutional provisions do not allow any change upto the year 2026, the present position may be maintained till then.

8. Strength of the Council of Ministers

Formation of the Ministry and strength of the Council of Ministers is the exclusive prerogative of the Chief Minister within the provisions of the Constitution.

9. Strengthening of the Democratic Process

Regular elections to democratic bodies including Panchayats and Municipalities etc. should be held.

10. Human Rights

The Human Right violations must not be tolerated and the State Government should take steps to strengthen institutions which are involved in safeguarding the human rights including the State Human Rights Commission.

Additional staff as recommended in the body of the report be sanctioned, which will work under the direct control of the Commission.

11. Right to Information Act and Accountability Commission

The positions vacant in the Accountability Commission may be filled up and the Commission should be made fully functional.

12. Armed Forces Special Powers Act

A group of Central Government and the State Government officers and peoples representatives may be constituted which will review the application of the Act to various parts of the State regularly to explore the possibility whether the Act can be withdrawn from any part of the State.

13. Issues relating to Kashmiri Migrants

The Central and State Governments must take all steps to implement the relief and rehabilitation packages sanctioned in this regard including the package announced by the present Prime Minister. The progress made should be regularly reviewed by a Group of Senior Officers from the Government of India and the State Government. Migrant employees should be encouraged to return to the Valley on guarantee of their children being admitted to educational/training institutions and they and their families be provided full security.

Large industrial units like ITI/HMT should be revived and migrants can also be housed in secure zones in these campuses, and also given employment.

Migrants within the Jammu Region may also be provided relief on the same pattern as the Kashmiri Migrants.

14. Issues relating to Refugees of 1947, 1965 and 1971 and other Migrants within Jammu Region

The recommendations of the Wadhwa Committee Report be implemented and an Empowered Group of Senior officers of Government of India/State Government be appointed to monitor the implementation of these recommendations and other measures as may be sanctioned by the State Government.

State Government may consider providing relief to the Refugees from West Pakistan as permissible under the Constitution. Otherwise an alternative package providing cash relief as one-time settlement be considered.

State Government may provide a limited number of seats to the children of the refugees from West Pakistan in technical institutions and the Government of India may provide employment to them in Central Government offices located in Jammu and Kashmir to the extent of 2%.

Other refugees and border migrants displaced as a result of conflict at international border/LOC be given suitable compensation and proper steps taken for their rehabilitation. Similarly those who were displaced in 1999 (after Kargil conflict) should be properly settled.

15. Under representation of Jammu in Legislative Assembly

Since there is Constitutional constraint to make any changes till the year 2026, as a new Delimitation Commission can be set up only thereafter, the present position may continue.

16. Discrimination against Jammu

The recommendations made by Gajendragadkar Commission and Sikri Commission may be kept in view while making out policies.

Planned Expenditure in the Jammu and Kashmir Regions and District sectors does not indicate any discrimination and this situation be maintained. (See detailed reasons)

The daily wage rate in all areas should be on the basis of 'Equal Pay for Equal Work' and there shall not be any discrimination.

State Government should take steps to ensure that viable projects under IRDF or any other scheme are prepared for consideration.

A Dogri Channel may be set up on the lines of Kashir Channel of the Doordarshan.

For improvement in technical education, the NIT at Srinagar and Government Engineering College at Jammu be upgraded to I IT level. Similarly the Central Government may also establish an MM in the State.

Steps be taken to promote IT Industry in both Jammu and Kashmir regions to open up the employment opportunities for technically qualified youth.

The Finance Commission recently set up by the State Government will be an appropriate forum to address any left out grievances of any regions of the State. The Scope of Work given to the Finance Commission needs to be effectively taken up for finding permanent solution.

Although the recommendations of The Gajendragadkar

Commission, The Sikri Commission and The Wazir Commission have largely been implemented, the State Government may examine if any further action is required so as to remove any apprehension about discrimination against any part of the state as brought out by some of the members.

The State Government may also look into the statement that the Civil Secretariate and H.O.D. offices have a proportionately high number of non-gazetted employees from The Kashmir Valley and if so this may be corrected through appropriate measure.

17. Union Territory Status for Ladakh

It is not recommended that the unity and integrity of the State of Jammu and Kashmir be compromised and the Union Territory Status for Ladakh is not recommended.

The functioning of Ladakh Autonomous Hill Development Council has been very successful and it may continue its commendable work.

Regarding higher cost of construction in Ladakh, the State Government/Finance Commission should make appropriate budget allocation for this region.

A separate university for Ladakh can be considered to be set up.

18. Position of Chief Minister, Dy. Chief Minister and Ministers from Ladakh

No specific recommendation is made except that the elected government should ensure that adequate representation is given to all regions of the State at appropriate levels, and may also consider the question of appointment of Dy. CM. either from Jammu/Kashmir or Ladakh depending on the region to which the Chief Minister belongs.

19. Representation in the Supreme Court

The High Court of Jammu and Kashmir has benches in both Jammu and Srinagar and are functional round the year, it will be appropriate and advisable in view of the Special Status of the State That Judges to the Supreme Court are elevated from both Jammu and Srinagar.

20. Regional Councils

The State may set up a State Planning and Development Board, which will be advisory in nature and could consider formulation of schemes for the state sector, assign priority to such schemes and also monitor their effective implementation. The Board will have MLAs, experts, representatives of backward regions as members.

21. Local Self-Governance

All Panchayati Raj institutions should be strengthened and the 73rd and 74th Amendments to the Constitution of India should be considered by the State for adaptation or making a similar provision in the State Constitution.

For backward areas, better infrastructure, road network and health and educational institutions should be provided. A special plan for backward areas within the overall State/District plans should be considered.

22. Reservation in services/promotions/professional institutions.

The Jammu and Kashmir State Backward Classes Commission will be the appropriate forum to deal with the issues of reservation for backward communities and backward areas.

The issue of providing reservation to the residents of areas adjoining international border at the same level as LOC may be considered by the State Government.

23. Other Issues

Certain other issues not within the terms of reference of the Working Group V, which were raised by various members, have been listed which may be considered for appropriate action.

This is only a summary of the recommendations made by the Working Group and for full appreciation of the recommendations and the background in which they have been made, the main report may be referred to.

APPENDIX II

Report of the State Autonomy Committee

Jammu, April 1999

CHAPTER I

Introduction

Centre-State relations have remained on centre stage of Indian political scenario for quite a length of time, before 1950 when the present Republican Constitution was adopted and enacted in its entirety on 26-01-1950 and even thereafter. Right from 1919, the future of India was seen as a Federal State. In fact Simon Commission put it on record unambiguously:

"Apart together from any question of an ultimate Federal Union between the Indian States and British India, there are, we think very strong reasons for the reconstruction of the Indian Constitution on a Federal basis. It is only in a Federal structure that sufficient elasticity can be obtained for the Union of elements of diverse internal conditions and the communities at very different stage of development and culture."

The developments till enactment of Government of India Act, 1935 ultimately led to constitutional framework for future federal polity of the country. The build up of this federal polity, of necessity, could not follow the pattern of formation of Federation of American States, Australia or Canada but, even so, the federal polity envisaged for India was to consist of Indian Provinces and Indian States, as units. The Joint Parliamentary Committee on Indian Reforms recorded as under:

"Federations have commonly resulted from an agreement between

independent or at least autonomous governments surrendering a definite part of their sovereignty to a new Central Organism . . . we are faced with the necessity of creating autonomous units and combining them into a Federation by one and the same Act."

The Federation was to consist of all British Provinces, till then centrally administered both in legislative as well as executive wings, and the Indian states which were to accede in respect of some subjects for legislative purposes to Federal/Union Legislature and to the extent of the surrender of those subjects to accept executive functioning of the Centre as well. States had the option to join or not to join the Federation. The Act of 1935 provided the instrumentality for exercise of this choice by providing for an Instrument of Accession.

The sequence of events after enforcement of 1935 Act in April 1937, elections in British provinces and formation of governments by Indian Parties, World War 1939-45. India's insistence on independence, equally shrill cries for partition of India, non-exercise of option by Indian States to join the Constituent Assembly, continued refusal of the Muslim League to sit in the Constituent Assembly, quick developments leading to departure of Lord Wavell and incoming of Lord the, preponing of the date of independence from 1948 to 1947 for the country, ultimate passage of the Indian Independence Act, 1947 on 4th July, 1947, declaring 15th August, 1947 as "appointed day" when Dominions of India and Pakistan were to be formed—all these developments took place at breathtaking pace. The Indian States had even so the option to join one or the other Dominion, India or Pakistan.

Indian States, with the lapse of paramountcy on the "appointed day", i.e. 15th August, 1947 as sovereign entities could go the way they chose to exercise the option. Their joining had to be voluntary and at the time of joining they were under no obligation to accept any future Constitution except by voluntary acceptance or supplementary agreement. They had the right to accept or not to accept provisions of the Constitution that either Dominion would adopt for itself.

Partition in 1947 did effect a slight change in the perception about future Constitution that would be adopted for the country. From truly federal polity, it took a turn towards making this federal polity such that Centre retains some extraordinary powers too. This seemingly was to ensure a strong Centre. It was regarded to be an "imperative necessity." In fact, even the Second Report of the Union Powers Committee placed on record the following:

> *"Now the partition is a settled fact. We are unanimously of the view that it would be injurious to the interests of the country to provide for a weak Central authority which would be uncapable of ensuring peace, in coordinating vital matters of common concern and of speaking effectively for the whole country in the international sphere."*

Earlier perception was creation, in a way, of the mandate of Cabinet Mission Plan which had discarded partition but partition having been announced the earlier perception was held to be non-binding. Indian Federation in the new context was to have a strong Centre, of course, retaining all the necessary features of a federal polity.

This primarily was the kind of difference in treatment which became inevitable in regard to Indian Provinces. Indian States who had to be part of either of the Dominions by their own choice were on a different footing. They constituted the real units choosing to be part of a federal system in that the unit, upon exercise of voluntary choice in favour of either of the two Dominions, would accept federal authority in some fields of governance.

How other Indian States exercised this choice, how they participated in Constitution framing and in what form did they adopt it, is not our concern today. This shall be referred to wherever necessary in the pages to follow. But it is relevant to mention here that whereas other Princely States signed the Instrument of Accession to India and subsequently the instruments of merger, the accession of J&K State was limited only to the areas of Defence, External Affairs and Communication.

Uniquely, Jammu and Kashmir State is the only one to have negotiated the terms of its membership of the Union. Right till the Delhi Agreement of 1952, it did not accept any provisions of the Constitution of India other than those agreed to in the Instrument of Accession and retained its autonomy.

Autonomy has remained, since the days of accession, the heart-beat of the people of the State. Today we find that the State has lost all resemblance to autonomy. Its erosion is the primary cause for Kashmir discontent. Keeping this in view, Shri Narasimha Rao, 'the then Prime Minister of India announced in 1995 that the Union Government would be prepared to consider autonomy "short of independence" for Jammu and Kashmir. Welcoming this on behalf of Jammu and Kashmir National Conference, Dr. Farooq Abdullah asked the Union Government to issue an order under Article 370 to restore the state's autonomy in terms of the Delhi Agreement of 1952. When this did not happen, the National Conference boycotted the Parliamentary poll in 1996.

Mr. Deve Gowda as Prime Minister, offered Jammu and Kashmir "maximum autonomy" which perusaded Dr. Farooq Abdullah and his party National Conference to participate in the Assembly elections. The Party fought these elections on autonomy plank and was returned with a thumping majority. Following the resumption of office as Chief Minister. Dr. Farooq Abdullah with the approval of his Cabinet promptly constituted a Committee to examine and recommend measures for the restoration of autonomy. This was exactly in accordance with the mandate given to him by the people of the State as also the assurances held out by the Union Government.

CHAPTER II

Constitution of State Autonomy Committee

The State Government set-up a Committee to examine the question of restoration of autonomy to the State of Jammu and Kashmir vide Government Order No. 1164-GAD of 1996 Dated 29-11-1996 with the following composition:

(1)	Dr. Karan Singh	Chairman
(2)	Sh. Mohi-ud-Din Shah	Member
(3)	Sh. Abdul Ahad Vakil	-do-
(4)	Sh. Abdul Rahim Rather	-do-
(5)	Sh. Piyaray Lal Handoo	-do-
(6)	Sh. Bodh Raj Bali	-do-
(7)	Molvi Iftikhar Hussain Ansari	-do-
(8)	Kushok Thiksay	-do-
(9)	Shri Teja Singh	-do-

By a subsequent Government Order No. 263-GAD of 1997

dated 21-02-1997, it was ordered that Shri Teja Singh shall be Member/Convernor of the above committee. Dr. Karan Singh resigned as Chairman on July 31, 1997 and vide Government Order No. 1303-GAD of 1997 dated 19-08-1997, Shri Ghulam Mohi-ud-Din Shah, PWD Minister. J&K Government was appointed as Chairman w.e.f. the date Dr. Karan Singh resigned. By another Government Order No. 1413 of 1997 dated 05-09-1997 Mirza Abdul Rashid, former Speaker of J&K Legislative Assembly was nominated as member of the Committee.

Terms of Reference

The terms of reference of the Committee are as follows:

(i) To examine and recommend measures for the restoration of autonomy to the State of Jammu and Kashmir consistent with the Instrument of Accession, the Constitution Application Order, 1950 and the Delhi Agreement of 1952.

(ii) To examine and recommend safeguards that be regarded necessary for incorporation in the Union/State Constitution to ensure that the Constitutional arrangement that is finally evolved in pursuance of the recommendations of this Committee is inviolable.

(iii) To also examine and recommend measures to ensure a harmonious relationship for the future between the State and the Union.

Four features of these terms of reference deserve particularly to be noted. First, implicit in the exercise is acknowledgement of the fact that the State's autonomy, guaranteed by Article 370 of the Constitution of India, was eroded in breach of its provisions, of those of the Instrument of Accession to which Article 370 gave full recognition of the Constitution (Application to Jammu and Kashmir) Order, made under Article 370, by the President of India on January 26, 1950, extending to the State specified provisions of the Constitution of India which had come into force on the same day, and of the Delhi Agreement of July, 1952. It is this erosion which has necessitated "the restoration of autonomy" to the State. As we shall point out, till now 94 of the 97 entries in the Union

List have been applied to the State, 26 entries in the Concurrent List have also been applied, 6 more with modifications. Even in 1954 the Concurrent List did not apply at all. The process did not cease. It was accelerated. The Constitutional relationship that was thus established was contrary to and went far beyond the Delhi Agreement.

Secondly, if this exercise is to be worthwhile, it would be necessary to devise appropriate effective constitutional safeguards against any repetition of that unfortunate phase of erosion in future. Any Constitutional arrangement that is evolved to this end must have finality and be "inviolable".

Thirdly, the exercise has a definite limit and a clear objective. It seeks in effect the full enforcement of the historic Delhi Agreement concluded between the Prime Minister of India, Pt. Jawaharlal Nehru, and the Prime Minister (as he was then called) of the State, Sheikh Mohammed Abdullah, the two foremost architects of the State's accession to the Union of India. Implementing their mutual pledges in that Agreement is, at once, the bottom line and the high ideal we have placed before ourselves.

Lastly, but not least, it follows necessarily from the foregoing that efforts in these directions will "ensure a harmonious relationship for the future between the State and the Union", of which it is a member, by redressing the grievances of the past and the strains they so needlessly created in the relationship. It will strengthen, not weaken, the relationship. Far from being inconsistent with each other, the autonomy of the State will strengthen the ties that bind it to the Union and, with them, the unity of India.

Our nation is rich in its diversities and we are justly proud of it as we are of the bonds that weld us into one nation. The Constitution of India reflects both the unity and the diversities. Besides the fundamental rights which protect all citizens, there are fundamental rights for the protection specifically of the "language, script or culture" of any section of the citizens (Article 29) and of the right of minorities as such "based on religion or language" to establish or administer educational institutions of their choice (Article 30).

There is a whole part (XVI) containing provisions for reservation of seats for Scheduled Castes, Scheduled Tribes and

Anglo-Indians in the Lok Sabha and in public services as well as provisions for the protection of Scheduled Tribes.

Regional diversities are reflected in special provisions with respect to the States of Nagaland (Article 371-A), Sikkim (Article 371-F), Mizoram (Article 371-G) and Arunachal Pradesh (Article 371-H) which confer "special status" on these states. There are other "special provisions" with respect to some states concerning certain areas within those states, for example. Article 371 relating to the States of Maharashtra and Gujarat. In respect of Nagaland and Mizoram, Parliament is barred not only from altering religious or social practices but also "customary law and procedure", "administration of civil and criminal justice" according to such law and ownership and transfer of land.

The State of Jammu and Kashmir is, thus, not the only one to enjoy "a special status" under Article 370. In turn, the State is a mosaic of diversities in its regions, groups and communities. Protection of minorities and regional interests is a prime duty. Mindful of this fact, the Government of the State appointed, simultaneously with this Committee, a Committee on Regional Autonomy.

The Report we submit to the Government, is addressed to the people of the State and, also, to the country. We have been fully alive to the hopes and expectations aroused by our work as well as the misgivings expressed in some quarters. The State has passed through a grim ordeal in the last decade. To any who honestly felt alienated or frustrated, for whatever reason, our Report will provide assurance that the democratic framework does provide avenues of redress.

We have heard a large cross-section of people within and outside the State and received memoranda from many persons and also held discussions with leaders of political parties, eminent jurists, journalists and members of Parliament from Jammu and Kashmir in November 1997. Their names are listed in Appendix I and II respectively. To all of them we express our deep gratitude. We have consulted pertinent literature on the State's constitutional history since independence in order to understand why and how things went wrong after the initial years of promise. It is our firm belief that that happy phase can yet be recalled and repeated if the mistakes and misjudgments that led to its termination are corrected. Our faith in the future of the State as a willing, content and enthusiastic member of the Union of India remains undiminished. We are beset with problems, misunderstandings and obstacles. We shall overcome them. All must cooperate earnestly in that endeavour.

CHAPTER III

Pre-Independence Scenario

Situation as it obtained on 14th and 15th August, 1947 in the State of Jammu and Kashmir was that a movement had been launched by the premier political party (National Conference) in May, 1946 and the slogan of "Quit Kashmir" had been echoed all over India. This slogan asked for transfer of power from the Ruler to the people of Jammu and Kashmir. The movement claimed the right of the people to end discontent and dissatisfaction created by enforcement of the undemocratic J&K Constitution Act of 1939 promulgated by the Maharaja of Jammu and Kashmir on September 7, 1939. It had gone underground after the desperate Ruler chose to ruthlessly suppress it. As in the past, Jenab Sheikh Mohammad Abdullah and other leaders of this movement were imprisoned. On the dawn of independence Jenab Sheikh Sahib was lodged in the State Army Cantonment in Badami Bagh, Srinagar, serving the sentence imposed by trial judge for sedition, other leaders of the movement were either in exile or underground.

India became independent on August 15, 1947. Section 1 of the Indian Independence Act, 1947 said that as from that date, "two independent Dominions shall be set-up in India, to be known respectively as India and Pakistan". It proceeded to define their territories. But they were confined to the provinces under direct British rule. Section 7(1)(b) declared that the suzerainty of the British Crown over the Indian States lapsed and with it all the treaties and agreements between them and the Crown. Section 8(2) of the Act provided that until the Constituent Assemblies of both States framed their respective constitutions, each of them "shall be governed as nearly as may be in accordance with the Government of India Act. 1935". Section 9(1)(c) empowered the Governor-General to make changes in the Act in its application to the separate new States.

Accordingly, on August 14, 1947, the Governor General made

the India (Provisional Constitution) order adapting the Government of India Act, 1935 as the interim Constitution of India with the changes specified in the Act. Section 6 of the Act provided that "an Indian State shall be deemed to have acceded to the Dominion if the Governor General has signified his acceptance of an Instrument of Accession executed by the Ruler thereof. It proceeded to lay down the minimum essential contents of such an Instrument. Simply put three matters were to be specified in the Instrument of Accession in order to conform to Section 6. First, acceptance of the functions of the central authorities as laid down in the Act; namely, the Governor General, the Dominion Legislature, the Federal Court and any other Dominion authority established by or under the Act. Secondly, the Ruler had to undertake to give effect to the provisions of the Government of India Act, 1935 within his State "so far as they are applicable therein by virtue of the Instrument of Accession". Lastly, the Instrument had to "specify the matters" which the Ruler accepted as ones with respect to which the Dominion Legislature may make laws for the State and correspondingly, the executive authority of the Dominion in the State. In respect of all the three the Instrument could specify the limitations as well.

The Indian Independence Act of 1947 enacted by the British Parliament leading to formation of the Indian Dominion and the Dominion of Pakistan had of necessity to recognise that with the surrender of imperial power their paramountcy over Indian States would, in the process, also lapse and with that lapse Indian states' rulers could become sovereign unto themselves. India faced yet another difficult period of history. The sub-continent had as many as 554 states known as native Indian states and fear and apprehensions were lurking in all minds keen to have a united India as to how the native rulers would behave in the event of freedom. March to Independence saw such fears gradually removed. Quite in good time hundreds of these native states by covenants/agreements got merged with the Indian Union giving up their right to freedom or to separate constitutions. They agreed to what the constitution would give to them via the Constituent Assembly of the Union.

After the adoption of the programme of "New Kashmir" (Naya Kashmir) in September, 1944 and its presentation to the Ruler, yet another experiment was launched by him to ensure popular association with the administration. In pursuance of a notification issued on 2nd October, 1944 a nominee of the National Conference and another member of Praja Sabha were appointed as Ministers in the Cabinet but this experiment did not last long. The experiment failed when the National Conference nominee resigned. It sharpened the struggle for ultimate changes in Kashmir. By the time this farce of dyarchy ended with resignation of National Conference nominee from the Cabinet, the Cabinet Mission was stated to arrive in India to negotiate transfer of power and the future constitution for the country. The premier political party in the State, All J&K National Conference, recognised that paramountcy of the British would lapse and that time had come when on such lapse the peoples' right to exercise the sovereign right for governance must take precedence over everything else. The party demanded that the Treaty of Amritsar dated 16th March 1846 signed between Maharaja Gulab Singh and the then British Government in India which was in the nature of a sale deed and was thus an insult to the people of the State must go lock, stock and barrel. This became the theme. The "Quit Kashmir" movement was launched in early 1946 (April-May). A memorial was submitted to the Cabinet Mission claiming the right to have sovereignty restored to the people rather than the Ruler.

Chapter IV

Accession to India

The State of Jammu and Kashmir acceded to the Dominion of India on October 26, 1947 when its Ruler, Maharaja Hari Singh, signed an Instrument of Accession and the Governor General of India, Lord Mountbatten, accepted the Instrument. The texts of the letters exchanged between the Maharaja and Lord Mountbatten and the Instrument of Accession as well as the circumstances in which they were executed are set out in the Government of India's White Paper on Jammu and Kashmir (1948). The three documents, viz. the Maharaja's letter and the Governor General's reply accepting the Instrument of Accession and the Instrument of Accession are appended as Appendix III.

By the Instrument of Accession, the Maharaja of Jammu and Kashmir accepted three subjects as ones on which the Dominion Legislature "may make laws for the State". They were: Defence,

External Affairs and Communications. A schedule to the Instrument listed precisely 16 topics of legislation that fell under those three heads. There was another section (D) in the Schedule on matters "Ancillary". Four were listed—elections to the Dominion Legislature, offences against laws made under the above subjects, inquiries and statistics concerning them; and "jurisdiction and powers of all courts with respect to any of the aforesaid matters but except with the consent of the Ruler of the Acceding State, not so as to confer any jurisdiction or powers upon any courts other than courts ordinarily exercising jurisdiction in or in relation to that State."

By the Instrument, the Maharaja also accepted, as Section 6 of the Act required, the functions conferred on the Dominion authorities by the Act, namely, the Governor General, the Dominion Legislature and the Federal Court.

For the federal machinery to function properly any document of adherence executed, either before or after the establishment of the federation, must specify the subjects it yields to the federal union and the provisions of the Constitution which it accepts. The Government of India Act, 1935 provided the basics of a federation. It was readily available for adaptation by all concerned. The Constitution of India is a more elaborate document. Article 370 had perforce to empower the President of India to make orders separately in order to specify both the Union subjects and provisions concerning the federal structure. The State was careful to ensure right till the Delhi Agreement that it did not accept all the provisions and retained its own institutions and its autonomy. Significantly, Clause 5 of the Instrument provided against any variation of its terms without the Ruler's consent. Clause 7 read thus: "Nothing in this Instrument shall be deemed to commit me in any way to acceptance of any future Constitution of India or fetter my discretion to enter into arrangements with the Government of India under any such future Constitution". Clause 8 said: "Nothing in this Instrument affects the continuance of my Sovereignty in and over this State, or, save as provided by or under this Instrument, the exercise of any powers, authority and rights now enjoyed by me as Ruler of this State or the validity of any law at present in force in this State".

The State of Jammu and Kashmir was then governed by the Jammu and Kashmir Constitution Act, 1939. Justice Dr. A.S.

Anand, a distinguished Judge of the Supreme Court, now Chief Justice of India opined in his book. The Development of the Constitution of Jammu and Kashmir: "The Government of Jammu and Kashmir did not accept the Constitution of India as a Constitution for the State. Despite the accession, the State was still to be governed by the old Constitution Act, 1939. This was because the Government of India had given an undertaking that the people of Kashmir could frame their own Constitution. The Government of India could not force the State to accept the Constitution (of India), for that would violate the agreed terms of the association of Kashmir with India. The State had voluntarily surrendered three matters only and the Government of India could not enlarge the sphere of its jurisdiction at its own discretion."[1] (Universal Book Traders, Delhi, Third Edition, 1994, page 99)

The Maharaja made an order on October 30, 1947 appointing Sheikh Mohammed Abdullah as "the Head of the Administration with power to deal with the emergency'" and appointed a twenty-three member Emergency Council "pending the formation of the Interim Government". By a proclamation issued on March 5, 1948 the Maharaja decided "to replace the Emergency Administration by a popular Interim Government and to provide for its powers, duties and functions, pending the formation of a fully democratic Constitution".

Sheikh Mohammed Abdullah was appointed Prime Minister. The Council of Ministers was to function "on the principle of joint responsibility." It was enjoined to convene "a National Assembly based upon adult suffrage" to frame a Constitution. The Assembly was to submit the Constitution "through the Council of Ministers for my acceptance."

This was a reference to a Constitution for the State. Right from the beginning in 1948, there was no doubt in any quarter that, regardless of the arrangements in respect of other former Indian States, the State of Jammu and Kashmir would have its own Constitution as a member of the Indian Union. Uniquely, the State is the only one to have negotiated the terms of its membership of the Union. The negotiations were spread over five months.

Negotiations on the provisions in the proposed Constitution

1. Justice A.S. Anand, The Development of the Constitution of Jammu & Kashmir, 3rd Edition, 1994, p. 99

of India that would embody the terms of the State's membership of the Union began when a conference of the leaders of the National Conference and of the leaders at the Centre was held in Delhi on May 15 and 16, 1949. Pt. Jawahar Lal Nehru recorded the issues discussed in a letter to Sheikh Saheb on 18th May. The State was to have its own Constitution and *"it will be for the Constituent Assembly of the State, when convened, to determine in respect of what other subjects the state may accede."* On May 27, 1949, a member of its Drafting Committee, Sir N. Gopalaswamy Ayyangar moved an amendment to the Assembly's Rules empowering "the Ruler of Kashmir on the advice of his Prime Minister" to nominate the State's four representatives to the Constituent Assembly of India. The State's legislature, the Praja Sabha, had not met since April 1947 and was now "dead". The National Assembly of the State was yet to be elected. On June 16, 1949 Sheikh Mohammad Abdullah, Mirza Mohammed Afzal Beg, Maulana Mohammed Saeed Masoodi and Moti Ram Baigra took the pledge and signed the Register of Members of the Constituent Assembly of India.

It must be mentioned at the outset in all fairness that the texts of Sheikh Mohammed Abdullah's letters of October 12 and 15, 1949 are not available, whereas those of Mr. Ayyangar and Sardar Vallabhbhai Patel's letters to him and to each other. On October 12, Sheikh Saheb complained to Mr. Ayyangar, as he recalled in his letter of 17th October, that the draft Article 306-A (with modifications, the present Article 370) which he had given to Mr. M.A. Beg "failed to implement the pledges given to us" and was, therefore, unacceptable. Two meetings followed on October 15. After the first, Mr. Ayyangar wrote to Sardar Patel enclosing his draft of the Article. It did not provide a finality to further acquisition of power by the Centre by stipulating that the concurrence of the State Government to such acquisition shall be ratified by the Constituent Assembly.

Mr. Ayyangar presented another draft later on October 15, which drew a protest from Patel and rejection by Sheikh Saheb, both, on 16th October. Mr. Ayyangar prepared yet another draft in consultation with Kashmir's representatives. It was finalized on the afternoon of October 16, 1949. On the assurance that the agreed draft would be moved, Mr. Beg withdrew his own amendment. Sheikh Mohammad Abdullah recorded the agreement in another letter of 16th October and thanked Ayyangar for his pains.

On October 16, 1949 a "Final Draft" of Article 306-A was settled between Mr. N. Gopalaswamy Ayyangar, Mirza Mohammed Afzal Beg and Mr. M.A. Shahmiri. It read thus:

Final Draft of Article 306-A (Jammu & Kashmir) as Settled Between the Hon'ble Shri N. Gopalswamy Ayyangar on the one side and Messers Beg and Shahmiri on the other on October 16, 1949.

306-A (1) Notwithstanding anything contained in this Constitution,

(a) the provisions of Article 211-A of this Constitution shall not apply in relation to the State of Jammu and Kashmir;

(b) the power of Parliament to make laws for the State shall be limited to—

(i) those matters in the Union List and the Concurrent List which, in consultation with the Government of State, are declared by the President to correspond to matters specified in the Instrument of Accession governing the accession of the State to the Dominion of India as the matters with respect to which the Dominion Legislature may make laws for the State; and

(ii) such other matters in the said Lists as with the concurrence of the Government of the State, the President may by order specify;

Explanation:—For the purposes of this article, the Government of the State means the person for the time being recognized by the Union as the Maharaja of Jammu and Kashmir acting on the advice of the Council of Ministers appointed under the Maharaja's Proclamation dated the 5th March 1948.

(c) the provisions of Article 1 of this Constitution shall apply in relation to the State;

(d) such of the other provisions of this Constitution and subject to such exceptions and modifications shall apply in relation to the State as the President may by order specify:

Provided that no such order which relates to the matters

specified in the Instrument of Accession of the State aforesaid shall be issued except in consultation with the Government of State:

Provided further that no such order which relates to matters other than those referred to in the preceding proviso shall be issued except with the concurrence of that Government;

(2) If the concurrence of the Government of the State referred to in sub-clause (b)(ii) or in the second proviso of sub-clause (d) of clause (1) was given before the Constituent Assembly for the purpose of framing the Constitution of the State is convened, it shall be placed before such Assembly for such decision as it may take thereon;

(3) Notwithstanding anything in the preceding clauses of this article, the President may, by public notification, declare that this article shall cease to be operative or shall be operative only with such exceptions and modifications and from such date as he may specify:

Provided that the recommendation of the Constituent Assembly of the State shall be necessary before the President issues such a notification.

This draft was finally agreed on October 16, 1949. What happened next day, October 17, 1949 in the Constituent Assembly was recorded immediately thereafter that very day by Sheikh Saheb in a letter to Mr. Gopalaswamy Ayyangar.

"This morning when we expected the final draft, which had appeared in the List of Amendments circulated by the Secretary of the Constituent Assembly, to come up before the Assembly, you and Mualana (Azad) Sahib came to me and asked me if I could accept an important change in the Explanation to Sub-clause (b) of Clause (1) of the draft Article 306-A, as appearing in the List of Amendments. After careful consideration of the proposed amendment in the Explanation, my colleagues and I told you both in the lobby that it was not possible for us to accept this change in the final draft and you and Mauiana Sahib left us while we were still discussing the matter in the lobby amongst ourselves, the draft Article 306-A was moved by you in the Constituent Assembly, and, when part of your speech was over, we were told by someone that the draft Article had been taken up by the Assembly, and, therefore, we took our seats in the Assembly Hall. We could not conceive that any amendment in the final draft, as circulated in the List of Amendments, would be made by you without conveying your final decision in the matter to us, and so we took it for granted that the final draft Article 306-A was presented before the Assembly in the form in which it had our consent; and, therefore, when it was passed by the Assembly, we did not take part in the debate. While Maulana Sahib and you came to us to discuss the matter with us in the lobby. I clearly told you that in the event of any change in the finalized draft Article 306-A. We should be at liberty to move the amendment, of which notice had been given by Mr. Beg and his two other colleagues and which had been withdrawn on the express assurance given by you yesterday. In these circumstances, it was not possible for us to move any amendment and we did not get an occasion to express our views on the matter before the open House."

Sheikh Saheb threatened to resign from the Constituent Assembly. Mr. Ayyangar replied on October 18. He did not deny that the draft had been unilaterally changed. "It is true that after having unsuccessfully attempted, alongwith Maulana Azad, to persuade you to agree willingly to the substitution of the words 'for the time being in office' for the word 'appointed', I did move the article with that amendment after obtaining the permission of the President to do so. He argued that it was "a trivial change" in response to the desire expressed by a large number of the leading Members of the House. The Prime Minister Pt. Nehru was abroad then. Mr. Ayyangar himself recorded that "the words in the Explanation as agreed to between us are Council of Ministers appointed under the Maharaja's Proclamation dated March 5, 1948." The words appearing in the Article as passed yesterday are "the Council of Ministers for the time being in office under the Maharaja's Proclamation dated March 5, 1948." His plea that "the change of words does not constitute the slightest change in sense or substance" was wrong. Under the agreed Explanation. Sheikh Saheb's dismissal in 1953 would have been a Constitutional impossibility.

In his letter to the Prime Minister Pt. Jawaharlal Nehru on November 3, 1949 on his return from the United States of America. Sardar Patel also admitted that the draft "was modified to cover not merely the first Ministry so appointed but any subsequent Ministries which may be appointed under that proclamation."

The Constituent Assembly adopted the Constitution of India

on November 26, 1949. (C.A.D.: Vol. 12, p. 995). It repealed the Government of India Act, 1935. Article 394 provided that most of its provisions would come into force from January 26, 1950. On November 25, 1949 the Maharaja of Jammu and Kashmir made a proclamation declaring that "the Constitution of India shortly to be adopted by the Constituent Assembly of India shall in so far as it is applicable to the State of Jammu and Kashmir, govern the Constitutional relationship between this State and the contemplated Union of India. . ."[1] On January 26, 1950 the President of India made the first Constitution (Application to Jammu and Kashmir) Order, 1950[2] under Article 370 of the Constitution of India. It conformed strictly to the Instrument of Accession.

CHAPTER V

Article 370 of the Constitution of India

Article 370 of the Constitution reads thus:

370. Temporary Provisions with respect to the State of Jammu and Kashmir—(1) Notwithstanding anything in this Constitution—

(a) the provisions of Article 238 shall not apply in relation to the State of Jammu and Kashmir;

(b) the power of Parliament to make laws for the said State shall be limited to—

(i) those matters in the Union List and the Concurrent List which, in consultation with the Government of the State, are declared by the President to correspond to matters specified in the Instrument of Accession governing the accession of the State to the Dominion of India as the matters with respect to which the Dominion Legislature may make laws for that State;

(ii) Such other matters in the said Lists, as, with the concurrence of the Government of the State, the President may by order specify.

Explanation:—For the purposes of this article, the Government of the State means the person for the time being recognised by the

1. (White paper on Indian States; Government of India, Ministry of States, New Delhi, 1950, p. 371).
2. See Appendix IV.

President as the Maharaja of Jammu and Kashmir acting on the advice of the Council of Ministers for the time being in office under the Maharaja's Proclamation dated the fifth day of March, 1948;

(c) the provisions of Article 1 and of this article shall apply in relation to that State;

(d) Such of the other provisions of this Constitution shall apply in relation to that State subject to such exceptions and modifications as the President may by order specify:

Provided that no such order which relates to the matters specified in the Instrument of Accession of the State referred to in paragraph (i) of sub-clause (b) shall be issued except in consultation with the Government of the State:

Provided further that no such order which relates to matters other than those referred to in the last preceding proviso shall be issued except with the concurrence of that Government.

(2) If the concurrence of the Government of the State referred to in paragraph (ii) of sub-clause (b) of clause (1) or in the second proviso to sub-clause (d) of that clause be given before the Constituent Assembly for the purpose of framing the Constitution of the State is convened, it shall be placed before such Assembly for such decision as it may take thereon.

(3) Notwithstanding anything in the foregoing provisions of this article, the President may, by public notification, declare that this article shall cease to be operative or shall be operative only with such exceptions and modifications and from such date as he may specify:

Provided that the recommendation of the Constituent Assembly of the State referred to in clause (2) shall be necessary before the President issues such a notification.

A careful study of the text reveals six special provisions for Jammu and Kashmir. First, it exempted the State totally from the provisions of the Constitution of India providing for the governance of the states. It was allowed to have its own Constitution within the Indian Union.

Second, Parliament's legislative power over the State was restricted to three subjects—defence, external affairs and communications. The President could extend to it other provisions of the Constitution to provide a constitutional framework if they related to the matters specified in the Instrument of Accession. For all this, only "consultation" with the State Government was required since the State had already accepted them in 1947 by the Instrument of Accession.

Third, if other "constitutional" provisions and other Union powers are to be extended to the State of Jammu and Kashmir the prior "concurrence" of the State Government was required.

The fourth feature is that even that concurrence alone did not suffice. It had to be ratified by the State's Constituent Assembly. This is often overlooked. Article 370 (2) says clearly: "If the concurrence of the Government of the State ... be given before the Constituent Assembly for the purpose of framing the Constitution of the State is convened, it shall be placed before such Assembly for such decision as it may take thereon."

The fifth feature is that the State Government's authority to give the "concurrence" lasts only till the State's Constituent Assembly is "convened". It is an "interim" power. Once the Constituent Assembly met, the State Government cannot give its own "concurrence". Still less, after the Assembly met and dispersed. Moreover, the President cannot exercise his powers to extend the Indian Constitution to Jammu and Kashmir indefinitely. The power has to stop at the point the State's Constituent Assembly drafted the State's Constitution and decided finally what additional subjects to confer on the Union and what other provisions of the Constitution of India it should get extended to the State rather than having their counterparts embodied in the State Constitution itself. Once the State's Constituent Assembly has finalized the scheme and dispersed the President's extending powers ended completely.

The sixth special feature, the last step in the process, is that Article 370(3) empowers the President to make an order abrogating or amending it. But for this, also "the recommendation" of the State's Constituent Assembly "shall be necessary before the President issues such a notification".

Article 370 cannot be abrogated or amended by recourse to the amending provisions of the Constitution which apply to all the other states because Article 368 has a proviso which says that no constitutional amendment "shall have effect in relation to the State of Jammu and Kashmir" unless applied by order of the President under Article 370. That requires first the concurrence of the State government and subsequent ratification by its Constituent Assembly.

Article 1(1) of the Constitution of India says that India shall be a Union of States. Sub-clause (2) adds that the states shall be specified in the First Schedule, this schedule mentions the State of Jammu and Kashmir. But, it is extended to the State only through Article 370(1)(c) which says: "The provisions of Article 1 and of this Article shall apply in relation to that State." This is not without legal significance and consequence. Mr. G.L. Nanda was, therefore, right in pointing out, as Union Home Minister, on 4th December, 1964 in the Lok Sabha, that it would be "totally wrong to assume that with the repeal of the Article all Constitutional provisions would automatically apply to Kashmir". Mr. S.B. Chavan made similar comments on March 1, 1993.

Article 370 was authoritatively explained by its mover in the Constituent Assembly. Mr. N. Gopalaswamy Ayyangar, contemporaneously and in 1952 by the President of the Assembly who became the first President of India, Dr. Rajendra Prasad.

Mr. Ayyangar said in the Constituent Assembly on October 17, 1949, "We have also agreed that the will of the people through the instrument of the Constituent Assembly will determine the Constitution of the State as well as the sphere of Union jurisdiction over the State ... You will remember that several of these clauses provide for the concurrence of the Government of Jammu and Kashmir State. Now, these relate particularly to matters which are not mentioned in the Instrument of Accession, and it is one of our commitments to the people and Government of Kashmir *that no such additions should he made except with the consent of the Constituent Assembly which may he called in the State for the purpose of framing its Constitution. In other words, what we are committed to is that these additions are matters for the determination of the Constituent Assembly of the State.*"

Mr. Ayyangar explained that, "the provision is made that when the Constituent Assembly of the State has met and taken its decision both on the Constitution for the State and on the range of federal jurisdiction over the State, the President may on the recommendation of that Constituent Assembly issue an order that this Article 306A shall either cease to be operative or shall be operative, only subject to such exceptions and modifications as may be specified by him. But before he issued any order of that kind the recommendation of the Constituent Assembly will be a condition precedent.

This unique process of Presidential orders altering Constitutional provisions by an executive order ends with the final decision of the State's Constituent Assembly. "When it has come to a decision on the different matters, it will make a recommendation to the President who will either abrogate Article 306A or direct that it shall apply with such modifications and exceptions as the Constituent Assembly may recommend." Mr. Ayyangar repeatedly said that the Government's concurrence alone will not do. "That concurrence should be placed before the Constituent Assembly when it meets and the Constituent Assembly may take whatever decisions it likes on those matters."[1]

The White paper on Indian States made an important exposition of the Constitutional changes in para 221 at page 113 in chapter XI entitled, "Indian States under the New Constitution". Referring to Article 370 it said, "Steps will be taken for the purpose of convenient a Constituent Assembly which will go into these matters in detail and when it comes to a decision on them, it will make a recommendation to the President who will either abrogate Article 370 or direct that it shall apply with such modifications and exceptions as he may specify." Thus, the State's Constituent Assembly's decision was to mark a finality to the exercise of the President's powers under Article 370.

On July 29, 1952 Sheikh Saheb wrote to Pt. Nehru to inform him that the Constituent Assembly proposed to elect the State's Head of the State on August 16, 1952 and he wished that the necessary Order under Article 370 should be issued by the President in time to make it possible. Pt. Nehru replied immediately that very day. His letter of July 29, 1952 is very instructive. It is reproduced below:

New Delhi
July 29, 1952

My dear Shaikh Saheb,

I have just received your letter of the 29th July about the Head of the State. I do not see how we can go through all the various processes about this matter before the 16th August. It is not a perfectly clear matter from the legal point of view how far the President can issue notifications under Article 370 several times. In any event, it would be desirable to include in one notification such present changes that we have decided

1. C.A.D., Vol. 8, pp. 424-427.

to make. To have repeated notifications following one another in fairly quick succession would be odd, apart from the possible difficulty about their legality. We are having this matter examined.

There is also the question of how the present Maharaja should be dealt with. The obviously easy and decorous course is for him to abdicate. I hope he will do so. If not, then it may become necessary for the President to take some steps. All this has to be thought out.

In this matter you will appreciate that we have to proceed with the concurrence of the President. The final decision, no doubt, is that of the Government. But we cannot hustle the President.

I am sending your letter to Dr. Katju and Gopalaswami Ayyangar.

Yours sincerely,
Jawaharlal Nehru

Evidently, the President, Dr. Rajendra Prasad, one of the leaders of the Patna Bar, had expressed his doubts about the legality of successive orders under Article 370. This impression, which Pt. Nehru's letter conveys, is fully borne out by Dr. Prasad's note to Pt. Nehru sent under a covering letter dated September 6, 1952. It was first published only in 1991.[1] In view of its high relevance we reproduce this authoritative document in full as Appendix VIII.

The President pointed out the uniqueness as well as the incongruity of amending a Constitution by mere executive order. *"Nowhere else, as far as I can see is there any provision authorizing the executive government to make amendments in the Constitution......"* The crucial issue was whether the President's power to make such orders under Article 370 "is exercisable from time to time or is exhausted by a single exercise thereof. *Judging by the language employed and by the very exceptional nature of the power conferred, I have little doubt myself that the intention is that the power is to be exercised only once, for then alone would it be possible to determine with precision which particular provisions should be excepted and which modified. The fact that the President is also required to specify the date from* which the notification is to take effect also lends to confirm this view."

1. Dr. Rajendra Prasad: Correspondence and Select Documents Edited by Valmiki Choudhary, Allied Publishers Ltd., New Delhi, Volume 15, pp. 104-08.

Precisely for this reason, the marginal note to Article 370 described its nature as "Temporary provisions with respect to the State of Jammu and Kashmir". They were temporary in point of time and not as a half way house to the State losing its special status, eventually. Elaborating on his reasoning the President concluded:

> "The correct view appears to be that recourse is to be had to this clause [(cl. 3) of Article 370] only when the Constituent Assembly of the State (sic. he meant clearly the Constitution) has been fully framed".

This interpretation accords with the terms of the provision, Article 370, with its author Mr. N. Gopalaswamy Ayyangar to exposition in the Constituent Assembly, with Prime Minister Jawaharlal Nehru's letter of July 29, 1952 and his other pronouncements, with Sheikh Mohammad Abdullah's understanding of Article 370, and, induced, with the entire process before and after the adoption of Article 370. On the other hand, not one contemporaneous document contradicts thus interpretation or supports the unconstitutional practice that later came into vogue. Pt. Nehru's letter to Sheikh Saheb on August 1, 1952 mentioned the aspect of propriety besides legality. "As I have written to you, there is doubt here as to whether we can issue a succession of President orders dealing with these questions piecemeal. Apart from the legality there is also the question of propriety"

Sheikh Saheb told the State's Constituent Assembly on August 11, 1952 that "the fact that Article 370 has been mentioned as temporary provision in the Constitution does not mean that it is capable of being abrogated, modified or replaced unilaterally. In actual fact, the temporary nature of this Article arises merely from the fact that *the power to finalise the Constitutional relationship between the State and the Union has been specifically rested in the Jammu and Kashmir Constituent Assembly.* This power ceases to be one of imparting finality if, even after the Assembly's dispersal, modifications to the Constitution and amassment of power by the Centre can take place with the concurrence of another executive body of the State Government. Later, orders under Article 370 were passed even with the concurrence of the Governor alone, who is removable from office by the Centre at any moment. He, thus, accorded "concurrence" to the centre at its bidding as, indeed, did some Chief Ministers of the State.

Sheikh Saheb continued: *"It follows that whatever modifications, amendments or exceptions that may become necessary either to Article 370, or any other Article in the Constitution of India in their application to the Jammu and Kashmir State, are subject to the decisions* of this sovereign body". Obviously, once this body disperses after completion of its task, no amendments to the Constitution of India could be made in their application to the State for the simple reason that the sovereign and appointed ratifying body no longer existed. Any other interpretation would reduce the terms of Article 370 to a naught and the entire exercise to a farce by making permanent what was meant to be a transitory arrangement till the Constituent Assembly of Jammu and Kashmir finalised (a) The State's Constitution, and (b) its corresponding recommendations to the President, as envisaged by Article 370.

Sheikh Saheb warned: "I would like to make it clear that any suggestions of altering arbitrarily this basis of our relationship with India would not only constitute breach of the spirit and letter of the Constitution, but it may invite serious consequences for a harmonious association of our State with India."

At its fourth session on August 20, 1952 the State's Constituent Assembly passed a detailed Resolution in implementation of its Resolution of June 10, 1952 on the Head of the State.

The President of India persisted with his objections till as late as November 7, 1952 insisting that the Constituent Assembly "should come to a decision on all matters relating to the State's Constitution...."[1] The Prime Minister of India was in bind. He had agreed with the President's views on the legality but termination of the royal dynasty was also part of the Delhi Agreement. He was under pressure from Sheikh Saheb and his colleagues. Pt. Nehru, therefore, wrote to the President on the same day, November 7, 1952: "I can only repeal what I have said above that we have considered every aspect of this question and come to certain conclusions which have to be given effect to now. We cannot reopen six month's discussions".

1. V. Choudhary; Vol. 20, p. 395, footnote 3.

Accordingly, on November 15, 1952 Constitution Order No. 44 was made by the President under Article 370: "In exercise of the powers conferred by this article the President, on the recommendation of the Constituent Assembly of the State of Jammu and Kashmir, declared that, as from the 17th day of November, 1952 the said Article 370 shall be operative with the modification that for the explanation in clause (I) thereof, the following explanation is substituted namely:

"*Explanation*—For the purposes of this article, the Government of the state means the person for the time being recognized by the President on the recommendation of the Legislative Assembly of the State as the Sadar-i-Riyasat of Jammu and Kashmir, acting on the advice of the council of Ministers of the state for the time being in office."[1]

CHAPTER VI

Convening of the J&K Constituent Assembly

After adoption of the Constitution of India and its application to the State of Jammu and Kashmir pursuant to proclamation dated 25th November, 1949 and enforcement of the Constitution on 26th of January, 1950 the constitutional relationship of the state with the Union of India was shaped by the Constitution (Application to Jammu and Kashmir) Order of 1950. This order specified matters corresponding to those in respect of which the State had acceded to the Indian Union according to the terms of the Instrument of Accession. These are given in the 1st Schedule to the aforesaid Order.

This Order further mentioned that in addition to the provisions of Article 1 and Article 370 of the Constitution the only other provisions of the Constitution shall apply in relation to the state of Jammu and Kashmir shall be those specified in the Second Schedule to this Order and shall so apply subject to the exceptions and modifications specified in the Second Schedule.

The jurisdiction of the Union Parliament to legislate with respect to our State was thus clearly defined consistently with the position that emerged as a result of having ceded the powers pursuant to Instrument of Accession. The rest of it was left for the

1. Ministry of Law Order No. C.O. 44, dated the 15th November, 1952.

State to take care of in its own Constitution.

While this was so, the need for a constitution for the State of Jammu and Kashmir was also very intensely fell not only for the reason of defining the state's legislative power but also for other reasons. Total uncertainty on the political horizon was eating into the vitals of the social fabric. The future of the ruling dynasty also required to be settled. Rightly had the Article 170 of Constitution of India consistent with the National Conference stand throughout in respect of the right of the Jammu and Kashmir State to frame its own constitution envisaged a Constituent Assembly. Kashmir has its own history of freedom movement and as we have seen above, "New Kashmir" programme had envisaged a National Assembly for the State of Jammu and Kashmir and attachment of the people with the perception was so well recognised that even in the declaration of 5th March 1948, the Maharaja of Jammu and Kashmir had proclaimed as under:

> "I have already appointed the popular leader of my people Sheikh Mohamad Abdullah as the Head of the Emergency Administration.
>
> It is now my desire to replace the emergency administration by a popular interim Government and to provide for its powers, duties and functions, pending the formation of a fully democratic constitution.
>
> My council of Ministers shall take appropriate steps, as soon as restoration of normal conditions has been completed, to convene a National Assembly based upon adult suffrage, having due regard to the principle that the number of representatives from each voting area should, as for as practicable, be proportionate to the population of the area.
>
> The constitution to be framed by the National Assembly shall provide adequate safeguards for the minorities and contain appropriate provisions guaranteeing freedom of conscience, freedom of speech and freedom of assembly".

Vuvraj Karan Singh functioning as Regent, therefore, issued a proclamation of 20th April, 1951 setting the ball rolling for the convening of the Constituent Assembly for the state of Jammu and Kashmir to decide the future Constitution of the State. The

Proclamation directed that the Constituent Assembly consisting of representatives of people elected on the basis of adult franchise shall be constituted for the purpose.

Elections were thus held in terms of the Proclamation, hopes rose high, Constituent Assembly met on 31st October, 1951.

In his inaugural speech in the State Constituent Assembly on 5th November, 1951 Jenab Sheikh Mohammad Abdullah, the then Prime Minister of Jammu and Kashmir State, echoing the aspirations of the people, made the following observations:

> "We must remember that our struggle for power has now reached its successful climax in the convening of this Constituent Assembly. It is for you to translate the vision of New Kashmir into reality and I would remind you of its opening words which will inspire our labours.
>
> 'We the people of Jammu, Kashmir, Ladakh and Frontier regions, including Poonch and Chenani illaqas commonly known as Jammu and Kashmir State in order to perfect our union in the fullest equality and self-determination, to raise ourselves and our children for ever from the abyss of oppression and poverty, degradation and suppression, from medieval darkness and ignorance into the sunlit valleys of plenty, ruled by freedom, science and honest toil, in worthy participation of the historic resurgence of the peoples of the East, and the working masses of the world, and in determination to make this our country a dazzling gem of the snowy bosom of Asia, do propose and propound the following Constitution of our State.'
>
> You are the sovereign authority in this State of Jammu and Kashmir; what you decide has the irrevocable force of law. The basic democratic principle of sovereignty of the nation, embodied ably in the American and French constitutions is once again given the shape in our midst. I shall quote the. famous words of Article 3 of the French Constitution of 1791.
>
> 'The source of all sovereignty resides fundamentally in the nation.... Sovereignty is one and indivisible, inalienable and imprescriptible. It belongs to the nation."
>
> We should be clear about the responsibilities that this power invests us with. In front of us lie decisions of the highest

national importance which we shall be called upon to take upon the correctness of our decisions depends not only the happiness of our land and people now, but the fate as well of generations to come."[1]

He set the following four tasks before the Constituent Assembly for deliberation:

(i) Devising Constitution for the future governance of the country which he called very difficult and a detailed one.

(ii) The future of the royal dynasty: The decision he said had to be taken with urgency and wisdom since on that decision depended the future form and the character of the State.

(iii) The third major issue which awaited deliberations of members of the Constituent Assembly arose out of the Land Reforms which the Government carried out with vigour and determination. A decision had also to be given by the members on the landowners' demand for compensation.

(iv) Fourth and what he called the final matter was to be reasoned conclusion of the Constituent Assembly regarding accession after full consideration of the three alternatives he would state later in the Assembly.

On each of these tasks he set the parameters in the inaugural speech itself.

He indicated that the future political set up had to be based on the highest principles of the democratic constitutions of the world and therefore the Assembly has to base its work on principles of equality, liberty, social justice, these being regarded as integral features of progressive constitutions. Rule of Law as in the rest of democratic would had to be the cornerstone of the political mechanism for governance of the State. Equality before law and independence of judiciary were vital to the whole fabric. Besides, freedom of the individual in the matter of speech, movement and association should be guaranteed. "Freedom of the press and opinion would also be features of our constitution", he

1. For full text of Sheikh Saheb's speech, see Appendix V.

said. Basis was provided in the outline embodied in "New Kashmir" programme. He described democracy as an "apparatus of social organisation wherein people govern through their own chosen representatives and are themselves guaranteed political and civil liberties".

In this regard we may place on record the following in relation to the then constitutional ties between the State and the Union of India:

> "The Constitution of India has provided for a federal union and in the distribution of sovereign powers has treated us differently from other constitutional units. With the exception of the items grouped under Defence, Foreign Affairs and Communications in the Instrument of Accession, we have complete freedom to frame our Constitution in the manner we like. In order to live and prosper as good partners in a common endeavour for the advancement of our peoples, I would advise that, while safeguarding our autonomy to the fullest extent so as to enable us to have the liberty to build our country according to the best traditions and genius of our people, we may also by suitable constitutional arrangements with the Union establish our right to seek and compel federal cooperation and assistance in this great task, as well as offer our fullest cooperation and assistance to the Union".

After describing the essential background that required to be taken into consideration in order to facilitate taking of final decision on the issues referred to above. Sheikh Saheb reminded the Hon'ble members of what he had said in the course of his trial for sedition at Badamibagh cantonment in the following words:

> 'The future constitutional set-up in the State of Jammu and Kashmir cannot derive authority from the old source of relationship, which was expiring and was bound to end soon. The set-up could only rest on the active will of the people of the state, conferring on the head of the State the title and authority drawn from the true and abiding source of sovereignty that is the people.'

From the above description of the task before the Constituent-

Assembly it is abundantly clear that Sheikh Saheb envisaged State Union relationship as "one of partners in common endeavour for the advancement of the people" and therefore, regarded "safeguarding of our autonomy to the fullest extent" and suitable "constitutional arrangement with the Union" as two cornerstones to ensure fullest cooperation and assistance between partners.

CHAPTER VII

Delhi Agreement of July, 1952

The Constituent Assembly, convened on 31st October, 1951, thus was not only to frame the Constitution for the State but was to give certain more important decisions regarding the future relationship of the State with the Union. It started its work in the right earnest and as days passed by, need for a decision on certain important matters relating to framing of the Constitution and any further application of the Union Constitution to the State was felt. Besides, questions arising out of the need to settle the future of the ruling dynasty and of arriving at a concrete solution about the fundamentals of the Constitution of the State as an integral part of India had also to be considered.

1952 proved a very important year in the State's constitutional evolution. It witnessed the conclusion of the historic Agreement between Pt. Jawahar Lal Nehru and Sheikh Saheb which was announced at a press conference in Delhi on July 24, 1952. It culminated in the President's second Order under Article 370 on November 15, 1952 but the first made on the recommendation of the Constituent Assembly of Jammu and Kashmir. Its constitutional significance emerges clearly if its background is borne in mind.

The National Conference led by Sheikh Saheb was pledged to radical programme covering a wide range of subjects such as land reforms. It included termination of hereditary rulership in the State. By 1952 it had ended in the other former princely States. Maharaja Hari Singh had virtually abdicated as ruler in favour of his son Yuvraj Karan Singh although the proclamation of June 9, 1949 merely said that since he was leaving the State for reasons of health his powers and functions shall he "exercisable" by the Yuvraj, thus making him Regent. Sheikh Saheb mentioned in his address to the Assembly that "another issue of vital import to the nation involves the future of the Royal Dynasty."

Events picked up speed in June. On June 10, 1952 the Basic Principles Committee submitted its Report to the State's Constituent Assembly. It provided *inter alia* that the "institution of hereditary Rulership shall be terminated" and that "the office of the Head of the State shall be elective." The Constituent Assembly accepted the Report on June 12, 1952.

It is against this background that the Delhi agreement was concluded after prolonged discussions; first, from June 14 to 20, 1952 and, next, from July 20 to 24, 1952.[1] Its terms were announced by Pt. Jawahar Lal Nehru in Lok Sabha on July 24, 1952[2] and in the Rajya Sabha on August 5, 1952.[3]

The terms of the agreement were explained to the Constituent Assembly of Jammu and Kashmir by the State's Prime Minister, Sheikh Mohammed Abdullah on August 11, 1952.[4]

Both leaders provided the background and highlighted the significance of the agreement. Pt. Nehru told the Lok Sabha:

> "The position since the Constitution was framed is thus contained in the Article 370 and in the President's Order following it. Article 370 was obviously of a transitional nature, and it allowed the President to make any additions to it, any variations to it, later on, the object being that if any change or addition was required, we need not have to go through the cumbrous process of amending our Constitution, but the President was given the authority to amend it in the sense of adding a subject, part of a subject, whatever, *it was to the other subjects, in regard to Kashmir. But in Article 370 the old principle was repeated and emphasized that all these changes or any change, required the approval of the Constituent Assembly of the Jammu and Kashmir State.*
>
> When this was put down in our Constitution, there was

1. S. Gopal (Editor), Selected works of Jawahar Lal Nehru, Vol. 19, p. 211.
2. Parliamentary Debates, Lok Sabha, Official Report Part II, Vol. III, No. 15, Cols. 4501-4521.
3. Rajya Sabha Debates, Vol. 1, Nos. 24-31 (July 28–August 5, 1952): Cols. 2970-2995.
4. For full text of Sheikh Saheb's speech see Appendix VI.

no Constituent Assembly of Jammu and Kashmir State, but we envisaged it. We had envisaged it for a long time. *And if the Constituent Assembly was not there, then it required the consent of the Jammu and Kashmir Government. So that was the position.*"[1]

The implication is plain. Additional subjects could be acquired by the Centre only with the approval of the State's Constituent Assembly.

Briefly the Delhi Agreement covered ten points. It was agreed that residuary powers would continue to vest in the State as provided in Article 370; within the ambit of Indian citizenship, the State legislature would have the power to regulate the rights and privileges of permanent residents or "State Subjects" as defined in a 1927 State Order, the Fundamental Rights chapter of the Indian Constitution be applied to the State with modifications and exceptions such as enabling transfer of land to the tiller without payment of compensation; the jurisdiction of the Supreme Court would extend to the State; the State flag would not be a rival to the national tricolour which would occupy a supremely distinctive place in the State, the power to grant reprieve and commute sentences would vest in the President of India; with the abolition of hereditary rulership, the Head of the State of Jammu and Kashmir shall be recognized by the President on the recommendations of the Legislative Assembly of the State; a financial arrangement between the State and the Union be evolved; with regard to emergency powers, Article 352 be modified to provide for its promulgation in case of external aggression but in case of internal disturbance only at the request of or with the concurrence of the State Government; and the Election Commission will conduct elections to Parliament and to the offices of President and Vice-President.

During the course of negotiations as had become necessary after the presentation of the interim report of the Basic Principles Committee in the circumstances referred to hereinbefore, certain agreements were arrived at, details of which were placed before the House by Jenab Sheikh Sahib on 11th of August, 1952. He said:

"The Government of India held the view that the fact that

1. For relevant extracts from Pt. Jawahar Lal Nehru's speech in the Lok Sabha on July 24, 1952 see Appendix VII.

J&K State was the Constituent Unit of the Union of India led inevitably to certain consequences in regard to certain matters, namely: (a) Residuary Powers, (b) Citizenship, (c) Fundamental Rights, (d) Supreme Court, (e) National Flag, (f) The President of India, (g) The Headship of the State, (h) Financial Integration, (i) Emergency Provisions, and (j) Conduct of Election to Houses of Parliament." Sheikh Saheb informed the House about its agreement arrived at in respect of each of them as follows:

Residuary Powers

It was agreed that while under the present Indian Constitution the Residuary Powers vested with the Centre in respect of all States other than Jammu and Kashmir, in the case of our State they vested in the State itself and should continue as such. In this regard, Sheikh Sahib observed as follows:

> "We have always held that the ultimate source of sovereignty resides in the people. *It is, therefore, from the people that all powers can flow. Under these circumstances, it is upto the people of Kashmir through this Assembly to transfer more powers for mutual advantage to the custody of the Union/Centre."*

Citizenship

In this connection, Sheikh Sahib informed the Assembly:

> "It was agreed that in accordance with Article 5 of the Indian Constitution persons who have their domicile in the Jammu and Kashmir State shall be the citizens of India. It was further agreed that the State Legislature shall have power to define and regulate the rights and privileges of the permanent residents of the State, more especially in regard to acquisition of immovable property, appointment to service and like matters. Till then the existing state law would apply."

> "It was also agreed that special provisions will be made in the laws governing citizenship to provide for the return of those permanent residents of J&K State who went to Pakistan in connection with the disturbances of 1947 or in fear of them as well as of those who have left for Pakistan earlier but could

not return. If they return, they should be entitled to the rights, privileges and obligations of citizenship".

Indicating the special reasons for the protection of State Subjects, he said as follows:

"Hon'ble Members are perhaps aware that in the late twenties people of J&K agitated for the protection of their bonafide rights against superior competing interests of the non-residents of the State. It was in response to this popular demand that the Government of the day promulgated a Notification in 1927 by which a strict definition of the term "State Subject" was provided. I am glad to say that Government of India appreciated the need for such a safeguard".

Fundamental Rights

In this regard, Sheikh Sahib observed as follows:

"It is obvious that while our Constitution is being framed the fundamental rights and duties of a citizen have necessarily got to be defined. It was agreed, however, that the Fundamental Rights, which are contained in the Constitution of India could not be conferred on the residents of J&K State in their entirety taking into account the economic, social and political character of our movement as enunciated in the New Kashmir Plan. The need for providing suitable modifications, amendments and exceptions as the case may be in the Fundamental Rights Chapter of the Indian Constitution in order to harmonize those provisions with the pattern of our principles was admitted".

The main point, Sheikh Sahib indicated, that remained to be determined was whether the Chapter of Fundamental Rights should form part of the Constitution of Jammu and Kashmir or that of the Union Constitution. On this aspect there was no agreement.

Supreme Court

It was agreed that Supreme Court should have original

jurisdiction in respect of disputes mentioned in Article 131 of the Constitution of India. It was further agreed that Supreme Court should have jurisdiction in regard to Fundamental Rights which are agreed to by the State. It was recommended on behalf of the Government of India that the Advisory Board in the State, designated as "His Highness's Board of Judicial Advisors" should be abolished and the jurisdiction exercised by it should be vested in the Supreme Court of India. The State Government felt that this would need a detailed examination and consequently it was agreed that it should have time to consider it further.

National Flag

For historical and other reasons connected with the freedom struggle in the State, the need for the continuance of the State flag was recognized. It was agreed that the Union Flag to which all owed allegiance as part of the Union will occupy supremely distinctive place in the State.

President of India

It was decided that powers to grant reprieve and commute death sentences, etc. should also belong to the President of the Union.

Headship of the State

The Government of India appreciated the principle proposed by the Basic Principles Committee as adopted by the Assembly in regard to the abolition of the hereditary rulership of the State. The following arrangement was mutually agreed upon in this regard:

(i) "The Head of the State shall be the person recognized by the President of the Union on the recommendation of the Legislature of the State.

(ii) He shall hold office during the pleasure of the President.

(iii) He may, by writing under his hand addressed to the President, resign his office.

(iv) Subject to the foregoing provisions the Head of the State shall hold office for a term of five years from the date he enters upon his office."

Financial Integration

It was recognized that while it would be necessary to evolve some sort of financial arrangement between the State and the Union, in view of the far-reaching consequences involved therein, it was agreed that a detailed examination of the subject would be necessary before doing that.

Emergency Powers

On behalf of the Government of India it was stated that Article 352 of the Constitution was necessary as it related to vital matters affecting the security of the State. The Government of India did run press for application of Article 356 or even Article 360. Item 1 in the Seventh Schedule relating to the defence of India applied and the Government of India would have full authority to take any steps in connection with defence, etc. The State representatives indicated that they were averse to internal disturbance being referred to in this connection as even petty internal disorder might be considered sufficient for application of Article 352. To meet the State's point of view it was therefore decided that Article 352 might be accepted with addition of the following words at the end of the first paragraph:

> "But in regard to internal disturbance at the request or with the concurrence of the Government of the State."

It was also agreed that the whole matter of application of Article 353, 354, 358 and 359 will be further examined.

Conduct of Elections to Houses of Parliament

Article 324 of the Indian Constitution was already applicable so far as it relates to elections to Parliament and in the offices of the President and the Vice-President of India.

This is how the leader of the Constituent Assembly Sheikh Mohammad Abdullah introduced the Delhi Agreement to the Assembly which was adopted unanimously on 19th August, 1952.

Consequent thereupon, the Drafting Committee of the State Constituent Assembly formed to work out and prepare proposals regarding termination of the hereditary rulership in the State presented its report.

Resolution for adoption by the House was introduced in the following words:

"Now, therefore, in pursuance of the resolution dated the 12th June, 1952, and having considered the report of the Drafting Committee the Assembly resolves:

1. (i) that the Head of the State shall be the person recognized by the President of the Union on the recommendations of the Legislative Assembly of the State;
   (ii) he shall hold office during the pleasure of the President;
   (iii) he may, by writing in his hand, addressed to the President, resign his office; and
   (iv) subject to the foregoing provisions, the Head of the State shall hold office for a term of five years from the date he enters upon his office:

   Provided that he shall, notwithstanding the expiration of his term, continue to hold the office until his successor enters upon his office;
2. that the recommendation of Legislative Assembly of the State in respect of the recognition of the Head of the State specified in sub-para (I) of paragraph 1, shall be made by election;
3. that the method of election to qualifications for and all other matters pertaining to the office of the Head of the State shall be prescribed, in the Constitution, and until these are so prescribed, shall be as set out in the rules contained in the schedule annexed to this resolution;
4. that the Head of the State shall be designated as the Sadar-i-Riyasat;
5. that the Sadar-i-Riyasat shall be entitled in such emoluments, allowances and privileges as may be prescribed in the Constitution and pending the framing of the Constitution, to such emoluments, allowances and privileges as may be decided by this Assembly by separate resolution;
6. that the Sadar-i-Riyasat shall exercise such powers and

perform such functions as may be prescribed in the Constitution to be framed by this Constituent Assembly, and until such Constitution is framed, he shall exercise such powers and perform such functions as have hitherto been exercised by His Highness under the Jammu and Kashmir Constitution Act, 1996, as amended by Act No. XVII of 2008;

7. That in the event of the occurrence of a casual vacancy in the office of the Sadar-i-Riyasat by reason of his death, resignation or otherwise, the powers and functions exercisable by the Sadar-i-Riyasat shall, until the assumption of office by the newly elected Sadar-i-Riyasat in accordance with the procedure laid down in this resolution, be exercised and performed by the person recommended by the State Government for recognition as officiating Sadar-i-Riyasat to the President of India; and
8. That this Assembly shall in due course provide a suitable remedy in respect of violation of the Constitution or gross misconduct by the person for the time being holding the office of the Sadar-i-Riyasal.

The Assembly further Resolves:

That the Prime Minister of Jammu and Kashmir State is authorized to communicate a copy of this resolution to "the Government of India for favour of appropriate action to enable its being given effect to."

This resolution was unanimously adopted after a formal amendment of changing the words, President of Union in sub-clause (1) of para 1 of the Resolution to President of India. Bill effecting the change based on this Resolution was introduced and passed on 10th November, 1952. This Act became Jammu and Kashmir Constitution Amendment Act of 2009.

CHAPTER VIII

Dismissal of Sheikh Mohammad Abdullah and its Aftermath

Then came the unfortunate and unconstitutional dismissal of Sheikh Mohammad Abdullah, the then duly elected Prime

Minister of the State on August 8, 1953 and his imprisonment simultaneously. This was without reference to the Legislature of the State that had exercised its right to elect its Sadar-i-Riyasal only a short time ago in pursuance of agreed proposition of Government of Jammu and Kashmir and Government of India. It is again grievously tragic in that the dismissal was not only of the Prime Minister without reference to the Legislature but also of the leader of the Constituent Assembly having sovereign task of framing the Constitution of the State as also of shaping the future relationship of Jammu and Kashmir State with the Indian Union. This happened at the hands of those in whom the people had reposed their trust and faith and while the Constitution-making process was still under way. This traumatic experience was the first major shock received by the people of the State after the new relationship. It justified the fears Sheikh Saheb had entertained on October 17, 1949 when an agreed draft was unilaterally altered by the leaders at the Centre. It also proved true, as later events showed, the warning he had delivered on August 11, 1952 against unilateral changes to Article 370. Sheikh Mohammad Abdullah was unconstitutionally dismissed from office as Prime Minister of the State of Jammu and Kashmir and put in prison along with his colleagues. A reign of terror was let loose. An era of corruption began. So did a phase of unconstitutionality.

The situation that followed this unfortunate event was neither in the national interest nor that of the State. During this period, besides what happened to the constitutional relationship between the Union and the State, India faced 1965 war followed by 1971 war and signed the Tashkent Agreement of 1966 and the Simla Agreement of 1972. Yet peace and development eluded it.

Highly controversial elections to the State legislative Assembly were held. Each election deepened the distress among the people and dislike for the managers of the election. Elections of 1957, the first held after the unfortunate incident of 1953, were internationally decried; 1962 elections were again on a similar pattern; rarely did these two so called general elections see anyone contesting or in any way being allowed to raise fundamental questions of why and how of developments of 1953. Elections of 1967 saw an additional change that had come about in Kashmir in that official National Conference had for the first time become a branch of the Indian National Congress in the State. In these elections, the people of the State lasted the first fruit and how bitter it was of the Congress entering into State politics as a substitute for the official National Conference. A dissident section of National Conference had by 1966 refused to continue to be part of the National Congress and constituted itself into Jammu and Kashmir National Conference over again. It sought to challenge the Indian National Congress in the battle for electoral confidence and having realized that the situation might become serious, a fraudulent drama of so-called scrutiny of papers was ensured on the table of the Returning Officer. Nomination papers of 22 contestants from as many Constituencies contesting against Indian National Congress candidates were rejected and Indian National Congress Candidates declared elected without having to ask for vote from these Constituencies. Curiously enough in Kashmir Valley in constituencies where contest was allowed. Congress cut a very sorry figure whether it was in the Parliamentary Constituency of Srinagar or Assembly Constituencies of Safakadal, Zadibal, Budgam, Banihal, Shopian and Tral. Of all the fifteen seats in Anantnag district only two seats were allowed to be contested not by National Conference but two young independent political activists and these were dismally lost by the Indian National Congress. This arbitrary and undemocratic manner of conduct of elections gravely shook the faith of the people.

The 1972 elections after Pakistan's debacle in Bangladesh had started assuming great importance because of widespread feeling that the erstwhile Jammu and Kashmir National Conference under the leadership of Jenab Sheikh Mohammad Abdullah was seriously considering that the public loss of faith in democratic process needs to be checked. But before this self-examination of various political options could be allowed to crystalize into a course of action decisively in favour of the people for regeneration of their faith, the Congress Government in the State inflicted a blow to this process of reappraisal by thoughtlessly enacting a law which banned participation in election by anyone who had at any time in the past been a member of a political party declined an unlawful association under the said law. In this way, they prevented the mass of the people from entering into the electoral process.

1972 election was over but it set in a realization that the

situation in Kashmir will not improve on any front whatsoever if Sheikh Saheb and all his loyal followers who spent most of the period from 1958 to 1975 in prisons did not become part of the national mainstream. Efforts to ensure this were set in motion. Negotiations continued for long. During the negotiations, an agonizing reappraisal of the sordid events of 1953 and onwards upto 1975—a long period of 22 years was undertaken. There were people who said the clock cannot be tuned back but there were also people who advocated that not only must the clock be turned back but it might be necessary to replace it if the purpose was to stem the rot that had set in after the arrest of Sheikh Saheb.

CHAPTER IX
Constitution (Application to Jammu & Kashmir) Order, 1954 and Beginning of Erosion of the State Autonomy

On February 11, 1954 Syed Mir Qasim presented to the Constituent Assembly the report of the Drafting Committee. The annexure to the Report indicated "in detail provisions of the Constitution of India which generally correspond to Defence, Foreign Affairs and Communications and such other matters as are considered essential concomitants of the fact of accession."

On February 15, 1954 the Constituent Assembly adopted the following resolution unanimously: Resolved that "(a) having adopted the report of the drafting committee this day, the 15th February, 1954, and (b) having thus given its concurrence to the application of the provisions for the Constitution of India in the manner indicated in the Annexure to the aforesaid report this Assembly authorize the Government of the State to forward a copy of the said Annexure to the Government of India for appropriate action".

This resolution was defective in form. It was not addressed to the President, as it should have been. But it was a substantial compliance with the requirement of a recommendation to him under Article 370. On May 14, 1954 the President made thereunder C.O. 48 the Constitution (Application to Jammu and Kashmir) Order, 1954. Its preamble says that it was made "with the concurrence of the Government of the State of Jammu and Kashmir". Once the Constituent Assembly was convened, the State government lost the power to accord any such concurrence.

However, the order may be said to be valid in so far as it conform to the Annexure to the report of the Constituent Assembly's Drafting Committee only, and, no further. The Order of 1954 does conform in the Annexure to the Report. This Order superseded the Order of 1950 and has been treated as the parent order to which subsequently amendments were made by Orders by the President under Article 370.

In view of its importance, the Order of May 14, 1954 is reproduced in full as Appendix VIII. The entries in the Union list I in the Seventh Schedule as applied to the State by this Order did not, unfortunately, conform strictly to the Instrument of Accession and the Delhi Agreement. However, the State List as well as the Concurrent List were entirely excluded. The State's right to all residuary subjects other than the ones in the Union List which were conferred on the Union was fully accepted. For the rest, certain provisions of the Constitution of India were applied in full; some with modifications, while the rest were omitted.

Before we proceed further and see how to evolve a consensus for action consistent with earnest desire to win back people solidly for participation in the national mainstream politics, it will be necessary to see how things had been allowed to go a drift after August 1953 till 1965 and after 1965 till 1975. It will be interesting to note that after inauguration of the Indian National Congress in the State when it substituted the National Conference and made it a branch of the National party with Sheikh Saheb and his colleagues still in jail and later facing alleged cases of conspiracy and treason, how maximum assault was launched upon Kashmir's special position, its autonomous character, its sovereign character and all this only to realise in 1975 that things had gone out of gear and people had lost whatever faith and confidence they had in the democratic relationship, issues deferred at the time of Delhi Agreement could not be negotiated any further till the Constituent Assembly itself was flawed by putting the real leadership of the people behind the bars arbitrarily and unconstitutionally. Even casual examination of the first Constitution (Application to Jammu and Kashmir) Order, 1954 that came into existence after these traumatic changes of 1953 will show that a path different from the one aspired to be chosen by the people of Kashmir State under the leadership of Sheikh Mohammad Abdullah was far different from the one envisaged by the Instrument of Accession and all that had gone with it. Jurisdiction of Union Parliament was extended from three subjects—Defense, External Affairs and Communications, to almost all the subjects—Defense, External Affairs and Communications, to almost all the subjects in the Union List. This constituted a first encroachment on the powers of legislation of the State by widening of those of the Union. We have seen the entries of the List 1 of Seventh Schedule which were made applicable by the Constitution Application Order of 1950 and also the entries which were not applicable to the State of Jammu and Kashmir. The Constitution Application Order of 1954 reversed the Order and made Union Parliament capable of legislating in respect of almost all the entries in the List, of course, with some exceptions and modifications. While the 1950 Order made some parts besides Articles 1 and 370 applicable—making exceptions and modifications also, 1954 Order made many more parts applicable with or without modifications. The important Article made thus applicable was Article 3 in which a proviso has been added for its modified application. The proviso required that "no bill for increasing or diminishing the area of Jammu and Kashmir or for altering the name of boundaries of the State shall be introduced in Parliament without the consent of the Legislature of the State." Part II of the Constitution of India now became applicable as a result of 1954 Order, with some modifications based upon letter and spirit of Delhi Agreement. Part III of the Constitution relating to Fundamental Rights was made applicable by 1954 Order. The question that remained to be determined was whether the chapter on Fundamental Rights of the Indian Constitution should form a part of the State Constitution or of the Constitution of India as applicable to the State. As it happened, a new Committee on Fundamental Rights was constituted after 9th August, 1953. The reconstituted committees both on Basic Principles as also on Citizenship and Fundamental Rights submitted their report to the Constituent Assembly on 3 February, 1954. The report of the Drafting Committee appointed by the Constituent Assembly in conformity with the recommendations of the two aforesaid committees was presented to the Assembly on 11th February, 1954. The annexure to that report indicated details of the provisions in the Constitution of India to be made applicable to the State. In accordance with the directions contained in the two reports, the sphere of Union jurisdiction was determined/refixed keeping intact all along the residuary powers of the State. It is this annexure to the report, which ultimately formed the Constitution (Application to J&K) Order of 1954 and made applicable parts of the Constitution of India to our State.

Part V dealing with Union had already been made applicable with some exceptions and modifications and additionally, Articles 54, 55, 73, 134, 139 and 150 were applied with modifications. Thereafter, from Part XI Article 246, 250, 251, 253, 254, 256, 261 were made applicable with modifications. Since this chapter deals with legislative powers of Parliament and residuary powers of legislation it may be worthwhile to notice changes brought about in the chapter in its application to the State of Jammu and Kashmir by 1954 Order.

Whereas under the 1960 Order, Parliament could make laws for the State in respect of only such matters in the Union list which correspond to the matters specified in the Instrument of Accession, by the 1954 Order, as a consequence of omission of the words "Subject to the provisions of paragraph 2", occurring in the 1950 Order, the Parliament could thereafter make laws in respect of all matters specified in the Union List. As if that was not enough, the Article was further modified in its application to the State vide C.O. No. 66 dated 28th September, 1963, enabling Parliament to make laws for the State in respect of matters in the Concurrent List also. Most important thing in the Seventh Schedule according to the Order of 1954 was continuance of what had been the feature of the earlier order of 1950 that the State List and the Concurrent List in their application to the State of Jammu and Kashmir were excluded. Regarding rest of the Articles from the important chapter dealing with legislative relations of the Union and the State it has been noted that the Articles 248 and 249 dealing with the residuary powers of the legislation and also power of Parliament to legislate in respect of matters in the State List in the national interest were not applicable to the State. Article 250 was also not applicable to the State under 1950 Order but was applied in a modified form by 1954 Order vesting the Parliament with the power to make laws for the State in respect of matters not enumerated in the Union List.

It may thus cover areas which are part of residuary powers of legislation or strictly powers of Legislature of the State. Article

251 in its application to Jammu and Kashmir State in view of non-application of Article 249 in the Order of 1954 had to remain confined to Article 250 alone in its application to the State. Vide Article 253 in its modified form it was made obligatory that after commencement of the Constitution (Application to J&K) Order of 1954 no decision affecting the disposition of the State of Jammu and Kashmir could be made by the Government of India without the consent of the Government of the State. Article 755 was omitted from application to Jammu and Kashmir State and Article 354 applied with modifications. The article as applicable to Jammu and Kashmir state at that time read as follows:

> "If any provision of law made by the Legislature of a State is repugnant to any provisions of law made by Parliament which Parliament is competent to enact, law made by Parliament whether passed before or after the law made by the Legislature of the State prevail and law made by the Legislature of the State shall to the extent of repugnancy be void."

Clause (2) of the Article as in the Union Constitution was omitted in relation to the J&K State.

From Chapter II of this Part dealing with Administrative Relations, while 1950 Order made Article 256 applicable to the State without any modifications or exceptions and applied Article 257 with the exceptions of clauses (3) and (4) thereof, Articles 260, 262 and 263 were excepted under the 1954 Order. Article 256 was renumbered as clause (1) of that Article and the following new clause (2) was added thereto, namely:

> "The State of Jammu and Kashmir shall so exercise its executive power as to facilitate the discharge by the Union of its duties and responsibilities under the Constitution in relation to that State; and in particular, the said State shall, if so required by the Union, acquire or requisition properly on behalf of and at the expense of the Union on such terms as may be agreed, or in default of agreement, as may be determined by an arbitrator appointed by the Chief Justice of India."

Article 259 in its application was omitted and Article 261 applied with minor modifications. In Clause (2) thereof the words 'made by Parliament' were ordered to be omitted. After this change, clause (2) of Article 261 in its application to J&K reads as under:

> "The manner in which and the conditions under which the acts, records and proceedings referred to in clause (1) shall be proved and the effect thereof determined shall be as provided by law.

The next chapter, namely Chapter XII deals with Finance, Property, Contracts and Suits. We have seen how Constitution Application Order of 1950 had dealt with this Chapter in its application to the State of Jammu and Kashmir. Exception was made in respect of Articles 264, 265, clause (2) of Articles 267, 268 and 281, clause (2) of Article 283, Articles 286 to 291, 293, 295, 296 and 297. Articles 266, 282, 284, 298, 299 and 300 were applied in modified form. 1954 Order did radically change the situation in so far as application of this chapter was concerned. This despite the fact that Delhi Agreement had not recorded any conclusions regarding financial relationship between the State and the Union and the matter had been deferred for final solution. The negotiations did not conclude at all between the real representatives of the State and the Government of India till introduction of the report of the Basic Principles Committee and Advisory Committee on Fundamental Rights in the Assembly in the manner described above. 1954 Order, however, affirmed omission of clause (2) of Article 267, clause (2) of Article 283 as in the 1950 Order and again repeated that Articles 266, 282, 284, 298, 299 and 300 would apply in identical terms as in 1950 Order. This would mean that reference in these Articles to State or States shall be construed as not including reference to the State of Jammu and Kashmir. In Article 277 and 295 commencement of Constitution was to be construed as commencement of Constitution (Application to J&K) Order of 1954.

The changes in Article 303, Part XIII deleted reference to any entry relating to trade and commerce in any list in Seventh Schedule as providing authority of restriction on legislative power of Union and of States in regard to trade and commerce and reference to Article 306 is not necessary since by now this provision stands deleted.

In Part XIV, provisions regarding All India Services (Art. 312) were not applicable to the State even under 1954 Order dated 14th May, 1954.

The next Part XV dealing with elections and Article 324 thereof was made applicable only in relation to elections to Parliament and to offices of President and Vice-President. Rest of the Articles 325, 326, 327, 328 and 329 were omitted from application to this State.

In Part XVI reference to Scheduled Tribes was omitted in relation to J&K. Articles 331, 332, 333, 336, 337, 339, 342 stood omitted and references to the State or States in Articles 334 and 335 were to be construed as not including references to the State of Jammu and Kashmir.

Part dealing with official languages, i.e. Part XVII in its application to State of Jammu and Kashmir had to remain related to:

(a) The official language of the Union;
(b) The official language for communication between one State and another, or between a State and the Union; and
(c) The Language of the proceedings in the Supreme Court.

That takes us to another important part namely Part XVIII relating to EMERGENCY PROVISIONS. Articles 352 to 360 are included in this Part.

This chapter was not mentioned in the Constitution (Application to J&K) Order of 1950. A new clause was added which became sub-clause (4) of Article 352 in the year 1954 as it then was. The sub-clause read as under:

> "No proclamation of emergency made on grounds only of internal disturbance or imminent danger thereof shall have effect in relation to the State of Jammu and Kashmir (except as respects Article 354) unless it is made at the request or with the concurrence of Government of that State."

Articles 356, 357 and 360 were omitted in their application to Jammu and Kashmir as per 1954 Order.

Thereafter comes Part XIX, MISCELLANEOUS (Articles 361-367). Exceptions was made in respect of Articles 362, 363, and 365 in the 1950 Order. Article 361 was applied with modification in that it would apply so far as it related to President and that article

364 would apply in so far as it related to the laws made by the parliament about major ports and aerodromes. Vide 1954 Order, however, situation had already been altered and after clause (4) of Article 361 clause (5) was added which read as under:

> "The provisions of this article shall apply in relation to the Sadar-i-Riyasat of Jammu and Kashmir as they apply in relation to a Rajpramukh, but without prejudice to the provisions of the Constitution of the State."

Articles 362 and 365 were omitted. In Article 366 clause (21) was omitted. This clause as it stood in the Indian Constitution in the year 1954 was finally deleted from the Constitution itself later in 1956.

A new clause was added to Article 367, i.e. clause (4) which read as under:

> "(4) For the purpose of this Constitution as it applies in relation to the State of Jammu and Kashmir:
>
> (a) Reference to this Constitution or to the provisions thereof shall be construed as references to the Constitution or the provisions thereof as applied in relation to the said State;
>
> (b) references to the Government of the said State shall be construed as including references to the Sadar-i-Rayasat acting on the advice of his Council of Ministers;
>
> (c) references to a High Court shall include references to a High Court of Jammu and Kashmir;
>
> (d) references the Legislature or the Legislative Assembly of the said State shall be construed as including references to the Constituent Assembly of the said State;
>
> (e) references to the permanent residents of the said State shall be construed as meaning persons who, before the commencement of the Constitution (Application to Jammu and Kashmir) Order, 1954, were recognised as State subjects under the law in force in the State or who are recognised by any law made by the Legislature of the State as permanent residents of the State; and
>
> (f) references to the Rajpramukh shall be construed as references to the persons for the time being recognised

by the President as the Sadar-i-Riyasat of Jammu and Kashmir and as including references to any person for the time being recognised by the President as being competent to exercise the powers of the Sadar-i-Riyasat."

The provisions of Article 368 which is a sole Article of Part XX relate to power of Parliament to amend the Constitution and procedure therefor. In its application to the State of Jammu and Kashmir the following proviso was added:

"Provided further that no such amendment shall have effect in relation to the State of Jammu and Kashmir unless applied by order of the President under clause (1) of Article 370."

From Part XXI, Articles 369, 371, 373, clauses 1, 2, 3 and 5 of Article 374. Article 376 and Article 392 were ordered to be omitted. This Part as earlier noted dealt with "Temporary, Transitional and Special Provisions" and this is the Part, which like other so-called transitory provisions, contains Article 370.

Article 370, part Article 372 and part Article 374 alone were applicable in the prescribed form to the State of Jammu and Kashmir. In Article 372, clauses (2) and (3) were to be deleted and references to laws in force in the territory of India would also include references to Hidayats, Ailans, Ishtihars, Circulars, Robkars, Irshad, Yadhasht, State Council Resolutions, Resolutions of the Constituent Assembly and other instruments having the force of law in the territory of the State of Jammu and Kashmir and reference to the commencement of the Constitution was construed to be reference to the commencement of the Application Order of 1954. In identical terms in Clause (4) of Article 374 the reference to the authority functioning as the Privy Council of a State was to be construed as a reference to the Advisory Board constituted under J&K Constitution Act Svt. 1996 and reference to the commencement of the Constitution here also was to be construed as reference to the commencement of the 1954 Order. From Part XXII, Articles 394 and 395 were omitted. The position regarding the application of Schedules appended to the Constitution that emerged as a result of the 1954 Order was as under:

(i) First Schedule	Applied
(ii) Second Schedule	Applied except paragraph 6

(iii)	Third schedule	Applied except Forms V, VI, VII and VIII
(iv)	Fourth Schedule Applied	
(v)&(vi)	Fifth and sixth Schedule	Not applied
(vii)	Seventh schedule	(a) Entries in the Union List as already noted above applied. (b) State list and the concurrent list stood omitted.
(viii)	Eighth Schedule	Applied
(ix)	Ninth Schedule	Applied

CHAPTER X

Erosion Continued Apace

The constitutional relationship between the State and the Union as it existed when the Constitution Application Order of 1950 was repealed and substituted by Constitution Application Order of 1954 has been detailed in the preceding chapter. There is no doubt that serious deviations were made and the position altered in some vital matters but for the time being we will only indicate what it is that had not been changed. In the legislative sphere of State-Union relationship, 1954 Order did not after the position insofar as non-application to the State of the Concurrent List and the State List of the Seventh Schedule was concerned. These two lists were completely excluded in their application in relation to the State of Jammu and Kashmir. This left Residuary Powers of legislation completely with the State Legislature and legislative power of the State was so extensive as to be capable of being available for all things not included in the Union List as applicable to the State of Jammu and Kashmir. Although the 1954 Order had increased the number of items to which the power of Parliament to legislate in respect of Jammu and Kashmir was extended but even so they were not as many as were subsequently added to it for effecting further erosion of autonomy by misuse of Article 370. The cumulative reading indicates that State's power to legislate on matters other than those ceded to the Union Parliament were quite wide and still left a great degree of autonomy with the State.

In Chapter II of Part XI dealing with administrative relations between the Union and the State. Article 256 was applied to the State in a modified form. This modification can be regarded as a normal and natural corollary of the State being a unit of the federation. This incidentally appears to be the spirit of clause 6 of the Instrument of Accession also.

Part VI did not apply with the result that State of Jammu and Kashmir was left free to frame its own Constitution for internal governance. This part also contained Chapter (V) which dealt with High Court in the States. The position in respect of the High Courts in the States also continued to be the same as it was at the time of passing of the 1950 Order. The continued non-application of this part of the Indian Constitution both in 1950 and 1954 Orders allowed the existing Constitution of Jammu and Kashmir State as amended upto 1950 to continue to remain a live document and also kept the prospect of State Constituent Assembly framing the Constitution of the State of Jammu and Kashmir alive and left the Constitution of the State as it was on 14th of May, 1954 undisturbed. It meant that the Head of the State and the Chief Executive continued to be Sadar-i-Riyasat and the Prime Minister respectively.

Provisions under Part XIV relating to services under the Union and the States were not applied to the State of Jammu and Kashmir either under 1950 or 1954 Order.

Likewise, provisions under Part XV regarding elections were restricted in their application to Jammu and Kashmir to the elections to parliament and offices of the President and Vice-President only. Also, provisions under Part XVI were restricted in their application to the J&K State to the Scheduled Castes only.

The next important Part that requires mention is Part XVIII. In this Part what was common between 1950 and 1954 Orders was non-application of Articles 356, 357 and 360. It, however, needs to be noted that the Order of 1954 did make Article 352 applicable in a modified form by addition of sub-clause (4) to Article 352 as mentioned earlier.

In the matter of financial relations many radical changes were made by the Constitution (Application to Jammu and Kashmir) Order, 1954. This inspite of the fact that no agreement could be reached in regard to the future financial relationship between the State and the Union under the Delhi Agreement of 1952.

Part XII (Articles 264-300) of the Indian Constitution was made applicable in essence as elaborated in the foregoing chapter.

The immenseness and the pace of erosion of State autonomy from 1953 onwards can be gauged from a perusal of the long list of Constitution Orders applying various provisions of the Indian Constitution to the State given below:

1. The Constitution (Application to J&K) Order, 1954 C.O. 48 Dated: 14.5.1954.
2. The Constitution (Application to J&K Amendment Order, 1956 C.O. 51 dated: 11.2.1956.
3. The Constitution (Application to J&K) Amendment Order, 1958 C.O. 55 dated: 16.1.1958.
4. The Constitution (Application to J&K) Second Amendment Order, 1958 C.O. 56 dated: 26.2.1958.
5. The Constitution (Application to J&K) Amendment Order 1959 C.O. 57 dated: 9.2.1959.
6. The Constitution (Application to J&K) Second Amendment Order, 1959 C.O. 59 dated: 23-04-1959.
7. The Constitution (Application to J&K) Amendment Order, 1960 C.O. 60 dated: 20-01-1960.
8. The Constitution (Application to J&K) Second Amendment Order, 1960 C.O. 61 dated: 22.6.1960.
9. The Constitution (Application to J&K) Amendment Order, 1961 C.O. 62 dated: 2.5.1961.
10. The Constitution (Application to J&K) Amendment Order, 1963 C.O. 66 dated: 28.9.1963.
11. The Constitution (Application to J&K) Amendment Order, 1964 C.O. 69 dated: 6.3.1964.
12. The Constitution (Application to J&K) Second Amendment Order, 1964 C.O. 70 dated: 2.10.1964.
13. The Constitution (Application to J&K) Third Amendment Order, 1964 C.O. 71 dated: 21.11.1964.
14. The Constitution (Application to J&K) Amendment Order, 1965 C.O. 72 dated: 17.5.1965.
15. The Constitution (Application to J&K) Second Amendment Order, 1965 C.O. 74 dated: 24.11.1965.
16. The Constitution (Application to J&K) Amendment Order, 1966 C.O. 75 dated: 29.6.1966.

17. The Constitution (Application to J&K) Amendment Order, 1967 C.O. 76 dated: 13.2.1967.
18. The Constitution (Application to J&K) Second Amendment Order, 1967 C.O. 77 dated: 5.5.1967.
19. The Constitution (Application to J&K) Third Amendment Order, 1967 C.O. 79 dated: 11.8.1967.
20. The Constitution (Application to J&K) Fourth Amendment Order, 1967 C.O. 80 dated: 26.12.1967.
21. The Constitution (Application to J&K) Amendment Order, 1968 C.O. 83 dated: 9.2.1968.
22. The Constitution (Application to J&K) Amendment Order, 1969 C.O. 85 dated: 17.2.1969.
23. The Constitution (Application to J&K) Second Amendment Order, 1969 C.O. 86 dated: 31.5.1969.
24. The Constitution (Application to J&K) Amendment Order, 1971 C.O. 89 dated: 24.8.1971
25. The Constitution (Application to J&K) Second Amendment Order, 1971 C.O. 90 dated: 8.11.1971
26. The Constitution (Application to J&K) Third Amendment Order, 1971 C.O. 91 dated: 29.11.1971
27. The Constitution (Application to J&K) Amendment Order, 1972 C.O. 92 dated: 24.2.1972.
28. The Constitution (Application to J&K) Second Amendment Order, 1972 C.O. 93 dated: 6.5.1972.
29. The Constitution (Application to J&K) Third Amendment Order, 1972 C.O. 94 dated: 2.8.1972.
30. The Constitution (Application to J&K) Fourth Amendment Order, 1972 C.O. 95 dated: 10.8.1972.
31. The Constitution (Application to J&K) Amendment Order, 1974 C.O. 97 dated: 1.5.1974.
32. The Constitution (Application to J&K) Second Amendment Order, 1974 C.O. 98 dated: 26.6.1974.
33. The Constitution (Application to J&K) Amendment Order, 1975 C.O. 100 dated: 29.6.1975.
34. The Constitution (Application to J&K) Second Amendment Order, 1975, C.O. 101 dated: 23.7.1975.
35. The Constitution (Application to J&K) Amendment Order, 1976 C.O. 103 dated: 2.3.1976.

36. The Constitution (Application to J&K.) Second Amendment Order, 1976 C.O. 104 dated: 25.5.1976.
37. The Constitution (Application to J&K) Third Amendment Order, 1976 C.O. 105 dated: 12.9.1976.
38. The Constitution (Application to J&K) Fourth Amendment Order, 1976 C.O. 106 dated: 31.12.1976.
39. The Constitution (Application to J&K) Amendment Order, 1977 C.O. 108 dated: 31.12.1977.
40. The Constitution (Application to J&K) Amendment Order, 1985 C.O. 122 dated: 4.6.1985.
41. The Constitution (Application to J&K) Second Amendment Order, 1985 C.O. 124 dated: 4.12.1985.
42. The Constitution (Application to J&K) Amendment Order, 1986 C.O. 129 dated: 30.7.1986.

Not all these Orders can be objected to. For instance, none can object to provision for direct elections to Parliament in 1966. Delimitation of Parliamentary constituencies, etc. It is the principle that matters. Constitutional limits are there to be respected, not violated. Amendments to the Constitution of India were extended as a matter of course to the State.

We have noticed above that in the eagerness to create an image of cementing closer relations, what followed 1954 is a series of Constitution (Application to J&K) Orders numbering 42 till now which were not conceived at any point of time either in 1950 or in 1952 or even later in May, 1954. Among the changes brought about the most important were in restricting the powers of legislature of the State, extension of powers of the Union Parliament, application to the State of financial provisions of the Constitution of India, provisions relating to emergency. All India Services, superintendence, direction and control of elections of the state legislature and several other matters.

The position having been so radically altered can be put in the following manner so as to indicate actual State-Union relationship which had emerged as a result of changes brought about.

(a) Almost all entries in the Union List are applicable to the State of Jammu and Kashmir with the result that Union Parliament's power to legislate extends to matters even beyond the three subjects on which the accession had originally been agreed upon. The list has gone far beyond 20 items of the list attached to the Instrument of Accession or even the Schedules to 1950 Order.

(b) Concurrent List of legislation in essence is applicable, even in regard to welfare legislation and essentially local matters.

(c) Most of the provisions about one of the wings of the State namely the Judiciary are now derivable or definable from the Country's Constitution rather than the Constitution of the State.

(d) Provision relating to All India Services is now applicable to the State.

(e) All the matters under Finance, Trade and Commerce are now applicable. Even the rudiments of financial autonomy have completely been swept away.

(f) Even the field of residuary legislation in the matter of law and order has been curtailed so far as the State is concerned and Entry 97 of the Union list too has been made applicable in curiously modified form to the detriment of the principle of political autonomy.

(g) All emergency powers including those in Article 356 and that too in their un-amended form and retrograde shape are applicable to the State and their misuse during the last eight to nine years has proved beyond doubt that apprehensions entertained in 1950's have come out to be true.

(h) Special provisions of Article 249 dealing with the Parliament's power of legislation in the State List have been extended to the State of Jammu and Kashmir quite surreptitiously in a brazen and clandestine manner by misinterpreting and misusing Article 370.

(i) Superintendence, direction and control of local elections now vests with the Central Election Commission.

Besides, some changes of far-reaching consequences including that of altering the mode of appointment of the Head of the State were effected in the Constitution of the State. The extent and the nature of autonomy which has been left with the

State as of now can be seen from the following table:

I.	Total No. of Articles	No. of Articles applied	Balance
	395	260	135*

*These relate to matters under Part VI of the Constitution of India which pertains to matters concerning the Executive, Legislature and High Courts of States of the Union and provisions whereof are identical to the provisions of the Constitution of Jammu and Kashmir.

II. Total No. of entries in the Union List	Entries applied	Balance
97	94	3*

*Entries 8.9 and 34 relating to CBI jurisdiction, preventive detention connected with Defence matters, and Courts of wards for the estates of Rulers of Indian States respectively.

III. Total No. of entries in the concurrent list	Entries applied	Balance
47	26	21*

*Entries 3, 5, 6, 7, 8, 9, 10, 14, 15, 17, 20, 21, 27, 28, 29, 31, 32, 37, 38, 41 and 44.

These entries relate mostly to matters of social legislation, charitable institutions, relief and rehabilitation of displaced persons, transfer of property etc.

IV.	Total No. of Schedules	No. of Schedules applied	Balance
	12	7	5*

*Schedule 5—Control of Scheduled Areas and S.T.

Schedule 6—Administration of Tribal Areas.

Schedule 10—Disqualification on grounds of defection except in so far it relates to members of Parliament.

Schedule 11—Powers of Panchayats (new provision of the Indian Constitution vide Seventy-third Amendment Act, 1992).

Schedule 12—Power and responsibilities of Municipalities (new provision of the Indian Constitution vide Seventy-fourth Amendment Act, 1992).

*Indicates provisions hithereto not applied to the State.

It is abundantly clear, therefore, that from 1953 onwards, especially in sixties, the process of erosion of the state autonomy was so rapid and on such a massive scale that entire Article 370 of the Constitution of India which was supposed to guarantee and preserve the special status of the State in the Indian Union was emptied of its substantive content with the result that the State's jurisdiction over the matters as envisaged by the Instrument of Accession of Oct. 1947 and the Delhi Agreement of 1952 was gradually diminished and systematically transferred to the Union.

Far from enjoying a special status, as Article 370 envisaged, the State was put in a status inferior to that of other States. One illustration suffices to demonstrate that Parliament had to amend the Constitution four times, by the 59th, 64th, 67th, 68th Constitution Amendments to extend President's rule imposed in Punjab on May 11, 1987. For the State of Jammu and Kashmir, the same result was accomplished by executive orders under Article 370.

The Union Home Minister. Mr. Gulzari Lal Nanda said on December 4, 1964 that Article 370 could well be used to serve as a "tunnel in the wall" in order to increase the Centre's powers. This was diametrically contrary to the clear intent underlying, and the objective of Article 370.

Another gross case illustrates the extent of misuse of Article 370. On July 30, 1986 the President made an Order under Article 370 extending to the State Article 249 of the Constitution in order to empower Parliament to legislate even on a matter in the State List on the strength of a Rajya Sabha resolution. "Concurrence" to this was given by the Centre's own appointee, Governor Jagmohan (*Indian Express*, August 17, 1986).

This is how C.O. 129 was made on July 30, 1986. It said that in Article 249, in clause (1) for the words "any matter enumerated in the State list specified in the resolution," the words "any matter specified in the resolution being a matter which is not enumerated in the Union List or in the concurrent list" shall be substituted. This was made "with the concurrence of the Government of the State of Jammu and Kashmir" when the State was under Governor's rule and no popular Government existed. This is a clear nullity.

Successive State governments had in the past accorded their "concurrence" for various reasons and under various political compulsions. No State would otherwise willingly accept curbs on its autonomy.

CHAPTER XI

Changes Effected in the Basic Structure of the State Constitution

This brings us to the perception which inspired both the State and the Union leadership in early fifties to envisage that the State of Jammu and Kashmir shall frame the Constitution of the State through a Constituent Assembly envisaged for it during the days of freedom struggle itself and recognised thereafter by a provision in the Constitution of India. This Constituent Assembly adopted a method of appointment of the Head of the State different from the one adopted by the Constituent Assembly of India in respect of the other States of the Union in as much as it provided for an elected Head (Sadar-i-Riyasat). Thus it brought to an end the era of hereditary rulership for all times to come and held out a promise for the future of a fully democratic Constitution for the State.

The Constitution finally adopted had the following features:

(a) An elected Head of the State.

(b) A chapter on Directive Principles ensuring equality, fraternity and social justice for all.

(A) An independent Judiciary.

(c) A Council of Ministers with a Prime Minister of the State at the Head.

(d) A Legislature consisting of two Houses with the Upper House based on absolute parity between the two regions of the State with very wide and effective powers.

(e) Another important feature of the Constitution adopted and enforced was and continues to be provided by Section 147. This section deals with power and procedure of amendment of the Constitution. This Section made some provisions of the Constitution of Jammu and Kashmir unalterable and among the unalterable provisions are the following:

(a) Section 147 itself.

(b) Section 3 defining the relationship of the State with the Union of India.

(c) Section 5 dealing with the extent of executive and legislative power of the State.

The State Constitution can be regarded as very rigid in this respect. This feature that it has provisions which are quite rigid and provisions which are flexible is not unique in the Constitution of the State alone. This is true of many Constitutions. Justice Anand has to say, in this regard, as follows:

> "The French Constitution declares that the Republican character of the Government cannot be changed and in the United States of America no federating State can secede and become independent."

In more than one ways, Sections 3, 4 and 5 in the Constitution of Jammu and Kashmir State can be regarded as the fundamental law on which in the words of His Lordship, Mr. Justice Adarsh Sen Anand, "the very structure of the Constitution has been erected".

Our purpose of making reference to these provisions of the Constitution of State of Jammu and Kashmir is to place on record how this fundamental law or the basic structure on which the Constitution is based has been subjected to changes. Even a casual study can indicate that despite the rigidity the requirement of the mandate of unalterable character of the provisions, politics has swayed someone to adopt measures which should not have been adopted at all.

The Amendment Acts of 1959 and 1965 were introduced respectively before and after the National Conference Party converted itself into a Pradesh Congress Committee, a branch in the State of Indian National Congress. The Constitution of Jammu and Kashmiri (Sixth Amendment) Act, 1960 introduced changes in Sections 2.27, 29, 30, 31, 32, 33, 51, 95, 100-A, 100-B and 126. As a result of the changes effected by this Amendment Act among various other provisions that suffered changes, was Section 147 also though declared by the Section itself as unalterable. Section 147 as it stood before the amendment was as follows:

> "An amendment of the Constitution may be initiated only by the introduction of a Bill for the purpose in the Legislative Assembly, and when the Bill is passed in the House by a majority of not less than two-thirds of the total membership of the House, it shall be presented to the Sadar-i-Riyasat for his assent and upon such assent being given to the Bill, the

Constitution shall stand amended in accordance with the terms of the Bill:

Provided that a Bill providing for the abolition of the Legislative Council may be introduced in the Legislative Assembly and passed by it by a majority of the total membership of the Assembly and by a majority of not less than two-thirds of the members of the Assembly present and voting.

Provided further that no Bill or Amendment seeking to make any change in—

(a) this section; or
(b) the provisions of Sections 3 and 5; or
(c) the provisions of the Constitution of India as applicable in relation to the State shall be introduced or moved in either House of the State Legislature."

Besides, an omnibus amendment in Section (2) by introduction of a sub-section (3) affected many other provisions. Sub-section (3) reads as under:

"Any reference in this Constitution to Sadar-i-Riyasat shall, unless the context otherwise requires, be construed as a reference to the Governor."

Section 147 vide Section (2) of the Sixth Amendment Act of the Constitution of Jammu and Kashmir State suffered change in that the word, 'Governor' was substituted for the word, 'Sadar-i-Riyasat' which could not have been made in view of the provision of the section. This amendment brings about fundamental changes in the core foundation of the Constitution of the State. This was done without considering the implication and so radically that the basic character of the Constitution was infringed upon just within eight years of its adoption and enforcement.

Incidentally, we may digress for a moment here and go to explanation part given at the end of sub-clause (b) of clause (1) of Article 370. This explanation originally was as under:

"For the purpose of this Article the Government of the State means the person for the time being recognised as Maharaja of Jammu and Kashmir acting on the advice of the Council of Ministers for the time being in office under Maharaja's proclamation dated 5th day of March, 1948."

The said explanation on the recommendation of the Constituent Assembly of the State of Jammu and Kashmir was changed by a Presidential Order vide C.O. 44 dated 17.11.1952 making Article 370 operative with a changed explanation with effect from 7th November, 1952. The substituted explanation reads as under:

> "For the purpose of this Order, the Government of the State means the person for the time being recognised by the President on the recommendation of the Legislative Assembly of the State as Sadar-i-Riyasat of Jammu and Kashmir acting on the advice of the Council of Ministers of the State for the time being in office".

So, the part dealing with Maharaja's proclamation of 5th March, 1948 became Sadar-i-Riyasat recognised as such by President of India and acting on the advice of the Council of Ministers of the State for the time being in office with effect from 17th November, 1952. What then is Article 370 after the word 'Sadar-i-Riyasat' is substituted by the word Governor after the Sixth Amendment Act of the Constitution of the State of Jammu and Kashmir if the substitution is not part of the Indian Constitution? The word Sadar-i-Riyasat continues to exist in Article 370 for any kind of change in Article 370 cannot be brought about by making change in Jammu and Kashmir State Constitution and in the way it was brought about.

The power of the State Legislature can next be found to have been impinged upon insofar as its legal right to elect the Head of State subject to the recognition by the President of India got obliterated. This deprivation cannot but be recorded as a serious assault on the autonomous character of this unit of the federation. The recommendation to have an elected Head as the substitute for the hereditary ruler had been made by the Basic Principles Committee for the Constituent Assembly as early as 1952. This was mutually agreed upon by the State and the Union leaders. Consequently, the Sadar-i-Riyasat was duly elected in 1952 and thereafter every five years till the Constitution of State was amended in 1965. Why it was necessary in 1965 to deprive the

State of electing its Sadar-i-Riyasat and provide for a nominee of the Central Government as Governor need not be dwelt upon at length but, however, reference to 1984, 1986 and 1990 interludes in history must indicate that but for events happening at the behest of nominated Governors, ground situation in the State of Jammu and Kashmir would in all probability have been different. Why and to satisfy whom did the State leadership after in-coming of Congress into the State embark upon this mis-adventure shall always be regretted.

During 1948-65 the word Prime Minister of Jammu and Kashmir did not raise any storm in any cup of tea nor did it even remotely lead to any confusion with that of the Prime Minister of the Union. It was there in the State prior to 1947, had continued to be thereafter Maharaja's declaration of March 5th, 1948 and again after the adoption of interim Constitution in 1952, till the dismissal of the first elected Prime Minister in 1953 and again till March 1965. What has been achieved after writing it off alongwith the principle of election of the Head of the State as also the nomenclature of Sadar-i-Riyasat can now be seen from what has happened in very recent history of the State particularly to State's relationship with the Union.

This assault on State Autonomy must be and has to be undone. For this purpose appropriate amendments shall have to be made in the Constitution of Jammu and Kashmir and also consequential changes in the provisions of the Constitution of India as applicable to the State.

This requires to be done speedily to restore the faith of the people in the path chosen by them through their representatives in the course of deliberations in the Constituent Assembly of the State way back in 1951-53.

CHAPTER XII

Return of Sheikh Mohammad Abdullah to Power in 1975 and After

After the dismissal of Jenab Sheikh Mohammad Abdullah from the office of the Prime Minister of Jammu and Kashmir on August 8, 1953 in an unconstitutional and undemocratic manner he was kept under detention for over two decades. However, in February, 1975 due to the pursuation of Mrs. Indira Gandhi, he agreed to take over the state administration pending the next elections of the State Assembly with the support of the then Congress members of the State Legislature, although he insisted on the holding of Assembly elections before taking office. But, as it happened, in March, 1977, much before the due date of Assembly elections, the Congress party withdrew its support to him.

The Janata Party which was then in power at the Centre ordered fresh and fair elections in the State in the same year and the Jammu and Kashmir National Conference under the leadership of Sheikh Saheb won a thumping majority as a result of the fairest ever elections held in Jammu and Kashmir till then after 1953. However, unfortunately even the Historically held elections were not made best use of to deepen the roots of national mainstream politics by enlightened national leadership and by yielding to the people of Kashmir what they needed most, what they held to be their birth right, their right to be a special state of the Indian Union with unbridled powers of legislation in matters other than those ceded under Instrument of Accession or powers incidental or ancillary thereto.

After Sheikh Saheb's death in 1982, fresh elections to the J&K Legislative Assembly were held in June, 1983 and the National Conference under the leadership of Dr. Farooq Abdullah again won the elections with comfortable majority. But in 1984 the Government headed by him was dismissed unconstitutionally and undemocratically and another Government under the leadership of Shri Ghulam Mohammad Shah was installed by engineering defections in the National Conference with Congress Party support from outside.

This experiment also did not succeed. Congress Party withdrew support in March, 1986 and the G.M. Shah Government had to be dismissed. Governor's rule was imposed. In the Assembly elections held in 1987 National Conference under the leadership of Dr. Farooq Abdullah won the elections again. In January 1990 the Central Government brought back a Governor in the State who was unacceptable to the popularly elected State Government with the result that it resigned. Then followed a blood bath and massacre on large scale of innocent persons. Even the mourners of late Mir Waiz Moulvi Mohammad Farooq carrying his dead body were not spared. The situation deteriorated to such an extent that only after four months the Governor had to be replaced.

There were massive demonstrations by the people in Srinagar followed by eruption of militancy, which the Central Government thought fit to curb under its own auspices but failed to do so. The demand for Azadi (independence) was raised by a section of the angry youth in Kashmir. It was, however, late in the day that even the Union leadership realised that what is needed for this unit of the Union is autonomy and that "Sky should be the limit" in terms of the then Prime Minister of the Union Shri P.V. Narasimha Rao. The declaration did not, however, go beyond promises having been made so piously.

The United Front Government recognised the need and followed it up only by means of declaration in the Common Minimum Programme in 1996 by holding the prospect of "Greater Autonomy" as a live issue for bringing people of Kashmir back to the era of normalcy and Kashmir's political scenario back into the national mainstream. However, on the assurance of the central Government that it would consider favourably the demand for restoration of autonomy to the State and was prepared to enter into a dialogue with the elected representatives of the State, the National Conference went to the polls in September, 1996 on the autonomy platform with the following manifesto:

> "We pledge that if we are elected our Party will be bound to accomplish the following:
>
> Dignified undiluted and meaningful autonomy which has been inspiring our people will be restored and made unalterable. We will strive to bring it to the shape which was kept before us at the time of the Accession. We will also demand credible guarantees from the federal centre to keep constitutional relationship with the State in its pristine form so that the tragic events through which we have had to pass are not repeated in future."

The people of the State returned the Party to power with a two-thirds majority. It is in pursuance of this mandate of the electorate and assurance of the Central Government that the State Government appointed this Committee to examine the question of restoration of autonomy to the State of Jammu and Kashmir.

CHAPTER XIII

Recommendations

Change in the title of Part XXI and heading of Article 370

The word 'temporary' has been used in the title of part XXI and heading of Article 370 of the Constitution of India. In this context it would be relevant to mention as to how and why it came to be used therein. This was because of the provision contained in clause (3) of this Article which came into being at a time when the Constituent Assembly of the State had yet to be convened.

This Article could cease to be operative if the President of the Republic were to issue a notification to this effect on the basis of a recommendation of the State Constituent Assembly. It could also be made operative with modifications and exceptions by a similar process and from such date as may be specified by the President.

The Constituent Assembly ceased to exist after the Constitution for the State was adopted by it in November, 1956. It did not make any recommendation for the removal of this Article.

So it should have been indicated as early as 1956 that it would be a misnomer to call Article 370 'Temporary provision'. In fact, it had then become and had to continue as a special provision of the Indian Constitution applicable to the State of Jammu and Kashmir.

It would be appropriate to quote Jenab Sheikh Sahib's views expressed in this regard while addressing the State Constituent Assembly on 11th August, 1952:

> "Here I would like to point out that the fact that Article 370 has been mentioned as a temporary provision in the Constitution does not mean that it is capable of being abrogated, modified or replaced unilaterally. In actual effect, the temporary nature of this Article arises merely from the fact that the *power to finalise the Constitutional relationship between the State and the Union of India has been specifically vested in the Jammu and Kashmir Constituent Assembly. It follows that whatever modifications, amendments or exceptions that may become necessary either to Article 370 or any other Article in the Constitution of India in their application to the Jammu and Kashmir State are subject to decisions of this Sovereign Body."*

Accordingly, it is recommended as under:

(i) That the word 'temporary' be deleted from the title of Part XXI of the Constitution of India; and

(ii) That the word 'temporary' occurring in the heading of Article 370 be substituted by the word 'special'.

Legislative Relations (Part XI)

We have at length described that breath and soul of State-Union relationship initially was the Instrument of Accession and later this was replaced by provisions of the Indian Constitution as and when these became applicable. The Instrument of Accession was to be the basis. The Instrument conceded powers of legislation to the Federal Union in the matter of Defence. External Affairs and Communications and vide clause (3) this Instrument itself specified matters in the "schedule" thereto with respect to which the Dominion legislature could make laws for the State of Jammu and Kashmir. These scheduled matters were 20 in number and were grouped under sub-heads:

(a) Defence.

(b) External Affairs.

(c) Communications.

(d) Ancillary.

Dominion Legislature, therefore, could legislate with respect to the State of Jammu and Kashmir in respect of matters specified in the schedule to the Instrument of Accession.

Articles 1 and 370 became applicable to our State straightway and our State became part of the scheme of distribution of legislative powers enshrined in the Constitution of India. Seventh Schedule to the Constitution itemised the legislative field of operation in the following manner:

List I	Union list.
List II	State list.
List III	Concurrent list.

With the enforcement of Indian Constitution on 26.1.1950 and simultaneously application of Article 370 to the State of Jammu and Kashmir, Presidential Order of 1950 came to be issued on this very date. With its application relevant Union List items with omissions, exceptions and modifications became applicable from that very date. This was consistent with original terms of accession, conceding powers of legislation to Union Parliament in matters on which State sovereign had acceded to the Union.

The Union thereafter could legislate on items included in the Schedule to 1950 Order. The items which were excluded from the ambit of legislative power of Parliament in respect of the State of Jammu and Kashmir were as under:

> 7, 8, 23, 24, 32, 33, 34, 35, 36, 37, 38, 40, 42 to 71, 78 to 92 and 97.

The entries 22 and 76 were applied with modification. A casual examination of these would show that these were rightly not applied being beyond the border line of ceded items of Defence, External Affairs, Communications and Ancillary.

At this stage it would be pertinent to mention that Article 246 in its original form clearly laid down that in relation to the State of Jammu and Kashmir reference to clauses (2) and (3) in clause (1) of the Article and clauses (2) (3) and (4) of the Article shall not apply. This made existence of State and Concurrent Lists only a matter of theoretical interest for our State. All that was yielded in Union List for federal legislation was thus known; rest of the powers were of the State and State alone. Such a decision was quite in keeping with the true spirit and context of federal polity. This is particularly so when application of Articles 248 and 249 were also excluded, the two having been completely omitted from the application to our State.

Their non-application ensured that residuary powers of legislation remained with the State unimpaired and Parliament could not legislate about any State matter even when there would have been a situation envisaged by Article 253.

It is note-worthy that all the entries made applicable particularly the substituted entry 97 read with modified Article 248 were not even remotely connected with Defence, External Affairs and Communications, nor can they in entirety or otherwise be regarded as ancillary to matters covered by these three subjects.

Changes from 1954 onwards, particularly in sixties were so

rapid that things started changing even beyond recognition. Encroachment on State jurisdiction was obvious, thereby reducing the State autonomy to a mockery.

Recommendations

In the legislative field, therefore, it is recommended as under:

(a) Matters in the Union list not connected with the three subjects of Defence, External Affairs and Communications and/or ancillary thereto but made applicable should be excluded from their application to the State.
(b) All modifications made in Article 246 in its application to the State subsequent to the 1950 Order should be rescinded.
(c) Articles 248, 249, 250 and 251 whether applied in original or substituted/modified form should be omitted in relation to the State.
(d) As in 1950 and 1954 List II (State) and List III (Concurrent) of the Seventh Schedule should not be applicable to the State.
(e) Article 254 be restored to the position it had in its application to our State in 1954.
(f) Articles 262 and 263 which were not applicable under 1950 Order but were subsequently extended to the State should cease to apply.

PART XV

Elections

(Articles 324 to 329)

Since elections to the State Legislature are held under laws made by the State Legislature, Article 324 should continue to apply in the manner and the way it was applicable in 1950/1954 Order. This is particularly so when the State Constitution had provisions relating thereto.

Recommendation

Therefore, change brought about in this Part after 1954 be reversed and consequential changes in other Articles in this Part be effected.

PART XVIII

Emergency Provisions

(Articles 352 to 360)

The following should be added to Clause 6 of Article 352.

Recommendation

(a) "provided that this request for concurrence of the Government of the State shall be subject to whatever decision the State Assembly may take within two months of declaration of emergency and failing any such decision, the proclamation of Emergency shall be deemed to have been revoked".

(b) Sub-clause (b) of clause (6) of this Article should be deleted.

(c) Articles 355, 356, 357, 358, 359 and 360 should be made non-applicable to the State of Jammu and Kashmir as was the position in 1954.

PART III

Fundamental Rights

(Articles 12 to 35)

Recommendation

This Part should be deleted. A separate chapter on Fundamental Rights needs to be included in the Jammu and Kashmir Constitution. Situation where Directive Principles do not apply and Fundamental Rights apply is not a happy one. Directive Principles in the State Constitution apply but in the absence of a provision these can hardly mean anything to Fundamental Rights which are enshrined in the Union Constitution. Fundamental Rights chapter in the State Constitution would add weight and worth to the organic law of the land and give the citizens satisfaction of even testing worth of Directive Principles for Legislation and for governance according to letter and spirit of law.

PART V

The Union

(Articles 52 to 151)

Very few Articles from this Part wer made applicable, in

1954 Order but the situation was changed with the passage of Constitution (Application to J&K) Order, 1960 and thereafter. Normally there can be no dispute now with the extended jurisdiction of the Supreme Court over matters in regard to our State, but it has got to be recorded that this aspect of State-Union relationship was not settled at the time of Delhi Agreement of 1952 and after the events of 1953 quick decisions were forced upon the flawed Constituent Assembly followed by a number of Constitution (Application to J&K) Orders. The position which ultimately has emerged is that the State of J&K has been accorded the same status as the rest of the States except for the above form of Articles 133 and 134 applied to the State. The judiciary of India has been unitary in character during the British rule and it remained so under the new Constitution of India adopted in 1950. Jammu and Kashmir too became part of it. notwithstanding the fact that strong views to have judicial autonomy were expressed during negotiations for Delhi Agreement, 1952. In any case divergent views were recorded.

The State had at that time a High Court whose judgements were subject to appeal/review before His Highness, advised in his judicial functions by a Board of Judicial Advisors consisting of eminent jurists/knowledgeable persons. That has not to be and reopening that chapter may not sound appropriate now except, of course, where adopting of provisions of the Union Judiciary for the State have in a way infringed upon the corresponding provisions of the State Constitution in regard to the State High Court.

Recommendation

(a) Article 72(1)(c), 72(3), 133, 134, 135, 136, 138, 145(1)(c) and 151(2) should be made non-applicable to the State as was the position in 1950 Order.

(b) Articles 149, 150 and 151 should apply to the State in the form in which they were in 1954.

PART VI

(Articles 152-237)

Article 124(4) of the Constitution of India mandates that a Supreme Court Judge shall not be removed from his office except by an Order of the President passed after an address by each

House of Parliament supported by a majority of the total membership of that House and by a majority of not less than two-thirds of the members of that House present and voting, has been presented to the President in the same session for such removal on the ground of proved misbehaviour or in capacity. Article 218 has in the course of time been applied to the J&K State. The position as it obtained prior to C.O. 60 was that under the State Constitution the removal of a judge of the High Court by the President for proved misbehaviour or incapacity could be on the basis of an address for removal supported by a majority of the total membership of each House of Legislature of the State and by the majority of not less than two-thirds of the members present and voting. But after the aforesaid application Order of 1960, the power to pass an address for such removal vests with the Parliament in accordance with Article 124 (4). Part VII of the State Constitutions deals with the State High Court. The Part starts with section 93 (Constitution of High Court) and ends with Section 108 (Officers and Servants of the High Court). Of these, we have Sec. 95 (Appointment and Tenure of Office of Judges) and Sec. 99 (Resignation and Removal of a Judge of the High Court). The aforementioned provision about removal till 1959 was sub-section (2) of section 99 of the State Constitution. The Constitution of Jammu and Kashmir (First Amendment) Act, 1959 vide its section 4 deleted this provision and the question of removal of a judge for proved misconduct or incapacity was left to be taken care of as in the rest of the country by resort to procedure in section 124 clause (4) thereof. This was so vide Constitution (Application to J&K) Order No. 60 of 1960.

All provisions about High Court having been retained in the State Constitution including one about administrative expenses, salaries, allowances and pensions continuing to remain a charge upon consolidated fund of the State, deletion of the above provision regarding removal by means of an address being the duty, right and obligation of State Legislature and not Parliament in terms of Section 124(4) is, to say the least, not justifiable. Article 218 conceded this right in respect of other High Courts to Parliament. It is because all other provisions like 93 to 108 of our State Constitution are in their case part of the Union Constitution itself. We would, therefore, recommend the following in this regard:

Recommendation

(i) Article 218 be omitted in its application to the State. That would enable the State Legislature to re-enact the provisions as they existed in sub-section (2) and (3) of Section 99 of the State Constitution before the enforcement of J&K Constitution (First Amendment) Act of 1959.

(ii) Articles 220, 222 and 226 should also be omitted in their application to J&K State.

PART XII

Finance, Property, Contracts and Suits
(Article 264 to 300 A)

We have seen that in 1952 during and after negotiations for Delhi Agreement that Article 266 (relating to the Consolidated Funds of India and public accounts of India and of the States), Articles 282 and 284 (relating to the Union or public account of India), Articles 298, 299 and 300 (relating only to the Union or Government of India) were applicable. Exception was made in respect of Articles 264 and 265, clause (2) of Article 267, Articles 268 to 281, Clause 2 of Article 283, Articles 286 to 291. Articles 293, 295, 296 and 297, C.O. 48 of 14th May 1954 made Articles 264, 265, 268, 272, 274-281, 285, 289, 293, 295 to 297 applicable to our State. Articles 269 and 286 were applied with amendments in 1958.

Law for imposition of tax burden is clearly laid down. The rule in federal polity generally is that if the Union levies a tax in respect of matters assigned to it, it retains the proceeds yielded by such imposition. Same is true of a unit in a federation. There are, however, a number of exceptions as under Articles 268 and 269 in the matter of distribution of income tax as also of whole or part of proceeds of excise duty. Our State also would collect excise and stamp duties as specified in entries 84 and 91 of list I and appropriate the net proceeds. Same is true as a result of application of Article 269 to our State in respect of levies collected thereunder. Even Article 270 applies to our State.

What has been incorporated in the Constitution of the State viz. Consolidated Fund and Contingency Fund of the State as also custody thereof, and Public Account of the State is covered by sections, 115, 116, 118 and 119 of the Constitution of our State. In fact the position that emerges from the application of various Constitution Orders is that the provisions of the Constitution of India identical to what has been incorporated in the State Constitution in sections 115, 116, 117, 118, 119, 120, 121, 122 and 123 do not apply and for the rest, by and large, provisions of Part XII of the Constitution of India apply to our State as to the rest of the States.

On the passage of Constitution (Application to J&K) Second Amendment Order 1958 (C.O. 56) jurisdiction of the Auditor General and Comptroller was extended. This brought entry 76 of list 1 into the picture in its application to the State.

Despite allocations available to the State at present, we are firmly of the opinion that in order that the State should be financially viable, it needs more financial resources and assistance. It may be recalled that during 1952 Delhi talks, the discussion on financial arrangement between the Union and the Sate remained inconclusive.

Recommendation

It is, therefore, recommended that the matter be discussed indepth between the State representatives and the Union Government.

PART XIV

Services under the Union and the States
(Articles 308-323)

Article 308 excluded application of this Part to our State. There is hardly any federation in the world where such provisions as those contained in Article 312 and legislative enactments thereunder are envisaged. These were not applicable to the State even in 1954 but have been made applicable thereafter.

Notwithstanding seemingly an attractive proposition one can say without any fear of contradiction that it has dwarfed local talent and made it difficult for local youth to aspire to compete for key civil posts on competitive basis. The weak-kneed attempt to organise Kashmir Civil Service is neither here nor there and increasing inflow of All India Services has meant pretty little in the field for which the services were apparently conceived. No imperial model of civil services in central cadre can be or could be a substitute for what the local youth could be expected to have, i.e. local patriotic feeling and passionate attachment for the service of those among whom they live. Ever since the application of these provisions of the Indian Constitution to our State the number of direct recruits from the State has been negligible. The problem has attained so unpleasant a shape, even in the national context, that demands of greater number of promotees from local services all over the country have assumed alarming proportions.

Recommendation

It is, therefore, recommended that in Article 312, the brackets and words "(including the State of Jammu and Kashmir)" inserted by the Constitution (Application to J&K) Order 1958 be omitted.

PART XVI

Special Provisions relating to certain classes

Articles 330 to 342

Article 339 regarding control of the Union over the administration of scheduled Areas and the Welfare of scheduled tribes was not applicable to the State till 1985. It was applied in a modified form to the State vide Constitution (Application to J&K) Order of 1985.

Likewise, Article 342 has been applied for the first time to the State in 1985.

Recommendation

(i) It is recommended that the powers in respect of aforesaid matters be restored to the State.

(ii) Articles 330, 331, 334, 335, 336 which were applied by 1950 Order should continue to be applicable Articles 338, 339, 340, 341 and 342 have been applied after 1950. Their application to the State should be omitted and corresponding provisions be made in the State Constitution.

PART XX

Amendment of the Constitution

(Article 368)

Needless to mention that unlike other states of the Union, the

State of Jammu and Kashmir has a Constitution of its own. Before the Constitution (Application to J&K) Second Amendment Order, 1975 (C.O. 101) the State Legislature had unfettered powers to amend it. But vide this Order Clause (4) was added to Article 368 of the Indian Constitution in its application to our State which reads as under:

"(4) No law made by the Legislature of the State of Jammu and Kashmir seeking to make any change in or in the effect of any provision of the Constitution of Jammu and Kashmir relating to—

(a) appointment, powers, functions, duties, emoluments, allowances, privileges or immunities of the Governor; or

(b) superintendence, direction and control of elections by the Election Commission of India, eligibility for inclusion in the electoral rolls without discrimination, adult suffrage and composition of the Legislative Council, being matters specified in sections 138, 139 and 50 of the Constitution of Jammu and Kashmir shall have any effect unless such law has, after having been reserved for the consideration of the President, received his assent."

The addition of this clause in the Indian Constitution has restricted the power of the State Legislature to amend its own Constitution. This uncalled for clog on the constituent powers of State Legislature needs to be removed lock, stock, and barrel.

Recommendation

It is therefore recommended that:

(i) clause (4) of Article 368 added vide C.O. 101 be deleted;

(ii) clause (2) of Article 368 should apply with the proviso already introduced by 1954 Order and Clause (1) thereof which was not in existence in 1954 and was introduced in 1971 should remain omitted in its application to the State.

PART XXII

(Schedules First to Twelve)

The Indian Constitution has 12 schedules only some of which apply to our State with or without modifications relatable to some of the Articles of the Constitution of India. Each Schedule which is applicable to the State of Jammu and Kashmir being fathered by a specific Article in the Constitution of the country will naturally suffer modification, change/substitution depending upon what that Article contains in regard to its application to the State of Jammu and Kashmir.

SEVENTH SCHEDULE

Seventh Schedule derives its character and quality from what Article 246 of the Constitution reads like. Its corresponding quality in respect of Jammu and Kashmir State naturally will depend upon the form and the content that Article 246 of the Constitution of India will assume in its relation to the State of Jammu and Kashmir. In 1950, Article 246 of the Constitution of India had one character and quality/content in its application to the State of Jammu and Kashmir and that was reflected in the number of entries in the Union List in the Seventh Schedule in their application to the State of Jammu and Kashmir. Later on, this Article suffered changes and consequently various entries in the Union List and the Concurrent List also suffered radical changes.

Recommendation

It is recommended that:—

(a) entries in the Union List which were applied to the State by 1950 Application Order should continue and all other entries made applicable to the State by subsequent orders should be omitted;

(b) Concurrent List was not applicable under 1950 Order and it was also agreed in the Delhi Agreement that this should not apply to the State. Hence all subsequent orders applying various entries from this list should be rescinded.

In sum, it is recommended that consistent with the above, requisite changes as may become necessary consequent upon change in the Articles of the Constitution of India in their application to the State of Jammu and Kashmir as a result of this report be effected in the Schedules concerned.

Changes Required in the State Constitution

In view of what has been stated in chapter XI ante, this Committee recommends the repeal of:

(i) The Constitution of Jammu and Kashmir (First Amendment) Act, 1959 relating to superintendence, direction and control of elections to the State Legislature and provisions relating to the State High Court; and

(ii) The Constitution of Jammu and Kashmir (Sixth Amendment) Act, 1965 relating to the mode of appointment and nomenclature of the Head of the State and nomenclature of the head of the Executive.

CHAPTER XIV

Summary of Recommendations

1. Temporary, Transitional and Special Provisions (Part XXI)

(i) The word 'Temporary' be deleted from the title of part XXI of the constitution of India and the word 'temporary' occurring in the heading of Article 370 be substituted by the word 'special'.

2. Legislative Relations (Part XI)

(a) Matters in the Union List not connected with the three subjects of Defence, External Affairs and Communications and/ or Ancillary thereto but made applicable should be excluded from their application to the State.

(b) All modifications made in Article 246 in its application to the State subsequent to the 1950 order should be rescinded.

(c) Articles 248, 249, 250 and 251 whether applied in original or substituted/modified form should be omitted from their application to the State.

(d) As in 1950 and 1954, List II (State) and List III (Concurrent) of the Seventh Schedule should not be applicable to the State.

(e) Article 254 should be restored to the position it had in its application to the State in 1954.

(f) Articles 262 and 263 which were not applicable under 1950 Order but were subsequently extended to the State should cease to apply.

3. Elections (Part XV)

Changes brought about in this Part be reversed and consequential changes in other Articles in this Part be effected.

4. Emergency Provisions (Part XVIII)

(a) The following should be added to Cl. 6 of Articles 352 in its application to the State:

> "Provided that this request for concurrence of the Government of the State shall be subject to whatever decision the State Assembly may take within two months of declaration of emergency and failing any such decision, the proclamation of emergency shall be deemed to have been revoked."

(b) Sub-clause (b) of Cl. (6) of this Article should be deleted.

(c) Articles 355, 356, 357, 358, 359 and 360 should be made non-applicable to the State as was the position in 1954.

5. Fundamental Rights (Part III)

This part should be deleted. A separate chapter on Fundamental Rights be included in the State Constitution.

6. The Union (Part V)

(a) Articles 72(1)(c), 72(3), 133, 134, 135, 136, 138, 145(1)(c) and 151(2) should be made non-applicable to the State as was the position in 1950 Order.

(b) Articles 149, 150 and 151 should apply to the State in the form in which they were in 1954.

7. The States (Part VI)

(i) Article 218 be omitted in its application to the State and the position as it existed before the J&K Constitution (First Amendment Act) of 1959 restored.

(ii) Articles 220, 222 and 226 should also be omitted in their application to Jammu and Kashmir State.

8. Finance, Property, Contracts and Suits (Part XII)

The matter be discussed between the State representatives and the Union Government as agreed to during the talks in 1952 (Delhi Agreement)

9. Services under the Union and the States (Part XIV)

In Article 312 the brackets and words "including the State of Jammu and Kashmir" inserted by the Constitution (Application to J&K) Order 1958 be omitted.

10. Special Provisions relating to certain classes (Part XVI)

Application of Articles 338, 339, 340, 341 and 342 to the State should be omitted and corresponding provisions made in the State Constitution.

11. Amendment of the Constitution of India (Part XX)

(i) Clause (4) of Article 368 added vide C.O. 101 be deleted.

(ii) Clause (2) of the Article should apply with the proviso already introduced by 1954 order and clause (1) thereof which was not in existence in 1954 and was introduced in 1971 should remain omitted in its application to the State.

12. Schedules

In the Seventh Schedule entries in the Union List not applied to the State by the Constitution (Application to J&K) Order, 1950 should be omitted. Concurrent List which was not applicable to the State in 1950 but was applied by subsequent orders should cease to apply to the State.

13. Changes in the State Constitution

All amendments in the Constitution of Jammu and Kashmir made vide:

(i) Constitution of Jammu and Kashmir (First Amendment) Act, 1959 insofar as they relate to superintendence, direction and control of elections to the State Legislature and to the State High Court; and

(ii) Constitution of Jammu and Kashmir (Sixth Amendment) Act, 1965 relating to change of nomenclature of the Head of the State and State Executive, mode of appointment of the Head of the State and other consequential amendments

should be repealed and the original provisions of the Constitution of Jammu and Kashmir restored.

To sum up the provisions of the Constitution of India specified in the Second Schedule and the matters specified in the first Schedule to the Constitution (Application to J&K) Order, 1950 and the matters agreed to by the representatives of the State and the Union vide Delhi Agreement of 1952 should continue to apply to the State subject to the same exceptions and modifications as are specified in the said Order and the Delhi Agreement. All Orders issued thereafter under clause (1) of Article 370 of the Constitution of India by the President, applying various provisions and matters of the Constitution of India to the State whether in full or in modified form or making any change in the provisions or matters already applied by 1950 Order or agreed to under Delhi Agreement, should be rescinded and the provisions or matters so applied to the State should cease to apply.

Also the changes made in the State Constitution vide Constitution of Jammu and Kashmir (First Amendment) Act, 1959 and Constitution of Jammu and Kashmir (Sixth Amendment) Act, 1965 be repealed and the original provisions of the Constitution of Jammu and Kashmir as adopted by the State Constituent Assembly on November 17, 1956 be restored.

CHAPTER XV

Safeguards for Future

In the preceding chapters we have discussed in detail the extent of erosion caused to the State autonomy from time to time and also suggested remedial measures. That completes the job assigned to us by first item of the terms of reference. There are, however, two other items which require our consideration. The first is to ensure the "inviolability" of the final settlement, and the other is to keep in mind the need to maintain "harmonious" relations with the Centre.

A suggestion has been made that Article 258 should be invoked for entrusting to the State "functions in relation to any matter to which the executive power of the Union extends." This would put a seal on the record of the past. "Functions" so "entrusted" can always be recalled back. The issue is not one of executive "functions" but legislative "powers" apportioned between the Union and the State under two solemn compacts between them, the Instrument of Accession in 1947 and the Delhi Agreement of 1952 to which the President's Order of May 14, 1954 gave constitutional sanction besides, of course, Article 370 itself. To them must we return if popular sentiment is to be respected and resentments assuaged. It is first and foremost a moral issue. It also has important constitutional and political aspects. In the nature of things redress can only be through another compact between the Union and the State. Once the basic principles are agreed, there will be discussion on procedure. Forty years of unconstitutional practice have created a mess. The best course is for the President to repeal all Orders which are not in conformity with Constitution (Application to Jammu and Kashmir) Order, 1950 and the terms of the Delhi Agreement of 1952.

Ever since, Article 370 has acquired a dangerously ambiguous aspect. Designed to protect the State's autonomy, it has been used systematically to destroy it. A compact is necessary between the Union and the State which makes ample redress and finalizes their relationship by declaring a "Constitutional Understanding" that Article 370 of the Constitution of India can no longer be used to apply to the State of Jammu and Kashmir any other provisions of the Constitution of India beyond the ones extended under 1950 Order and the Delhi Agreement, 1952. This could be embodied in a new Article that specifies the agreement as part of the unamendable basic structure of the Indian Constitution.

Such constitutional understandings have been formulated in other democracies. The complexities of our situation render it the best, perhaps the only, course for removing the debris of an unhappy past and building, in its place, a relationship between the State of Jammu and Kashmir and the Union of India which reflects the most vital aspect of federalism -mutual trust and respect.

(Gh. Mohi-ud-Din Shah)
Chairman

(Abdul Ahad Vakil)
Member

(Abdul Rahim Rather)
Member

(Piyaray Lal Handoo)
Member

(Bodh Raj Bali)
Member

(Molvi I.H. Ansari)
Member

(Kushok Thiksay)
Member

(Mirza Ab.Rashid)
Member

(S.Teja Singh)
Member-Convenor

APPENDIX II—1

Names of Individuals and Organisations from whom Memorandums and Letters have been Received in Response to the State Autonomy Committee's Notification No. D 18/J-27/96 dated 14.12.1996

1. C.R. Khamitkar, consulting Engineer Journalist, Mysore sales D.B. Mahinderkar Building: Shroff Bassaweshwar Road, Bijapur-586101.
2. Rev. Dr. Kodumutti A.J. Nadar, MBBS, M. Divinity 7, Palaniappa Nagar, Salem-636007, India.
3. S. Sunil Kumar S/O P.S. Nair Indira Bhawan. Chambayil Road. Neyyattinkar. P.O. Pin No. 695-121, Trivandrum District, State Kerela.
4. A.A. Syed, Managing Director Sir Syed and Sons Engineering (P) Ltd., Room No. 67. 3rd Floor Development Cooperative Bank Building; Paltun Road, Crawford Market Bombay-400001.
5. President Social and Cultural Welfare Society, Portroad Shaynam, Leh 194101.
6. President of Educational and Cultural Organisation, Tukcha Leh-194101 (Ladakh) J&K State.
7. President of Ladakh Budhist Association.
8. G.M. Khan, R/O Aribal Shalimar, Srinagar.
9. Ladakh People's Forum.
10. President of Youth Wing L.B.A., Tashis Gatsal Chowlamsar, Leh Ladakh.
11. T.N. Saraf (IAS Retd) FAO Representative at the United Nations (Retd).
12. President of Ladakh, Budhist Association, Youth Wing, Leh Ladakh.
13. President of Lamdon Social Welfare Society, Leh-194101, Ladakh, J&K, India.
14. Ashwani Kumar, Convenor Panun Kashmir Movement (PKM).
15. President of Gonpathundal Tsogspa, Cultural and Welfare Society, Leh-Ladakh.

16. P.N. Tengloo, Organising Secretary All State Kashmiri Pandit Conference.
17. Pyari Lal Sharma of Baramulla, C/O Sanjay Sharma, 32-R. Rani Park, Jammu Tawi-180001.
18. Hari Om, Ph.D. Professor and Head of the Department of History and Centre for History and Culture.
19. Vinayak G. Madhavi, Usha V. Madhavi, Miss Sharmila V. Madhavi, Advocates High Court, Swami Nivas, Opp. Dena Bank, 315/3, Thakurdwar, Bombay-400002.
20. Jammu Mukti Morcha.
21. Tsering Samphel, President District Congress Committee (I), Leh, 194101. Ladakh, J&K.
22. Harbajan Singh S/O Kartar Singh, R/O Rafiabad, Tehsil Sopore, VIII, Sialkote, Distt. Baramulla.
23. Jammu and Kashmir Bhartiya Janta Party, PT, Prem Nath Dogra Bhawan, Kachi Chawani.
24. President Lothun Tsogspa, Phey Village Leh-Ladakh.
25. President of Nyamuthun Society Mane-Tselding, Leh-Ladakh.
26. Mr. Yog R. Sharma, 2329 B-l N, 11th St. Arlington VA 22201 USA.
27. President of Chang Thang Youth Welfare Association, Nyoma Block, Ladakh (J&K), India.
28. Dr. R.S. Kanwar, 245-L, Model Town, Jalandhar.
29. M.I. Ansari Compound, Agra Rd. Narpoli, Bhiwandi-421305, Distt. Thane, Mumbai.
30. Prof. M.L. Kapur, 342-Jiwan Shah Street, Shahidi Chowk, Jammu.
31. Bansi Lal Kaul, Chairman Committee to build response on Autonomy constituted by Kashmiri Pandit Global Smit, 232-C, Ram Vihar, Old Janipura, Jammu-180007.
32. Lawers of Jammu Mubark Mandi, Jammu.
33. Panun Kashmir C/o Raman and Pawan Steel Works, new Plots, Jammu-180005.
34. Syed Shahabuddin, IPS (Retd) Ex-MP, Advocate, Supreme Court of India
35. Shri Justice V.M. Tarkunde.
36. Swami Raj Sharma, IAS, (Retd) Advocate, J&K High Court, Jammu.

37. R.D. Kewal Ramani, Advocate, Supreme Court of India, 65 Lawyer's Chamber, Tilak Marg, New Delhi-110001.
38. Satish Sharma, S/10-6, Akhnoor.
39. Abdul Rehman, Tukro Secretary, Kashmir Council of Communist Party of India.
40. V. Veulcate Reddy, d2-76, K.R. Palem Seellureipate.
41. Contours of Autonomy of the State of Jammu and Kashmir by witness.

APPENDIX II—2

List of Members of Political Parties, Journalists, Jurists and other Eminent Persons with whom discussions were held in New Delhi in November, 1997

1. Shri Sharad Yadav, President Janta Dal Party, Janta Dal Party Office, 7-Jantar-Mantar Road, New Delhi.
2. Shri Harkrishan Singh Surjit, General Secretary, CPI(M).
3. Justice V.M. Tarkunde.
4. Congress M.P's.
   i. Shri G.R. Kar,
   ii. Shri P. Namgial
   iii. Shri Janak Raj Gupta, Ex-M.P.
5. CPI Secretaries
   i. Shri D. Raja
   ii. Shri Atulkumar Anjaan
   iii. Shri Shamim Faizi.
6. Shri A.G. Noorani.
7. Shri B.G. Verghese, Journalist.
8. Shri Shahab-ud-din, Ex-M.P.
9. Shri S.R. Kesri, President, Indian National Congress, 7-Purana Qila Road, New Delhi.
10. Shri Mulayam Singh Yadav, 2-Menon Road, New Delhi.
11. Justice V.R. Krishana Iyer, Former Judge, Supreme Court at Kerela House, New Delhi.

APPENDIX II—3-A

Maharaja of J&K's Letter Dated 26-10-1947 to Lord Mountbatten

My dear Lord Mountbatten,

I have to inform Your Excellency that a grave emergency has arisen in my State and request immediate assistance of your Government.

As your Excellency is aware the State of Jammu and Kashmir has not acceded to the Dominion of India or to Pakistan. Geographically my State is contiguous to both the Dominions. It has vital economic and cultural links with both of them. Besides my State has a common boundary with the Soviet Republic and China. In their external relations the Dominions of India and Pakistan cannot ignore this fact.

I wanted to take time to decide to which Dominion I would accede, or whether it is not in the best interests of both the Dominions and my State to sand independent, of course with friendly and cordial relations with both.

I accordingly approached the Dominions of India and Pakistan to enter into Standstill Agreement with my State. The Pakistan Government accepted this Agreement. The Dominion of India desired further discussions with representatives of my Government. I could not arrange this in view of the developments indicated below. In fact, the Pakistan Government are operating Post and Telegraph system inside the State.

Though we have got a Standstill Agreement with the Pakistan Government they have permitted steady and increasing strangulation of supplies like food, salt and petrol to my State.

Afridis, soldiers in plain clothes, and desperadoes with modern weapons have been allowed to infilter into the State at first in Poonch and then in Sialkot and finally in mass area adjoining Hazara District on the Ramkot side. The result has been that the limited number of troops at the disposal of the State had to bedispersed and thus had to face the enemy at several points simultaneously, that it has become difficult to stop the wanton destruction of life and property and lotting. The Mahora powerhouse which supplies the electric current to the whole of Srinagar has been burnt. The number of women who have been kidnapped and raped makes my heart bleed. The wild forces thus let loose on the State are marching on with the aim of capturing

Srinagar, the summer Capital of my Government, as first step to over running the whole State.

I hereby declare that I accede to the Dominion of India on the assurance that if an agreement is made between the Governor-General and the Ruler of this State whereby any function in relation to the administration in this State of any law of the Dominion Legislature shall be exercised by the Ruler of this State, then any such agreement shall be deemed to form part of this Instrument and shall be so construed and have effect accordingly.

The terms of this my Instrument of Accession shall not be varied by any amendment of the Act or the Indian Independence Act, 1947, unless such amendment is accepted by me by an Instrument supplementary to this Instrument.

Nothing in this Instrument shall empower the Dominion Legislature to make any law for this State authorising the compulsory acquisition of land for any purpose, but I hereby undertake that should the dominion for the purposes of a Dominion law which applies in this State deem it necessary to acquire any land, I will at their request acquire the land at their expense or if the land belongs to me transfer it to them on such terms as may be agreed, or, in default of agreement, determined by an arbitrator to be appointed by the Chief Justice of India.

Nothing in this Instrument shall be deemed to continue in anyway to acceptance of any future Constitution of India or to fetter my discretion to enter into arrangements with the Government of India under any such future constitution.

Nothing in this Instrument affects the continuance of my sovereignty in and over this State, or, save as provided by or under this Instrument, the exercise of any powers, authority and rights now enjoyed by me as Ruler of this State or the validity of any law at present in this State.

I hereby declare that I execute this Instrument on behalf of this State and that any reference in this Instrument to me or the Ruler of the State is to be construed as including a reference to my heirs and successors.

Given under my hand this 26th day of October, nineteen hundred and forty-seven.

HARI SINGH
Maharajadhiraj of
Jammu and Kashmir State

APPENDIX II—3B

Instrument of Accession of Jammu and Kashmir State

Whereas, the Indian Independence Act, 1947, provides that as from the fifteenth day of August, 1947, there shall be set-up an independent Dominion known as INDIA, and that the Government of India Act, 1935, shall with such omissions, additions, adaptations and modifications as the Governor-General may by order specify, be applicable to the Dominion of India;

And whereas the Government of India Act, 1935, as so adapted by the Governor-General provides that an Indian State may accede to the Dominion of India by an Instrument of Accession executed by the Ruler thereof;

Now, therefore, I Shriman Indar Mahandar Rajrajeshwar Maharajadhiraj Shri Had Singhji Jammu Kashmir Naresh Tatha Tibbet adi Deshadhipathi, Ruler of JAMMU AND KASHMIR State in the exercise of my sovereignty in and over my said State do hereby execute this my Instrument of Accession and—

1. I hereby declare that I accede to the Dominion of India with the intend that the Governor-General of India, the Dominion Legislature, the Federal Court and any other Dominion authority established for the purposes of the Dominion shall, by virtue of this my Instrument of Accession, but subject always to the terms thereof, and for the purposes of the Dominion, exercise in relation to the State of Jammu and Kashmir (hereinafter referred to as "this State") such functions as may be vested in them by or under the Government of India Act, 1935, as in force in the Dominion of India on the 15th day of August, 1947 (which Act as so in force is hereinafter referred to as "the Act").
2. I hereby assume the obligation of ensuring that due effect is given to the provisions of the Act within this State so far as they are applicable therein by virtue of this my Instrument of Accession.
3. I accept the matters specified in the Schedule hereto as

the matters with respect to which the Dominion Legislature may make laws for this State.

4. I hereby declare that I accede to the Dominion of India on the assurance that if an agreement is made between the Governor-General and the Ruler of this state whereby any functions in relation to the administration in this state of any law of the Dominion Legislature shall be exercised by the ruler of this State, then any such agreement shall be deemed to form part of this Instrument and shall be construed and have effect accordingly.
5. The terms of this my Instrument of Accession shall not be varied by any amendment of the Act or of the Indian independence Act, 1947, unless such amendment is accepted by an Instrument supplementary to this Instrument.
6. Nothing in this Instrument shall empower the Dominion Legislature to make any law for this State authorising the compulsory acquisition of land for any purpose, but I hereby undertake that should the Dominion for the purpose of a Dominion law which applied in this state deem it necessary to acquire any land, I will at their requisite acquire the land at their expense or if the land belongs to me transfer it to them on such terms as may be agreed, or in default of agreement, determined by an arbitrator to be appointed by the chief Justice of India.
7. Nothing in this Instrument shall be deemed to commit me in any way to acceptance of any future Constitution of India or to fetter my discretion to enter into arrangements with the Government of India under any such future constitution.
8. Nothing in this Instrument affects the continuance of my sovereignty in and over this State, or save as provided by or under this Instrument, the exercise or any powers, authority and rights now enjoyed by me as Ruler of this State or the validity of any law at present in force in this State.
9. I hereby declare that I execute this Instrument on behalf

of this State and that any reference in this Instrument to me or to the Ruler of the State is to be construed as including a reference to my heirs and successors.

Given under my hand this 26th day of October Nineteen Hundred and Forty-Seven.

(Sd.) HARI SINGH
Maharajadhiraj of Jammu and Kashmir State.

APPENDIX II—3C

Acceptance of Accession

Lord Mountbatten's Reply to Maharaja Sir Hari Singh, Dated 27th October 1947

My dear Maharajah Sahib,

Your Highness's letter, dated the 26th October, has been delivered to me by Mr. V.P. Menon. In the special circumstances mentioned by Your Highness, my Government have decided to accept the accession of Kashmir State to the Dominion of India. Consistent with their policy that, in the case of any State where the issue of accession has been the subject of dispute, the question of accession should be decided in accordance with the wishes of the people of the State, it is my Government's wish that, as soon as law and order have been restored in Kashmir and her soil cleared of the invader, the question of the State's accession should be settled by a reference to the people. Meanwhile, in response to your Highness's appeal for military aid, action has been taken today to send troops of the Indian Army to Kashmir to help your own forces to defend your territory and to protect the lives, property and honour of your people.

My Government and I note with satisfaction that your Highness has decided to invite Sheikh Abdullah to form an Interim Government to work with your Prime Minister.

Yours sincerely,
Sd/- Mountbatten of Burma

New Delhi
October 27, 1947.

APPENDIX II—4

[1]The Constitution (Application to Jammu and Kashmir) Order, 1950

C.O. 10

In exercise of the powers conferred by clause (1) of Article 370 of the Constitution of India, the President, in consultation with the Government of the State of Jammu and Kashmir, is pleased to make the following Order, namely:

1. (1) This Order may be called the Constitution (Application to Jammu and Kashmir) Order, 1950.

(2) It shall come into force at once.

2. For the purposes of sub-clause (b)(i) of clause (1) of article 370 of the Constitution, the matters specified in the First Schedule to this Order, being matters in the Union List, are hereby declared to correspond to matters specified in the Instrument of accession governing the accession of the State of Jammu and Kashmir to the Dominion of India as the matter with regard to which the Dominion Legislature may make laws for that State; and accordingly, the Power of Parliament to make laws for that State shall be limited to the matters specified in the said First Schedule.

3. In addition to the provisions of article 1 and article 370 of the Constitution, the only other provisions of the Constitution which shall apply in relation to the State of Jammu and Kashmir shall be those specified in the Second Schedule to this Order; and shall so apply subject to the exceptions and modifications specified in the said Schedule[2] and to the modification that all references in the said provisions to the Rajpramukh shall be construed as references to the Sadar-i-Riyasat of Jammu and Kashmir.

THE FIRST SCHEDULE
(See paragraph 2)

[Note—The number of each entry in this Schedule is the number of the corresponding entry in the Union List.]

1. Published with the Ministry of Law Notification No. C.O. 10, dated the 26th January, 1950, Gazette of India, Extraordinary, 1950, Part II, Section 3(i), page 673, superseded by CO. 48.
2. Added by C.O. 43 dated 15th November, 1952.

1. Defence of India and every part thereof including preparation for defence.
2. Naval, military and air forces; and other armed forces of the Union.
3. Delimitation of cantonment areas, local self-government in such areas the constitution and powers within such areas of cantonment authorities and the regulation of house accommodation (including the control of rents) in such areas.
4. Naval, military and air force works.
5. Arms, firearms, ammunition and explosives.
6. Atomic energy for the purpose of defence and mineral resources necessary for its production.
9. Preventive detention for reasons connected with Defence, Foreign Affairs or the security of India.
10. Foreign Affairs; all matters which bring the Union into relation with any foreign country.
11. Diplomatic, consular and trade representation.
12. United Nations Organisation.
13. Participation in international conferences, associations and other bodies and implementing of decisions made thereat.
14. Entering into treaties and agreements with foreign countries, and implementing of treaties, agreements and conventions with foreign countries.
15. War and peace.
16. Foreign jurisdiction.
17. Naturalisation and aliens.
18. Extradition.
19. Admission into, and emigration and expulsion from India; passports and visas.
20. Pilgrimages to places outside India.
21. Piracies and crimes committed on the high seas or in the air, offences against the law of nations committed on land or on the high seas or in the air.
22. Railways, but as respects any railway owned by the State of Jammu and Kashmir, and either operated by that State or operated on its behalf otherwise than in accordance with a contract with the State by the Government of India, limited to a regulation thereof in respect of safety, maximum and minimum rates and fares, station and service terminal charges, interchange of traffic and the responsibility of the

railway administrtion as carriers of goods and passengers, and as respects any railway which is wholly situate within the State and does not form a continuous line of communication with a railway owned by the Government of India, whether of the same guage or not, limited to the regulation thereof in respect of safety and the responsibility of the railway administration as carriers of goods and passengers.

25. Maritime shipping and navigation, including shipping and navigation on tidal waters; provision of education and training for the mercantile marine and regulation of such education and training provided by states and other agencies.
26. Light houses, including lightships, beacons and other provision for the safety of shipping and aircraft.
27. Ports declared by or under law made by Parliament or existing law to be major ports, including their delimitation, and the constitution and powers of ports authorities therein.
28. Port quarantine, including hospitals connected therewith; seamen's and marine hospitals.
29. Airways; aircraft and air navigation; provision of aerodromes; regulation and organisation of air traffic and of aerodromes; provision for aeronautical education and training and regulation of such education and training provided by States and other agencies.
30. Carriage of passengers and goods by railway, sea or air.
31. Posts and telegraphs, telephones, wireless, broadcasting and other like forms of communication.
41. Trade and commerce with foreign countries.
72. Elections to Parliament, and the offices of President and Vice-President; the Election Commission.
73. Salaries and allowances of members of Parliament, the Chairman and of the House of the People.
74. Powers, privileges and immunities of each House of Parliament and of the members and the committees of each House; enforcement of attendance of persons for giving evidence of producing documents before committees of Parliament or commissions appointed by Parliament.
75. Salaries and allowances of the Ministers for the Union; the salaries, allowances, and rights in respect of leave of absence

and other conditions of service of the Comptroller and Auditor-General.

76. Audit of the account of the Union.

77. Constitution and organisation of the Supreme Court, and the fees taken therein; persons entitled to practise before the Supreme Court.

80. Extension of the powers and jurisdiction of members of a police force belonging to any State to railway areas outside that State.

93. Offences against laws with respect to any of the matters aforesaid.

94. Inquiries and statistics for the purpose of any of the matters aforesaid.

95. Jurisdiction and powers of all courts, except the Supreme Court, with respect to any of the matters aforesaid, but, except with the consent of the State Government, not so as to confer any jurisdiction or powers upon any courts other than courts ordinarily exercising jurisdiction in, or in relation to, the State; admiralty jurisdiction.

96. Fees in respect of any of the matters aforesaid, but not including fees taken in any court.

THE SECOND SCHEDULE

(See paragraph 3)

Provisions of the Constitution applicable	*Exceptions*	*Modifications*
Part-V	Articles 72(1)(c), 72(3), 133, 134, 135, 136, 138, 145(1)(c) and 151 (2).	1) Articles 80 & 81 shall apply subject to the modification that the representatives of the State in the Council of States and the House of the People respectively, shall be chosen by the President in consultation with the Government of the State. [1](1A) Articles 54 & 55 shall apply subject to the modifications: (a) that the references therein to

1. Ins. by C.O. 39, dated 20th March, 1952.

		the elected members of both Houses oi Parliament and to each elected member of either House of Parliament shall be deemed to include, respectively, a reference to the representatives of the State in those Houses and to each such representative. (b) that the references to the elected members of the Legislative Assemblies of the States and to each such elected member shall be deemed to include, respectively, a reference to the members of the Constituent Assembly of the State and to each such member, and (c) that the population of the State shall be deemed to be forty-four Lakhs and ten thousands. (2) Articles 149 and 150 shall apply subject to the modification that the references therein to the State shall be construed as not including the State of Jammu and Kashmir.
Part XI	Articles 247 to 252, clauses (3) and (4) of article 257 and articles 260, 262 and 263.	(1) Clause (1) of article 246 shall apply subject to the provisions of paragraph (2) of this Order and clauses (2) and (3) of article 246 shall not apply in relation to the State. (2) Clause (1) of article 259 shall apply subject to the modification that after the words "until Parliament by law otherwise provides", the words "and the concurrence of the State to such law has been obtained" shall be deemed to be inserted.

Part XII	Articles 264 and 265, clause (2) of article 267, articles 268 to 281, clause (2) of article 283, articles 286 to 291, 293, 295, 296 and 297.	(1) Articles 266 shall apply only in so far as it relates to the Consolidated Fund of India and the public account of India. (2) Articles 282 and 284 shall apply only in so far as they relate to the Union or the public account of India. (3) Articles 298. 299 and 300 shall apply only in so far as they relate to the Union or the Government of India.
Part XV	Articles 325 to 329	Article 324 shall apply only in so far as it relates to elections to Parliament and to the offices of the President and Vice President.
Part XVI	Articles 332, 333 and 337 to 342	(1) Article 330 shall apply only in so far as it relates to seats reserved for Scheduled Castes. (2) Article 334 shall apply only in so far as it relates to the House of the People. (3) Article 335 shall apply only in so far as it relates to the Union.
Part XVII	Nil	The provisions of this Part shall Apply only in so far as they relate to the official language of the Union and to proceedings in the Supreme Court.
Part XIX	Articles 362, 363 and 365[1] and clause (21) of article 366].	(1) Article 361 shall apply only in so far as it relates to the President. (2) Article 364 shall apply only in so far as it relates to the Laws made by Parliament.
Part XX	Nil	Article 368 shall apply subject to the additional proviso: "Provided further that no such amendment shall have effect in relation to the State of Jammu and Kashmir unless applied by order of the President under clause (1) of article 370."

1. Inserted by C.O. 43 *infra*.

Part XXI	Articles 369, 371 and 373, clause (4) of article 374, articles [1]376, 378 and 386 and clause (2) of article 388.	(1) In clause (3) of article 379 after the words "Minister for any such State", the words "other than the State of Jammu and Kashmir" shall be deemed to be inserted. (2) Article 389 shall apply only in so far it relates to Bills pending in the Dominion Legislature. (3) Article 390 shall apply only in so far as it relates to the Consolidated Fund of India.
Part XXII	Nil	Nil
First Schedule	Nil	Nil
Second Schedule	Paragraph 6	Nil
Third Schedule	Forms V, VI, VII and VIII	Nil
Fourth Schedule	Nil	Nil
Eighth Schedule	Nil	Nil

1. Substituted *ibid*. for "376 and 378".

ANNEXURE II—5

Inaugural Speech made by Sher-I-Kashmir Sheikh Mohammad Abdullah in the Jammu and Kashmir Constituent Assembly on 5th November, 1951

"Mr. President:

Today is our day of destiny. A day which comes only once in the life of a nation. A day on which to remember the hosts of those gone before us, and of those yet to come, and we are humbled by the greatness of this day.

After centuries, we have reached the harbour of our freedom, a freedom, which, for the first time in history, will enable the people of Jammu and Kashmir, whose duly elected representatives are gathered here, to shape the future of their country after wise deliberation, and mould their future organs of Government. No person and no power stand between them and the fulfilment of this—their historic task. We are free, at last to shape our aspirations as people and to give substance to their ideals, which have brought us together here.

We meet here today, in this palace hall, once the symbol of unquestioned monarchial authority, as free citizens of the New Kashmir for which we have so long struggled.

I see about me in this hall, many companions—Hindus, Muslims, Buddhists, Harijans and Sikhs, who first trod with me that path which has brought us to this Constituent Assembly of 1951. We fought as one against tyranny and oppression. We survived privations and bitter struggles. The Jails of Hari Parbat, Bahu, Baderwah and those other jails, which only imprisoned our bodies but could not crush our spirit.

When we took back on these years, we see how our footsteps have taken us not among the privileges, but into the homes of the poor and downtrodden, we fought their battle against privilege and oppression and against these darker powers in the background which sought to set man against man on the ground of religion. Our movement grew and thrived side by side with the Indian National Congress and gave strength and inspiration to the people of the Indian States.

I may be forgiven if I feel proud that once again in the history of this State, our people have reached a peak of achievement through what I might call the classical Kashmiri genius for synthesis, born of toleration and mutual respect. Throughout the long tale of our history, the highest pinnacles of our achievement have been scaled when religious bigotry and intolerance ceased to cramp us and we have breathed the wider air of brotherhood and mutual understanding.

Our movement to freedom has been enacted against the background of this same old struggle. We stood for the brotherhood of men of all creeds and strengthened our union on the basic of common work and sacrifice. Against us were ranged the forces of religious bigotry centered in the Muslim League and its satellites, and the Hindu communalists from within and without the State. Ranged against us and often in alliance with communalism were the forces of the autocratic States, backed up on the one hand by British Imperialism, the paramount power, and on the other, by the rich Landowners and other beneficiaries of Court patronage.

We must remember that our struggle for power has now reached its successful climax in the convening of this Constituent Assembly. It is for you to translate the vision of New Kashmir into reality, and I would remind you of its opening words, which will inspire our labours:

> "We the people of Jammu, Kashmir, Ladakh and the Frontier regions, including Poonch and Chenani Illaqas—commonly known as Jammu and Kashmir State—in order to perfect our union in the fullest equality and self-determination, to raise ourselves and our children for ever from the abyss of oppression and poverty, degradation and superstition, from medieval darkness and ignorance, into the Sunlit Valleys of plenty, ruled by freedom, science and honest toil, in worthy participation of the historic resurgence of the peoples of the East, and the working masses of the world, and in determination to make this our country a dazzling gem of the snowy bosom of Asia, do propose and propound the following Constitution of our State."

This was passed at the 1944 Session of the National Conference in Srinager. Today, in 1951, embodying such aspirations, men and women from the four corners of the State in this Constituent Assembly has become the repository of its sovereign authority. This Assembly, invested with the authority of a constituent body, will be the fountain-head of basic laws, laying the foundation of a just social order and safeguarding the democratic rights of all the citizens of the State.

You are the sovereign authority in this State of Jammu and Kashmir; what you decide has the irrevocable force of law. The basic democratic principle of sovereignty of the nation, embodied ably in the American and French Constitution, is once again given shape in our midst. I shall quote the . . . famous words of Article 3 of the French Constitution of 1791:

> "The source of all sovereignty resides fundamentally in the nation... Sovereignty is one and indivisible, inalienable and imprescriptable. It belongs to the nation."

We should be clear about the responsibilities that this power invests us with. In front of us lie decision of the highest national importance, which we shall be called upon to take. Upon the correctness of our decisions depends not only the happiness of our land and people now, but the fate as well of generation to come.

What then are the main functions that this Assembly will be called upon to perform!

One great task before this Assembly will be to devise a constitution for the future governance of the country, Constitution-making is a difficult and detailed matter. I shall only refer to some of the broad aspects of the Constitution, which should be the product of the labours of this Assembly.

Another issue of vital importance to the nation involves the future of the Royal Dynasty. Your decision will have to be taken both with urgency and wisdom for on that decision rests the future form and character of the State.

The third major issue awaiting your deliberations arises out of the Land Reforms which the Government carried out with vigour and determination. Our "land to the tiller" policy brought light into the dark homes of the peasantry; but, side by side, it has given rise to the problem of the landowner's demand for compensation. The nation being the ultimate custodian of all wealth and resources, the representatives of the nation are truly the best jury for giving a just and final verdict on such claims. So in your hand lies the power of this decisior

Finally, this Assembly will after full consideration of three alternatives that I shall state later, declare its reasoned conclusion regarding accession. This will help us to canalise our energies resolutely and with greater zeal in direction in which we have already started moving for the social and economic advancement of our country.

To take our first task, that of Constitution-making we shall naturally be guided by the highest principles of the democratic constitution of the world. We shall base our work on the principles of equality, liberty, and social justice, which are an integral feature of all progressive Constitution. The rule of law as understood in the democratic countries of the world should be the cornerstone of our political structure. Equality before the law and the independence of the Judiciary from the influence of the Executive or vital to use. The freedom of the individual in the matter of speech, movement and association should be guaranteed; freedom of the Press and of opinion would also be features of our Constitution. I need not refer in great detail to all those rights and obligations, already embodied in NEW KASHMIR, which are integral parts of democracy which has been defined as "an apparatus of social organization wherein people govern through their chosen representatives and are themselves guaranteed political and civil liberties."

You are no doubt aware of the scope of our present constitutionalities with India. We are proud to have our bonds with India, the goodwill of whose people and Government is available to us in unstinted and abundant measure. The Constitution of India has provided for a federal union and in the distribution of sovereign powers has treated us differently from other constitutional units. With the exception of the items grouped under Defence, Foreign Affairs and Communication in the Instrument of Accession, we have complete freedom to frame our constitution in the manner we like. In order to live and prosper as good partners in a common endeavour for the advancement of our peoples. I would advise that, while safeguarding our autonomy to the fullest extent so as to enable us to have the liberty to build our country according to the best traditions and genius of our people, we may also by suitable constitutional arrangements with the Union establish our right to seek and compel federal cooperation and assistance in this great task, as well as offer our fullest cooperation and assistance to the Union.

Whereas it would be easy for you to devise a document calculated to create a framework of law and order, as also a survey of the duties and rights of citizens, it will need more arduous labour to take concrete decision with regard to the manner in which we propose to bring about the rapid economic development of the State and more equitable distribution of our national income among the people to which we are pledged. Our National conference avows its faith in the principal that there is one thing common to meet of all castes and creeds, and that is their humanity. That being so, the one ailment which is ruthlessly sapping the vitality of human beings in Jammu and Kashmir is their appalling poverty, and if we merely safeguard their political freedom in solemn terms, it will not affect their lives materially unless it guarantees them economic and social justice.

NEW KASHMIR contains a statement of the objectives of our social policy. It given broadly a picture of the kind of life that we hope to make possible for the people of Jammu and Kashmir and manner in which the economic organization of the country will be geared to the purpose. These ideals you will have to integrate with the political structure which you will devise.

The future political set-up which you decide upon for Jammu and Kashmir must also take into consideration the existence of various sub-national groups in our State. Although culturally diverse, history has forged an uncommon unity between them; they all are pulsating with the same hopes and aspirations, sharing in each others joys and sorrows. While guaranteeing this basic unity of the State, our constitution must not permit the concentration of power and privilege in the hands of any particular group or territorial region. It must afford the fullest possibilities to each of these groups to grow and flourish in conformity with their cultural characteristics, without detriment to the integral unity of the state or the requirement of our social and economic policies.

Now let us take up an issue of basic importance which involves the fundamental character of the State itself. As an instrument of the will of a self-determining people who have now become sovereign in their own right, the Constituent Assembly will now re-examine and decide upon the future of the present ruling dynasty, in respect of its authority.

The present House of the Rulers of our state based its claim to authority on the treaty Rights granted to it by the British Government in 1846. To throw light on the nature of these rights it will be helpful to recall that the British power, in its drive for territorial expansion, achieved its objectives through a network of alliances with the Indian Princes, subsidiary and subordinate offensive and defensive. This mutually helpful arrangement enabled the British to consolidate their power and strengthened the grip of the princes, giving them military help in the event of rebellion by their exploited subjects. The Butler Committee Report on Treaty Rights in 1929, bears ample testimony to this save.

"The duty of the Paramount Power to protect the State against rebellion and insurrection is derived from the clause of treaties and snads from usage and from the promise of the King Emperor to maintain unimpaired the privileges, rights and dignities of the Princes. . . . The promise of the King Emperor to maintain unimpaired the privileges, rights and dignities of the Princes carries with it a duty to protect the Prince against attempt to eliminate him and substitute another form of Government."

In recognition of their services to the British Crown, the Indian Princess earned the rewards of a limited sovereignty over their States under the Protection and suzerainty of the Paramount power. It was in this way that their right, privileges and prerogatives were preserved.

Thus the pioneers of the British imperialism subjugated India, aided by the Indian Princes. This was hardly diplomacy it amounted to fraud and deceit: Mutual agreements arrived at for such ignoble purposes were invested with the sanctity of treaties. And it is from such "treaties that the Princes claimed their right to rule. Our own stage provides a classic example of this. One glance at a page of our history will lay bare the truth.

The State of Jammu and Kashmir came to be transferred to Maharaja Gulab Singh in 1846 after the Sikh Empire began to disintegrate. His failure to render competent assistance to the Sikh armies was duly noticed by the British as also his willingness to acknowledge their authority. This paved the way for the total occupation of Northern India by the British who were nor slow in recognizing Maharaja Gulab Singh's services to them in reward they sold him the territory of Jammu and Kashmir for 75 lakhs of rupees, and in the Treaty of Amritsar, the British Government made over the entire country independent possession of Maharaja Gulab Singh and the heirs mail of his body. In this way, the entire population of Jammu and Kashmir state came under his absolute authority. The peculiar indignity of the transaction naturally offended the national self-respect of our people who resisted the occupation of their country. But the direct intervention of the British troops helped the Maharaja to take possession of the territory.

This event in the history of the State had catastrophic consequences for the people. The old feudal order, which was bad enough, gave way to more exacting rule, in which the Maharaja assumed all proprietary rights over land. The entire state was plunged into a chaotic economic condition, aggravated by a heavy state of taxation, tributes and levies which were required to make up for the money given by the Maharaja to the British. This unrelieved despotism reduced the bulk of the people to the level of serials. There was general impoverishment in 1948, some 4000 artisans started on a trek to Lahore, with the object of permanently setting there. Even the British counseled the Maharaja to loosen his grip so as to avoid a total collapse of his administration. Perhaps the forefathers of the great poet philosopher son of Kashmir Iqbal, where also part of the same trail of migrants who left the State at this time. When his agony over the fate of the people of his homeland bruit out in immortal verse, his feelings are echoed in the heart of every Kashmiri:

> "O Wind, if you pass through Geneva, give this message to the comity of the people of the world. They sold the peasant, his field, his property and the roof over his head, in fact, they sold the entire nation and for what a paltry price."

Invested with this absolute authority acquired in 1846 the present ruling dynasty was in power for one hundred years. This sad and stern century of servitude has stultified the growth of our people, leaving them in the backwaters of civilization. While in British India, and even in some of the Indian States, many a measure of reform was introduced to alleviate the misery of the people, in this state the unenlightened absolutism of the Rulers drove them deeper and deeper into poverty and degradation. The conditions became increasingly intolerable they made determined efforts to wrest power from the hands of the Ruler.

By 1947, India had achieved independence and reached one of her historical watersheds. It was clear that with the withdrawal of the Paramount Power, the treaty rights of the Indian Princes would cease Sovereignty in that case should revert to the people: they wished, therefore, to be consulted about the arrangements to be made with regard to the transfer of power. But a strange situation arose. The Cabinet Mission, while admitting the claims of the Indian National Congress and the Muslim League in British India, completely refused a similar representation of the States people, who would not allow the right of the princes to speak on their behalf.

In our own state the National Conference had made it clear as early as February 10, 1946 that it was against any further continuance of the treaty rights of the princes which had been made in times and under circumstances which do not obtain now and which have been framed without seeking in consent of the state peoples. Under such circumstances no treaties or engagements which act as dividing wall between their progress and that of their brethren in British India, can be binding on the people.

It was in this connection that I invited the attention of the Cabinet Mission to the standing inquiry of the Treaty of Amritsar and sought its termination. I wrote to the Cabinet Delegation that:

> "As the mission is at the moment reviewing the relationship of the princes with the Paramount Power with reference to treaty rights, we wish to submit that for us in Kashmir re-examination of this relationship is a vital matter because a hundred years ago in 1846, the land and people of Kashmir were sold away by the British for 50 lakhs of British Indian Rupees. The people of Kashmir are determined to mould their destiny and we appeal to the Mission to recognise the justice and strength of our cause."

In the Memorandum submitted to the Cabinet Mission later by the National Conference the demand for independence from autocracy was reiterated. Today the National demand of the people of Kashmir is not merely the establishment of responsible

Government, but their right to absolute freedom from autocratic rule. This immensity of the wrong done to our people by the sale deed of 1646 can only be judged by looking into the actual living conditions of the people. It is the depth of our torment that has given strength to our protest.

The indifferent attitude of the Cabinet Mission to the claims of the States people convinced us that freedom would not be given to a hundred million people who were to be left to groan under the heel of autocratic rulers. Consequently the National Conference gave a call to the people to prepare themselves for fresh ordeals and new responsibilities in the final bid for the capture of power from the hands of autocracy. This call came on the eve of the transfer of power in India and was therefore in keeping with the spirit of the times.

The partition of India in 1947 brought many new problems and developments in its wake in Kashmir, the very foundations of the administration began to shake and the Government made frontal efforts to patch up the cracking structure its incompetence had become glaring with the tribal raids on the State in October, 1947, it was obvious that the Maharaja's authority had ceased to function and the real power lay in the hands of the peoples' organization, the National Conference even at this hour of grave national danger, the Ruler failed to see the wisdom of taking this organization into his confidence and he preferred escape to the dignity of a formal surrender. When the situation became critical, the unprecedented pressure of the people, forced him to call upon the representatives of the National Conference to deal with the emergency, when he himself had failed to handle the affairs of the State effectively.

The emergency Administration in the state marked in effect a revolutionary transfer of power from the Ruler to the people.

It was, however, the proclamation of March 5, 1948, which constituted the first step towards the completion of National emancipation. On this day, I, as leader of the largest party of the State, was entrusted with its Government being assisted by a cabinet with full powers to run the administration. The Maharaja's authority was limited to that of a constitutional ruler, making it imperative upon him to consult his Government on an issues relating to the governance of the State.

This was obviously an interim measure. The cabinet of the

peoples' representatives thus chosen functioned with the support and cooperation of the National Conference, but with the passage of time it became clear that the Maharaja could not reconcile himself to this democratic system of Government. He put positive impediments in the way of the Government. These threatened to block much needed reforms in various spheres of administration. It was, therefore, natural that following disagreement between him and the Government on matters of policy, that he should disconnect himself from the administration and leave the state. His young son Yuvaraj Karan Singh thereupon became the Regent and has functioned since as constitutional head of the state.

Today the Constituent Assembly having met, the time has come for the people's representatives to make fundamental decision about the future position of the present dynasty.

It is clear that this dynasty can no longer exercise authority, on the basis of an old discredited Treaty. During my trial for sedition in the "Quit Kashmir" movement I had clarified the attitude of my party when I said:

> "The future constitutional set-up in the State of Jammu and Kashmir cannot derive authority from the old source of relationship which was expiring and was bound to end soon. The set-up could only rest on the active will of the people of the State, conferring on the Head of the State the title and authority drawn from the true and abiding source of sovereignty, that is the people".

On this occasion, in 1946 I had also indicated the basis on which an individual could be entrusted by the people with the symbolic authority of a Constitutional head.

"The State and its Head represent the constitutional circumference and the centre of this sovereignty respectively, the Head of the State being the symbol of the authority with which the people may invest him for the realisation of their aspirations and the maintenance of their rights."

In consonance with these principles, and in supreme fulfilment of the peoples, aspirations, it follows that a constitutional Head of the state will have to be chosen to exercise the functions which this Assembly may choose to entrust to him.

So far as my party is concerned, we are convinced that the

institution of monarchy is incompatible with the spirit and needs of modern times which demand an egalitarian relationship between one citizen and an other. The supreme test of a democracy is the measure of equality of opportunity that it affords to its citizens to rise to the highest point of authority and position. In consequence, monarchies are fast disappearing from the world picture, as something in the nature of feudal anachronisms. In India, too, where before the partition, six hundred and odd princes exercised rights and privileges of rulership, the process of democratisation has been taken up and at present hardly ten of them exercise the limited authority of Constitutional Head of State.

After the attainment of complete power by the people, it would have been an appropriate gesture of goodwill to recognize Maharaja Hari Singh as the first constitutional head of the state. But I must say with regret that he has completely forfeited the confidence of every section of the people. His incapacity to adjust himself to changed conditions and his antiquated views on vital problems constitute positive disqualifications for him to hold the high office of a democratic Head of the State. Moreover, his past actions as a ruler have proved that he is not capable of conducting himself with dignity, responsibility and impartiality. The people still remember in with pain and regret this failure to stand by them in times of crisis, and his incapacity to afford protection to a section of his people in Jammu.

Saint Thomas Aquinas, as early as the thirteenth century described the consequences of a king refusing to realise his responsibilities in these wise words:

> "A king who is unfaithful to his duty forfeits the claim to obedience. It is not rebellion to depose him for he is himself a rebel whom the nation has a right to put down. But it is better to abridge his power that he may be unable to abuse it. All political authority is derived from the people, and all laws ought to be made by them or their own representation. There is no security for us so long as we depend upon the will of another man".

Because of his background, it would, therefore, be impossible to think of his being associated again with the administration of the State.

I am sure none of us is interested in a personal controversy with the Maharaja's family. In the conduct of public affairs, it is necessary that an impartial view of every individuals deeds should be taken. Our judgement should not be wrapped by ill will or personal rancour. During our association with Yuvaraj Karan Singh these last few years, I and my colleagues in the Government have been impressed by his intelligence, his broad outlook and his keen desire to serve the country. These qualities of the Yuvaraj singh prove him as a fit choice for the honour of being chosen the first Head of the State.

There is no doubt that Yuvaraj Karan Singh in his capacity as a citizen of the State, will prove a fitting symbol of the transition to a democratic system in which the ruler of yesterday becomes the first servant of the people, functioning under their authority and on their behalf.

The next issue before us is that of the compensation which we should or should not grant to those landowners who have been expropriated during the putting into operation of the land to the tiller legislation under which land was given, or given back to the man who actually cultivates it.

It is not possible for you to consider this question dispassionately unless you understand something of the history of land tenure in the state. For us the well-being of the peasants who from the vast majority of the population of this country is a top priority; we realize that on a sound organization of agriculture, and the elimination of debit and the evils of landlordism their ultimate welfare depends. We sincerely believe that our body politic cannot be healthy as long as their exists here an army of men doing little or no work and getting easy remuneration for it, and as long as we perpetuate the dangerous age old class division of our society that landlordism breeds. Our attempt has been to make our land-dwellers contented. We set about these fundamental reforms in the following way.

On Martyrs day, the 13th of July, 1950 the Government declared its policy of liquidating the big landed estates and transferring land to the tillers of the soil. On the 17th of October, 1950 was enacted the Big Landed Estates Abolition Act. By this Act, the right of ownership in respect of lands in excess of 22/34 acres of land excluding orchards, grass and fuel reserves was abolished and such land was decreed to be transferred to the actual tillers to the extent of their possession. In this way, the right of the cultivator to the ownership of land in his possession was recognized and enforced and no new class of intermediaries or rent receivers was allowed to come into being. The abolition of landlordism is thus an accomplished fact and, there is no going back on the decision already taken. The big landed Estates Abolition Act, however, provides for the Constituent Assembly to settle the question of compensation with respect to the land from which expropriation has taken place, that question is now before you for decision.

The system of individual ownership of land is of modern growth and originally, the land belonged in common to communities of kinsmen or to the State Before the British rule, the proprietors were by no means the real owners of the soil and of all method for the collection of revenue during that time, the most noteworthy was that of collecting it direct from the cultivators through the Headmen of the villages. There is very little evidence to show that in Mughal and Sikh times, there were many rent paying tenants. The Ain-I-Akbari not only contains no regulations about tenants, but also recognise no intermediary between the cultivator and the State. Nevertheless there were some types of intermediaries in the pre-British period and also in later times, and it is the existence......of these intermediaries, which led to the development of landlordism in the State. The revenue farmers were on class of such intermediaries and so were the different privileged classes of assignees, Jagirdars, muafidars and mukarraridars, all enjoying feudal concession, which were created during the Mughal and Sikh times and also during the Dogra Rule.

In the Jammu Province, ownership of land was granted by State Deeds during the Sikh Rule and the earlier period of the Dogra Rule. In the Kashmir Province, the ownership of land was held by the Ruler since 1846 when Maharaja Gulab Singh purchased Kashmir from the British. It was in 1933 as a result of the pressure of public opinion than proprietary right in land was conferred on the landholders in the Kashmir province including the Frontier Districts, but this concession to mass demand for transfer of proprietorship of land to the actual cultivators was reduced to a fiction inasmuch as large tracts of land, granted by earlier Rulers to influential persons. Rajas and Dewiness by state Deeds were construed and acted upon as grants of the right of proprietorship in land in this manner were created big proprietors who did not cultivate their land themselves, but had tenants who paid them rent in cash and kind. The small peasant proprietor who cultivated land with his own hands also existed, but there were cases where the cultivators who had originally acquired holders', right and were recorded as such were relegated to the position of tenants by the right of land holding being granted by the Ruler to some of his favourites who did not cultivate the land themselves and where pure and simple rent receivers.

While the land settlement in the State was rightly made with the peasant proprietors, the settlement with the peasant proprietors, the settlement with the intermediary proprietors was not made on their recognition as proprietors of the soil, but because of certain political and financial reasons. It was well understood, even by the successive settlement officers and Settlement Commissioner in the State that though the intermediary proprietors were to be declared the proprietors of the soil, their tenants really were no ordinary tenants, but were in most cases, the original and hereditary possessors of the soil. The First Regular Settlement conducted in the state had perhaps nothing to do with the determination of the historical and accurate theory of the intermediary proprietors' position, nor was its function to confer on the proprietors a position comparable to what they originally were. It appears that the task of the settlement authorities was only to legalize all the original acts of illegality and usurpation by which intermediary revenue framers or rent receivers had assumed great power and influence in the period or disorder, before a proper Revenue Administration came to the country.

At the first Regular Settlement the area of land not under cultivation was very large. In 1891 AD when the later Sir Walter Lawrence was in the State, every inducement was given to the cultivators to till the land and in this way large tracts of State land where brought under cultivation. But even such lands as had been reclaimed and brought under the plough by the cultivators where gifted away in proprietary right to influential person. There were grants of land known as Chaks made under orders No. 5 and 6, otherwise known as the Pratap Code. All these grants were subject to substantial concession in land revenue. There were grants in different kind, as for instance. State Official's Grants in perpetuity, Hindu, Grants and others. The vast majority of these concessionist landholders obtained their grants by virtue of the high positions they had acquired. The grants under the Pratap Code were entirely made to the clan and the kinsmen of the Royal House in whose favour were also released some State Forest Reserves and cultivable areas in some Game Reserves. With the demarcation of forests in the Suite, several areas where excluded from the forests and let out for cultivation and for purposes of agriculture. State lands were similarly permitted to be used as Grazing Ground. The reclaimed land out of the Wular Lake and in and around the Dal Lake, which was owned by the State, was also released for cultivation. And then under Raj Tilak Room No. 4 about 26 years ago. State waste lands were granted as Village Commons equivalent to the aggregate cultivated land of each village, with the same rights as the landholders enjoyed in respect of their existing holdings. Even after the First Regular Settlement, many estates were sold to speculators or given over to those who were prepared to meet the land revenue demand in cases where default was made by actual cultivators, and the right to own land was recognized as that of the revenue payer as against the actual cultivator who defaulted. The no cultivating land owners leased out their interests and the middlemen leased it out in turn, creating a long chain of rent receivers and rent payers, who intervened between the state and the actual cultivators.

It will thus be seen that a substantial portion of the landed property came to be owned from such land as was the property of the state before and in every case the acquisition of land was free from any encumbrance or payment of any consideration. It is in the light of this historical background, therefore that the Hon'ble Members of this House shall have to consider whether there is any justification for payment of any compensation to such land owners for lands from which they are expropriated under the Big landed Estates Abolition Act.

Finally, we come to the issue, which has made Kashmir an object of world interest, and has brought her before the forum of the United Nations. This simple issue has become so involved that people have begun to ask themselves, after three and a half years of tense expectancy. "Is there any solution?" Our answer is in the affirmative. Everything hinges round the genuineness of the will to find a solution. If we face the issue straight, the solution is simple.

The problem may be posed in this way. Firstly was Pakistan's action invading Kashmir in 1947 morally and legally correct, judged by any norm of international behaviour? Sir Owen Dixon's verdict on this issue is perfectly plain. In unambiguous terms he declared Pakistan an aggressor. Secondly, was the Maharaja is accession to India legally valid or not? The legality of the accession has not been seriously questioned by an irresponsible or independent person or authority.

These two answers are obviously correct. Then where is the justification of treating India and Pakistan at par in matters pertaining to Kashmir? In fact, the force of logic dictates the conclusion that the aggressor should withdraw his armed forces, and the United Nations should see that Pakistan gets out of the State.

In that event, India herself anxious to give the people of the state a chance to express their will freely would willingly cooperate with any sound plan of dimilitarization. They would withdraw their forces, only garrisoning enough posts to ensure against any repetition of that earlier treacherous attack from Pakistan.

These two steps would have gone a long way to bring about a new atmosphere in the State. The rehabilitation of displaced people, and the restoration of stable civic conditions would have allowed people to express their will and take the ultimate decision.

We as a Government are keen to let our people decide the future of our land in accordance with their own wishes. If these three preliminary processes were accomplished we should be happy to have the assistance of international observers to ensure fair play and the requisite conditions for a free choice by the people.

Instead invader and defender have been put on the same plan. Under various grabs, attempts have been made to side track the main issues. Sometimes, against all our ideals of life and way of living attempts to divide our territories have been made in the form of separation of our State religion-wise with ultimate plans of further disrupting its territorial integrity once an offer was made to police our country with Commonwealth forces, which threatens to bring in impartial control by the back door. Besides, the repugnance which our people have however, to the idea of inviting foreign troops on their soil, the very presence of Commonwealth troops could have reacted suspicion among our neighbours that we were allowing ourselves to be used as a base of possible future aggression against them. This could easily have made us in a second Korea.

We have watched all this patiently but we cannot be indifferent to the growing sufferings of our people we cannot any longer tolerate being banded about and left with an indefinite future. Not only has our patience been tried to its limits but our self-respect has been challenged by allegation that we are the stooges of India. And nobody in our own land that our influence rests on Indian bayonets that we are running a police state and various other taunts and fantastic allegations.

We, therefore, thought if best to call upon our own people to declare what future they seek. At last we, in October, 1950 decided to convoke a Constituent Assembly, which would pronounce upon the future affiliations of our state. We were, and are, convinced that whatever some groups or individuals in the world outside might have to say about this decision of ours, there are in every country many people who have faith in justice and straightforward dealing.

I have no doubt that our considered views will be understood and supported by freedom-losing, peace-loving and democratic minded people all over the world. I am sure too that Almighty God who guards all just causes will bestow. His blessings upon us and guide our footsteps towards correct and honest ends.

The problem, then of accession has to be considered against the background of history in particular, of the immediate past consequent on the British quitting India disappearance of the paramount power. The end of the war brought to ahead the question of Indian freedom. Let me recapitulate. The Cabinet Mission was sent to India to hammer out plans for the transfer of power. This mission had a series of consultations with parties and leaders of opinion in British India, but refused to agree to the people of the Indian States being represented by their popular leaders and instead backed up their old allies, the Indian princes and my colleagues had at that time raised our voice against this attitude in the following words of our Memorandum:

"The fate of the Kashmiri nation is in the balance and in this hour of decision we demand our basic democratic right to send our selected representatives to the constitution-making bodies that will construct the framework of Free India. We emphatically repudiate the right of the Princely Order to represent the people of the Indian States of their right to nominate their personnel representatives as our spokesmen."

I have no doubt in my mind that if popular representatives from the Indian States had been included in the discussions they would have certainly helped in having many controversial issues resolved fairly and smoothly. But that was not to be. To our misfortune, and to the misfortune of millions of people in India and Pakistan, the Cabinet Mission as well as the Indian political parties seemed to have been swayed by various conflicting considerations, with the result that the Indian sub-continent which had acquired an organic unity through ages of social, cultural and economic intercourse, was suddenly vivisected into the two Dominions of India and Pakistan. I need not relate here the horrors that followed this unnatural operation. Millions of hearts in both countries still ache with wounds that will not heal.

The agony of this change over became all the more intense as a result of the position in which the Indian States were left under the Indian independence Act of the Brilish parliament the paramountcy of the British Crown, against which the princes had been leaning, lapsed, and it was made clear that it would not be transferred to either of the succeeding Dominions. There were three alternative courses open to them. They could accede to either of the two Dominions or remain independent. This gave the princes, themselves the option to decide the fate of their States.

Following the announcement of the 'Mountbaten plan' on June 3, some of the Indian States acceded to Pakistan and some to India by means of Instruments of Accession executed through their princes. There were also some who entered into stand still Agreements with either or both pending finalization of their decisions.

"The betrayal of the interests of the State' people had been expected following the rejection of the Memorandum of the National Conference, and so we in Kashmir decided to place the issue before the people themselves.

This is how our well-known "Quit Kashmir" agitation began. The National Conference once again led the people through a great struggle, and once again the Ruler tried to curb it, this time with unprecedented severity. But when a whole people is on the move, it is not possible to repress them and they do not stop until they wrest freedom and justice for themselves from the unwilling hands of those above them.

The crucial date of Indian and Pakistani independence therefore, came when I and my colleagues were still behind prison bars. The whole sub-continent was in a state of high tension and disturbance. If at that time, the head of the State of Jammu and Kashmir had even the slightest sense of realism or a proper awareness of the danger lurking in the situation, he would have immediately taken the people into his confidence. By associating their representatives with administration, I am sure many of the complications that arose later could have been avoided.

Instead of that, the Maharaja's Government entered in Stand Still Agreement with Pakistan, and this was accepted without question by that Dominion. A similar arrangement was suggested to India, also but it is noteworthy that the Government of India insisted that it could not consider any agreement entered into by the Government of the State valid until it had the approval of the people's representatives.

While the leaders constantly refused to recognise vital issue of accession without first securing the approval of his people, the Muslim League and the Pakistan government supported the claims of the Rulers to speak for their States. The late Mr. Jinah took the position that after the lapse of Paramountcy, the Princes were completely independent and that they could themselves determine what relations they should have with the two Dominions. Throughout the struggles that the people of Kashmir waged against autocracy we should never forget that the Muslim League leadership had completely disassociated itself from them and that, during the upsurge of 1946 their local party organs had assisted the administration to suppress the movement.

At this crucial time, then, Pakistan was under strict cover of secrecy perfecting her own plans, and the Dawn, the Muslim League official organ in Karachi, was appealing to the Maharaja to accede to Pakistan on the grounds that he would have far greater freedom there than in India.

It was at this stage taking advantage of the isolation of the Kashmiris from the rest of the world, that Pakistan imposed an economic blockade upon us with a view to starving us into submission. Attempts were made even to excite communal hatred to disrupt our peaceful civic life. Even in the face of such provocation, the National Conference, I am proud to say, took an objective and democratic stand. Immediately on my release from imprisonment, I clarified the issue at a mass meeting in Srinagar. The first and fundamental issue before us was the establishment of a popular Government. Our objective might be summarised a "Freedom First." Then alone could we as a free people decide our future associations through accession. I also made it clear that the National Conference would consider this issue without prejudice to its political friends and opponets, and strictly in accordance with the best interests of the country as a whole. I said that in the state of tension and conflict that obtained both in India and Pakistan, it was difficult for the people here and now to predict what the final shape of both would be.

You will realize, therefore, that we could not be accused of being partial to one side or the other. During that period we openly discussed the matter with representatives of the Muslim League who had come to Srinagar for this purpose. We even sent one of our representatives to Lahore to acquaint the authorities in Pakistan, with our point of view. We were thus still struggling against autocracy and for freedom when the state was suddenly invaded from the state of Pakistan.

The overwhelming pressure of this invasion brought about a total collapse of the armed forces of the State as well as its administrative machinery, leaving the completely defenseless people at the mercy of invaders. It was not an ordinary type of invasion, inasmuch as no canons of warfare were observed. The bribement tribesmen who attacked the state in thousands, killed, burned, looted and destroyed whatever came their way and in this savagery no section of the people could escape. Even the nuns and nurses of a Catholic Mission were either killed, or brutally maltreated. As these raiders advanced towards Srinagar, the last vestige of authority, which lay in the person of the Maharaja, suddenly disappeared from the Capital. This created a strange vacuum, and would have certainly led the occupation of the whole state by Pakistani troops and tribesmen, if, at this supreme hour of crisis, the entire people of Kashmir had not risen like a solid barrier against the aggressor. They halted his onrush, but could not stop him entirely as the defenders, had not enough experience, training and equipment to fight back effectively. There is no doubt that some of them rose to great heights of heroism during these fateful days. Who can help being moved by the saga of crucified Sherwani. Abdul Aziz, Brigadier Rajendra Singh, Prempal Sardar Rangil Singh early Militia boys like Punshkar Nath Zadoo, Somnath Bira, Ismail among scores of other named and unnamed heroes of all communities. But we though rich in human material lacked war equipment and trained soldiers.

When the raiders were fast approaching Srinagar, we could think of only one way to save the State from total annihilation by asking for help from a friendly neighbour. The representative of the National Conference, therefore, flew to Delhi to seek help from the Government of India. But the absence of any constitutionalities between our State and India made it impossible for her to render us any effective assistance in meeting the aggressor. As I said earlier, India had refused to sign a standstill agreement with the State for the ground that she could not accept such an agreement until it had the approval of the people. But now, since the people's representatives themselves sought an alliance, the Government of India showed readiness to accept it. Legally the instrument of Accession had to be signed by the Ruler of the State. This the Maharaja did. While accepting that accession, the Government of India said that she wished that "as soon as law and order have been restored in Kashmir and her soil cleared of the invader, the question of the States accession should be settled by reference to the people."

Actuated by a sincere desire to avoid bloodshed and further conflict, the Government of India approached the Security Council in 1948 with a plant against Pakistan. The request was simple. The contention of India was that Pakistan was responsible for the invasion of Kashmir and was continuing to help the raiders who had been employed as mercenaries for this purpose. And it was further said that legally bound as India was to clear the Jammu and Kashmir State of raiders. She might be constrained to pursue the invaders to their bases in Pakistan, which might lead to a still bigger conflagration. India, therefore, wanted the Security Council to dispose of the case as quickly as possible in the interest of peace.

If this had been done, condition would have ifso facto came into being when the people of Jammu and Kashmir would have expressed their will with regard to the continuance of the accession to the Dominion they had joined. This was not to be.

This is the essential background, which we must fully take into account. Now I shall indicate some of the considerations which should be kept in view when you the Hon'ble Members of this august Assembly, shoulder the grave responsibility of giving your considered opinion on this issue of accession which effects not only the present generation of our people but generations yet to come.

The Cabinet Mission Plan has provided for three courses which may be followed by the Indian states when determining their future affiliations. A state can either accede to India or accede to Pakistan but, failing to do either, it still can claim the right to remain independent. These three alternatives are naturally open to our state, while the intention of the British Government was to secure the privileges of the Princes: the representatives of the people must have the primary consideration of promoting the greatest good of the common people. Whatever steps they take must contribute to the growth of a democratic social order wherein all invidious distinctions between group and creeds are absent. Judged by this supreme consideration, what are the advantages and disadvantages of our states accession to either India or Pakistan, or of having an independent status?

As a realist I am conscious that nothing is all black or all white, and there are many facts to each of the proposition before us. I shall first speak on the merits and demerits of the State's accession to India. In the final analysis, as I understand it, it is the kinship of ideals, which determines the strength of ties between two States. The Indian National Congress has consistently supported the cause of the State's Peoples' freedom. The autocratic rule of the Princes has been done away with the representative Governments have been entrusted with the administration. Steps towards democratization have been taken and these have raised the people's standard of living, brought about much needed social reconstruction, and, above all built up their very independence of spirit. Naturally, if we accede to India there is no danger of a revival of feudalism and autocracy. Moreover, during last four years, Government of India has never tried to interfere in our internal autonomy. This experience has strengthened our confidence in them as a democratic State.

The real character of a State is revealed in its Constitution. The Indian Constitution has set before the country the goal of secular democracy based upon justice freedom and equality for all without distinction. This is the bedrock of modern democracy. This should meet the argument that the Muslims of Kashmir cannot have security in India, where the large majority of the populations are Hindus. Any unnatural cleavage between religious groups is the legacy of Imperialism, find no Modern State can at ford to encourage artificial divisions if it is to achieve progress and prosperity. The Indian Constitution has amply and finally repudiated the concept of a religious State, which is a throwback to medievalism, by guaranteeing the equality of rights of all citizens irrespective of their religion, colour, caste and class.

The national movement in our State naturally gravitates towards these principles of secular democracy. The people here will ever accept a principle, which seeks to favour the interests of one religion or social group against another. This affinity in political principles, as well as in past association, and our common path of suffering in the cause freedom, must be weighed properly while deciding the future of the State.

We are also intimately concerned with the economic well-being of the people of this State. As I said before while referring to constitution-building, political ideals are often meaningless unless linked with economic plans. As a State, we are concerned mainly with agriculture and trade. As you know, and as I have detailed before, we have been able to put through our "land to the tiller" legislation and make of it a practical success. Land and all it means is an inestimable blessing to our peasants who have dragged along in servitude to the landlord and his allies for centuries without number. We have been able under present conditions to carry these reforms through; are we sure that in alliance with landlord ridden Pakistan, with so many feudal privileges intact, that these economic reforms of ours will be tolerated? We have already heard that news of our Land Reforms has travelled to the peasants of the enemy-occupied area of our State who vainly desire a like status, and like benefits. In the second place, our economic welfare is bound up with our arts and crafts. The traditional markets for these precious goods, for which we are justly known all over the world, have been centered in India. The volume of our trade, in spite of the dislocation of the last few years, shows this. Industry is also highly important to us. Potentially we are rich in minerals, and in the raw materials of industry; we need help to develop our resources in India, being more highly industrialized than Pakistan, can give us equipment, technical services and materials. She can help us too in marketing. Many goods also which it would not be partical for us to produce here for instance, sugar, cotton, cloth and otherwise essential commodities can be got by us in large quantities from India. It is around the efficient supply of such basic necessities that the standard of living of the man-in-the-street depends.

I shall refer now to the alleged disadvantages of accession to India.

To begin with, although the land frontiers of India and Kashmir are contiguous, an all-weather road-link as dependable as the one we have Pakistan does not exist. This must necessarily hamper trade and commerce to some extent, particularly during the snowy winter months. But we have studied this question, and with improvements in modern engineering, if the State wishes to remain with India the establishment of an all weather stable system of communication is both feasible and easy. Similarly, the use of the State rivers as a means of timber transport is impossible if we turn to India, except in Jammu where the river Chenab still carries logs to the plans. In reply to this argument, it may be pointed out that accession to India will open up possibilities of utilizing our forest wealth for industrial purposes and that, instead of timber, finished goods which will provide work for our carpenters and labourers, can be exported to India where there is a ready market for them. Indeed in the presence of our fleets of timber-carrying trucks, river transport is a crude system which inflicts a loss of some 20% to 35% in transit.

Still another factor has to be taken into consideration. Certain tendencies have been asserting themselves in India, which may in the future convert it into a religious State wherein the interests of Muslims will be jeopardized. This would happen if a communal organization had a dominant hand in the Government, and Congress ideals of the equality of all communities were made to give way to religious intolerance. This continued accession of Kashmir to India should, however, help in defeating this tendency.

From my experience of the last four years, it is my considered judgement that the presence of Kashmir in the Union of India has been the major factor in stabilizing relations between the Hindus and Muslims of India. Gandhiji was not wrong when he uttered words before his death which para-phrase; "I lift up mine eyes unto the hills, from whence cometh my help."

As I have said before, we must consider the question of accession with an open mind, and not let our personal prejudices stand in the way of balanced judgement. I will now invite you to evaluate the alternative of accession to Pakistan.

The most powerful argument, which can be advanced in her favour, is that Pakistan is a Muslim State, and a big majority of our people being Muslim the State must acceded to Pakistan. This claim of being a Muslim State is of course only a camouflage. It is a screen to dupe the common man, so that he may not see clearly that Pakistan is a feudal State in which a clique is trying by these methods to maintain itself in power. In addition to this, the appeal to religion constitutes a sentimental and a wrong approach to the question. Sentiment has its own place in life, but often it leads to irrational action. Some argue, as supposedly natural corollary to this that our acceding to Pakistan our annihilation or survival depends. Facts have disproved this. Right thinking men would point out that Pakistan is not an organic unity of all the Muslims in this sub-continent. It has on the contrary, caused the dispersion of the Indian Muslims for whose benefit it was claimed to have been created. There are two Pakistanis at least a thousand miles apart from each other. The total population of Western Pakistan which is contiguous to our state, is hardly 25 million, while the total number of Muslims resident in India is as many as 40 million. As one Muslim is as good as another, the Kashmiri Muslim if they are worried by such considerations should choose the forty millions living in India.

Looking at the matter too from a more modern political angle, religious affinities alone do not and should not normally determine the political alliances of State. We do not find a Christian bloc, a Buddhist bloc, or even a Muslim bloc, about which there is so much talk now-a-days in Pakistan. These day's economic interests and a community of political ideals more appropriately influence the policies of States.

We have another important factor to consider, if the State

decide to make this the predominant consideration. What will be the fate of the one million non-Muslims now in our State? As things stand at present, there is no place for them in Pakistan. Any solution which will result in the displacement or the total subjugation of such a large number of people will not be just or fair, and it is the responsibility of this House to ensure that the decision that it takes an accession does not militate against the interests of any religious group.

As regards the economic advantages, I have mentioned before the road and river links with Pakistan. In the last analysis, we must however remember that we are not concerned only with the movement of people but also with the movement of goods and the linking up of markets. In Pakistan there is a chronic dearth of markets for our products. Neither, for that matter, can she help us with our industrialization, being herself industrially backward.

On the debit side we have to take into account the reactionary character of her politics and State politics. In Pakistan, we should remember that the lot of the State subjects has not changed and they are still helpless and under the heel of their Rulers, who wield the same unbridled power under which we used to suffer here. This clearly runs counter to our own aspirations for freedom.

Another big obstacle to dispassionate evaluation of her policies is the lack of a constitution in Pakistan. As it stands at present, this state enjoys the unique position of being governed by a Constitution enacted by an outside Parliament which gives no idea whatsoever of the future shape of civic and social relations. It is reasonable to argue that Pakistan cannot have the confidence of a freedom loving and democratic people when it has failed to guarantee even fundamental rights of its citizens. The right of self-determination for nationalities is being consistently denied and those who fought against Imperialism for this just right are being suppressed with force. We should remember Badshah Khan and his comrades who laid down their all for freedom, also Khan Abdus Samad Khan and other fighters in Baluchistan. Our national movement in the State considers this right of self-determination inalienable, and no advantage however great, will persuade our people to forego it.

The third course open to us has still to be discussed. We have to consider the alternative of making ourselves an Eastern Switzerland, of keeping aloof from both States, but having friendly relations with them. This might seem attractive in that it would appear to pave the way out of the present deadlock. To us as a tourist country it could also have certain obvious advantages. But in considering independence we must not ignore practical consideration. Firstly, it is not easy to protect sovereignty and independence in a small country, which has not sufficient to strength, defend itself on our long and difficult frontiers bordering so many countries. Secondly, we must have the good will of all our neighbours. Can we find powerful guarantors among them to pull together always in assuring us freedom from aggression? I would like to remind you that from August 15 to October 22, 1947, our State was independent and the result was that our weakness was exploited by the neighbour with whom we had a valid standstill Agreement. The State was invalid. What is the guarantee that in future we may not be victims of a similar aggression?

I have now put the pros and cons of the three alternatives before you. It should not be difficult for men of discrimination and patriotism gathered in this Assembly to weigh all these in the scales of our national good and pronounce where the true well-being of the country lies in the future.

Mr. President, it will be fitting here if I on this solemn occasion remember the last words of one of our martyrs which still ring in my ears. In 1931, the State Police had fired on our demonstrators, and many lay wounded and dying in the grounds of the Jammu Mosque. One man, supported by his old mother and young wife, was nearing his last breath, and he comforted them in their misery, forgetting his own. Then he called for me. When I came to him he looked me straight in the eyes and said. "We have done our duty. Now it is for you and the nation to carry it through to a successful end." Perhaps the spirit of that hero is in this Hall today to see one fulfilment of his dreams of this land of Kashmir. Today is a day of fulfilment for all—a day when we finally and triumphantly assert our right to decide our own future, free from threats of force and outside dictation.

On this historic day, we remember the Prime Minister of India, our cherished friend and never failing comrade on this difficult journey and, besides, an illustrious son of Kashmir, the many friends in India and some even in Pakistan, who in the years before partition, helped us forward. We remember the Ahrars who went to jail in their thousands for us; Badshah Khan and our friends of the frontier, now in jails and fighting for their own freedom. Nor can we ever forget our kith and kin across the cease-fire line who are at present living under the heel of the enemy. There welfare is always dear to us and we shall continue to regard them as an integral part of ourselves.

For twenty years, Mr. President, we have journeyed to this day and our criterion in all we do must be the welfare of our people. This consideration alone must guide our decision.

Now again, I have put my deepest thoughts before you and may God, in His merey, lead us all forward on the right path.

ANNEXURE II—6

Constitutional Relationship between the Jammu and Kashmir State and the Indian Union

[1]*Speech made by Jenab Sheikh Mohammad Abdullah in Jammu and Kashmir Constituent Assembly on 11 August, 1952*

Sir, I crave permission to make a statement before the House in regard to constitutional relationship between the Jammu and Kashmir State and the Indian Union. As the Hon'ble Members are aware, during the last Session of the Constituent Assembly, the Basic Principles Committee had submitted a report making certain specific recommendations about the future Head of the State. The Drafting Committee will, no doubt, submit its report to the House during this Session.

Since the changes proposed by this Assembly involved corresponding adjustments in the Indian Constitution, the Government of India desired that it should have time to discuss with our representatives the proposals pending in this Assembly. Accordingly, a Delegation headed by Hon'ble M.A. Beg was sent by us to Delhi. The Government of India also availed of this opportunity to discuss with our representatives other matters pertaining to the constitutional relationship, it became necessary for me and some of my other colleagues in the Government to participate in the talks. I am now in a position to inform the House that certain broad principles have been laid down and certain decisions have been tentatively arrived at between the two Governments.

Before I apprise this House of the details of these tentative decision, I wish to review briefly the background of our relationship with India. For sometime past, there has been a good deal of discussions on this important question both here as well as outside. In the heat of public controversy, which this question aroused, the points at issue were sometime obscured.

May I mention here the developments which led to the establishment of our relationship with India in October, 1947?

1. Jammu & Kashmir Constituent Assembly (debates), Part I, Ist Vol. 1951-55, pp. 485-97.

After the Independence Act of 1947 was passed by the British Parliament, the Dominion Status was conferred on India and Pakistan; and the British Parliament having lapsed the Indian States became Independent. They were however, advised to join either of these two Dominions. It is a tragic commentary on these arrangements proposed by the British Government that the position of these Indian States, comprising one-fourth of the total population of the entire Indian sub-continent, was left absolutely vague and nebulous with the result that the future of the States people came to be subjected to the vagaries of their respective rules. Many of them acceded to either of the two Dominions after a good deal of procrastination while others hesitated and delayed the final decision to the detriment of the interests of the people living in these States.

The Jammu and Kashmir State was one of the States whose ruler had not taken a decision in regard to accession. While the State was in the condition of uncertainty and indecision and while the national movement was seeking transfer of complete power to the representatives of the people and the then State Government was indulging in repression in certain areas of the State particularly in Poonch, the State was suddenly invaded. Thousands of tribesmen from Pakistan as well as Pakistan nationals, launched a savage attack against the people of this State. The administration then in charge of its affairs proved singularly ineffective to cope with the grave emergency and consequently it collapsed all of a sudden. At that critical movement in the history of the State, the National Conference stepped into avert what looked like total annihilation at the hands of the raiders from Pakistan who were later proved to have been abetted by the Pakistan Government. The National Conference once mobilized all sections of the population in an effort to prevent conditions of chops and dislocation from spreading to the entire State. This factor was mainly responsible for the splendid moral displayed by the people of Kashmir who were inspired to heroic deeds in their resistance against the invaders.

It was, however, obvious that in face of the overwhelming number of the well armed raiders, unarmed people of Kashmir could not hold out for long. Consequently, it became urgently necessary for us to seek the assistance of the friendly neighbour which alone would enable us to throw back the invaders. In that critical moment, we could turn only to India where the Government and the people had demonstrated their sympathies for the ideals for which we were fighting the raiders.

But legal complications came in the way of India rendering the State any immediate help for its defence against aggression. The Government of India could send their army only if the State would acceded to that Dominion. In accordance with the Indian Independence Act of 1947, the Instrument of Accession had to be executed by the Ruler of the State in order to make it legally valid. Consequently, with the backing of the most popular organization in the country, the Maharaja signed the Deed of Accession on the 26th of October, 1947, and the State of Jammu and Kashmir became part of the Indian Dominion.

The basis of our relationship with India is the Instrument of Accession which enable our State to enter into a union with India. In accordance with the terms of the Instrument, certain powers were transferred to the Centre. The principle matters specified for this purpose in respect to which the Dominion Legislature could make laws for this State were:

(a) Defence,
(b) External Affairs, and
(c) Communications.

This arrangement involved a division of sovereignty which is the normal feature of a Federation. Beyond the powers transferred by it to the Dominion, the State enjoyed complete residuary Sovereignty.

These terms of the association of our State with the Dominion of India were maintained; and, subsequently, when the Constituent Assembly of India was charged with the task of framing a constitution, this overriding consideration was kept in view in determining the position of the State in the proposed Constitution earlier to this, it had been agreed between the two Governments that "in view of the special problems arising in respect of this State and the fact that the Government of India have assured its people that they would themselves finally determine their political future", a special position should be accorded to Jammu and Kashmir in the future Constitution so that a limited field of the Union Powers over the State is ensured. Four representatives were nominated from the Jammu and Kashmir State to the Constituent Assembly of India. These representatives participated in the deliberations of the Constituent Assembly of India at a time when the bulk of the Indian Constitution had already been adopted. It was at this stage that the constitutional position of the State was determined in the Constitution of India. The representatives of the Jammu and Kashmir State reiterated their views that our association with India should be based on the terms of the Instrument of Accession. It was also made clear that while the accession of the Jammu and Kashmir State with India was complete in fact and in law to the extent of the subjects enumerated in this instrument, the autonomy of the State with regard to all other subjects outside the ambit of the Instrument of Accession should be preserved.

Taking into account the special circumstances in which this State was placed, a special constitutional arrangement was evolved and provided in Article 370 of the Constitution which defines the position of Jammu and Kashmir as follows:

"Notwithstanding anything in this Constitution—

(a) the provisions of Article 238 shall not apply in relation to the State of Jammu and Kashmir;

(b) the power of parliament to make laws for the said States shall be limited to;

  (i) those matters in the Union list and the Concurrent list which, in consultation with the Government of the State, are declared by the President to correspond to matters specified in the instrument of Accession governing the accession of the State to the Dominion of India as the matters with respect to which the Dominion legislature may make laws for that State; and

  (ii) such other matters in the said lists as with the concurrence of the Government of the State, the President may by order specify.

Explanation: For the purposes of this Article; the Government of the State means the person for the time being recognized by the President as the Maharaja of

Jammu and Kashmir acting on the advice of the Council of Ministers for the time being in office under the Maharaja's proclamation dated: the fifth day of March, 1948;

(c) the provisions of Article 1 and of this article shall apply in relation to that State;

(d) such of the other provisions of this Constitution shall apply in relation to that State subject to such exceptions and modifications as the president may by order specify: Provided that no such order which relates to the matters specified in the Instrument of Accession of the State referred to in paragraph (1) of sub-clause (b) shall be issued except in consultation with the Government of the State:

Provided further that no such order which relates to matters other than those referred to in the last preceding proviso shall be issued except with the concurrence of the Government.

(2) If the concurrence of the Government of the State referred to in paragraph (ii) of sub-clause (b) of clause (1) or in the second proviso to sub-clause (d) of that clause be given before the Constituent Assembly for the purpose of framing the Constitution of the State is convened, it shall be placed before such Assembly for such decision as it may take thereon.

(3) Notwithstanding anything in the foregoing provisions of the Article, the President may by public Notification, declare that this Article shall cause to be operative or shall be operative only with such exceptions and modifications and from such date as he may specify:

Provided that the recommendation of the Constituent Assembly of the State referred to in clause (2) shall be necessary before the President issues such a Notification."

While the State of Jammu and Kashmir is included in the list of States in Part B of Schedule 1 of the Constitution, it is apparent from a perusal of this Article that the provisions of Article 238 relating to the Constitution of the States in Part B shall not apply to the State of Jammu and Kashmir. In view of the special position and character of the State and with a view to regulate the relationship of the State with the Union of India, Article 370 was devised.

The other important feature of this constitutional set-up is that the matters specified in the Instrument of Accession shall apply in relation to the Jammu and Kashmir State in consultation with the Government of Jammu and Kashmir State and all other matters which do not fall within the terms of the Instrument of Accession shall not apply in relation to our State except with the final concurrence of the Jammu and Kashmir Constituent Assembly.

Here I would like to point out that the fact that Article 370 has been mentioned as a temporary provision the Constitution does not mean that it is capable of being abrogated, modified or replaced unilaterally. In actual effect, the temporary nature of this Article arises merely from the fact that the power to finalize the Constitutional relationship between the State and the Union of India has been specifically vested in the Jammu and Kashmir Constituent Assembly. It follows that whatever modifications, amendments or exceptions that may become necessary either to Article 370 or any other Article in the Constitution of India in their application to the Jammu and Kashmir State are subject to decisions of this Sovereign Body.

Since a good deal of confuted thinking and uninformed criticism is indulged in by some interested people. I would like to point out here that the Constitution has confined the scope and jurisdiction of the Union Powers to the terms of Instrument of Accession with the proviso that they may be extended to such other matters also as the President may by order specify with the concurrence of the Jammu and Kashmir Constituent Assembly. The special problems facing the State were thus taken into account and under the Constitution the relationship approximated to that subsisting under the Instrument of Accession.

The Constitution of the Indian Union, therefore, clearly envisaged the convening of a Constituent Assembly for the Jammu and Kashmir State which would be finally competent to determine the ultimate position of the State in respect of the sphere of its accession which would be incorporated as in the shape of permanent provisions of the Constitution.

This briefly, is the position which the Constitution of India has accorded to our State. I would like to make it clear that any suggestions of altering arbitrarily this basis of our relationship with India would not only constitute a breach of the spirit and letter of the constitution, but it may invite serious consequences for a harmonious association of our State with India. The formula evolved with the agreement of the two Governments remains as valid today as it was when the Constitution was framed and reasons advanced to have this basis changed seem completely devoid of substance.

In arriving at this arrangement the main consideration before our Government was to secure a position for the State which would be consistent with the requirements of maximum autonomy for the local organs of State Power which are the ultimate source of authority in the State while discharging obligations as a unit of the Federation.

I would, therefore, plead that the validity of such constitutional arrangement should not be appraised academically but in the proper context of the extraordinary circumstances through which the State has been passing for the last five years or so. Since the State was invaded in 1947, the situation here has been bristling with such compelling urgencies as needed drastic administrative and economic changes. The revolutionary conditions prevailing in our State could be coped with only through extraordinary measures. The Government of the State was, therefore, called upon to take vital decisions which could not wait. Accordingly, it enacted laws which were calculated to transform the social and economic fabric of the common people. With the improvement in the internal situation of the country, the necessity for a legislature become obvious. Consequently, it was decided to convince a Constituent Assembly for the State elected on the basis of adult franchise. This Assembly accordingly came into being in October, 1951.

The Hon'ble members are aware that as the Leader of the National Conference Party, I indicated in my inaugural address the scope of the decisions which I felt the Constituent Assembly would have to take. I listed the four main issues as pertaining to the main functions to the Assembly, viz., the future of the Ruling Dynasty, payment of compensation for the land transferred to cultivators under the Big Landed Estates Act, Ratification of the State's accession to India as well as the framing of a Constitution for the State. While discussing these in my address to this House, I had given clear indications of my party views in regard to them. I had also an occasion to place my point of view on these issues before the representatives of the Government of India and I had the satisfaction that they approved of it.

When the Constituent Assembly commenced its labours, it had to tackle these issues in course of time. It took decisions in regard to payment of compensation to landlords and it came to the conclusion that no compensation was justified.

The Constituent Assembly has, at present, under its consideration the future of the Ruling Dynasty. In this connection the Basic Principles Committee recommended that the Institution of hereditary rulership in the State should be abolished and in future the office of the Head of the State should be elective. While accepting the recommendations of the Basic Principles Committee this Assembly charged the Drafting Committee to place before this House appropriate proposals for the implementation of these recommendations.

As I said in the beginning of my statement, such a fundamental decision involved corresponding adjustments in the Indian Constitution and in order to finalize the position in respect of this issue and other matters pertinent to it. I and my colleagues had discussions with the representatives of the Government of India as a result of which we arrived at some tentative agreements, the details of which I wish to place before the House.

The Government of India hold the view that the fact that the Jammu and Kashmir State was the constituent unit of the Union of India led inevitably to certain consequences in regard to some important matters, namely:

(a) Residuary powers;
(b) Citizenship;
(c) Fundamental Rights;
(d) Supreme Court of India;
(e) National Flag;
(f) The president of India;
(g) The Headship of the State;
(h) Financial Integration;
(i) Emergency Provisions; and
(j) Conduct of election to Houses of Parliament.

Permit me, Mr. President, now to deal with each one of these items and also the agreement arrived at between the Jammu and Kashmir Government and the Government of India in relation to them.

Residuary Powers

It was agreed that while under the present Indian Constitution, the Residuary Powers vested in the Centre in respect of all States other than Jammu and Kashmir, in the case of our State, they vested in the State itself. This position is compatible with Article 370 of the Indian Constitution and the Instrument of Accession on which this Article is based. We have always held that the ultimate source of sovereignty resides in the people. It is, therefore, from the people that all powers can flow. Under these circumstances, it is up to the people of Kashmir through this Assembly to transfer more powers for mutual advantage to the custody of the Union Centre.

Citizenship

It was agreed that in accordance with Article 5 of the Indian Constitution persons who have their domicile in the Jammu and Kashmir State shall be the citizens of India. It was further agreed that the State Legislature shall have power to define and regulate the rights and privileges of the permanent residents of the State, more especially in regard to acquisition of immovable property, appointments to services and like matters. Till then the existing State law would apply. It was also agreed that special provisions should be made in the laws governing citizenship to provide for the return of those permanent residents of Jammu and Kashmir State, who went to Pakistan in connection with the disturbances of 1947 or in fear of them as well as of those who have left for Pakistan earlier but could not return. If they returned, they should be entitled to the rights, and privileges and obligations of citizenship.

There are historic reasons which necessitate such constitutional safeguards as for centuries part, the people of the State have been victims of exploitation at the hands of their well-to-do neighbours. The Hon'ble Members are perhaps aware that in the late twenties, the people of Jammu and Kashmir agitated for the protection of their bonafide right against the superior competing interest of the non-residents of the State. It was in response to this popular demand that the Government of the day promulgated a Notification in 1927 by which a strict definition of the term "State Subject" was provided. I am glad to say that the Government of India appreciated the need for such a safeguard. No definition of the special rights and privileges of the residents of the State can afford to remain static. The need may arise at one stage or the other to liberalize such a definition. The importance of the fact that the State Legislature shall retain powers to be able to effect such modifications becomes obvious in this context.

There is yet another class of State Subjects whose interests had to be safeguarded. The Hon'ble Members of this House are aware that on account of the disturbances of 1947 and also as a consequence of the invasion of this country by Pakistan, large number of the residents of this State suffered dislocation. We have therefore, to visualize the possibility of their return to their homes and hearths as soon as normal conditions are restored. It has been suggested in certain quarters that this protection has been provided only for those residents of the State who are at present stranded in Pakistan. I would like to make it clear, as I have stated earlier, that this protection will operate only when the conditions are normal and such conditions naturally presume that the resettlement of the dislocated population, whether Muslims or Non-Muslims cannot be one sided or unilateral.

FUNDAMENTAL RIGHTS

It is obvious that while our Constitution is being framed, the Fundamental Rights and duties of a citizen have necessary got to be defined. It was agreed, however, that the Fundamental Rights, which are contained in the Constitution of India could not be conferred on the residents of Jammu and Kashmir State in their entirety taking into account the economic, social and political character of our movement as enunciated in the New Kashmir Plan. The need for providing suitable modification amendments and exceptions as the case may be in the Fundamental Rights Chapter of the Indian Constitution in order to harmonize those provisions with the pattern of our principles was admitted.

Particular care would have to be taken to preserve the basic character of the decisions taken by this House on the question of land compensation as well as the laws relating to the transfer of land to the tiller and other matters. The main point to be determined is whether the Chapter of our Fundamental Rights should form a part of the Kashmir Constitution on that or that of the Union Constitution.

Supreme Court

It was agreed that the Supreme Court should have original jurisdiction in respect of disputes mentioned in Article 131 of the Constitution of India. It was further agreed that the Supreme Court should have jurisdiction in regard to Fundamental Rights which are agreed to by the State.

On behalf of the Government of India, it was recommended that the Advisory Board in the State, designated "His Highness's Board of Judicial Advisors" should be abolished and the jurisdiction exercised by it should be vested in the Supreme Court of India. That is to say that the Supreme Court should be the final Court of Appeal in all civil and criminal matters as laid down in the Constitution of India.

We, however, felt that this would need a detailed examination and consequently it was agreed that we should have time to consider it further.

National Flag

We agreed that in view of the clarifications issued by me in my public statements while interpreting the resolution of this House according to which the old State flag was substituted by a new one. It was obvious that the new State flag was in no sense a rival of the National Flag. But for historical and other reasons connected with the freedom struggle in the State, the need for the continuance of this flag was recognized. The Union Flag to which we continue our allegiance as part of the Union will occupy the supremely distinctive place in the State.

President of India

It was agreed that the powers to grant reprieve commute

death sentences, etc. should also belong to the President of the Union.

Headship of the State

I am glad to inform this House that the Government of India have appreciated the principle proposed by the Basic Principles Committee as adopted by this Assembly in regard to the abolition of the hereditary rulership of the State. In order to accommodate this principle, the following arrangement was mutually agreed upon:

(i) The Head of the State shall be the person recognized by the President of the Union on the recommendation of the Legislature of the State;
(ii) He shall hold office during the pleasure of the President;
(iii) He may, by writing under his hand addressed to the President, resign his office; and
(iv) Subject to the foregoing provisions, the Head of the State shall hold office for a term of five years from the date he enters upon his office.

Financial Integration

In regard to this subject, we agreed that it would be necessary to evolve some sort of financial arrangement between the State and the Indian Union. But as this involved far reaching consequences, it was felt that a detailed and objective examination of this subject would be necessary.

Emergency Powers

On behalf of the Government of India, it was stated that the application of Article 352 of the Constitution was necessary as it related to vital matters affecting the security of the State. They did not press for the application of Article 356 or 360.

On behalf of the Kashmir Delegation, it was stated that the application of Article 352 to the State was not necessary. In the event of war on external aggression, item 1 in the Seventh Schedule relating to the defence of India applied and the Government of India would have full authority to take any steps in connection with defence, etc. In particular, we were averse to internal disturbance being referred to in this connection as even some petty internal disorder might be considered sufficient for the application of Article 352.

In reply it was pointed out that Article 352 could only be applied in a state of grave emergency and not because of some small disorder or disturbance.

In order to meet our view point, it was suggested on behalf of the Government of India that Article 352 might be accepted as it is with the addition at the end of the first paragraph (1) of the following words:

> "but in regard to internal disturbance at the request or with concurrence of the Government of the State".

We generally accepted this position, but wanted some time to consider the implications and consequences as laid down in Article 353, 358 and 359, which on the whole accepted. In regard to Article 354, we wanted to examine it further before expressing our opinion.

Conduct of Elections to Houses of Parliament

Article 324 of the Indian Constitution already applies to the State in so far as it relates to elections to Parliament and to the offices of the President and the Vice-President of India.

I have put before this House the broad indications of the agreement arrived at between us and the Government of India. As the Hon'ble Members will, no doubt, observe, the attitude of the Government of India has been most helpful. A satisfactory position has emerged and we are now able to assess the basic issues of our constitutional relationship with India in clearer terms. There has been a good deal of accommodation of our respective points of view. Both the representatives of Government of India and the Kashmir Delegation have been impelled by the desire to strengthen future the existing relationship to remove all security and vagueness. We are convinced, as ever before, that we have the full support both of the Government and the people of India in the fulfilment of our democratic ideals and the realization of our objectives.

This good will and amity, I am sure, will result in the consolidation of freedom and democracy in our country. I may however, emphasize, that the supreme guarantee of our relationship with India is the identity of the democratic and secular aspirations, which have guided the people of India as well as those of Jammu and Kashmir in their struggle for emancipation and before which all constitutional safeguards will take a secondary position.

It is of course, for the Constituent Assembly which is seized of these matters to determine the extent and scope of the State's accession to India. The Assembly may agree to continue this relationship on the present basis or extend its scope as it might like and consider feasible and proper. In the course of framing the Constitution for the State, the Hon'ble Members of this Assembly will have an opportunity of discussing these agreements and expressing their views thereon.

I thank you Sir, for affording me this opportunity to place before the Hon'ble Members of the House the result of our recent talks with the representatives of the Government of India.

APPENDIX II—7

[1]Statement of Pt. Jawahar Lal Nehru, Prime Minister of India in the House of People on July 24, 1952

"... Now, the position since the Constitution was framed, is thus contained in Article 370 and in the President's Order following it. Article 370 was obviously of a transitional nature, and it allowed the President to make any additions to it, any variations to it, later on, the subject being that if any change or addition was required, we need not have to go through the cumbrous process of amending our Constitution, but the President was given authority to amend it in the sense of adding a subject, part of a subject, whatever it was to the other subjects in regard to Kashmir. But in Article 370, the old principle was repeated and emphasized that all these changes or any change required the approval of the Constituent Assembly of Jammu and Kashmir State. . . ."

"... Now in regard to the talks we have had, the position, obviously the admitted position, is that the Jammu and Kashmir State is a constituent part or unit of the Indian Republic. It is a unit of India and is therefore a part of the territory of India. That is the basic position.

The question of citizenship arose obviously. Full citizenship applies there. But our friends from Kashmir were very apprehensive about one of two matters. For a long time past. In the Maharaja's time, there had been laws there preventing any outsider, that is, any person from outside Kashmir, from acquiring or holding land in Kashmir, if I may mention it in the old days the Maharaja was very much afraid of a large number of Englishmen coming and settling down there. Because the climate is delectable, and acquiring property. So, although most of their rights were taken away from the Maharaja under the British rule, the Maharaja stuck to this that nobody from outside should acquire land there. And that continues. And in the State Subjects notification by the Maharaja, they have defined four grades of subjects. Class number one, class two, class three and class four.

1. As per press release issued by Press Information of Bureau, Government of India dated July 24, 1952.

And unless you come in one of these classes, you just cannot acquire land there, or any immovable property. So the present Government of Kashmir is very anxious to preserve that right because, they are afraid, and I think rightly afraid, that Kashmir would be over run by people whose sole qualification might be the possession of too much money and nothing else, who might buy up and get the delectable places. Now they want to vary the old Maharaja's law to liberalize it, but nevertheless to have checks on the acquisition of lands by persons from outside. So far as we are concerned, I agree that under article 19, clause (5) of our Constitution we think it is clearly permissible both in regard to the existing law and any subsequent legislation. However, we agreed that this should be cleared up. The old State's subjects definition gave certain privileges regarding the acquisition of land, the services, and other minor things, I think, state scholarships and the rest. So, we agreed and noted down this.

The State Legislature shall have power to define and regulate the rights and privileges of the permanent residents of the State, more especially in regard to the acquisition of immovable property appointments to services and like matters. Till then the existing State law should apply.

Then there was another matter relating to citizenship because owing to these troubles in Kashmir since 1947 and little before and after there have been large number of people who have gone out of Kashmir but want to return. So there must be provision made for them to return. In fact in our own Constitution, some provision has been made and I might inform the House that this question was raised early this year or last year about the inclusion of a large number of migrants from East Bengal. We could not include them in our electoral rolls, because they came too late. We are including them now. Those that fulfil the conditions will all come in. So those who had gone away from Kashmir to Pakistan or elsewhere and who normally speaking might not be eligible for citizenship should be provided for, if they want to return so we said:

Special provision should be made in the laws governing citizenship for the return of those permanent residents of Jammu and Kashmir State, who went to Pakistan in connection with the disturbances of 1947 or earlier in fear of them, and could not return if they return they should be entitled to the rights and privileges and obligations of citizenship.

Then came the question of fundamental rights. Now there was general agreement that there should fundamental rights and these fundamental rights should apply to the State. But again there were great apprehensions in the minds of our friends from Kashmir. First of all, the question was how far these fundamental rights might not conic in the way of their land legislation now or any later development of it. Certainly we did not want them to come in the way of their land legislation. We like their land legislation. We thought it was very good, in fact it is quite impossible to upset a thing that has been done, but we said the matter should be cleared.

The second thing was this. Owing to all this business of invasion of Kashmir State, war, cease fire, all kinds of continuing tensions, difficulties due to infiltration, etc., constant attempts are made by infiltration, espionage cases are repeatedly heard. There is sabotage and the rest; but if you go to that State, you find normalcy there, that is to say, the state is functioning adequately normally, but behind that normalcy there is this tension, constant tension of an enemy trying to come in to create trouble, to disturb and all that. And the State Government has to be wary and watchful all the time and so we were told that it was possible that some part of the fundamental rights provisions might very well hamper the activities of the State Government from taking these precautions and these measures. We agreed that it was essential and in the interests of Kashmir situated as the State is now that the State Government should have that authority. So subject to this, further consideration can be given to it as to how this could be done, so that a fuller consideration of this and like matters was necessary so that the fundamental rights might be applied with such modifications and exceptions as might be considered necessary from this point of view, and agreed upon.

Then in regard to the Supreme Court it was agreed that the Supreme Court should have original jurisdiction in respect of disputes mentioned in Article 131 of the constitution of India. It was further agreed that the Supreme Court should have jurisdiction in regard to fundamental rights, which are applied to that State. On behalf of the Government of India we recommended that the advisory tribunal in the State which is designated as His Highness's Board of Judicial Advisors should be abolished and the jurisdiction exercised by it should be vested in the Supreme

Court of India that is to say that the Supreme Court should be the final Court of Appeal in all civil and criminal matters as laid down in the Constitution of India. The Kashmir Government delegation had no objection to this. They were prepared to agree but they said they would like to consider the matter in some detail further.

Now I come to the question which has been much discussed and referred to in the newspapers, the question of the Head of the State.

I might mention that apart from past history when this Constituent Assembly met in Kashmir the inaugural address to that Assembly stated quite clearly some of the policies that they were going to pursue, and among these policies was the election, by democratic process, of the head of the State. That has been the declared policy of the National Conference Organization in Kashmir for a long time. We had no objection with regard to the enunciation of that principle then. Now after careful consideration because we have always had to consider two matters: firstly, to give effect to the wishes of the people of the State, and secondly, to give effect to our own Constitution. We have come to an agreed formula. Of course, you will not attach too much importance to the language. A word here or there. For legal and constitutional purposes the words may be changed, but it describes the way we have been thinking and what we have agreed to. Now it was agreed (1) that the Head of the State shall be the person recognized by the President on the recommendation of the legislature of the State. How the Legislature of the state recommends is a matter for the Legislature. Whether it is by the process of election or not it is for them to decide; it may be by the process of a majority or two-thirds majority, it is entirely for them to decide. Anyhow they recommend and then it is for the President to recognize, (2) He that is Head of the State, shall hold office during the pleasure of the President, (3) He the Head of the State may by writing under his hand addressed to the President. Resign his office, and (4) Subject to the foregoing provisions of this article, the Head of the State shall hold office for a term of five years from the date he enters upon his office provided that he shall notwithstanding the expiration of his term, continue to hold office until his successor enters upon his office. That is so-far as the Head of the State is concerned.

Then there has been a good deal of misunderstanding in regard to the National Flag. This has been cleared up, I think, adequately by public statements made. Nevertheless, we thought that this should be further cleared up. Sheikh Abdullah, the Prime Minister of Jammu and Kashmir State had stated publicly that the question did not arise so far as they were concerned. Because the National Flag was the supreme flag and it had exactly the same status and position in the Jammu and Kashmir state as in any other part of India. The State flag was in no sense a rival to the National flag but for historical and sentimental reasons connected with their struggle for freedom in Kashmir, they wanted this state symbol to continue. This was agreed. It was added that this should be made clear in a formal manner, preferably by the Constituent Assembly of the State.

Thus in regard to the President of India, it was agreed that the powers to reprieve and commute death sentences, etc. should belong to the President of India.

There has been some talk about financial integration. It was decided that such financial arrangements between the State and the Government of India should be considered further and details worked out. The position as I said, is a dynamic changing one. Matters have to be gone into in some detail; so whatever the financial arrangements might be, we shall gradually work them out.

Then there is the question of emergency powers contained in our Constitution, more especially in our article 352 of the Constitution, it was agreed to; I will remind the House what article 352 is in case of invasion, external danger or internal disturbances, the President has power to declare a state of emergency and then various consequences flow from it. This parliament is then seized of the position. Now this was agreed to; but the friends from Kashmir were slightly apprehensive of what internal disturbances meant there. For the rest they have said, of course, if there is a grave emergency this should happen. So, with regard to adding some words to clear up, not to clear up that matter but rather to bring in the fact that in the case of internal disturbances any action taken should be with the concurrence of the Government of the State. It was agreed that article 352 of the Constitution should apply to the State with the addition at the end of the first paragraph of the following words:

"but in regard to internal disturbances, at the request or with the concurrence of the Government of the State."

That is the state of emergency will be declared with the concurrence of the Government of the State.

These are the principal things that have been discussed and I think that we have arrived at very satisfactory decisions, agreements which are in consonance with the wishes of the people of Kashmir and in consonance with our Constitution.

ANNEXURE II—8

Dr. Rajendra Prasad's note to Shri Jawahar Lal Nehru dated September 6, 1952

Rashtrapati Niwas
Simla
6th September 1952

My dear Prime Minister,

When you last saw me, I promised to send you a note on the legal and Constitutional aspect of the proposal to substitute a system of elected head for the Jammu and Kashmir State in place of the existing Rajpramukh. I now enclose a note for your consideration. In view of the complexity and importance of the issues involved, I have no doubt that the Attorney General and the Law Minister will be consulted.

I have received a memorial from the Maharaja, a copy of which, I understand, has also been received by you. Presumably, the Minister for States has also received a copy. I shall be glad in due course to have the comments of yourself and the Minister for States on this memorial.

I am leaving Simla on the morning of Sunday, the 7th September for places in the interior of Himachal Pradesh, but will be back by the evening of Tuesday, the 9th September.

I am sending copies of this letter with enclosure to the Ministers for Education, Defence and States.

Yours sincerely,

Rajendra Prasad

Shri Jawaharlal Nehru
Prime Minister

Enclosure:

The Prime Minister of Jammu and Kashmir has forwarded a copy of the resolution of the Constituent Assembly of the Jammu and Kashmir State relating to the substitution of a system of elected head of the state in place of Rajapramukh as at present with a request to the Government of India to take action to enable effect being given to the resolution. Along with the resolution two draft notifications to be issued by the President, one under clause (1) of that Article, have also been received. The former draft involves amendment of a provision of the Constitution of India and the latter contemplates a modification of two other provisions of the Constitution in its application to the State of Jammu and Kashmir. The proposal raises questions of considerable importance concerning the Constitutional scope of the proposed notifications and also about the competence of the President to have repeated recourse to the extraordinary powers conferred on him by the Article in question.

Before I take up this question it is very necessary to know whether any steps are being taken to amend the present Constitution of the State of Jammu and Kashmir. It appears from paragraph 6 of the resolution that there is already in existence the Jammu and Kashmir Constitution Act of 1996, which has been amended by Act No. XVII of 2008. Under this Constitution the Maharaja is presumably the head of the State, and it would obviously be necessary, as a first step, to amend that Constitution if it is decided to give immediate effect to the proposal now under consideration. Not having a copy of the Jammu and Kashmir Constitution Act, I am not in a position to say whether provision exists in that Constitution for its amendment, but inasmuch as it has been amended as recently as the Hindu Year 2008, I believe such provision does exist. I suggest that this question needs looking into.

The first draft notification enclosed with the letter of the Prime Minister of Jammu and Kashmir purports to be issued under clause (3) of Article 370. This clause is of a peculiar and exceptional nature in as much as it authorises amendments of Constitution by an executive act of the Government of India as distinguished from Parliament. The Constitution of India contemplates and lays down, apart from this article, two methods for its amendment. An amendment proper of the Constitution can be effected by the special procedure laid down in Article 368. There are certain other provisions in the Constitution in regard to which it is specially and specifically laid down that Parliament, by ordinary legislation can effect changes. In both these cases, it is the Parliament alone which can effect amendments. In the first case, ever the power of Parliament to amend the Constitution is limited in as much as it can do so only if the special procedure in Article 368 is followed. In the second group of cases the Parliament is left free to pass legislation which may amount to amendment of the Constitution laid down. Nowhere else, as far as I can see is there any provision authorising the executive Government to make amendments in the Constitution, the temporary provisions contained in the Articles 391 and 392 having come to an end. There can be no doubt that Article 370, and particularly clause (3) thereof, is of an exceptional nature. While it safeguards in clause (2) the right of the Constituent Assembly of Jammu and Kashmir to revise or annul any action taken by the Government of that State in giving concurrence under clause 1(b)(ii) and the second proviso to clause l(d) of Article 370, it excludes altogether the Parliament of India from having any say regarding the Constitution of Jammu and Kashmir and places full power in the hands of the government including the power to amend the Constitution of India. It is therefore, necessary to examine the wording of this peculiar clause with some care for a correct appreciation of the comprehensive terms that:

> "Notwithstanding anything in the foregoing provisions of this article, the President may, by public notification, declare that this article shall cease to be operative or shall be operative only with such exceptions and modifications and from such date he may specify:
>
> "Provided that the recommendation of the Constituent Assembly of the State referred to in clause (2) shall be necessary before the President issues such a notification."

Clause (1) of this Article lays down that:

(a) the provisions of Article 238 shall not apply in relation to the State of Jammu and Kashmir;

(b) that the power of Parliament to make laws for the said State shall be limited to:

  (i) those matters in the Union list and the concurrent list which, in consultation with the Government of State, arc declared by the President to correspond to matters specified in the instrument of Accession governing the accession of the ate to the Dominion of India as the matter with respect to which the Dominion Legislature may make laws for that State; and

(ii) such other matters in the said Lists as with the concurrence of the Government of the State the President may by order specify.

Then follows explanation of the term "Government of the State" namely, the person for the time being recognized by the President as the Maharaja of Jammu and Kashmir acting on the advice under the Maharaja's proclamation dated the fifth day of March 1948.

The Article proceeds further to lay down in paragraph (c) and (d) of clause (1) that the provision(s) of Article 1 and of the Article shall apply in relation to that State; and that such of the other provisions of the Constitution shall apply in relation to that state subject to such exceptions and modifications as the President may by order specify: Provided that no such order which relates to the matter specified in the Instrument of Accession of the State referred to in paragraph (1) of sub-clause (b) shall be issued except in consultation with the Government of the State: and provided further that no such order which relates to matters other than those referred to in the last proceeding provision shall be issued with the concurrence of that Government.

The present proposal is to amend the Explanation in clause (1) by substituting for the words "as the Maharaja of Jammu and Kashmir acting the advice of the Council of Ministers for the time being in office under the Maharaja's Proclamation dated the fifth of March 1948." The word "as the Sadar-i-Riyasat of Jammu and Kashmir acting on the advice of the Council of Minister for the time being in office."

It is worthnothing that, while the proviso to clause (3) of Article 370 lays down that the recommendation of the Constituent Assembly of the State is a condition precedent to the issue of any notification by the President under the substantive provisions of the clause, it does not make it obligatory for the President to issue a notification to give effect to any recommendation that he may receive from the Constituent Assembly. Presumably it is deliberately so worded in order that the recommendation of the

Constituent Assembly could be examined on its merits before the President is advised to issue a notification under that clause. It is also worthnoting that the clause envisages two alternatives for the President, namely, either to declare that the whole of Article 370 shall cease to be operative or to declare that the whole of only with exceptions and modifications. In either case the President is further required to specify the date from which the notification is to take effect.

As I have already observed, the scope of this Article, if literally intercepted is exceedingly wide. Suppose the first alternative is adopted and whole of the Article is declared to be inoperative, what will be the result? One view would be that the Article being in the nature of an exception to the application of the Constitution of the State of Jammu and Kashmir, abrogation of the Article would result in the whole Constitution becoming applicable to the State of Jammu and Kashmir without any exception or modification. But the Article itself has been very peculiarly worded, for paragraph (c) of clause (I) of that Article expressly applies the provision of Article and of that Article to the State. In fact, it is because of this application of Article 1 to the State that the State is included within the territories of the Union. The abrogation of Article 370 abrogates along with the application of Article 1 to the State with the result that the State ceases to be part of the territory of India. I do not think that this could have been the intention of the framers of the Constitution for nowhere is the President empowered to exclude any portion of the territories of India from the Union. As a matter of fact, Article 2 contemplates the admission of fresh territories into the Union or the establishment of new States, but nowhere does the Constitution contemplate the exclusion of any territory from the territories of the Union.

Further, under the second alternative envisaged in clause (3), extensive power is conferred on the President to apply the Constitution to the State with such exceptions and modifications as may be specified in the notification and the question at once arises whether such an extensive power is exercisable from time to time or is exhausted by a single exercise thereof, judging by the language employed and by the very exceptional nature of the power conferred. I have little doubt myself that the intention is that the power is to be exercised only once, for then alone would it be possible to determine with precision which particular provisions should be excepted and which modified. The fact that President is also required to specify the date from which the notification is to take effect also tends to confirm this view. Although the phrase "exceptions modification" is used, there can be no doubt that what is involved is really an amendment by executive order of the Constitution in relation to the State of Jammu and Kashmir. Parliament could never have intended that such an extraordinary power of amending the Constitution by executive order was to be enjoyed without any limitation as to the number of times on which it could be exercised or as to the period within which it was exercisable or as to the scope and extent of the modifications and exceptions that could be made. It cannot be seriously maintained that for all time to come the application of our Constitution to Jammu and Kashmir would derive its authority from Article 370 to the complete exclusion of Parliament. The marginal note to Article 370 itself describes the nature of the Article as "Temporary Provision with respect to the State of Jammu and Kashmir". The conclusion, therefore, seems to me to be irresistible that clause (3) of Article 370 was not intended to be used from time to time. The correct view appears to be that recourse is to be had to this clause only when the Constituent Assembly of the State has been fully framed.

APPENDIX II—9

[1]The Constitution (Application to Jammu and Kashmir) Order, 1954 C.O. 48

In exercise of the powers conferred by clause (1) of article 370 of the Constitution, the President, with the concurrence of the Government of the State of Jammu and Kashmir, is pleased to make the following Order:

1. (1) This Order may be called the Constitution (Application to Jammu and Kashmir) Order, 1954.
   (2) It shall come into force on the fourteenth day of May 1954, and shall thereupon supersede the Constitution (Application to Jammu and Kashmir) Order, 1950.

2. The provisions of the Constitution which in addition to article 1 and article 370, shall apply in relation to the State of Jammu and Kashmir and the exceptions and modifications subject to which they shall so apply shall be as follows:

1. The preamble.
2. Part I: To article 3, there shall be added the following further proviso namely:

"Provided further that no Bill providing for increasing or diminishing the area of the State of Jammu and Kashmir or altering the name or boundary of that State shall be introduced in Parliament without the consent of the Legislature of that State."

3. Part II: (a) This part shall be deemed to have been applicable in relation to the State of Jammu and Kashmir as from the 26th day of January, 1950.

(b) To article 7, there shall be added the following further proviso namely:

1. Published in the Gazette of India, Extraordinary, Part II, Section 3, dated 14th May, 1954.

"Provided further that nothing in this article shall apply to a permanent resident of the State of Jammu and Kashmir who after having so migrated to the territory now included in the Pakistan, returns to the territory of that State under a permit for resettlement in that State or permanent return issued by or under the authority of any law made by the Legislature of that State, and every such person shall be deemed to be a citizen of India".

4. Part III: (a) In article 13, references to the commencement of the Constitution shall be construed as reference to the commencement of this Order.

(b) In clause (4) of article 15, the reference to Schedule Tribes shall be omitted.

(c) In clause (3) of article 16, the reference to the State shall be construed as not including a reference to the State of Jammu and Kashmir.

(d) In article 19, for a period of five years from the commencement of this order:

(i) in clauses (3) and (4), after the words "in the interest of" the words "the security of the State or" shall be inserted;

(ii) in clause (5) for the words "or for the protection of the interests of any Scheduled Tribes" the words "or in the interests of the security of the State" shall be substituted; and

(iii) the following new clause shall be added, namely:
'(7) The words "reasonable restrictions" occurring in clauses (2), (3), (4) and (5) shall be construed as meaning such restrictions as the appropriate Legislature deems reasonable'.

(e) In clauses (4) and (7) of article 22, for the word "Parliament", the words "the Legislature of the State" shall be substituted.

(f) In article 31, clauses (3), (4) and (6) shall be omitted; and for clause (5) there shall be substituted the following clause, namely:

"5 Nothing in clause (2) shall effect—

(a) the provisions of any existing law; or

(b) the provisions of any law which the State may hereafter make—

(i) for the purpose of imposing or levying any tax or penalty; or

(ii) for the promotion of public health or the prevention of danger to life or property; or

(iii) with respect to property declared by law to be evacuee property".

(g) In article 31-A, the proviso to clause (1), shall be omitted; and for sub-clause (a) of clause (2), the following sub-clause shall be substituted, namely:

'(a) "estate" shall mean land which is occupied or has been let for agricultural purposes or for purposes subservient to agriculture, or for pasture, and includes—

(i) sites of buildings and other structures on such land;

(ii) trees standing on such land;

(iii) forest land and wooded waste;

(iv) area covered by or fields floating over water;

(v) sites of jandars and gharats;

(vi) any jagir, inam, muafi or mukarrari or other similar grant; but does not include—

(i) the site of any building in any town, or town area or village abadi or any land appurtenant to any such building or site;

(ii) any land which is occupied as the site of a town or village; or

(iii) any land reserved for building purposes in a municipality or notified area or cantonment or town area or any area which a town planning scheme is sanctioned".

(h) In article 32, clause (3) shall be omitted; and after clause (2) the following new clause shall be inserted, namely:

"(2-A) Without prejudice to the powers conferred by clauses (1) and (2), the High Court shall have power throughout the territories in relation to which it exercises jurisdiction to issue to any person or authority, including in appropriate cases any Government within those territories, directions or orders or writs, including writs in the nature of *habeas corpus*, *mandamus*, prohibition, *quo warranto* and *certiorari*, or any of them, for the enforcement of any of the rights conferred by this Part."

(i) In article 35—

(i) references to the commencement of the Constitution shall be construed as reference to the commencement of this Order;

(ii) in clause (a) (i), the words, figures and brackets "clause (3) of article 16, clause (3) of article 32" shall be omitted; and

(iii) after clause (b), the following clause shall be added namely:

"(c) no law with respect to preventive detention made by the Legislature of the State of Jammu and Kashmir, whether before or after the commencement of the Constitution Application to Jammu and Kashmir) Order, 1954, shall be void on the ground that it is unconsistent with any of the provisions of this part, but any such law shall, to the extent of such unconsistency, cease to have effect on the expiration of five years from the commencement of the said Order, except as respects things done or omitted to be done before the expiration thereof.

(j) After article 35, the following new article shall be added namely:

'35-A. Saving of laws with respect to permanent residents and their right: Notwithstanding anything contained in this Constitution, no existing law in force in the State of Jammu and Kashmir, and no law hereafter enacted by the Legislature of the State,—

(a) defining the classes of persons who are, or shall be, permanent residents of the State of Jammu and Kashmir; or

(b) conferring on such permanent residents any special right and privileges or imposing upon other persons any restrictions as respects—

(i) employment under the State Government;
(ii) acquisition of immovable property in the State;
(iii) settlement in the State; or
(iv) right to scholarships and such other forms of aid as the State Government may provide,

shall be void on the ground that it is inconsistent with or takes away or abridges any rights conferred on the other citizens of India by any provision of this Part".

5. Part V: (a) In articles 54 and 55, references to the elected members of the House of the people and to each such member shall include references to the representatives of the State of Jammu and Kashmir in that House; and the population of the State shall be deemed to be forty-four lakhs and ten thousand.

(b) In the proviso to clause (1) of article 73, the words "or in any law made by Parliament" shall be omitted.

(c) Article 81 shall apply subject to the modification that the representatives of the State in the House of the people shall be appointed by the President on the recommendation of the Legislature of the State.

(d) In article 134, clause (2), after the words "Parliament may", the words "on the request of the Legislature of the State" shall be inserted.

(e) Articles 135, 136 and 139 shall be omitted.

(f) In articles 149 and 150, references to the States shall he construed as not including the State of Jammu and Kashmir.

(g) In article 151, clause (2) shall be omitted.

6. Part XI: (a) In article 246, the words, brackets and figures "Notwithstanding anything in clauses (2) and (3)" occurring in clause (1) and clauses (2), (3) and (4) shall be omitted.

(b) Articles 248 and 249 shall be omitted.

(c) In article 250, for the words "to any of the matters enumerated in the State List", the words "also to matters not enumerated in the Union List" shall be substituted.

(d) In article 251, for the words and figures, "articles 249 and 250", the word and figures "article 250" shall be substituted, and the words "under this Constitution" shall be omitted; and for the words "under either of the said articles", the words "under the said article" shall be substituted.

(e) To article 253, the following proviso shall be added, namely:

"Provided that after the commencement of the Constitution (Application to Jammu and Kashmir) Order, 1954, no decision affecting the disposition of the State of Jammu and Kashmir shall be made by the Government of India without the consent of the Government of that State".

(f) In article 254, the words, brackets and figure "or to any provision of an existing law with respect to one of the matters enumerated in the Concurrent List, then, subject to the provisions of clause (2)" and the words "or as the case may be, the existing law", occurring in clause (1), and the whole of clause (2) shall be omitted.

(g) Article 255 shall be omitted.

(h) Article 256 shall be renumbered as clause (1) of that article, and the following new clause shall be added thereto, namely:

"(2) The State of Jammu and Kashmir shall so exercise its executive power as to facilitate the discharge by the Union of its duties and responsibilities under the Constitution in relation to that State; and in particular, the said State shall, if so required by the Union, acquire or requisition property on behalf and at the expense of the Union, or if the property belongs to the State, transfer it to the Union on such terms as may be agreed, or in default of agreement, as may be determined by an arbitrator appointed by the Chief Justice of India."

(i) Article 259 shall be omitted.

(j) In clause (2) of Article 261, the words "made by Parliament" shall be omitted.

7. Part XII: (a) Clause (2) of article 267, article 273, clause 2 of article 283, articles 290 and 291 shall be omitted.

(b) In articles 266, 282, 284, 298, 299 and 300, references to the State or States shall be construed as not including references to the State of Jammu and Kashmir.

(c) In articles 277 and 295, references to the commencement of the Constitution shall be construed as references to the commencement of this Order.

8. Part XIII: (a) In clause (1) of article 303, the words "by virtue of any entry relating to trade and commerce in any of the Lists in Seventh Schedule" shall be omitted.

(b) In article 306, references to the commencement of the Constitution shall be construed as references to the commencement of this Order.

9. Part XIV: In article 308, after the words "First Schedule", the words "other than the State of Jammu and Kashmir" shall be added.

10. Part XV: (a) Article 324 shall apply only in so far as it relates to elections to Parliament and to the offices of President and Vice-President.

(b) Articles 235, 326, 327, 328 and 329 shall be omitted.

11. Part XVI: (a) In article 330, references to the "Scheduled Tribes" shall be omitted.

(b) Articles 331, 332, 333, 336, 337, 339 and 342 shall be omitted.

(c) In articles 334 and 335 references to the State or States shall be construed as not including references to the State of Jammu and Kashmir.

12. Part XVII: The provisions of this Part shall apply only in so far as they relates to—

(i) the official language of the Union;

(ii) the official language for communication between one State and another, or between a State and the Union; and

(iii) the language of the proceedings in the Supreme Court.

13. Part XVIII: (a) To article 352, the following new clause shall be added, namely:

"(4) No proclamation of Emergency made on grounds only of internal disturbance or imminent danger thereof shall have effect in relation to the State of Jammu and Kashmir (except as respects article 354) unless it is made at the request or with the concurrence of Government of that State."

(b) Articles 356, 357 and 360 shall be omitted.

14. Part XIX: (a) In article 361, after clause (4), the following shall be added, namely:

"(5) The provisions of this article shall apply in relation to the Sadar-i-Riyasat of Jammu and Kashmir as they apply in relation to a Rajpramukh, but without prejudice to the provisions of the Constitution of that State".

(b) Articles 362 and 365 shall be omitted.

(c) In article 366, clause (21) shall be omitted.

(d) To article 367, there shall be added, the following clause, namely:

(4) For the purposes of this Constitution as it applies in relation to the State of Jammu and Kashmir—

(a) references to this Constitution or to the provisions thereof shall be construed as references to the Constitution or the provisions thereof as applied in relation to the said State;

(b) references to the Government of the said State shall be construed as including references to the Sadar-i-Riyasat acting on the advice of his Council of Ministers;

(c) references to a High Court shall include references to the High Court of Jammu and Kashmir;

(d) references to the Legislature or the Legislative Assembly of the said State shall be construed as including references to the Constituent Assembly of the said State;

(c) references to the permanent residents of the said State shall be construed as meaning persons who, before the commencements of the Constitution (Application to Jammu and Kashmir) Order, 1954, were recognised as State subject under the law in force in the State or who are recognised by any law made by the Legislature of the State as permanent residents of the State; and

(f) references to the Rajpramukh shall be construed as references to the persons for the time being recognized by the President as the Sadar-i-Riyasat of Jammu and Kashmir and as including references to any person for the time being recognised by the President as being competent to exercise the powers of the Sadar-i-Riyasat".

15. Part XX: To article 368, the following proviso shall be added, namely:—

"Provided further that no such amendment shall have effect in relation to the State of Jammu and Kashmir unless applied by order of the President under clause (I) of Article 370".

16. Part XXI: (a) Articles 369, 371, 373, clauses (1), (2), (3) and (5) of article 374 and articles 376 to 392 shall be omitted.

(b) In article 372—

(i) clauses (2) and (3) shall be omitted;

(ii) references to the laws in force in the territory of India shall include references, to Hidayats, Ailans, Ishtihars, circulars, Robkars, Irshads, Yadashts, State, Council Resolutions, Resolutions of the Constitution Assembly, and other instruments having the force of law in the territory of the State of Jammu and Kashmir; and

(iii) references to the commencement of the Constitution shall be construed as references to the commencement of this Order.

(c) In clause (4) of article 374, the reference to the authority functioning as the Privy Council of a State shall be construed as a reference to the Advisory Board constituted under the Jammu and Kashmir Constitution Act, 1996, and references to the commencements of the Constitution shall be construed as references to the commencement of this Order.

17. Part XXII: Articles 394 and 395 shall be omitted.

18. First Schedule.

19. Second Schedule: Paragraph 6 shall be omitted.

20. Third Schedule: Forms V, VI, VII & VIII shall be omitted.

21. Fourth Schedule.

22. Seventh Schedule: (a) In the Union List—

(i) for entry 3, the entry "3. Administration of cantonments" shall be substituted;

(ii) entries 8, 9, 33 and 34, the words "trading corporations including" in entry 43, entries 44, 50, 52, 54, 55, 60, 67, 69, 78 and 79, the words "inter-State migration"' in entry 81, and entry 97 shall be omitted.

APPENDIX III

Gajendragadkar Commission Report

November 1968

CHAPTER I

SCOPE OF THE INQUIRY

1.01. The Jammu and Kashmir Commission of Inquiry was appointed by the Government of Jammu and Kashmir, in consultation with the Union Government, by their Order No. 878-D of 1967, dated 6 November 1967. Its terms of reference were as follows:

"(i) To make an assessment of the development programmes apportioned to the various regions of the State and to recommend measures necessary to give assurance that the resources available to the State Government are being shared equitably and also to convey a feeling of equal participation in the integrated development of the State.

"(ii) To examine the recruitment policies of Government and to recommend measures for giving an equitable share in Government employment to the various regions and communities, having special regard to the claim of the Scheduled Castes and other economically, educationally and socially backward communities, classes and groups among the citizens of the State consistently with the maintenance of efficiency of administration.

"(iii) To examine the policies of the State Government

regarding admissions to institutions of higher education and the schemes of assistance by way of scholarships and loans, with a view to ensuring an equitable distribution of the available facilities to the various regions and communities, and having special regard to the claims of the Scheduled Castes and other economically, educationally and socially backward communities, classes and groups among the citizens of the State.

"(iv) To consider generally the causes that lead to irritations and tensions and to recommend remedial measures."

1.02. In considering the above matters, the Commission was required to take note of the provisions contained in Part III "Fundamental Rights", as well as other provisions of the Constitution of India as made applicable to the State of Jammu and Kashmir and of the Directive Principles of State Policy laid down in Part IV of the Constitution of Jammu and Kashmir and particularly of Section 23 thereof.

1.03. It took some time to secure the services of a senior and experienced officer to work as Secretary to the Commission. Mr. B.P. Bagchi, ICS, joined the Commission as its Secretary on 4 December 1967 and we held our first meeting in Delhi on the same day. We decided to call by public notice for memoranda from all parties, groups, associations, institutions, societies and individuals interested in the problems referred to the Commission, by 31 January 1968. We also decided that after the contents of the memoranda had been analysed, examined and collated, the Commission should visit Jammu and Srinagar for recording oral evidence. A Press-note to this effect was issued and paid advertisements published in most of the leading English dailies of the country and the local papers of the Jammu and Kashmir State.

1.04. In January 1968, the President of the Jammu and Kashmir Plebiscite Front wrote to the Chairman that his party "could not get necessary time to determine its attitude towards the Commission of Inquiry" or "to collect material required for submission to the Commission." He, therefore, requested that the last date for the submission, of memoranda be extended. Similar requests were received from the National Conference and from

Shri Kushak Bakula on behalf of the people of Ladakh and others. Many asked for an extension of time on grounds of the inclemency of the weather and the unusual severity of the winter in parts of the Jammu and Kashmir State which made them practically inaccessible. As these grounds were legitimate, the last date for the submission of memoranda was extended to 31 March 1968.

1.05. At three meetings held in Delhi on 15 December 1967, 5 and 6 January 1968 and 19 April 1968, we settled the various details pertaining to the functioning of the Commission's Secretariat and the programme and procedure of the Commission. The main decisions were:—

(i) That the Commission should first visit Srinagar for recording evidence and then go to Jammu. Later, the Commission should visit the Valley again for recording further evidence. The evidence of the parties belonging to the Valley and Ladakh should be recorded at Srinagar in June and that of the parties of Jammu in the second half of August. The Commission should also visit such other areas, including Ladakh... as it might consider necessary.

(ii) That the hearings by the Commission should be held in camera; but in order to expedite the collection of evidence the State Government should be requested to depute a senior officer to be present at the sittings so that he could immediately take steps to furnish such information as might be required.

(iii) That copies of memoranda received by the Commission should be supplied on payment of copying charges to those who had filed memoranda themselves and wished to give evidence before it.

1.06. We received in all 93 memoranda from different associations, groups and individuals. The list of those who submitted memoranda is given in Part A of Appendix 1. Certain parties first appeared before the Commission and subsequently submitted memoranda of supplementary memoranda or additional information, some of whom are listed in Part B of Appendix 1.

1.07. We also received a number of complaints or representations of a personal character. Some of these we referred to the State Government for such remedial action as they considered necessary and in response to certain others informed the persons concerned that the Commission was not going to deal with individual cases except those that might have relevance to its terms of reference.

1.08. Climatic conditions made it difficult for us to meet at Srinagar earlier than in June 1968. We held sittings daily at Srinagar from 6 June to 18 June 1968 (except on Sundays, 9 and 16 June) and heard the oral evidence of the associations, groups and individuals from Kashmir and Ladakh who had submitted memoranda and also of certain legislators and other individuals whom we had specially invited. A list of those who gave evidence at Srinagar is given in Appendix 2.

1.09. Sittings were held at Jammu daily from 22 August to 27 August 1968 for recording similar evidence. A list of those who appeared before us at Jammu is given in Appendix 3.

1.10. We assembled once again at Srinagar from 14 to 18 September 1968, mainly to hear, and hold discussions with, the Chief Minister and other Cabinet-Ministers of the State and senior officers of the State Government. A list of those who appeared before us during this session is given in Appendix 4.

1.11. Certain representatives from remote areas desired us to visit them to get a first-hand knowledge of the conditions there and their disabilities. It was not possible for the Commission as a whole to visit these areas. One of us, however, paid a visit to Ladakh in June 1968 and heard many officials and non-officials both at Leh and at Kargil. Two of us paid a brief visit to Poonch and Rajouri in August 1968 and to Doda, Kishtwar and Bhadarwah in September 1968 where they met certain local individuals and groups. Some memoranda and representations, dealing mainly with local problems, were also presented to them on these visits which have been considered by the Commission.

1.12. We finally met at Bombay from 25 to 29 November 1968 to complete our Report.

1.13. We received to utmost courtesy, co-operation and consideration from the Government of Jammu and Kashmir and we have pleasure in placing on record our appreciation and thanks to them. Our thanks are also due to the Union Government for their co-operation and assistance. Finally, we should like to thank to political parties, local organizations and associations and individuals who took the trouble to submit memoranda to us and to assist us by a frank discussion of the matters in issue. We are particularly grateful to those who, at considerable personal inconvenience, came from far-off places in the interior to place their views on the subjects before us.

CHAPTER II

Pleadings before the Commission

2.01. Of the 93 memoranda received by us, a little over one-third were from the Kashmir region, 51 from the Jammu region, four from Ladakh and six from outside the State. Only five (two from Jammu City, one each from Udhampur, Poonch and Srinagar) were from political parties while 12 were submitted by communal bodies. Of the rest, a little less than one-third were from associations, unions and communities, while the bulk of the remaining 47 were from individuals or groups of individuals. Forty memoranda were of a general nature and spoke only about the regions while 28 had a communal bias. In addition 12 were more or less unrelated to our terms of reference; 11 were from backward or depressed classes and the remaining two from Ex-Army personnel. Some parties who appeared before us subsequently presented memoranda or additional memoranda to supplement their oral evidence.

2.02. An analysis of the memoranda and the oral evidence recorded by the Commission shows that the grievances put forward by the memorialists and the witnesses can be broadly classified under four major Heads pertaining to (i) Development, (ii) Employment, (iii) Education, and (iv) Conditions giving rise to irritations and tensions. They can all be directly related to our terms of reference. Certain other grievances which fall in categories such as economic, fiscal, social and political, or those which pertain to a miscellaneous variety of subjects, such as tenancy laws, corruption in administration, breakdown of law and order, elections, discrimination in the issue of rations, etc. also have an inferential bearing on our terms of reference as causes tending to create irritations and tensions among the people.

2.03. *Development.—The* main complaint of several parties in regard to developmental matters was that planning was defective; that it showed a marked regional bias, as a result of which certain regions or areas, notably the Jammu region, Ladakh and the hilly, inaccessible areas of the State, had received altogether inadequate attention and their development had suffered in consequence. The alleged neglect of the tourist spots in the Jammu region was another grievance frequently voiced. It was represented that although the area of cultivable land in the Jammu region was larger than that in the Kashmir region, fewer irrigation schemes were taken up there for implementation and the expenditure incurred on them was disproportionately low. There were complaints that proper attention was not being paid towards the construction of roads and bridges in the backward areas of Jammu and Ladakh and that even drinking water facilities were not available in the Kandi areas of Jammu. The inadequacy of medical facilities, particularly the absence of mobile dispensaries, in the districts of Poonch and Kathua, was another grievance. The representatives from Ladakh pleaded that Ladakh was a delicate strategic area and needed special care and deft handling. Transport facilities, the prime need of this area, were woefully inadequate. They also stressed the need for providing enough electricity on a stable basis and for devising a suitable method whereby the funds allocated to Ladakh for developmental purposes were properly utilized and did not lapse. A suggestion was also made that the status of Ladakh in the State of Jammu and Kashmir should be formally recognized by including the word 'Ladakh' in the name of the State.

2.04. *Employment*.—Regarding employment in Government services, the complaints were of discrimination on communal and regional grounds in recruitment, favouritism and nepotism in promotions and lack of reservations for the Scheduled Castes and backward classes. Instances of unjust supersessions in the matter of promotions were cited. Many Jammu representatives felt aggrieved that the Jammu region was inadequately represented in the Secretariat and in various Government departments, and that frequently even peons, forest guards and Patwaries from Kashmir were posted in the Jammu region as though qualified persons to fill such posts could not be found locally: while, actually, it was alleged that Kashmiries with inferior qualifications were being preferred to better qualified persons of Jammu. Aspersion was also cast on the impartiality and fairness of the Public Service Commission. It was suggested that its members should be recruited from outside the State. Whereas region-wise representation in the services was advocated by the political parties, communal bodies wanted reservation to be made on a communal basis. Communities such as the Gujjars, Rajputs, Shias, Christians, etc. all desired special quotas and reservations of appointments for themselves on the ground of their backwardness.

2.05. *Education.*—The pleadings under the head 'Education' related to a lack of educational facilities in general; discrimination on the basis of regions and religions in the matter of admissions to higher educational and professional institutions; the lack of professional colleges in the Jammu region; discrimination in the grant of scholarships and selections for training abroad and an almost complete lack of encouragement to the backward classes to acquire higher education. Several parties from the Jammu region, particularly the Students' Congress, complained that all the technical colleges were located in Kashmir and pleaded for the establishment of such colleges in their own legion. A suggestion was also made by the Students' Congress for the establishment of a separate University in Jammu. The representatives from Ladakh pointed out that as the matriculation examination was held in Ladakh long after it was held in the rest of the State, their boys lost a whole term in the process of seeking admission to institutions of higher studies. They desired that something should be done to eliminate this loss of time.

2.06. *Causes of irritations and tensions.* Most of the representatives from Jammu and Ladakh complained that their legitimate regional aspirations were being ignored and that they had little share in the political power of the State. They stated that their regions were discriminated against in most matters, such as in the allocation of developmental funds, the provision of educational facilities, employment in Government services, etc.

2.07. No representative or individual who wrote to, or appeared before us questioned the constitutional or legal position of the State as an integral part of the Indian Union, or made out that this was a cause leading to the creation of tensions and irritation among the people. All of them on the contrary were at pains to emphasize that even the proposals or suggestions that they were making for greater decentralization of power to, or autonomy for, the various regions of the State; were subject to the overall consideration that they should in no way imperil or impair the unity and integrity of the State on the maintenance of which they laid great emphasis. Only one solitary organization, namely the Dogra Mandal, suggested the division of the State and the merger of the Jammu region with Himachal Pradesh.

2.08. Some parties pleaded for the abrogation of Article 370 of the Constitution which conferred a special status on the Jammu and Kashmir State, while certain others pressed for its continuance.

2.09. A number of parties were bitter that the general elections held in the past in the State had not been free and fair. We were also told that the elections to local bodies such as municipalities, town area committees, etc. had not been held for many years with the result that these bodies were no longer representative.

2.10. Representatives of the Zamindari and agriculturist interests were foud in their complaints about the iniquitous and anomalous features of the land and tenancy laws by which land had been expropriated without the payment of any compensation; a uniform ceiling for holdings had been fixed without reference to the quality and productivity of the land; and different rates had been prescribed for the sharing of the produce by land-holders owning more than 100 *Kanals* or less. Another cause of irritation pointed out by them was the great delay in the disposal of ejectment applications. They also complained that though the provisions of Section 45 of the Jammu and Kashmir Tenancy Act enabled the landlord to eject his tenant in possession on the ground that he required the land for personal cultivation, applications made by the landlords to enforce this right had been stayed, for the time being, till 31 December 1968 by a statutory notification. They urged that the notification should be rescinded.

2.11. Representatives of certain communities, such as Jats, Gujjars, Shias, Sikhs, Buddhists and Christians pleaded for adequate representation in the Cabinet, the legislature and the Public Service Commission.

2.12. A number of parties from the Jammu region were aggrieved that there was discrimination in the fixation of the quantum of rations and issue prices of foodgrains. Representatives from Ladakh complained of the lack of rationing facilities for the general population in their area, and of discrimination made between Ladakhi Government servants and others.

2.13. Several organizations of the Jammu region represented before us that all the State toll barriers were located in the Jammu region and that this had adversely affected its economy. Goods and traffic could, on the other hand, flow freely from any part of the Kashmir region to any other place within it.

2.14. Different views were expressed about the six-monthly move of the headquarters of the State Government between Srinagar and Jammu. Several representatives thought that the practice was inevitable even while conceding that it caused dislocation of work and waste of time.. A few representatives from Kashmir desired the discontinuance of this practice on the ground that it gave a feeling of isolation and neglect to Kashmir during the winter months when the Valley was snow-bound.

CHAPTER III

THE STATE OF JAMMU AND KASHMIR—A GENERAL BACKGROUND

3.01. In this Chapter we are giving some background information, gleaned from published and authentic sources, about the State of Jammu and Kashmir—the land and its people, their past history, the religions they follow, the languages they speak and the occupations they pursue. This may help to bring about a better understanding of the matters which fall within the scope of our inquiry.

3.02. State of Jammu and Kashmir occupies a position of great strategic importance in the north-west of India. It is separated from the rest of the country by mountains and uneven terrain. The State is composed of three distinct cultural units—Jammu, Ladakh and the Valley. It is the meeting place of the Hindu, Muslim and Buddhist cultures as living, co-existent forces. The Valley of Kashmir, apart from being justly famous for its natural scenery, has the distinction of possessing an ancient Sanskrit historical record. The ancient history of Jammu Province, however, is shrouded in mystery. There is no chronicle which throws light on the happenings thereof the period prior to the 18th century.

3.03. *Hindu Period.*—Till the 14th century, Kashmir was ruled by a series of Buddhist and Hindu dynasties whose annals are related in the celebrated versified Sanskrit chronicle known as 'Rajatarangini' by Kalhana. Its later chapters give a fairly reliable record of events from the 7th century to the middle of the 12th century. Kalhana's chronicles are continued by Pandit Jonaraja, who takes us to the beginning of the 15th century, and by Srivara and Prajyabhatta who bring the narration down to the Moghul conquest of Kashmir in 1586. The later history of the Valley can be found in the works of Birbal Kacheri and Diwan Kirpa Ram and certain British and European scholars noteworthy among them being Lawrence and Younghusband.

3.04. After the phase of local kings and rulers who extended their rule beyond the Valley into India and Central Asia, Asoka introduced Buddhism into Kashmir in the 3rd century B.C. This was later strengthened by Kanishka. In the early 6th century the control of the Valley passed to the Huns. The Valley regained freedom in 530 A.D., but soon after that came under the sway of the Ujjain Empire. Later, on the decline of the Vikramaditya dynasty, it once again had its own ruler, and there was a fusion of Hindu and Buddhist cultures. Lalitaditya (697-738 A.D.), who extended his hold up to Bengal in the east, Konkan in the south, Turkistan in the north-west and Tibet in the north-east, was the most famous of its Hindu rulers. While Lalitaditya was known for his building activity, King Avantivarman (855-83 A.D.), his successor, is remembered for the great progress in irrigation and drainage in the Valley made during his reign. By the beginning of the 14th century, "the Hindu kings had become incapable of their office" and Kashmir came to have Muslim rulers when Sinha Dev, the Hindu King, fled before a Tartar invasion.

3.05. *Muslim Period.*—Zainul Abedin (1417-69), Sikandar's second son, was not only the most famous of the Muslim rulers but the most illustrious ruler that Kashmir has known. Father and son were of entirely different temperaments; while the father was cruel and intolerant, the son was tolerant, wise and kind. When Zainul Abedin came to power, he completely reversed the policy of Sikandar. A man of secular outlook, he patronized all faiths and religions alike. He brought new life to the tortured Valley by putting an end to his father's rule of persecution and forcible conversions. He recalled those Hindus who had fled to distant places during Sikandar's regime and got the temples rebuilt and repaired. He banned cow-slaughter and removed the prohibition on the performance of Sati. In Zainul Abedin's time, handicrafts were introduced or stimulated, literature and the arts were pationized, canals and bridges were built and taxes were reduced. The reign of this enlightened ruler had an unhappy end for there was a struggle amongst his sons for succession to the throne. Eventually, his weak son, Haider Shah, fell a prey to the aggressive tribes from the north known as the Chaks. Sunni Muslims and Hindus alike were persecuted by the Chaks and they looked towards the Moghul Empire in India for a redress of their grievances. The Chak dynasty continued to rule till 1587 when Akbar invaded Kashmir and made it an apanage of the Moghul Empire; Kashmir then became the summer residence of Mughal Emperors for nearly 200 years. Akbar was followed by Jahangir, Shahjahan and Aurangzeb. Aurangzeb's successor was a weak ruler and in 1752, Kashmir passed from the feeble control of the Moghul emperor into the powerful grasp of Ahmed Shah Abdali of Afghanistan. For the next 67 years, it was held for the Pathans by a series of governors who were more or less independent of their kings and who behaved like tyrants.

3.06. *Sikh Rule.*—By the beginning of the 18th century, Sikh power had risen in the Punjab. The Kashmiris, harassed and exploited by the Pathan kings and unable to secure relief from their tyranny by their own efforts, sought outside assistance and looked forward to a Sikh invasion. In 1814, Ranjit Singh attempted an invasion by the Pir Panjal route, but was repulsed. A further personal appeal to him by Birbal Dai, a Brahmin who managed to escape from Srinagar to Lahore, resulted in another attack by the Sikhs. Misar Diwan Chand, one of Ranjit Singh's most competent generals, who was accompanied by Gulab Singh, was in command of the Sikh forces which in 1819 expelled the Afghans and brought Kashmir under the rule of the Sikhs.

3.07. *Dogra Rule.*—Till 1846, Kashmir remained under the Sikhs and was administered by their governors. The important governors during the Sikh regime were Moti Ram, Kirpa Ram, Sher Singh, Mian Singh, Ghulam Mohi-ud-Din and Imam-ud-Din, but all of them did not command the same respect in Kashmir. In fact the last two actually ruled after the death of Ranjit Singh but were too weak to assert themselves, and the decaying Sikh power, as one writer puts it, "exploded, disappearing in fierce but fading flames." Events leading to the transfer of Kashmir into the hands of the Dogras are closely related to the later history of the Sikhs, especially the prominent role played by Gulab Singh, who had earlier been a minister at Ranjit Singh's court. Gulab Singh belonged to a Rajput family. He was one of the three great-grand nephews of Ranjit Deva, a Dogra Chief of Rajput descent who ruled Jammu in the latter half of the 18th century.

3.08. As already stated, no record is available of the history of Jammu before the 18th century. It appears that during the 12th century when Mohammad Ghori had invaded India and overrun the Punjab, Rajputs, had taken refuge in the mountainous tracts of Jammu province and carved out separate estates and principalities such as Jammu, Kishtwar, Bhadarwah, Basohli, Reasi, etc. which they ruled as independent sovereigns. Very little information is available about the successive regimes which dominated the different regions of the province from time to time until Raja Ranjit Deva, son of Dhruv Deva, proclaimed himself as the ruler of the principality of Jammu in 1730 A.D.

3.09. On the death of Ranjit Deva in 1780, there ensued a struggle for succession. This gave the Sikhs an opportunity of turning Jammu and the neighbouring Hill tracts into a dependency. Gulab Singh, by then, had entered the service of Maharaja Ranjit Singh and had rendered such distinguished service that the Maharaja conferred the principality of Jammu on him with the hereditary title of Raja. During Ranjit Singh's lifetime, Gulab Singh remained loyal to the Lahore Court. However, on the death of Ranjit Singh and the consequent anarchy in the Sikh Court British penetration into north-western regions of India began. In subduing the Sikh power, they sought and secured the co-operation of Gulab Singh. In 1846, at the close of the first Sikh war, Gulab Singh appeared on the scene as a mediator between the British and the Lahore Durbar. On the condition of paying the war indemnity asked for by the British, Gulab Singh was made an independent ruler of Jammu and Kashmir. A separate treaty embodying this arrangement was concluded at Amritsar on 16 March 1846, under which Gulab Singh acknowledged the supremacy of the British-Government. This treaty thus marks the commencement of the history of the Jammu and Kashmir State as a political entity.

3.10. The treaty put Gulab Singh as Maharaja, in possession of all the hill country between the Indus and the Ravi, including Kashmir, Jammu, Ladakh and Gilgit, but excluding Lahaul, Kulu and certain other areas which, for strategical purposes, it was considered advisable to retain and for which a remission of Rs. 25 lakhs was made from the crore demanded, leaving Rs. 75 lakhs as the final amount to be paid by Gulab Singh. Gulab Singh had some difficulty in obtaining actual possession of the province of Kashmir. The last governor appointed by the Sikhs, Imamuddin, successfully resisted his efforts for a time, and it was only at the end of 1846 that Maharaja Gulab Singh with the aid of British troops was established in Kashmir.

3.11. No subsidiary force was imposed on Gulab Singh. Political relations between the Government of India and the State commenced in the year 1849 but these were conducted by the Punjab Government through the Maharaja's agent at Lahore and no representative of the Government of India was stationed in the State. It was not until the year 1852 that the first 'Officer on Special Duty' in the State was appointed. This officer resided in Kashmir only during the summer months. Maharaja Gulab Singh died in 1857 and was succeeded by his son Ranbir Singh. In 1885, after the death of Ranbir Singh and the accession to the *gaddi* of Maharaja Partap Singh, the designation of the 'Officer on Special Duty' was changed to 'Resident in Kashmir', who was permanently stationed at Srinagar. Partap Singh died in 1925 and was succeeded by his nephew, Hari Singh, the ruler who wielded authority till 1948.

3.12. *Independence.*—With the lapse of British Paramountcy on 15 August 1947, the Jammu and Kashmir State became free. It did not decide upon the issue of accession for more than two months after the British withdrawal from the sub-continent. The Maharaja, however, entered into a standstill agreement with Pakistan in order to ensure a free flow of trade and communications as before with the areas that constituted Pakistan. While negotiations for a standstill agreement with India were going on, Pakistan imposed an economic blockade to put pressure on the Maharaja into signing an Instrument of Accession in favour of Pakistan. This was supplemented by a massive armed tribal attack on the State. The people of Jammu and Kashmir, however, offered heroic resistance to the invaders. The invasion from Pakistan precipitated the issue of accession, and on 26 October 1947 the Government of India accepted the Instrument of Accession signed by the Maharaja with the popular backing of the people of the State led by Sheikh Mohammad Abdullah. Jammu and Kashmir thus became legally an integral part of India with overwhelming popular support.

3.13. *Location.—The* present State of Jammu and Kashmir presents a challenging subject for the study of economists, planners and social scientists of the country. Forming the northern most fringe of the country with a good part of the State separated from the rest of India by mountains and uneven terrain, it presents many special problems of its own, Lying between latitude 32.30 degree and 37.00 degree North and longitude 72.50 degree and 80.20 degree East, it forms the North-Western part of India. Its boundaries in the north are Soviet Turkistan and Chinese Sinkiang. In the west and the south-west, it is bounded by Afghanistan and Pakistan and in the east by Tibet while Himachal Pradesh and Punjab form the southern boundaries of the State.

3.14. *Physical features.—The* State falls into four natural regions described below:

(i) The Sub-montane and Semi-mountainous Tracts

This region consists of the plains bordering the Punjab and the broken mass of the foot-hills known locally as the 'Kandi' areas. The average height of this region is about 2,000 feet above sea-level. The river Chenab flows' through it. But on account of its being mostly stony and arid, cultivation here is scanty, scattered and wholly dependent on rain. The whole of Jammu district and a part of Kathua district fall in this tract.

(ii) The Outer Hills Region

The rest of Jammu province (i.e., the districts of Udhampur, Poonch, Doda and part of Kathua) falls in this region. It consists of low hills lying roughly to the south of the Pir Panjal range which separates the two provinces of Jammu and Kashmir. A large part of this area lies between 2,000 and 4,000 feet above sea-level. The river Chenab passes through this area also. Except in the fertile valleys formed by the river and its tributaries, cultivation is scarce and scattered and is done on small patches.

(iii) Jhelum Valley or Kashmir Valley Region

This region consists of the administrative districts of Anantnag, Srinagar and Baramulla. It is known as the Kashmir Valley. The river Jhelum with its numerous tributaries, pursuing a zigzag course, flows through the whole length of the Valley bisecting it almost into two-halves. The average height of the Valley is 5,500 feet above sea-level, while the mountains surrounding, it average 12,000 feet with a dip to about 9,000 feet, at Banihal pass. The region has a rich alluvial soil and paddy and fruit grow extensively there.

(iv) Indus Valley or Tibetan or Semi-Tibetan Tract

This area consists almost entirely of snow-capped mountains with plateaus, glaciers, rocky river valleys and wastes. The Indus is the main river of this region. There are a number of mountains over 20,000 feet in height. At present, it comprises Kargil and Leh divisions of the frontier district of Ladakh in Kashmir province. The whole of the area is dry and almost rainless. The cultivation of such crops as barley, maize and millets is, however, undertaken in this region with the help of irrigation from small canals known as 'Kuhls' which are fed by melting snow.

3.15. Administratively the State consists of three units, viz. Jammu, Kashmir and Ladakh—Doda, Udhampur, Jammu, Kathua and Poonch forming Jammu province and Anantnag, Srinagar and Baramulla the province of Kashmir, while Ladakh forms the frontier district of the State. The State comprises 6,726 villages and 43 towns of which Jammu and Srinagar are the most important industrial centres.

3.16. *Area and Population.*—According to the 1961 Census, the State has an area of about 139,000 square kilometres and a total population of 35.61 lakhs, giving a density of 26 per square kilometre, the lowest of all the States of the Indian Union, except for a few Union territories. The low density is explained by the fact that the frontier district of the State constitutes more than two-thirds of the area but has less than 2.5 per cent of the population. If the area and population of this district are excluded, the density would go up to 84 per square kilometre. In other words, the density of population for the residual area would be higher than that of Madhya Pradesh and Rajasthan. The fact, however, remains that the density of the State has been rising from decade to decade all along in the past.

3.17. The distribution of the area, population and density in the three administrative units is as under:—

Area, Population and Density—Based on 1961 Census

	Area		*No. of Towns*	*No. of Villages*	*Population*	*Density (Population)*	
	sq. miles	*sq. kms.*				*per sq. mile*	*per sq. km.*
1	*2*	*3*	*4*	*5*	*6*	*7*	*8*
Jammu	10073.1	26089.4	24	3485	1572887	156	60
Doda	4380.2	11344.7	6	661	268403	61	24
Udhampur	1731.6	4484.9	4	627	254061	147	57
Jammu	1248.6	3233.8	7	1050	516932	414	160
Kathua	1023.6	2651.2	4	585	207430	203	78
Poonch	1689.1	4374.8	3	562	326061	193	75
Kashmir	5838.0	15120.3	18	3003	1899438	325	126
Anantnag	2096.9	5430.9	6	1222	654368	312	120
Srinagar	1205.4	3121.2	3	714	640411	531	205
Baramulla	2536.0	6568.2	9	1067	604659	238	92
Ladakh	37753.8	97782.4	1	238	88651	2	0.9
Total	53664.9	138992.1	43	6726	3560976	66	26

Note: The figures exclude the area under unlawful occupation of Pakistan and China, where census could not be taken, and its population.

3.18. *Religions.*—The Jammu and Kashmir State presents a picture of a multi-racial society professing a variety of religions, speaking different languages and heir to a composite culture and customs. The State is inhabited by Hindus, Muslims, Sikhs, Christians, Buddhists and Jains. Muslims comprise about 68 per cent of the population, Hindus a little over 28 per cent, and Sikhs and Buddhists 1.8 arid 1.4 per cent respectively, while the total number of Christians is 2,848 and of Jains only 1,427. The percentage of population of Hindus and Muslims in Jammu province is 58:7 and 38.1 respectively. The districts of Udhampur, Jammu and Kathua have a concentration of Hindu population (78.9 per cent); Doda and Poonch have more of Muslims (72.9 per cent). Sikhs live mostly in Jammu and Poonch, and form 6.3 per cent of the population of Jammu and 2.5 per cent of that of Poonch. Kashmir has a majority of Muslims (94.4 per cent), the percentage in Anantnag, Srinagar and Baramulla being 95.4, 90.7 and 97.3 respectively. Hindus in the Valley constitute 4.7 per cent of the population. The maximum proportion of Hindus in the Valley (8.3 per cent) is found in Srinagar. Out of a total of 304 Christians, 230 live in Srinagar alone. About 54 per cent Buddhists and 45 per cent Muslims, besides about one per cent of Hindus and Sikhs, inhabit the territory of Ladakh. The district-wise distribution of population by religion is given in the table below:—

Percentage Distribution of Population by Religion—Based on 1961 Census

Region/ Religion	*Hindus*	*Muslims*	*Sikhs*	*Christians*	*Buddhists*	*Jains*	*Total*
1	2	3	4	5	6	7	8
Jammu	58.7	38.1	2.9	0.2	—	0.1	100.0
Doda	34.6	65:0	0.2	—	0.2	..	100.0
Udhampur	65.1	33.9	0.9	0.1	..	..	100.0
Jammu	83.0	10.0	6.3	04	—	0.3	100.0
Poonch	18.0	79.5	2.5	—	..	..	100.0
Kathua	85.7	13.0	1.2	0.1	..	—	100.0
Kashmir	4.7	94.4	0.9	—	—	—	100.0
Anantnag	3.7	95.4	.0.9	—	..	—	100.0
Srinagar	8.3	90.7	1.0	—	—	—	100.0
Baramulla	2.0	97.3	0.7	—	_	..	100.0
Ladakh	.0.7	45.4	0.1	—	53.8	..	100.0
Total	28.4	68.3	1.8	0.1	1.4	—	100.0

. . Nil.
—Negligible.

3.19. *Scheduled Castes.*—With the introduction of the Constitution of India, envisaging the establishment of a secular democracy, the 1961 Census for the first time dispensed with the details of the castes and sub-castes under the different religions, except for persons belonging to the Scheduled Castes. There are no Scheduled Tribes in the State and even the Scheduled Castes are found only in the five districts of Jammu province. The total population of the Scheduled Castes in the province is 2,84,131 (2,63,236 in rural areas and 20,895 in the urban areas). The district-wise proportion to population is given on next page.

Percentage of Scheduled Castes to Population

District	*Persons*	*Males*	*Females*
1	*2*	*3*	*4*
Doda	9.22	9.09	9.37
Udhampur	19.91	19.89	19.93
Jammu	29.31	29.53	29.06
Kathua	22.88	23.06	22.69
Poonch	3.01	2.94	3.10

The 1961 Census shows that the number of Scheduled Castes professing the Sikh religion is very small and that they mostly belong to the Basith, Chamar or Ramdasis and Megh or Kabirpanthi castes. All the others profess Hinduism. In fact, the population of Hindu Scheduled Castes is much larger than the entire population in the State of those professing Sikhism or Buddhism. It is six times that of the latter and more than four times the population of Sikhs. In the State as a whole, Hindu Scheduled Castes claim 28 per cent of the total Hindu population. The following table gives the percentage of Hindu Scheduled Castes to the total Hindu population and the total number of persons belonging to Sikh Scheduled Castes in Jammu province and its districts:—

	Percentage of Hindu Scheduled Castes Population to Total Hindu Population	*Total number of persons belonging to Sikh Scheduled Castes*
J & K State	28.0	168
Jammu Province	30.7	168
Doda District	26.7	10
Udhampur District	30.6	17
Jammu District	35.3	97
Kathua District	26.7	. .
Poonch District	16.6	44

3.20. *Languages*—A number of languages are spoken in the State. The important languages spoken are Kashmiri in Kashmir; Dogri, Punjabi and Pahari-unspecified in Jammu and Ladakhi, Balti, Budhi and Tibetan in Ladakh. As the Valley is predominantly inhabited by Kashmiris, the mother tongue of over 90 per cent is Kashmiri, the other important languages spoken there are Punjabi (1.7 per cent) and Gojri (3.4 per cent). Although on the whole a little over 55 per cent speak Dogri in Jammu province, not less than 80 per cent in Jammu district, 77 per cent in Udhampur and 92 per cent in Kathua speak the same language.

In the whole of Jammu province, Punjabi is the mother tongue of only 5 per cent; 12 per cent speak Punjabi in Jammu district and 2.5 per cent in Poonch. There are only 11 per cent people in whole of Jammu province whose mother tongue is Kashmiri; in Doda, however, over 44 per cent of the people speak Kashmiri. Gojri is the mother tongue of 10 per cent of population in Udhampur and 9.3 per cent in Doda. Cher 26 per cent speak Gojri in Poonch, where the other important languages are Pahari-unspecified and Dogri which are spoken by 48.3 per cent and 13.2 per cent respectively. In Ladakh, over 56 per cent speak Ladakhi while the mother tongue of 37.1 percent is Balti and of 2.4 per cent Budhi; Tibetan is the mother tongue of only 2 per cent people in Ladakh. A few persons speak Kashmiri (0.7 per cent), Punjabi (0.2 per cent), and Dogri (0.2 per cent) as well. The region-wise proportion of languages spoken is given in the table below:—

Percentage Distribution of Population by Languages Spoken—Based on 1961 Census

Region/ Language	*Kashmiri*	*Punjabi*	*Dogri*	*Ladakhi*	*Budhi*	*Bakar-wali*	*Gojri*	*Others*	*Total*
1	2	3	4	5	6	7	8	9	10
Jammu	11.3	4.9	55.1	—	0.1	0.4	9.2	19.0	100.0
Doda	44.5	0.3	7.0	..	0.2	0.2	9.3	38.5*	100.0
Udhampur	8.8	1.4	77.6	..	..	1.0	10.0	1.2	100.0
Jammu	2.1	11.6	80 6	—	..	0.1	1.1	4.5	100.0
Kathua	1.8	1.9	92.3	..	..	0.3	1.6	2.1	100.0
Poonch	6.6	2.5	13.2	..	..	0.5	26.2	51.0†	100.0
Kashmir	90.4	1.7	0.1	—	—	..	3.4	4.4	100.0
Anantnag	93.3	1.1	0.1	—	—	..	4.2	1.3	100.0
Srinagar	95.1	1.6	0.1.	—	—	..	2.2	1.0	100.0
Baramulla	82.3	2.5	—	—	..	..	3.9	11.3	100.0
Ladakh	0.7	0.2	0.2	56.2	2.4	..	..	40.3‡	100.0
Total	53.3	3.1	24.4	1.4	0.1	0.2	5.9	11.6	100.0

. . Nil. —Negligible.

*Bhadrawahi 12.3 per cent; Pahari-unspecified 6.0 per cent. Siraji-Kashmiri 7.4 per cent; Kishtwari 4.3 per cent.

†Pahari-unspecified 48.3 per cent; Urdu 1.9 per cent.

‡Balti 37.1 per cent; Tibetan 2.1 per cent.

3.21. *Natural Resources.*—Of the natural resources of Kashmir Valley, forests need special mention. The forests of the State are renowned all over India for their grandeur; their lofty fir, deodar and pine trees; and varied flora and fauna. These forests are a very important source of revenue and yield large quantities of timber, firewood and minor forest products. They add grandeur to the landscape and are a means of protecting the land against erosion and ensuring the regular flow of water. It is estimated that out of the total forest area, about 28 per cent consists of coniferous forests and the rest of miscellaneous forests including high level pasturages. Of these the commercially exploitable forests comprise only 20 per cent; the rest are inaccessible at present. The other important natural resources of Jammu and Kashmir consist of minerals although only a small portion of the known deposits has as yet been surveyed in detail. It is now known, however, that the State has considerable deposits of gypsum and limestone and a geological survey reveals the existence of copper, lead and zinc also. In spite of the fact that the State occupies an important position because of its mineral resources in the whole of northwest India, its mineral industry has nevertheless remained undeveloped due to lack of suitable transport and power facilities.

3.22. *Literacy.* The basic problem of Kashmir for long has been its low income, poverty, disease, ignorance and unemployment. The State has all along been very backward, having the lowest incidence of literacy among all the States of India. According to the 1961 census, there are only 3.9 lakh literate persons in the State giving a literacy percentage of about 13 against the national average of 28 per cent. Urban areas, where greater facilities for education are available, however, claim a literacy percentage of 32.8 while in rural areas the literacy percentage is only 8.9. The largest number of literate persons is found in the cities of Jammu and Srinagar, the percentages being 45.0 and 24.8 respectively. The districts of Jammu and Srinagar have the highest percentage of literacy—22.3 for Jammu and 16.8 for Srinagar. The percentage of literacy in the various regions and districts of the State is indicated in the table on next page.

Percentage of Literacy*—Based on 1961 Census

Region	Rural			Urban			Total		
	M	*F*	*T*	*M*	*F*	*T*	*M*	*F*	*T*
Jammu	16.8	2.6	10.1	54.8	35.6	46.3	21.8	6.5	14.6
Doda	15.0	1.1	8.5	49.3	22.4	37.4	17.1	2.3	10.2
Udhampur	13.5	2.1	8.1	56.5	36.6	47.5	16.4	4.2	10.7
Jammu	21.4	4.5	13.4	56.2	39.2	48.7	30.7	12.8	22.3
Kathua	19.0	3.9	11.9	47.0	25.3	37.0	21.2	5.4	13.8
Poonch	13.7	1.2	7.8	55.2	29. 7	43.6	15.9	2.6	9.6
Kashmir	13.5	1.2.	7.9.	36.4	14.9	26.5	18.3	4.1	11.8
Anantnag	14.6	1.3	8.5	30.3	7.2	20.0	15.7	1.7	9.3
Srinagar	11.4	1.1	6.7	38.4	17.0	28.5	23.7	8.5	16.8
Baramulla	13.7	1.1	7.9	30.8	9.6	21.2	15.3	1.9	9.2
Ladakh	16.2	0.9	8.7	42.0	7.6	24.9	17.3	1.2	9.4
Total	15.1	1.8	8.9	42.4	21.3	32.8	19.8	5.1	13.0

M: Males; F: Females; T: Total.
*Excludes population in age group 0-4.

3.23. *Economic*—Agriculture has been the main occupation of the State's population, the rural/urban ratio of population being 83:17; the proportion of workers to the total population is about 43 per cent according to the 1961 census. Over three-fourths of the workers are cultivators and agricultural labourers. About 6 per cent are engaged in household industries, 2 per cent each in manufacturing (other than household industry) and trade and commerce, while 9 per cent of the workers derive their livelihood from other services. The percentage distribution of workers in the different industries is given in the table on next page.

3.24. Agriculture is the mainstay of the State's economy, about 90 per cent of the population depending for their living on land. Rice is the staple food in the Kashmir Valley while in Jammu province people eat wheat, maize, barley and rice. A variety of fruit grow in the State: apples, pears, plums, cherry, etc. Walnuts, almonds and saffron are also among the other important products of the State. The produce of the various districts of the State, however, varies according to their altitude.

3.25. The cottage industries of the Jammu and Kashmir State like wood carving, wool weaving, shawl making, etc. are famous all over the world. Silk is found in abundance and silk goods are

Proportion of Workers in Different Industries—Based on 1961 Census

Region	*Total workers as per cent of population*	*As cultivator*	*As Agricultural labourer*	*Mining, quarrying etc.*	*Household industry*	*Manufacturing other than household industry*	*Construction*	*Trade and commerce*	*Transport, Storage and Communications*	*Other services*
Jammu	41.5	75.8	1.1	1.9	7.0	1.0	0.8	2.2	0.7	9 5
Doda	55.3	83.7	0.4	2.5	8.8	0.3	0.3	0.7	0.1	3 2
Udhampur	50.8	80.4	0.4	1.4	10.6	0.3	0.3	1.4	0.2	5.0
Jammu	32.3	58.1	2.6	1.3	3.0	3.0	1.9	5.1	2.1	22.9
Kathua	40.8	75.9	1.2	3.0	7.1	0.7	0.8	1.9	0.6	8.8
Poonch	38.0	85.4	0.7	1.8	6.3	0.4	0.2	0.9	0 2	4.1
Kashmir	42.7	74.9	1.3	1.5	5.6	3.3	0.4	2.3	1.1	9.6
Anantnag	43.9	81.8	1.5	1.4	6.8	4.2	0.4	1.7	0.5	4.7
Srinagar	37.9	56.2	1.0	1.5	6.4	8.3	0.6	4.3	2.6	19.1
Baramulla	46.7	84.1	1.4	1.6	3.8	1.0	0.2	1.3	03	6.3
Ladakh	66 1	85 .3	0.5	1.3	7.6	0.3	1.1	0.7	0.1	3.1
Total	42.8	75.7	1.2	1.7	6.3	2.2	0.6	2.2	0.8	9.3

a major export of Kashmir. The most important industry of the State is, however, Tourism. It is its main source of revenue. With beautiful tourist spots both in Jammu and Kashmir, the State attracts tourists from all over India and the world. The additional amenities provided by the Government in recent years for tourists have made for a substantial increase in their number.

3.26. The income of the State in 1965-66 (at 1955-56 prices) is estimated to be about Rs. 93 crores giving a per capita income of about Rs. 250. Agriculture, etc. constitute about 41.5 per cent of the State income while mining and manufacturing provide about 25.0 per cent. The contribution of commerce and transport is 9.1 per cent while other services absorb about 24.4 per cent of the State's income. Though the First and Second Five Year Plans witnessed a rise of 4 to 5 per cent per annum in the State's income, during the period, of the Third Five Year Plan the income, which was showing an annual growth of about 2.4 per cent till 1964-65, showed a decline of about 1/6 per cent in 1965-66 on account of a serious decline in agricultural production throughout the country caused by adverse weather conditions. With the better agricultural production expected in subsequent years, it is likely that the income growth may equal that prevailing in the First and the Second Five Year Plan periods. The State income at 1955-56 prices by industry of origin is shown in the table below:—

State Income at 1955-56 Prices by Industry of Origin

(In lakhs of rupees)

Industry	*1950-51*	*1955-56*	*1960-61*	*1965-66**	*1966-67†*
1. Agriculture, Animal Husbandry, Forestry, Fishing, etc.	2,605.5	3,374.1	4,084.3	3,876.0	4,464.2
2. Mining, Manufacturing and Small Enterprises	1,353.2	1,546.8	2,018.1	2,326.5	2,367.9
3. Commerce and Transport	635.4	689.2	764.8	853.6	865.3
4. Other services	960.2	1,187.3	1,736.5	2,272.6	2,409.0
5. Total	5,554.3	6,797.4	8,603.7	9,328.6	10,106.4
6. Per capita income (Rs.)	188.4	216.5	252.6	250.4	265.8

*Partially revised. †Preliminary.

Source: Directorate of Economics and Statistics, Jammu and Kashmir.

CHAPTER IV

Development Programmes

4.01. Our first term of reference requires us "to make an assessment of the development programmes apportioned to the various regions of the State and to recommend measures necessary to give assurance that the resources available to the State Government are being shared equitably and also to convey a feeling of equal participation in the integrated development of the State."

As is inevitable with any inquiry that involves making regional comparisons, each region tries to substantiate its claim that its interests have been neglected and that the other regions have prospered unduly over the years at its expense. We, therefore, took oral evidence and checked the statements made in evidence by reference to the statistical information obtained from the State Government and also other relevant material. The complaints of neglect were made mostly in the memoranda submitted by representatives from the Jammu Division and Ladakh though there were also some from the Kashmir Division. Besides, from the same region, allegations we're made that the urban areas had received more attention while the needs of the rural, hilly and inaccessible areas had been comparatively neglected.

4.02. *Resources of the Stole.* Before proceeding to discuss the apportionment of development programmes to the different regions, and the sharing of resources, by them, we propose to examine the budgetary resources, first of the State as a whole and then of the regions separately. The budgetary resources of a State are made up of the revenue receipts of the State and the grants-in-aid and loans given to it by the Centre in pursuance of the constitutional provisions as also for meeting its specific Plan needs. The resources of the State of Jammu and Kashmir are admittedly quite inadequate for its needs and the Union Government have had to supplement them to a considerable extent by giving grants-in-aid and loans. The following table, prepared for six consecutive years, gives an idea of how the revenue receipts of the State compare with the amount of Central assistance received by it in the form of grants and loans:

(In crores of rupees)

Year	Revenue Receipts of the State	Central Grants	Central Loans	Total
1960-61	12.58	3.14	5.31	21 03
1961-61	12.59	9.48	6.64	28 71
1962-63	17.64	7.68	10 36	35.68
1963-64	18.36	8.19	9.07	35.62
1964-65	18.02	8.51	11.68	38.21
1965-66	19.76	11.91	12.83	44.50

Thus, Central assistance was nearly equal to the revenue receipts of the State in 1962-63 and 1963-64 and substantially exceeded the State's revenue in the years 1964-65 and 1965-66. The principal sources of revenue are: (a) forests, (b) road toll, (c) land revenue, (d) sales tax, and (e) excise.

4.03. *Allocation of resources to different regions.*—We shall now proceed to attempt an analysis of the regional breakdown of the State's revenue. This will give an idea of the revenue-earning capacity of each of the regions, viz., Jammu, Kashmir and Ladakh, and the contribution that each makes to the total revenue of the State. In arriving at the regional breakdown, certain assumptions have, however, to be made. This is be cause the figures relating to the State's revenue are not maintained region-wise. The apportionment of certain items of revenue to the regions is also not possible, for the point of collection of a tax may fall in one region while its incidence may fall in another. The receipts from road toll provide an illustration of this. The State of Jammu and Kashmir has a fairly extensive road system and road toll is an important source of revenue. Although the incidence of road toll is spread over the entire State, the collection points are all located in the Jammu region. It would thus be incorrect to show the entire receipts on this account as having been earned by the Jammu region merely because the toll barriers are all located there. There are a few other items of revenue also where the correct apportionment to the regions presents similar difficulties. There are still others where such apportionment is not possible at all. Nevertheless, after excluding such items as well as Central assistance and making suitable assumptions about the allocation of some of the other items of revenue to the regions, the State

Government have, at our request, made an analysis of the regional budgetary resources. This has been done for a few selected years, the years being 1960-61, 1963-64 and 1965-66. In overall, terms, the regional breakdown of resources for the years for which the analysis has been made; is as follows:

(In lakhs of rupees)

	1960-61	*1963-64*	*1965-66*
Jammu	389 21	462 51	453.98
Kashmir	322.94	490.38	46190
Ladakh	2.89	5.04	5.72
Total	715.04	957.93	921.60

The detailed breakdown for the three years in terms of individual items of revenue and the assumptions made in allocating them to the different regions are given in Appendix 5. The figures given above show that the resources of the Jammu region and the Kashmir region are about equal. No such large variation exists between them as would entitle one region to claim distinct superiority over the other in this respect. Ladakh is, however, in quite a different category. Its scanty resources require a great deal of additional support from the State and the Union Government.

4.04. *Apportionment of development programmes and expenditure.—We* now come to the development programmes of the State. Like the budgetary resources discussed in the preceding paragraph, the accurate apportionment of development programmes and developmental expenditure to the different regions is difficult. Many developmental schemes transcend regional boundaries and cannot be allocated to particular regions. Attempts have, however, been made by the State Government to allocate developmental expenditure to the different regions to the extent practicable and where it has not been possible to do so, they have shown such expenditure as common to two or more regions.

4.05. Development programmes in the State have been financed mainly out of its Plan budgets and only, to a limited extent out of its non-Plan budgets. We shall first consider the Plan budgets and then proceed to discuss the non-Plan budgets in so far as they relate to development.

4.06. The total Plan expenditure on development in the entire

State, during the three Plan periods, has been Rs. 10.681.25 lakhs. The expenditure on each Plan was as follows:—

(In lakhs of rupees)

First Five-Year Plan (1951-52 to 1955-56)	1,151.71
Second Five-Year Plan (1956-57 to 1960-61)	3,120.20
Third Five-Year Plan (1961-62 to 1965-66)	6,409.34
Total	10,681.25

As mentioned earlier, the resources of the State are quite inadequate for its needs and therefore the Union Government have had to make substantial assistance available to the State Government in the form of grants and loans for financing the State Plans. The quantum of assistance for the three Plans was as follows:—

(In lakhs of rupees)

	Total Plan expenditure	*Central assistance*	*Percentage of Central assistance to Plan expenditure*
First Plan	1,151.71	1,000.00	87
Second Plan	3,120.20	2,000.00	64
Third Plan	6,409.34	6,200.00	97
Total	10,681.25	9,200.00	86

Thus, the State Plans have largely been financed by the Union Government. A statement is given in Appendix 6 showing the quantum of Central assistance received by each State of the Union for each of the three Five-Year Plans, for purposes of comparison.

4.07. The apportionment of the Plan expenditure to the regions has been done by the State Government at our request. In respect of the First Plan however, it has not been possible to do so in the absence of sufficient details. It may be stated that the First Plan of the State did not represent any major developmental effort, the total expenditure during the five years being only Rs. 1,151.71 lakhs. The Second and the Third Plans were much larger and the per capita expenditure on development went up from Rs. 37.25 in the First Plan to Rs. 196.37 in the Third-Plan.

4.08. The expenditure under each Head of Development in the Second and Third Plans has been apportioned to the regions after taking into account the expenditure on the schemes included under that Head and the region that each such scheme is intended to serve. As stated in paragraph 4.04, in respect of certain schemes it has, however, not been possible to determine the particular region which derives benefit from them, and so such expenditure has been shown as common to the two regions of Jammu and Kashmir. Worked out thus, the allocation of expenditure on the Second and the Third Plan to the different regions would be as follows:

(In lakh of rupees)

	Total Plan expenditure	*Jammu region*	*Kashmir region*	*Common to Jammu and Kashmir regions*	*Ladakh region*
Second Plan	3,120.20	1.385,23	1,472.62	175.70	86.65
Third Plan	6,409.34	2,119.69	2,796.78	1,345.51	147.36
Total	9,529.54	3,504.92	4.269.40	1,521.21	234.01

This shows that Ladakh has received a much smaller share than either the Jammu or the Kashmir region and that as between the Jammu and Kashmir regions, the share of the latter in so far as Plan expenditure is concerned, has been about twenty-two per cent higher than that of the former. During the Second Five Year Plan period, the levels of expenditure in the Jammu and Kashmir regions were not markedly different and it was only in the Third Plan period that a substantially higher expenditure was incurred in the Kashmir region.

4.09. The details of Plan expenditure under each Head of Development for each region are given in Appendix VII. A scrutiny of the expenditure under these Heads of Development shows that the major regional disparities occur in a few of them as, for instance 'Agriculture', 'Irrigation', 'Power', 'Transport and Communication', 'Education' and 'Health and Family Planning'. The physical achievements in each of these will be discussed in later paragraphs.

4.10. Apart from the Plan expenditure, there is also a certain amount of non-Plan expenditure incurred on developmental schemes. The bulk of this expenditure has been incurred on the construction of roads. The allocation of non-Plan expenditure to the regions during the Second and the Third Plan periods is as follows:—

(In lakhs of rupees)

	Jammu region	*Kashmir region*	*Common to Jammu and Kashmir regions*	*Ladakh region*	*Total*
Second Plan	245.22	153.25	—	—	398.47
Third Plan	1,006.79	390.88	153.48	949.36	2,500 51
Total	1,252.01	544.13	153.48	949.36	2,898.98

The details of non-Plan expenditure under each Head of Development for each region are also given in Appendix VII.

4.11. If we take both Plan and non-Plan developmental expenditure into account, the overall position relating to expenditure on the different regions would be as follows:

(In lakhs of rupees)

	Jammu region	*Kashmir region*	*Common to Jammu and Kashmir regions*	*Ladakh region*	*Total*
A. SECOND PLAN					
Plan Expenditure	1,385.23	1,472.62	175.70	86.65 3.	120.20
Non-Plan Expenditure	245.22	153.25			398.47
Total 'A' (Plan + Non-Plan Expenditure)	1,630.45	1,625,87	175.70	86.65 3	518.67
B. THIRD PLAN					
Plan Expenditure	2,119.69	2796.78	1.345.51	147.36	6,409.34
Non-Plan Expenditure	1,006.79	390,88	153.48	949.36	2,500.51
Total 'B' (Plan + Non-Plan Expenditure) .	3,126.48	3.187.66	1,498.99	1,096.72	8.909.85
Grand Total: 'A' + 'B' (Plan+ Non-Plan Expenditure	4,756.93	4,813.53	1,674.69	1,183.37	12,428.52

Thus, on an overall assessment and leaving out of account the unallocable part of the expenditure, the development programmes during the Second and Third Plan periods, expressed in terms of expenditure, cannot be said to have been unequally shared between the Jammu and Kashmir regions. There does not, therefore, seem to be justification for the complaint of there having been deliberate discrimination exercised against either region. Ladakh's share has only been about one-fourth of that of the Jammu or Kashmir region; and besides, out of the total developmental expenditure of Rs. 1,183.37 lakhs there, one single item—construction of roads—accounts for as much as Rs. 934.44 lakhs.

4.12. Before drawing any conclusions, however, we should like to invite attention to the table that follows, giving certain statistical data relating to the State of Jammu and Kashmir and its three regions.

	Item	*Jammu region*	*Kashmir region*	*Ladakh region*	*Total J&K State*
1	*Geographical Area* (Sq Miles)	10,073.1	5,836.0	37,753.8	53,664.9
2	*Population* (Mid Plan) *(Figures in lakhs)*				
	First Plan (Projected)	12.78	17.32	0.82	30.92
	Second Plan (Projected)	14. 70	18.42	0.86	33.98
	Third Plan (Projected)	16.73	20.06	0.95	37.74
3	*Actual Development Expenditure* (excluding items common to Jammu and Kashmir regions)				
					(In Lakhs of rupees)
	First Plan period		Not available		1,151.71
	Second Plan period				
	Plan	1,3.85.23	1,47.62	86.65	2,944.50
	Non-Plan	245.22	153.2		398.4
	Total—Second Plan period (Plan+Non-Plan Expenditure)	1,630.45	1,625.87	86.65	3,342.97*

(In Lakhs of rupees)

	Item	Jammu region	Kashmir region	Ladakh region	Total J&K State
	Third Plan period:				
	Plan	2,119.69	2,796.78	147.36	5,063.83
	Non-Plan	1.006.79	190.88	949.36	2.347.03
	Total—Third Plan period (Plan+Non-Plan Expenditure)	3,126-48	3,187,66	1,096.72	7,410.86
4	*Per Capita Expenditure*		*(In rupees)*		
	First Plan				37.25
	Second Plan	110.91	88.27	100.75	98.38*
	Third Plan	186.87	158.91	1,154.44	196.37
5	*Expenditure per sq mile*		*(In rupees)*		
	First Plan				2,146
	Second Plan	16,186	27,850	229	6,229
	Third Plan	31,038	54,602	2,905	13,809

1. The figures exclude area under unlawful occupation of Pakistan and China and its population.
2. The figures marked with an asterisk do not take into account the developmental expenditure on items common to Jammu and Kashmir regions.

These figures show that the Jammu region's share of the total developmental expenditure has attained a certain parity with that of the Kashmir region. It does not, however, necessarily follow from this that in terms of actual performance also, the situation in the Jammu region is comparable to that in the Kashmir region. Similarly, the high per capita expenditure on Ladakh in the Third Plan period may not have much significance if the extremely low density of population of the area is kept in view.

4.13. The per capita developmental expenditure during the Third Plan period was Rs. 158.91 in the Kashmir region and Rs. 186.87 in the Jammu region while the developmental expenditure per square mile was Rs. 54,602 and Rs. 31,038 respectively. As an indication of development, the expenditure per unit of area is not a relevant factor in most sectors though it may have some relevance in those like Agriculture, Communication, etc. The lower figure per square mile for the Jammu region perhaps only indicates that the sparsely populated and under-developed area is larger in the Jammu region than in the Kashmir region. To obtain an integrated view of the progress made in different sectors of development, the foregoing data have to be related to other relevant information, such as the physical achievements made in each of the sectors of development. These are discussed below for the following sectors.

(a) Agricultural Programmes;
(b) Irrigation;
(c) Power;
(d) Industries;
(e) Transport and Communications;
(f) Education; and
(g) Health and Family Planning.

4.14. *Agricultural Programmes.*—The expenditure incurred during each of the Second and the Third Plan periods on Agricultural Programmes in the Jammu and Kashmir regions was as follows:

(In lakhs of rupees)

	Jammu region	*Kashmir region*	*Common to Jammu and Kashmir regions*	*Ladakh region*	*Total*
Second Plan period	66.49	88.10	12.11	2.77	16.9.47
Third Plan period	165.02	269.99	24.86	28.93	479.80
Total	231.51	349.09	36.97	31.70	649.27

Under Agricultural Programmes, the activities included are: Agriculture, Horticulture, Animal Husbandry, Sheep, Breeding and Wool Development, Dairying and Milk Supply, Fisheries and Forests and Soil Conservation. The figures shown above for the Second and Third Plans pertain to expenditure incurred on all these activities. These figures show that the expenditure during the period of the Second and Third Plans on Agricultural Programmes in the Kashmir region was approximately fifty per cent more than in the Jammu region. The activities included in Agricultural Programmes are discussed separately below:—

(i) Agriculture (including Horticulture).—The expenditure incurred on Agriculture in the Jammu and Kashmir regions during the Second and Third Plan periods was as follows:—

(In lakhs of rupees)

	Jammu region	*Kashmir region*	*Common to Jammu and Kashmir regions*	*Ladakh region*	*Total*
Second Plan period	15.00	30.97	7.48	—	53.45
Third Plan period	73.68	103.31	—	4.74	181.73
Total	88.68	134.28	7.48	4.74	235.I8

The area under cultivation in each of these regions in the years 1950-51 and 1964-65 was as follows:—

	Unit	*Year*	*Jammu region*	*Kashmir region*	*Ladakh region*	*Total*
1. Gross area under cultivation	000 acres	1950-51	780	780	40	1600
		1964-65	1211	863	42	2116
2. Net area under cultivation		1950-51	746	753	37	1536
		1964-65	797	819	42	1658

Thus, while the gross area under cultivation in the Jammu region increased considerably between 1950-51 and 1964-65 it increased only marginally in the Kashmir region. In Ladakh it remained almost static. Further, while the gross area under cultivation in the Jammu region is much larger than in the Kashmir region, the investment in Agriculture in the former has been substantially less than in the latter.

(ii) *Animal Husbandry (including Sheep Breeding and Wool Development, Dairying and Milk Supply)*.—A considerable section of the population of the State is engaged on sheep breeding and cattle-rearing. The State Government made the investments, indicated below, on Animal Husbandry in each of the regions during the Second and the Third Plan periods:

(*In lakhs of rupees*)

	Jammu region	*Kashmir region*	*Common to Jammu and Kashmir regions*	*Ladakh region*	*Total*
Second Plan period	15.59	11.57	4.63	2.77	34.56
Third Plan period	33.16	68.98	4.95	16.21	123.30
Total	48.75	80.55	9.58	18.98	157.86

The progress achieved during the period of the three Plans is summarized in the following statement, which indicates the position immediately before the First Plan was launched and that at the end of the Third-Plan period:

Year	*Indicator*	*Unit of measure-ment*	*Jammu region*	*Kashmir region*	*Ladakh region*	*Total*
1950-51	1. Livestock population	Lakhs numbers	16.32	14.41	1.56	32.29
	2. Veterinary Hospitals and Dispensaries	Numbers	28	25	2	55
	3. Other Animal Husbandry Units	Numbers	3	2		5
1965-66	1. Livestock population	Lakhs numbers	23.50	14.86	2.43	40.79
	2. Veterinary Hospitals and Dispensaries	Numbers	65	71	4	142
	3. Other Animal Husbandry Units	Numbers	14	29	4	47

This table shows that though the livestock population in the Kashmir region is considerably smaller than in the Jammu region, the veterinary hospital facilities are better in the former and very much larger sums of money have been spent there than in the Jammu region or Ladakh.

(iii) *Forests and Soil Conservation*.—The activities of the State Government in this field of development can be judged from the following statistical tables:—

Expenditure

(In lakhs of rupees)

	Jammu region	*Kashmir region*	*Common to Jammu and Kashmir regions*	*Ladakh region*	*Total*
Second Plan period	34.39	40.54			74.93
Third Plan period	57.98	82.91	17.47	7.56	165.92
Total	92.37	123.45	17.47	7.56	240.85

Physical Achievements

	Unit of measurement	*Year*	*Jammu region*	*Kashmir region*	*Ladakh region*	*Total*
1. Sowing and planting of economic and industrial species	Acres	1956-57 to 1960-61	2,140	2,660	300	5,100
		1961-62 to 1965-66	1,039	4,654	N.A.	5,693
2. (a) Rehabilitation of degraded forest	Number of plants planted	1956-57 to 1960-61	35,000	65,000		100,000
(b) -do-	Acres	1961-62 to 1965-66	791	800		1,591
3. Soil Conservation on water-shed basis	Acres	1956-57 to 1960-61	40,862	13,381	660	54,903
		1961-62 to 1965-66	28,243	20,012	N.A.	48,255

N.A.: Not available.

Thus, in the field of forestry, the Kashmir region has received more attention than the Jammu region. In Jammu the emphasis has been on soil conservation. One wishes that more attention was paid to afforestation in Ladakh.

(iv) *Fisheries.*— The expenditure on Fisheries during the Second and the Third Plan periods in the different regions was as follows:—

(In lakh of rupees)

	Jammu region	*Kashmir region*	*Common to Jammu and Kashmir regions*	*Ladakh region*	*Total*
Second Plan period	1.51	5.02	—	—	6.53
Third Plan period	0.20	5.79	2.44	0.42	8.85
Total	1.71	10.81	2.44	0.42	15.38

Thus much higher investment was made in the Kashmir region than in either of the other two regions. In fact, in the Jammu region; there was a sharp decline in the investment during the Third Plan period. The higher expenditure in the Kashmir region is perhaps attributable to the fact that the scope for development of fisheries there was much greater than in the other regions.

4.15. *Irrigation.*—The amounts invested during the Second and the Third Five-Year Plan periods on irrigation and the results, as at the end of the Third Five-Year Plan period are as follows:

	Jammu region	*Kashmir region*	*Common to Jammu and Kashmir regions*	*Ladakh region*	*Total*
Expenditure during Second Plan period (In lakhs of rupees)	115.11	250.45	Nil	1.48	367.04
Expenditure during third Plan period (In lakhs of rupees)	169.05	527.16	120.98	4.07	821.26
Gross area under irrigation at the end of 1964-65 (In thousands of acres)	212	519		42	773

In irrigation, therefore, the Kashmir region is much better served than Jammu or Ladakh.

4.16. *Power:*—The expenditure incurred by the State Government on the development/purchase of power during the Second and the Third Five-Year Plan periods was as follows:

(In lakhs of rupees)

	Jammu region	*Kashmir region*	*Common to Jammu and Kashmir regions*	*Ladakh region*	*Total*
Second Plan period	152.68	219.06			371.74
Third Plan period	539.53	379 05	40.85		959.43
Total	692.21	598.11	40.85		1,331.17

The acutal achievement at the end of the Third Five-Year Plan period can be summarized thus:

	Unit of measure-ment	*Jammu region*	*Kashmir region*	*Ladakh region*	*Total*
Installed capacity	000 KW	3.50	24.00	Negligible	27.50
Electricity purchased	-do-	8.66	. .	. .	8.66
Towns and villages electrified	Actual number	177	349	Negligible	526

At the end of the Third Plan period, therefore, the availability of power in the Kashmir region was considerably more than in the Jammu region. In Ladakh it was almost negligible. The number of towns and villages electrified in the Kashmir region was almost double the number of those electrified in the Jammu region. The major Thermal/Hydel Projects under execution in the State are mentioned below:—

Jammu

(1) Chenani Hydro Electric Project with an ultimate capacity of 24 MW.

(2) Kalakote Thermal Power Project which is proposed to generate 22.5 MW.

Kashmir

(1) Lower Jehlum Hydro-Electric Project—Installed capacity 96 MW.

(2) Upper Sindh Hydel Project—intended to generate 34.5 MW

4.17. *Industries:*—There are certain natural disadvantages in setting up industries in this State. Cheap transport power and intrepreneurship are all lacking and the Government have had, therefore, to take the initiative in laying the foundation of its industrialization. Two companies were set-up in the public sector, viz., 'The Jammu and Kashmir Minerals Ltd.' and 'The Jammu and Kashmir Industries Ltd.' The following factories, arranged region-wise are functioning at present:

J&K Minerals Ltd.	*J&K Industries Ltd.*
Jammu	
1. Thermal Power Station, Kalakote	1. Sericulture
2. Mining of Coal at Kalakote	2. Knitting Factory
3. Padder Sapphire Mining Project	3. Kashmir Willows
	4. Rosin and Turpentine Factory
	5. Sole Leather Plant
	6. Arts Emporium
Kashmir	
1. Wuyan Cement Factory	1. Sericulture
2. Spun Pipe Factory	2. Woollen Mills
3. Prestressed Concrete Factory	3. Silk Weaving Factory
	4. Handloom Silk Weaving Factory
	5. Spinning Mill
	6. Joinery Mill
	7. Match Factory
	8. Pharmaceutical Works
	9. Leather Tanneries
	10. Bricks and Tiles Factory
	11. Arts Emporium

In addition, the following projects of the J&K Minerals Ltd. are under consideration:—

1. The Rayon Grade Pulp & Yarn Factory, Kashmir.
2. Cement Factories at Reasi and Basohli, Jammu.
3. A Paper Plant in Kashmir.

No factory has so far been located in Ladakh.

An idea of the performance of the six factories functioning under the J&K Minerals Ltd. can be had from Appendix 8 which is based on a note furnished by them.

There is not much industrial activity in the State and it is difficult to come to any definite, conclusions about it from the data furnished by the State Government in this region. The expenditure incurred on Industries during the Second Plan period has been split up by the State Government region-wise to some extent but the entire investment during the Third Plan period has been shown as being common to the two regions of Jammu and Kashmir. The expenditure during the two Plan periods was as follows:

(In lakhs of rupees)

	Jammu region	*Kashmir region*	*Common to Jammu and Kashmir regions*	*Ladakh region*	*Total*
Second Plan period	18.90	79.33	103.46		201.69
Third Plan period			864.07		864.07

The only conclusion that can be drawn from these figures is that Ladakh has not participated at all in the industrial development of the State.

The State Government have furnished some other information regarding the number of factories set-up in each region and the number of workers employed in them. The relevant data are reproduced below:—

	Jammu region		*Kashmir region*	
	1952	*1965*	*1952*	*1965*
Number of factories	19	78	27	113
Number of workers engaged	1,067	4,034	4,742	5,826

This shows that the Jammu region has received less attention than the Kashmir region in industrial development.

4.18. *Transport and Communications.—The* expenditure incurred on Transport and Communications in the Second and the Third Plan periods in the three regions of the State was as follows:

(In lakhs of rupees)

	Jammu region	*Kashmir region*	*Common to Jammu and Kashmir regions*	*Ladakh region*	*Total*
Second Plan period	693.77	449.11	6.52	63.74	1,213.14
Third Plan period	1,192.28	866.95	250.49	934.44	3,244.16
Total	1,886.05	1,316.06	257.01	998.18	4,457.30

Thus, considerable expenditure has been incurred by the State Government in this sector of development. Roads (including National Highways) and Bridges account for a substantial part of this expenditure. The important roads of the State are at present in the charge of three agencies, viz. the State Public Works Department, the Central Public Works Department and the Border Roads Development Board under the Ministry of Transport, Government of India. The financial outlays on the construction of roads and bridges in the Second and the Third Plan periods in the different regions of the State were as follows:

(In lakhs of rupees)

	Jammu region	*Kashmir region*	*Ladakh region*	*Total*
Second Plan period	487.12	245.48	63.74	796.34
Third Plan period	864.80	45.27	934.44	2,344.51
Total	1,351.92	790.75	998.18	3,140.85

The progress achieved in respect of roads under the State Public Works Department is shown on next page.

(In miles)

	Road milage at the beginning of the First Plan period			*Road milage at the end of the Third Plan period*		
	Jammu region	*Kashmir region*	*Ladakh region*	*Jammu region*	*Kashmir region*	*Ladakh region*
Motorable road milage (including jeepable roads)						
(i) Surlaccd	N.A.	416	—	715	1,201	Nil
(ii) Unsurfaced	N.A.	207	—	594	487	229
Total	432	623	—	1,309	1,168	229

N.A. : Not available.

These figures do not include the many miles of roads throughout the State which are in the charge of Central Government agencies.

In both the Jammu and Kashmir regions a number of places have been opened up and connected by new roads and the Suite and the Union Governments have applied themselves with vigour to this developmental activity. Much leeway has, however, still to be made up in the hilly and inaccessible areas of both the regions. In Ladakh, much road building activity has taken place recently but the Ladakhi people have not derived much benefit from them for lack of adequate civil transport facilities.

4.19. *Education.*—One significant feature of education in the Jammu and Kashmir State is that it is free from the kindergarten to the university stage. This has resulted in substantial growth in the education budget. The regional allocation of the State Government's expenditure on education during the last two Plan periods was as follows:—

(In lakhs of rupees)

	Jammu region	*Kashmir region*	*Common to Jammu and Kashmir regions*	*Ladakh region*	*Total*
Second Plan period	94.05	99.98	18.43	5.55	218.01
Third Plan period	234.99	325.61		12.33	572.93
Total	329.04	425.59	18.43	17.88	790.94

The progress made by the State Government in the matter of setting up of schools, colleges, professional institutions, etc. in the three regions during the period of the last three Plans may be judged from the following table showing the number of various types of educational institutions and the enrolment of students belonging to the different age groups in the years 1950-51 and 1965-66:—

Year 1950-51	*Jammu region*	*Kashmir region*	*Ladakh region*	*Total*
1. Primary Schools	647	510	25	1,182
2. Middle Schools	26	122	1	149
3. High and Higher Secondary Schools	16	26	2	44
4. Colleges (other than Medical, Engineering, Agricultural and Teachers' Training)	1	6		4
5. Teachers' Training:				
(a) T.T. Colleges	1	1	. .	2
(b) T.T. Schools	N.A.	N.A.	N.A.	N.A.
6. Enrolment				
(a) 6-11- years age	20,000	35,000	1,000	56,000
(b) 11-14 years age	3,000	18,000	100	21,100
(c) 14-17 years age	4,000	3,000	20	4,020
Year 1965-66				
1. Primary and Basic Schools	1,937	2,355	212	4,504
2. Middle Schools	522	582	27	1,131
3. High and Higher Secondary Schools	190	223	9	422
4. Colleges (other than Medical, Engineering, Agricultural and Teachers' Training)	7	9		16
5. Teachers' Training:				
(a) T.T. Colleges	1	1		2
(b) T.T. Schools	6	4	2	12
6. Enrolment:				
(a) 6-11 years age	1,42,000	1,44,000	5,000	2,91,000
(b) 11-14 years age	38,000	48,000	1,000	87,000
(c) 14-17 years age	16,000	25,000	300	41,300

N.A.: Not available.

It would also be worthwhile to compare the student-teacher ratios in high schools and colleges in the various regions:

	Jammu region	*Kashmir region*	*Ladakh region*	*Tolal*
High and Higher Secondary Schools:				
Year 1965-66:				
1. Number of High and Higher Secondary	190	223	9	422
2. Enrolment	63,867	65,606	935	1,30,408
3. Number of Teachers	2,734	3,363	77	6,174
4. Teachers per Institution	14.4	15.0	8.6	14.6
5. Students per Teacher	23	20	12	21
Colleges:				
Year 1965-66:				
1. Number of Colleges	7	9	..	16
2. Number of Teachers	245	367.	..	612
3. Enrolment	3.813	6840	..	10,653
4. Teachers per Institution	35	41	..	38
5. Students per Teacher	16	19	..	17

The data given above indicate the progress made in this vital field of development. They also show that in education, the Kashmir region has done better than the other regions. The student-teacher ratio for high, and higher secondary schools is smaller in the Kashmir region than in the Jammu region, though for colleges it is higher in the former. Enrolment in colleges is much higher in the Kashmir region—almost twice the enrolment in the Jammu region, though the former has only two more colleges. Professional institutions also are located mostly in the Kashmir region. The Agriculture College at Ranbirsinghpura in the Jammu Division has since been ordered to be closed.

4.20. *Health arid Family Planning.*—The steps taken by the State Government to improve the conditions of public health, which at the beginning of the First Five-Year Plan period were far from satisfactory, are summarized on next page.

(In lakhs of rupees)

	Jammu region	*Kashmir region*	*Common to Jammu and Kashmir regions*	*Ladakh region*	*Total*
Second Plan period	79.03	72.32	17.70	1.62	170.67
Third Plan period	140.13	208.43	8.41	6.51	363.48
Total	219.16	280.75	26.11	8.13	534.15

Physical Achievements:

Indicator	*Year*	*Jammu region*	*Kashmir region*	*Ladakh region*	*Total*
Number of Hospitals	1950-51	4	4	Nil	8
	1965-66	10	9	1	20
Number of Dispensaries		N.A.	N.A.	N.A.	11
		269	236	9	514
Number of Primary Health Centres		Nil	Nil	Nil	Nil
		23	30	Nil	53
Bed Strength		150	450	Nil.	600
		1,540	2,224	50	3,814
Number of Family Planning Centres		Nil	Nil	Nil	Nil
		8	10	1	19
Number of Doctors		86	98*	N.A.	184
		298	471	19	788

NA: Not available.
The figure marked with an asterisk includes the number of doctors in Ladakh region.

These tables show that at the end of the Third Plan period there was no great disparity between the Jammu and Kashmir regions in regard to the number of Hospitals, Dispensaries, Family Planning Centres and Primary Health Centres set-up. The number of Doctors was, however, almost 60 per cent more in the Kashmir region than in the Jammu region at the end of the Third Five-Year Plan period. It is also to be noted that even though the Kashmir region had only 9 hospital at the end of the Third Plan period as against 30 in the Jammu region, the bed-strength in the former was about 50 per cent more than in the latter. In Ladakh the facilities available appear to be extremely poor.

4.21. *Conclusions:* Thus, as we have said in paragraph 4.08, so far as developmental expenditure within the Plans is concerned, the expenditure incurred in the Kashmir-region has been about twenty-two per cent more than that incurred in the Jammu region. But it is only by taking into account the developmental, expenditure incurred outside the Plans also that some kind of arithmetical parity, between the two regions can be established. When we consider the items that constitute non-Plan developmental expenditure, we do not think that one should attach much importance to such parity. Appendix 7 shows that the non-Plan items are: Transport and Communications, National Highways and Colonies (Rehabilitation of Displaced Persons). In so far as: 'Transport and Communications' and 'National Highway' are concerned, it is difficult to say to what extent these may be deemed to serve purely regional needs and interests. It is doubtful whether the expenditure on the rehabilitation of displaced persons can be treated as developmental expenditure in the ordinary sense of the term. We have noticed that in most of the sectors of development discussed in paragraphs 4.14 to 4.20, judged by the physical achievements, the Kashmir region has done better than the other regions.

4.22. In absolute terms it is very difficult to define equitability as applied to the sharing of resources by different regions of a State and perhaps even more difficult to achieve it in practice. In judging this, several factors have to be taken into account such as population, area, specific needs, potential available, etc. Irrespective of the criteria that are adopted for the purpose, it is important that the people of each region should have a feeling of equal participation in the integrated development of the State. From the various memoranda and the oral evidence, we came to realize how strongly Jammu nurses a feeling of being discriminated against in developmental matters. It is not possible to ignore this feeling of dissatisfaction even allowing for the fact that much of it seems to be psychological. The position of Ladakh is somewhat similar. From the statistical and other data which we have examined in this Chapter; the conclusion seems fairly clear that the Kashmir region has on the whole received more attention than the other regions during the period of the three Plans. Even so, we do not think that on the basis of the material available to us, we would be justified in concluding that the State Government have deliberately discriminated against either Jammu or Ladakh.

4.23. In oral testimony as also in a number of memoranda, it was represented to us that within both the Jammu and Kashmir regions there are certain pockets which have remained much more backward than the rest of the region. These are the hilly and inaccessible parts of the State. It has not been possible to assess the extent of development, or the lack of it in these areas as district-wise details of development programmes and developmental expenditure are not maintained by the State Government. From the evidence produced before us, however, we feel that these areas deserve special attention and the Government should address themselves urgently to the task of developing them speedily.

4.24. The development in Ladakh during the period of the three plans has been inadequate. True, a number of roads have been constructed in the area but the public transport facilities still remain unsatisfactory. We feel that a vitally important border area like Ladakh should receive greater attention from both the State Government and the Union Government and that the Ladakhis should not be allowed to nurse a feeling that they are being left out in the State's march to prosperity.

4.25. *Recommendations.*—We have given thought to the question of how best to ensure that the resources available to the State Government are shared equitably by the regions so that they have a feeling of equal-participation in the integrated development of the State. It is not easy to lay down a rigid formula for the purpose nor do we think it is necessary to devise one. We should, however, like to visualize an arrangement whereby the regions can have the maximum opportunity to draw up their own developmental programmes and to implement them subject to the interests of the State as a whole.

4.26. We would suggest that there should be a statutory State Development Board and statutory Regional Development Boards for the three regions—Jammu, Kashmir and Ladakh. Each of the Regional Boards should be headed by the Chief Minister or the Planning Minister and should consist of legislators from the regions, economists, experts and concerned officials. . . The regions should be adequately represented on State Development Board which should be headed by the Chief Minister.

4.27. The functions of the Regional Development Boards should be:

(a) to draw up the regional Plans;
(b) to assign priority to schemes and projects included in the regional Plans; and
(c) to supervise the implementation of the regional Plans.

In discharging these functions it should be the special responsibility of the Regional Development Boards to look after the special needs of the backward areas in their respective regions.

4.28. The regional Plans prepared by the Regional Development Boards should be placed before the State Development Board which should carefully scrutinize them. The State Development Board should also prepare a residuary Plan of such schemes and projects as transcend regional boundaries or happen to be of an all-State, as opposed to regional, interest. With the regional Plans and the residuary Plan before it, the State Development Board should allocate Plan funds equitably (after taking into account the population, area and the specific, needs of each region) to the regional Plans and the residuary Plan of all-State interest.

4.29. We consider it very important that the general population should be kept correctly and adequately informed of the progress of development programmes and developmental expenditure. We would accordingly suggest that the State Development Board and each of the Regional Development Boards should prepare at the end of each year a report of their respective activities giving, details of the progress of the Plan programmes and Plan expenditure. At the end of each Plan, similar detailed reports should be prepared by the Boards indicating the physical and financial targets and the physical and financial achievements. All these reports should be laid before the Legislature as soon as may be after they are prepared.

CHAPTER V

RECRUITMENT Pounds

5.01. *Introduction.*—We shall now examine the recruitment policies of the State Government as required by our second term of reference. We have also to "recommend measures for giving an equitable share in the Government employment to the various regions and communities, having special regard to the claims of the Scheduled Castes and other economically, educationally and socially backward communities, classes and groups.

Several memorialists and representatives have complained that in the matter of recruitment to Government services there is discrimination on communal or religious grounds, or a lack of reservation for the Scheduled Castes and for those who claim to be economically educationally and socially backward. The question of giving an equitable representation in the services to the various communities of the State has a rather long history. In the late twenties and early thirties there were complaints that the Muslims, who formed the great majority of the population were not adequately represented in the State services and that this was also true of certain minority communities of the State.

5.02. *Glancy Commission.*—In November 1931, a Commission was appointed consisting of 4 non-official members, presided over by a European member, Mr. Bertrand J. Glancy of the Indian Civil Service (seconded to the then Indian Political Service), who was lent to the Jammu and Kashmir State by the Government of India, to enquire into and report on the various complaints, of religious or general nature already submitted to the State Government and also such complaints as might be directly laid before the Commission. It was from his name that the Commission derived its popular title of "the Glancy Commission."

5.03. *Recommendations.*—On the question of employment in the public services of the State, the Glancy Commission found that, generally the Muslims and certain minority communities were inadequately represented in the services. It made certain

1. Chapter IV of the Report of the Commission appointed under the Orders of His Highness the Maharaja Bahadur, dated the 13th November, 1931, to inquire into Grievances & Complaints, 2nd Edition, 1933 (hereafter referred to as the Report of the Glancy Commission).

recommendations with a view to achieving a more equitable method of recruitment to the services and affording to every community a fair chance of representation. Its principal recommendations on the subject are summarized below:

(i) While there need not be different standards for different communities, the standard should not be more exacting than efficiency demanded and those who possessed qualifications in excess of that standard should not be held to deserve appointment as a matter of right.

(ii) There was no need to change the age limit which was then thirty years.

(iii) Appointments and scholarships should be properly advertised and given as wide publicity as possible.

(iv) Due regard should be paid to the legitimate interests of every community in the matter of recruitment to Government services and the grant of scholarships for training provided that suitable candidates were forthcoming.

5.04. In regard to the claim that the Muslims, who constituted 78 per cent of the State's population, should be given a corresponding reservation in Government appointments, the Commission observed that it rested with the Muslims to work up the number of their representatives in State services by availing themselves of the opportunities to be pro-vided. It also observed that the hereditary occupation of a vast number of Muslims was agriculture and it was reasonable to suppose that the great majority of agriculturists would continue to prefer that occupation to any other. While no community should be allowed to acquire a stranglehold on State employment, the Commission wanted it to be recognized that certain communities were far in advance of others in [2]education.

5.05. It was claimed before the Glancy Commission that although no scholarships had been specifically reserved for Kashmiri Pandits, over 50 per cent of their numbers were literate (a far higher percentage than in any other community), that ministerial work had been their hereditary occupation and that they had no other means of subsistence readily available. The Commission recognized the force of this contention and

2. Page 24 of the Report of the Glancy Commission.

recommended that the need for other openings that could be legitimately provided for those who could not/be absorbed in State departments should receive the sympathetic attention of the Government. It should be carried out to the best of the Government's ability, for example, in the [3]field of industrial development, etc.

5.06. These recommendations of the Commission were accepted the then Ruler of the [4]State.

5.07. *Recruitment Rules Committee.*— The recommendations of the Glancy Commission did not bring about a final solution to the problem. A few years later a Committee was appointed to formulate proposals for recruitment to and training for, the services, the Recruitment Rules Committee was presided over by Mr. P.C. Mogha then Revenue Minister, and its members were the Chief Justice. Use Chief Secretary and the Accountant General of the State, besides Mr. M. Afzal Khan, Revenue Commissioner and later Home Minister of the State. The report of the Committee on the gazetted services was published in 1939 and that on the non-gazetted services in 1941.

5.08. *Main recommendations of the Committee.*—The Committee made detailed proposals regarding the classification of each service, gazetted and non-gazetted into classes and categories, the method of recruitment of each class and category and the qualifications required of the candidates. The main recommendations of the Committee which involved a departure from, or improvement on, the position under the Glancy Commission's Report are summarized below:—

(i) For direct recruitment the age limit should be reduced to 28 years, except for gazetted appointments in such departments as the Judicial, Education and Medical Departments where higher educational qualifications were required. In the Judicial and Education Departments, an age limit of 30 years was recommended and in the case of the Medical Department a still higher age limit of 32 years was [5]proposed.

3. Page 23 of the Report of the Glancy Commission.
4. Orders on the recommendations mentioned in the Report of the Glancy Commission.
5. Page 1 of the Interim Report of the Recruitment, Rules Committee re: Gazetted Services, 1939.

(ii) For gazetted services the normal method of recruitment should be by a competitive examination. Direct recruitment by nomination was provided for in most of the services but the Committee did not consider it desirable to fix a ratio between nomination and recruitment by competition as it thought that recruitment by nomination should be resorted to only exceptionally and should not be regarded as a normal method. The Committee recommended a proportion between direct appointments and promotions, including transfer, varying from 50 to 75 per cent according to the circumstances of each department. One consideration on recruitment was that it would give a better chance for regulating communal [6]represeniation.

(iii) For non-gazetted services the Committee recommended five methods of recruitment, namely, selection, nomination, competitive examination, promotion from a lower category or grade and transfer from another class. Recruitment partly by one method and partly by another was also recommended. The Report also indicated the proportion in which recruitment should be made direct, i.e., by selection, nomination or competitive examination, and by promotion or transfer. For technical departments such as the Medical and Public Works Departments, recruitment by competitive examination was not considered necessary and nomination or selection was considered [7]sufficient.

5.09. The Report of the Committee indicates that though no definite orders existed at the time on the subject of communal representation, 50 per cent representation for the Muslim community was supposed to be the [8]aim. This Committee also

6. Page 2 of the Interim Report of the Recruitment Rules Committee re: Gazetted Services, 1-939.
7. Pages 1-3 of the Report of the Committee appointed to formulate proposals for recruitment to Government services (Non-Gazetted Services), 1941.
8. Page 3 of the Interim Report of the Recruitment Rules Committee re: Gazetted Services, 1939.

suggested rules for the various competitive examinations recommended by it and detailed syllabuses for each of them.

5.10. *Position after introduction of popular rule.*—After the introduction of popular rule in the State in 1947, there was large expansion of the services as a result of accelerated developmental activities of the State Government. We have been advised by the State Government that between 1947 and 1953, recruitment was made in some Departments after observing the usual formalities but "there were cases where this 'was not done". In explanation, it has been stated that "recruitment could not probably be made strictly under the rules which were sanctioned as far back as in 1941". We have also been informed that immediately after 1947, some appointments in the higher ranks were also made from political cadres, though the number of such appointments was small.

5.11. *Jammu and Kashmir Public Services Reorganization Committee.*—To enable measures being taken towards the establishment of a State Public Service Commission as a statutory body, the State Government set-up.

The Committee does not seem to have submitted a report; the State Government have informed it that no copy of such a report is traceable.

5.12. *Jammu and Kashmir Public Service Recruitment Board:*—By an Order dated 31 December 1954 the Government appointed a Recruitment Board for recruitment to the superior services of the State. The powers and functions of this Board, designated as the Jammu and Kashmir Public service Recruitment Board, were laid down in a subsequent Order dated 2 May, 1955. It was required to advise the Government on the method, manner and principles governing direct recruitment to gazetted services and such non-gazetted superior services as might be specified by the Government from time to time, in accordance with the qualifications, standards, and other requirements laid down in the recruitment rules and other rules issued in that behalf. The activities of the Board were thus confined to cases of direct recruitment and promotion cases did not fall within its purview. We have been told by the State Government that while the Board made recommendations regarding direct recruitment to gazetted services from time to time, very few cases of non-gazetted establishment were referred to it. On the esta'·lishment of a Public

Service Commission in the State, the Recruitment Board was abolished on 2 September 1957.

5.13. *The Jammu and Kashmir Civil Services (Classification, Control and Appeal) Rules, 1956.* In June 1956, the State Government promulgated the Jammu and Kashmir Civil Services (Classification, Control and Appeal) Rules. These rules were originally framed in exercise of the powers conferred on the Government by the Jammu and Kashmir Civil Servants (Removal of Doubts and Declaration of Rights) Ordinance, 1956. When the Ordinance was replaced by a regular Act of the Legislature, the Jammu and Kashmir Civil Services (Classification, Control and Appeal) Rules were saved and they are still in force. Various representatives have complained that certain provisions of the Jammu and Kashmir Civil Services (Classification, Control and Appeal) Rules are being ignored or applied in such a way as to cause irritation and result in undue discrimination, the provisions which are alleged to be generally ignored are those relating to the prescription of qualifications for recruitment, seniority and promotions. Those which are alleged to be misused are the ones, relating to the reservation of posts for the backward classes and the provision that enables the Government to declare that the Jammu and Kashmir (Classification, Control and Appeal) Rules, 1956, shall not apply in whole or in part to a particular person or group of persons or to relax in individual cases and for reasons to be recorded in writing, any of those rules or any rules made thereunder if the Government is satisfied that a strict application of the rules would cause hardship to the individual concerned or confer undue benefit on him.

5.14. In order to judge whether the provisions of the rules of the Jammu and Kashmir Government have any unusual characteristics, they have been compared with the corresponding rules of the Union Government and of a few other States in the country. It has been found that so far as the procedure for consultation with the Public Service Commission is concerned the position in the Jammu and Kashmir State is on the whole similar to the position obtaining elsewhere. The differences, where they exist, are marginal. The only point which may be considered to make some difference is the exclusion of all appointments, promotions and transfers to non-gazetted services in Jammu and Kashmir from the purview of the Public Service Commission of the [9]State. But it is relevant to point out here that several categories of posts which would be included in the non-gazetted category in other States, are included in the gazetted category in Jammu and Kashmir.

5.15. In regard to the provisions of the Classification, Control and Appeal Rules also the position in Jammu and Kashmir does not appear to be materially different from the position at the Centre or in some other States.

5.16. The regulations relating to their Public Service Commission or the Jammu and Kashmir Civil Services (Classification, Control and Appeal) Rules do not, therefore, by themselves allow special scope for discrimination in the matter of recruitment, transfers, etc. of the State Government staff.

5.17. Coming to the complaints mentioned in paragraph 5.13, it may be mentioned that up-to-date recruitment rules do not exist for several services and posts. The absence of such rules has been the subject of criticism by the State Public Service Commission. They have complained that for a large majority of posts referred to them proper recruitment rules have not been framed and among those that exist, some are obsolete and require revision. They have also observed that for a large number of posts, qualifications have not been prescribed nor have the posts been [10]classified. This criticism has appeared in more than one Report of the Commission. The State Government are aware of this unsatisfactory position and steps are being taken to frame proper recruitment rules. According to available information, proper recruitment rules exist in the case of 4 State services only; for one service the rules require to be brought up to date; for 5 services the rules are still in the draft stage and for 10 other services no rules have been drafted so far. The progress of framing the recruitment rules needs to be speeded up.

5.18. *Results of competitive examinations.*—Here we should like to mention that some representatives demanded that the detailed subject-wise results of the competitive examinations held by the State Public Service Commission should be published for general information as was the practice before 1947. They thought that

9. Regulation 4 of the Jammu and Kashmir Public Service Commission (Limitation of Functions) Regulations, 1957.
10. Annual Reports of the Jammu and Kashmir Public Service Commission for the years 1963-64 and 1965-66.

such publication would remove any possible doubts with regard to the results and would also enable the public to judge whether or not the appointments had been made strictly on the basis of merit. In the course of his evidence before us, the Chairman of the State Public Service Commission stated that the Commission only published the aggregate marks of the candidates and that if it was the practice of the Union Public Service Commission to publish the detailed results, subject-wise, in respect of the examinations held by it, the State Public Service Commission would also consider doing so. He, however, added that a considerable time-lag in the publication of the detailed results would be unavoidable. In order to allay any misgivings in the mind of the public, we should like to recommend that the results, complete in all details, of all competitive examinations held by the State Public Service Commission, and any other Recruitment Board that may be set-up, should be published. These results should be sent to all the candidates who have taken the examination or, if this is not always feasible, they should at least be made available for scrutiny on request.

5.19. *Seniority Lists.*—The Annual Reports of the Public Service Commission also indicate that proper seniority lists are not always being [11]maintained. We have been told that the State Government are drawing up seniority lists, service by service. The State Government are having difficulty in doing so because of past neglect. It is needless to say that the drawing up of correct seniority lists and maintaining them up to date is a *sine qua non* for being able to deal with cases of promotion on a fair basis.

5.20. *Confidential rolls.*—Another defect pointed out in the Annual Reports of the Public Service Commission is that the confidential rolls of the members of the services are not always [12]submitted. When a question of supersession is involved this naturally makes it difficult for the Commission to judge whether the supersession is justified or not. Some of the memoranda presented to us have expressed the fear and suspicion that the remarks actually recorded in the character rolls were influenced

11. Annual Report of the Jammu and Kashmir Public Service Commission for the year 1964-65 and 1965-66.
12. Annual Report of the Jammu and Kashmir Public Service Commission for the year 1964-65.

by extraneous considerations. It is obviously necessary that the annual confidential rolls should be written up regularly and objectively and that provision should be made for review of the rolls by an authority superior to the reporting officer wherever such a provision does not already exist. We presume that adverse entries recorded in the confidential rolls of Government servants are communicated to them in accordance with the general practice in this matter. A procedure should be prescribed for dealing properly with representations of Government servants against such adverse entries.

5.21. *Viva Voce Tests.*—Complaints have been made to us that in the matter of recruitment to Government services, undue weightage is being given to *viva voce* tests, and that this leads to discrimination. No party, however, has been able to substantiate this charge. We obviously cannot recommend that *viva voce* tests should be dispensed with, nor do we consider that the weightage given by the State Government to such tests is disproportionately large.

5.22. *Communal Reservation.*—Our terms of reference require us to recommend measures for giving an equitable share in Government employment to the various regions and communities, having special regard to the claims of the Scheduled Castes and other economically, educationally and socially backward communities, classes and groups among the citizens of the State consistently with the maintenance of efficiency of administration. It has been enjoined on us that in considering this matter we should take note of the provisions contained in Part III—"Fundamental Rights" as well as other provisions of the Constitution of India as made applicable to the State of Jammu and Kashmir and of the Directive Principles of State Policy laid down in Part IV of the Constitution of Jammu and Kashmir and particularly of Section 23 thereof. As mentioned at the outset of this Chapter, the problem of affording equitable representation to the various communities of the State in the services is not a new one. Even the Glancy Commission and the Recruitment Rules Committee had occasion to deal with the matter many years ago.

5.23. The irritations and tensions mentioned in our fourth term of reference and which are likely to arise from various causes, including those that have given rise to our other three terms of reference, are not confined to the State of Jammu and Kashmir.

Irritations and tensions arising from similar causes exist in the minds of different communities and groups of citizens in other parts of India too; and it is the urgent and paramount duty of Indian democracy to remove the causes of such irritations and tensions. This problem has become more acute with the passage of time, the growth of population, the adoption-of the Welfare State ideology and the spread of mass education. Unless the socially and economically weaker sections of the Indian community, including the Scheduled Castes and the backward classes, as well as the members of linguistic and religious minorities residing in all parts of India, feel that the concept of equality of opportunity and justice—political, social and economic—has become a reality in their lives, these tensions and irritations are likely to continue. The goal set by the Constitution of India before Indian, democracy to afford equality before law to all citizens and to create a social and economic structure in which every citizen will be able to enjoy fully life, liberty, and happiness yet remains to be attained and it must be the earnest endeavour of Indian democracy to reach that goal as early as possible. We would like to emphasize, here that in the matter of irritations and tensions, whatever happens in the rest of India is bound to haw an immediate impact on the State of Jammu and Kashmir and *vice-versa*.. These general observations will apply to the further discussion of the problems which have been referred to us. How the causes for irritations and tensions existing in the minds of groups of citizens in the rest of India should be removed is a matter with which we are not concerned in the present inquiry.

5.24. We have obtained from the State Government statistical data regarding the communal and regional composition of the State Government staff as on 1 April 1967 as well as the communal and regional composition of the persons recruited to the State Government services, year by year, from 1961-62 to 1965-66. We have also had before us the statistical data furnished by the State Government to the High Court of Jammu and Kashmir in regard to the regional and communal composition of the gazetted and non-gazetted staff of the State Government as on 10 September 1963 in the case of Triloki Nath and another *Vs*. State of Jammu and Kashmir and others, a case to which we will make further reference in the subsequent paragraphs of this Chapter. Appendix IX is a summary of the data as compiled in the

Commission's Secretariat. It will be seen that region-wise, the position in the Kashmir Valley, taking both the rate of annual recruitment and the total strength of the staff, has improved while the corresponding position in Jammu has deteriorated. Though the Kashmir region's population is 53.3 per cent of the total population of the State, its share in the services as on 1 April 1967 was 60.9 per cent. The Jammu region's population is 44.2 per cent of the total population of the State but its share in the services on 1 April 1967 was only 36.1 per cent. The rate of recruitment of Ladakhis has shown a decline from 2.5 per cent in 1961-62 to 1.4 per cent in 1965-66. Their total share in the services as on 1 April 1967, however, was slightly in excess of the proportion of the population of Ladakh to the total population of the State. Community-wise the position of Muslims has shown an improvement though their total share in the services on 1 April 1967 was appreciably less than what it should be oh the basis of population. The position of Hindus has shown a decline though their share in the services as on 1 April 1967 was substantially higher than what was due to them according to their population. The annual intake of Buddhists has also shown a fall. The recruitment of Sikhs in the services has been fluctuating from year to year but their share on 1 April 1967 was considerably in excess of what was due to them on a population basis.

5.25. *Constitutional provision.*—Prior to the coming into force of the Constitution of India, reservations in the services, the legislatures, etc. in the country were made on the basis of religion. The recommendations of the Glancy Commission also seem to have followed the same pattern. Article 370 of the Constitution of India, which, came into force on 26 January 1950, makes a special provision with respect to the State of Jammu and Kashmir. The President issued an order under that Article on 14 May 1954 extending the application of the provisions of the Constitution of India to Jammu and Kashmir and indicating the exceptions and modifications subject to which they should [13]apply. This order made Article 15 of the Constitution, prohibiting discrimination on grounds of religion, race, caste, sex or place of birth, and Article 16, guaranteeing equality of opportunity in matters of public employment, applicable to the State of Jammu and Kashmir,

13. The Constitution (Application to Jammu and Kashmir) Order, 1954.

subject to the following modifications:—

(i) The reference to Scheduled Tribes in clause (4) of Article 15 is to be omitted; and

(ii) the reference to State in clause (3) of Article 16 is to be construed as not including a reference to the State of Jammu and Kashmir.

Article 29 dealing with protection of minorities became applicable without any modification. Section 10 of the Constitution of Jammu and Kashmir, which came into force on 17 November 1956, guarantees to the permanent residents of the State all the rights guaranteed to them under the Constitution of India, including the provisions, of Articles 15, 16 and 29. In Section 23, the Constitution of Jammu and Kashmir lays down a directive principle that the State shall guarantee to the socially and educationally backward sections of the people special care in the promotion of their educational, material and cultural interests and protection against social injustice.

5.26. *Position of Scheduled Castes and Scheduled Tribes.*—Apparently no tribe in Jammu and Kashmir is treated as a Scheduled Tribe. No special constitutional safeguards have been made for such tribes. For Scheduled Castes, the only Article—Article 335—in the Constitution of India dealing with the claims of the Scheduled Castes to services and posts has been rendered inapplicable to services and posts in connection with the affairs of the Jammu and Kashmir State by virtue of sub-para (11) of paragraph 2 of the Constitution (Application to Jammu and Kashmir) Order, 1954.

5.27. *Implementation of the Constitutional provisions by the State Government.*—The Government of Jammu and Kashmir do not appear to be following any clear-cut policy either in the classification of backward classes or in the matter of special benefits to be given to them. In February 1956 they issued a notification in which certain classes were recognized as 'backward classes'. The list has been amended from time to time. A copy of the list as it stands now is attached at Appendix 10. As far as we have been able to understand, this list, has been used only for the limited purpose of granting special scholarships to students belonging to the classes. In June 1956 the State Government issued the Jammu at Kashmir Civil Services (Classification, Control and

Appeal) Rules in which a clause was included to enable the State Government to make operations in Government services in favour of any backward class which, in the opinion of the Government, was not adequately represented in the services. It appears, however, that the term "backward classes" used for the purpose of recruitment did not have the same meaning as the one mentioned in the notification of February 1956, as amended from time to time. In fact the State Government do not appear to have issued any clear-cut orders, statutory or other, specifying which are the backward classes for the purpose of being accorded special facilities in the matter of recruitment to Government services. They have had some working rule which has been subject to modification from time to time to suit particular situations. The latest working rule, as it emerged from at affidavit filed by the State Government in a [14]writ petition submitted by two teachers to the Supreme Court, is apparently that 50 per cent of the posts are to be filled by Muslims from the entire State of Jammu and Kashmir and 40 per cent of them are to be filled by Jammu Hindus. The State Government sought to justify this working rule in the Supreme Court on the ground that Muslims as a community in the whole of the State of Jammu and Kashmir formed a "backward class" of citizens and they were not adequately represented in the services in the State; and that similarly; Hindus from the province of Jammu formed "a backward community" and were not adequately represented in the services of the State. Accordingly, reservation in the matter of appointments to posts and promotions in the services of the State was made in respect of both these classes.

5.28. *Supreme Court's Rulings.*—The Supreme Court examine the position at great length and observed as [15]follows:

> "Clause (4) of Art. 16 undoubtedly empowers the State to make reservation of appointments or posts in favour of any backward class of citizens so as to give the class an adequate representation in the services under the State. The provision

14. Writ Petition No. 107 of 1965 in the Supreme Court of India.
15. Judgement of the Supreme Court in Writ Petition No. 107 of 1965—Triloki Nath and another *Vs.* State of Jammu and Kashmir and others—delivered 23 April 1968.

making such reservation need not be by a statutory enactment; it may be made by an executive order or direction. But there is not even a formal executive order expressly dealing with reservation of posts and appointments in the Education Department. On behalf of the State it is claimed that as a matter of State Policy, in making appointments and promotions, reservations in fact have been made by the State as alleged by the petitioners with some variations. . . .

The expression backward class is not used as synonymous with 'backward caste' or 'backward community'. The members of an entire caste or community may in the social, economic and educational scale of values at a given time be backward and may on that account be treated as a backward class, but that is not because they are members of a caste or community, but because they form a class. In its ordinary connotation the expression 'class' means a homogeneous section of the people grouped together because of certain likenesses or common traits, who are identifiable by some common attributes such as the states, rank, occupation, residence in a locality, race, religion and the like. But for the purpose of Art. 16(4) in determining whether a section forms a class, a test solely based on caste, community, race, religion, sex, descent, place of birth or residence cannot be adopted, because it would directly offend the Constitution.

"In the voluminous evidence produced before the High Court a formal order making a provision for reservation of appointments or posts in favour of any backward class of citizens does not find a place. The only evidence to which our attention has been invited is the statement of Malik Ghulam Nabi, who deposed that the policy laid down by the Government in matters of the employment to the State services is that 50 per cent of the vacancies are reserved for the Muslims of Kashmir (for the entire State). Out of the remaining 50 per cent, 40 per cent are reserved for the Jammu Hindus and 10 per cent for the Kashmiri Hindus. There are a number of Government orders by which this policy has been laid down, but due to the short time at my disposal, I have been able to get only one copy of such order, which is signed by the Chief Secretary, whose handwriting I know and identify. In cross-examination Malik Ghulam Nabi stated that the order produced by him applied to all kinds of services under the State and it was being implemented even now and was still in force. The witness was unable to speak to the criteria on the basis of which the order was issued. . . It was recorded in paragraph-4 of the order that a Selection Board consisting of four Secretaries to the Government was set-up and they were asked to prepare a Select List on the basis of merit-*cum*-seniority, keeping in view the policy of adequate representation of such elements as are not adequately represented in the services and to pay due regard to provincial proportions. There is no reference in any of the clauses of the order to selection of officers on the basis that they belong to backward classes. The injunction to the Secretaries to select candidates keeping in view the policy of adequate representation of such elements as were not adequately represented in the services is not a provision making reservation of appointments or posts in favour of backward classes. Selections made, assuming that similar orders were passed enjoining the making of promotions to the gazetted, cadre in the Educational Service, could not be deemed to have been made on the basis of backwardness of the class to which they belonged.

"The State of Jammu and Kashmir had, it is admitted, from time to time framed lists of backward communities. . . But it is not claimed that in making promotions to the gazetted cadre in the Educational Service, the authorities acted in pursuance of the List. . . As already observed the normal rule contemplated by the constitutional provision is equality between aspirants to public employment, but in view of backwardness of certain classes it would be open to the State to make a provision for reservation of appointments or posts in their favour. When the State proceeds not to make reservations in favour of any backward class, but to distribute the total number of posts or appointments on the basis of community or place or residence, no reservation permitted by cl. (4) of Art. 16 can be said to be made. In effect the State policy which Malik Ghulam Nabi spoke to was a policy not of reservation of some appointments or posts: it was a scheme of distribution of all the posts community-wise. Distribution of appointments, posts or promotions made in implementation of that State policy is contrary to the constitutional guarantee under Art. 16(1) and (2) and is not saved by cl. (4).

"The promotions granted to respondents 3 to 83 are accordingly declared contrary to the provisions of Art. 16(1) and (4) of the Constitution and therefore void."

5.29. The Supreme Court had also occasion to examine the legality of reservation on a regional basis, in connection with a series of writ petitions filed against the policy of the Madras Government of allocating the seats in the Medical Colleges of the State to the various districts in the ratio of the population of each district to the total population of the State. It has [16]held that the allocation of seats on district-wise basis is *ultra vires* of Article 14 of the Constitution of India and has accordingly struck down the policy of the Madras Government. The principle enunciated by the Supreme Court in that case will, in our opinion, hold good in the case of recruitment to Government services and posts as well and any recommendation for fixing quotas for recruitment on a purely regional basis will be *ultra vires* of Article 16 of the Constitution of India as made applicable to the Jammu and Kashmir State.

5.30. The Muslims of the entire State together with the Hindus of Jammu province form 94.2 per cent of the total population of the State. When practically the entire population is treated as backward, there is bound to be considerable difference in the degree of backwardness between one class and another included in that population. The really backward classes which need protection have, therefore, to compete with those which are more advanced. This is bound to shut out the classes which are really backward from the services and we believe that this is what has happened in the State.

16. Judgement of the Supreme Court in Writ Petitions 194 of 1967 etc. and Civil Appeal No. 1456 of 1965—Minor P. Rajendran *Vs.* the State of Madras & others etc.—delivered on 17 January 1968.

5.31. While passing orders striking down the promotions of teachers in the Education Department, referred to in paragraphs 5.27 and 5.28, the Supreme Court has observed that its orders would not prevent the State Government from devising a scheme, consistent with the Constitutional guarantees, for the reservation of appointments, posts or promotions in favour of any backward class of citizens which in the opinion of the State is not adequately represented in the services under the State. In our opinion, the immediate requirement is to draw up afresh the list of backward classes in the State. The adoption of a single criterion or test of community, caste or region to which the persons concerned belong will be *ultra vires* of the Constitution. For identifying the backward classes in the State, therefore, a multiple test will have to be adopted; in other words, several criteria relating to economic, educational and social backwardness will have to be applied for determining which classes are really backward. Several witnesses who gave evidence before us were also of the same view.

5.32. Here, we should like to draw attention to the fact that clause (4) of Article 16 is in the nature of an exception, made in favour of the backward classes, to the basic principle enunciated in Article 14 and clauses (1) and (2) of Article 16, guaranteeing equality of opportunity to all citizens in matters relating to employment or appointment to any office under the State. In giving effect to the provisions of this clause, therefore, it is necessary to determine, for every State, which are the socially and educationally backward classes within its boundaries that deserve the protection of that clause. In India, some States are relatively advanced, socially and educationally, while certain others are comparatively backward. Even for a State that is relatively backward, socially and educationally, it is not permissible, in terms of Article 16(4), to treat the whole of the State as "backward" or a whole community as a community as "backward", without the application of the multiple test referred to in the previous paragraph. The attempt to identify the socially and educationally backward sections which deserve the protection of clause (4) of Article 16, involves making a comparison between different classes of citizens. Only such classes of citizens in the State can justifiably claim the protection of that clause as constitute socially and educationally the weakest section of the community. What we have stated here in relation to public employment applies equally to clause (4) of Article 15, which was introduced by way of a constitutional amendment in 1951; it provides for an exception to the basic principle contained in Article 14 and clauses (1) and (2) of Article 15, prohibiting, discrimination on grounds of religion, race, caste, sex or place of birth. This exception has been "made as a measure of protection to the backward classes and the Scheduled Castes and the Scheduled Tribes."

5.33. *Multiple criteria for determining backwardness.*—The problem of determining which are the backward classes is not simple. In its Report submitted to the Union Government in March 1955, the Backward Classes Commission has attempted to lay down certain criteria for general guidance in the matter. The tests recommended by the Commission, however, appeared to the Government to be too vague and wide to be of much practical value. It has been held by the Supreme Court in Balaji *Vs.* State of Mysore (A 1963 S.C. 649) that the appointment or recommendation of the Backward Classes Commission under Article 340 is not a condition precedent for the State to make special provisions for the backward classes under Article 15(4). In other words, the State is competent to classify classes of persons as "backward" by executive or legislative action so long as this has not already been determined after investigation by the Commission. This judgement of the Supreme Court indicates broadly, the factors that may be taken into account or the tests that may be applied in determining the social and educational backwardness of groups or classes of citizens. In considering social and educational backwardness, there is no escape from considering economic backwardness also. As the Backward Classes Commission has stated, "the economic backwardness had also to be kept in view in order to find out the ability of a community to take advantage of the available opportunities as also the recent trends in its advancement as a result of various measures initiated by State Governments during the last one or two decades." The Supreme Court has also, in the judgement referred to above, stated that "social backwardness is in the ultimate analysis the result of poverty to a very large extent. The classes of citizens who are deplorably poor automatically become socially backward." It follows, therefore, that the "means test" is one of the important tests for determining backwardness. The occupations of citizens may also contribute to make classes of citizens socially backward. To quote again, from the Supreme Court judgement: "There are some occupations which are treated as inferior, according to conventional beliefs and classes of citizens who follow these occupations are apt to become socially backward. The place of habitation also plays not a minor part in determining the backwardness of a community of persons". Thus, the occupation of citizens, and the place of their habitation are two other criteria for determining backwardness. As regards educational backwardness, a suitable criterion for determining it would be to consider the average of student population, per thousand in a particular class of citizens and to consider the class "backward" if this average is substantially below the State average. Moreover, in the case of certain classes, caste may also become a relevant factor in considering their backwardness although this cannot be made the sole or dominant test for the purpose.

5.34. To sum up, therefore, the following criteria should, in our opinion, be suitable for determining whether a certain class of citizens is socially and educationally backward:

(1) The economic backwardness of the class. [For this purpose, a suitable *ad hoc* figure of annual income may be adopted.]

(2) The occupation or occupations pursued by that class of citizens.

(3) Their place of habitation.

(4) The average of student population per thousand in that class. [This should be substantially below the State average.]

(5) Caste, in relation to Hindus.

5.35. *Revision of the list of backward classes.*—We recommended that the determination of classes which are backward on the basis of multiple criteria of the kind suggested in the previous paragraph be entrusted to high-powered Committee that would command general respect. On a Committee of this calibre there should at least be one or two persons who have expert knowledge and past experience of the subject. The reservation of posts and appointments in the services of the State Government should be made, available only to those classes that are included in the fresh list of backward classes drawn up on the basis of the Committee's recommendations. The percentage of posts and appointments so reserved should not exceed the proportion that the total population of the backward classes so listed form of the total population of the State, subject, however, to the condition that the total number of vacancies reserved for all classes of persons should not ordinarily exceed fifty percent. All direct recruitment to reserved vacancies, as well as to the general vacancies should be made strictly on the basis of merit from amongst the persons eligible for recruitment to the respective categories of vacancies.

5.36. *Reservation for Scheduled Castes.*—Representatives belonging to the Scheduled Castes have suggested to us that no vacancies in Government service are separately reserved for them and hence their representation in Government service is very low. As mentioned in paragraph 5.26, the provisions of Article 335 of the Constitution of India are not applicable to the Jammu and Kashmir State. Until recently no posts or vacancies in Government service seem to have been reserved for the Scheduled Castes as such. In July 1966, the State Government ordered that "all appointing authorities should know the district-wise population of Harijans in the State and while making appointments keep this in mind. If the post relates to a district or region the percentage of population in the district or region may be considered for fixing number of appointments to be reserved for Harijans. If it relates to the State as a whole, the percentage of population in the whole State may be considered." For admissions to technical and other institutions, the heads of the institutions and the selecting authorities have been similarly ordered to keep this ratio in view. A copy of the State Government's orders is at Appendix 11.

5.37. The above mentioned orders are not precise and they do not contain a clear directive. The position has, however, since been rectified to some extent by the issue of a notification by the State Government specifically providing for reservation for the Scheduled Castes in the services and posts in the State which shall, "as nearly as may be", be 5 per cent of the available vacancies, and for regulation of appointments to such services and posts accordingly. A copy of the notification is at Appendix 12.

5.38. We note that in order to provide for the reservation in services and posts for the Scheduled Castes, the State Government have had to include such Castes among the "backward classes of citizens of the State". Apparently, this was found necessary because the provisions of Article 335 of the Constitution of India relating to the claims of the Scheduled Castes to services and posts are not applicable to the Jammu and Kashmir State. We do not think that the conditions of the Scheduled Castes in the Jammu and Kashmir State are different from those of the Scheduled Castes in the other parts of the country. We, therefore, recommend that the provisions of Article 335 of the Constitution of India be made applicable to the Jammu and Kashmir State as well.

5.39. According to the 1961 census, the Scheduled Castes of the Jammu and Kashmir State formed 7.98 per cent of the total population of the State. Their share in the services of the Government is very much lower than is justified on the basis of their population. We consider that the reservation for the permanent resident Scheduled Castes in the services and posts under the State Government should be made in proportion to their population.

CHAPTER VI

Educational Policies

6.01. *Introduction.*—In this Chapter we propose to deal with the policies of the State Government regarding admissions to institutions of higher education and their schemes of assistance by way of scholarships and loans. The third of our terms of reference requires us to examine these policies "with a view to ensuring an equitable distribution of the available facilities to the various regions and communities, having special regard to the claims of the Scheduled Castes and other economically, educationally and socially backward communities, classes and groups among the citizens of the State."

Like the recruitment policies of the State Government discussed in the previous Chapter, these policies have also been the subject of much criticism. Complaints have been made to us of discrimination being exercised on the basis of regional and religious considerations in regard to admissions to higher educational and professional institutions and the grant of scholarships and selection for training abroad. There have also been complaints that no professional colleges are located in the

Jammu region and that the backward classes are not given any encouragement or facilities to pursue higher studies or receive professional training.

6.02. Complaints against the educational policies of the State are again not of recent origin. Of all the complaints made to the Glancy Commission (appointed in November 1931), one of the most widespread and insistent, according to it, was to the effect that certain communities, specially, the Muslim community, had not been given a fair chance in the matter of education. Some sixteen years prior to the appointment of the Glancy Commission, Mr. Sharp, Educational Commissioner with the Government of India, had visited Jammu arid Kashmir on the invitation of the State authorities and had advised them on the improvements required to be made in the Education Department of the State. While drawing attention to the suggestions of Mr. Sharp, the Glancy Commission recommended, *inter alia,* that care should be taken to see that the Muslims received all practicable encouragement in the matter of education; that the Principal of Shri Pratap Singh College, Srinagar, should be careful to see that Muslims were given a fair chance of admission to the science classes; that the special Mohammadan scholarships should be equated in value with merit scholarships; that in the matter of free studentships a due proportion should be allotted to all communities, care being taken to see that the rules prescribed were fairly carried out in practice, that the number of Muslim teachers and professors in High Schools and Colleges should be interviewed; that the post of Inspector for Mohammadan Education which had remained vacant should be revived and that the propagation of education among the depressed classes should receive due [1]attention.

6.03. In regard to Kashmiri Pandits, the Glancy Commission made the following observations:

> "It has been represented by the Kashmiri Pandits that special treatment should be afforded to them in the matter of technical training on the ground that as the proportion of clerical appointments falling to their community decreases they most have recourse to other outlets for employment. The Pandits like all other communities should be given a fair

1. Chapter III of the Report of the Glancy Commission.

chance in this matter and might receive special encouragement if they manifest an increased tends to take advantage of technical education for there are many reasons to suppose that they will not be in a position to compare successfully with other [2]students."

6.04. *Progress of education.*—The State of Jammu and Kashmir has been very backward in literacy and education. As late as 1941 the literacy percentage of the State was 6.9 only and the total number of women literates was less than 36,000. Since Independence and with the implementation of the Five Year Plans there has been great improvement. Education is now free throughout the State from the kindergarten to the university standard. The number of educational institutions and enrolment therein have registered marked progress, as the following table will [3]show:—

Sl. No.	*Heading*	*Position in 1950-51*	*Position in 1965-66*
1.	Number of Primary Schools	1,182	4,504
2.	Number of Middle Schools	149	1,131
3.	Number of High and Higher Secondary Schools	44	422
4.	Enrolment		
	(a) 6-11 years of age	56,000	2,91,000
	(b) 11-14 years of age	21,100	87,000
	(c) 14-17 years of age	4,020	41,300

6.05. Before Independence there were only 3 colleges in the State. The number of colleges has now risen to 17. The University of Jammu and Kashmir, which was established in 1948, started as a mere examining body. Now it is a full-fledged teaching University with several departments. It has two divisions, one at Jammu and the other at Srinagar. Both divisions provide for post-graduate studies in several subjects.

6.06. The percentage of literacy in the State rose to [4]13 (19.8 for males and 5.1 for females) by 1961. Even so, the percentage of literacy in Jammu and Kashmir is the lowest in the country.

2. Page 14 of the Report of the Glancy Commission.
3. Paragraph 4-19.
4. Page 133 of the Statistical Pocket Book of the Indian Union, 1966.

6.07. *Scholarships and Study Loans.*—Besides making education free from the kindergarten to the university stage, the State Government have also been granting scholarships and study loans on a liberal scale. The scholarships' are available to members of the Scheduled Castes and backward classes and to those of the remaining students who belong to the "lower income group" as defined by the Government of India. Educational loans are granted to students who are selected or nominated for various training and technical courses in and outside the State in terms of the Educational Loans Rules promulgated by the State Government in 1964. These loans are granted to hereditary State subjects "for courses of study, education or any other training approved by them". They carry no interest. The rate of loan admissible is normally Rs. 1,500 per annum for diploma courses, Rs. 2,500 per annum for technical/professional degree or post-graduate courses and Rs. 1,500 per annum for other courses. The initial grant of loan is also dependent upon the income of the parents or guardians of the students and the number of children dependent on them. Students whose parents or guardians have a monthly income exceeding Rs. 1,000 are not generally eligible for study loans. Loans are also granted to students who secure admissions privately in various courses of studies such as medicine, engineering and post-graduate courses in science subjects. The payment to the loanees is generally made for a period between 2 and 5 years, while the period for recovery of the loans extends up to 12 years. The following table shows the expenditure incurred by the State Government on this scheme during the last three years for which figures are available:

Year	*Amount*
1964-65	Rs. 29,95,536.10
1965-66	Rs. 34,74,790.32
1966-67	Rs. 38,02,363.80

6.08. So far as education at the school level or in the arts faculties at the university level is concerned, there is hardly any problem of finding places for intending scholars. Almost everyone who wants to join these courses is admitted. The position in professional and technical institutions is, however, different. The number of students seeking admission to such institutions is in excess of the number of places available in them and it has become necessary for the State to adopt a system of selection from among the eligible candidates.

4.09. *System of selection for admission.*—In 1963 and subsequent years, the practice followed by the State Government in respect of admissions, nominations to institutions for higher learning in and outside the State was as follows:

(i) For places reserved in institutions outside the State for degree and post-graduate degree courses in engineering, the Public Service Commission invited applications and submitted a merit list for final selection by the Chief Minister.

(ii) For places available for engineering courses in the Regional Engineering College, Srinagar, the Principal of the College invited applications and submitted a merit list for final selection by the Chief Minister.

(iii) For places available in the M.B.B.S., B.D.S., B.V.Sc., Ayurvedic and Unani courses and in the Polytechnics, whether within the State or outside, applications were invited by the Principals concerned and a Selection Committee selected the candidates. The list of candidates so selected was submitted to the Chief Minister for final approval.

(iv) For B.Sc. (Agri), the concerned Principals invited applications and submitted a merit list to the Agriculture Department for approval.

6.10. The procedure was modified in June 1966 and a Committee of two members was constituted for the selection of candidates for all the courses of training within and outside the State. It was open to the Committee to co-opt as adviser(s) any or all of the following:

(i) the Principal of the concerned institution;

(ii) the Secretary of the concerned Department of Government;

(iii) any person who might be considered suitable to act as an Adviser for the particular course of instruction.

The Committee scrutinised the applications of the candidates for each particular training course in accordance with the conditions governing admissions to the particular institution and thereafter interviewed the candidates to judge their physical fitness, personality, general knowledge and aptitude for the particular profession or it held a written test on general subjects "prescribed by a notification by the Committee." It was open to the Committee to hold the interview as well as the written test if it so desired. It then drew up the final list of the candidates to be selected for each course in order of merit of the candidates for each of the two regions, namely Jammu and Kashmir, having regard to the results of the interview and/or the written test and submitted the list to the Chief Minister for issuing orders in accordance with its recommendations. One hundred marks were assigned for the interview and the same number of marks for the written test.

6.11. The matter was reviewed again in July 1967 and instead of one Selection Committee for all the courses a separate Selection Committee was appointed for each of the technical courses such as Medicine, Ayurveda, Agriculture, Veterinary Science, Engineering, Polytechnic, Post-graduate education, etc. These Committees scrutinize the applications of the candidates in accordance with the conditions governing admissions to the particular institution and interview the candidates for judging their physical fitness, personality, general knowledge and aptitude for a particular profession. The Committees then draw up the final list of candidates to be selected for each of the two regions, namely, Jammu and Kashmir, in order of merit, having regard to the results of the interview and their academic merit as revealed by their performance in the basic qualifying examination, and submit the list to the Chief Minister for issuing orders in accordance with their recommendations. The interview carries 50 marks, allotted equally for physical fitness, personality, general knowledge and aptitude. One hundred marks are allotted for academic merit. The Regional Engineering College, Srinagar, being an autonomous body, was kept out of the purview of this procedure. Selection for admission to this institution is being made by an Admission Board set-up for the purpose by the Governing Body of the Regional Engineering College.

6.12. The revised procedure introduced in July 1967 for selection of candidates appears to us unexceptionable if the interview is conducted in a fair and objective manner. The selection of candidates on a regional basis, however, will offend the provisions of Article 14 of the Constitution of India, as indicated in paragraph 5.29. We shall have occasion to refer to this subject again later in this Chapter. If the procedure is correctly followed and the selection of candidates made strictly on merit, there is no justification for submitting such lists to the Chief Minister for approval.

6.13. *Reservation for backward classes and Scheduled Castes.*—We note that the State Government have made no formal provision for the reservation of places in educational and professional institutions either for backward classes or for the Scheduled Castes. This has also been pointed out by the High Court of Jammu and Kashmir State while delivering judgement in the case of Lalita Shuri Tikku *Vs.* State of Jammu and Kashmir and others (Writ Petition No. 66 of 1965 and allied Writ Petitions) relating to admissions to the Srinagar Medical College The relevant extract from the judgement is reproduced below:—

> "On the other hand, the Advocate General submitted that in the instant case, the selection was made on the basis of classification contemplated by Article 15(4) of the Constitution of India. He drew our attention to the affidavits of the Chief Secretary in various petitions which show that the selection was made, firstly, on the basis of candidates who were drawn from socially and educationally backward classes, secondly, of candidates who were residents of Jammu and thirdly, of candidates who were drawn from scheduled castes. It was, therefore, contended by the Advocate General that the affidavits of the Chief Secretary should be construed as a special provision falling within the permissible limits of Article 15 sub-clause 4 of the Constitution of India. We are, however, unable to agree with this argument.
>
> "Article 15(4) as already indicated, clearly contemplates that there must be a special provision for the classes mentioned in that Article, such a provision need not be made by a Legislative enactment and it can be made also by an executive order, but there must be some order or notification to show that the State having applied its mind to the various factors and the statistics of a particular class of citizens

considers it to be a socially and educationally backward class for whose benefit provision has to be made. In the instant ease, no such provision at all appears to have been made by the State. For the first time, in answer to the petitions, the stand taken by the Chief Secretary, is that the selection has been made after taking into consideration the nature of the socially and educationally backward classes of citizens and of Scheduled Castes. Even in the affidavits, the Chief Secretary has hot disclosed the data statistics or the factors which go to make a particular class as a socially and educationally backward one. It has not even been indicated as to which is the class of citizens which has been declared to be socially and educationally backward. In these circumstances, therefore, we are constrained to hold that since no provision under Article 15(4) has been made, the selection has been made on a purely discriminatory basis."

6.14. In the course of our inquiry we came across instances where the selection of students for the technical and professional courses had been made in an arbitrary or discriminatory manner. There have been critical comments on such selections by the High Court of Jammu and Kashmir. In the case of Lalita Shuri Tikku *Vs.* State of Jammu and Kashmir and others, referred to in paragraph 6.13, the High Court made the following observations:

"It is, therefore, manifest that a discrimination between members of the Scheduled Castes has also been made by the State and Kumari Bilori to have been subjected to hostile discrimination instead of her being considered on merits."

In another writ petition concerning admission to the Srinagar Medical College, filed before them in 1968 by Subash Mohan Jalali and others, the Court has observed as follows:

"There appears to be discrimination in selecting the candidates even with respect to petitioner's belonging to same class namely residents of Jammu and those of Kashmir Province. . . . Thus it would appear that the selection has been made by the Committee either consciously or unconsciously in such a way as to discriminate (between) candidates even belonging to the same class of citizens."

6.15. We have scrutinized the statistical data pertaining to admissions of students to institutions of higher education furnished by the State Government. An abstract of these data is given in Appendix 13. We note that as between the Jammu region and the Kashmir region, the number of students belonging to Jammu selected for study in higher institutions was much smaller than the number of those belonging to Kashmir, but the share of Hindus has been much larger than that of Muslims in all the important courses of study.

6.16. It is unfortunate that the State Government do not maintain a separate record of admissions of students belonging to the backward classes. We are, therefore, unable to make any observation as to the extent to which the Directive Principles of State Policy laid down in Section 23 of the Constitution of Jammu and Kashmir have been followed by the State Government.

6.17. *Regional communal allocation of seats:*—The question whether any special provisions can be made in the matter of educational facilities on the basis of religion or region to which the persons concerned belong, has come up before the High Courts and the Supreme Court on a number of occasions and the Courts have given authoritative rulings. We should like to invite attention to the judgements in the following cases:

(i) M.R. Balaji *Vs.* State of Mysore in the Supreme Court;

(ii) R. Chitralekha *Vs.* State of Mysore in the Supreme Court;

(iii) Minor P. Rajendran *Vs.* State of Madras and other similar writ petitions in the Supreme Court; and

(iv) Lalita Shuri Tikku *Vs.* State of Jammu and Kashmir and other connected writ petitions in the High Court of Jammu and Kashmir.

6.18. It seems that special concessions, quotas or reservations for admission to educational and professional institutions can be made available only to the socially and educationally backward classes of citizens or to the Scheduled Castes and Scheduled Tribes: It is also clear that the classification of people as backward on the basis of their religion or region alone is repugnant to the provisions relating to fundamental rights in the Constitution of India as made applicable to Jammu and Kashmir. The remedy, therefore, is to draw up a list of backward classes on the basis of a multiple test as suggested by us in paragraphs 5.31 to 5.34, and provide for admission quotas or reservations for them in institutions of higher learning, which should not exceed the proportion that the population of the backward classes as a whole bears to the total population of the State. Similarly, reservations should also be made for the Scheduled Castes in proportion to their population. The total percentage of reservation for the backward classes and the Scheduled Castes should not, however, ordinarily exceed fifty. Subject to the reservation for the backward classes and the Scheduled Castes, the selection for admissions to educational institutions should be made strictly and solely on merit. Merit should also be the sole criterion for filling the seats reserved for the backward classes and the Scheduled Castes.

6.19. *Scholarships and study loans.*—We have not heard any serious complaints about the inadequacy of the scholarships or study loans granted by the State Government. On the other hand, complaints have been voiced by several parties that in the matter of distribution of the scholarships and study loans considerable discrimination is practised between the Jammu region and the Kashmir region and between one community and another. We have examined the statistical data made available to us by the State Government pertaining to the study loans given to students for study in institutions of higher education, during the three Five-Year Plan periods. An abstract of the data is given at Appendix 14. We note that region-wise, the students belonging to the Kashmir region have received a much larger amount, by way of study loans than the students belonging to the Jammu region. Community-wise, however, the Hindus have received a much larger share of study loans than the Muslims. The members of the Scheduled Casles have received no study loans whatsoever in the course of the entire period of the three Plans. Details of the study loans given to backward classes are not available as the figures for backward classes are included in those of their parent community.

6.20. As we have suggested for admissions, a certain proportion of the provision available for the grant of scholarships and study loans should be set apart for the backward classes and the Scheduled Castes. The provision should be separate for each of them and should not be less than the proportion that either of them bears to the total population of the State. The balance should be made available to the rest of the student population. In giving scholarships or loans, the means of the parent or guardian should be an important factor for determining the eligibility of the applicant and, other things being equal, merit should be the sole criterion for granting, them.

CHAPTER VII

Irritations and Tensions Remedies

7.01. *Introduction.*—We now come to the fourth and last of our terms of reference. This requires us "to consider generally the causes that lead 10 irritations and tensions and to recommend remedial measures." We shall begin by referring to certain recent facts of history which are responsible for some of the major irritations and tensions now existing among certain sections of the population.

7.02. We have mentioned in paragraphs 3.07 to 3.09 how Dogra rule came to be established in the Jammu and Kashmir State. Dogra rule was personal in character but several important developments in the State took place during this period. The Legislative Assembly, which was created in 1934, had thirty-five of its seventy-five members nominated by the Ruler and the electorate comprised only eight per cent of the population. In 1939, several constitutional reforms were carried out and the Constitution. Act came into force. It was, however, specifically provided in the Constitution that "nothing contained in this or any other act shall affect or be deemed to have affected the right and prerogative of His Highness to make laws, and issue proclamations, orders, and ordinances by virtue of his inherent authority". Besides, the legislature had no jurisdiction over a number of important matters which were included in the list of the Maharaja's reserved powers. In spite of the authoritarian nature of Dogra rule, certain sections of the population flourished and prospered during this period. The State Army was composed almost entirely of Dogra Rajputs for whom it provided the main source of employment. The educated and advanced Kashmiri Pandit community came gradually to monopolize the ministerial posts in the Government and occupy positions of influence in the civil administration after the State Government had yielded in 1925 to the pressure from the inhabitants of the State, and accepted the principle of recruiting only State subjects to Government posts,

These two communities were the main beneficiaries of Dogra rule along with a large number of Jagirdars, Chakdars and Shahukars (moneylenders).

7.03. With the introduction of democracy and popular rule in the State a complete break with the autocratic rule of the previous regime was inevitable. One of the first acts of the popular Government under Sheikh Mohammed Abdullah and one of its greatest achievements from the viewpoint of the peasants and the landless, who formed the overwhelming majority of the population, was to implement the programme of social and agrarian reforms as envisaged in the "New Kashmir" Plan. The new land reform laws which were introduced in the State meant not only the abolition of intermediary rights but also the redistribution of land and protection of the tenants. These land reforms dealt a heavy blow to the important and prosperous class of landholders, many of whom have not been able to reconcile themselves to this day to the altered situation. The expropriation of their land in excess of 182 *kanals* without payment of compensation was understandably a source of great distress and dissatisfaction to this class. Besides, in the haste with which the new land laws were enacted a number of serious anomalies crept into them and these have acted as additional irritants.

7.04. As we have already mentioned in paragraph 5.10, there was a large expansion of the services after the introduction of popular rule in the State in 1947. There were instances, as a result, where recruitment was made without observing the usual formalities; besides, some appointments in the higher ranks were also made from political cadres. We were told that the non-observance of the recruitment rules which started immediately after the introduction of popular rule adversely affected the people of the Jammu region in particular and was a source of irritation to that region. In evidence before us Bakshi Ghulam Mohammed unequivocally stated that merit could not be the only criterion in these matters, for merit were made the sole criterion there would be no place for Muslims, Jammu Dogras and other backward people in the State. He, therefore, introduced communal and regional representation for filling' Government posts and making admissions to educational institutions. When the Public Service Commission was established in 1957, it was also advised to keep these considerations in view and to suggest an equal number of candidates from the Jammu and Kashmir regions and also an equal number of candidates belonging to the Muslim and non-Muslim communities for filling vacancies in Government service. As a result of these new policies, the Kashmiri Pandit community lost its pre-eminent position in Government services. Since their main occupation was Government service, they could not easily adjust themselves to the changed situation and qualify themselves for the pursuit of other occupations for a living. Similarly, the Jammu Dogras who had traditionally sought, their career in the armed forces of the State lost this source of employment after Independence when the State Army, ceased to exist as a separate entity. They seem to have been caught unprepared by the change and did not equip themselves for other forms of employment.

7.05. The foregoing analysis shows how irritations and tensions have grown in certain communities and classes of the population because of their background and historical reasons. The Kashmiri Pandits seem to look back when they had almost a monopoly of the State services. Similarly, the Dogras of Jammu hark back to the days, when the ruler of the State belonged to their clan and they had a virtual, monopoly in the armed forces of the State. Neither of these communities, finds it easy to appreciate that with the establishment of democratic rule in the State the employment pattern in the public services was bound to change and that it was necessary to prepare oneself for other occupation. In Chapters V and VI, we have recommended reservation of posts in the services and admissions to institutions of higher education for the genuinely backward classes only, classified on the basis of certain multiple criteria. We venture to hope that when this is done and the rest of the employment and educational opportunities are made available on the basis of merit alone such grievances as these communities now have, will be largely removed.

7.06. We now proceed to deal with the causes of irritations and tensions which have been represented before us in the written memoranda and oral evidence. The alleged imbalance in development programmes and the policies-pursued by the State Government in the matter of recruitment to services and the provision of educational facilities are themselves some of the principal causes of irritation and tension. We have examined them in the three preceding chapters. In this Chapter we shall confine ourselves to the other matters. They are of varying degrees of importance. They range from such matters as the doubt and uncertainty which disturbs the minds of some people about the political future of their State or the bitterness which is engendered by real or imagined grievances of regional discrimination or the inequitable aspects of the land laws to the persistent complaints of general administrative inefficiency and corruption or such petty demands as the upgrading of a naib tehsil to a tehsil or the opening of a school here or a dispensary there. Some persons have also tried to ventilate their individual grievances in the garb of general complaints of irritation and tension. We propose to ignore petty and individual grievances and to deal in the paragraphs which follow only with those causes of irritation and tension which appear to us to be of consequence.

Political

7.07. *Ambivalence in regard to political policy.*—The people of the State, particularly those living in the Valley, feel that there is a certain degree of ambivalence about the political policy of the Union Government towards the State. Constant hostile propaganda from the other side of the sub-continent, the secessionist doctrines propagated by certain political leaders and parties of the State and the attempts of some political leaders of India to mediate in Jammu and Kashmir affairs, have created doubts in the mind of the people of the State about their political future. All the parties which appeared before us were however, unequivocal in their stand that the accession of the State to the Indian Union was final and irrevocable. Nevertheless, the effect of the propaganda carried on in the State by some elements which have not adjusted themselves to the realities of the situation cannot be ignored. Such propaganda is likely to create in the mind of the people in the Valley a general feeling of political uncertainty which is clearly a cause for creating tensions and irritations. The common man in the Valley as well as in Jammu and Ladakh is naturally vitally interested in his own betterment and in reaching a stage of economic development in which, he would be able to enjoy life, liberty and the pursuit of happiness more fully. This aim is undoubtedly hindered by the sense of uncertainty created by anti-Indian propaganda in the State. In judging the effect of this hostile propaganda in Jammu and Kashmir one has to bear in mind that

Pakistan has been ceaselessly challenging the validity of the State's accession to the Indian Union.

7.08. We noted with satisfaction that notwithstanding the delicate nature of the subject, the present State Government have allowed ample scope to freedom of expression to the citizens and have deliberately decided to deal with the challenge posed by these subversive treads in the State on a political plane. Our hope is that the public at large will extend their moral help to the State Government through the creation of sound public opinion to meet this challenge.

7.09. It would not be inappropriate to add here that the teachers in the University and the schools of Jammu and Kashmir, who form a cosmopolitan and progressive group and believe in the sense of values on which Indian democracy is founded and which form the basis also of the Constitution of Jammu and Kashmir, should play their legitimate role in guiding the impressionable minds of the younger generation in the State. If the intellectuals and educationists help the democratic forces in the State to tackle the situation created by subversive propaganda, the liberal policy adopted by the State Government is bound to be successful.

7.10. We gathered the impression that the University students in the Jammu and Kashmir State as in the rest of India and, indeed, in many parts of the world today, are unhappy and restive: Elements hostile to Indian democracy may well be tempted to exploit this frustration and restiveness. It should, we think, be possible for the teachers in the universities by means of close contact, and for the intellectuals in and outside the State through fruitful discussions, to assist in the process of inculcating in the minds of the students in Jammu and Kashmir an abiding faith in the basic values of life for which our Constitution stands, namely, justice—political, social and economic—secularism and the rule of law.

7.11. *Article* 370 *of the Constitution of India.*—Some parties feel that the special status conferred on the Jammu and Kashmir State by Article 370 of the Constitution of India is a major cause of irritation and tension. They desire that the provisions of that Article should be abrogated

They consider that this Article is being used to legalize unconstitutional acts by the State Government and that it encourages arbitrariness on their part. The validation of some of the State statutes, such as the Big Landed Estates Abolition Act, 1950, which provides for the expropriation of land without compensation, by the issue of a Presidential order under this Article of the Constitution is cited as an example. They also point out that its provisions are meant to be temporary and the Article is not meant to be a permanent feature of our Constitution.

On the other hand, another section considers that it is what it alleges to be the systematic erosion of the autonomy of the State guaranteed by this Article, that causes irritation and tension. It desires that the provisions of this Article should be strictly observed and that the Union Government should guarantee that, irrespective of which party is in power at the Centre, the special status conferred on the State by this Article should not be tampered with. The irredentism, chauvinism and revivalism preached by certain political and religious parties in other parts of the country have caused a genuine fear in the mind of this section about this.

7.12. Article 370, as its title itself indicates, is a temporary provision with respect to the State of Jammu and Kashmir. By means of this Article, the provisions in the Constitution of India relating to the Government of the States have been made inapplicable to the State of Jammu and Kashmir and a separate Constitution framed by the Constituent Assembly of the State has been enforced. The power of Parliament to make laws for the State of Jammu and Kashmir is limited to —

"(i) those matters in the Union List and in the Concurrent List which, in consultation with the Government of the State, are declared by the President to correspond to matters specified in the Instrument of Accession governing the accession of the State to the Dominion of India as the matters with respect to which the Dominion Legislature might make laws for that State; and

(ii) such other matters in the said Lists as, with the concurrence of the Government of the State, the President may by order specify."

It also provides for the application of such other provisions of the Constitution of India to the State of Jammu and Kashmir as the President may by order specify. The order may indicate the exceptions or modifications subject to which these provisions should be made applicable. Before issuing any such order, however, the President is required to consult the State Government in certain cases and obtain their concurrence in the other cases. For easy reference the full text of this Article is reproduced in Appendix 15.

7.13. It would be observed that the Jammu and Kashmir State has been granted by the Constitution of India a much larger measure of Autonomy within the Indian Union than the other States. There were reasons for according such-special treatment. According to the late N. Gopalaswami Ayyanger, who piloted the Article in the Constituent Assembly in 1949, "that particular State is not yet ripe for this kind of integration. It is the hope of everybody, here that in due course even Jammu and Kashmir will become ripe for the same sort of integration as has taken place in the case of other states". It was, however, inevitable that in course of time Article 370 should have been used to bring about uniformity of the State of Jammu and Kashmir with the rest of the country in matters of vital importance to the rights of individual citizens and the enforcement of the rule of law. But this has always been done in strict compliance with the letter and spirit of that Article.

7.14. Federal Financial Integration which had taken place in 1950 in the case of other Part B States was practically fully achieved in the Jammu and Kashmir State in 1954 as a result of the State Government agreeing to the application of a large number of items of the Constitution to that State. Consequently; Union Departments, like Customs, Central Excise, Posts and Telegraphs, Civil Aviation, All India Radio, etc. had their operation expended to the State just as to other States. The functions of the Comptroller and Auditor-General of India were extended to the State in 1958. In matters involving the interpretation of the Constitution, the Supreme Court has the same jurisdiction in respect of Jammu and Kashmir as in respect of the other States. The functions of the Election Commission of India now extend to Jammu and Kashmir not only for elections to Parliament and to the office of the President and of the Vice-President, but also for elections to the State Legislature. In December 1964, Articles 356 and 357 of the Constitution of India, containing provisions relating to the failure of the constitutional machinery in the States, were applied to Jammu and Kashmir. This brief and illustrative narration of the operation of Article 370 would show that the process adopted so far is consistent with the declared objectives of the Constitution of India and the Constitution of Jammu and Kashmir.

7.15. Article 370 has been introduced in the Constitution of India on account of the historical facts which led to the accession of the Jammu and Kashmir State to India. As we have already indicated, this Article guarantees to Jammu and Kashmir a very much larger measure of autonomy than is enjoyed by any other State. Arguments are often heard in India, and were repeated before us, both for repealing this Article and for retaining it. If the Article is repealed, it may raise nice questions of constitutional law as to the effect of such a step on the Constitution of Jammu and Kashmir. This may itself created, in the present circumstances, additional tensions in the mind of the majority community in the Valley. This is a consideration that has been emphasized before us by parties which want Article 370 to continue. On the other hand, those that want the Article to be removed from the Constitution have urged that it indirectly retards the process of the complete integration of the State of Jammu and Kashmir in the Indian Union which must be the ultimate objective. They stated that the time had come for abrogating his Article and placing the State of Jammu and Kashmir on the same footing as the other States in the Union. Those who advocated this view expressed their disapproval of the fact that citizens in India were not able to acquire property in Jammu and Kashmir unless they were permanent residents of the State as defined in Part III of the Constitution of Jammu and Kashmir while the persons belonging to the State were entitled to acquire property anywhere in the rest of India. It was also urged that no other State had an independent Constitution of its own and the existence of an independent Constitution for Jammu and Kashmir had an adverse, if indirect effect upon the process of complete integration of the State in the Indian Union.

7.16. We have given anxious consideration to this problem. We think that a present it would be inadvisable to recommend that Article 370 be abrogated. Keeping in view the progress which has already been made over the years in the integration of Jammu and Kashmir with the rest of India, we feel that it would be prudent to leave it to the Government and the people of the State of Jammu and Kashmir themselves to decide when this Article should be abrogated.

7.17. *Elections.*—Some representatives who appeared before us have cast doubts on the manner in which the elections have been conducted in the State in the past, particularly about the fairness of the last General Election. They have pointed out that at the last General Election, 141 nomination papers were rejected and 26 members were returned unopposed to the State Legislative Assembly and that the whole of Anantnag District failed to get an opportunity to go to the polls for electing its representatives to Parliament or to the State Legislature. These persons feel that all the elections held so far were systematically interfered with by the State authorities and that this has undermined the faith of the common man in democracy. The conduct of the elections, however, is now a matter which concerns the Election Commission and it is not for us to go into the question whether the last General Election was in fact interfered with. The proper forum to deal with it are the Election Tribunals and the Supreme Court. We were informed that a number of election petitions had been filed before the Election Tribunals in Jammu and Kashmir and some had already been disposed of. Some elections have been set aside by the Tribunals while certain others have been upheld by them. Though, as we have just observed, the forum to decide whether the elections were properly held or not is the Election Tribunals, we have mentioned this matter to indicate that a feeling does exist in the minds of some citizens that the elections were not free and fair. We should like to add that we have had an opportunity to examine 29 judgements delivered by the High Court of Jammu and Kashmir in Election Petitions filed before it. Out of these 29 petitions, 6 have been allowed while the rest have failed. It seems to us significant that in 12 out of these 29 cases, the nomination papers of non-Congress candidates were rejected on the ground that the said candidates had not subscribed and made the oath as required by law. In one case (Election Petitions Nos. 1 and 10 of 196: Ghulam Qadir Mir *V.* Ghulam Moh'd Rajpuri and others and Moh'd Shan Simnani *V.* Ghulam Moh'd Mir Rajpuri). Mr. Justice Anant Singh came to the conclusion that Mr. Kumar, the Returning Officer, and Mr. Safaya, the Assistant Returning Officer, appeared to have entered into a conspiracy to reject nomination papers of non-Congress candidates improperly with a view to facilitating the uncontested return of Mr. Rajpuri, who was a Congress candidate. According to the Judge, these two officers did not stop short of fabricating and tampering with the evidence. The Judge also felt that there was reasonable ground to suspect that Mr. Rajpuri, who was once a sitting Minister of Tourism under whom Mr. Safaya was working at Srinagar, had influenced the said two officers in that behalf. As a consequence of this finding, the Judge has directed that proceedings should be taken against the two officers under section 476 of the Criminal Procedure Code. The decisions of the High Court to which we have just referred are, of course, subject to appeal to the Supreme Court.

This is a cause of irritation and tension and a note of this feeling has to be taken. We should, therefore, like to add that as the Jammu and Kashmir State occupies a strategic area, it is necessary to nurture the faith of the common man in democracy and democratic institutions in the State. We hope that the State Government will do all they canto build up and sustain that faith.

7.18. We were told that the elections to local bodies such as Panchayats, town area committees, notified area committees and municipalities are long overdue and that these bodies are no longer, representative in character. Some parties have alleged that besides depriving the public of their fundamental right of franchise, this has resulted in the Government managing to have their own candidates elected to the Legislative Council from the local bodies constituencies. We think that it is necessary that the State Government should immediately take all steps to arrange for the holding of the elections to the local bodies as early as possible. We should also like to add that these elections should he held regularly in future.

7.19. *Civil liberties.*—We have heard complaints of the suppression of civil liberties in the State. For instance, it is alleged that the provisions of Section 144 of the Criminal Procedure Code are in force throughout the State that no public meeting can be held without prior permission of the Government authorities, and that the opposition Press has been muzzled. Discrimination is also alleged to be exercised in granting permission for holding public meetings. It is stated that while the ruling party gets the permission for the asking, the opposition parties find it difficult to secure it. We are not satisfied that these allegations are true.

We have been informed that the allegation that the provisions of Section 144 of the Criminal Procedure Code are in force throughout the State, is wrong. It is well known that the leaders of opposition parties are addressing public meetings in various parts of the State and are making statements to the Press. Some of them are very critical of the Government and some even question the finality of accession of the State to the Indian Union.

7.20. It seems appropriate at this stage to make a passing reference to the Kashmir Suite People's Convention held at Srinagar in October last. At this convention divergent opinions were freely and fully expressed. Some of the views which were ardently advocated appear to be plainly inconsistent with the correct constitutional position under the Constitution of India and the Constitution of Jammu and Kashmir. We feel that it is a tribute to the democratic way of life adopted by India, and by the State of Jammu and Kashmir as an integral part of the Union of India, that a Convention of this kind should have been called and such views openly, freely and fearlessly canvassed. We have already referred to the present State Government's decision—and we think the decision is correct and consistent with the democratic spirit of the Constitution—to allow full freedom of expression even to parties that do not see eye to eye with them or are opposed to their political ideology and commitments. Political trends, however, subversive they may appear to be, have necessarily to be countered on a political plane, and in a democratic country freedom of expression has to be granted to every citizen. This freedom does not mean the freedom to express views only in favour of the established order; it also means the freedom to express dissent so long as it is within the limits prescribed by the Constitution and the relevant provisions of the law. The fact that freedom of expression has been allowed to be exercised uninterruptedly in such a sensitive area as Jammu and Kashmir speaks volumes for the spirit and strength of Indian democracy.

7.21. *Autonomy of the State within the Union.—We* would now like to deal with the demand for a larger measure of autonomy for the State of Jammu and Kashmir within the Indian Union as such a demand was made before us. In dealing with it, several considerations have to be taken into account. The first consideration is that the demand for a larger measure of autonomy for the State of Jammu and Kashmir has not been made before us directly by any party from Jammu or Ladakh. Even amongst the parties belonging to the Valley that appeared before us only one or two raised the subject. We note, however, that some participants at the Convention, referred to in the preceding paragraph, made such a claim but it seems reasonable to conclude that the demand for a larger measure of autonomy for the State does not have the support of a substantial section of the population even of the Valley and has received little, if any, support from Jammu or Ladakh. While it may be conceded that this demand may give rise to certain tensions in the regions, it is one of those internal problems which arise between the Union Government and constituent States and in which no third party can have a *locus standi*. In fact, in any federal structure stresses and strains often occur between the federal Government and the constituent units and they have to be tackled in a democratic way by the parties concerned by evolving proper and healthy federal conventions.

7.22. The second consideration which is relevant in this connection is that the State of Jammu and Kashmir enjoys, as we have pointed out already, a much larger measure of autonomy than the other States in the Union of India. We have also indicated that this autonomy flows from Article 370 of the Constitution of India and have expressed the view that it should be for the Government and the people of the Jammu and Kashmir State to decide when this Article should be abrogated. In view of this constitutional position, we do not see any justification for considering the demand for an even larger measure of autonomy for the State in isolation without reference to the other States. The Centre-State relations which have emerged as a result of the fourth General Election held in 1967 has posed the question whether the Constitution of India should be amended to confer larger authority on the constituent States. Some of the State Governments have been pleading for a re-examination of the relevant provisions of the Constitution with a view to conferring greater authority on the States. It seems to us that if the Union Government decide to consider this question in the context of the newly evolving pattern of political life in this country, the case of the Jammu and Kashmir State should receive due consideration along with that of the other constituent States. Even in that event, as we have just indicated, the best way of dealing with such a problem in a democracy is to evolve appropriate conventions and traditions.

7.23. *Representation in Cabinet/Legislature.*—Several communities have complained to us that they are not adequately represented in the State Cabinet or the State Legislature or have no representation in them at all. The first comment that we should like to make on this demand is that with the exception of the Scheduled Castes and, in respect of nomination to the Legislative Council, of the backward classes, the suggestion that the communities as such are entitled in representation in the Cabinet or the Legislature is inconsistent with the provisions of the Constitution of India and the Constitution of Jammu and Kashmir. Besides, the number of communities in the State is large. Within the small size of the Cabinet or of the State Legislature it would be almost impossible to satisfy the demands of every community. It is for these communities to join the mainstream of politics of the State and avail themselves of the political advantages that this may offer.

Regional Aspirations

7.24. In the preceding chapters and the earlier paragraphs of this Chapter, we have dealt with several matters that agitate the minds of the people of the State. Even if all the matters were equitably settled, we feel that there would still be a measure of discontent unless the political aspirations of the different regions of the State were satisfied. In fact, we consider that the main cause of irritation and tension is the feeling of political neglect and discrimination real or imagined, from which certain regions of the State suffer.

7.25. Although the Jammu and Kashmir State has been a single political entity for over a hundred years, it cannot be denied that geographically, ethnically, culturally and historically, it is composed of three separate homogeneous regions, namely, Jammu, Kashmir and Ladakh. In fact, the Pir Panjal range forms a natural dividing line between the Jammu and Kashmir regions.

7.26. *Regional autonomy.*—We are glad to note that notwithstanding these differences and the regional political aspirations, no party or individual who has submitted a memorandum to us or appeared before us in person, with the solitary exception of the Dogra Mandal, has suggested a division of the State or the creation of a sub-State within the State. Even the idea of autonomy for the regions of the State is unacceptable to most of them. The Jammu Autonomy Forum is the sole protagonist from the Jammu region of regional autonomy for Jammu, Kashmir and Ladakh. The two individuals from Kashmir who supported autonomy for the regions also pleaded strongly for a greater measure of autonomy for the State as a whole within the Indian Union. The Dogra Mandal suggested that the Jammu region be merged with Himachal Pradesh.

7.27. We have given consideration to the proposal which was elaborately and ably presented before us by the delegation of the Jammu Autonomy Forum. It may theoretically be conceded that if the proposal represents the aspirations of a large majority of the population of the Jammu region—and we do not think that it does the satisfaction of their legitimate expectation in good time may lead to greater consolidation of the region with the rest of the State. On the other hand, it is quite likely that any recognition of the autonomy of a region of the State may whet its appetite for greater autonomy and accentuate separatist tendencies which may ultimately lead to the disintegration of the State itself. Besides, in dealing with the question of autonomy for the Jammu region, as in considering the question of autonomy for the State as a whole within the Indian Union, we cannot treat as irrelevant the impact that such a step is likely to have on the other regions constituting the State. This point is relevant and valid as all the parties which appeared before us, with one solitary exception, were agreed that nothing should be done that would impair or injure the unity and integrity of the State. On the basis of the evidence tendered before us, we have no doubt that the acceptence of the demand for autonomy made by the Jammu Autonomy Forum would make an adverse impact on the minds of the residents of the Kashmir region. Although there was general agreement among the parties which appeared before us for the establishment of Regional Development. Boards for developmental purposes, only two persons from the Kashmir region supported the demand for regional autonomy, and none from Ladakh supported it. As already stated, the Jammu Autonomy Forum was the only party from Jammu that advocated autonomy for the regions. After careful consideration of all the relevant factors, we have come to the conclusion that the demand made before us by the Jammu Autonomy Forum should not be accepted.

7.28. We have also given careful thought to the desirability of introducing a system of Regional Committees of the State Legislature of the type envisaged for certain States in Article 371 of the Constitution of India. Such Regional Committees existed for the Punjabi-speaking and the Hindi-speaking areas of the former Punjab State. The experiment did not work satisfactorily and the establishment of these Regional Committees did not prevent the eventual division of the former Punjab State into the new States of Punjab and Haryana. The reasons that we have already given for recommending the rejection of the demand made by the Jammu Autonomy Forum hold good also for rejecting the idea of introducing the system of Regional Committees of the State Legislature.

7.29. In paragraphs 4.25 to 4.29 we have suggested the establishment of a statutory State Development Board and statutory Regional Development Boards for the three regions—Jammu, Kashmir and Ladakh. This and certain other measures which we shall discuss in the subsequent paragraphs will, we hope, go a long way in satisfying the regional aspirations of the people of the State.

7.30. *Convention regarding composition of Cabinet.*—A convention should be established, that if the Chief Minister belongs to one region, there should be a Deputy Chief Minister belonging to the other region. By another convention, the number of Cabinet Ministers belonging to the two regions should be equal. There should also, in addition, be a full-fledged Cabinet Minister belonging to Ladakh.

7.31. *Decentralization of administration.*—The functions of each Head of Department should be divided on a regional basis in other words, each Department should have a Head and an Additional Head, one of them functioning in one region and the other in the other region. The Head of Department or Additional Head of Department, as the case may be will be responsible for all programmes in his region. The Additional Head of Department may correspond with the Secretariat direct on all matters concerning his region. He will, however, send copies of such correspondence to the Head of Department for record. Orders passes by the Government on the proposals of the Additional Head of Department will be sent to him direct with copies to the Head of Department. Matters of common interest and those requiring inter-regional coordination will be dealt with by Head of Department. It is understood that in certain departments, such as the Public Works Department there is a Chief Engineer for each region. What is suggested by us here is an extension of the principle to the other departments.

7.32. So far as the High Court of Jammu and Kashmir is concerned, when it functions at Srinagar, there should be at least one High Court Judge stationed at Jammu to dispose of matters that may arise in the Jammu region. Similarly, when the High Court functions at Jammu, there should be at least one High Court Judge stationed at Srinagar to deal with the cases arising in the Kashmir region.

7.33. *Regionalization of cadres.*—We are given to understand that all the service cadres of the State of whatever grade are State cadres and officials of every rank or class are liable to be transferred from any part of the State to any other part where there are posts of that rank or class in the service. For instance, we have been told that a peon or Patwari or forest guard may be transferred not only from one district to another but even from one region to another. It has been represented that when officers, particularly the low-paid ones, belonging to one region are posted to the other; they generally tend to count their days until they can get themselves transferred back to their own region and that, as a result, they fail to put their heart in their work in the other region. We feel that such transfers of low-paid staff are likely to cause hardship to them without any compensating administrative advantage. We would suggest that the posts in the various services should, where possible, be divided into three cadres; namely, a district-based cadre, a region-based cadre and a State-based cadre. Speaking in general terms, the inferior and non-gazetted (other than supervisory) posts should be district-based. In district-based cadres, transfers should be permissible only within the district. Supervisory non-gazetted posts, both clerical and non-clerical, and class III and class IV gazetted posts should generally form the regional cadre. In region-based cadres, transfers should be permissible only within the region. Members of State-based cadres alone should be liable to transfer anywhere within the State. Although we are recommending the division of the posts into three cadres—a district-based cadre, a region-based cadre and a State-based cadre—we should like to make it clear that the residents of the entire State will be eligible for appointment to the posts included in any of the cadres.

7.34. Members of district-based cadres on promotion to posts in the regional, cadre will become transferable anywhere within the region. Similarly, a person on promotion from a post in a regional cadre, to a post in the State cadre will become transferable to a place anywhere in the State.

7.35. The Kashmir Administrative Service, the Kashmir Civil Service (Judicial) and the Kashmir Police-Service are feeder services for the All India Services and the higher judiciary. Their incumbents should therefore, have wide experience of State administration. Members of these services and such other State services as the State Government may consider appropriate should in our opinion, be liable to work for a minimum specified period (say, five years) in one or two spells in each of the three regions, namely, Jammu, Kashmir and Ladakh.

7.36. *Regional and District Recruitment Boards.*—As a corollary to the proposal for the decentralization of cadres, a Regional Recruitment Board should be set-up for the Jammu region and another for the Kashmir region, and a District Recruitment Board for each district in the State, including Ladakh. The function of the Regional Recruitment Board should be to make recruitment to the regional cadres and that of the District Recruitment Boards to make recruitment to the district cadres. These Boards will concern themselves with filling only those posts which are outside the purview of the Public Service Commission. They could function on a part-time basis and be manned by suitable officers drawn from the regions or the districts, as the case may be.

Regional Discrimination

7.37. *Separate Universities for Jammu region and Kashmir region.*— We have heard complaints that the Jammu region has been discriminated against by being denied an equal number of University faculties and by not starting any technical and professional colleges there. We have compared the list of faculties existing on the Srinagar campus of the Jammu and Kashmir University with that of the faculties available on the Jammu campus. The former consists of one faculty more than the latter. We do not, therefore, agree that there has been any deliberate discrimination in the matter. There is, however, another matter which is stated to be agitating the mind of the student community in the Jammu region. We learn that the main university examinations in the Jammu region are held when the Kashmir region has its supplementary examinations and that its supplementary examinations are held when the Kashmir region has its main examinations. We would suggest that there should be a full-fledged university for each of Jammu and Kashmir regions. One of them should immediately start a faculty of law. Perhaps this could be done at Jammu first as there are no professional colleges there. We believe that it would soon become necessary to start law classes in the other university as well.

7.38. *Opening of technical and professional colleges.*— We note that technical and professional colleges, such as the Medical College, the Engineering College and the Agricultural College, are all located in the Kashmir region and the only professional college which were located in the Jammu region, namely, the Agricultural College at Ranbirsinghpura, has been closed down. This has caused some regional bitterness. As the existing professional colleges are all located in the Kashmir region; we consider that it would be appropriate to open a new Medical College at Jammu. The question of starting an Engineering College in the Jammu region may also be considered subsequently when the need for having a larger number of engineering graduates is felt.

7.39. *Matriculation examination.*— Another complaint of a regional nature that we have heard is that while the Matriculation Examination is held simultaneously in the Jammu region and the Valley, the dates on which the examination is held in Ladakh are different as a result of which the students of Ladakh lose a whole term when proceeding for higher studies. We would have recommended that the feasibility of holding the examination simultaneously in Jammu, Kashmir and Ladakh be examined by the State Government, had we not been informed by them that henceforth all the annual examinations of the Board of Secondary Education would be held, in the Jammu and Kashmir regions in March or April and in Ladakh district in April or May. We have also informed that with this change in dates, the Ladakhi students will not have to lose an academic session.

7.40. *Discrimination in rates of foodgrains.*—Several representatives from the Jammu and Ladakh regions have drawn our attention to the alleged discrimination in the sale of foodgrains at subsidized rates. The subsidized rates of foodgrains sold in

Srinagar City are lower than the corresponding rates in Jammu city. The State Government have explained to us that this is because' the prices of foodgrains, particularly rice, which is the staple food of the people of the Kashmir region have been traditionally low in the Valley; and that the procurement prices of paddy there are lower than elsewhere. We find it difficult to understand the explanation given by the State Government because the issue, prices of food-grains in the town and mofussils (other than Srinagar City) in the Valley are higher than the corresponding prices in the towns and mofussils of the Jammu region. We do not also understand the significance of the State Government's observation that the procurement prices of paddy in the Valley are lower. The procurement prices should, as far as possible, be linked with the cost of production; otherwise, there would be no incentive to the farmer to increase production. We recommend that the State Government should review their whole price policy, both for the procurement and for the issue of foodgrains, and introduce uniform issue prices for them throughout the two regions. We were told that the State Government were trying to fix a uniform price for coarse rice and also a higher uniform price for Basmati rice throughout the State.

7.41. *Quantum of rations.*—There is also some regional discrimination in the quantum of foodgrain rations that are issued. The quantum of monthly cereal ration in Srinagar City, is 11 kilograms of rice and 2 kilograms of Atta, making a total of 13 kilograms, while that in Jammu City is 3.45 kilograms of rice and 6.90 kilograms of Atta, making a total of 10.35 kilograms. The State Government explained this difference on the ground that rice is less nutritious (and made more so "by unscientific cooking") than wheat Atta and that on account of the colder climate of Srinagar the consumption of food is higher in Srinagar City than in Jammu City. So far as we are aware neither of such grounds would be tenable in any other part of the country for justifying a different scale of rations in rice-eating areas of in colder climates. We suggest that the quantum of rations at Srinagar and Jammu should be the same.

7.42. So far as the Ladakh district is concerned, it is not a statutorily rationed area. Rations are issued only to Government servants, both "locals" and "non-locals". The State Government have said that special rations are distributed in Ladakh on permits on the occasion of festivals or to needy persons. The scale of rations in the Ladakh district is stated to be uniform for both local and non-local Government servants, the scale being 14 kilograms per head per mensem. Out of the 14 kilograms, the "non-locals" get 9 kilograms of rice while no rice is issued to Government servants who belong to Ladakh. The State Government explained this distinction by saying that the local people take wheat Atta while "non-locals" generally consume only rice. We are not convinced by this explanation. We recommend that there should be no discrimination made between "non-locals" and "locals". If, however, non-locals want to take the whole or part of the rice ration in the form of wheat Atta they should be permitted to do so. If there is any similar discrimination made in the issue of relief rations to the indigent and needy, the State Government should examine the desirability of removing it.

7.43. The representatives of the State Government explained to us that as the staple food of the local population was grim barley (a cross between wheat and barley), there was no rationing in Ladakh for the general public and that a rationed supply of rice was likely to act as a disincentive to production. As, however, the district of Ladakh is deficit in foodgrains, some supplementary rationing should be introduced in the towns, of Ladakh, namely, Leh and Kargil, on a basis similar to that adopted for the towns of the Jammu and Kashmir regions, other than the cities of Srinagar and Jammu.

7.44. *Toll barriers.*—At present, all the State toll barriers are located in the Jammu region. There is not a single toll barrier in the entire Kashmir region. Representatives of Jammu complained that this was an instance of regional discrimination. The State Government have explained this by saying that the toll barriers have been so located as to make the collection of the tax convenient and evasion difficult. But as things stand the tell becomes payable in respect of goods and traffic moving within the Jammu region itself they have to cross any toll barrier while no toll is payable for movement anywhere within the Kashmir region. This is bound to place the economy of the Jammu region at a disadvantage. The State Government have informed us that they are considering the question of imposing a goods tax on goods moving within the Kashmir region and of those areas of the Jammu region that are not at present covered by toll barriers.

We recommend that the system of collection of tolls and the location of the toll barriers should be re-examined and rationalized so that neither region is placed at a disadvantage compared to the other.

Position of Ladakh

7.45. *Difficulties of Ladakh.* Ladakh District is in a somewhat unhappy position. It is one of the remotest districts of the country. It is cut off from the rest of the country for the major part of the year. Even when it is not so cut-off, access to it is difficult because of the inadequacy of means of transport. The number of civilian buses and trucks plying between Srinagar and Leh is indequate and the interior places in Ladakh are virtually unconnected. Government servants from other regions posted to the district try to get away from it as quickly as possible because of the rather forbidding terrain and climate. An adequate number of quilified Ladakhis for manning the services in the District is not yet available. We were told that few Ministers and senior officers of the State Government visit the District. In former days it used to have an appreciable trade and commerce with Tibet and the adjoining parts of China. This has now come to an end. There is not a single degree college in the whole of this far-flung district. By all accounts, therefore, the conditions in the Ladakh District are difficult, and its people have a feeling of isolation and neglect.

7.46. *Suggested remedies.*—We are conscious that both the State Government and the Union Government have done and are doing a great deal to improve these conditions. The people of Ladakh are appreciative of these efforts. But something special seems called for to remove the feeling of isolation and neglect from which Ladakh suffers. We recommend the following measures:—

(i) A degree College should be established immediately at Leh. Subsequently, a second college should be established at Kargil.

(ii) The transport facilities available to Ladakhi should be improved; in particular, the number of buses and trucks plying between Srinagar and Leh should be substantially increased and transport facilities made available to the interior places in Ladakh.

(iii) Suitable arrangements should be made for the stay at Kargil of persons travelling between Leh and Srinagar.

(iv) Stable and satisfactory arrangements for providing electricity to Leh and Kargil and other places of importance in Ladakh should be made.

(v) The single-line administration which was introduced in Ladakh some time ago should be revived in its entirety. The post of Development, Commissioner should be merged with that of the Deputy Commissioner and the incumbent of the post should function as the Head of all Departments in Ladakh, and the Ladakh Affairs Secretary should be the Secretary for all subjects so far as Ladakh is concerned. He should work under the Ladakhi Minister who could hold charge of the portfolio of Ladakh Affairs.

(vi) The headquarters of the Ladakh District (in area, one of the largest in India) lacks even the ordinary amenities and attributes of a district headquarters town. It is necessary that its status should be accorded due recognition by the construction of suitable buildings and roads, improving sanitary arrangements and such other measures. It would be appropriate if the old Raja's Palace were made into a museum for Ladakhi antiquities and arts and crafts.

7.47. It was represented to us that the procedure for sanctioning roads, irrigation and hydel schemes for Ladakh was extremely lengthy and dilatory and that such schemes had to pass through numerous stages before they could be implemented. We have had case studies made of a few such schemes and it does appear that they are undfit, delayed at certain stages both in the State Government and in the Central Government. It is doubtful, however, whether any of the stages can be eliminated altogether. Until recently, all such schemes of more than Rs. 3 lakhs had to be laid before the Council of Ministers for according administrative approval and this entailed delay. By a welcome amendment of the relevant Rules of Business administrative approval to schemes of over Rs. 20 lakhs can now be accorded with the Chief Minister's approval and to those of less with the approval of the Minister-in-charge. We were happy to observe that, in the cases which were studied by us, where more than one authority had to be consulted about any matter, action had generally been taken to consult them simultaneously and not successively. In the circumstances, as the working season in Ladakh is short and the need for speedy disposal great, we would recommend that all authorities concerned in the State and the Central Governments should be instructed to deal as expeditiously as possible with the schemes relating to Ladakh.

7.48. Incidentally, we may mention that some representatives of Ladakh painted out to us that in earlier times the State was referred to in certain documents as 'Jammu, Kashmir, Ladakh and Tibet-ha', 'Tibet-ha' being a Persian adaptation of Little Tibet. Subsequently, this usage seems to have fallen into disuse and reference to Ladakh and Tibet-ha was dropped. They, therefore, suggested that Ladakh should get its due place in the formal name of the State. We recommend that this plea should be taken into consideration by the State Government and some change made to meet the sentiments of the residents of Ladakh.

Land Reforms

7.49. *Wazir Committee recommendations.*—The subject which seems to be agitating the mind of people in the State most, irrespective of the region to which they may belong, concerns the abolition of big landed estates and the working of the provisions of the tenancy laws. Party after party which appeared before us had bitter things to say about them. There has been agitation in some form or other ever since the Big Landed Estates Abolition Act, 1950, and the amendments to the Tenancy Act came into force. In 1953, the State Government appointed a Committee to examine the working of land reforms and certain other matters under the chairmanship of Mr. Justice Janki Nath Wazir. In its report submitted the same year, the Committee pointed out several inconsistencies, anomalies and iniquities in the land reforms adopted by the State Government. We have been informed that no action was taken by the State Government on the recommendations of the Committee on matters relating to land reforms.

7.50. *Land Commission.*—The agitation seems to have continued. In 1963, the State Government appointed a Land Commission to go into the whole question of land reforms, including the conduct of settlement, the consolidation of holdings and the prevention of fragmentation and co-operative farming. We understand that the Land Commission has since submitted its report to the State Government.

7.51. *Removal of anomalies.*—We do not propose to go into the question of land reforms in detail. The expropriation of property without the payment of compensation and holding the landlord liable for mortgages on the land so expropriated are indeed unusual provisions. But they have been legally validated. Moreover, these provisions came into force eighteen years ago. Their operation can harldy be reversed now because that would lead to a fresh upheaval.

7.52. It should, however, be possible for the State Government, to remove some of the obvious anomalies. We suggest that the State Government should give due consideration to the recommendation of the Wazir Committee relating to land reforms and also to the recommendations of the subsequent Land Commission and take action to remove the anomalies, wherever possible. For instance, it is anomalous that if the extent of tenancy or tenancies under one landlord is not more than 100 *kanals* the rent payable by the tenant should be one-half, but as soon as the tenancy exceeds 100 *kanals,* the rent should be one-fourth in respect of the entire land including the first 100 *kanals.* This would mean that a landlord having more than 100 *kanals* under tenancy will in fact get less than what a landlord having 100 *kanals* will get. On the other hand, if a landlord owning singly more than 100 *kanals* dies and is succeeded by two or more heirs, the extent of the ownership of each heir and consequently the extent of the tenancy under each will be less than 100 *kanals.* In such cases, the heirs should be enabled to collect rent at the same rate at which any other landlord, owning less than 100 *kanals* can get under the law. But as the law stands, they can get a rent of only one-fourth. If, however, they are to get a rent of one-half, the tenant of tenants will be hard hit for no fault of theirs. We feel that the proper remedy is to fix a uniform rate of rent on a scientific basis.

7.53. *Applications for ejectment of tenancy.*—According to Section 44 of the Jammu and Kashmir Tenancy Act, 1923, a tenant can, subject to certain conditions, be ejected on any of the following grounds, namely:—

(i) that he has used the land comprised in the tenancy in a

manner which renders it unfit for the purpose for which it was let;

(ii) when rent is payable in kind, that he has without sufficient cause, failed to cultivate the land in the manner or to the extent customary in the locality in which the land is situate;

(iii) that a decree for arrears of rent in respect of the tenancy has been passed against him and remains unsatisfied without sufficient cause;

(iv) that being a tenant other than an occupancy tenant for a fixed term, he has sublet the land; and

(v) that the landlord requires the land for his personal cultivation.

We were told that though the applications for ejectment made in accordance with the above-mentioned provisions are meant to be disposed of in a summary manner by the revenue courts they drag on for long period's resulting in needless harassment to the landlords. We were also told that a very large number of such applications are awaiting disposal. Besides, action on about 5,000 applications made for ejectment of tenants on grounds of resumption for personal cultivation by the landlords has been stayed till 31 December 1968 by a statutory notification. We recommend that the notification staying the disposal of these applications should be rescinded, the Act under which, the notification has been issued be repealed and all pending applications for ejectment be disposed of as expeditiously as possible.

7.54. *Six-monthly move of the Secretariat.*—It has been pointed out to us that the practice of the six-monthly move of the headquarters of the State Government causes dislocation of work and is wasteful. We agree that this practice does cause dislocation and results in a waste of time. It would perhaps be logical to let the Secretariat of the State Government function at one place throughout the year allowing only a camp office to move to the other place for a limited period. If such a course were adopted, the permanent headquarters would probably be at Srinagar and the camp office would move to Jammu during the winter. Apart from other considerations, however, this arrangement would not be practicable for a long time to come for want of adequate heating arrangements which would be required in the office buildings and also at the residences of the officers and staff at Srinagar. Besides, in dealing with this question the impact of the proposed change on the minds of the residents of the Jammu region cannot be ignored. This arrangement has been in existence for very many years. For the reasons already indicated, therefore; we would not recommend its discontinuance.

7.55. *Rehabilitation of refugee's from non-liberated areas.*—The refugees who have migrated from the non-liberated areas of Jammu and Kashmir to the other part of the State have complained to us that they have not been properly rehabilitated though a period of twenty-one years has elapsed since they were uprooted. They contend that many of them were residents of Muzaffarabad and Uri which belong to Kashmir Province and that they should have been settled in the Kashmir region. They have stated that this was not done and that they were unjustifiably moved to the Jammu region. They have alleged that when lands were allotted to them, a sum of Rs. 2,500 per evacuee family was withheld from the rehabilitation grant, but they have not been given proprietary rights over their lands yet. They also desire that the registration of their claims for property left behind in the non-liberated areas of the State should be undertaken without further delay so that when there is an eventual political settlement their claims do not go by default for want of evidence. The problem requires to be handled with sympathy and understanding. We hope that the State Government will do all that they can to allay the apprehensions of these refugees.

7.56. *Clean and efficient administration.*—We have heard complaints of corruption, inefficiency and political interference in the State's administration. We are not directly concerned with these complaints. We have taken note of them only in so far as they tend to contribute to the irritations and tensions in the State. The allegations made before us were mostly of a general nature. We have no cause to think that the position in Jammu and Kashmir is worse than in many other parts of the country. The need for giving the people a clean and efficient administration cannot be over-emphasized, but as the Jammu and Kashmir State occupies a strategic area and there are already several other matters which are causing irritations and tensions in the State, the need for this in Jammu and Kashmir is even greater. We hope that the State Government will address themselves urgently to this important matter and that in this endeavour they will receive the unstinted support of the Services.

7.57. We have stressed the need forgiving the State of Jammu and Kashmir a clean and efficient administration which may inspire the faith of the common man in the impartiality and incorruptibility of its officers. It is obvious that in securing a clean and efficient administration for the State, its Services will have to play an important role. The members of the Services should be men of character and integrity who are able to act independently and fearlessly without running the risk of incurring the displeasure of their official superiors or political bosses. In order to give them a greater sense of security we should like to make certain specific recommendations.

7.58. We consider that fresh appointments to posts should as a rule be made only on the recommendation of the Public Service Commission or the Regional/District Recruitment Boards, the establishment of which we have recommended in paragraph 7.36. The tendency to make *ad hoc* appointments against newly created posts should be discouraged for such appointments cause dissatisfaction; besides, an *ad hoc* appointee gains an advantage over other candidates at the time of regular selection having worked against the post for some time and acquired the requisite experience. One method of eliminating such *ad hoc* appointments would be to ask the Public Service Commission and the proposed Regional District Recruitment Boards to maintain panels of eligible candidates for the common categories of posts. For the less common categories, the Commission or the Boards could make recommendations by issuing short-term advertisements and expediting the process of selection if an appointment to a post within the purview of the Public Service Commission has to be made in an emergency pending selection by the Commission, a temporary promotion from a panel prepared earlier by the concerned Departmental Promotion Committee may be made in preference to the *ad hoc* appointment of an outside candidate. In exceptional cases, however, when an *ad hoc* appointment of an outside candidate is unavoidable, the post should be filled as soon as possible by due selection in accordance with the relevant recruitment rules; no attempt should be made to get the *ad hoc* appointment "regularized" by the Public Service Commission in relaxation of the recruitment rules.

7.59. Regular meetings of the Departmental Promotion Committees, presided over by a Member of the Public Service Commission, should be held so that up-to-date panels of officers eligible for promotion to posts within the purview of the Commission are always available. *Ad hoc* promotions pending the approval of the Public Service Commission should be avoided. With a view to introducing greater objectivity in their deliberations and greater uniformity in the manner of their functioning, the Departmental Promotion Committees, whether presided over by a Member of the Public Service Commission or not, should invariably have a representative of the Services Department as a member.

7.60. The basic problem of the State as in several other parts of India has long been poverty, disease, ignorance and unemployment. In spite of the completion of three Five-Year Plans, the lot of the common man in the State does not seem to have substantially improved. Complaints were made before us that the large funds received from the Union Government over the years for the implementation of the State's developmental programmes had not been properly utilized and that the formulation and execution of many schemes and projects had been haphazard and defective. We feel that if developmental plans and programmes are formulated with due regard to the actual economic needs of the people and are implemented with vigour and efficiency, they would lead to their economic betterment and that would help the State Government to overcome the basic problem.

CHAPTER VIII

Recommendations

Development Programmes

1. There should be a statutory State Development Board and statutory Regional Development Boards for the three regions—Jammu, Kashmir and Ladakh. The Regional Boards should be headed by the Chief Minister or the Planning Minister and should consist of legislators from the regions, economists, experts and concerned officiate. The regions should be adequately represented on the State Development Board which should be headed by the Chief Minister.

The functions of the Regional Development Boards wiil be—

(a) to draw up the regional Plans;
(b) to assign priority to schemes and projects included in the regional Plans; and
(c) to supervise the implementation of the regional Plans.

In discharging these functions it should be the special responsibility of the Regional Development Boards to pay due regard to the special needs of the backward areas of their respective regions.

The State Development Board will scrutinize the regional Plans, prepare a residuary Plan of schemes and projects which transcend regional boundaries or happen to be of an all-State interest and allocate Plan funds equitably (after taking into account the population, area and the specific needs of each region) to the regional Plans and the residuary Plan of all-State interest. [Paragraphs 4.26 to 4.28]

2. The State Development Board and each of the Regional Development Boards will prepare at the end of each year a report of their respective activities giving details of the progress of the Plan programmes and Plan expenditure. At the end of each Plan, similar detailed reports should be prepared by the Boards indicating the physical and financial targets and the physical and financial achievements. All these reports should be laid before the Legislature as soon as may be after they are prepared. [Paragraph 4.29]

Recruitment Policies

3. Recruitment rules for all the State services for which they do not exist at present should be framed and promulgated as early as possible. Recruitment rules for other services also should be speedily framed. [Paragraph 5.17]

4. Complete, tabulated results of all competitive examinations held by the Public Service Commission and any other Recruitment Board that may be set-up, should be published. These results should be sent to all candidates who have taken the examination or, if this is not always feasible, the results should at least be made available for scrutiny on request. [Paragraph 5.18]

5. Seniority lists for ail services should be drawn up correctly and maintained up to date. [Paragraph 5.19]

6. The annual confidential reports on all Government servants should be written up regularly and objectively and maintained properly There should be provision for the review of the confidential rolls by an authority superior to the reporting officer. A proper procedure should be prescribed for dealing with representations of Government servants against adverse entries in their confidential rolls. [Paragraph 5.20]

7. The following-multiple criteria should be adopted for determining which classes should be treated as backward:

(1) The economic backwardness of the class.
(2) The occupation or occupations pursued by that class of citizens.
(3) Their place of habitation.
(4) The average of student population per thousand in that class.
(5) Caste, in relation to Hindus.

[Paragraphs 5.33 and 5.34]

8. The existing list of backward classes should be revised and a fresh list drawn up by a high-powered committee after applying the multiple criteria, mentioned above, relating to social, educational and economic backwardness. [Paragraph 5.35]

9. Article 335 of the Constitution of India should be made applicable to the Jammu and Kashmir State and reservation for the Scheduled Castes made in the services in proportion to their population. [Paragraphs 5.38 and 5.39]

10. Reservation in the services should also be made for the backward classes, as freshly determined, in proportion to their population, subject, however, to the condition that the total reservation for the backward classes and the Scheduled Castes should not ordinarily exceed fifty per cent.

The balance of the posts should be filled strictly and solely on the basis of merit. In filling the posts reserved for the backward classes and the Scheduled Castes, persons belonging to each of these categories should be selected on the basis of merit. [Paragraph 5.35]

Educational Policies

11. Reservation of places in educational and professional institutions should be made for the backward classes and the

Scheduled Castes in proportion to their respective population, subject to the condition that the total reservation does not ordinarily exceed fifty per cent. The balance of the places in such institutions should be filled strictly and solely on the basis of merit. In filling the places reserved for the backward classes and those reserved for the Scheduled Castes, merit should be the criterion for selecting the persons in each of these categories. [paragraph 6.18]

12. A certain proportion of the provision available for the grant of scholarships and study loans should be set apart for the backward classes and the Scheduled Castes. The provision should be separate for each of them and should not be less than the proportion that either of them bears to the population of the State. [Paragraph 6.20]

13. The balance of the provision for the grant of scholarships and study loans should be made available to the rest of the student population. In giving scholarships or loans, the means of the parent or guardian should be an important factor for determining the eligibility of the applicant and, other things being equal, merit should be the sole criterion for granting them. [Paragraph 6.20]

Irritations and Tensions

14. The Government and the people of the State of Jammu and Kashmir may themselves decide when Article 370 of the Constitution of India should be abrogated. [Paragraph 7.16]

15. The State Government should immediately take all steps to arrange for the holding of elections to the local bodies as early as possible. These election's should be held regularly in future. [Paragraph 7.18]

16. A convention should be established that if the Chief Minister belongs to one region, there should be a Deputy Chief Minister belonging to the other region. By another convention, the number of Cabinet Ministers belonging to the two regions should be equal. There should also be a full-fledged Cabinet Minister belonging to Ladakh. [Paragraph 7.30]

17. The functions of each Head of Department should be divided on a regional basis; in other words, each Department should have a Head and an Additional Head, one of them functioning in one region and the other in the other region. The Department will be under the overall control of the main. Head

who will also be responsible for the coordination of work between him and the Additional Head. [Paragraph 7.31]

18. When the High Court of Jammu and Kashmir functions at Srinagar, there should be at least one High Court Judge stationed at Jammu to dispose of the cases there. Similarly, when the High Court is functioning at Jammu, there should be at least one High Court Judge stationed at Srinagar to deal with the cases arising in Kashmir. [Paragraph 7.32]

19. Some of the cadres should be district-based, certain others region-based and the balance State-based. In district-based cadres transfers should be permissible only within the district and in region-based cadres transfers should be permissible only within the region. Members of State-based cadres alone should be transferable anywhere within the State. Generally speaking, the incumbents of inferior and non-gazetted (other than supervisory) posts should be district-based. Supervisory non-gazetted posts, both clerical and non-clerical, should belong to the regional cadres. Class III and Class IV gazetted posts should also generally be in the regional cadres. The residents of the entire State shall be eligible for appointment to the posts included in any of these cadres. [Paragraph 7.33]

20. The incumbent of a district-based post on promotion to a post in the regional cadre will become transferable anywhere within the region. Similarly, a person on promotion from a post in a regional cadre to a post in art all-State cadre will become liable to transfer to a place-anywhere in the State. [Paragraph 7.34]

21. Members of the Kashmir Administrative Service, the Kashmir Civil Service (Judicial) the Kashmir Police Service and such other State services as the State Government may consider necessary, shall be liable to serve for a minimum specified period say, 5 years in each of the three regions of Jammu, Kashmir and Ladakh. [Paragraph 7.35]

22. A Regional Recruitment Board should be set-up for each of the Jammu and Kashmir regions and a District Recruitment Board for each district in the State including Ladakh. The function of the Regional Recruitment Board will be to make recruitment to the regional cadres, and that of the District Recruitment Boards to make recruitment to the district cadres. These Boards will concern themselves with filling those posts which are outside the purview of the Public Service Commission. These Boards could

function part-time and be manned by suitable officers drawn from the regions or districts, as the case may be. [Paragraph 7.36]

23. There should be a separate full-fledged university in both the Jammu and Kashmir regions. One of them, preferably the one in Jammu, should immediately start a faculty of law. Subsequently, law classes will also have to be started in the other university. [Paragraph 7.37]

24. As all the professional colleges are located in Kashmir (the Agricultural College at Ranbirsinghpura also having been closed down recently) it will be proper to open a new-medical college at Jammu. The question of starting an engineering college in the Jammu region may also be considered when the need for turning out a larger number of engineering graduates is felt. [Paragraph 7.38]

25. The State Government should, review the entire policy of food-grain prices, both for procurement and for issue, and introduce uniform prices for foodgrains throughout the Jammu and Kashmir regions. [Paragraph 7.40]

26. The quantum of rations issued at Srinagar and Jammu should be the same. [Paragraph 7.41]

27. In the matter of rations issued to Government servants in the Ladakh District, no distinction should be made between "locals" and "non-locals"; if, however, non-locals want to take the whole or part of the rice ration in the form of wheat Atta, this should be permitted. [Paragraph 7.42]

28. Some supplementary rationing of foodgrains should be introduced at Leh and Kargil on a basis similar to that adopted for the towns of the Jammu and Kashmir regions other than the cities of Srinagar and Jammu. [Paragraph 7.43]

29. The system of collection of tolls and the location of the toll barriers in the State should be re-examined and rationalized so that neither the Jammu region nor the Kashmir region is placed at a disadvantage compared to the other. [Paragraph 7.44]

30. A degree college should be established immediately at Leh. Subsequently, a second college should be established at Kargil. [Paragraph 7.46]

31. The transport facilities available to Ladakh should be improved. In particular the number of buses and trucks plying between Srinagar and Leh should be substantially increased and transport facilities made available for access to the interior places, in Ladakh. [Paragraph 7.46]

32. Suitable arrangements should be made for the stay at Kargil of persons travelling between Leh and Srinagar. [Paragraph 7.46]

33. Stable and statisfactory arrangement's for providing electricity to Leh and Kargil and other places of importance in Ladakh should be made. [Paragraph 7.46]

34. The single-line administration which was introduced in Ladakh some time ago should be revived in its entirety. The post of Development Commissioner should be merged with that of the Deputy Commissioner and the incumbent of the post should function as the Head of all. Departments in Ladakh and the Ladakh Affairs Secretary should be the Secretary for all subjects so far as Ladakh is concerned. He should work under the Ladakhi Minister who could hold charge of the portfolio of Ladakh Affairs. [Paragraph 7.46]

35. The status of Leh should be accorded due recognition as the headquarters of a vast region by the construction of suitable buildings and roads, improving sanitary arrangements and other such measures. [Paragraph 7.46]

36. The sanctioning of roads, irrigation and hydel schemes for Ladakh entails much delay as they have to pass through several stages both in the State Government and in the Central Government. As the passage through these different stages is unavoidable, all the authorities concerned in the State and Central Government should be instructed to deal as expeditiously as possible with the schemes relating to Ladakh. [Paragraph 7.47]

37. The State Government should consider the request of the people of Ladakh for giving 'Ladakh' its due place in the formal name of the State. [Paragraph 7.48]

38. There are some obvious anomalies in the Big Landed Estates Abolition Act and the Tenancy Act. The Wazir Committee had in 1953 made certain recommendations for dealing with some of them. The Land Commission appointed in 1963 has recently submitted its report. The State Government should consider the recommendations of the Wazir Committee and the Land Commission and take action to remove the anomalies, wherever possible. [Paragraph 7.52]

39. The notification staying the disposal of applications made by the land-holders on grounds of resumption for personal cultivation should be rescinded, the Act under which the

notification has been issued should be repealed and all pending applications for ejectment should be disposed of as expeditiously as possible. [Paragraph 7.53]

40. The outstanding problems of refugees from non-liberated areas of the Jammu and Kashmir State should be examined sympathetically so that their apprehensions may be allayed. [Paragraph 7.55]

41. Fresh appointments to posts should, as a rule, be made only on the recommendation of the Public Service Commissionor the Regional/District Recruitment Boards and the tendency to make *ad hoc* appointments against newly created posts should be discouraged. [Paragraph 7.58]

42. Regular meetings of the Departmental Promotion Committees, presided over by a Member of the Public Service Commission, should be held so that panels of officers eligible for promotion to posts within the purview of the Commission are always available. *Ad hoc* promotions-pending the approval of the Public Service Commission should be avoided. The Departmental Promotion Committees should invariably have a representative of the Services Department as a member. [Paragraph 7.59]

Before we conclude we wish to express our sense of appreciation for the very valuable assistance given to us by Mr. B.P. Bagchi, the Secretary of the Commission, in organizing the work of the Commission and drafting the Report. We also wish to express our appreciation for the meritorious work done by the officers of the Commission, particularly Mr. R. Subrahmanian, who was of great help to the Secretary in the drafting of the Report. We also wish to thank the staff of the Commission for their help and co-operation.

P.B. GAJENDRAGADKAR
Chairman
SHANKAR PRASADA
Member
BADR-UD-DIN TYABJ
Member

(B.P. BAGCHI)
Secretary
Bombay
November 29, 1968.

Appendices

Appendix 1

Part A

Names of Bodies Associations/Individuals who submitted written Memoranda to the Commission

1. Shri Abdul Aziz Shawl, Ex-MLA, P.O. Rajouri
2. Shri A. Bhatt, Rainawari, Srinagar
3. Shri Ali Mohd. Sheikh, Kakran, P.O. Kulgam, Kashmir
4. All J&K Backward Classes Union, Jammu
5. All J&K Bohra Sudhar Sabha, Srinagar
6. All J&K Christian Association, Jammu
7. All Jammu and.Kashmir National Conference, Srinagar
8. All J&K National Integration Front, Jammu
9. All Kashmir Hindu Action Committee
10. Anjuman Islamia, Jammu
11. Shri Badri Nath Parihar of Village Hadyal, Tehsil Kishtwar
12. Shri Bansi Lal Kohistani, Jammu
13. Beopar Mandal, Jammu
14. Bharatiya Depressed Classes League, Jammu
15. "Citizen of India", West Bengal
16. Congress Committee, Rajouri
17. Constructional Contractors Welfare Association, Srinagar
18. Shri D.C. Dubgotra, Palam Village, Delhi
19. District National Congress Committee, Udhampur
20. Dogra Mandal, Jammu
21. Dogra United Front, Jammu
22. Shri Durga Nath Raina, Chowgam, Tehsil Kulgam
23. Shri D. N. Raina, Chandigarh
24. Ex-Officers of the J & K Forces who retired before 1957, Jammu
25. Ex-Servicemen of J & K State, Jammu
26. Sofi Ghulam Ahmed Gash, Srinagar

27. Shri Ghulam Mohammad Wani, Nadihal-Bandipore, Member Kashmir Political Conference
28. Shri Ghulam Mohi-ud-Din, Srinagar
29. Shri Ghulam Rasool Matto, Srinagar
30. Government Officers belonging to Ladakh District
31. Gujar Samaj Sudhar Sabha, Poonch District
32. "Illegible (Kashmir)"
33. Choudhri Iqbal Azeem (Bakarwal), P.O. and Village Bhimri, Jammu
34. Jammu Autonomy Forum
35. Jammu Citizen's Council, Jammu
36. Janta Adhikar Raksha Samiti, Jammu
37. J & K Agriculturists' Association, Jammu
38. Jammu and Kashmir Ravidas Sabha, Jammu
39. J & K Shia United Front, Srinagar
40. Jammu and Kashmir State Gujjar Samaj Sudhar Sabha, Jammu
41. Jammu and Kashmir Students Congress (Shri K. Sharma)
42. Jammu and Kashmir Students Congress (Shri Preetam Singh)
43. Shri J.L.K. Jalali, Retired Assistant Governor, Srinagar
44. Shri J. R. Sethi of Jammu
45. Jat Sudhar Sabha, J & K State, Jammu
46. S/Shri Jivan Ram and Chabilal Kapoor of Village Chakcharat Ram, Baramulla
47. Kashmir Chamber of Commerce and Industry, Srinagar
48. Kashmir Fruit Association, Srinagar
49. "Kashmiri Hindus"
50. Kashmir Rajput Sabha, Mirhama, Kulgam (Kashmir)
51. (Two Memoranda)
52. Shri Khurshid Anwar Dogra, Jammu
53. Kisan Conference Doda, Jammu
54. Kshatriya Community of Jammu and Kashmir, Jammu
55. Ladakh Buddhist Association, Leh
56. Shri Mela Ram, Advocate, Jammu
57. S/Shri Mohan Lal and others, Clerks Dehat Sudhar Sabha, J&K Government
58. Shri Mohan Lal Motial, Jammu
59. Shri Mulk Raj Acharya, Jammu
60. Muslims Committee, Udhampur

61. Shri Nanak Chand Hieuntal, Border Security Force, Srinagar
62. Nehru Ekata Committee, Jammu
63. Shri Niranjan Nath Kaul, Batapura, Shopian (Kashmir)
64. "Observer"
65. Oilmen of Sopore town
66. Pleading Committee, Ladakh National Congress
67. Shri Poshkar Nath Dhar, Anantnag
68. Shri Prabhu Shoor, Poonch
69. Praja Socialist Party, Jammu and Kashmir State, Jammu
70. Shri Prathvi Nath, Srinagar
71. President, Nyaya-Bhavan, P.O. Banat, District Muzaffarnagar, U.P.
72. "Public" of Doda District
73. Raksha Samiti, Poonch
74. Shri Ram Chander Khajuria, Billawar, District Jammu
75. Refugees from Pakistan, District Kathua
76. Residents of Tehsil Biliawar
77. Rural Kashmiri Pandits, Kulgam
78. Secretary, Naya Bhawan, Jammu
79. Shri Shabbir Ahmed Salaria, Advocate, Jammu
80. Shri Shamim Ahmed Shamim, MLA, Srinagar
81. Shri Shiv Kumar Sharma, Sakhi Dafar, 7th Bridge, Srinagar
82. Singh Sabha, Jagir Sialkot, Village Balhama, Tehsil Sopore, District Baramulla
83. Siri Guru Singh Sabha Jammu, Akali Dal Jammu Province and Sikh Minority Board, Jammu and Kashmir, Jammu
84. Shri S. Norbo, MLC, Leh.
85. Shri Suraj Parkash Malgotra, Jammu
86. Shri Suresh Chander, Srinagar
87. Shri Tek Singh Dua, Jammu
88. "Traders of Gilgit etc."
89. "Uprooted Muslims of Tehsil Ramnagar, District Udhampur (Jammu)"
90. Walnut Dealers' Association, Srinagar
91. Without name and date
92. Shri Zafar Hussain, Jammu (Tawi)
93. Zamindara Association, Jammu

Part B

Parties/Associations/Individuals who Submitted Memoranda or Supplementary Memoranda Later

1. Shri Ali Mohd. Sheikh, P.O. Kulgam
2. All J&K Bhora Sudhar Sabha, Srinagar.
3. All Kashmir Hindu Action Committee
4. Anjuman Islamia, Jammu
5. Shri Bansi Lal Kohistani, Jammu
6. Beopar Mandal, Jammu
7. Dogra Mandal, Jammu
8. Dogra United Front, Jammu
9. Ex-J&K Militia Personnel
10. Ex-officers of the J&K Forces who retired before 1957
11. Ex-servicemen of J&K State, Jammu
12. Shri Ghulam Nabi Khyal, Srinagar
13. Shri Harbans Singh Azad, Chairman, Village and Khadi Industries Board, Srinagar
14. J&K Agriculturists' Association, Jammu
15. Jammu and Kashmir State Gujjar Samaj Sudhar Sabha, Jammu
16. Janta Adhikar Raksha Samiti, Jammu
17. Jat Sudhar Sabha, J&K State, Jammu
18. Kashmir Chamber of Commerce and Industry, Srinagar
19. Shri Mohan Lal Motial, Jammu
20. Major Piarsingh, MLC, P.O. Janglot (Kathua)
21. Oilmen of Sopore town
22. Pradesh Congress Refugee Advisory Committee, Jammu
23. President, Action Committee, Landless Jagirdars of Kashmir
24. Shri Guru Singh Sabha, Jammu, Akali Dal, Jammu Province, and Sikh Minority Board, Jammu and Kashmir, Jammu
25. Sharnarthi Action Committee, Jammu
26. Sharnarthi Pratinidhi Board, Jammu
27. Shri S. Norbo, MLC Leh
28. Mtr. Zainab Begum, Gagribal, Srinagar
29. Zamindara Association, Jammu

APPENDIX 2

Names or Parties/Associations/Individuals who gave Oral Evidence before the Commission at Srinagar

6 June 1968

1. Shri H.S. Azad, Chairman, Khadi and Village Industries Board, Srinagar
2. Shri Mohammad Muzaffar Khan, MLA, Tehsil Uri (Kashmir)
3. Shri Mohammad Younis, MLA, Tangdar (Kashmir)
4. The Jammu and Kashmir Shia United Front, Srinagar,
5. Shri Ali Mohammad Sheikh and other landowners of Kulgam (Kashmir)

7 June 1968

1. Syed Mir Qasim, President; Jammu and Kashmir Pradesh Congress
2. Shri R.K. Pandit, M.A., R/o Kakran, P.O. Kulgam (Kashmir) and others
3. The Kashmir Chamber of Commerce and Industry, Srinagar (Kashmir)

8 June 1968

1. Shri Mohammad Shafi, Deputy Minister for Animal Husbandry, Jammu and Kashmir
2. All Jammu and Kashmir National Conference, Srinagar
3. Shri Ghulam Rasool Matto, Srinagar
4. Singh Sabha, Village Balhama (Baramulla)

10 June 1968

1. Shri Ghulam Nabi 'Khayal', Editor 'Watan' and Secretary Swatantra Forum
2. Shri Jiwan Ram and Shri Chabilal Kapoor, Village Chakcharat Ram, Baramulla (Kashmir)

11 June 1968

All Jammu and Kashmir National Conference, Srinagar

12 June 1968

1. The Jammu and Kashmir State Gujjar Samaj Sudhar Sabha, Jammu
2. The Traders of Gilgit
3. Oilmen's Industrial Cooperative Society, Sopore
4. Shri Nanak Chand Hieuntal, Inspector, Border Security Force
5. (i) Shri Guru Singh Sabha, Jammu and Kashmir
   (ii) The Sikh Minority Board, and
   (iii) Sikh Riyasati Akali Dal, Jammu

13 June 1968

1. Shri G.R. Kar, Minister of State for Forests and Irrigation
2. Shri S.K. Kaul, MLA, Srinagar
3. Shri Motilal Misri, Secretary, Communist Party of India, Kashmir Branch, Srinagar
4. All Jammu and Kashmir Bhora Sudhar Sabha, Srinagar
5. Shri Soft Ghulam Ahmed Gash, Pleader, Bar Association, Srinagar
6. Shri Saifudin Soze, President, Backward Classes League, Baramulla
7. Kumari Veena Dhar

14 June 1968

All Kashmir Hindu Action Committee

15 June 1968

1. Mohtarma Zainab Begum, Srinagar
2. Agha Syed Ahmed, M.P., Srinagar
3. Professor D.N. Raina, Chandigarh
4. Shri Shamim Ahmed Shamim, MLA, Srinagar

17 June 1968

The Pleading Committee, Ladakh National Congress, Leh

18 June 1968

1. Shri Sonam Narboo, MLC, Leh
2. Kacho Mohammad Ali Khan, MLA, Kargil
3. Ladakh Buddhist Association, Leh

APPENDIX 3

Names of Parties/Associations/Individuals who gave Oral Evidence before the Commission at Jammu

22 August 1968

1. Shri Beli Ram, Deputy Speaker, Legislative Assembly
2. Shri Dharam Pal, MLA
3. Zamindara Association, Jammu
4. Shri Mohan Lal Motial, Jammu, and Others
5. Agriculturists' Association, Jammu
6. Janta Adhikar Raksha Samiti, Jammu

23 August 1958

1. Shri Parmanand, Deputy Minister, Transport
2. Shri Bhagat Chajoo Ram; MLA
3. Shri Guran Ditta Mal, MLA
4. Major Piarsingh, MLC
5. Shri Lachman Singh, MLC
6. Anjuman Islamia, Jammu
7. Jammu Citizens' Council, Jammu

24 August 1968

1. Shri Prem Nath Dogra, MLA
2. Shri Ram Nath Bhalgotra, MLA
3. Jammu and Kashmir Ex-Servicemens' Association, Jammu
4. Ex-Army Officers of Jammu and Kashmir State, Jammu
5. Jammu Autonomy Forum, Jammu
6. Raksha Samiti, Poonch
7. Shri Zaffar Hussain, Jammu
8. Ex-Jammu and Kashmir Militia personnel

25 August 1968

1. Shri Trilochan Dutta, MLA

2. Shri Bansi Lal Kohistani, MLA
3. Distt. National Congress Committee, Udhampur
4. Gujjar Samaj Sudhar Sabha, Jammu
5. Praja Socialist Party, Jammu and Kashmir State, Jammu
6. Shri Phulel Singh, Doda

26 August 1968

1. All J&K National Integration Front, Jammu
2. All J&K Backward Classes Union, Jammu
3. J&K Ravidas Sabha, Jammu
4. Shri Prabhu Shoor, Village Kangri, Distt. Rajouri
5. Jat Sudhar Sabha, Jammu and Kashmir State, Jammu
6. All J&K Kshatriya Sadar Sabha
7. Dogra Kashtriya Sadar Sabha, Jammu
8. Khukhran Bradri (Kashatriya Khukhran), Jammu
9. Beopar Mandal
10. Convener, Pradesh Congress Refugee Advisory Committee, Jammu

27 August 1968

1. Dogra United Front, Jammu
2. Dogra Mandal, Jammu
3. J & K Students Congress, Jammu
4. J & K Students Congress, Jammu
5. Residents of Tehsil Billawar/Basholi
6. All J&K Christian Association, Jammu

In addition to the persons mentioned above, Dr. Karan Singh, Union Minister for Tourism and Civil Aviation, met the Commission informally on 24 August 1968 at Jammu.

Appendix 4

List of Persons who Appeared before the Commission at Srinagar, in September, 1968

14 September 1968

1. Thakur Ranjit Singh, Minister of Works and Transport
2. Pir Gias-ud-Din, Minister of Industries and Power
3. Shri M.A. Khan, Minister of Health

15 September 1968

1. Chairman, Public Service Commission
2. Chief Secretary; Commissioner, Planning and Development Finance Secretary; Food Commissioner; Revenue Secretary; Additional Secretary, Education

16 September 1968

1. Shri G.L. Dogra, Minister of Revenue
2. Shri S.N. Fotedar, Chairman, Legislative Council

In addition to the persons mentioned above, the following persons met the Commission informally:

1. Shri Bhagwan Sahay, Governor of Jammu and Kashmir
2. Shri G.M. Sadiq, Chief Minister, Jammu and Kashmir
3. Shri Janki Nath Wazir, Retired Chief Justice of Jammu and Kashmir High Court

APPENDIX 5

Breakdown of Budgetary Resources

I. 1960-61

(In Lakhs of Rupees)

Sl. No.	*Head*	*Jammu*	*Kashmir*	*Ladakh*	*Total*
1.	Forests	190.72	171.13	0.16	362.01
2.	Excise	30.78	10.72	..	41.50
3.	Entertainment Tax	2.81	2.16	..	4.97
4.	Show Tax	..	..	..	..
5.	Road Toll Basic	24.6.6	16.43	..	41.09
6	Road Toll Addl.	27.29	32.41	1.71	61.41
7.	Sales Tax (Gen)	*5.60*	4.83	..	10.43
8	Sales Tax (Motor Spirit)	9.27	4.92	..	14.19
9.	Passenger Tax	..	..	..	..
10.	Property Tax	..	..	..	..
11.	Stamps	5.38	7.82	0.05	13.25
12.	Electricity	6.56	6.56	..	..
13.	Irrigation	4.44	1.00	..	5.44
14.	Rents and Misc. P.W.D. Receipts	2.35	12.03	..	14.38
15.	Land Revenue	24.65	42.10	0.97	67.72
16.	Fees under Motor Vehicles Act	0.52	1.77	..	2.29
17.	Taxes under Motor Vehicles Taxation Act	4.05	3.10	..	7.15
18.	Transport	46.73	15.58	..	62.31
19.	Water Rates	3.40	3.50	..	6.90
	Total	389.21	322.94	2.89	715.04

(Contd.)

APPENDIX 5 (*Contd.*)

II. 1963-64

(In Lakhs of Rupees)

Sl. No.	*Head*	*Jammu*	*Kashmir*	*Ladakh*	*Total*
1.	Forests	167.10	203.50	N.A.	370.60
2.	Excise	48.65	15.55	..	64.20
3.	Entertainment Tax	4.06	3.03	..	7 06
4.	Show Tax	0.37	0.23	..	0.60
5:	Road Toll Basic	36.84	24.56	..	61.40
6	Road Toll Addl.	59.22	70.34	3.70	133.26
7.	Sales Tax (Gen)	27.89	15.03	..	42.92
8.	Sales Tax (Motor Spirit)	15.84	12.94	..	28.78
9.	Passenger Tax	4.76		..	12.53
10.	Property Tax	0.56	23	..	0.79
11.	Stamps	8.46	11.47	0.14	20.07
12.	Electricity	(–)3.40	36.24	..	32.84
13.	Irrigation	3.12	2.23	..	5.35
14.	Rents and Misc. P.W.D. Receipts	4.27	13.55	..	17.82
15.	Land Revenue	25.51	33.06	1.20	59.77
16.	Fees under Motor Vehicles Act	2.23	7.90	..	10.13
17.	Taxes under Motor Vehicles Taxation Act	6.91	5.93	..	12.84
18.	Transport	48.54	25.10	..	73.64
19.	Public Health	1.58	1.75	..	3.33
	Total	462.51	490.38	5.04	957.93

(*Contd.*)

APPENDIX 5 (*Contd.*)

III. 1965-66

(In Lakhs of Rupees)

Sl. No.	*Head*	*Jammu*	*Kashmir*	*Ladakh*	*Total*
1.	Forests	137.19	177.40	N.A.	314.59
2.	Excise	72.63	17.96	..	90.59
3.	Entertainment Tax	4.22	3.26	..	7.48
4.	Show Tax	0.38	0.22	..	0.60
5.	Road Toll Basic	51.37	34.25	..	85.62
6.	Road Toll Addl.	71.30	8.4.64	4.46	160.40
7.	Sales Tax (Gen)	35.44	16.10	..	51.54
8.	Sales Tax (Motor Spirit)	13.36	13.50	..	26.86
9.	Passenger Tax	4.72	6.35	..	11.07
10.	Property Tax	1.07	0.92	..	1.99
11.	Stamps	7.63	13.20	0.11	20.94
12.	Electricity	3.30	32.03	..	35.33
13.	Irrigation	3.47	2.00	..	5.47
14	Rents and Misc. P.W.D. Receipts	6.25	10.70	..	16.95
15.	Land Revenue	18.29	24.27	1.08	43.64
16.	Fees under Motor Vehicles Act	6.23	9.13	..	15.36
17.	Taxes Under Motor Vehicles Taxation Act	9.17	7.59	..	16.76
18.	Transport	5.83	6.19	0.07	12.09
19.	Public Health	2.13	2.19	..	4.32
	Total	453.98	461^90	5.72	921.60

(*Contd.*)

Appendix 5 (*Contd.*)

IV. Allocation of Resources: Assumptions

(a) The allocation of total resources to different regions has by and large, been made on the basis of the point of collection, though there is no bar to remitting the revenue of one region in the Treasury of another region.

(b) For 'road toll' which is a significant item of revenue of the State, the points of collection are all located in Jammu, though the incidence of the toll is spread all over the State. The location of the toll points is done after taking into account the convenience of collection and ensuring that all possible points of leakage are plugged. The allocation of road-toll has been done by the State Government on the following basis:

(1) *Basic Toll:* 60 percent for Jammu and 40 percent for Kashmir.

(2) *Additional Toll* has been allocated to three regions in proportion to the population of each region.

(c) In respect of receipts under the 'Electricity Department', which is a commercial department, the figures have been worked out by deducting from the gross receipts collected in each region, the working expenses incurred in that region.

(d) With regard to receipts under the Transport Department, (which is also a commercial department) the net receipts for the entire State have been worked out by deducting from the gross receipts the working expenses of the year. The net receipts so arrived at have been allocated to the different regions in the proportion of gross receipts 'collected from each region.' While doing so, the receipts accruing from Pathankot have been added to those of Jammu region even though these receipts are on account of services rendered to the Army for carriage of goods from Pathankot to places in the Kashmir Division or Ladakh District. The same procedure has been followed in the case of foodgrains transported from Pathankot to Srinagar.

APPENDIX 6

Plan Outlay and Central Assistance—State-wise

(In crores of Rupees)

State		First Plan			Second Plan			Third Plan (Provisional)		
		Plan outlay	*Central Assistance*	*Col. (3) as % of Col. (2)*	*Plan. outlay*	*Central Assistance*	*Col. (6) as % of Col. (5)*	*Plan outlay*	*Central Assistance*	*Col. (9) as % of Col. (8)*
1	2	3	4	5	6	7	8	9	10	11
1.	Andhra Pradesh	107	61	57.0	181	96	53.0	349	220	63.0
2.	Assam	28	22	78 6	63	31	49.2	132	100	75.8
3.	Bihar	102	55	53.9	177	84	47.5	332	216	65.4
4	Gujarat	99	32	32.3	147	50	34.0	240	112	46.7
5.	Jammu & Kashmir	11.52	10	86.8.	31.20	20	64.1	64.09	62	967
6.	Kerala	44	24	54.5	79	38	48.1	182	122	67.0
7.	Madhya Pradesh	94	61	64.9	145	96	66.2	287	219	76.3
8.	Madras	85	42	49.4	187	95	50.8	342	187	54.7
9.	Maharashtra	125	48	.38.4	214	74	34.6	435	167	38.4
10.	Mysore	94	47	50.0	139	67	48.2	264	156	59.1
11.	Nagaland	..	..	..	..	..	..	11	11	100.0
12.	Orissa	85	77	90.6	89	66	74.2	224	137	61.2
13.	Punjab	163	141	86.5	151	88	58.3	252	134	53.2
14.	Rajasthan	66	60	90.9	109	59	59. 0	213	161	75.6
15.	Uttar Pradesh	166	87	52.4	223	121	53.1	557	356	63.9
16.	West Bengal	154	113	73.4	156	73	46.8	305	155.	.50.8

Note: The figures of Plan outlay shown for Jammu and Kashmir have been furnished by the State Government. The figures for the other States are those furnished by the Union Ministry of Finance.

Appendix 7

Development Programme (Plan): Second Five Year Plan

Sl. No.	Head of Development	Total Plan Outlay	Jammu Region	Kashmir Region	Common to Jammu and Kashmir Region	Ladakh Region	Total
1	2	3	4	5	6	7	8
1.	Agricultural Programme	267.74	66.49	88.10	12.11	..	166.70
2.	Co-operation and C.D.	228.78	170.00	173.81	2.99	..	346.80
3.	Irrigation	495.45	115.11	250.45	..	..	365.56
4.	Power	329.24	152.68	219.06	..	..	371.74
5.	Village and Small Scale-Industries	341.24	18.90	79.33	103.46	..	201.69
6.	Industry and Mining						
7.	Transport and Communications	665.00	502.31	295.86	6.52	..	804.69
8.	Education	281.68	94.05	99.98	18.43	..	212.46
9.	Health	285.00	79.03	72.32	17.70	..	169.05
10.	Water Supply (Rural)	81.07	59.47	21.63	..	..	81.10
11.	Urban Water Supply		19.62	15.12	..	..	34.74
12.	Housing	95.00	43.46	58.60	..	..	102.06
13.	Labour and Labour Welfare	9.97	4.66	4.94	..	..	9.60
14.	Welfare of Scheduled Castes and other Backward Classes	38.95	33.32	4.85	..	..	38.17
15.	Social Welfare	21.47	1.79	1.74	..	..	3.53
16.	Development of backward area	94.73	..	23.67	..	86.65	110.32
17.	Local Bodies	132.05	24.34	63.16	..	..	87.50
18.	Plan Publicity	15.20	..	..	11.43	..	11.43
19.	Statistical Schemes	9.50	..	..	3.06	..	3.06
	Total	3392.07	1385.23	1472.62	175.70	86.65	3120.20

(Contd.)

APPENDIX 7 *(Contd.)*

Development Expenditure Outside Plan: Second Five-Year Plan (1956-61)

(In lakhs of Rupees)

Sl. No.	*Head of Development*	*Jammu Region*	*Kashmir Region*	*Common to Jammu and Kashmir Region*	*Ladakh Region*	*Total*
1	2	3	4	5	6	7
1.	Transport and Communications	120.46	88.52	..	..	208.98
2.	National Highways	71.00	64.73	..	..	135.73
3.	Colonies (Rehabilitation of Displaced Persons)	53.76	—	..	..	53.76
	Total	245.22	153.25	..	..	398.47

(Contd.)

APPENDIX 7 *(Contd.)*

Development Programme (Plan): Third Five Year Plan

(In lakhs of Rupees)

Sl. No.	*Head of Development*	*Total Plan Outlay*	*Jammu Region*	*Kashmir Region*	*Common to Jammu and Kashmir Region*	*Ladakh Region*	*Total*
1	2	3	4	5	6	7	8
1.	Agriculture Programmes excluding minor irrigation	675.40	165.02	260.99	24 .86	..	450.87
2.	Co-operation and C.D.	513.51	156.18	142.76	168.83	..	467.77
3.	Irrigation (including minor irrigation)	1625.00	169.05	527.16	120.98	..	817.19

1	2	3	4	5	6	7	8
4.	Power	997.00	539.53	379.05	40.85	..	959.43
5.	Village and Small Scale Industries }	906.00	..	..	864.07	..	864.07
6.	Industry and Mining }						
7.	Transport and Communications	9.31.59	412.05	494.51	97.00	..	1003.57
8.	Education (including Cultural activities)	498.02	234.99	325.61	..	..	560.60
9.	Health and Family Planning	351.00	140.13	208.43	8..41	..	156.97
10.	Water Supply						
	(a) Rural	227.44	117.26	122.98	..	..	240.24
	(b) Urban	..	61.32	84.98	..	..	146.30
11.	Housing	200.00	54.32	126.84	..	..	181.16
12.	Labour and Labour Welfare	30.00	15.29	11.78	..	..	27.07
13.	Welfare of	24.00	30:68	12.46	..	..	..
	Scheduled Castes and other Backward Classes	24.00	30.68	12.46	..	..	43.14
14.	Social Welfare	13.69	4.03	2.30	..	..	6.33
15.	Public Co-operation	4.45	0.29	..	..	..	0.29
16.	Area Development	402.00		50.35 (Sonawari)		147.36	197.71
17.	Local Bodies	75.00	17.74	45.23		..	62.97
18.	Plan Publicity	13.00			8.48	..	8.48
19.	Government Presses	5.00	1.81	1.35		..	3.16
20.	Statistical Schemes	7.90	..	..	1.47	..	1.47
21.	Metric Systems of weights	..	..	..	10.55	..	10.55
	Total	7500.00	2119.69	2796.78	1345.51	147.36	6409.34

(*Contd.*)

APPENDIX 7 *(Contd.)*

Development Expenditure Outside Plan: Third Five-Year Plan (1961-66)

(In lakhs of Rupees)

Sl. No.	*Head of Development*	*Jammu Region*	*Kashmir Region*	*Common to Jammu and Kashmir Region*	*Ladakh Region*	*Total*
1	2	3	4	5	6	7
1.	Transport and Communications	618.61	285.95	153.48	934.44	1992.03
2.	National Highways	162.07	86.49	..	..	248.56
3.	Local Bodies	16.64	18.44	..	..	29.08
4.	Ladakh Development	..	..	..	14.92	44.92
5.	Colonies (Rehabilitation of displaced Persons)	215.92	..	..	..	215.92
	Total	1006.79	390.88	153.48	949.36	2500.51

APPENDIX 8

A Note on J & K Minerals Ltd.

J & K Minerals Ltd. was established in February, 1960 for exploration of mineral resources in the State of J & K and for the development of mineral-based industries including generation of thermal power, etc.

The projects which are being managed by the Corporation at present and the targets and achievements of each are given below:—

(i) Wuyan Cement Factory

Investment:		Rs. 136.64 lakhs
Installed capacity:		18,000 tonnes per year
Production:		
1963-64	=	14,554.42 tonnes
1964-65	=	9,756.95 tonnes
1966-67	=	8,845.90 (clinker)
	=	8,030.98 (Cement)
1967-68	=	7,660.24 (clinker)
	=	5,826.01 (Cement)
Target production for 1968-69		12,000 tonnes of cement.

The factory was set-up in February, 1963 with an initial production capacity of 60 tonnes per day. The plant installed in the factory is the only plant of its type and size in Asia. The factory meets the bulk of the requirements of cement in the Kashmir Valley and the sale price has been so fixed that it is slightly lower than the price of cement obtained from the plains. Because of frequent shut-downs of electricity and low voltage, the production of the factory has remained low. The Corporation has recently purchased its own 860 KVA generating set to reduce: the effect of the power shut-downs and low voltage. It is proposed to expand the production capacity of the factory to 120 tonnes per day as the demand for cement in the valley is said to be on the increase. During 1968-69, the target production of cement in the factory is expected to be 12,000 tonnes.

(ii) Spun Pipe Factory

Investment:		Rs. 6,61,277
Installed capacity: 6′	=	100% efficiency— 9600 Nos.—57,600 rft.
8′	=	100% efficiency — 8640 Nos.—69,120 rft.
Production: 1964-65	=	41,344 rft.
1965-66	=	51,648 rft.
1966-67	=	66,832 rft.
1967-68	=	74,152 rft.
Target for 1968-69	=	75,000 rft.

The factory went into commercial production on 1-4-1964 and its performance is stated to be satisfactory. Since the demand for spun pipes in the valley is said to be steadily on the increase, the production capacity of the factory is proposed to be expanded so as to obtain a capacity, of 2.5 to 3 lacs rft. of pipes per annum. During financial year 1968-69, the target production of 75,000 rft. of pipes has been fixed for the factory.

(iii) Prestressed Concrete Factory

Investment	=	Rs. 12,93,266
Installed capacity	=	Capacity as per project report
		30′/350 lb — 3,700 Nos. Poles
		32′/380 lb — 3,300 " "
		36′/400 lb— 2,000 " "
Actual Capacity	=	22′/250 lb — 1,725 " "
		27′/400 lb — 1,494 " "
		30′/350 lb — 1,264 " "
		32′/500 lb — 632 " "
		34′/400 lb — 575 " "

Production

	22'/250	27'/400	32'/500	30'/350	30'/500	34'/400	Total
1962-63	60	52	66	..	..		178
1963-64	960	182	66	66	..	198	1.472
1964-65	..	52	..	814	100	..	966
1965-66	720	416	..	44	80	..	1,260
1966-67	720	104	22	572	60	..	1,478
1967-68	175	252	..	..	20	..	453
Target for—1968-69 — 2.000 poles							

The factory with a capacity for manufacturing 9,000 P.C.C. poles, per-year went into production on 1-4-1963. The factory, which was mainly designed for the manufacture of P.C.C. poles for the State Electrical-Department has been facing considerable difficulties from us very inception, due to lack of orders from that Department. The State Government has been apprised of the problem from time to time. Plans are stated, to be under preparation for utilisation of the idle capacity of the factory by diverting some of its sheds for manufacture of some other P.C.C. products.

(iv) Thermal Power Stations — Kalakot

Investment = Rs. 365.76 lakhs fending March, 1966)

Capacity = 22.5 M.W.

The power house is under construction at Kalakot and the first 7.5 M.W. has been commissioned on trial basis recently.

(v) Padder Saphire Mining Project

Production =	1963-64	50,000 grams
	1964-65	2,00,000 grams
	1965-66	2,24,839 grams
	1966-67	1,84,950 grams
	1967-68	1,88,672 grams

The extraction of saphire made at present is mainly from the debris. It is expected that operations connected with the extraction of saphire corundums from Padder area will be taken-up on a larger scale during the year 1968-69.

(vi) Mining of Coal at Kalakot

Bergoa Mining Project:

Investment: Rs. 61.59 lakhs (ending March, 1966)

Production:	1962-63	=	17,458 tonnes
	196.3-64	=	19,717 tonnes
	1964-65	=	8,558 tonnes inclusive of Metka and Jangalgali
	1965-66	=	743.5 tonnes

The coal extracted from Bergoa mines is being, reserved. For Thermal Power Station, Kalakot. It is stated that other connected mines, i.e., Melka and Chakkar coalfields are under study at present, and some exploratory mining is being done

(vii) New Projects

The Corporation has also been entrusted with setting up of new units, subject to economic and technical feasibility, like Rayon Grade Pulp and Yarn Plant in Kashmir Valley, and cement plants at Reasi and Basholi in Jammu Province. It is stated that detailed investigations regarding these projects have already been taken up in hand and a firm of consultants namely, M/s. C.M.D.C. are busy at present in preparing the project reports of these projects. The report for the Reasi Cement-Plant has already been received from the Consultants and is under detailed scrutiny at present. The project reports for other schemes are expected to be submitted by the Consultant during the year 1968-69. Besides, the Government has also entrusted the work of preparation of a project report for a paper plant of a capacity of 10 tonnes per day to M/s. National Industrial Development Corporation.

Appendix 9

Recruitment of Government Employees during 1961-62 to 1965-66 and Position as on 10-9-1963 and 1-4-1967

I. Regional Composition

(Based on material supplied by the State Government upto 22-11-68)

	Jammu				*Kashmir*				*Ladakh*				*Outside the State*				*Total*			
	G	*NG*	*CIV*	*T*	*G*	*NG*	*CIV*	*T*	*G*	*NG*	*CIV*	*T*	*G*	*NG*	*CIV*	*T*	*G*	*NG*	*CIV*	*T*
1961-62	116	1943	519	2578	234	3164	661	4049	3	105	63	173	12	30	..	32	355	1212	1235	..
Percentage	32.7	37.1	41.7	37.7	63.1	60.5	53.1	59.3	0.8	2.0	5.2	2.5	3.4	0.4		0.5	100.0	100.0	100.0	100.0
1962-63	140	1356	368	2554	232	2768	645	3670	..	103	47	150	12	60	42	64	390	..	72.2	..
Percentage	30.6	38.7	45.9	39.7	66.1	58.1	50.3	57.0	..	2.2	3.7	2.3	3.3	4.0	0.1	1.0	100.0	100.0	100.0	100.0
1963-64	133	1601	517	2114	280	3175	669	4124	..	56	46	102	8	41	24	..	828	138	1234	..
Percentage	31.6	32.4	41.9	34.1	66.5	65.7	54.3	63.7	..	1.1	3.7	1.5	1.9	6.8	0.1	6.7	100.0	100.0	100.0	100.1
1964-65	255	2771	711	3639	315	3981	369	4874	1	92	400	198	2	12	1	45	475	..	..	..
Percentage	33.3	42.2	42.3	41.7	66.3	56.4	51.7	55.8	0.2	1.5	5.9	2.3	0.4	0.2	0.1	0.2	100.0	100.0	100.0	100.0
1965-66	249	3456	900	4635	432	7912	956	9305	3	126	72	511	..	2	..	2	684	1154	..	..
Percentage	25.4	39.2	46.7	32.8	63.2	68.7	49.6	65.8	0.4	1.1	3.7	1.4	..	..	..	..	100.0	100.0	100.0	100.0
10-9-1963	762	15612	4353	21727	1424	25749	6108	33281	NA	NA	NA	NA	177	7	21	235	2363	4238	1342	..
Percentage	32.2	39.2	41.5	39.3	60.3	60.7	58.3	69.2	NA	NA	NA	NA	7.5	0.1	0.2	0.5	100.0	100.0	100.0	100.0
1-4-1967	1074	23673	5250	29927	2038	40512	7986	50526	27	1750	543	7290	58	54	36	145	3112	65836	12285	..
Percentage	32.2	35.9	38.1	36.1	65.1	61.4	57.9	69.9	0.9	2.7	3.7	2.8	1.8	..	0.3	0.2	100.0	100.0	100.0	100.0
				1572387				1899438				88651								
Percentage				44.2				53.3				2.5								100.0

G: Guaranted; NG: Non-Guaranteed; CIV: Class IV; T: Total; NA: Not applicable.

APPENDIX 9 (*Contd.*)

II. Communal Composition

(Based on material supplied by the State Government upto 22-11-68)

	Muslims			*Hindus*				*Sikhs*				*S. Castes*							
												Hindus				*Sikhs*			
	NG	*CIV*	*T*	*G*	*NG*	*CIV*	*T*	*G*	*NG*	*CIV*	*T*	*G*	*NG*	*CIV*	*T*	*G*	*NG*	*CIV*	*T*
1961-62	2559	716	3411	202	2145	377	2724	16	302	48	366	..	155	63	218	..	4	..	4
Percentage	48.9	57:5	49.9	56.9	41.0	30 3	39 9	4.5	5.8	3.9	5.3	..	3.0	5.0	3.2	..	0.1	..	0.1
1962-63	2264	753	3156	202	2070	392	2664	18	259	69	346	..	124	37	161	..	18	..	18
Percentage	47.2	58.7	49.0	56.3	43.1	30.6	41.4	5.0	.5.4	5.4	5.4	..	2.6	2.9	2.5	..	0.4	..	0.3
1963-64	2667	717	3557	232	2004	379	2615	16	335	49	400	..	89	43	132	..	5	..	5
Percentage	51.9	58.1	52.4	55.1	39.0	30.7	38.5	3.8	6.6	4.6	5.9	..	1.7	3.8	1.9	..	0.1	..	0.1
1964-65	3379	96.3	4530	263	2758	514	3535	23	251	59	333	..	120	68	188	..	8	1	9
Percentage	51.4	57.3	51.9	55.4	42.0	30.6	40.5	4.8	3.8	3.5	3.8	..	1.8	4.0	2.2	..	0.1	0.1	0 1
1965-66	7197	1068	8498	405	3615	567	4587	33	446	45	524	6	181	120	307	..	12	..	12
Percentage	62.4	55.4	60.1	59.2	31.3	29.5	32.4	4.8	3.9	2.3	3.7	0.9	1.6	6.2	2.2	..	0.1	..	0.1
10-9-1963	19115	5955	25963	1175	19878	3682	24735	106	2454	387	2947	NA	NA	NA	NA	NA	NA	NA	NA
Percentage	45.1	56.8	47.0	49.7	46.9	35.1	44.8	4.5	5.8	3.7	5.3								
1-4-1967	34300	7810	43441	1565	26305	4412	32282	180	3255	451	3886	12	1142	694	1848	..	77	6	83
Percentage	52.0	56.7	52.4	50.2	39.9	32.0	38.9	5.8	4.9	3.3	4.7	0.4	1.7	5.0	2.2	..	0.1	..	0.1
			243267				729,230				62,901				283963				168
Percentage			68.3				20.4				3.8				8.0				—

G: Guaranted; NG: Non-Guaranteed; CIV: Class IV; T: Total; NA: Not applicable.

APPENDIX 9 (*Contd.*)

II. Communal Composition

(Based on material supplied by the State Government up 22-11-68)

	Buddhists				*Others*				*Total*			
		NG	*CIV*	*T*	*G*	*NG*	*CIV*	*T*	*G*	*NG*	*CIV*	*T*
1961-62	..	41	26	67	1	26	15	42	355	5232	1245	68.32
Percentage	..	0.7	2.1	1.0	0.3	0.5	1.2	0.6	100.0	100.0	100.0	100.0
1962-63	..	39	15	54	..	23	16	39	359	47.7	128.2	6438
Percentage	..	0.8	1.2	0.8	..	0.5	1.2	0.6	100.0	100.0	100.0	100.0
1963-64	..	25	27	52	..	11	18	29	431	51.36	1233	6790
Percentage	..	0.5	2.2	0.8	..	0.2	1.5	0.4	100.0	100.0	100.0	100.0
1964-65	1	36	40	77	..	18	36	54	475	6520	1681	8726
Percentage	0.2	0.6	2.4	0.9	..	0.3	2.1	0.6	100.0	100 0	100.0	100.0
1965-66	3	56	27	86	4	24	101	129	684	11551	1928	14143
Percentage	0.4	0.5	1.4	0.6	0.6	0.2	5.2	0.9	100.0	100 0	100.0	100.0
10-9-1963	NA	NA	NA	NA	189	951	458	1598	2363	42398	10482	55243
Percentage					8.0	2.2	4.4	2.9.	100.0	100.0	100.0	100.0
1-4-1967	10	591	198	799	19	316	214	549	3117	65986	13785	82885
Percentage	0.3	0.9	1.4	1.0	9.6	0.5	1.6	0.7	100.0	100.0	100.0	100.0
				48.360				4287				3560976
Percentage				1.4				.0.1				100.0

G: Guaranted; NG: Non-Guaranteed; CIV: Class IV; T: Total; NA: Not applicable.

APPENDIX 10

List of Backward Classes other than Scheduled Castes Recognized in the State of Jammu and Kashmir

Acharji; Arikasha (Sawer); Alqa (Patigur); Aknoon (Maktab teacher)

Bhjojki; Bafand (Weaver); Baba Fquir; Beggar; Bede* and Bon (Drum and flute player); Bhands; Bazigar; Banjara; Biloch; Bawria; Bakarwals; Bharmunje; Bohrees (Kashmir Hindus)

*Champas (Nomadic people of Chushul)

Dubduba; Dhobi; Dosali; Derazi (Village Darzi)

Kul Faqir (Gypsies)

*Guraj (blacksmith); Gujjars; Gharate (Kashmir Pohol); Gorkahn (Grave digger); Geseoni; Gaddis; Gosains

Hajam

Jhiwar; Jullaha; Jogi

Kamboh; Kumar; Kanwai (village Nanwai) Kaligar (village Kaligar) Kawaj

Lohar; Lubhana

Madari; Mirasi; Mochi; Manjie (including Gad Hanjis); Malyar; Markban

Nalband; Nadar (Kashmir Doom)

Pakhtoons; Pathira (Khist saz); Pandit Goar

Qasab

Reshi (Maliyar); Rangreez; Razire

*Ladakh District.

Sansi; Sikligar; Shaksar; Sheer Gujar; Sangtrash (stone-cutter); Shaw Faqir; Shippies; Sochies

Teli; Tarkhans; Thanthur

Watal (Sweepers, Shupri Watal); Waza (village Waza)

Zalooger (Durkigar); Zargar (village Zargar)

List of Scheduled Castes

1. Barwals
2. Basith
3. Batwal
4. Chamar or Ramdasia
5. Chura
6. Phyar
7. Doom or Mahasha
8. Gardi
9. Jolaha
10. Megh or Kabirpanthi
11. Ratal
12. Saryara
13. Watal

Appendix 11

Government of Jammu and Kashmir General Department

Circular

Rule 19 of Civil Services (Classification, Control and Appeal Rules provide for securing of adequate representation of various communities in the State in services. In pursuance of this Rule, Government have been contemplating to determine certain reservation of posts for Scheduled Castes. It has now been decided that with a view to achieve this purpose:—

1. all appointing authorities should know the district-wise population of Harijans in the State and while making appointments keep this in mind. If the post relates to a district or region the percentage of population in the district or region may be considered for fixing number of appointments to be reserved for Harijans. If it relates to the State as a whole the percentage of population in the whole State may be considered;
2. for this purpose the population figures as given in the Census Report 1961 are brought to the notice of appointing authorities.

State/Division/District	*Total Population (in lakh)*	*Scheduled Castes*
Jammu and Kashmir	35.67	2.84
lammu Division	15.72	2.84
Udhampur, District	2.54	0.51
Doda District	2.68	0.25
Jammu District	5.17	1.52
Kathua District	2.07	0 47
Poonch Rajouri District	3.26	0.09

Similarly in the case of allotment of seats for technical or other institutions, heads of the institutions and the selecting authorities should keep the above ratio in view.

The undersigned is directed that the above policy should be strictly followed while making appointments.

(Sd). E.N. Mangat Rai,
Chief Secretary to Government.

APPENDIX 11 *(Contd.)*

No. GD(ADM) 4/65-SW(i) Dated: -7-1966

Copy for information and necessary action forwarded to the:

1. All Secretaries to Govt.
2. Secretary to Governor.
3. Secretary to Chief Minister.
4. Secretary Public Service Commission.
5. All Head of Departments.
6. All Provincial Heads.
7. Superintendent Govt. Press for publication in the three consecutive issues of the Govt. Gazette.

APPENDIX 12

Government of Jammu and Kashmir Civil Secretariat—General Department

NOTIFICATION

No. 1034-D of 1968 Dated 20-7-1968

Whereas on the basis of the facts, figures and data given in the Census Report and those available from other sources including public records, the Government is of the opinion that the permanent residents of Ladakh District and the permanent resident Scheduled Castes are backward classes of citizens of the State and are not adequately represented in the services under the State:

Now, therefore, the Government hereby directs that reservations shall be made in the services and posts under the State in favour of these classes which shall, as nearly as may be, bear such proportion to the available vacancies as is specified below against each such class and appointment to such services and posts shall be regulated accordingly:

(a)	Permanent residents Scheduled Caste	5%
(b)	Permanent residents of Ladakh Distt.	2%

Provided that if a sufficient number of candidates belonging to any class specified above is not available for filling up the available vacancies reserved for such classes, the remaining vacancies shall lapse and shall be filled up on merit from amongst other candidates.

This order shall apply to all cases in which recruitment action has not been completed.

Explanation:—For purposes of this order "available vacancies", means the vacancies in the service or in respect of posts under the State which are to be filled.

By Order of the Government of Jammu and Kashmir.

(Sd.) (Isher Dass Gupta)
Deputy Secretary to Government,
General Department.

APPENDIX 12 *(Contd)*

No. GD (Adm.) 382/68-SW dated 20-7-1968.

Copy for information and necessary action forwarded to the:

1. All Secretaries to Government.
2. All Heads of Departments.
3. Divisional Commissioner, Kashmir/Jammu.
4. Secretary, Public Service Commission.
5. Secretary to Governor, Jammu and Kashmir State.
6. Secretary, Legislative Assembly.
7. Secretary, Legislative Council.
8. Manager, Government Press, Srinagar for publication in the Government Gazette.

Index